The
Selected Stories
of
Patricia
Highsmith

The
Selected Stories
of
Patricia
Highsmith

With a Foreword by G<small>RAHAM</small> G<small>REENE</small>

W. W. Norton & Company

NEW YORK · LONDON

Frontispiece: Patricia Highsmith, 1964. Photograph © Jerry Bauer.

The text of this book is composed in Bembo
with the display set in Bembo Italic OsF
Composition by Allentown Digital Services Division
Manufacturing by The Haddon Craftsmen, Inc.
Book design by Brooke Koven
Production manager: Andrew Marasia

Library of Congress Cataloging-in-Publication Data

Highsmith, Patricia, 1921–
[Short stories, Selections]
The selected stories of Patricia Highsmith / foreword by Graham Greene.
p.   cm.
ISBN 0-393-02031-2
1. Detective and mystery stories, American.   2. Psychological fiction, American.   I. Title.
PS3558.I366 A6 2001
813'.54—dc21

2001030878

W. W. Norton & Company, Inc., 500 Fifth Avenue, New York, N.Y. 10010
www.wwnorton.com

W. W. Norton & Company Ltd., Castle House, 75/76 Wells Street, London W1T 3QT

1 2 3 4 5 6 7 8 9 0

Contents

SLOWLY, SLOWLY IN THE WIND

THE BLACK HOUSE

MERMAIDS ON THE GOLF COURSE

Foreword

BY GRAHAM GREENE

Miss Highsmith is a crime novelist whose books one can reread many times. There are very few of whom one can say that. She is a writer who has created a world of her own—a world claustrophobic and irrational which we enter each time with a sense of personal danger, with the head half turned over the shoulder, even with a certain reluctance, for these are cruel pleasures we are going to experience, until somewhere about the third chapter the frontier is closed behind us, we cannot retreat, we are doomed to live till the story's end with another of her long series of wanted men.

It makes the tension worse that we are never sure whether even the worst of them, like the talented Mr. Ripley, won't get away with it or that the relatively innocent won't suffer like the blunderer Walter or the relatively guilty escape altogether like Sydney Bartleby in *A Suspension of Mercy*. This is a world without moral endings. It has nothing in common with the heroic world of her peers, Hammett and Chandler, and her detectives (sometimes monsters of cruelty like the American Lieutenant Corby of *The Blunderer* or dull sympathetic rational characters like the British Inspector Brockway) have nothing in common with the romantic and disillusioned private eyes who will always, we know, triumph finally over evil and see that justice is done, even though they may have to send a mistress to the chair.

Nothing is certain when we have crossed *this* frontier. It is not the world as we once believed we knew it, but it is frighteningly more real to us than the house next door. Actions are sudden and impromptu and the motives sometimes so inexplicable that we simply have to accept them on trust. I believe because it is impossible. Her characters are irrational, and they leap to life in their very lack of reason; suddenly we realize how unbelievably rational most fictional characters are as they lead their lives from A to Z, like commuters always taking the same train. The motives of these characters are never inexplicable because they are so drearily obvious. The characters are as flat as a mathematical symbol. We accepted them as real once, but when we look back at them from Miss Highsmith's side of the frontier, we realize that our world was not really as rational as all that. Suddenly with a sense of fear we think, "Perhaps I really belong *here*," and going out into the familiar street we pass with a shiver of apprehension the offices of the American Express, the center, for so many of Miss Highsmith's dubious men, of their rootless European experience, where letters are to be picked up (though the name on the envelope is probably false) and travelers' checks are to be cashed (with a forged signature).

Miss Highsmith's short stories do not let us down, though we may be able sometimes to brush them off more easily because of their brevity. We haven't lived with them long enough to be totally absorbed. Miss Highsmith is the poet of apprehension rather than fear. Fear after a time, as we all learned in the Blitz, is narcotic, it can lull one by fatigue into sleep, but apprehension nags at the nerves gently and inescapably. We have to learn to live with it. Miss Highsmith's finest novel to my mind is *The Tremor of Forgery,* and if I were to be asked what it is about I would reply, "Apprehension."

In her short stories Miss Highsmith has naturally to adopt a different method. She is after the quick kill rather than the slow encirclement of the reader, and how admirably and with what field-craft she hunts us down.

The Animal-Lover's Book of Beastly Murder

Chorus Girl's Absolutely Final Performance

They call me Chorus Girl—shouts of "Chorus Girl" go up when I stand and swing my left leg, then my right, and so on. Before that, however, maybe ten, twenty years ago, I was "Jumbo Junior," mostly "Jumbo." Now it's Chorus Girl entirely. My name must be written on the wooden board at the front of my cage, along with "Africa." People stare at the board, sometimes say "Africa," then start calling me "Chorus Girl!—Hey, Chorus Girl!" If I swing my legs, a small cheer goes up.

I live alone. I never saw another creature like myself, in this place at any rate. I remember when I was small, though, following my mother everywhere, and I remember many creatures like myself, much bigger, a few even smaller. I remember following my mother up a sloping wooden board on to a boat, the boat a bit unsteady. My mother was led and prodded away, back the same board, and I was on the boat. My mother, wanting me to join her, lifted her trunk and bellowed. I saw ropes flung about her, ten or twenty men tugging to hold her back. Someone fired a gun at her. Was it a deadly gun or a dope gun? I will never know that. The smell is different, but the wind was not blowing towards me that day. I only know my mother collapsed after a little while. I was on the deck, screaming shrilly like a baby. Then I was shot with a dope gun. The boat finally moved, and after a very long time during which I mainly slept and ate in semidarkness in a box, we arrived in another land where there were no forests, no grass. Into another box I went, more movement, another place with cement underfoot, hard stone everywhere, bars, and foul-smelling people. Worst of all, I was alone. No little creatures my own age. No mother, no friendly grandfather, no father. No play. No baths in a muddy river. Alone with bars and cement.

But the food was all right, and there was plenty of it. Also a nice man took care of me, a man named Steve. He carried a pipe in his mouth, but almost never did he light it, just held it between his teeth. Even so he could talk and I could soon understand what he said, or at least what he meant.

"Kneel, Jumbo!" and a tap on my knees meant to get down on my knees. If I held my trunk up, Steve would clap his hands once in appreciation, and toss some peanuts or a small apple into my mouth.

I liked it when he got astride my back and I would get up, and we would walk around the cage. People seeing this would clap their hands, especially little children would clap.

Steve kept the flies off my eyes in summer by means of a string fringe which he fixed around my head. He would hose the cement floor, the shady part, so I could lie down and keep cool. He would hose me. When I became bigger, Steve would sit on my trunk and I would lift him into the air, being careful not to tip him, because he had nothing to hold on to except the end of my trunk. Steve took special care of me in winter also, making sure I had enough straw, even sometimes blankets if it was very cold. One particularly bad winter, Steve brought me a little box with a cord attached which blew warm air on to me. Steve nursed me through an illness caused by the cold.

The people here wear large hats. Some of the men carry short guns on their belts. Once in a while one pulls a gun and fires it into the air to try to scare me or the gazelles who live next door to me and whom I can see through the bars. The gazelles react violently, leap into the air, then huddle together in a far corner of their cage. A pitiable sight. By the time Steve or one of the caretakers arrives, the man who fired the shot has put his gun back in his belt, and looks like all the other men—who are laughing and won't point out the man who did it.

This reminds me of one of my pleasanter moments. There was a red-faced fat fellow about five years ago who on two or three Sundays fired his loud gun into the air. It annoyed me, though I would never have dreamt of showing my annoyance. But the third or fourth Sunday when this particular fellow fired his gun, I quietly took a snoutful of water from my trough and let him have it full force through the bars. I hit him in the chest and he went over backwards with his boots in the air. Most of the crowd laughed. A few of the people were surprised or angry. Some threw a few stones at me—which didn't hurt, or missed entirely, or hit the bars and bounced in another direction. Then Steve came trotting up, and I could see that Steve (having heard the shot) knew exactly what had happened. Steve laughed, but he patted the shoulder of the wet man, trying to calm him down. The man was probably denying having fired the shot. But I saw Steve give me a nod which I took for approval. The gazelles came forth timidly, staring through the bars at the crowd and also at me. I fancied they were pleased with my action, and I felt proud of myself that day. I dreamt even of seizing the wet man, or a man like him, of squeezing his soft body until he died, then of trampling him under my feet.

During Steve's time with me, which must have been thirty years, we would occasionally take a walk in the park and children, sometimes three at a time, would ride on my back. This was at least amusing, a nice change. But the park is anything but a forest. It is just a few trees growing from rather hard, dry soil. It is almost never wet. The grass is close cut, and I was not allowed to pull any grass up, not that I much wanted to. Steve managed everything, managed me, and carried a stick made of woven leather with which he prodded me to make me turn in a certain direction, kneel, stand up, and at the end of the outing stand on my hind legs. (More cheering.) Steve did not need the stick, but it was part of the show, like my turning in a couple of stupid circles before standing on my hind legs at the end. I could also stand on my front legs, if Steve asked me to. I remember my temper was better in those days, and I would avoid without Steve's telling me the low branches of some of the trees so the children on my back would not be knocked off. Given a chance, I am not sure I would be that careful any more. What have people, except Steve, ever given me? Not even grass under my feet. Not even companionship of another creature like myself.

Now that I am older, my legs heavier, my temper shorter, there are no more rides for children, though the band still plays on summer Sunday afternoons—"Take Me Out to the Ball Game" and lately "Hello, Dolly!" Sometimes I wish I could take a walk again, with Steve again, wish I could be young again. And yet, what for? For more years in this place? Now I spend more time lying down than standing up. I lie in the sun, which doesn't seem as hot as it used to. The people's clothing has changed a little, not so many guns and boots, but still the same broad-brimmed hats on the men and some of the women. Still the same tossed peanuts, not always shelled, that I used to stick my trunk through the bars for so eagerly when I was younger and had better appetite. Still the same popcorn and sweet Cracker Jack. I don't always bother getting on my feet Saturday and Sunday. This infuriates Cliff, the new young keeper. He wants me to do my stuff, as in the old days. It is not that I am so old and tired, but I don't like Cliff.

Cliff is tall and young, with red hair. He likes to show off, cracking a long whip at me. He thinks he can make me do things according to certain jabs and commands. There is a sharp point of metal on his stick, which is annoying, although it doesn't break my skin by any means. Steve approached me as one creature to another, making acquaintance with me and not assuming I was going to be what he expected. That is why we got along. Cliff doesn't really care about me, and does nothing to help me against the flies in summer, for instance.

Of course when Steve retired, I continued to go through the Saturday and Sunday rounds with the children, once in a while with adults on my back. One man (another trying to show off) dug his spurs into me one Sunday, whereupon I put on a very little speed of my own accord and did not duck under a low branch but deliberately trotted under it. It was too low for the man to duck, and he was swept neatly off my back, landed on his knees and howled with pain. This caused a lot of disturbance, the man groaned for a while, and what was worse Cliff took the man's side, or tried to placate the man, by yelling and prodding at me with the pointed stick. I snorted with rage myself—and was gratified to see the crowd fall back in terror of me. I was nowhere near charging them, which I'd have liked to do, but responded to Cliff's prods and headed back to my cage. Cliff was muttering at me. I took a snoutful of water, and Cliff saw it. Cliff retreated. But he came back after nightfall when the park gates were closed, and gave me a whipping and a lecture. The whipping did not hurt at all, but must have exhausted Cliff who was staggering when he finished.

The following day Steve turned up in a wheelchair. His hair had become white. I had not seen him in four or five years, perhaps, but he was really the same, with his pipe in his mouth, the same kind voice, the same smile. I swung my legs with joy in my cage, and Steve laughed and said something pleasant to me. He had brought some small red apples to give me. He came in his wheelchair into the cage. This was pretty early one morning, so there was hardly any of the public in the park as yet. Steve said something to Cliff and gestured towards Cliff's pointed stick, so that I knew Steve meant that Cliff should get rid of it.

Then Steve made a sign to me. "Up! Lift me up, Chorus Girl!"

I knew what he meant. I knelt, and stuck my trunk under the seat of Steve's wheelchair, sideways, so he could grab the end of my trunk with his right hand and with his other hand press against my head for balance. I did not get to my feet for fear of toppling Steve's chair, but I lifted him off the cement by quite a distance. Steve laughed. I set the chair down gently.

But that was years ago, Steve's visit. It was not his last visit. He came two or three times in his wheelchair, but never on the two days of the week when there were the most people. Now I have not seen Steve in about three years. Is he dead? This possibility makes me sad whenever I think of it. But then it is equally sad to expect, to hope for Steve to appear some morning of the quiet days, when just a few people straggle in, and Steve is not among them. Sometimes I raise my trunk and bellow my chagrin and disappointment because Steve doesn't come. It seems to amuse people, my bellowing—just as my mother bellowed on the dock when she couldn't reach me. Cliff pays no attention, only sometimes puts his hands over his ears, if he happens to be near.

This brings me close to the present time. Just yesterday, Sunday, there was the usual crowd, even more than usual. There was a man in a red suit with a white beard ringing a bell in his hand, walking about talking to everyone, especially to children. This man appears every now and then. People had peanuts and popcorn to give me through the bars. As usual, I held my snout through the bars, and my mouth was open also, in case someone aimed a peanut correctly. Someone threw a round object into my mouth, and I thought it was a red apple until I crunched on it, whereupon it started stinging my mouth horribly. I immediately took some water into my trunk, rinsed my mouth and spat. I had not swallowed any of the stuff, but the whole inside of my mouth was burning. I took more water, but it did little good. The pain made me shift from foot to foot, and at last I trotted around my cage in agony. The people laughed and pointed. I became angry, furious. I took as big a snoutful of water as I could manage and walked rather casually to the front of my cage. Standing a little way back from the bars so I could hit them all, I forced the water through my snout with all my power.

No one quite fell, but more than twenty people staggered, fell back against each other, choking and blinded for a few seconds. I went to my trough and took on more water, and not a moment too soon, because the crowd had armed itself also. Rocks and sticks came flying at me, empty Cracker Jack boxes, anything. I aimed at the biggest man, knocked him down, and used the rest of the water to spray the whole assembly again. A woman was screaming for help. Others retreated. A man pulled his gun, shot at me and missed. Another gun was being drawn, although the first man who had shot was at once jumped on by another man. A bullet hit me in the shoulder, not going through but rather skimming the surface. A second bullet knocked off the end of my right tusk. With the last of my trough water in my snout, I attacked one of the gunmen squarely in the chest. It should have been enough to break his bones. At any rate he flew backward and knocked a woman down as he fell. Feeling I had won that set-to, in spite of my burning mouth, I withdrew prudently to my sleeping quarters (also of cement) where no bullets could hit me. Three more shots rang out, echoing in empty space. I don't know what they hit, but they did not hit me.

I could smell blood from my shoulder. I was still so angry, I was snorting instead of breathing, and almost to my own surprise, I found myself barricading the entrance to my sleeping quarters with the bales of hay which lined the place. I pulled the bales down from their stacks against the walls, shoved and kicked them, and with my trunk managed to boost one up on to the top of the heap of eight or nine, thereby closing the doorway except at the very top. This was bulletproof, anyway. But the bullets had ceased. Now I could hear Cliff outside, shouting to the crowd.

"Take it easy there, Chorus Girl!" Cliff's voice said.

I was familiar with the phrase. But I had never heard the fear, like a shaking, in Cliff's voice before. The crowd was watching him, of course. Cliff had to show himself powerful, able to control me. This thought plus my dislike of Cliff set me off again, and I butted my head against the barricade I'd made. Cliff had been pulling at the top bale, but now the whole heap fell on him.

The crowd gave a cry, a scream of shock.

I saw Cliff's legs, his black boots kicking underneath the bales.

A shot sounded, and this time I was hit in the left side. Cliff had a gun in his hand, but it was not his gun that had gone off. Cliff was not moving now. Neither was I. I expected another shot from the crowd, from someone in the crowd.

The crowd only stared back at me. I glared at them, with my mouth slightly open: the inside of my mouth was still burning.

Two uniformed men of the place arrived via the side door of my cage. They carried long guns. I stood still and did nothing, barely looked at them. Crazy and excited as they were, they might have shot me at once out of fear, if I had shown any sign of anger. My self-possession was returning. And I thought Cliff might be dead, which gave me pleasure.

But no, he wasn't. One man bent over him, pulled a bale of hay off him, and I saw Cliff's red-haired head move. The other man prodded me rudely with the point of his gun towards my sleeping quarters. He was yelling something at me. I turned and strolled, not hurrying, into my cement room which was now bestrewn with hay and bales in disorder. Suddenly I was not feeling well, and my mouth still hurt. A man stood in the doorway with his gun pointed at me. I regarded him calmly. I could see Cliff getting up. The other man was talking with Cliff in an angry tone. Cliff was talking and waving his hands, though he didn't look like himself at all. He looked unsteady on his feet, and he kept feeling his head.

Then a man with grayish hair, not as gray as Steve's, came to the gate with another man who carried a bag. They were let into the cage. Both of them came quite close to me and looked at me. Blood was dripping from my left side on to the cement. Then the gray-haired man spoke to Cliff angrily, kept on talking when Cliff interrupted—a string of words from both of them. The gray-haired man pointed to the cage door, a sign for Cliff to leave. The next moments are vague to me, because the man with the bag put a cloth over my snout and tied it firmly. He also gave me a prod with a needle. By now, during the loud talk, I had lain down. The cloth smelt cool but awful, and I went into a frightening sleep in which I saw animals like huge cats leaping about, attacking me, my mother, my family. I saw green trees again, high grass. But I felt that I was dying.

When I awakened, it was dark, and there was some kind of grease in my mouth. My mouth no longer hurt, and my side hurt only a little. Was this death? But I could smell the hay in my room. I got to my legs and felt sick. I threw up a little.

Then I heard the side gate clang as someone closed it. I recognized the step of Cliff, though he was walking softly in his boots. I considered going out of the small sleeping-room, which was like a trap with no other exit but the door, but I was too sleepy still to move. I could barely see Cliff kneeling with a bag like the one the man had carried. Then I smelt the same sweet, thin smell that the man had put over my nose. Even Cliff snorted, and turned his head away, then he came at me with a rush, tossing the cloth around my nose and pulling it tight at once with a rope. I flicked my snout and knocked Cliff down with a blow against his hip. I beat my trunk against his fallen form, trying more to get the cloth off than to hurt Cliff, who was writhing and groaning. The rope loosened, and with a toss I managed to shake off the cloth. It fell on Cliff's chest and part of his legs—stinking, evil, dangerous. I went out into the purer air of my cage.

Cliff was getting to his feet, gasping. He too came out for air, then rushed back, muttering, seized the cloth and came at me again. I rose a little on my hind legs and pivoted away from him. Cliff nearly fell. I gave Cliff the merest bump with my trunk and it lifted him off his feet. He fell his whole length on to the cement. Now I was angry. It was a fight between the two of us, Cliff with the evil-smelling cloth still in his hand. Cliff was getting to his knees.

I gave Cliff a kick, hardly more than a prod, with my left foot. I caught him in the side, and I heard a cracking sound like the breaking of tree branches. After that Cliff did not move again. Now there was the awful smell of blood mixed with the sweet and deadly smell. I went to the front corner of my cage, as far from the cloth as possible and lay down, trying to recover in the fresher air. I was cold, but that was of little importance. Slowly I began to feel calmer. I could breathe again. I had one brief desire to go and stomp a foot on Cliff, but I hadn't the energy. What I felt was rage. And little by little even the rage went away. But I was still too upset to sleep. I waited in my cement corner for the dawn.

And this is where I am now, lying in a corner of the cement and steel cage where I have spent so many years. The light comes slowly. First there is the familiar figure of the old man who feeds the two musk oxen. He pushes a cart, opens another cage where there are more horned animals. At last he passes my cage, glances twice at me, and says something with "Chorus Girl" in it, surprised to see me lying where I am. Then he sees Cliff's form.

"Cliff?—Hey, Cliff! What's the matter?"

The cage isn't locked, it seems, and the old man comes right in, bends over Cliff, says something, holds his nose and drags the big white cloth out of the cage. Then he runs off, yelling. I get to my feet. The cage door is slightly open. I walk past Cliff's body, nudge the gate wider and walk out.

There is no one in the park. It is pleasant to walk on the ground again, as I haven't done since they stopped the weekend rides so long ago. The dry ground even feels soft. I pause to raise my trunk, pull some green leaves off a branch, and eat them. The leaves are tough and prickly, but at least they are fresh. Here is the round fountain, that I was never allowed to pause at, or drink from, on the weekend outings. Now I take a long cool draft.

Behind me there are excited voices. The voices are no doubt back at my cage, but I don't even bother looking. I enjoy my freedom. Above me is the great blue sky, a whole world of emptiness overhead. I go into a thicket of trees growing so close that they scrape both my sides. But there are so few trees, I am immediately out again, and on a cement path where apes and monkeys in cages stared goggle-eyed and chatter in amazement as I stroll by. A couple of them huddle at the back of their cage, little hairy fellows. Gray monkeys yell shrilly at me, then turn their blue behinds at me and scamper to the far corner of their cage. But perhaps some of them would like to ride on my back? From somewhere I remember that. I pull some flowers and eat them, just for amusement. The black monkeys with long arms are grinning and laughing, holding on to their bars, jerking the bars up and down and making a clatter.

I stroll over, and they are only a little afraid, much more curious than afraid, as I stick my trunk around two of the bars and pull the bars towards me. Then a third bar, and there is room for the black monkeys to scramble out.

They scream and titter, leaping along the ground, using their hands to boost them. One grabs my tail mischievously. Two of them take to a tree with delight.

But now there are footsteps from somewhere, sounds of running feet, shouts.

"There she is! By the monkeys!"

I turn to face them. A monkey scrambles on to my back, using my tail to get up. He slaps my shoulders, wanting a ride. He seems to weigh nothing at all. Two men, the same as yesterday, with the long guns, come running towards me, then halt, skidding, and raise their guns. Before I can lift my trunk in a gesture that might indicate friendliness, before I can kneel even, three shots go off.

"Don't hit the monkey!"

But they hit me.

Bang!

Now the sun is coming up and the tops of the trees are greenish, not all the trees being bare. My eyes go up and up. My body sinks. I am aware of the monkey leaping nimbly from my back to the ground, loping off, terrified by the gunshots. I feel very heavy suddenly, as if falling asleep. I mean to kneel and lie down, but my body sways sideways and I strike the cement. Another shot jolts my head. That was between the eyes, but my eyes are still open.

Men scamper round me as the monkeys did, kicking me, shouting to one another. Again I see the huge cats leaping in the forest, leaping on me now. Then through the blur of the men's figures I see Steve very clearly, but Steve as he was when he was young—smiling, talking to me, with his pipe in his teeth. Steve moves slowly and gracefully. So I know I am dying, because I know Steve is dead. He is more real than the others. There is a forest around him. Steve is my friend, as always. There are no cats, only Steve, my friend.

Djemal's Revenge

Deep in the Arab desert lived Djemal, with his master Mahmet. They slept in the desert, because it was cheaper. By day, they trudged (Mahmet riding) to the nearest town, Elu-Bana, where Djemal gave rides to tourists, squealing women in summer dresses and nervous men in shorts. It was about the only time that Mahmet walked.

Djemal was aware that the other Arabs didn't care for Mahmet. A faint groan came from other camel drivers when he and Mahmet approached. There was much haggling over prices, dinars, between Mahmet and the other drivers who would at once pounce upon him. Hands would fly and voices rise madly. But no one exchanged dinars, only talked about them. Finally Mahmet would lead Djemal to the group of staring tourists, tap Djemal and yell a command for him to kneel.

The hair on Djemal's knees, front legs and back, was quite worn off, so his skin looked like old leather there. As for the rest of him, he was shaggy brown with some clotted patches, other patches nearly bare, as if moths had been at him. But his big brown eyes were clear, and his generous, intelligent lips had a pleasant look as if he were constantly smiling, though this was far from the truth. At any rate, he was only seventeen, in the prime of life, and unusually large and strong. He was shedding now because it was summer.

"Ooooooh!—Eeeeeek!" a plump lady screamed, jolted from side to side as Djemal stood up to his impressive full height. "The ground looks miles away!"

"Don't fall! Hang on! That sand's not as soft as it looks!" warned an Englishman's voice.

Little filthy Mahmet, in dusty robes, tugged at Djemal's bridle, and off they went at walking pace, Djemal slapping his broad feet down on the sand and gazing about wherever he wished, at the white domes of the town against the blue sky, at an automobile purring along the road, at a yellow mountain of lemons by the roadside, at other camels walking or loading or unloading their human cargo. This woman, any human being, felt like no weight at all, nothing like the huge sacks of lemons or oranges he often had to carry, or the sacks of plaster, or even the bundles of young trees that he transported far into the desert sometimes.

Once in a while, even the tourists would argue in their hesitant, puzzled-sounding voices with Mahmet. Some argument about price. Everything was price. Everything came down to dinars. Dinars, paper and coin, could make men whip out daggers, or raise fists and hit each other in the face.

Turbaned Mahmet in his pointed, turned-up-toed shoes and billowing old djellaba, looked more like an Arab than the Arabs. He meant himself to be a tourist attraction, photogenic (he charged a small fee to be pho- tographed) with a gold ring in one ear and a pinched, sun-tanned visage which was almost hidden under bushy eyebrows and a totally untended beard. One could hardly see his mouth in all the hair. His eyes were tiny and black. The reason the other camel drivers hated him was because he did not abide by the set price for a camel ride that the others had estab- lished. Mahmet would promise to stick to it, then if a tourist happened to approach him with a pitiable attempt to bargain (as Mahmet knew they had been advised to do), Mahmet would lower the price slightly, thus get- ting himself some business, and putting the tourist in such a good mood for having succeeded in bargaining, that the tourist often tipped more than the difference at the end of the ride. On the other hand, if business was good Mahmet would up his price, knowing it would be accepted—and this sometimes in the hearing of the other drivers. Not that the other dri- vers were paragons of honesty, but they had informal agreements, and mostly stuck to them. For Mahmet's dishonesty, Djemal sometimes suf- fered a stone thrown against his rump, a stone meant for Mahmet.

After a good tourist day, which often went on till nearly dark, Mahmet would tie Djemal up to a palm tree in town and treat himself to a meal of couscous in a shack of a restaurant which had a terrace and a squawking parrot. Meanwhile Djemal might not have had any water even, because Mahmet took care of his own needs first, and Djemal would nibble the tree leaves that he could reach. Mahmet ate alone at a table, eschewed by the other camel drivers who sat at another table together, making a lot of merry noise. One of them played a stringed instrument between courses. Mahmet chewed his lamb bones in silence and wiped his fingers on his robes. He left no tip.

Maybe he took Djemal to the public fountain, maybe he didn't, but he rode while Djemal walked into the desert to the clump of trees where Mahmet made his camp every night. Djemal could not always see in the darkness, but his sense of smell guided him to the bundle of clothing of Mahmet, the rolled up tent, the leather water bags, all of which were permeated with Mahmet's own sweaty, sharp scent.

In the early mornings, it was usually lemon-hauling in the hot summer months. Thank Allah, Mahmet thought, the Government had established "camel ride" hours for the tourists, 10–12 in the mornings, 6–9 evenings, so it left the drivers free to earn money in the daytime, and to do all the tourist business in concentrated hours.

Now as the big orange sun sank on the horizon of sand, Mahmet and Djemal were out of hearing of the muezzin in Elu-Bana. Besides, Mahmet had his transistor on, a little gadget not much bigger than his fist, which he could prop on his shoulder amid folds of djellaba. Now it was a wailing and endless song, with a man singing in falsetto. Mahmet hummed, as he spread a tattered rug on the sand and threw down some more rags upon this. This was his bed.

"Djemal!—Put yourself there!" said Mahmet, pointing to a side he had discovered was windward of the place where he intended to sleep. Djemal gave out considerable heat, as well as blocking the gritty breeze.

Djemal went on eating dry brush several yards away. Mahmet came over and whacked him with a braided leather whip. It did not hurt Djemal. It was a ritual, which he let continue for a few minutes before he tore himself away from the dark green shrubs. Fortunately he wasn't thirsty that night.

"Oy-yah-yah-yah . . ." said the transistor.

Djemal knelt down, turning himself slightly against the wishes of Mahmet, so that the light wind nearly stuck him straight in the tail. Djemal didn't want sand up his nose. He stretched his long neck out, put his head down, almost closed his nostrils, and closed his eyes completely. After a while, he felt Mahmet settling against his left side, tugging at the old red blankets in which he wrapped himself, settling his sandaled heels in the sand. Mahmet slept as he rested, almost sitting up.

Sometimes Mahmet read a bit in the Koran, mumbling. He could read hardly at all, but he knew a lot of it by heart, since childhood. His school had consisted, as the schools consisted even now, of a roomful of children sitting on the floor repeating phrases uttered by a tall man in a djellaba who prowled among them, taking long strides over their heads, reading phrases from the Koran. This wisdom, these words were like poetry to Mahmet—pretty enough when one read it, but of no use in everyday life. This evening, Mahmet's Koran—a chunky little book with curled corners and nearly obliterated print—remained in his woven knapsack along with sticky dates and a stale hunk of bread. Mahmet was thinking of the forthcoming National Camel Race. He scratched a flea somewhere under his left arm. The camel race started tomorrow evening, and lasted for a week. It went from Elu-Bana to Khassa, a big port and a major city of the country, where there were even more tourists. The drivers camped out at night, of course, and were supposed to carry their food and water supplies, and make a stop at Souk Mandela, where the camels were to drink, then push on. Mahmet went over his plans. No stop at Souk Mandela, for one thing. That was why he was making Djemal go dry now. When Djemal tanked up tomorrow, and just before the race started in the evening, he could go seven days, Mahmet thought, without water, and Mahmet hoped to make it in six, anyway.

Traditionally, the Elu-Bana to Khassa race was very close, drivers flogging their camels at the finish. The prize was three hundred dinars, quite enough to be interesting.

Mahmet pulled the red blanket over his head, and felt secure and self-sufficient. He hadn't a wife, he hadn't even a family—rather he had one in a faraway town, but they disliked him, and he them, so Mahmet never thought about them. He'd stolen as a boy, and the police had come a few times too often to his family's house, warning him and his parents, so Mahmet had left aged thirteen. From then on, he'd led a nomadic existence, shining shoes in the capital, working for a while as waiter until he was caught stealing out of the till, then picking pockets in museums and mosques, then as assistant pimp for a chain of bordellos in Khassa, then as runner for a fence during which time he'd been winged in the calf by a policeman's bullet, giving him a limp. Mahmet was thirty-seven or thirty-eight, maybe even forty, he wasn't quite sure. When he won the National Camel Race money, he intended to make a down payment on a little house in Elu-Bana. He'd seen the two-room white house with running cold water and a tiny fireplace. It was up for sale cheap, because the owner had been murdered in his bed, and nobody wanted to live there.

The next day, Djemal was surprised by the relative lightness of his work. He and Mahmet cruised along the lemon mountains on the out-skirts of Elu-Bana, and Djemal's two huge sacks were loaded and unloaded four times before the sun went down, but that was nothing. Ordinarily, Djemal would have been prodded much faster along the roads.

"Ho-ya! Djemal!" someone shouted.

". . . Mahmet! . . . F-wissssss!"

There was excitement, Djemal didn't know why. Men clapped their hands. Praise or disapproval? Djemal was aware that no one liked his mas-ter, and Djemal took some of this ill-feeling, therefore apprehension, upon himself. Djemal was ever wary against a sneaky blow, something thrown at him, meant for Mahmet. The huge trucks pulled out, loaded with lemons brought by scores of camels. Drivers sat resting, leaning against their camels' bellies or squatting on their heels. As Djemal walked out of the compound, one camel for no reason stretched his head forward and nipped Djemal's rump.

Djemal turned quickly and lifted a protruding upper lip, baring pow-erful long front teeth, and snapped back, not quite catching the camel's nose. The driver on the other camel was nearly thrown by his camel's recoil, and cursed Mahmet roundly.

". . . !" Mahmet gave back as good as he got.

Though Djemal was already full of water, Mahmet led him again to the town trough. Djemal drank a little, slowly, pausing to lift his head and sniff the breeze: he smelt the perfume of tourists from afar. And he also heard loud music, not unusual as transistors blared all day from every direc-tion, but this music was bigger and more solid. Djemal felt a wallop on his left hind leg. Mahmet was walking, in front of him now, pulling his rein.

There were flags, a grandstand, tourists, and a couple of loudspeakers whence the music came. All this at the edge of the desert. Camels were lined up. A man was speaking, his voice unnaturally loud. The camels looked good. Was it a race? Djemal had once been in a race with Mahmet riding him, and Djemal remembered that he had run faster than the oth-ers. That was last year, when Mahmet had acquired Djemal. Djemal had a fleeting recollection of his first master, who had trained him. This man had been tall, kind, and rather old. He had argued with Mahmet, doubtless over dinars, and Mahmet had won. That was how Djemal saw it. Mahmet had taken Djemal away with him.

Djemal was suddenly in a line with the other camels. A whistle blew. Mahmet whacked him, and Djemal loped ahead, taking a minute or two to get into stride. Then he was galloping straight into the setting sun. He was ahead. It was easy. Djemal began to breathe regularly, settling down to keep the pace for a long time, if necessary. Where were they going? Djemal could not smell leaves or water, and he was unfamiliar with the terrain.

Ka-pa-la-pop, ka-pa-la-pop . . . The hoof beats of the camels behind Djemal faded out of hearing. Djemal went a trifle slower. Mahmet did not whack him. Djemal heard Mahmet chuckle a little. The moon rose, and they kept on, Djemal walking now. He was a little tired. They stopped, Mahmet drank from his watersack, ate something, and bundled himself up against Djemal's side as usual. But there was no tree, no shelter where they lay that night. The land was flat and wide.

The next morning, they set off at dawn, Mahmet having had a mug of sweet coffee brewed on his spirit lamp. He switched on his transistor, and held it in the crook of his leg, which was cocked over Djemal's shoulder. Not a camel was in sight behind him. Nevertheless, Mahmet urged Djemal on at a fair pace. Judging from Djemal's firm hump behind him, he was good for four or five days more without showing any sign of flagging. Still Mahmet looked to right and left for any lines of trees, any kind of foliage that could give shelter from the sun, however brief. When noon came, they had to stop. The heat of the sun had begun to penetrate even Mahmet's turban, and sweat ran into his eyebrows. For the first time, Mahmet threw a cloth over Djemal's head to shelter it from the sun, and they rested till nearly four in the afternoon. Mahmet had no watch, but he could tell time quite well by the sun.

The next day was the same, except that Mahmet and Djemal found some trees—but no water. Mahmet knew the territory vaguely. Either he had been over it years before, or someone had told him about it, he couldn't quite remember. There was no water except at Souk Mandela, where the contestants were supposed to stop. That was a detour off the straight course, and Mahmet had no intention of stopping there. On the other hand, he thought it best to give Djemal an extra long rest at midday and to make up for this by traveling far into the night. This they did. Mahmet navigated a bit by the stars.

Djemal could have done all right for five days without water, with moderate pace and load, but Djemal was often loping. By the noonday rest of the sixth day, Djemal was feeling the strain. Mahmet mumbled the Koran. There was a wind, which blew Mahmet's coffee brewer flame out a couple of times. Djemal rested with his tail directly towards the wind, his nostrils open just enough to breathe.

It was the edge of a windstorm, not the storm itself, Mahmet saw. He patted Djemal's head briefly. Mahmet was thinking that the other camels and their drivers were in the worst of the storm, since the gloom lay in the direction of Souk Mandela to the north. Mahmet was hoping they'd all be seriously delayed.

Mahmet was wrong, as he discovered on the seventh day. This was the day they'd been supposed to finish the race. Mahmet started at dawn, when the sand was so whirling around him, he didn't bother trying to prepare coffee; instead he chewed a few coffee beans. Mahmet began to think that the storm had moved down to him, on his direct route to Khassa, and that his competitors had perhaps not done too badly by stopping at Souk Mandela for water, then resuming a direct course to Khassa, because this would put them at the northern edge of the storm, not the middle.

It was difficult for Djemal to make good progress, since he had to keep his nostrils half shut against the sand, and consequently couldn't breathe well. Mahmet, riding on his shoulders and leaning over his neck, flogged him nervously to go ever faster. Djemal sensed that Mahmet was scared. If Djemal couldn't see or smell where he was going, how could Mahmet? Was Mahmet out of water? Maybe. Djemal's right shoulder became sore, then bleeding from Mahmet's whip. It hurt worse there, which was why Mahmet didn't try the other shoulder, Djemal supposed. Djemal knew Mahmet well by now. He knew that Mahmet intended to be paid somehow for his efforts, Djemal's efforts, or Mahmet wouldn't be putting himself to such discomfort. Djemal also had a vague notion that he was in competition with the other camels he had seen at Elu-Bana, because Djemal had been forced to do other "races" in the form of running faster than other camels towards a group of tourists which Mahmet had spotted half a mile away.

"Hay-yee! Hay-yee!" Mahmet cried, bouncing up and down and wielding the whip.

At least they were getting out of the sandstorm. The pale haze of the sun could be seen now and then, still a long way above the horizon. Djemal stumbled and fell, tossing Mahmet off. Djemal got a mouthful of sand inadvertently, and would have loved to lie there for several minutes, recovering, but Mahmet flogged him up, shouting.

Mahmet had lost his transistor, and went scrambling and scuffling about for it in the sand. When he found it, he kicked Djemal hard in the rump to no immediate avail, then kicked him unmercifully in the anus, because Djemal had lain down again.

Mahmet cursed.

Djemal did likewise, blowing his breath out and baring his two formidable front teeth before he gradually hauled himself up with a slow, bitter dignity. Stupefied by heat and thirst, Djemal saw Mahmet fuzzily, and was exasperated enough to attack him, except that he was weak from fatigue. Mahmet whacked him and gave him the command to kneel. Djemal knelt, and Mahmet mounted.

They were moving again. Djemal's feet became ever heavier, and dragged in the sand. But he could now smell people. Water. Then he heard music—the ordinary wailing music of Arabian transistors, but louder, as if several were playing in unison. Mahmet whacked Djemal again and again on the shoulder, shouting encouragement. Djemal saw no reason to exert himself, since the goal was plainly in sight, but he did his best to walk fast, hoping that this would make Mahmet ease up on the whip.

"Yeh-yah!" The cheers grew louder.

Djemal's mouth was now open and dry. Just before he reached the people, his eyesight failed him. So did his leg muscles. His knees, then his side hit the sand. The hump on his back sagged limp, empty like his mouth and his stomach.

And Mahmet beat him, yelling.

The crowd both moaned and yelled. Djemal didn't care. He felt he was dying. Why didn't someone bring him water? Mahmet was now lighting matches under Djemal's heels. Djemal barely twitched. He would have bitten through Mahmet's neck with pleasure, but he hadn't the strength. Djemal lost consciousness.

With fury and resentment, Mahmet saw a camel and its driver walk across the finish line. Then another. The camels looked tired, but they were not playing dead-tired like Djemal. There was no room for pity in Mahmet's mind. Djemal had failed him. Djemal who was supposed to be so strong.

When a couple of the camel drivers jeered at Mahmet and made nasty remarks about his not having given his camel water—a fact which was obvious—Mahmet cursed them back. Mahmet threw a bucket of water on to Djemal's head, and brought him to. Then Mahmet watched, grinding his teeth, as the winner of the race (a fat old swine who had always snubbed Mahmet in Elu-Bana) received his prize in the form of a paper check. Naturally the Government wasn't going to hand out that money in cash, because it might be stolen in the crowd.

Djemal drank water that night, and ate a bit also. Mahmet did not give him food, but there were bushes and trees where they spent the night. They were on the edge of the city of Khassa. The next day, having taken on pro-visions—bread, dates and water and a couple of dry sausages for himself—Mahmet started off with Djemal across the desert again. Djemal was still a little tired and could have rested for a day with profit. Was Mahmet going to stop somewhere for water this time? Djemal hoped so. At least they weren't racing.

Near noon, when they had to rest under shade, Djemal's right front leg gave under him as he was kneeling for Mahmet to dismount. Mahmet tumbled on to the sand, then jumped up and struck Djemal a couple of times on the head with his whip handle.

"Stupid!" Mahmet shouted in Arabic.

Djemal bit at the whip and caught it. When Mahmet lunged for the whip, Djemal bit again and got Mahmet's wrist.

Mahmet shrieked.

Djemal got to his feet, inspired to further attack. How he hated this smelly little creature who considered himself his "master"!

"Aaaah! Back! Down!" Mahmet yelled, and brandished the whip, retreating.

Djemal walked steadily towards Mahmet, teeth bared, and his eyes big and red with fury. Mahmet ran and took shelter behind the bending trunk of a date tree. Djemal circled the tree. He could smell the sharp stink of Mahmet's terror.

Mahmet was snatching off his old djellaba. He pulled off his turban also, and flung both these things towards Djemal.

Surprised, Djemal bit into the smelly clothes, shaking his head as if he had his teeth in Mahmet's neck and was shaking him to death. Djemal snorted and attacked the turban, now unwound in a long dirty length. He ate part of it, and stomped his big front feet on the rest.

Mahmet, behind his tree, began to breathe more easily. He knew that camels could vent their wrath on the clothes of the man they hated, and that was the end of it. He hoped so. He didn't fancy walking back to Khassa. He wanted to go to Elu-Bana, which he considered "home."

Djemal at last lay down. He was tired, almost too tired to bother putting himself in the patchy shade under the date tree. He slept.

Mahmet prodded him awake, carefully. The sun was setting. Djemal nipped at him, missing. Mahmet thought it wise to ignore it.

"Up, Djemal! Up—and we go!" said Mahmet.

Djemal plodded. He plodded on into the night, feeling the faint trail more than seeing it in the sand. The night was cool.

On the third day, they arrived at Souk Mandela, a busy market town, though small. Mahmet had decided to sell Djemal here. So he made for the open market where braziers, rugs, jewelry, camel saddles, pots and pans, hairpins and just about everything was for sale and on display on the ground. Camels were for sale too, at one corner. He led Djemal there, walking himself and being careful to look over his shoulder and to walk far enough ahead so that Djemal would not bite him.

"Cheap," Mahmet said to the dealer. "Six hundred dinars. He's a fine camel, you can see that. And he just won the Elu-Bana to Khassa race!"

"Oh yes? That's not the way we heard it!" said a turbaned camel driver who was listening, and a couple of others laughed. "He collapsed!"

"Yes, we heard you didn't stop for water, you crooked old bastard!" said someone else.

"Even so—" Mahmet began, and dodged as Djemal's teeth came at him.

"Ha! Ha! Even his camel doesn't like this one!" said one old beard.

"Three hundred!" Mahmet screamed. "With the saddle!"

A man pointed to Djemal's beaten shoulder, which was still bloody and on which flies had settled, as if it were a serious and permanent defect, and proposed two hundred and fifty dinars.

Mahmet accepted. Cash. The man had to go home to get it. Mahmet waited sullenly in some shade, watching the dealer and another man leading Djemal to the market water trough. He had lost a good camel—lost money, even more painful—but Mahmet was damned glad to be rid of Djemal. His life was worth more than money, after all.

That afternoon, Mahmet caught an uncomfortable bus to Elu-Bana. He was carrying his gear, empty watersacks, spirit lamp, cooking pot and blanket. He slept like the dead in an alley behind the restaurant where he often ate couscous. The next morning, with a clear vision of his bad luck, and the stinging memory of the low price he had got for one of the best camels in the country, Mahmet pilfered one of the tourists' cars. He got a plaid blanket and a bonus beneath it—a camera—a silver flask from the glove compartment, and a brown-paper-wrapped parcel which contained a small rug evidently just bought in the market. This theft took less than a minute, because the car was unlocked. It was in front of a shabby bar, and a couple of barefoot adolescent boys sitting at a table in the sand merely laughed when they saw Mahmet doing it.

Mahmet sold his loot before noon for seventy dinars (the camera was a good German one) which made him feel slightly better. With his own cache of dinars which he carried with him, sewn into a fold of blanket, Mahmet now had nearly five hundred. He could buy another camel of sorts, not as good as Djemal who had cost him four hundred dinars. And he would have enough to put something down on the house he wanted. The tourist season was on, and Mahmet needed a camel to earn money, because camel driving was the only thing he knew.

Meanwhile, Djemal had fallen into good hands. A poor but decent man called Chak had bought him to add to his string of three. Chak mainly hauled lemons and oranges and did other kinds of transport work with his camels, but in the tourist season, he gave camel rides too. Chak was delighted with Djemal's grace and willingness with the tourists. Because Djemal was so tall, he was often preferred by the tourists who wanted "a view."

Djemal was now quite healed of his sore shoulder, well fed, not over-worked, and very content with his new master and his life. His memory of Mahmet was growing dimmer, because he never encountered him for one thing. Elu-Bana had many routes in and out of it. Djemal often worked miles away, and Chak's home was a few miles outside of town; there Djemal slept with the other camels under a shelter near the house where Chak lived with his family.

One day in early autumn, when the weather was a trifle cooler and most of the tourists had gone, Djemal picked up the scent of Mahmet. Djemal was just then entering the big fruit market in Elu-Bana, carrying a heavy load of grapefruit. Huge trucks were being loaded with boxes of dates and pineapples, and the scene was noisy with men talking and yelling and transistors everywhere blaring different programs. Djemal didn't see Mahmet, but the hair on his neck rose a little, and he expected a blow out of nowhere. He knelt at Chak's command, and the burdens slipped from his sides.

Then he saw Mahmet just a camel's length in front of him. Djemal got to his feet. Mahmet saw Djemal also, took a second or two to make sure he was Djemal, then Mahmet jumped and stepped back. He pushed some paper dinars into his djellaba somewhere.

"So—your old camel, eh?" another camel driver said to Mahmet, jerking a thumb towards Djemal. "Still afraid of him, Mahmet?"

"I never was afraid of him!" Mahmet came back.

"Ha-ha!"

A couple of other drivers joined the conversation.

Djemal saw Mahmet twitch, shrug his shoulders, talking all the while.

Djemal could smell him well, and his hatred rose afresh. Djemal moved towards Mahmet.

"Ha! Ha! Watch out, Mahmet!" laughed a turbaned driver, who was a little drunk on wine.

Mahmet retreated.

Djemal followed, walking. He continued to walk, even though he heard Chak calling him. Then Djemal broke into a lope, as Mahmet vanished behind a truck. When Djemal reached the truck, Mahmet darted towards a small house, a shed of some kind for the market drivers.

To Mahmet's horror, the shed door was locked. He ran behind the shed.

Djemal bore down and seized Mahmet's djellaba and part of his spine in his teeth. Mahmet fell, and Djemal stomped him, stomped him again on the head.

"Look! It's a fight!"

"The old bastard deserves it!" cried someone.

A dozen men, then twenty gathered around to watch, laughing, at first urging one another to go in and put a stop to it—but nobody did. On the contrary, someone passed a jug of red wine around.

Mahmet screamed. Djemal now came down with a foot in the middle of Mahmet's back. Then it was over really. Mahmet stopped moving, anyway. Djemal, just getting his strength up for the task, bit through the exposed calf of Mahmet's left leg.

The crowd howled. They were safe, the camel wasn't going to attack *them,* and to a man they detested Mahmet, who was not only stingy but downright dishonest, even with people whom he led to think were his friends.

"What a camel! What's his name?"

"Djemal! Ha-ha!"

"Used to be Mahmet's camel!" someone repeated, as if the whole crowd didn't know that.

At last Chak burst through. "Djemal! Ho! Stop, Djemal!"

"Let him have his revenge!" someone yelled.

"This is terrible!" cried Chak.

The men surrounded Chak, telling him it wasn't terrible, telling him they would get rid of the body, somewhere. No, no, no, there was no need to call the police. Absurd! Have some wine, Chak! Even some of the truck drivers had joined them, smiling with sinister amusement at what had happened behind the shed.

Djemal, head high now, had begun to calm down. He could smell blood along with the stench of Mahmet. Haughtily he stepped over his victim, lifting each foot carefully, and rejoined his master Chak. Chak was still nervous.

"No, no," Chak was saying, because the men, all a bit tipsy now, were offering Chak seven hundred and more dinars for Djemal. Chak was shaken by the events, but at the same time he was proud of Djemal, and wouldn't have parted with him for a thousand dinars at that moment.

Djemal smiled. He lifted his head and looked coolly through his long-lashed eyes towards the horizon. Men patted his flanks, his shoulders. Mahmet was dead. His anger, like a poison, was out of his blood. Djemal followed Chak, without a lead, as Chak walked away, looking back and calling to him.

There I Was,
Stuck with Bubsy

Yes, here he was, stuck with Bubsy, a fate no living creature deserved. The
Baron, aged sixteen—seventeen?—anyway aged, felt doomed to spend
his last days with this plump, abhorrent beast whom the Baron had detested
almost since he had appeared on the scene at least ten or twelve years ago.
Doomed unless something happened. But what would happen, and what
could the Baron make happen? The Baron racked his brain. People had said
since he was a pup that his intelligence was extraordinary. The Baron took
some comfort in that. It was a matter of strengthening Marion's hand, difficult for a dog to do, since the Baron didn't speak, though many a time his
master Eddie had told him that he did speak. That was because Eddie had
understood every bark and growl and glance that the Baron ever gave.

The Baron lay on a tufted polka-dot cushion which lined his basket.
The basket had an arched top, and even this was lined with tufted polka-
dot. From the next room, the Baron could hear laughter, jumbled voices,
the *clink* of a glass or bottle now and then, and Bubsy's occasional "Haw-
ha-*haw*!" which in the days after Eddie's death had made the Baron's ears
twitch with hostility. Now the Baron no longer reacted to Bubsy's guffaws.
On the contrary, the Baron affected a languor, an unconcern (better for his
nerves), and now he yawned mightily, showing yellowed lower canines,
then he settled his chin on his paws. He wanted to pee. He'd gone into the
noisy living room ten minutes ago and indicated to Bubsy by approaching
the door of the apartment that he wanted to go out. But Bubsy had not
troubled himself, though one of the young men (the Baron was almost
sure) had offered to take him downstairs. The Baron got up suddenly. He
couldn't wait any longer. He could of course pee straight on the carpet
with a damn-it-all attitude, but he still had some decency left.

The Baron tried the living room again. Tonight there was more than usually a sprinkling of women.

"O-o-o-oh!"

"Ah-h-h! There's the Baron!"

"Ah, the Baron!" said Bubsy.

"He wants to go out, Bubsy, for Christ's sake! Where's his leash?"

"I've just had him out!" shrieked Bubsy, lying.

"When? This morning? . . ."

A young man in thick, fuzzy tweed trousers took the Baron down in the elevator. The Baron made for the first tree at the curb, and lifted a leg slightly. The young man talked to him in a friendly way, and said something about "Eddie." The name of his master made the Baron briefly sad, though he supposed it was nice of people, total strangers, to remember his master. They walked around the block. Near the delicatessen on Lexington Avenue, a man stopped them and in a polite tone asked a question with "the Baron" in it.

"Yes," said the young man who held the Baron's leash.

The strange man patted the Baron's head gently, and the Baron recognized his master's other name "Brockhurst . . . Edward Brockhurst . . ."

They went on, back towards the awning of the apartment house, towards the awful party. Then the Baron's ears picked up a tread he knew, then his nose a scent he knew: Marion.

"Hello! Excuse me . . ." She was closer than the Baron had supposed, because his ears were not what they used to be, nor his eyes for that matter. She talked with the young man, and they all rode up in the elevator.

The Baron's heart was pounding with pleasure. Marion smelled nice. Suddenly the whole evening was better, even wonderful, just because Marion had turned up. His master had always loved Marion. And the Baron was well aware that Marion wanted to take him away to live with her.

There was quite a change in the atmosphere when the Baron and the young man and Marion walked in. The conversation died down, and Bubsy walked forward with a glass of his favorite bubble in his hand, champagne. The young man undid the Baron's leash.

"Good evening, Bubsy . . ." Marion was speaking politely, explaining something.

Some people had said hello to Marion, others were starting up their conversation again in little groups. The Baron kept his eyes on Marion. Could it be possible that she was going to take him away *tonight*? She was talking about him. And Bubsy looked flustered. He motioned for Marion to come into one of the other rooms, Bubsy's bedroom, and the Baron followed at Marion's heels. Bubsy would have shut the Baron out, but Marion held the door.

"Come in, Baron!" Marion said.

The Baron disliked this room. The bed was high, made higher still by pillows, and at the foot of it was the contraption Bubsy used when he had his fits of wheezing and gasping, usually at night. There were two chromium tanks from which a rubber pipe came out, flexible metal pipes also, and the whole thing could be wheeled up to Bubsy's pillows.

"...friend...vacation..." Marion was saying. She was pleading with Bubsy. The Baron heard his name two or three times, Eddie's name once, and Bubsy looked at the Baron with the angry, stubborn expression that the Baron knew well, knew since years, even when Eddie had been alive.

"Well, no..." Bubsy went on, making quite an elaborate speech.

Marion began again, not in the least discouraged.

Bubsy coughed, and his face darkened a little. He repeated his "No... no..."

Marion dropped on her knees and looked into the Baron's eyes and talked to him. The Baron wagged his cropped tail. He trembled with joy, and could have flung his paws up on Marion's shoulders, but he didn't, because it was not the right thing to do. But his front paws kept dancing off the floor. He felt years younger.

Then Marion began talking about Eddie, and she grew angrier. She drew herself up a little when she talked about Eddie, as if he were something to be proud of, and it was evident to the Baron that she thought, she might even be saying, that Bubsy wasn't worth as much. The Baron knew that his master had been someone of importance. Strangers, coming to the house now and then, had treated Eddie as if he were their master, in a way, in those days when they had lived in another apartment, and Bubsy had served the drinks and cooked the meals like one of the servants on the ships the Baron had traveled on, or in the hotels where the Baron had stayed. Now suddenly Bubsy was claiming the Baron as his own dog. That was what it amounted to.

Bubsy kept saying "No" in an increasingly firm voice. He walked towards the door.

Marion said something in a quietly threatening tone. The Baron wished very much that he knew exactly what she had said. The Baron followed her through the living room towards the front door. He was prepared to sneak out with her, leap out leashless, and just stay with her.

Marion paused to talk with the young man in the fuzzy tweed trousers who had come up to her.

Bubsy interrupted them, waving his hands, wanting to put an end to the conversation.

Marion said, "Good night . . . good night . . ."

The Baron squeezed out with her, loped in the hall towards the elevators. A man laughed, not Bubsy.

"Baron, you can't . . . darling," said Marion.

Someone caught the Baron by the collar. The Baron growled, but he knew he couldn't win, that someone would give him a warning slap, if he didn't do what *they* wanted. Behind him, the Baron heard the awful *clunk* that meant the elevator door had closed on Marion, and she was gone. Some people groaned as the Baron crossed the living room, others laughed, as the din began again, louder and merrier than ever. The Baron made straight for his master's room which was across the hall from Bubsy's. The door was closed, but the Baron could open it by the horizontal handle, providing the door wasn't locked. The Baron couldn't manage the key, which stuck out below the handle, though he had often tried. Now the door opened. Bubsy had perhaps been showing the room to some of his guests tonight. The Baron went in and took a breath of the air that still smelled faintly of his master's pipe tobacco. On the big desk was his master's typewriter, now covered with a cloth of a sort of polka-dot pattern like the lining of his basket-bed in the spare room. The Baron was just as happy, even happier, sleeping on the carpet here near the desk, as he had often done when his master worked, but Bubsy, nastily, usually kept the door of his master's room locked.

The Baron curled up on the carpet and put his head down, his nose almost touching a leg of his master's chair. He sighed, suddenly worn out by the emotions of the last ten minutes. He thought of Marion, recalled happy mornings when Marion had come to visit, and his master and Bubsy had cooked bacon and eggs, or hotcakes, and they had all gone for a walk in Central Park. The Baron had used to retrieve sticks that Marion threw into a lake there. And he remembered an especially happy cruise, sunlight on the decks, with his master and Marion (pre-Bubsy days), when the Baron had been young and spry and handsome, popular with the passengers, pampered by the stewards who brought whole steaks to his and Eddie's cabin. The Baron remembered walks in a white-walled town full of white houses, with smells he had never known before or since . . . And a boat ride with the boat tossing, and spray in his face, to an island where the streets were paved with cobblestones, where he got to know the whole island and roamed where he wished. He heard again his master's voice talking calmly to him, asking him a question . . . The Baron heard the ghostly click of the typewriter . . . Then he fell asleep.

He awakened to Bubsy's coughing, then his strained intake of air, with a wheeze. The house was quiet now. Bubsy was walking about in his room. The Baron got to his feet and shook himself to wake up. He went out of the room, so as not to be locked in for the rest of the night, walked towards the living room, but the smell of cigarette smoke turned him back. The Baron went into the kitchen, drank some water from his bowl, sniffed at the remains of some tinned dog food, and turned away, heading for the spare room. He could have eaten something—a bit of leftover steak, or a lambchop bone would have been nice. Lately, Bubsy dined out a lot, didn't take the Baron with him, and Bubsy fed him mostly from tins. Now his master would have put a stop to that! The Baron curled up in his basket.

Bubsy's machine was buzzing. Now and again it made a *click-click* sound. Bubsy blew his nose—a sign he was feeling better.

Bubsy didn't go to work, didn't work at all in the sense that Eddie had worked several hours a day at his typewriter, in some periods every day of the week. Bubsy got up in midmorning, made tea and toast, and sat in his silk dressing gown reading the newspaper which was still delivered every morning at the door. It would be nearly noon before Bubsy took the Baron out for a walk. By this time Bubsy would have telephoned at least twice, and then he would go out for a long lunch, perhaps, or anyway he seldom came back before late afternoon. Bubsy had used to have something to do with the theater, just what the Baron didn't know. But when his master had met Bubsy, they had visited him a couple of times in the busy backstage part of a New York theater. Bubsy had been nicer then, the Baron could remember quite well, always ready to take him out for a walk, to brush his ears and the clump of curly black hair on the top of his head, because Bubsy had been proud to show him off on the street in those days. Yes, and the Baron had won a prize or two at Madison Square Garden in his prime, so many years ago. Oh, happy days! His two silver cups and two or three medals occupied a place of honor on a bookshelf in the living room, but the maid hadn't polished them in weeks now. Eddie had shown them sometimes to people who came to the apartment, and a couple of times, laughing, Eddie had served the Baron his morning biscuits and milk in one of the cups. The Baron recalled that at the moment there were no biscuits in the house.

Why did Bubsy hang on to him, if he didn't really like him? The Baron suspected it was because Bubsy was thus able to hang on to his master, who had been a more important man—which meant loved and respected by a lot more people—than Bubsy. In the awful days during his master's illness, and after his death, the person the Baron had clung to was Marion, not Bubsy. The Baron thought that his master wished, probably had made it clear, that he wanted the Baron to live with Marion after he died. Bubsy had always been jealous of the Baron, and the Baron had to admit that he had been jealous of Bubsy. But whether he lived with Bubsy or Marion, that was what the fight was about. He was no fool. Marion and Bubsy had been fighting ever since Eddie's death.

Down on the street, a car rattled over a manhole. From Bubsy's room, the Baron heard wheezing inhalations. The machine was unplugged now. The Baron was thirsty, thought of getting up to drink again, then felt too tired, and merely flicked his tongue over his nose and closed his eyes. A tooth was hurting. Old age was a terrible thing. He'd had two wives, so long ago he scarcely remembered them. He'd had many children, maybe twelve, and the pictures of several of them were in the living room, and one on his master's desk—the Baron with three of his offspring.

The Baron woke up, growling, from a bad dream. He looked around, dazed, in the darkness. It had *happened*. No, it was a dream. But it had happened, yes. Just a few days ago. Bubsy had waked him from a nap, leash in hand, to take him out, and the Baron—maybe ill-tempered at that moment because he'd been awakened—had growled in an ominous way, not raising his head. And Bubsy had slowly retreated. And later that day, again with the leash in his hand, doubled, Bubsy had reminded the Baron of his bad behavior and slashed the air with the leash. The Baron had not winced, only watched Bubsy with a cool contempt. So they had stared at each other, and nothing had come of it, but Bubsy had been the first to move.

Would he be able to get anywhere by fighting? The Baron's old muscles grew tense at the thought. But he couldn't figure it out, couldn't see clearly into the future, and soon he was asleep again.

In the evening of that day, the Baron was surprised by a delicious meal of raw steak cut into convenient pieces, followed by a walk during which Bubsy talked to him in amiable tones. Then they got into a taxi. They rode quite a distance. Could they be going to Marion's apartment? Her apartment was a long way away, the Baron remembered from the days when Eddie had been alive. But Bubsy never went to Marion's house. Then when the taxi stopped and they got out, the Baron recognized the butcher's shop, still open, that smelled of spices as well as meat. They *were* at Marion's building! The Baron's tail began to wag. He lifted his head higher, and led Bubsy to the right door.

Bubsy pushed a bell, the door buzzed, then they went in and climbed three flights, the Baron pulling Bubsy up, panting, happy.

Marion opened the door. The Baron stood on his hind legs, careful not to scratch her dress with his nails, and Marion took his paws.

"Hello, Baron! Hel-*lo,* hello!—Come in!"

Marion's apartment had a high ceiling and smelled of oil paint and turpentine. There were big comfortable sofas and chairs which the Baron knew he was allowed to lie on if he wished to. Now there was a strange man who stood up from a chair as they went in. Marion introduced Bubsy to him, and they shook hands. The men talked. Marion went into the kitchen and poured a bowl of milk for the Baron, and gave him a steak bone which had been wrapped in wax paper in the refrigerator. Marion said something which the Baron took to mean, "Make yourself at home. Chew the bone anywhere."

The Baron chose to chew it at Marion's feet, once she had sat down in a chair.

The conversation grew more heated. Bubsy whipped some papers out of his pocket, and now he was on his feet, his face pinker, his thin blond curls tossing.

"There is not a *thing* . . . No . . . *No.*"

Bubsy's favorite word, "No."

"That is not the *point,*" Marion said.

Then the other man said something more calmly than either Marion or Bubsy. The Baron chewed on his bone, sparing the sore tooth. The strange man made quite a long speech, which Bubsy interrupted a couple of times, but Bubsy finally stopped talking and listened. Marion was very tense.

"No . . . ?"

"No . . . now . . ."

That was a word the Baron knew. He looked up at Marion, whose face was a little flushed also, but nothing like Bubsy's. Only the other man was calm. He had papers in his hand, too. What was going to happen *now?* The Baron associated the word with rather important commands to himself.

Bubsy spread his hands palm down and said, *"No."* And many more words.

A very few minutes later, the Baron's leash was attached to his collar and he was dragged—gently but still dragged—towards the door by Bubsy. The Baron braced all four feet when he realized what was happening. He didn't want to go! He'd hardly begun to visit with Marion. The Baron looked over his shoulder and pled for her assistance. The strange man shook his head and lit a cigarette. Bubsy and Marion were talking to each other at the same time, almost shouting. Marion clenched her fists. But she opened one hand to pat the Baron, and said something kind to him before he was out in the hall, and the door shut.

Bubsy and the Baron crossed a wide street, and entered a bar. Loud music, awful smells, except for a whiff of freshly broiled steak. Bubsy drank, and twice muttered to himself.

Then he yanked the Baron into a taxi, yanked him because the Baron missed his footing and sprawled in an undignified way, banging his jaw on the floor of the taxi. Bubsy was in the foulest of moods. And the Baron's heart was pounding with several emotions: outrage, regret he had not spent longer with Marion, hatred of Bubsy. The Baron glanced at the windows (both nearly closed) as if he might jump out of one of them, though Bubsy had the leash wrapped twice around his wrist, and the buildings on either side flashed by at great speed. Bubsy let out the leash a little for the benefit of the doormen who always greeted the Baron by name. Bubsy was so out of breath, he could hardly speak to the doormen. The Baron knew he was suffering, but had no pity for him.

In the apartment, Bubsy at once flopped into a chair, mouth open. The Baron's leash trailed, and he walked dismally down the hall, hesitated at his master's door, then went in. He collapsed on the carpet by the chair. Back again. How brief had been his pleasure at Marion's! He heard Bubsy struggling to breathe, undressing in his room now—or at least removing his jacket and whipping off his tie. Then the Baron heard the machine being plugged in. *Buzz-zz . . . Click-click.* The groan of a chair. Bubsy was doubtless in the chair by his bed, holding the mask over his face.

Thirsty, the Baron got up to go to the kitchen. His leash, the hand loop part of it, caught under the door and checked him. The Baron patiently entered the room again, pulled the leash out, and went out with his shoulder near the right door jamb so the same accident wouldn't happen again. It reminded him of nasty tricks Bubsy had used to play when the Baron had been younger. Of course the Baron had played a few tricks, too, tripping Bubsy adroitly while he (the Baron) had been ostensibly only cavorting after a ball. Now the Baron was so tired, his hind legs ached and he limped. Several teeth were hurting. He had chewed too enthusiastically on that bone. The Baron drank all his bowl—it was only half full and stale—then on leaving the kitchen, the Baron caught his leash in the same manner under the kitchen door. Bubsy just then lurched out of his room, coughing, heading for the bathroom, and stepped hard on the Baron's front paw. The Baron gave an agonized cry, because it had really hurt, nearly broken his toes!

Bubsy kicked at him and cursed.

The Baron—as if a mysterious spring had been released—leapt and sank his teeth through Bubsy's trousers into his lower leg.

Bubsy screamed, and swatted the Baron on the head with his fist. This made the Baron turn loose, and Bubsy kicked at him again, missing. Bubsy was gasping. The Baron watched Bubsy go into the bathroom, knowing he was going to get a wet towel for his face.

The Baron was suddenly full of energy. Where had it come from? He stood with forelegs apart, his aching teeth bared, trapped by his leash which was stuck under the kitchen door. When Bubsy emerged with the dripping towel clamped against his forehead, the Baron growled his deepest. Bubsy stumbled past him into his room, and the Baron heard him flop on the bed. Then the Baron went back into the kitchen slowly, so as not to make his leash predicament worse. The leather was tightly wedged this time, and there was not enough space, if the Baron moved towards the sink, to tug it out. The Baron caught the leash in his back teeth and pulled. The leash slipped through his teeth. He tried the other side of his jaw, and with one yank freed the leash. This was the worse side of his jaw, and the pain was awful. The Baron cringed on the floor, eyes shut for a moment, as he would never have cringed before Bubsy or anyone else. But pain was pain. Terrible. The Baron's very ears seemed to ring with his agony, but he didn't whine. He was remembering a similar pain inflicted by Bubsy. Or was that true? At any rate, the pain reminded him of Bubsy.

As the pain subsided, the Baron stood up, on guard against Bubsy who might come to life at any moment. The Baron carefully walked towards the living room, dragging his leash straight behind him, then turned so that he was facing the hall. He sank down and put his chin on his paws and waited, listening, his eyes wide open.

Bubsy coughed, the kind of cough that meant the mask was off and he was feeling better. Bubsy was getting up. He was going to come into the living room for some champagne, probably. The Baron's hind legs grew tense, and he really might have moved out of the way if not for a fear in the back of his mind that his leash would catch on something again. Bubsy approached coughing, pushing himself straight with a hand against a wall. Bubsy made a menacing gesture with his other hand, and ordered the Baron to get out of the way.

The Baron expected a foot in his face, and without thinking hurled himself at Bubsy's waistline and bit. Bubsy came down with a fist on the Baron's spine. They struggled on the floor, Bubsy hitting and missing most of his blows, the Baron snapping and missing also. But the Baron was still on the living room side, and Bubsy retreated towards his room, the Baron after him. Bubsy grabbed a vase, and hit the Baron on top of the head. The Baron's sight was knocked out, and he saw only silvery lights for a few seconds. As soon as his vision came back a little, he leapt for Bubsy whose legs now dangled over the side of the bed.

The Baron fell short, and his teeth clamped the rubber tube, not Bubsy's leg. The Baron bit and shook his head. The tube seemed as much Bubsy and Bubsy's own flesh. Bubsy loved that tube, depended on it, and the thick rubber was yielding slowly, just like flesh. Bubsy, with the mask over his face, kicked at the Baron, missing. Then the tube broke in two and the Baron slid to the floor.

Bubsy groped for the other end of the tube, started to put it in his mouth, but the end was frayed and full of holes. Bubsy gave it up, and lay back on the bed, panting like a dog himself. Blood was trickling through the hair above the Baron's eyes. The Baron staggered towards the door and turned, his tongue hanging out, his heartbeats shaking his body. The Baron lay down on the floor, and his eyes glazed over until he could hardly see the bed and Bubsy's legs over the side, but the Baron kept his eyes open. The minutes passed. The Baron's breathing grew easier. He listened, and he could not hear anything. Was Bubsy asleep?

The Baron half-slept, instinctively saving every bit of strength that he had left. The Baron heard no sound from Bubsy, and finally the hackles on the Baron's neck told him that he was in the presence of something dead.

At dawn, the Baron withdrew from the room, and like a very old dog, head hanging, legs wobbling, made his way to the living room. He lay on his side, more tired than ever. Soon the telephone began to ring. The Baron barely lifted his head at the first ring, then paid no more attention. The telephone stopped, then rang again. This happened several times. The top of the Baron's head throbbed.

The woman who cleaned the apartment twice a week arrived in the afternoon—the Baron recognized her step in the hall—and rang the bell, although she had a key, the Baron knew. At the same time, another elevator opened its door, and some steps sounded in the hall, then voices. The apartment door opened, and the maid whose name was something like Lisa entered with two men friends of Bubsy's. They all seemed surprised to see the Baron standing in the living room with his leash on. They were shocked by the patch of blood on the carpet, and the Baron was reminded vaguely of the first months of his life, when he had made what his master called mistakes in the house.

"Bubsy!"

"Bubsy, are you here?"

They found Bubsy in the next seconds. One man rushed back into the living room and picked up the telephone. This man the Baron recognized as the one who had worn fuzzy trousers and had aired him at Bubsy's last party. No one paid any attention to the Baron, but when the Baron went into the kitchen, he saw that Lisa had put down some food for him and filled his water bowl. The Baron drank a little. Lisa undid his leash and said something kind to him. Another man arrived, a stranger. He went into Bubsy's bedroom. Then he looked at the Baron but didn't touch him, and he looked at the blood on the carpet. Then two men in white suits arrived and Bubsy was carried out, wrapped in a blanket, on a stretcher—just as his master had been carried out, the Baron recalled, but his master had been alive. Now the Baron felt no emotion at all on seeing Bubsy depart in the same manner. The young man made another telephone call. The Baron heard the name Marion, and his ears pricked up.

Then the man put the telephone down, and he smiled at the Baron in a funny way: it was not really a happy smile. What was the man thinking of? He put the Baron's leash on. They went downstairs and took a taxi. Then they went into an office which the Baron knew at once was a vet's. The vet jabbed a needle into him. When the Baron woke up, he was lying on his side on a different table, and he tried to stand up, couldn't quite, and then he threw up the bit of water he had drunk. The friend of Bubsy's was still with him, and carried the Baron out, and they got into another taxi.

The Baron revived in the breeze through the window. The Baron took more interest as the ride went on and on. Could they possibly be going to Marion's?

They were! The taxi stopped. There was the butcher's shop again. And there was Marion on the sidewalk outside her door! The Baron wriggled from the man's arms and fell on the sidewalk outside the cab. Silly! Embarrassing! But the Baron got on his wobbly legs again, and was able to greet Marion with tail wagging, with a lick of her hand.

"Oh, Baron! Old Baron!" she said. And the Baron knew she was saying something reassuring about the cut on his head (now bandaged, the bandage going under his chin, too), which the Baron knew was not serious, was quite unimportant compared to the fact that he was with Marion, that he was going to stay with Marion, the Baron somehow felt sure. Marion and the man were talking—and sure enough, the man was taking his leave. He patted the Baron on the shoulder and said, "Bye-bye, Baron," but in a tone that was merely polite. After all, he was more a friend of Bubsy's than the Baron's. The Baron lifted his head, gave a lick of his tongue towards the man's hand, and missed.

Then Marion and the Baron walked into the butcher's shop. The butcher smiled and shook the Baron's paw, and said something about his head. The butcher cut a steak for Marion.

Marion and the Baron climbed the stairs, Marion going slowly for the Baron's sake. She opened the door into the apartment with the high ceiling, with the sharp smell of turpentine that he had come to love. The Baron ate a bit of steak, and then had a sleep on one of the big sofas. He woke up and blinked his eyes. He'd just had a dream, a not so nice dream about Bubsy and a lot of noisy people, but he had already forgotten the dream. *This* was real: Marion standing at her worktable, glancing at him now because he had raised his head, but gazing back at her work—because for the moment she was thinking more about her work than about him. Like Eddie, the Baron thought. The Baron put his head down again and watched Marion. He was old, he knew, very old. People even marveled about how old he was. But he sensed that he was going to have a second life, that he even had a fair amount of time before him.

Ming's Biggest Prey

Ming was resting comfortably on the foot of his mistress's bunk, when the man picked him up by the back of the neck, stuck him out on the deck and closed the cabin door. Ming's blue eyes widened in shock and brief anger, then nearly closed again because of the brilliant sunlight. It was not the first time Ming had been thrust out of the cabin rudely, and Ming realized that the man did it when his mistress, Elaine, was not looking.

The sailboat now offered no shelter from the sun, but Ming was not yet too warm. He leapt easily to the cabin roof and stepped on to the coil of rope just behind the mast. Ming liked the rope coil as a couch, because he could see everything from the height, the cup shape of the rope protected him from strong breezes, and also minimized the swaying and sudden changes of angle of the *White Lark,* since it was more or less the center point. But just now the sail had been taken down, because Elaine and the man had eaten lunch, and often they had a siesta afterward, during which time, Ming knew, that the man didn't like him in the cabin. Lunchtime was all right. In fact, Ming had just lunched on delicious grilled fish and a bit of lobster. Now, lying in a relaxed curve on the coil of rope, Ming opened his mouth in a great yawn, then with his slant eyes almost closed against the strong sunlight, gazed at the beige hills and the white and pink houses and hotels that circled the bay of Acapulco. Between the *White Lark* and the shore where people plashed inaudibly, the sun twinkled on the water's surface like thousands of tiny electric lights going on and off. A water-skier went by, skimming up white spray behind him. Such activity! Ming half dozed, feeling the heat of the sun sink into his fur. Ming was from New York, and he considered Acapulco a great improvement over his environment in the first weeks of his life. He remembered a sunless box with straw on the bottom, three or four other kittens in with him, and a window behind which giant forms paused for a few moments, tried to catch his attention by tapping, then passed on. He did not remember his mother at all. One day a young woman who smelled of something pleasant came into the place and took him away—away from the ugly, frightening smell of dogs, of medicine and parrot dung. Then they went on what Ming now knew was an airplane. He was quite used to airplanes now and rather liked them. On airplanes he sat on Elaine's lap, or slept on her lap, and there were always tidbits to eat if he was hungry.

Elaine spent much of the day in a shop in Acapulco, where dresses and slacks and bathing suits hung on all the walls. This place smelled clean and fresh, there were flowers in pots and in boxes out front, and the floor was of cool blue and white tile. Ming had perfect freedom to wander out into the patio behind the shop, or to sleep in his basket in a corner. There was more sunlight in front of the shop, but mischievous boys often tried to grab him if he sat in front, and Ming could never relax there.

Ming liked best lying in the sun with his mistress on one of the long canvas chairs on their terrace at home. What Ming did not like were the people she sometimes invited to their house, people who spent the night, people by the score who stayed up very late eating and drinking, playing the gramophone or the piano—people who separated him from Elaine. People who stepped on his toes, people who sometimes picked him up from behind before he could do anything about it, so that he had to squirm and fight to get free, people who stroked him roughly, people who closed a door somewhere, locking him in. *People!* Ming detested people. In all the world, he liked only Elaine. Elaine loved him and understood him.

Especially this man called Teddie Ming detested now. Teddie was around all the time lately. Ming did not like the way Teddie looked at him, when Elaine was not watching. And sometimes Teddie, when Elaine was not near, muttered something which Ming knew was a threat. Or a command to leave the room. Ming took it calmly. Dignity was to be preserved. Besides, wasn't his mistress on his side? The man was the intruder. When Elaine was watching, the man sometimes pretended a fondness for him, but Ming always moved gracefully but unmistakably in another direction.

Ming's nap was interrupted by the sound of the cabin door opening. He heard Elaine and the man laughing and talking. The big red-orange sun was near the horizon.

"Ming!" Elaine came over to him. "Aren't you getting *cooked*, darling? I thought you were *in!*"

"So did I!" said Teddie.

Ming purred as he always did when he awakened. She picked him up gently, cradled him in her arms, and took him below into the suddenly cool shade of the cabin. She was talking to the man, and not in a gentle tone. She set Ming down in front of his dish of water, and though he was not thirsty, he drank a little to please her. Ming did feel addled by the heat, and he staggered a little.

Elaine took a wet towel and wiped Ming's face, his ears and his four paws. Then she laid him gently on the bunk that smelled of Elaine's perfume but also of the man whom Ming detested.

Now his mistress and the man were quarreling, Ming could tell from the tone. Elaine was staying with Ming, sitting on the edge of the bunk. Ming at last heard the splash that meant Teddie had dived into the water. Ming hoped he stayed there, hoped he drowned, hoped he never came back. Elaine wet a bathtowel in the aluminum sink, wrung it out, spread it on the bunk, and lifted Ming on to it. She brought water, and now Ming was thirsty, and drank. She left him to sleep again while she washed and put away the dishes. These were comfortable sounds that Ming liked to hear.

But soon there was another *plash* and *plop,* Teddie's wet feet on the deck, and Ming was awake again.

The tone of quarreling recommenced. Elaine went up the few steps on to the deck. Ming, tense but with his chin still resting on the moist bathtowel, kept his eyes on the cabin door. It was Teddie's feet that he heard descending. Ming lifted his head slightly, aware that there was no exit behind him, that he was trapped in the cabin. The man paused with a towel in his hands, staring at Ming.

Ming relaxed completely, as he might do preparatory to a yawn, and this caused his eyes to cross. Ming then let his tongue slide a little way out of his mouth. The man started to say something, looked as if he wanted to hurl the wadded towel at Ming, but he wavered, whatever he had been going to say never got out of his mouth, and he threw the towel in the sink, then bent to wash his face. It was not the first time Ming had let his tongue slide out at Teddie. Lots of people laughed when Ming did this, if they were people at a party, for instance, and Ming rather enjoyed that. But Ming sensed that Teddie took it as a hostile gesture of some kind, which was why Ming did it deliberately to Teddie, whereas among other people, it was often an accident when Ming's tongue slid out.

The quarreling continued. Elaine made coffee. Ming began to feel better, and went on deck again, because the sun had now set. Elaine had started the motor, and they were gliding slowly towards the shore. Ming caught the song of birds, the odd screams, like shrill phrases, of certain birds that cried only at sunset. Ming looked forward to the adobe house on the cliff that was his and his mistress's home. He knew that the reason she did not leave him at home (where he would have been more comfortable) when she went on the boat, was because she was afraid that people might trap him, even kill him. Ming understood. People had tried to grab him from almost under Elaine's eyes. Once he had been suddenly hauled away in a cloth bag, and though fighting as hard as he could, he was not sure he would have been able to get out, if Elaine had not hit the boy herself and grabbed the bag from him.

Ming had intended to jump up on the cabin roof again, but after glancing at it, he decided to save his strength, so he crouched on the warm, gently sloping deck with his feet tucked in, and gazed at the approaching shore. Now he could hear guitar music from the beach. The voices of his mistress and the man had come to a halt. For a few moments, the loudest sound was the *chug-chug-chug* of the boat's motor. Then Ming heard the man's bare feet climbing the cabin steps. Ming did not turn his head to look at him, but his ears twitched back a little, involuntarily. Ming looked at the water just the distance of a short leap in front of him and below him. Strangely, there was no sound from the man behind him. The hair on Ming's neck prickled, and Ming glanced over his right shoulder.

At that instant, the man bent forward and rushed at Ming with his arms outspread.

Ming was on his feet at once, darting straight towards the man, which was the only direction of safety on the rail-less deck, and the man swung his left arm and cuffed Ming in the chest. Ming went flying backwards, claws scraping the deck, but his hind legs went over the edge. Ming clung with his front feet to the sleek wood which gave him little hold, while his hind legs worked to heave him up, worked at the side of the boat which sloped to Ming's disadvantage.

The man advanced to shove a foot against Ming's paws, but Elaine came up the cabin steps just then.

"What's happening? *Ming!*"

Ming's strong hind legs were getting him on to the deck little by little. The man had knelt as if to lend a hand. Elaine had fallen on to her knees also, and had Ming by the back of the neck now.

Ming relaxed, hunched on the deck. His tail was wet.

"He fell overboard!" Teddie said. "It's true, he's groggy. Just lurched over and fell when the boat gave a dip."

"It's the sun. Poor *Ming!*" Elaine held the cat against her breast, and carried him into the cabin. "Teddie—could you steer?"

The man came down into the cabin. Elaine had Ming on the bunk and was talking softly to him. Ming's heart was still beating fast. He was alert against the man at the wheel, even though Elaine was with him. Ming was aware that they had entered the little cove where they always went before getting off the boat.

Here were the friends and allies of Teddie, whom Ming detested by association, although these were merely Mexican boys. Two or three boys in shorts called "Señor Teddie!" and offered a hand to Elaine to climb on to the dock, took the rope attached to the front of the boat, offered to carry *"Ming!—Ming!"* Ming leapt on to the dock himself and crouched, waiting for Elaine, ready to dart away from any other hand that might reach for him. And there were several brown hands making a rush for him, so that Ming had to keep jumping aside. There were laughs, yelps, stomps of bare feet on wooden boards. But there was also the reassuring voice of Elaine warning them off. Ming knew she was busy carrying off the plastic satchels, locking the cabin door. Teddie with the aid of one of the Mexican boys was stretching the canvas over the cabin now. And Elaine's sandaled feet were beside Ming. Ming followed her as she walked away. A boy took the things Elaine was carrying, then she picked Ming up.

They got into the big car without a roof that belonged to Teddie, and drove up the winding road towards Elaine's and Ming's house. One of the boys was driving. Now the tone in which Elaine and Teddie were speaking was calmer, softer. The man laughed. Ming sat tensely on his mistress's lap. He could feel her concern for him in the way she stroked him and touched the back of his neck. The man reached out to put his fingers on Ming's back, and Ming gave a low growl that rose and fell and rumbled deep in his throat.

"Well, well," said the man, pretending to be amused, and took his hand away.

Elaine's voice had stopped in the middle of something she was saying. Ming was tired, and wanted nothing more than to take a nap on the big bed at home. The bed was covered with a red and white striped blanket of thin wool.

Hardly had Ming thought of this, when he found himself in the cool, fragrant atmosphere of his own home, being lowered gently on to the bed with the soft woolen cover. His mistress kissed his cheek, and said something with the word hungry in it. Ming understood, at any rate. He was to tell her when he was hungry.

Ming dozed, and awakened at the sound of voices on the terrace a couple of yards away, past the open glass doors. Now it was dark. Ming could see one end of the table, and could tell from the quality of the light that there were candles on the table. Concha, the servant who slept in the house, was clearing the table. Ming heard her voice, then the voices of Elaine and the man. Ming smelled cigar smoke. Ming jumped to the floor and sat for a moment looking out of the door towards the terrace. He yawned, then arched his back and stretched, and limbered up his muscles by digging his claws into the thick straw carpet. Then he slipped out to the right on the terrace and glided silently down the long stairway of broad stones to the garden below. The garden was like a jungle or a forest. Avocado trees and mango trees grew as high as the terrace itself, there were bougainvillea against the wall, orchids in the trees, and magnolias and several camellias which Elaine had planted. Ming could hear birds twittering and stirring in their nests. Sometimes he climbed trees to get at their nests, but tonight he was not in the mood, though he was no longer tired. The voices of his mistress and the man disturbed him. His mistress was not a friend of the man's tonight, that was plain.

Concha was probably still in the kitchen, and Ming decided to go in and ask her for something to eat. Concha liked him. One maid who had not liked him had been dismissed by Elaine. Ming thought he fancied barbecued pork. That was what his mistress and the man had eaten tonight. The breeze blew fresh from the ocean, ruffling Ming's fur slightly. Ming felt completely recovered from the awful experience of nearly falling into the sea.

Now the terrace was empty of people. Ming went left, back into the bedroom, and was at once aware of the man's presence, though there was no light on and Ming could not see him. The man was standing by the dressing table, opening a box. Again involuntarily Ming gave a low growl which rose and fell, and Ming remained frozen in the position he had been in when he first became aware of the man, his right front paw extended for the next step. Now his ears were back, he was prepared to spring in any direction, although the man had not seen him.

"*Ssss-st!* Damn you!" the man said in a whisper. He stamped his foot, not very hard, to make the cat go away.

Ming did not move at all. Ming heard the soft rattle of the white necklace which belonged to his mistress. The man put it into his pocket, then moved to Ming's right, out of the door that went into the big living room. Ming now heard the clink of a bottle against glass, heard liquid being poured. Ming went through the same door and turned left towards the kitchen.

Here he meowed, and was greeted by Elaine and Concha. Concha had her radio turned on to music.

"Fish?—Pork. He likes pork," Elaine said, speaking the odd form of words which she used with Concha.

Ming, without much difficulty, conveyed his preference for pork, and got it. He fell to with a good appetite. Concha was exclaiming "Ah-eee-ee!" as his mistress spoke with her, spoke at length. Then Concha bent to stroke him, and Ming put up with it, still looking down at his plate, until she left off and he could finish his meal. Then Elaine left the kitchen. Concha gave him some of the tinned milk, which he loved, in his now empty saucer, and Ming lapped this up. Then he rubbed himself against her bare leg by way of thanks, and went out of the kitchen, made his way cautiously into the living room en route to the bedroom. But now Elaine and the man were out on the terrace. Ming had just entered the bedroom, when he heard Elaine call:

"Ming? Where are you?"

Ming went to the terrace door and stopped, and sat on the threshold.

Elaine was sitting sideways at the end of the table, and the candlelight was bright on her long fair hair, on the white of her trousers. She slapped her thigh, and Ming jumped on to her lap.

The man said something in a low tone, something not nice.

Elaine replied something in the same tone. But she laughed a little.

Then the telephone rang.

Elaine put Ming down, and went into the living room towards the telephone.

The man finished what was in his glass, muttered something at Ming, then set the glass on the table. He got up and tried to circle Ming, or to get him towards the edge of the terrace, Ming realized, and Ming also realized that the man was drunk—therefore moving slowly and a little clumsily. The terrace had a parapet about as high as the man's hips, but it was broken by grills in three places, grills with bars wide enough for Ming to pass through, though Ming never did, merely looked through the grills sometimes. It was plain to Ming that the man wanted to drive him through one of the grills, or grab him and toss him over the terrace parapet. There was nothing easier for Ming than to elude him. Then the man picked up a chair and swung it suddenly, catching Ming on the hip. That had been quick, and it hurt. Ming took the nearest exit, which was down the outside steps that led to the garden.

The man started down the steps after him. Without reflecting, Ming dashed back up the few steps he had come, keeping close to the wall which was in shadow. The man hadn't seen him, Ming knew. Ming leapt to the terrace parapet, sat down and licked a paw once to recover and collect himself. His heart beat fast as if he were in the middle of a fight. And hatred ran in his veins. Hatred burned his eyes as he crouched and listened to the man uncertainly climbing the steps below him. The man came into view.

Ming tensed himself for a jump, then jumped as hard as he could, landing with all four feet on the man's right arm near the shoulder. Ming clung to the cloth of the man's white jacket, but they were both falling. The man groaned. Ming hung on. Branches crackled. Ming could not tell up from down. Ming jumped off the man, became aware of direction and of the earth too late, and landed on his side. Almost at the same time, he heard the thud of the man hitting the ground, then of his body rolling a little way, then there was silence. Ming had to breathe fast with his mouth open until his chest stopped hurting. From the direction of the man, he could smell drink, cigar, and the sharp odor that meant fear. But the man was not moving.

Ming could now see quite well. There was even a bit of moonlight. Ming headed for the steps again, had to go a long way through the bush, over stones and sand, to where the steps began. Then he glided up and arrived once more upon the terrace.

Elaine was just coming on to the terrace.

"Teddie?" she called. Then she went back into the bedroom where she turned on a lamp. She went into the kitchen. Ming followed her. Concha had left the light on, but Concha was now in her own room, where the radio played.

Elaine opened the front door.

The man's car was still in the driveway, Ming saw. Now Ming's hip had begun to hurt, or now he had begun to notice it. It caused him to limp a little. Elaine noticed this, touched his back, and asked him what was the matter. Ming only purred.

"Teddie?—Where are you?" Elaine called.

She took a torch and shone it down into the garden, down among the great trunks of the avocado trees, among the orchids and the lavender and pink blossoms of the bougainvilleas. Ming, safe beside her on the terrace parapet, followed the beam of the torch with his eyes and purred with content. The man was not below here, but below and to the right. Elaine went to the terrace steps and carefully, because there was no rail here, only broad steps, pointed the beam of the light downward. Ming did not bother looking. He sat on the terrace where the steps began.

"Teddie!" she said. *"Teddie!"* Then she ran down the steps.

Ming still did not follow her. He heard her draw in her breath. Then she cried:

"Concha!"

Elaine ran back up the steps.

Concha had come out of her room. Elaine spoke to Concha. Then Concha became excited. Elaine went to the telephone, and spoke for a short while, then she and Concha went down the steps together. Ming settled himself with his paws tucked under him on the terrace, which was still faintly warm from the day's sun. A car arrived. Elaine came up the steps, and went and opened the front door. Ming kept out of the way on the terrace, in a shadowy corner, as three or four strange men came out on the terrace and tramped down the steps. There was a great deal of talk below, noises of feet, breaking of bushes, and then the smell of all of them mounted the steps, the smell of tobacco, sweat, and the familiar smell of blood. The man's blood. Ming was pleased, as he was pleased when he killed a bird and created this smell of blood under his own teeth. This was big prey. Ming, unnoticed by any of the others, stood up to his full height as the group passed with the corpse, and inhaled the aroma of his victory with a lifted nose.

Then suddenly the house was empty. Everyone had gone, even Concha. Ming drank a little water from his bowl in the kitchen, then went to his mistress's bed, curled against the slope of the pillows, and fell fast asleep. He was awakened by the *rr-rr-r* of an unfamiliar car. Then the front door opened, and he recognized the step of Elaine and then Concha. Ming stayed where he was. Elaine and Concha talked softly for a few minutes. Then Elaine came into the bedroom. The lamp was still on. Ming watched her slowly open the box on her dressing table, and into it she let fall the white necklace that made a little clatter. Then she closed the box. She began to unbutton her shirt, but before she had finished, she flung herself on the bed and stroked Ming's head, lifted his left paw and pressed it gently so that the claws came forth.

"Oh, Ming—Ming," she said.

Ming recognized the tones of love.

In the Dead
of
Truffle Season

S amson, a large white pig in the prime of life, lived on a rambling old farm in the Lot region, not far from the grand old town of Cahors. Among the fifteen or so other pigs on the farm was Samson's mother Georgia (so named because of a song the farmer Emile had heard once on the television) but not Samson's grandmother, who had been hauled away, kicking and squealing, about a year ago, and not Samson's father, who lived many kilometers away and arrived on a pick-up car a few times a year for brief visits. There were also countless piglets, some from Samson's mother, some not, through whom Samson disdainfully waded, if they were between him and a feed trough. Samson never bothered shoving even the adult pigs, in fact, because he was so big himself, he had merely to advance and his way was clear.

His white coat, somewhat thin and bristly on his sides, grew fine and silky on the back of his neck. Emile often squeezed Samson's neck with his rough fingers when boasting about Samson to another farmer, then he would kick Samson gently in his larded ribs. Usually Samson's back and sides bore a grey crust of sun-dried mud, because he loved to roll in the mud of the unpaved farmyard court and in the thicker mud of the pig pen by the barn. Cool mud was pleasant in the southern summer, when the sun came boiling down for weeks on end, making the pig pen and the court-yard steam. Samson had seen two summers.

The greatest season of the year for Samson was the dead of winter, when he came into his own as truffle-hunter. Emile and often his friend René, another farmer who sometimes took a pig, sometimes a dog with him, would stroll out with Samson on a rope lead of a Sunday morning, and walk for nearly two kilometers to where some oak trees grew in a small forest.

"*Vas-y!*" Emile would say as they entered the forest's edge, speaking however in the dialect of the region.

Samson, perhaps a bit fatigued or annoyed by the long promenade, would take his time, even if he did happen to smell truffles at once at the base of a tree. An old belt of Emile's served as his collar, very little of its end hanging, so big was Samson's neck, and Samson could easily tug Emile in any direction he chose.

Emile would laugh in anticipation, and say something cheery to René, or to himself if he were alone, then pull from a pocket of his jacket the bottle of Armagnac he took along to keep the cold out.

The main reason Samson took his time about disclosing any truffles was that he never got to eat any. He did get a morsel of cheese as a reward, if he indicated a truffle spot, but cheese was not truffles, and Samson vaguely resented this.

"Huh-*wan-nk!*" said Samson, meaning absolutely nothing by it, wasting time as he sniffed at the foot of a tree which was not an appropriate tree in the first place.

Emile knew this, and gave Samson a kick, then blew on his free hand: his woolen gloves were full of holes, and it was a damned freezing day. He threw down his Gauloise, and pulled the collar of his turtleneck sweater up over his mouth and nose.

Then Samson's nostrils filled with the delicate, rare aroma of black truffles, and he paused, snorting. The hairs on his back rose a little with excitement. His feet of their own accord stomped, braced themselves, and his flat nose began to root at the ground. He drooled.

Emile was already tugging at the pig. He looped the rope a few times around a tree some distance away, then attacked the spot cautiously with the fork he had been carrying.

"Ah! A-hah!" There they were, a cluster of crinkly black fungus as wide as his hand. Emile put the truffles gently into the cloth knapsack that was swung over his shoulder. Such truffles were worth a hundred and thirty new francs the *livre* in Cahors on the big market days, which were every other Saturday, and Emile got just a trifle less where he usually sold them, at a Cahors delicacy shop which in turn sold the truffles to a pâté manufacturer called Compagnie de la Reine d'Aquitaine. Emile could have got a bit more by selling direct to La Reine d'Aquitaine, but their plant was the other side of Cahors, making the trip more expensive because of the cost of petrol. Cahors, where Emile went every fortnight to buy animal feed and perhaps a tool replacement, was only ten kilometers from his home.

Emile found with his fingers a bit of gruyère in his knapsack, and approached Samson with it. He tossed it on the ground in front of Samson, remembering Samson's teeth.

"*Us-ssh!*" Samson inhaled the cheese like a vacuum cleaner. He was ready for the next tree. The smell of truffles in the knapsack inspired him.

They found two more good spots that morning, before Emile decided to call it a day. They were hardly a kilometer from the Café de la Chasse, on the edge of Emile's home town Cassouac, and the bar-café was on the way home. Emile stomped his feet a few times as he walked, and tugged at Samson impatiently.

"Hey, fatso! Samson!—Get a move on! Of course you're not in a hurry with all that lard on you!" Emile kicked Samson on a back leg.

Samson pretended indifference, but condescended to trot for a few steps before he lapsed into his oddly dainty, I'll-take-my-time gait. Why should he hurry, why should he do everything to suit Emile? Also Samson knew where they were heading, knew he'd have a long wait outside in the cold while Emile drank and talked with his friends. There was the café in view now, with a few dogs tied up outside it. Samson's blood began to course a little faster. He could hold his own with a dog, and enjoyed doing so. Dogs thought they were so clever, so superior, but one lunge from Samson and they flinched and drew back as far as their leads permitted.

"Bonjour, Pierre! . . . Ha-ha-ha!" Emile had encountered the first of his cronies outside the café.

Pierre was tying up his dog, and had made some risible remark about Emile's *chien de race.*

"Never mind, I've got nearly a *livre* of truffles today!" Emile countered, exaggerating.

The barks of more dogs sounded as Emile and Pierre went into the small café. Dogs were allowed in, but some dogs who might snarl at the others were always tied outside.

One dog nipped playfully at Samson's tail, and Samson turned and charged in a leisurely way, not going far enough to make his rope taut, but the dog rolled over in his effort to escape. All three dogs barked, and to Samson it sounded derogatory—towards him. Samson regarded the dogs with a sullen and calm antipathy. Only his pinkish little eyes were quick, taking in all the dogs, daring them or any one of them to advance. The dogs smiled uneasily. At last Samson collapsed by leaning back and letting his legs fold under him. He was in the sun and comfortable enough despite the cold air. But he was hungry again, therefore a bit annoyed.

Emile had found René in the café, drinking pastis at the bar. Emile meant to linger until there was just time to walk home and not annoy his wife Ursule, who liked Sunday dinner to start not later than a quarter past noon.

René wore high rubber boots. He'd been cleaning a drain of his cowbarn, he said. He talked about the truffle-hunting contest that was to take place in two weeks. Emile had not heard of it.

"Look!" said René, pointing to a printed notice at the right of the door. La Compagnie de la Reine d'Aquitaine offered a first prize of a cuckoo clock plus a hundred francs, a second prize of a transistor radio (one couldn't tell the size from the picture), a third prize of fifty francs to the finders of the most truffles on Sunday, January 27. Judges' decisions to be final. Local newspaper and television coverage was promised, and the town of Cassouac was to be the judges' base.

"I'm giving Lunache a rest this Sunday, maybe next too," René said. "That way she'll have time to work up a truffle appetite."

Lunache was René's best truffling pig, a black and white female. Emile smiled a little slyly at his friend, as if to say, "You know very well Samson's better than Lunache!" Emile said, "That should be amusing. Let's hope it's not raining."

"Or snowing! Another pastis? I invite you." René put some money on the counter.

Emile glanced at the clock on the wall and accepted.

When he went out ten minutes later, he saw that Samson had chased the three tied-up dogs to the extremity of their leads, and was pretending to strain at his rope—a sturdy rope, but Samson might have been able to break it with a good tug. Emile felt rather proud of Samson.

"This monster! He needs a muzzle!" said a youngish man in muddy riding boots, a man Emile didn't recognize. He was patting one of the dogs in a reassuring way.

Emile was ready to return a spate of argument: hadn't the dog been annoying the pig first? But it crossed his mind that the young man might be a representative of La Reine d'Aquitaine come to look the scene over. Silence and a polite nod was best, Emile thought. Was one of the dogs bleeding a little on the hind leg? Emile didn't tarry to look more closely. He untied Samson and ambled off. After all, Emile was thinking, he'd had Samson's lower tusks sawed off three or four months ago. The tusks had started to grow higher than his snout. His upper tusks were still with him, but they were less dangerous because they curved inward.

Samson, in a vaguer though angrier way, was also thinking about his teeth at that moment. If he hadn't been mysteriously deprived of his rightful lower tusks long ago, he could have torn that dog up. One upward sweep of his nose under the dog's belly, which in fact Samson had given ... Samson's breath steamed in the air. His four-toed feet, only the two middle toes on each foot touching the ground, bore him along as if his great bulk were light as a white balloon. Now Samson was leading like a thoroughbred dog straining at the leash.

Emile, knowing Samson was angry, gave him serious and firm tugs. Emile's hand hurt, his arms were growing tired, and as soon as they neared the open gate of the farm's court, Emile gladly released the rope. Samson went trotting directly towards the pig pen where the food was. Emile opened the low gate for him, followed Samson's galloping figure, and unbuckled the belt collar while Samson guzzled potato peelings.

"*Oink!*—Oink-oink!"

"Whuff-f!"

"*Hwon-nk!*"

The other pigs and piglets fell back from Samson.

Emile went into the kitchen. His wife was just setting a big platter of cold diced beets and carrots, sliced tomatoes and onions in the center of the table. Emile gave a greeting which included Ursule, their son Henri and his wife Yvonne and their little one Jean-Paul. Henri helped a bit on the farm, though he was a full-time worker in a Cahors factory that made Formica sheets. Henri was not fond of farm work. But it was cheaper for him and his family to live here than to take an apartment or buy a house just now.

"Good truffling?" asked Henri, with a glance at the sack.

Emile was just emptying the contents of the sack into a pan of cold water in the sink. "Not bad," said Emile.

"Eat, Emile," said Ursule. "I'll wash them later."

Emile sat down and began eating. He started to tell them about the truffle-hunting contest, then decided it might be bad luck to mention it. There were still two weeks in which to mention it, if he felt like it. Emile was imagining the cuckoo clock fixed on the wall in front of him, striking about now the quarter hour past twelve. And he would say a few words on the television (if it was true that there'd be television), and he'd have his picture in the local newspaper.

The main reason Emile did not take Samson truffling the following weekend was that he did not want to diminish the amount of truffles in that particular forest. This forest was known as "the-little-forest-down-the-slope" and was owned by an old man who didn't even live on his land any more but in a nearby town. The old man had never objected to truffle-hunting on his land, nor had the current caretakers who lived in the farm-house nearly a kilometer away from the forest.

So Samson had a leisurely fortnight of eating and of sleeping in the scoop of hard-packed hay in the pig shed, which was a lean-to against the main barn.

On the big day, January 27, Emile shaved. Then he made his way to the Café de la Chasse in his village, the meeting point. Here were René and eight or ten other men, all of whom Emile knew and nodded a greeting to. There were also a few boys and girls of the village come to watch. They were all laughing, smoking, pretending it was a silly game, but Emile knew that inside each man with a truffle-dog or truffle-pig was a determination to win first prize, and if not first then second. Samson showed a desire to attack Georges's dog Gaspar, and Emile had to tug at him and kick him. Just as Emile had suspected, the young man of two weeks ago, again in the riding boots, was master of ceremonies. He put on a smile, and spoke to the group from the front steps of the café.

"Gentlemen of Cassouac!" he began, then proceeded to announce the terms of the contest sponsored by La Reine d'Aquitaine, manufacturers of the best *pâté aux truffes* in all France.

"Where's the television?" a man asked, more to raise a laugh from his chums than to get an answer.

The young man laughed too. "It'll be here when we all come back—a special crew from Toulouse—around eleven-thirty. I know all of you want to get home soon after noon so as not to annoy your wives!"

More good-natured "Ha-ha's!" It was a frosty day, sharpening every-one's edge.

"Just for formality," said the young man in riding boots, "I'll take a look in your sacks to see that all's correct." He stepped down and did so, and every man showed a clean bag or sack except for apples and bits of cheese or meat which were to be rewards for their animals.

One of the onlookers made a side bet: dogs against pigs. He had man-aged to find a pig man.

Final *petits rouges* were downed, then they were off, straggling with dogs and pigs down the unpaved road, fanning off into favorite fields, towards cherished trees. Emile and Samson, who was full of honks and oinks this morning, made for the-little-forest-down-the-slope. He was not the only man to do so: François with his black pig was going there too.

"Plenty of room for both of us, I think," said François pleasantly.

That was true, and Emile agreed. He gave Samson a kick as they entered the forest, letting the cleats of his boot land solidly on Samson's backside, trying to convey that there was a greater urgency about the truffle-hunting today. Samson turned irritably and made a feint at Emile's legs, but bent to his work and snuffled at the foot of a tree. Then he abandoned the tree.

François, quite a distance away among the trees, was already digging with his fork, Emile saw. Emile gave Samson his head and the pig lumbered on, nose to the ground.

"Hwun-nf!—Ha-wun-nf! Umpf!" Samson had found a good cache and he knew it.

So did Emile. Emile tied Samson up, and dug as fast as he could. The ground was harder than a fortnight ago.

The aroma of truffles came stronger to Samson as Emile unearthed them. He strained at his rope, recoiled and charged forward again. There was a dull snap—and he was free! His leather collar had broken. Samson plunged his snout into the hollowed earth and began to eat with snorts of contentment.

"Son of a bitch!—Merde!" Emile gave Samson a mighty kick in his right ham. Goddamn the old belt! Emile had no choice but to waste precious minutes untying the rope from the tree and tying it again around the neck of Samson, who made every effort to evade him. That was to say, Samson rotated in a circle around the truffle hoard, keeping his muzzle on the same spot, eating. Emile got the rope tied, and at once tugged and cursed with all his might.

François's distant but loud laughter did not make Emile feel any more kindly towards Samson. Damn the beast, he'd eaten at least half the find here! Emile kicked Samson where his testicles would have been, if Emile had not had them removed at the same time as Samson's lower tusks.

Samson retaliated by charging Emile at knee level. Emile fell forward over the rushing pig, and barely had time to protect his face from the ground. The pain in his knees was agonizing. He was afraid for a few seconds that his legs had been broken. Then he heard François yelling with indignation. Samson was loose again and was invading François's place.

"Hey, Emile! You're going to be disqualified! Get this goddamn pig away from me! Get him—or I'll *shoot* him!"

Emile knew that François had no gun. Emile got to his feet carefully. His legs were not broken, but his eyes felt awful from the shock, and he knew he'd have a pair of prize shiners by tomorrow. "*Damn* you, Samson, get the hell away!" Emile yelled, trudging towards François and the two pigs. François was now whacking at Samson with a tree branch he had found, and Emile couldn't blame François.

"A hell of a way to . . ." François's words were lost.

Emile had never been very chummy with François Malbert, and he knew François would try to disqualify him, if he possibly could, mainly because Samson was an excellent truffler and presented a threat. This thought, however, concentrated Emile's anger more on Samson for the moment than on François. Emile pulled at Samson's rope, yanked it hard, and François came down at the same time with the branch on Samson's head, and the branch broke.

Samson charged again, and Emile, suddenly nimble in desperation, looped the end of the rope a couple of times around a tree. Samson was jerked off his feet.

"No use digging any more here! That's not fair!" François said, indicating his half-eaten truffle bed.

"Ah, oui? It's an *accident!*" Emile retorted.

But François was trudging away, in the direction of the Café de la Chasse.

Emile now had the little forest to himself. He set about gathering what was left of François's truffle find. But he was afraid he was going to be disqualified. All because of Samson.

"Now get to work, you bastard!" Emile said to Samson, and hit him on the rump with a short piece of the branch that had broken.

Samson only stared at Emile, facing him, in case another blow was coming.

Emile groped for a piece of cheese in his sack, and tossed it on the ground as an act of appeasement, also to whet Samson's appetite, perhaps. Samson did look as angry as a pig could look.

Samson snuffed up the cheese.

"Let's go, boy!" Emile said.

Samson got moving, but very slowly. He simply walked. He wasn't even sniffing the ground. Emile fancied that Samson's shoulders were hunched in anger, that he was ready to charge again. But that was absurd, he told himself. Emile pulled Samson towards a promising birch tree.

Samson smelled the truffles in Emile's sack. His saliva was still running from the truffles he had gobbled up from the hole in the ground. Samson turned with agility and pressed his nose against the sack at Emile's side. Samson had stood up a little on his hind legs, and his weight knocked

Emile down. Samson poked his nose into the sack. What a blissful smell! He began to eat. There was cheese too.

Emile, on his feet now, jabbed at Samson with his fork, hard enough to break the skin in three places where the tines sank. *"Get away, you bastard!"*

Samson did leave the sack, but only to rush at Emile. *Crack!* He hit Emile's knees again. The man lay on the ground, trying to bring his fork into position for striking, and in a flash Samson charged.

Somehow the pig's belly hit Emile in the face, or the point of his chin, and Emile was knocked half unconscious. He shook his head, and made sure he still had a good grip on his fork. He had suddenly realized that Samson could and might kill him, if he didn't protect himself.

"Au secours!" Emile yelled. *"Help!"*

Emile brandished the fork at Samson, intending to scare the pig off while he got to his feet.

Samson had no intention, except to protect himself. He saw the fork as an enemy, a very clear challenge, and he blindly attacked it. The fork went askew and dropped as if limp. Samson's front hooves stood triumphant on Emile's abdomen. Samson snorted. And Emile gasped, but only a few times.

The awful pink and damp nose of the pig was almost in Emile's face, and he recalled from childhood many pigs he had known, pigs who had seemed to him as gigantic as this Samson now crushing the breath out of him. Pigs, sows, piglets of all patterns and coloring seemed to combine and become this one monstrous Samson who most certainly—Emile now knew it—was going to kill him, just by standing on him. The fork was out of reach. Emile flailed his arms with his last strength, but the pig wouldn't budge. And Emile could not gasp one breath of air. Not even an animal any longer, Emile thought, this pig, but an awful, evil force in a most hideous form. Those tiny, stupid eyes in the grotesque flesh! Emile tried to call out and found that he couldn't make as much noise as a small bird.

When the man became quiet, Samson stepped off his body and nuzzled him in the side to get at the truffle sack again. Samson was calming down a bit. He no longer held his breath, or panted, as he had done alternately for the last minutes, but began to breathe normally. The heavenly scent of truffles further soothed him. He snuffled, sighed, inhaled, ate, his snout and tongue seeking out the last morsels from the corners of the khaki sack. And all his own gleanings! But this thought came not at all clearly to Samson. In fact, he had a vague feeling that he was going to be shooed away from his banquet, yet who was there to shoo him away now?

This very special sack, into which he had seen so many black truffles vanishing, out of which had come measly, contemptible crumbs of yellow cheese—all that was finished, and now the sack was his. Samson even ate some of the cloth.

Then, still chewing, he urinated. He listened, and looked around, and felt quite secure and in command of things—at least of himself. He could walk anywhere he chose, and he chose to walk away from the village of Cassouac. He trotted for a bit, then walked, and was sidetracked by the scent of still more truffles. It took Samson some time to dig them up, but it was glorious work, and his reward was his own, every gritty, superb crinkle. Samson came to a stream, a little crusty at the edges with ice, and drank. He went on, dragging his rope, not caring where he went. He was hungry again.

Hunger impelled him towards a group of low buildings, whence he smelled chicken dung and the manure of horses or cows. Samson strolled a little diffidently into the cobbled courtyard where some pigeons and chickens walked about. They made way for Samson. Samson was used to that. He was looking for a feed trough. He found a trough with some wet bread in it, a low trough. He ate. Then he collapsed against a stack of hay, half sheltered by a roof. It was now dark.

From the two lighted windows in the lower part of the house near by came music and voices, sounds of an ordinary household.

As dawn broke, the wandering, pecking chickens in the courtyard and near Samson did not really awaken him. He dozed on, and only opened one eye sleepily when he heard the gritty tread of a man.

"Ho-ha! What have we got here?" murmured the farmer, peering at the enormous pale pig lying in his hay. A rope dangled from the pig's neck, a good sturdy rope, he saw, and the pig was an even more splendid specimen of his kind. Whom did he belong to? The farmer knew all the pigs in the district, knew their types, anyway. This one must have come from a long way. The end of the rope was frayed.

The farmer Alphonse decided to keep his mouth shut. After more or less hiding Samson for a few days in a back field which was enclosed, Alphonse brought him forward once more and let him join the pigs he had, all black ones. He wasn't concealing the white pig, he reasoned, and if anyone came looking for such a pig, he could say the pig had simply wandered on to his land, which was true. Then he would give the pig back, of course, after being sure the inquirer knew that the pig's lower tusks had been sawn off, that he'd been castrated and so forth. Meanwhile Alphonse debated selling him on the market or trying him out at truffle-hunting before the winter was over. He'd try the truffling first.

Samson grew a little fatter, and dominated the other pigs, two sows and their piglets. The food was slightly different and more abundant than at the other farm. Then came the day—an ordinary working day, it seemed to Samson from the look of the farm—when he was taken on a lead to go to the woods for truffles. Samson trotted along in good spirits. He intended to eat a few truffles today, besides finding them for the man. Somewhere in his brain, Samson was already thinking that he must from the start show this man that he was not to be bossed.

The Bravest Rat
in Venice

The household at the Palazzo Cecchini on the Rio San Polo was a happy, lively one: husband and wife and six children ranging from two to ten years of age, four boys and two girls. This was the Mangoni family, and they were the caretakers. The owners of the Palazzo Cecchini, an English-American couple named Whitman, were away for three months, and probably longer, in London, staying at their townhouse there.

"It's a fine day! We'll open the windows and sing! And we'll *clean* up this place!" yelled Signora Mangoni from the kitchen as she untied her apron. She was eight months' pregnant. She had washed up the breakfast dishes, swept away the breadcrumbs, and was facing the crisp, sunny day with the joy of a proprietress. And why not? She and her family had the run of every room, could sleep in whatever beds they wished, and furthermore had plenty of money from the Whitmans to run things in a fine style.

"Can we play downstairs, mama?" asked Luigi, aged ten, in a perfunctory way. Mama would say *"No!"* he supposed, and he and a couple of brothers and maybe his sister Roberta would go anyway. Wading, slipping, falling in the shallow water down there was great fun. So was startling the passing gondoliers and their passengers just outside the canal door by suddenly opening the door and heaving a bucket of water—maybe on to a tourist's lap.

"No!" said mama. "Just because today is a holiday—"

Luigi, Roberta and their two brothers Carlo and Arturo went to school officially. But they had missed a lot of days in the last month since the Mangoni family had full possession of the Palazzo Cecchini. It was more fun than school to explore the house, to pretend to own everything, to be able to open any door without knocking. Luigi was about to give a hail to Carlo to join him, when his mother said:

"Luigi, you promised to take Rupert for a walk this morning!"

Had he? The promise, if made, did not weigh much on Luigi's conscience. "This afternoon."

"No, this morning. Untie the dog!"

Luigi sighed and went in a waddling, irritated way to the kitchen corner where the Dalmatian was tied to the foot of a tile stove.

The dog was growing plump, and that was why his mother wanted him or Carlo to walk him a couple of times a day. The dog was plump because he was given risotto and pasta instead of the meat diet recommended by Signor Whitman, Luigi knew. Luigi had heard his parents discussing it, and the discussion had been brief: with the price of meat what it was, why feed a *dog* bistecca? It was an absurdity, even if they had been given the money for it. The dog could just as well eat stale bread and milk, and there was some fish and clam bits after all in the risotto leftovers. A dog was a dog, not a human being. The Mangoni family were now eating meat.

Luigi compromised by letting Rupert lift his leg in the narrow street outside the front door of the palazzo, summoned Carlo who was strolling homeward with a half-finished soda pop in hand, and together they went, with the dog, down the steps behind a door of the front hall.

The water looked half a meter deep. Luigi laughed in anticipation, pushed off his sandals and removed his socks on the steps.

Schluck-slosh! The dark water moved, blindly lapped into stone corners, rebounded. The big, empty square room was semi-dark. Two slits of sunlight showed on either side of the loose door. Beyond the door were more stone steps which went right down into the water of the rather wide canal called the Rio San Polo. Here for several hundred years, before the palazzo had sunk so much, gondolas had used to arrive, discharging well dressed ladies and gentlemen with dry feet into the marble-floored salon where Luigi and Carlo now splashed and slipped in water nearly up to their knees.

The dog Rupert shivered on one of the steps the boys had come down. He was not so much chilly as nervous and bored. He did not know what to do with himself. His routine of happy walks three times a day, milk and biscuits in the morning, a big meal of meat around 6 P.M.—all that was gone. His life now was a miserable chaos, and his days had lost their shape.

It was November, but not cold, not too cold for Luigi's and Carlo's informal game of push-the-other. First man down lost, but was rewarded by applause and laughter from the others—usually Roberta and little sister Benita were wading too, or watching from the steps.

"A rat!" Luigi cried, pointing, lying, and at that instant gave Carlo a good push behind his knees, causing Carlo to collapse on his back in the water with a great hollow-sounding splash that hit the walls and peppered Luigi with drops.

Carlo scrambled to his feet, soaked, laughing, making for the steps where the trembling dog stood.

"Look! There's a real one!" Luigi said, pointing.

"Ha-ha!" said Carlo, not believing.

"There it *is!*" Luigi slashed the surface of the water with his hand, trying to aim the water at the ugly thing swimming between him and the steps.

"Sissi!" Carlo shrieked with glee and waded towards a floating stick.

Luigi snatched the stick from him and came down with it on the rat's body—an unsatisfactory blow, rather sliding off the rat's back. Luigi struck again.

"Grab him by the tail!" giggled Carlo.

"Get a knife, we'll kill it!" Luigi spoke with bared teeth, excited by the fact the rat might dive and nip one of his feet with a fatal bite.

Carlo was already splashing up the stairs. His mother was not in the kitchen, and he at once seized a meat knife with a triangular blade, and ran back with it to Luigi.

Luigi had battered the rat twice more, and now with the knife in his right hand, he was bold enough to grab the rat's tail and whirl him up on to a marble ledge as high as Luigi's hips.

"Ah-i-i! Kill 'im!" Carlo said.

Rupert whined, lifting his head, thought of going up the steps, since his lead dangled, and could not come to any decision, because he had no purpose in going up.

Luigi made a clumsy stab at the rat's neck, while still holding its tail, missed the neck and struck an eye. The rat writhed and squealed, showing long front teeth, and Luigi was on the brink of releasing its tail out of fear, but came down once more with a blow he intended to be decapitating, but he cut off a front foot instead.

"Ha-ha-ha!" Carlo clapped his hands, and wildly splashed water, more on Luigi than the rat.

"Bastard rat!" cried Luigi.

For a few seconds the rat was motionless, with open mouth. Blood flowed from its right eye, and Luigi came down with the blade on the rat's right hind foot which was extended with splayed toes, vulnerable against the stone. The rat bit, caught Luigi in the wrist.

Luigi screamed and shook his arm. The rat fell off into the water, and began to swim wildly away.

"Oooh!" said Carlo.

"Ow!" Luigi swished his arm back and forth in the water and examined his wrist. It was merely a pink dot, like a pinprick. He'd been wanting to exaggerate his prowess to his mother, have her nurse his wound, but he'd have to make do with this. "It *hurts!*" he assured Carlo, and made his way through the water towards the steps. Tears had already come to his eyes, though he felt no pain at all. *"Mama!"*

The rat scrabbled with one stump of a forepaw and his other good paw against a mossy stone wall, keeping his nose above water as best he could. Around him the water was pinkening with blood. He was a young rat, five months old and not fully grown. He had never been in this house before, and had come in at the street side via a dry alley or slit along one side of the wall. He had smelled food, or thought he had, rotting meat or some such. A hole had led through the wall, and he had tumbled into water before he knew it, water so deep he had had to swim. Now his problem was to find an exit. His left foreleg and right hind leg smarted, but his eye hurt worse. He explored a bit, but found no hole or slit of escape, and at last he clung to slimy threads of moss by the claws of his right forefoot and was still, rather in a daze.

Some time later, chill and numb, the rat moved again. The water had gone down a little, but the rat was not aware of this, because he still had to swim. Now a narrow beam of light showed in a wall. The rat made for this, squeezed through, and escaped from the watery dungeon. He was in a kind of sewer in semi-darkness. He found an exit from this: a crack in a pavement. His next hours were a series of short journeys to an ashcan's shelter, to a doorway, to a shadow behind a tub of flowers. He was, in a circuitous way, heading for home. The rat had no family as yet, but was indifferently accepted in the house or headquarters of several rat families where he had been born. It was dark when he got there—the cellar of an abandoned grocery store, long ago plundered of anything edible. The cellar's wooden door was falling apart, which made entry easy for the rats, and they were in such number no cat would have ventured to attack them in their lair, which had no escape route for a cat but the way the cat would have come.

Here the rat nursed his wounds for two days, unassisted by parents who did not even recognize him as offspring, or by relatives either. At least he could nibble on old veal bones, moldy bits of potato, things that rats had brought in to chew in peace. He could see out of only one eye, but already this was making him more alert, quicker in darting after a crumb of food, quicker in retreating in case he was challenged. This period of semi-repose and recuperation was broken by a torrent of hose water early one morning.

The wooden door was kicked open and the blast of water sent baby rats flying up in the air, smashed a few against the wall, killing them by the impact or drowning them, while adult rats scrambled up the steps past the hose-holder to be met by clubs crashing on their heads and backs, huge rubber-booted feet stamping the life out of them.

The crippled rat remained below, swimming a bit finally. Men came down the steps with big nets on sticks, scooping up corpses. They dumped poison into the water which now covered the stone floor. The poison stank and hurt the rat's lungs. There was a back exit, a hole in a corner just big enough for him to get through, and he used it. A couple of other rats had used it also, but the rat did not see them.

It was time to move on. The cellar would never be the same again. The rat was feeling better, more self-assured and more mature. He walked and crept, sparing his two sore stumps. Before noon, he discovered an alley at the back of a restaurant. Not all the garbage had fallen into the bins. Pieces of bread, a long steakbone with meat on it lay on the cobblestones. It was a banquet! Maybe the best meal of his life. After eating, he slept in a dry drainpipe, too small for a cat to enter. Best to keep out of sight in daylight. Life was safer at night.

The days passed. The rat's stumps grew less painful. Even his eye had ceased to hurt. He regained strength and even put on a little weight. His gray, slightly brownish coat became thick and sleek. His ruined eye was a half-closed, grayish splotch, a bit jagged because of the knife's thrust, but it was no longer running either with blood or lymph. He discovered that by charging a cat, he could make the cat retreat a bit, and the rat sensed that it was because he presented an unusual appearance, limping on two short legs, one eye gone. The cats too had their tricks, puffing their fur up to make themselves look bigger, making throaty noises. But only once had an old ginger tomcat, mangy and with one ear gone, tried to close his teeth on the back of the rat's neck. The rat had at once attacked a front leg of the cat, bitten as hard as he could, and the cat had never got a grip. When the rat had turned loose, the cat had been glad enough to run away and leap to a windowsill. That had been in a dark garden somewhere.

The days came and went and grew ever colder and wetter, days of sleep in a patch of sun if possible, more often not, because a hole somewhere was safer, nights of prowling and feeding. And day and night the dodging of cats and the upraised stick in the hands of a human being. Once a man had attacked him with a dustbin, slammed it down on the stones, catching the rat's tail but not cutting any of it off, only giving him *pain* such as he had not known since the stab in his eye.

The rat knew when a gondola was approaching. "Ho! Aye!" the gondoliers would shout, or variations of this, usually when they were about to turn a corner. Gondolas were no threat. Sometimes the gondolier jabbed at him with an oar, more out of playfulness than to kill him. Not a chance had the gondolier! Just one stab that always missed, and the gondolier had glided past in his boat.

One night, smelling sausage from a tied-up gondola in a narrow canal, the rat ventured on board. The gondolier was sleeping under a blanket. The sausage smell came from a paper beside him. The rat found the remains of a sandwich, ate his fill, and curled up in a coarse, dirty rag. The gondola bobbed gently. The rat was an expert swimmer now. Many a time he had dived underwater to escape a cat that had been bold enough to pursue him into a canal. But cats didn't care to go below the surface.

The rat was awakened by a bumping sound. The man was standing up, untying a rope. The gondola moved away from the pavement. The rat was not alarmed. If the man saw him and came at him, he would simply jump overboard and swim to the nearest wall of stones.

The gondola crossed the Canale Grande and entered a widish canal between huge palaces which were now hotels. The rat could smell the aromas of fresh roasting pork, baking bread, orange peel and the sharper scent of ham. Some time later, the man maneuvered the gondola to the steps of a house, got out and banged on a door with a round ring of a knocker. From the gunwale, the rat saw a decaying portion of the embankment that would offer foothold, jumped into the water and made for it. The gondolier heard the splash and stomped towards him, yelling "*Aye*-yeh!" So the rat didn't climb up at that spot, but swam on, found another accessible place and got to dry pavement. The gondolier was back at the door, knocking again.

That day the rat met a female, a pleasant encounter in a rather damp alley behind a dress shop. It had just rained. Pushing on, the rat found a trail, almost, of sandwich ends, dropped peanuts, and hard corn kernels which he didn't bother with. Then he found himself in a large open area.

It was the Piazza San Marco, where the rat had never been. He could not see all its vastness, but he sensed it. Pigeons in greater number than he had ever seen walked about on the pavement among people who were tossing grain to them. Pigeons sailed down, spread their wings and tails and landed on the backs of others. The smell of popcorn made the rat hungry. But it was broad daylight, and the rat knew he must be careful. He kept to the angle made by the pavement and the walls of the buildings, ready to duck into a passageway. He seized a peanut and nibbled it as he hobbled along, letting the shell fall, keeping the peanut in his mouth, retrieving the other half of the peanut which held a second morsel.

Tables and chairs. And music. Not many people sat in the chairs, and those who did wore overcoats. Here were all manner of croissant crumbs, bread crusts, even bits of ham on the stone pavement among the chairs.

A man laughed and pointed to the rat. "Look, Helen!" he said to his wife. "Look at that rat! At this time of day!"

"Oh! What a *creature!*" The woman's shock was genuine. She was nearly sixty, and from Massachusetts. Then she laughed, a laugh of relief, amusement, and with a little bit of fear.

"Good God, somebody's cut his feet off!" the man said in almost a whisper. "And one eye's gone! Look at him!"

"Now *that's* something to tell the folks back home!" said the woman. "Hand me the camera, Alden!"

The husband did so. "Don't do it now, the waiter's coming."

"Altro, signor?" asked the waiter politely.

"No, grazie. Ah, sì! Un caffè latte, per piacere."

"Alden—"

He wasn't supposed to have more than two coffees a day, one morning, one evening. Alden knew. He had only a few months to live. But the rat had given him a curious zest, a sudden joy. He watched the rat nosing nervously in the forest of chair legs just three feet away, peering with his good eye, darting for the crumbs, eschewing the small, the inferior, the already crushed. "Do it now before he goes," said Alden.

Helen lifted the camera.

The rat sensed the movement, one of potential hostility and glanced up.

Click!

"I think that'll be good!" Helen whispered, laughing with a gentle happiness as if she'd just taken the sunset at Sounion or Acapulco.

"In this rat," Alden began, also speaking softly, and interrupted himself to pick with slightly trembling fingers the end of a dainty frankfurter from the buttery little bun in front of him. He tossed it towards the rat, which drew back a little, then darted for the sausage and got it, chewed it with one foot—the stump—planted on it. Suddenly the sausage vanished from view, and the plump jowls worked. "Now that rat has fortitude!" Alden said finally. "Imagine what he's been through. Like Venice itself. And he's not giving up. Is he?"

Helen returned her husband's smile. Alden looked happier, better than he had in weeks. She was pleased. She felt grateful to the rat. Imagine being grateful to a rat, she thought. When she looked again, the rat had vanished. But Alden was smiling at her.

"We're going to have a splendid day," he said.

"Yes."

Daily the rat grew stronger, bolder about venturing out in the daytime, but he was also learning more about protecting himself, even against people. He might make a dash as if to attack a person who was lifting a broom, a stick, a crate to smash him, and the person, man or woman, would retreat a step, or hesitate, and in that instant the rat could run in any direction, even past the person, if that direction meant escape.

More female rats. When in the mood, the rat had his pick of the females, because other males were afraid of him, and their challenges, if any, never came to a real fight. The rat with his heavy, rolling gait and his evil, single eye had a menacing air, a look that said nothing would stop him but death. He thrust his way through the maze of Venice, at seven months rolling like an old sea captain, sure of himself and sure of his ground. Mothers pulled their small children away from him in horror. Older children laughed and pointed. Mange attacked his stomach and head. He rolled on cobblestones to relieve the itching sometimes, or plunged into water despite the cold. He ranged from the Rialto to San Trovaso, and was familiar with the warehouses on the Ponte Lungo which bordered the broad Canale della Giudecca.

The Palazzo Cecchini lay between the Rialto and the cusp of land which held the warehouses. One day Carlo was returning from the local grocery store with a big cardboard carton meant for the Dalmatian Rupert to sleep in. Rupert had caught a cold, and Carlo's mother was worried. Carlo spied the rat emerging from between two wooden crates of fish and ice outside a shop.

It was the same rat! Yes! Carlo remembered vividly the two feet cut off, the stabbed eye. Not hesitating more than a second, Carlo slammed the carton upside down on the rat, and sat on the carton. He had him! Carlo sat gently but firmly.

"Hey, Nunzio!" Carlo yelled to a chum who happened to be passing. "Go call Luigi! Tell him to come! I've caught a rat!"

"A rat!" Nunzio had a fat loaf of bread under his arm. It was after six, getting dark.

"A special rat! Call Luigi!" Carlo yelled more forcefully, because the rat was hurling himself against the sides of the carton and soon he'd start chewing.

Nunzio ran.

Carlo got off the carton and pressed the bottom down hard, and kicked at the sides to discourage the rat from gnawing. His big brother would be impressed, if he could keep the rat till he got here.

"What're you doing there, Carlo, you're in the *way!*" yelled the fishmonger.

"I gotta rat! You oughta gimme a kilo of scampi for catching one of your rats!"

"*My* rats?" The fishmonger made a gesture of menace, but was too busy to shoo the boy off.

Luigi came on the run. He had picked up a piece of wood on the way, a square end of a crate. "A rat?"

"Same rat we had before! The one with the feet off! I swear!"

Luigi grinned, set his hand on the carton and gave its side a good kick. He raised the carton a little at one side, his piece of wood at the ready. The rat darted out, and Luigi came down on its shoulders.

The rat was breathless, and hurt. Another blow fell on his ribs. The rat's legs moved, and he wanted frantically to escape, but he could not get to his feet. He heard the boys' laughter. He was being borne away, in the big carton.

"Let's throw him downstairs! Drown 'im!" said Carlo.

"I want to see him. If we found a cat, we could see a good fight. That black and white cat—"

"She's never around. The water's high. Drown 'im!" The downstairs room fascinated Carlo. He had fantasies of gondolas floating through the door, dumping passengers who would drown in that awful semi-darkness, and finally cover the marble floor with their corpses, which would be seen only when the tide ran out. The ground floor of the Palazzo Cecchini might become another gruesome attraction of Venice, like the dungeons past the Ponte dei Sospiri.

The boys climbed the front steps and entered the Palazzo Cecchini whose tall wooden doors were slightly ajar. Their mama was singing in the kitchen where the transistor played a popular song. Carlo kicked the door shut, and their mother heard it.

"Come and eat, Luigi, Carlo!" she called. "We're going to the *cine,* don't forget!"

Luigi cursed, then laughed. *"Subito, mama!"*

He and Carlo went down the steps that led to the ground floor.

"You got the carton?" yelled their mother.

"*Si, si!*—Gimme the wood!" Luigi said to his brother. Luigi grabbed the square of wood and tipped the carton at the same time. Luigi remembered the bite on his wrist, and had a particular fear of this rat. The rat tumbled into the water. Yes, it was the same! Luigi saw the two stumps of his legs. The rat sank at once, and barely felt the clumsy blow that Luigi gave with the edge of the wood.

"Where is he?" asked Carlo. He was ankle-deep in water, standing on the first step, not caring about sandals and socks.

"He'll be up!" Luigi, on the step above, held the wood poised, ready to throw it when he saw the rat surface for air. The boys scanned the dark water that now heaved because of some motor boat that had just passed beyond the door.

"Let's go down! Scare 'im up!" Carlo said, with a glance at his brother, and Carlo at once went down into water up to his knees, and began kicking to make sure the rat didn't come near him.

"Luigi!" their mother shrieked. "Are you down below? You'll get a beating if you don't come up *now!*"

Luigi twisted around to shout a reply, mouth open, and at that instant saw the rat clumsily climbing the top step into the first floor of the house. "Mama mia!" he whispered, pointing. "The rat's gone up!"

Carlo grasped the situation at once, though he didn't see the rat, raised his eyebrows, and silently climbed the steps. They couldn't tell their mother. They'd have to follow the wet trail of the rat and get him out of the house. Both the boys understood this without speaking. When they entered the front hall, the rat had vanished. They peered about for a wet trail, but saw no sign of drops on the gray and white marble floor. Two salon doors were open. The downstairs toilet door was ajar. The rat could even have gone upstairs—maybe.

"Are you coming? The spaghetti is on the plates! Hurry!"

"Sissi, subito, mama!" Luigi pointed to Carlo's wet feet, and jerked a thumb to the upstairs, where Carlo's clothing mostly was.

Carlo dashed up the stairs.

Luigi took a quick look in the toilet. They couldn't tell their mother what had happened. She'd never leave the house or let them go to the film tonight, if she knew there was a rat loose. Luigi looked in one of the salons, where six chairs stood around an oval table, where more chairs stood beside wine tables near the walls of the room. He stopped, but still he saw no rat.

Carlo was back. They went down some steps into the kitchen. Papa had nearly finished his spaghetti. Then came bistecca. The plump dog watched with his muzzle on his paws. He salivated. He was tied again to a foot of the tile stove. Luigi looked around, covertly, for the rat in the corners of the kitchen. Before the meal was over, Maria-Teresa, the baby-sitter, arrived. She had two books under her arm. She smiled broadly, unbuttoned her coat and loosened the scarf that covered her head.

"I am early! I am sorry!" she said.

"No-no! Sit down! Have some torta!"

The dessert was a delicious open-faced pie with peach slices. Who could resist, especially with the appetite of a seventeen-year-old? Maria-Teresa sat and had a slice.

Papa Mangoni had a second piece. Like Rupert he was putting on weight.

Then the family was off, in a hurry, the smallest child in papa's arms, because they'd be four minutes late, by papa's calculations, even if they ran. Papa liked the advertisements that preceded the feature, and he liked saying hello to his chums.

The television set had been moved from the parents' bedroom into the room where the two-month-old Antonio lay as if in state in a cradle high off the ground and covered in white lace which hung nearly to the floor. The cradle was on wheels. Maria-Teresa, humming a song softly, saw that the baby was asleep, and rolled the cradle farther away from the television, which was in a corner, then switched the set on with the volume low. The program didn't look interesting, so she sat down and opened one of her novels, a love story whose setting was the American West of the last century.

When Maria-Teresa looked at the television screen several minutes later, her eye was caught by a moving gray spot in the corner. She stood up. A rat! A big, horrible-looking thing! She moved to the right, hoping to shoo it towards the door on her left, which was open. The rat advanced on her, slowly and steadily. It had one eye only. One of its front feet had been cut off. Maria-Teresa gave a little cry of panic, and ran out of the door herself.

She had no intention of attempting to kill the thing. She hated rats! They were the curse of Venice! Maria-Teresa went at once to the telephone in the downstairs hall. She dialed the number of a bar-café not far away, where her boy friend worked.

"Cesare," she said. "I want to speak with Cesare."

Cesare came on. He heard the story and laughed.

"But can you *come?* The Mangonis went to the cinema. I'm all alone! I'm so scared I want to run out of the house!"

"Okay, I'll come!" Cesare hung up. He swung a napkin over his shoulder, grinning, and said to one of his colleagues, a bar-man, "My girl-friend's baby-sitting and there's a rat in the house. I'm supposed to go over and kill it!"

"Ha-ha!"

"That's a new one! What time you coming back, Ces?" asked a customer.

More laughter.

Cesare didn't bother telling his boss he was leaving for a few minutes, because the Palazzo Cecchini was one minute away if he trotted. From the pavement outside, Cesare picked up an iron bar four feet long which went across the inside of the door when they closed up. It was heavy. He trotted, and imagined stabbing the bar at a cornered rat, killing it, and imagined the gratitude, the rewarding kisses he would get from Maria-Teresa.

Instead of the door being opened by an anxious girl, his beloved whom he would comfort with a firm embrace, words of courage before he tackled the little beast—instead of this, Cesare was met by a girl crumpled in tears, trembling with terror.

"The rat has eaten the baby!" she said.

"What?"

"Upstairs—"

Cesare ran up with the iron bar. He looked around in the nearly empty, formally furnished room for the rat, looked under a double bed which had a canopy.

Maria-Teresa came in. "I don't know where the rat is. Look at the baby! We've got to get a doctor! It just happened—while I was telephoning you!"

Cesare looked down at the shockingly red, blood-covered pillow of the baby. All the baby's nose—It was horrible! There *wasn't* any nose! And the cheek! Cesare murmured an invocation of aid from a saint, then turned quickly to Maria-Teresa. "The baby's *alive?*"

"I don't know! *Yes,* I think!"

Cesare timidly stuck a forefinger into the baby's curled hand. The baby twitched, gave a snuffling sound, as if he were having trouble breathing through blood. "Shouldn't we turn him over? Turn him on his side! I'll—I'll telephone. Do you know any doctor's number?"

"No!" said Maria-Teresa who was already imagining concretely the blame she was going to get for letting this happen. She knew she should have fought the rat out of the room instead of telephoning Cesare.

Cesare after one vain attempt to reach a doctor whose name he knew and whose number he looked up in the telephone book, rang the main hospital of Venice, and they promised to arrive at once. They came via a hospital boat which docked on the Canale Grande some fifty yards away. Cesare and Maria-Teresa even heard the noise of the fast motor. By this time Maria-Teresa had wiped the baby's face gently with a damp face towel, mainly with an idea of facilitating the baby's breathing. The nose was gone, and she could even see a bit of bone there.

Two young men in white gave the baby two injections, and kept murmuring *"Orribile!"* They asked Maria-Teresa to make a hot water bottle.

The blood had gone from Cesare's usually ruddy cheeks, and he felt about to faint. He sat down on one of the formal chairs. Gone was his idea of a passionate embrace with Maria-Teresa. He couldn't even stand on his legs.

The interns took the baby away in the boat, the baby wrapped in a blanket with the hot water bottle.

Cesare recovered a bit of strength, went down to the kitchen and after a search found half a bottle of Strega. He poured two glasses. He was keeping an eye out for the rat, but didn't see it. The Mangonis were due back soon, and he would have preferred to be elsewhere—back at his job—but he reasoned that he ought to stand by Maria-Teresa, and that this excuse would be a good one for his boss. A baby nearly killed, maybe dead now—who knew?

The Mangoni family arrived at 10:40 P.M., and there was instant chaos.

Mama screamed. Everyone talked at once. Mama went up to see the bloody cradle, and screamed again. Papa was told to telephone the hospital. Cesare and the oldest three of the brothers and one of the sisters went on a complete search of the house, armed with empty wine bottles for bashing, knives, a wooden stool from the kitchen, a flat iron, and Cesare had his iron bar. No one saw a rat, but several pieces of furniture received nicks inadvertently.

Maria-Teresa was forgiven. Or was she? Papa could understand her telephoning for help to her boyfriend who was near. The hospital reported that the baby had a fifty-fifty chance to live, but could the mother come at once?

The rat had escaped via a square drain in the kitchen wall at floor level. His jump had put him in the Rio San Polo nearly three meters below, but that was no problem. He swam with powerful thrusts of his two good legs, all his legs, plus sheer will power, to the nearest climbing point, and got on to dry land feeling no diminution of his energy. He shook himself. The taste of blood was still in his mouth. He had attacked the baby out of panic, out of fury also, because he hadn't at that point found an exit from the accursed house. The baby's arms and fists had flailed feebly against his head, his ribs. The rat had taken some pleasure in attacking a member of the human race, one with the same smell as the big ones. The morsels of tender flesh had filled his belly somewhat, and he was now deriving energy from them.

He made his way in the darkness with a rolling gait, pausing now and then to sniff at a worthless bit of food, or to get his bearings with an upward glance, with a sniff at the breeze. He was making for the Rialto, where he could cross by means of the arched bridge, pretty safe at night. He thought to make informal headquarters around San Marco, where there were a lot of restaurants in the area. The night was very black, which meant safety for him. His strength seemed to increase as he rolled along, belly nearly touching the dampish stones. He stared at, then sprang at a curious cat which had dared to come close and size him up. The cat leapt a little in the air, then retreated.

Engine Horse

When the big mare, Fanny, heard the rustle in the hay, she turned her head slowly, still chomping with unbroken rhythm, and her eyes, which were like large soft brown eggs, tried to look behind her and down. Fanny supposed it was one of the cats, though they seldom came close. There were two cats on the farm, one ginger, one black and white. Fanny's looking back had been casual. A cat often came into the stable in search of a quiet spot to nap in.

Still munching hay from her trough, Fanny looked for a second time and saw the little gray thing near her front foot. A tiny cat it was. Not one of the household, not one of the small cats belonging to either of the larger cats, because there weren't any just now.

It was sunset in the month of July. Gnats played around Fanny's eyes and nose, and made her snort. A small square window, closed in winter, was now open and the sun flooded directly into Fanny's eyes. She had not done much work that day, because the man called Sam, whom Fanny had known all her twelve years, had not come, either today or yesterday. Fanny had not done anything that she could remember except walk with the woman Bess to the water tank and back again. Fanny had a long period of munching in daylight, before she lay down with a grunt to sleep. Her vast haunch and rib cage, well covered with fat and muscle, hit the bed of hay like a carefully lowered barrel. It became cooler. The little gray kitten, which Fanny could now see more clearly, came and curled herself up in the reddish feathers behind Fanny's left hoof.

The little cat was not four months old, an ash-gray and black brindle, with a tail only the length of a king-sized cigarette, because someone had stepped in the middle of it when she was younger. She had wandered far that day, perhaps three or four miles, and turned in at the first shelter she had seen. She had left home, because her grandmother and great-grandmother had attacked her for an uncountable time, one time too many. Her mother had been killed by a car just a few days ago. The little cat had seen her mother's body on the road and sniffed it. So the little kitten, with an instinct for self-preservation, had decided that the great unknown was better than what she knew. She was already wiry of muscle, and full of pluck, but now she was tired. She had investigated the farmyard and found only some muddy bread and water to eat in the chickens' trough. And even at that hour in July the little cat was chilly. She had felt the warmth coming from the huge bulk of the red-brown mare, and when the horse lay down, the kitten found a nook, and collapsed.

The mare was somehow pleased. Such a dainty little creature! That size, that weight that was nothing at all!

The horse and the kitten slept.

And in the white, two-story farmhouse, the people argued.

The house belonged to Bess Gibson, a widow for the last three years. Her grandson Harry had come with his bride Marylou, a few days ago, for a visit, Bess had thought, and to introduce Marylou. But Harry had plans also. He wanted some money. His mother hadn't enough, or had refused him, Bess gathered. Bess's son Ed, Harry's father, was dead, and Harry's mother in California had remarried.

Now Harry sat in the kitchen, dressed in cowboy clothes, a toothpick alternating with a cigarette between his lips, and talked about the restaurant-drive-in-bar-and-café that he wanted to buy his way into.

"If you could only see, Gramma, that this farm isn't even paying its way, that the money's sitting here doing nothing! What've you got here?" He waved a hand. "You could get a hundred and twenty thousand for the house and land, and think for a minute what kind of apartment in town you could have for a fraction of that!"

"That's true, you know?" Marylou parroted. She was dawdling over her coffee, but she'd whipped out a nailfile and was sawing away now.

Bess shifted her weight in the wooden chair, and the chair gave a creek. She wore a blue and white cotton dress and white sandals. She suffered from dropsy. Her hair had gone completely white in the last couple of years. She realized that Harry meant an apartment in town, and town was Danville, thirty miles away. Some poky little place with two flights of stairs to climb, probably belonging to someone else to whom she'd have to pay rent. Bess didn't want to think about an apartment, no matter how many modern conveniences it might have. "This place pays its way," Bess said finally. "It's not losing money. There's the chickens and ducks—people come to buy them or their eggs. There's the corn and the wheat. Sam manages it very well—I don't know about the immediate future, with Sam gone," she added with an edge in it, "but it's home to me and it's yours when I'm gone."

"But not even a tractor? Sam still uses a plow. It's ridiculous. That one horse. What century are you living in, Gramma?—Well, you could *borrow* on it," Harry said not for the first time, "if you really want to help me out."

"I'm not going to leave you or anybody a mortgaged house," Bess replied.

That meant she was not completely convinced of the safety of what he wanted to do. But since Harry had been over this ground, he was too bored to go over it again. He merely exchanged a glance with Marylou.

Bess felt her face grow warm. Sam, their handyman—hers and her husband Claude's for seventeen years, a real member of the family—had left two days ago. Sam had made a speech and said he just couldn't stand Harry, he was sorry. Sam was getting on in years, and Harry had tried to boss him around, as if he were a hired hand, Bess supposed. She wasn't sure, but she could imagine. Bess hoped Sam would write to her soon, let her know where he was, so she could ask him back when Harry left. When she remembered old Sam with his best jacket on and his suitcase beside him, hailing the bus on the main road, Bess almost hated her grandson.

"Gramma, it's as simple as this," Harry began in the slow, patient voice in which he always presented his case. "I need sixty thousand dollars to buy my half with Roscoe. I told you Roscoe's just a nickname for laughs. His name is Ross Levitt."

I don't care what his name is, Bess thought, but she said a polite "Um-hm."

"Well—with sixty thousand dollars each, it's a sure thing for both of us. It's part of a chain, you know, twelve other places already, and they're all coining money. But if I can't put up my part in a few days, Gramma—or can't give a promise of the money, my chances are gone. I'll pay you back, Gramma, naturally. But this is the chance of a lifetime!"

To use such words, Bess was thinking, and to be only twenty-two! Harry had a lot to learn.

"Ask your lawyer if you're in doubt, Gramma," Harry said. "Ask any banker. I'm not afraid of the facts."

Bess recrossed her thick ankles. Why didn't his mother advance the money, if it was so safe? His mother had married a well-to-do man. And here was her grandson, married, at twenty-two. Too early for Harry, Bess thought, and she didn't care for Marylou or her type. Marylou was pretty and silly. Might as well be a high school crush, not a wife. Bess knew she had to keep her thoughts to herself, however, because there was nothing worse than meddling.

"Gramma, what fun is it here for you any more, all alone in the country? Both the Colmans dead in the last year, you told me. In town, you'd have a nice circle of friends who could . . ."

Harry's voice became a drone to Bess. She had three or four good friends, six or eight even in the district. She'd known them all a long time, and they rang up, they came to see her, or Sam drove her to see them in the pick-up. Harry was too young to appreciate what a home meant, Bess thought. Every high-ceilinged bedroom upstairs was handsome, everyone said, with curtains and quilts that Bess or her own mother had made. The local newspaper had even come to take photographs, and the article had been reprinted in the . . .

Bess was stirred out of her thoughts by Harry's getting up.

"Guess we'll be turning in, Gramma," he said.

Marylou got up with her coffee cup and took it to the sink. All the other dishes were washed. Marylou hadn't much to say, but Bess sensed a terrible storm in her, some terrible wish. And yet, Bess supposed, it probably wasn't any worse or any different from Harry's wish, which was simply to get his hands on a lot of money. They could live on the grounds behind the restaurant, Harry had said. A fine house with swimming pool all their own. Bess could imagine Marylou looking forward to that.

The young people had gone up to the front bedroom. They'd taken the television set up there, because Bess had said she didn't often watch it. She did look at it nearly every night, but she'd wanted to be polite when Harry and Marylou first arrived. Now she wished she had the set, because she could have done with a little change of thoughts, a laugh maybe. Bess went to her own sleeping quarters, which in summer was a room off the back porch with screened windows against mosquitoes, though there weren't ever many in this region. She turned on her transistor radio, low.

Upstairs, Harry and Marylou talked softly, glancing now and then at the closed door, thinking Bess might knock with a tray of milk and cake, as she had done once since they'd been there.

"I don't think she'll be coming up tonight," Marylou said. "She's sort of mad at us."

"Well, that's too bad." Harry was undressing. He blew on the square toes of his cowboy boots and passed them once across the seat of his Levi's to see if the shine came up. "Goddamn it, I've heard of these situations before, haven't you? Some old person who won't turn loose of the dough—which is really *coming* to me—just when the younger people damn well need it."

"Isn't there someone else you know who could persuade her?"

"Hell—around here?" They'd all be on his grandmother's side, Harry was thinking. Other people were the last thing they needed. "I'm for a small snort. How about you?" Harry pulled from a back corner of the closet a big half-empty bottle of bourbon.

"No, thanks. I'll have a sip of yours, if you're going to put water in it."

Harry splashed some water from the porcelain pitcher into his glass, handed the glass to Marylou for a sip, then added more bourbon for himself, and drank it almost off. "You know Roscoe wanted me to call him up yesterday or today? With an answer?" Harry wiped his mouth. He wasn't expecting a reply from Marylou and didn't get one. *I damn well wish she was dead now*, Harry thought, like a curse that he might have said aloud to get the resentment and anger out of his system. Then suddenly it came to him. An idea. Not a bad idea, not a horrible idea. Not too horrible. And safe. Well, ninety percent safe, if he did it wisely, carefully. It was even a simple idea.

"What're you thinking?" Marylou asked, propped up in bed now with the sheet pulled up to her waist. Her curly reddish hair glowed like a halo in the light of the reading lamp fixed to the bed.

"I'm thinking—if Gramma had something like a hip injury, you know—those things old people always get. She'd—" He came closer to the bed and spoke even more softly, knowing already that Marylou would be with him, even if his idea were more dangerous. "I mean, she'd have to stay in town, wouldn't she—if she couldn't get around?"

Marylou's eyes swam in excited confusion, and she blinked. "What're you talking about?" she asked in a whisper. "Pushing her down the stairs?"

Harry shook his head quickly. "That's too obvious. I was thinking of—maybe going on a picnic, the way she says she does, you know? With the horse and wagon. A watermelon, sandwiches and all and—"

"And beer!" Marylou said, giggling nervously knowing the climax was coming.

"Then the wagon turns over somewhere," Harry said simply, shrugging. "You know, there's that ford by the stream. Well, *I* know it, anyway."

"Wagon turns over. What about us? If we're in it?"

"You don't have to be in it. You could've jumped off to lay the cloth, some damn thing. I'll do it."

A pause.

"You're serious?" Marylou asked.

Harry was thinking, with his eyes almost closed. Finally he nodded. "Yes. If I can't think of anything else. Anything better. Time's getting short, even for promises to Roscoe. Sure. I'm serious." Then abruptly Harry went and switched on the television.

To THE LITTLE gray cat, Fanny the horse had become a protectress, a fortress, a home. Not that Fanny did anything. Fanny merely existed, giving out warmth in the cold of the night before dawn. The gray kitten's only enemies were the two older cats, and fortunately these chose to be simply huffy, ready with a spit, a swipe of a paw full of claws. They made life unpleasant, but they were not out for the kill, or even to drive her off the premises, which was something.

The kitten spent not much time in the stable, however. She liked to play in the ducks' and the chickens' yard, to canter towards a chick as if with evil intent, then to dodge the lunge, the terrible beak of the mother hen. Then the kitten would leap to an upright of the wooden fence and sit, washing a paw, surveying alertly the area in front of her and the meadow behind her. She was half-wild. She was not tempted to approach the back door of the house. She sensed that she wouldn't be welcome. She had never had anything but ill-treatment or indifference at best from the creatures that walked on two legs. With her grandmother and great-grandmother, she had eaten the remains of their kills, what was left of rats, birds, now and then a small rabbit, when her elders had eaten their fill. From the two-legged creatures came nothing reliable and abundant, maybe a pan of milk and bread, not every day, not to be counted on.

But the big red horse, so heavy, so slow, the gray kitten had come to recognize as a reliable friend. The kitten had seen horses before, but never any as huge as this. She had never come close to a horse, never touched one before. The kitten found it both amusing and dangerous. The kitten loved to feel amused, to feel as if she were playing tricks on other creatures (like the chickens) and on herself, because it eased the realities of existence, the fact that she could be killed—in a flash, as her mother had been—if the gigantic horse happened to step on her, for instance. Even the horse's big feet had metal bottoms: the kitten had noticed this one evening when the horse was lying down. Not soft, like the horse's long hair there, but hard, able to hurt.

Yet the kitten realized that the horse played with her too. The horse turned its great head and neck to look at her, and was careful not to step on her. Once when the horse was lying down, the kitten in a nervous rush of anxiety and mischief dashed up the horse's soft nose, up the bony front, and seized an ear and nipped it. Then at once the kitten had leapt down and crouched, fearing the worst in retaliation. But the horse had only tossed its head a little, showed its teeth and snorted—disturbing some nearby wisps of hay—as if it were amused also. Therefore the gray kitten pranced without fear now on the horse's side and haunch, leapt to tackle the coarse hair of the horse's tail, and dodged the tail's slow flick with ease. The horse's eyes followed her. The kitten felt those eyes a kind of protection, like her mother's eyes which the kitten remembered. Now the kitten slept in the warm place under the horse's shoulder, next to the great body which radiated heat.

One day the fat woman caught sight of the little kitten. Usually the kitten hid at the first glimpse of a human figure coming from the house, but the kitten was caught unawares while investigating a well-pecked chicken bone outside the stable. The kitten crouched and stared at the woman, ready to run.

"Well, well! Where'd you come from?" said Bess, bending to see better. "And what's happened to your tail?—You're a tiny little thing!" When Bess moved closer, the kitten dashed into the raspberry bushes and disappeared.

Bess carried the bucket of oats into Fanny's stable—poor Fanny was standing and doing nothing now—set the oats on the corner of the trough, and led Fanny out for water. When Fanny had drunk, Bess opened a fence gate, and led Fanny into an enclosed meadow.

"You're having a fine holiday, aren't you, Fanny? But we're going on a picnic today. You'll pull the wagon. Down to the old brook where you can cool your feet." She patted the mare's side. The top of Fanny's back was on a level with Bess's eyes. A huge creature she was, but she didn't eat a lot, and she worked willingly. Bess remembered Harry at thirteen or so, sitting astride Fanny for his picture to be taken, legs all bowed out as if he were sitting on a barrel. Bess didn't like to recall those days. Harry had been a nicer boy then. Engine Horse, Harry had called Fanny, impressed by her strength, as who wouldn't be, seeing her pull a wagonload of wheat sacks.

Bess went into the stable, poured the oats into Fanny's trough, then went back to the house, where she had a peach pie in the oven. She turned the oven off, and opened the oven door so it stayed ajar about four inches. Bess never measured or timed things, but her baking came out right. She ought to give the little kitten a roast beef rib to chew on, Bess thought. She knew the type this kitten was, half-wild, full of beans, and she—or maybe it was a he—would make a splendid mouser, if it could hold its own against the pair of cats here till it grew up a little. Bess took the plate of leftover roast beef from the refrigerator and with a sharp knife cut off a rib about fourteen inches long. If she could manage to give it to the kitten without the other cats noticing and stealing it, it would do the kitten a power of good.

The ham and cheese sandwiches were already made, and it was only a quarter to twelve. Marylou had deviled half a dozen eggs this morning. Where was she now? They were both upstairs talking, Bess supposed. They did a lot of talking. Bess heard a floorboard squeak. Yes, they were upstairs, and she decided to go out now and see if she could find the kitten.

Bess approached the chicken yard in her waddling gait, calling, "Here kitty-kitty-kitty!" and holding the bone out. Her own two cats were away hunting now, probably, and just as well. Bess even looked in the stable for the little one, but didn't see her. Then when she glanced at Fanny in the meadow—Fanny with her head down, munching clover—Bess caught sight of the little kitten, gamboling and darting in the sunlight around Fanny's hooves, like a puff of smoke blown this way and that. The kitten's lightness and energy held Bess spellbound for a few moments. What a contrast, Bess was thinking, with her own awful weight, her slowness, her *age!* Bess smiled as she walked towards the gate. The kitten was going to be pleased with the bone.

"Puss-puss?" she called. "What'll we name you—if you stay?" Bess breathed harder, trying to walk and talk at the same time.

The kitten drew back and stared at Bess, her ears erect, yellow-green eyes wary, and she moved nearer the horse as if for protection.

"Brought you a bone," Bess said, and tossed it.

The kitten leapt backward, then caught the smell of meat and advanced, nose down, straight towards her objective. An involuntary, primal growl came from her small throat, a growl of warning, triumph and voraciousness. With one tiny foot on the great bone, in case an intruder would snatch it, the kitten tore at the meat with baby teeth. Growling and eating at the same time, the kitten circled the bone, glancing all around her to see that no enemy or rival was approaching from any direction.

Bess chuckled with amusement and gratification. Certainly old Fanny wasn't going to bother the little cat with her bone!

Marylou was already loading the wagon with baskets and thermoses and the blankets to sit on. Bess pulled a fresh tablecloth out of the kitchen cabinet.

Harry went out to hitch up Fanny. He strode like a cowboy in his high-heeled boots, grabbed the curved brim of his Stetson and readjusted it to reassure himself, because he was not an expert at throwing a collar over a horse's head.

"*Whoa,* Fanny!" he yelled, when the mare drew back. He'd missed. Damnit, he wasn't going to call for Bess to help him, that'd be ridiculous. The mare circled Harry, facing him, but drawing back every time he tried to slip the heavy collar on. Harry jumped about like a bullfighter—except that the collar was getting damned heavy in his hands, not like something a bullfighter had to carry. He might have to tie up the beast, he thought. He seized the bridle, which dangled from a halter. She hadn't even a bit in as yet. "Engine hoss! *Whoa,* girl!"

Fortified and exhilarated by her half-eaten banquet, the little gray kitten leapt about also, playing, pretending she had to guard her bone, though she knew the man hadn't even seen her.

"Whoa, I *said*!" Harry yelled, and lunged at Fanny and this time made it with the collar. Harry turned his ankle and fell to the ground. He got up, not at all hurt by the fall, and then he heard a cry, a rhythmic cry like something panting.

Harry saw the little gray animal, thought at first it was a rat, then realized it was a kitten with half its bowels out. He must have stepped on it, or the horse had. Or maybe he'd fallen on it. He'd have to kill it, that he saw right away. Annoyed and suddenly angry, Harry stepped hard on the kitten's head with the heel of his cowboy boot. Harry's teeth were bared. He was still getting his own breath back. His Gramma probably wouldn't miss the kitten, he thought. She usually had too many of them. But Harry picked the kitten up by its oddly short tail, swung it once and hurled it as far as he could across the meadow, away from the house.

The mare followed the movement with her eyes, until the kitten— even before it landed on the ground—was lost to her vision. But she had seen the kitten smashed by the man falling on it. Fanny followed docilely as Harry led her towards the gate, towards the house. Fanny's awareness of what had happened came slowly and ponderously, even more slowly than she plodded across the meadow. Involuntarily, Fanny turned her head and tried to look behind her, almost came to a stop, and the man jerked her bridle.

"Come on, come on, Engine!"

THE BROOK, SOMETIMES called Latham's Brook, was about two miles from Bess's farm. Harry knew it from his childhood visits with his grandmother. It crossed his mind that the wooden bridge might be different—wider, maybe with a rail now—and he was relieved to see that it was the same: a span of hardly twenty feet, and maybe eight or nine feet wide, not wide enough for two cars, but a car seldom came here, probably. The road was a single-lane, unpaved, and there were lots of better roads around for cars.

"There's the old spot," said Bess, looking across the brook at the green grass, pleasantly sheltered by a few trees, where the family had come for years to picnic. "Hasn't changed, has it, Harry?" Bess was seated on a bench that let down from a side of the wagon, the right side.

Harry had the reins. "Nope. Sure hasn't."

This was where Marylou was to get down, and according to plan, she said, "Let me walk across, Harry! Is it shallow enough to wade?"

Harry tugged Fanny to a halt, sawing on her bit, and Fanny even backed a little, thinking that was what he wanted. "I dunno," said Harry in a frozen tone.

Marylou jumped down. She was in blue jeans, espadrilles, and a red-checked shirt. She trotted across the bridge, as if feeling happy and full of pep.

Harry clucked up Fanny again. He'd go over the right side of the bridge. He tugged Fanny to the right.

"Careful, Harry!" said Bess. "*Harry,* you're—"

The horse was on the bridge, the two right wheels of the wagon were not. There was a loud bump and scrape, a terrible jolt as the axles hit the edge of the bridge. Bess was thrown backward, balanced for a second with the wagon side in the small of her back, then she fell off into the water. Harry crouched, prepared to spring to safety, to jump towards the bank, but the falling wagon gave him nothing solid to leap from. Fanny, drawn backwards and sideways by the weight of the wagon, was suddenly over the edge of the bridge, trapped in her shafts. She fell on Harry's shoulders, and Harry's face was suddenly smashed against stones, underwater.

Fanny threshed about on her side, trying to regain her feet.

"*Har-ry!*" Marylou screamed. She had run onto the bridge. She saw a red stream coming from Harry's head, and she ran to the bank and waded into the water. *"Harry!"*

The crazy horse was somehow sideways in the wagon shafts, trampling all over Harry's legs now. Marylou raised her fists and shouted.

"Back, you idiot!"

Fanny, dazed with shock and fear, raised her front feet, not high, and when they came down, they struck Marylou's knees.

Marylou screamed, gave a panic-stricken, brandishing movement of her right fist to drive the horse off, then sank into the water up to her waist, gasping. Blood, terrifying blood, poured from her knees, through her torn blue jeans. And the stupid horse was now pitching and stomping, trying to get out of the shafts. Again the hooves came down on Harry, on his body.

It all happened so slowly. Marylou felt paralyzed. She couldn't even cry out. The horse looked like something in a slow-motion film, dragging now the broken wagon right across Harry. My God! And was it Bess yelling something now? Was it? Where? Marylou lost consciousness.

Bess was struggling to get to her feet. She'd been knocked out for a few minutes, she realized. What on earth had happened? Fanny was trying to climb the bank opposite, and the wagon was wedged between two trees. When Bess's eyes focused a bit better, she saw Harry almost covered by water, and then Marylou, who was nearer. Clumsily Bess waded into the deeper water of the brook, seized Marylou by one arm, and dragged her slowly, slowly over the stones, until her head was on the bank, clear of the water.

But Harry was face down and underwater! Bess had a horrible moment, had a desire to scream as loudly as she could for help. But all she did was wade towards Harry, hands outstretched, and when she reached him, she took as hard a grip as she could on his shirt, under his arm, and tugged with all her strength. She could not move him, but she turned him over, held his head in the air. His face was a pink and red blur, no longer a face. There was something wrong with his chest. It was crushed.

"Help!" Bess yelled. *"Please!—Help!"*

She waited a minute, and shouted again. She sat down finally on the grass of the bank. She was in shock, she realized. She shivered, then she began to tremble violently. A chill. She was soaking wet. Even her hair was wet. See about Marylou, she told herself, and she got up again and went to Marylou who was on her back, her legs twisted in an awful way, as if they were broken. But Marylou was breathing.

Bess made herself move. She unhitched Fanny. Bess had no purpose.

She felt she was in some kind of nightmare, yet she knew she was awake, that it had all happened. She held on to a brass ring of Fanny's collar, and Fanny pulled her up the slope, on to the bridge. They walked slowly, the woman and the horse, back the way they had come. It was easily nearly a mile to any house, Bess thought. The Poindexter place, wasn't that the next?

When the Poindexter house was in sight, Bess saw a car approaching. She raised her arm, but found she hadn't strength to yell out loudly enough. Still, the car was coming, slowing down.

"Go to the bridge. The brook," Bess told the bewildered looking man who was getting out of his car. "Two people—"

"You're hurt? You're bleeding," said the man, pointing to Bess's shoulder. "Get in the car. We'll go to the Poindexters' house. I know the Poindexters." He helped Bess into the car, then he took Fanny's dangling reins and pulled her into the long driveway of the Poindexters' property, so the horse would be off the road. He went back and drove the car into the driveway, past the horse, on to the house.

Bess knew the Poindexters too. They were not close friends, but good neighbors. Bess had enough of her wits about her to refuse to lie down on the sofa, as Eleanor Poindexter wished her to do, until they'd put newspapers down on it. Her clothes were still damp. Eleanor made her some tea. The man was already on the telephone. He came back and said he'd asked for an ambulance to go at once to the ford.

Eleanor, a gentle, rather pretty woman of fifty, saw to Bess's shoulder. It was a cut, not serious. "Whatever made your grandson go over the edge?" he said for the second time, as if in wonderment. "That bridge isn't all that narrow."

It was two or three days before Bess felt anything like her usual self. She hadn't needed to go into a hospital, but the doctor had advised her to rest a lot at home, which she had done. And Eleanor Poindexter had been an angel, and driven Bess twice to visit Marylou in the Danville hospital. Marylou's legs had been broken, and she'd need an operation on both knees. She might always walk with a limp, one doctor told Bess. And Marylou was strangely bitter about Harry—that shocked Bess the most, considering they were newlyweds, and Bess assumed much in love.

"Stupid—selfish—so-and-so," Marylou said. Her voice was bitter.

Bess felt Marylou might have said more, but didn't want to or didn't dare. Harry's body had been sent to California, to Harry's mother. After the brook, Bess had never seen Harry.

One day that same week, Bess took Fanny into the meadow for grazing. Bess was feeling a little happier. She'd had a letter from Sam, and he was willing to come back, providing Harry's visit was over (Sam didn't mince words), and Bess had just replied to him in a letter which the mailman would take away tomorrow morning.

Then Bess saw the dry and half-eaten body of the little gray cat, and a shock of pain went through her. She'd supposed the kitten had wandered on somewhere. What had happened to it? Crushed somehow. By what? A car or tractor never came into this meadow. Bess turned and looked at Fanny, whose thick neck was bent towards the ground. Fanny's lips and teeth moved in the grass. Fanny couldn't have stepped on the little thing, the kitten was much too quick, had been. Fanny had liked the kitten, Bess had seen that the morning she'd given the kitten the rib bone. And there, just a few feet away, was the long bone, stripped clean now by birds. Bess bent and picked it up. How the little kitten had loved this bone! Bess, after bracing herself, lifted the kitten's body up too. Hadn't Harry harnessed Fanny in the meadow that day? What had happened? What had happened to make Fanny so angry that day at the brook? It was Harry's hands that had driven the wagon over the edge. Bess had seen it. Fanny would never have gone so near the edge, if she hadn't been tugged that way.

In the afternoon, Bess buried the kitten in an old, clean dishtowel in a grave she dug in the far meadow, beyond the chickens' and the ducks' yard. It hadn't seemed right to dispose of the kitten in the garbage, even if she'd wrapped the body well. The kitten had been so full of life! Harry had somehow killed the kitten, Bess felt sure. And Fanny had seen it. Bess knew too that Harry had meant to kill her. It was horrid, too horrid to think about.

The Day of
Reckoning

John took a taxi from the station, as his uncle had told him to do in case
they weren't there to meet him. It was less than two miles to Hanshaw
Chickens, Inc., as his Uncle Ernie Hanshaw now called his farm. John
knew the white two-story house well, but the long gray barn was new to
him. It was huge, covering the whole area where the cow barn and the
pigpens had been.

"Plenty of wishbones in that place!" the taxi driver said cheerfully as
John paid him.

John smiled. "Yes, and I was just thinking—not a chicken in sight!"

John carried his suitcase towards the house. "Anybody home?" he
called, thinking Helen would probably be in the kitchen now, getting
lunch.

Then he saw the flattened cat. No, it was a kitten. Was it real or made
of paper? John set his suitcase down and bent closer. It was real. It lay on its
side, flat and level with the damp reddish earth, in the wide track of a tire.
Its skull had been crushed and there was blood there, but not on the rest of
the body which had been enlarged by pressure, so that the tail looked
absurdly short. The kitten was white with patches of orange, brindle and
black.

John heard a hum of machinery from the barn. He put his suitcase on
the front porch, and hearing nothing from the house, set off at a trot for the
new barn. He found the big front doors locked, and went round to the
back, again at a trot, because the barn seemed to be a quarter of a mile
long. Besides the machine hum, John heard a high-pitched sound, a din of
cries and peeps from inside.

"Ernie?" John yelled. Then he saw Helen. "*Hello,* Helen!"

"John! Welcome! You took a taxi? We didn't hear any car!" She gave him a kiss on the cheek. "You've grown another three inches!"

His uncle climbed down from a ladder and shook John's hand. "How're you, boy?"

"Okay, Ernie. What's going on here?" John looked up at moving belts which disappeared somewhere inside the barn. A rectangular metal container, nearly as big as a boxcar, rested on the ground.

Ernie pulled John closer and shouted that the grain, a special mixture, had just been delivered and was being stored in the factory, as he called the barn. This afternoon a man would come to collect the container.

"Lights shouldn't go on now, according to schedule, but we'll make an exception so you can see. Look!" Ernie pulled a switch inside the barn door, and the semi-darkness changed to glaring light, bright as full sun.

The cackles and screams of the chickens augmented like a siren, like a thousand sirens, and John instinctively covered his ears. Ernie's lips moved, but John could not hear him. John swung around to see Helen. She was standing farther back, and waved a hand, shook her head and smiled, as if to say she couldn't bear the racket. Ernie drew John farther into the barn, but he had given up talking and merely pointed.

The chickens were smallish and mostly white, and they all shuffled constantly. John saw that this was because the platforms on which they stood slanted forward, inclining them towards the slowly moving feed troughs. But not all of them were eating. Some were trying to peck the chickens next to them. Each chicken had its own little wire coop. There must have been forty rows of chickens on the ground floor, and eight or ten tiers of chickens went up to the ceiling. Between the double rows of back-to-back chickens were aisles wide enough for a man to pass and sweep the floor, John supposed, and just as he thought this, Ernie turned a wheel, and water began to shoot over the floor. The floor slanted towards various drain holes.

"All automatic! Somethin', eh?"

John recognized the words from Ernie's lips, and nodded appreciatively. "Terrific!" But he was ready to get away from the noise.

Ernie shut off the water.

John noticed that the chickens had worn their beaks down to blunt stubs, and their white breasts dripped blood where the horizontal bar supported their weight. What else could they do but eat? John had read a little about battery chicken farming. These hens of Ernie's, like the hens he had read about, couldn't turn around in their coops. Much of the general flurry in the barn was caused by chickens trying to fly upward. Ernie cut the lights. The doors closed after them, apparently also automatically.

"Machine farming has really got me over the hump," Ernie said, still talking loudly. "I'm making good money now. And just imagine, one man—me—can run the whole show!"

John grinned. "You mean you won't have anything for me to do?"

"Oh, there's plenty to do. You'll see. How about some lunch first? Tell Helen I'll be in in about fifteen minutes."

John walked towards Helen. "Fabulous."

"Yes. Ernie's in love with it."

They went on towards the house, Helen looking down at her feet, because the ground was muddy in spots. She wore old tennis shoes, black corduroy pants, and a rust-colored sweater. John purposely walked between her and where the kitten lay, not wanting to mention it now.

He carried his suitcase up to the square, sunny corner room which he had slept in since he was a boy of ten, when Helen and Ernie had bought the farm. He changed into blue jeans, and went down to join Helen in the kitchen.

"Would you like an old-fashioned? We've got to celebrate your arrival," Helen said. She was making two drinks at the wooden table.

"Fine.—Where's Susan?" Susan was their eight-year-old daughter.

"She's at a—Well, sort of summer school. They'll bring her back around four-thirty. Helps fill in the summer holidays. They make awful clay ashtrays and fringed money-purses—you know. Then you've got to praise them."

John laughed. He gazed at his aunt-by-marriage, thinking she was still very attractive at—what was it? Thirty-one, he thought. She was about five feet four, slender, with reddish blonde curly hair and eyes that sometimes looked green, sometimes blue. And she had a very pleasant voice. "Oh, thank you." John accepted his drink. There were pineapple chunks in it, topped with a cherry.

"Awfully good to see you, John. How's college? And how're your folks?"

Both those items were all right. John would graduate from Ohio State next year when he would be twenty, then he was going to take a post-graduate course in government. He was an only child, and his parents lived in Dayton, a hundred and twenty miles away.

Then John mentioned the kitten. "I hope it's not yours," he said, and realized at once that it must be, because Helen put her glass down and stood up. Who else could the kitten have belonged to, John thought, since there was no other house around?

"Oh, Lord! Susan's going to be—" Helen rushed out of the back door.

John ran after her, straight for the kitten which Helen had seen from a distance.

"It was that big truck this morning," Helen said. "The driver sits so high up he can't see what's—"

"I'll help you," John said, looking around for a spade or a trowel. He found a shovel and returned, and prized the flattened body up gently, as if it were still alive. He held it in both his hands. "We ought to bury it."

"Of course. Susan mustn't see it, but I've got to tell her.—There's a fork in back of the house."

John dug where Helen suggested, a spot near an apple tree behind the house. He covered the grave over, and put some tufts of grass back so it would not catch the eye.

"The times I've brought that kitten in the house when the damned trucks came!" Helen said. "She was barely four months, wasn't afraid of anything, just went trotting up to cars as if they were something to play with, you know?" She gave a nervous laugh. "And this morning the truck came at eleven, and I was watching a pie in the oven, just about to take it out."

John didn't know what to say. "Maybe you should get another kitten for Susan as soon as you can."

"What're you two doing?" Ernie walked towards them from the back door of the house.

"We just buried Beansy," Helen said. "The truck got her this morning."

"Oh." Ernie's smile disappeared. "That's too bad. That's really too bad, Helen."

But at lunch Ernie was cheerful enough, talking of vitamins and antibiotics in his chicken feed, and his produce of one and a quarter eggs per day per hen. Though it was July, Ernie was lengthening the chicken's "day" by artificial light.

"All birds are geared to spring," Ernie said. "They lay more when they think spring is coming. The ones I've got are at peak. In October they'll be under a year old, and I'll sell them and take on a new batch."

John listened attentively. He was to be here a month. He wanted to be helpful. "They really do eat, don't they? A lot of them have worn off their beaks, I noticed."

Ernie laughed. "They're de-beaked. They'd peck each other through the wire, if they weren't. Two of 'em got loose in my first batch and nearly killed each other. Well, one did kill the other. Believe me, I de-beak 'em now, according to instructions."

"And one chicken went on eating the other," Helen said. "Cannibalism." She laughed uneasily. "Ever hear of cannibalism among chickens, John?"

"No."

"Our chickens are insane," Helen said.

Insane. John smiled a little. Maybe Helen was right. Their noises had sounded pretty crazy.

"Helen doesn't much like battery farming," Ernie said apologetically to John. "She's always thinking about the old days. But we weren't doing so well then."

That afternoon, John helped his uncle draw the conveyor belts back into the barn. He began learning the levers and switches that worked things. Belts removed eggs and deposited them gently into plastic containers. It was nearly 5 P.M. before John could get away. He wanted to say hello to his cousin Susan, a lively little girl with hair like her mother's.

As John crossed the front porch, he heard a child's weeping, and he remembered the kitten. He decided to go ahead anyway and speak to Susan.

Susan and her mother were in the living room—a front room with flowered print curtains and cherrywood furniture. Some additions, such as a bigger television set, had been made since John had seen the room last. Helen was on her knees beside the sofa on which Susan lay, her face buried in one arm.

"Hello, Susan," John said. "I'm sorry about your kitten."

Susan lifted a round, wet face. A bubble started at her lips and broke. "Beansy—"

John embraced her impulsively. "We'll find another kitten. I promise. Maybe tomorrow. Yes?" He looked at Helen.

Helen nodded and smiled a little. "Yes, we will."

The next afternoon, as soon as the lunch dishes had been washed, John and Helen set out in the station wagon for a farm eight miles away belonging to some people called Ferguson. The Fergusons had two female cats that frequently had kittens, Helen said. And they were in luck this time. One of the cats had a litter of five—one black, one white, three mixed—and the other cat was pregnant.

"White?" John suggested. The Fergusons had given them a choice.

"Mixed," Helen said. "White is all good and black is—maybe unlucky."

They chose a black and white female with white feet.

"I can see this one being called Bootsy," Helen said, laughing.

The Fergusons were simple people, getting on in years, and very hospitable. Mrs. Ferguson insisted they partake of a freshly baked coconut cake along with some rather powerful homemade wine. The kitten romped around the kitchen, playing with gray rolls of dust that she dragged out from under a big cupboard.

"That ain't no battery kitten!" Frank Ferguson remarked, and drank deep.

"Can we see your chickens, Frank?" Helen asked. She slapped John's knee suddenly. "Frank has the most *wonderful* chickens, almost a hundred!"

"What's wonderful about 'em?" Frank said, getting up on a stiff leg. He opened the back screen door. "You know where they are, Helen."

John's head was buzzing pleasantly from the wine as he walked with Helen out to the chicken yard. Here were Rhode Island Reds, big white Leghorns, roosters strutting and tossing their combs, half-grown speckled chickens, and lots of little chicks about six inches high. The ground was covered with claw-scored watermelon rinds, tin bowls of grain and mush, and there was much chicken dung. A wheelless wreck of a car seemed to be a favorite laying spot: three hens sat on the back of the front seat with their eyes half closed, ready to drop eggs which would surely break on the floor behind them.

"It's such a wonderful *mess!*" John shouted, laughing.

Helen hung by her fingers in the wire fence, rapt. "Like the chickens I knew when I was a kid. Well, Ernie and I had them too, till about—" She smiled at John. "You know—a year ago. Let's go in!"

John found the gate, a limp thing made of wire that fastened with a wooden bar. They went in and closed it behind them.

Several hens drew back and regarded them with curiosity, making throaty, skeptical noises.

"They're such stupid darlings!" Helen watched a hen fly up and perch herself in a peach tree. "They can see the sun! They can fly!"

"And scratch for worms—and eat watermelon!" John said.

"When I was little, I used to dig worms for them at my grandmother's farm. With a hoe. And sometimes I'd step on their droppings, you know—well, on purpose—and it'd go between my toes. I loved it. Grandma always made me wash my feet under the garden hydrant before I came in the house." She laughed. A chicken evaded her outstretched hand with an *"Urrr-rrk!"* "Grandma's chickens were so tame, I could touch them. All bony and warm with the sun, their feathers. Sometimes I want to open all the coops in the barn and open the doors and let ours loose, just to see them walking on the grass for a few minutes."

"Say, Helen, want to buy one of these chickens to take home? Just for fun? A couple of 'em?"

"No."

"How much did the kitten cost? Anything?"

"No, nothing."

SUSAN TOOK THE kitten into her arms, and John could see that the tragedy of Beansy would soon be forgotten. To John's disappointment, Helen lost her gaiety during dinner. Maybe it was because Ernie was droning on about his profit and loss—not loss really, but outlay. Ernie was obsessed, John realized. That was why Helen was bored. Ernie worked hard now, regardless of what he said about machinery doing everything. There were creases on either side of his mouth, and they were not from laughing. He was starting to get a paunch. Helen had told John that last year Ernie had dismissed their handyman, Sam, who'd been with them seven years.

"Say," Ernie said, demanding John's attention. "What d'you think of the idea? Start a battery chicken farm when you finish school, and hire *one man* to run it. You could take another job in Chicago or Washington or wherever, and you'd have a steady *separate* income for life."

John was silent. He couldn't imagine owning a battery chicken farm.

"Any bank would finance you—with a word from Clive, of course."

Clive was John's father.

Helen was looking down at her plate, perhaps thinking of something else.

"Not really my lifestyle, I think," John answered finally. "I know it's profitable."

After dinner, Ernie went into the living room to do his reckoning, as he called it. He did some reckoning almost every night. John helped Helen with the dishes. She put a Mozart symphony on the record player. The music was nice, but John would have liked to talk with Helen. On the other hand, what would he have said, exactly? *I understand why you're bored. I think you'd prefer pouring slop for pigs and tossing grain to real chickens, the way you used to do.* John had a desire to put his arms around Helen as she bent over the sink, to turn her face to his and kiss her. What would Helen think if he did?

That night, lying in bed, John dutifully read the brochures on battery chicken farming which Ernie had given him.

. . . The chickens are bred small so that they do not eat so much, and they rarely reach more than 3½ pounds . . . Young chickens are subjected to a light routine which tricks them into thinking that a day is 6 hours long. The objective of the factory farmer is to increase the original 6-hour day by leaving the lights on for a longer period each week. Artificial Spring Period is maintained for the hen's whole lifetime of 10 months . . . There is no real falling off of egg-laying in the natural sense, though the hen won't lay quite so many eggs towards the end . . . [Why, John wondered. And wasn't "not quite so many" the same as "falling off"?] At 10 months the hen is sold for about 30¢ a pound, depending on the market . . .

And below:

Richard K. Schultz of Poon's Cross, Pa., writes: "I am more than pleased and so is my wife with the modernization of my farm into a battery chicken farm operated with Muskeego-Ryan Electric equipment. Profits have quadrupled in a year and a half and we have even bigger hopes for the future . . ."

Writes Henry Vliess of Farnham, Kentucky: "My old farm was barely breaking even. I had chickens, pigs, cows, the usual. My friends used to laugh at my hard work combined with all my tough luck. Then I . . ."

John had a dream. He was flying like Superman in Ernie's chicken barn, and the lights were all blazing brightly. Many of the imprisoned chickens looked up at him, their eyes flashed silver, and they were struck blind. The noise they made was fantastic. They wanted to escape, but could no longer see, and the whole barn heaved with their efforts to fly upward. John flew about frantically, trying to find the lever to open the coops, the doors, anything, but he couldn't. Then he woke up, startled to find himself in bed, propped on one elbow. His forehead and chest were damp with sweat. Moonlight came strong through the window. In the night's silence, he could hear the steady high-pitched din of the hundreds of chickens in the barn, though Ernie had said the barn was absolutely soundproofed. Maybe it was "daytime" for the chickens now. Ernie said they had three more months to live.

John became more adept with the barn's machinery and the fast artificial clocks, but since his dream he no longer looked at the chickens as he had the first day. He did not look at them at all if he could help it. Once Ernie pointed out a dead one, and John removed it. Its breast, bloody from the coop's barrier, was so distended, it might have eaten itself to death.

Susan had named her kitten "Bibsy," because it had a white oval on its chest like a bib.

"Beansy and now Bibsy," Helen said to John. "You'd think all Susan thinks about is food!"

Helen and John drove to town one Saturday morning. It was alternately sunny and showery, and they walked close together under an umbrella when the showers came. They bought meat, potatoes, washing powder, white paint for a kitchen shelf, and Helen bought a pink-and-white striped blouse for herself. At a pet shop, John acquired a basket with a pillow to give Susan for Bibsy.

When they got home, there was a long dark gray car in front of the house.

"Why, that's the doctor's car!" Helen said.

"Does he come by just to visit?" John asked, and at once felt stupid, because something might have happened to Ernie. A grain delivery had been due that morning, and Ernie was always climbing about to see that everything was going all right.

There was another car, dark green, which Helen didn't recognize beside the chicken factory. Helen and John went into the house.

It was Susan. She lay on the living room floor under a plaid blanket, only one sandaled foot and yellow sock visible under the fringed edge. Dr. Geller was there, and a man Helen didn't know. Ernie stood rigid and panicked beside his daughter.

Dr. Geller came towards Helen and said, "I'm sorry, Helen. Susan was dead by the time the ambulance got here. I sent for the coroner."

"What *happened*?" Helen started to touch Susan, and instinctively John caught her.

"Honey, I didn't see her in time," Ernie said. "She was chasing under that damned container after the kitten just as it was lowering."

"Yeah, it bumped her on the head," said a husky man in tan work-clothes, one of the delivery men. "She was running out from under it, Ernie said. My *gosh,* I'm sorry, Mrs. Hanshaw!"

Helen gasped, then she covered her face.

"You'll need a sedative, Helen," Dr. Geller said.

The doctor gave Helen a needle in her arm. Helen said nothing. Her mouth was slightly open, and her eyes stared straight ahead. Another car came and took the body away on a stretcher. The coroner took his leave then too.

With a shaky hand, Ernie poured whiskeys.

Bibsy leapt about the room, and sniffed at the red splotch on the carpet. John went to the kitchen to get a sponge. It was best to try to get it up, John thought, while the others were in the kitchen. He went back to the kitchen for a saucepan of water, and scrubbed again at the abundant red. His head was ringing, and he had difficulty keeping his balance. In the kitchen, he drank off his whiskey at a gulp and it at once burnt his ears.

"Ernie, I think I'd better take off," the delivery man said solemnly. "You know where to find me."

Helen went up to the bedroom she shared with Ernie, and did not come down when it was time for dinner. From his room, John heard floorboards creaking faintly, and knew that Helen was walking about in the room. He wanted to go in and speak to her, but he was afraid he would not be capable of saying the right thing. Ernie should be with her, John thought.

John and Ernie gloomily scrambled some eggs, and John went to ask Helen if she would come down or would prefer him to bring her something. He knocked on the door.

"Come in," Helen said.

He loved her voice, and was somehow surprised to find that it wasn't any different since her child had died. She was lying on the double bed, still in the same clothes, smoking a cigarette.

"I don't care to eat, thanks, but I'd like a whiskey."

John rushed down, eager to get something that she wanted. He brought ice, a glass, and the bottle on a tray. "Do you just want to go to sleep?" John asked.

"Yes."

She had not turned on a light. John kissed her cheek, and for an instant she slipped her arm around his neck and kissed his cheek also. Then he left the room.

Downstairs the eggs tasted dry, and John could hardly swallow even with sips of milk.

"My God, what a day," Ernie said. "My God." He was evidently trying to say more, looked at John with an effort at politeness, or closeness.

And John, like Helen, found himself looking down at his plate, wordless. Finally, miserable in the silence, John got up with his plate and patted Ernie awkwardly on the shoulder. "I am sorry, Ernie."

They opened another bottle of whiskey, one of the two bottles left in the living room cabinet.

"If I'd known this would happen, I'd never have started this damned chicken farm. You know that. I meant to earn something for my family— not go limping along year after year."

John saw that the kitten had found the new basket and gone to sleep in it on the living room floor. "Ernie, you probably want to talk to Helen. I'll be up at the usual time to give you a hand." That meant 7 A.M.

"Okay. I'm in a daze tonight. Forgive me, John."

John lay for nearly an hour in his bed without sleeping. He heard Ernie go quietly into the bedroom across the hall, but he heard no voices or even a murmur after that. Ernie was not much like Clive, John thought. John's father might have given way to tears for a minute, might have cursed. Then with his father it would have been all over, except for comforting his wife.

A raucous noise, rising and falling, woke John up. The chickens, of course. What the hell was it now? They were louder than he'd ever heard them. He looked out of the front window. In the pre-dawn light, he could see that the barn's front doors were open. Then the lights in the barn came on, blazing out on to the grass. John pulled on his tennis shoes without tying them, and rushed into the hall.

"*Ernie!—Helen!*" he yelled at their closed door.

John ran out of the house. A white tide of chickens was now oozing through the wide front doors of the barn. What on earth had happened? "Get *back!*" he yelled at the chickens, flailing his arms.

The little hens might have been blind or might not have heard him at all through their own squawks. They kept on flowing from the barn, some fluttering over the others, and sinking again in the white sea.

John cupped his hands to his mouth. "Ernie! The *doors!*" He was shouting into the barn, because Ernie must be there.

John plunged into the hens and made another effort to shoo them back. It was hopeless. Unused to walking, the chickens teetered like drunks, lurched against each other, stumbled forward, fell back on their tails, but they kept pouring out, many borne on the backs of those who walked. They were pecking at John's ankles. John kicked some aside and moved towards the barn doors again, but the pain of the blunt beaks on his ankles and lower legs made him stop. Some chickens tried to fly up to attack him, but had no strength in their wings. *They are insane,* John remembered. Suddenly frightened, John ran towards the clearer area at the side of the barn, then on towards the back door. He knew how to open the back door. It had a combination lock.

Helen was standing at the corner of the barn in her bathrobe, where John had first seen her when he arrived. The back door was closed.

"What's *happening*?" John shouted.

"I opened the coops," Helen said.

"Opened them—why?—Where's Ernie?"

"He's in there." Helen was oddly calm, as if she were standing and talk-ing in her sleep.

"Well, what's he *doing*? Why doesn't he close the place?" John was shaking Helen by the shoulders, trying to wake her up. He released her and ran to the back door.

"I've locked it again," Helen said.

John worked the combination as fast as he could, but he could hardly see it.

"Don't open it! Do you want them coming *this* way?" Helen was sud-denly alert, dragging John's hands from the lock.

Then John understood. Ernie was being killed in there, being pecked to death. Helen wanted it. Even if Ernie was screaming, they couldn't have heard him.

A smile came over Helen's face. "Yes, he's in there. I think they will fin-ish him."

John, not quite hearing over the noise of chickens, had read her lips. His heart was beating fast.

Then Helen slumped, and John caught her. John knew it was too late to save Ernie. He also thought that Ernie was no longer screaming.

Helen straightened up. "Come with me. Let's watch them," she said, and drew John feebly, yet with determination, along the side of the barn towards the front doors.

Their slow walk seemed four times as long as it should have been. He gripped Helen's arm. "Ernie *in* there?" John asked, feeling as if he were dreaming, or perhaps about to faint.

"In there." Helen smiled at him again, with her eyes half closed. "I came down and opened the back door, you see—and I went up and woke Ernie. I said, 'Ernie, something's wrong in the factory, you'd better come down.' " He came down and went in the back door—and I opened the coops with the lever. And then—I pulled the lever that opens the front door. He was—in the middle of the barn then, because I started a fire on the floor."

"A fire?" Then John noticed a pale curl of smoke rising over the front door.

"Not much to burn in there—just the grain," Helen said. "And there's enough for them to eat outdoors, don't you think?" She gave a laugh.

John pulled her faster towards the front of the barn. There seemed to be not much smoke. Now the whole lawn was covered with chickens, and they were spreading through the white rail fence on to the road, pecking, cackling, screaming, a slow army without direction. It looked as if snow had fallen on the land.

"Head for the house!" John said, kicking at some chickens that were attacking Helen's ankles.

They went up to John's room. Helen knelt at the front window, watching. The sun was rising on their left, and now it touched the reddish roof of the metal barn. Gray smoke was curling upward from the horizontal lintel of the front doors. Chickens paused, stood stupidly in the doorway until they were bumped by others from behind. The chickens seemed not so much dazzled by the rising sun—the light was brighter in the barn—as by the openness around them and above them. John had never before seen chickens stretch their necks just to look up at the sky. He knelt beside Helen, his arm around her waist.

"They're all going to—go away," John said. He felt curiously paralyzed.

"Let them."

The fire would not spread to the house. There was no wind, and the barn was a good thirty yards away. John felt quite mad, like Helen, or the chickens, and was astonished by the reasonableness of his thought about the fire's not spreading.

"It's all over," Helen said, as the last, not quite the last chickens wobbled out of the barn. She drew John closer by the front of his pajama jacket.

John kissed her gently, then more firmly on the lips. It was strange, stronger than any kiss he had ever known with a girl, yet curiously without further desire. The kiss seemed only an affirmation that they were both alive. They knelt facing each other, tightly embracing. The cries of the hens ceased to sound ugly, and sounded only excited and puzzled. It was like an orchestra playing, some members stopping, others resuming instruments, making a continuous chord without a tempo. John did not know how long they knelt like that, but at last his knees hurt, and he stood up, pulling Helen up, too. He looked out of the window and said:

"They must be all out. And the fire isn't any bigger. Shouldn't we——" But the obligation to look for Ernie seemed far away, not at all pressing on him. It was as if he dreamed this night or this dawn, and Helen's kiss, the way he had dreamed about flying like Superman in the barn. Were they really Helen's hands in his now?

She slumped again, and plainly she wanted to sit on the carpet, so he left her and pulled on his blue jeans over his pajama pants. He went down and entered the barn cautiously by the front door. The smoke made the interior hazy, but when he bent low, he could see fifty or more chickens pecking at what he knew must be Ernie on the floor. Bodies of chickens overcome by smoke lay on the floor, like little white puffs of smoke themselves, and some live chickens were pecking at these, going for the eyes. John moved towards Ernie. He thought he had braced himself, but he hadn't braced himself enough for what he saw: a fallen column of blood and bone to which a few tatters of pajama cloth still clung. John ran out again, very fast, because he had breathed once, and the smoke had nearly got him.

In his room, Helen was humming and drumming on the windowsill, gazing out at the chickens left on the lawn. The hens were trying to scratch in the grass, and were staggering, falling on their sides, but mostly falling backwards, because they were used to shuffling to prevent themselves from falling forward.

"Look!" Helen said, laughing so, there were tears in her eyes. "They don't know what grass is! But they like it!"

John cleared his throat and said, "What're you going to say?—What'll we say?"

"Oh—say." Helen seemed not at all disturbed by the question. "Well— that Ernie heard something and went down and—he wasn't completely sober, you know. And—maybe he pulled a couple of wrong levers.—Don't you think so?"

Notes from a
Respectable Cockroach

I have moved.

   I used to live at the Hotel Duke on a corner of Washington Square. My family has lived there for generations, and I mean at least two or three hundred generations. But no more for me. The place has degenerated. I've heard my great-great-great—go back as far as you like, she was still alive when I spoke to her—talk about the good old days when people arrived in horse-drawn carriages with suitcases that smelled of leather, people who had breakfast in bed and dropped a few crumbs for us on the carpet. Not purposely, of course, because we knew our place then, too, and our place was in the bathroom corners or down in the kitchen. Now we can walk all over the carpets with comparative impunity, because the clients of the Hotel Duke are too stoned blind to see us, or they haven't the energy to step on us if they did see us—or they just laugh.

   The Hotel Duke has now a tattered green awning extending to the curb, so full of holes it wouldn't protect anyone from the rain. You go up four cement steps into a dingy lobby that smells of pot smoke, stale whiskey, and is insufficiently lighted. After all, the clientele now doesn't necessarily want to see who else is staying here. People reel into each other in the lobby, and might thereby strike up an acquaintance, but more often it's an unpleasant exchange of words that results. To the left in the lobby is an even darker hole called Dr. Toomuch's Dance Floor. They charge two dollars admission, payable at the inside-the-lobby door. Juke box music. Puke box customers. Egad!

   The hotel has six floors, and I usually take the elevator, or the lift as people say lately, imitating the English. Why climb those grimy cement air shafts, or creep up staircase after staircase, when I can leap the mere half-inch gap between floor and lift and whisk myself safely into the corner beside the operator at the controls? I can tell each floor by its smell. Fifth floor, that's a disinfectant smell since more than a year, because a shoot-up occurred and there was lots of blood-and-guts spilt smack in front of the lift. Second floor boasts a worn-out carpet, so the odor is dusty, faintly mingled with urine. Third floor stinks of sauerkraut (somebody must have dropped a glass jar of it, the floor is tile here) and so it goes. If I want out on the third, for instance, and the elevator doesn't stop there, I just wait for the next trip, and sooner or later I make it.

I was at the Hotel Duke when the U.S. Census forms came in in 1970. What a laugh. Everybody got a form, and everybody was laughing. Most of the people here probably haven't any homes to begin with, and the census was asking, "How many rooms in your house?" and "How many bathrooms have you?" and "How many children?" and so forth. And what is your wife's age? People think that roaches can't understand English, or whatever is the going lingo in their vicinity. People think roaches understand only a suddenly turned-on light, which means "Scram!" When you've been around as long as we have, which is long before the *Mayflower* got here, you dig the going yak. So I was able to appreciate many a comment on the U.S. Census, which none of the cruds at the Duke bothered filling out. It was amusing to think of myself filling it out—and why not? I was more of a resident by hereditary seat than any of the human beasts in the hotel. I am (though I am not Franz Kafka in disguise) a cockroach, and I do not know my wife's age or for that matter how many wives I have. Last week I had seven, in a manner of speaking, but how many of these have been stepped on? As for children, they're beyond count, a boast I've heard my two-legged neighbors make also, but when it comes to the count, if the count is what they want (the more the merrier, I assume), I will bet on myself. Only last week I recall two egg capsules about to be delivered from two of my wives, both on the third (sauerkraut) floor. Good God, I was in a hurry myself, off in pursuit—I blush to mention it—of food which I had smelled and which I estimated to be at a distance of one hundred yards. Cheese-flavored potato chips, I thought. I did not like to say "Hello" and "Good-bye" so quickly to my wives, but my need was perhaps as great as theirs, and where would they be, or rather our race be, if I could not keep my strength up? A moment later I saw a third wife crunched under a cowboy boot (the hippies here affect Western gear even if they are from Brooklyn), though at least she wasn't laying an egg at that time, only hurrying along like me, in an opposite direction. Hail and farewell!—though, alas, I am sure she did not even see me. I may never again see my parturient wives, those two, though perhaps I saw some of our offspring before I left the Duke. Who knows?

When I see some of the people here, I count myself lucky to be a cockroach. I'm at least healthier, and in a small way I clean up garbage. Which brings me to the point. There used to be garbage in the form of breadcrumbs, an occasional leftover canapé from a champagne party in a room. The present clientele of the Hotel Duke doesn't eat. They either take dope or drink booze. I've only heard about the good old days from my great-great-great-great-grandmothers and -fathers. But I believe them. They said you could jump into a shoe, for instance, outside the door, and be taken into a room along with the tray by a servant at eight in the morning, and thus breakfast on croissant crumbs. Even the shoe-polishing days are gone, because if anybody put shoes outside his room these days, they'd not only not be polished, they'd be stolen. Nowadays it's all you can hope for that these hairy, buckskin-fringed monsters and their see-through girls will take a bath once in a while and leave a few drops of water in the tub for me to drink. It's dangerous drinking out of a toilet, and at my age I won't do it.

However, I wish to speak of my newfound fortune. I'd just about had enough last week, what with another young wife squashed before my eyes by a lurching step (she had been keeping out of the *normal* path, I remember), and a moronic roomful of junkies licking up—I mean this—food from the floor as a kind of game. Young men and women, naked, pretending to be handless for some insane reason, trying to eat their sandwiches like dogs, strewing them all over the floor, then writhing about together amid salami, pickles and mayonnaise. Plenty of food this time, but unsafe to dart among those rolling bodies. Worse than feet. But to see sandwiches at all was exceptional. There's no restaurant anymore, but half the rooms in the Hotel Duke are "apartments," meaning that they have refrigerators and small stoves. But the main thing people have in the way of food is tinned tomato juice for vodka Bloody Marys. Nobody even fries an egg. For one thing, the hotel does not furnish skillets, pans, can openers or even a single knife or fork: they'd be pinched. And none of these charmers is going to go out and buy so much as a pot to heat soup in. So the pickings is slim, as they say. And that isn't the worst of the "service" department here. Most of the windows don't shut tightly, the beds look like lumpy hammocks, straight chairs are falling apart at the joints, and the so-called armchairs, maybe one to a room, can inflict injury by releasing a spring in a tender

place. Basins are often clogged, and toilets either don't flush or keep flushing maniacally. And robberies! I've witnessed a few. A maid gives the
passkey and someone's in, absconding with suitcase contents under an arm,
in pockets, or in a pillowcase disguised as dirty laundry.

Anyway, about a week ago I was in a temporarily vacant room at the
Duke, scrounging about for a crumb or a bit of water, when in walked a
black bellhop with a suitcase that smelled of *leather*. He was followed by a
gentleman who smelled of aftershave lotion, plus of course tobacco, that's
normal. He unpacked, put some papers out on the writing table, tried the
hot water and muttered something to himself, jiggled the running toilet,
tested the shower which shot all over the bathroom floor, and then he rang
up the desk. I could understand most of what he was saying. He was essen-
tially saying that at the price he was paying per day, this and that might be
improved, and could he change his room, perhaps?

I lurked in my corner, thirsty, hungry, but interested, knowing also that
I would be stepped on by this same gentleman if I made an appearance on
the carpet. I well knew that I would be on his list of complaints if he saw
me. The old French window blew open (it was a gusty day) and his papers
went in all the four corners. He had to close the window by propping the
back of a straight chair against it, and then he gathered his papers, cursing.

"Washington Square!—Henry James would turn in his grave!"

I remember those words, uttered at the same time as he slapped his
forehead as if to hit a mosquito.

A bellhop in the threadbare maroon livery of the establishment arrived
stoned and fiddled with the window to no avail. The window leaked cold
air, made a terrible rattle, and everything, even a cigarette pack, had to be
anchored down or it would have blown off a table or whatever. The bellhop in looking at the shower managed to drench himself, and then he said
he would send for "the engineer." The engineer at the Hotel Duke is a joke
on his own, which I won't go into. He didn't turn up that day, I think
because the bellhop made the final bad impression, and the gentleman
picked up the telephone and said:

"Can you send someone sober, if possible, to carry my suitcases
down? . . . Oh, keep the money, I'm checking out. And get me a taxi,
please."

That was when I made up my mind. As the gentleman was packing, I
mentally kissed good-bye to all my wives, brothers, sisters, cousins, children
and grandchildren and great-grandchildren and then climbed aboard the
beautiful suitcase that smelled of leather. I crawled into a pocket in the lid,

and made myself snug in the folds of a plastic bag, fragrant of shaving soap and the aftershave lotion, where I would not be squashed even when the lid was closed.

Half an hour later, I found myself in a warmer room where the carpet was thick and not dusty-smelling. The gentleman has breakfast in bed in the mornings at 7:30. In the corridor, I can get all sorts of things from trays left on the floor outside the doors—even remnants of scrambled eggs, and certainly plenty of marmalade and butter on rolls. Had a narrow squeak yesterday when a white-jacketed waiter chased me thirty yards down the hall, stomping with both feet but missing me every time. I'm nimble yet, and life at the Hotel Duke taught me plenty!

I've already cased the kitchen, going and coming by lift, of course. Lots of pickings in the kitchen, but unfortunately they fumigate once a week. I met four possible wives, all a bit sickly from the fumes, but determined to stick it out in the kitchen. For me, it's upstairs. No competition, and plenty of breakfast trays and sometimes midnight snacks. Maybe I'm an old bachelor now, but there's life in me yet if a possible wife comes along. Meanwhile I consider myself a lot better than those bipeds in the Hotel Duke, whom I've seen eating stuff I wouldn't touch—or mention. They do it on bets. Bets! All life is a gamble, isn't it? So why bet?

Eddie and
the Monkey Robberies

Eddie's job was to open doors. Formerly, he had been cup-shaker for a record-player named Hank, a young man who hadn't been able to subsidize his poetry writing sufficiently by tootling, and it had been difficult to keep Eddie in the face of complaining landlords, so Hank had passed Eddie on to a girlfriend called Rose, to whom he had just said good-bye, and had taken a job. And Rose knew Jane, and Jane was an ex-convict, which was why Eddie was now opening doors of strange houses.

Being a young and clever Capuchin, Eddie had learned his new job quickly, and often approached doors gaily waltzing and swinging himself from any nearby object, such as a newel post or the back of a straight chair, towards his goal: the knob of a Yale lock, a button that undid a bolt, maybe a chain and bolt also. His nimble fingers flew, undoing everything, or experimenting until they could.

Thus he would admit the husky blonde woman called Jane, whose ring or knock he had usually already heard. Sometimes Eddie had the door open when Jane was still climbing the front steps or walking up the front path, her reticule in hand. Eddie would have got in through a window. Jane always paused for a moment on the threshold, and mumbled something, as if addressing someone standing in the house. Then she would come in and close the door.

Ka-*bloom!* This particular house was a solid one, and had a pleasant smell to Eddie, for there was a big cluster of yellow roses in a vase in the downstairs hall.

From the pocket of her loose coat, Jane produced a banana, its partly opened peel limp and blackening. Eddie gave a squeak of thanks, ripped the rest of the peel off and handed it back to Jane, who pocketed it. Jane was already walking towards the back of the house, towards the kitchen and dining room.

She opened a drawer in the dining room, then a second before she found what she wanted, and at once began loading her reticule with handfuls of silver spoons, forks and knives. She took a silver salt and pepper set from the dining room table. Then she went into the living room, went at once to the telephone table, where a silver-framed photograph stood. This she put into her bag, and also a handsome paper knife which had what looked like a jade handle. By now barely three minutes had passed, Eddie had finished his banana, Jane whispered his name, opened her coat, and Eddie leapt. He clung to her big sweatered bosom with his twenty fingers and toes, aided also by his long tail, as he had clung to his mother when he was small.

They were out of the house. To Eddie, the hum of the car grew louder, then they were inside the car, Jane sat down with a thump, and the car moved off. The women talked.

"Easy, very easy, that one," Jane said, getting her breath back. "But I didn't bother with the bedrooms."

"Silver?"

"You bet! Ha-ha!—Ah, a nice whiskey'll taste good!"

Rose, younger than Jane, drove prudently. This was their seventh or eighth robbery this summer. Rose was twenty-one, divorced from a first marriage, and she'd fallen out with her boyfriend two months ago. Someone like Jane, a little crazy excitement, had been just what she needed. But she had no intention of doing a stretch in prison, as Jane had done, if she could help it. "So? The Ponsonby place now?"

"Yep," said Jane, enjoying a cigarette. For two weeks, they had made telephone calls now and then to the Ponsonby house, and no one had ever answered. Two or three times in the last week, Jane and Rose had cruised past the big house, and had not seen any sign of life. Tommy, their fence, hadn't watched the house, hadn't had the time, he said. Jane thought the people were away on vacation. It was July. Lots of people were away, with only one neighbor or maybe a cleaning woman coming in to water the plants. But had the Ponsonbys a burglar alarm, for instance? It was a very swank section. "Maybe we ought to phone one more time," Jane said. "Got the number handy?"

Rose had. She stopped the car in the parking area of a roadside bar-and-steakhouse.

"You stay here, Eddie," Jane said, sticking Eddie under a disorder of plastic shopping bags and a raincoat on the back seat. She gave him a rap with her heavily ringed fingers to let him know she meant it.

The rap caught Eddie on the top of the head. He was only slightly annoyed. The two women were back before long, before it became unpleasantly hot in the car, and they drove on for a while, then stopped again. Eddie was still sitting on the back seat, hardly conspicuous in the debris except for the white cap of fur on the crown of his head. He watched as Rose got out. This was the way things always went when he had a job to do: Rose got out first, came back, then Jane put him under her coat and took him out of the car.

Jane hummed a tune to herself and smoked a cigarette.

Rose came back and said, "No window open and the ones in back are locked. Nobody home, because I rang the bell and knocked front and back.—What a house!" Rose meant that it looked rich. "Maybe breaking a back window is best. Let Eddie in that way."

The neighborhood was residential and expensive, the lawns generous, the trees tall. Rose and Jane were parked, as usual, around the corner from the house they were interested in.

"Any sign of life in the garage?" Jane asked. They had thought that there might be a servant sleeping there without a telephone, or with a different telephone from the Ponsonbys'.

"Of course not or I'd have told you," said Rose. "Have you emptied the tapestry bag yet?"

Jane and Rose did this, using the old gray raincoat to wrap the lot of silverware and the other objects up in, and this they put on the back seat, without themselves leaving the front seat.

"Why don't we try Eddie down a chimney?" Jane asked. "It's so quiet here, I don't like the idea of breaking a window."

"But he doesn't like chimneys," Rose said. "This house has three storys. Pretty long chimneys."

Jane thought for a moment, then shrugged. "What the hell? If he doesn't like going all the way down, he can come up again."

"And suppose he just stays up there—on the roof?"

"So—we've lost a good monkey," said Jane.

A few weeks ago, they had practiced with Eddie at a Long Island house which belonged to a friend of Jane's. The chimney top had been only twelve feet from the ground because it was a one-story cottage. Eddie hadn't liked going down the chimney, but he had done it two or three times, with Rose on a ladder encouraging him, and Jane waiting to give him raisins and peanuts when he unlocked the front door for her. Eddie had coughed and rubbed his eyes, and made a lot of chattering noises. They'd tried him again the next day, tossing him onto the roof and pointing to the chimney and talking to him, and he'd done it well then, had come down and opened the door. But Rose remembered the worry wrinkles around his brows that had made him look like a little old man, remembered how pleased he was when she'd given him a bath and a brushing afterward. Eddie had given her a most endearing smile and clasped her hands. So Rose hesitated, wondering about Eddie, worried about herself and Jane.

"Well?" said Jane.

"Chi-chi," said Eddie, knowing something was up. He scratched an ear, and looked attentively from one to the other of the women. He preferred to listen to Rose, her voice being gentler, though he lived with Jane.

Things got moving, but slowly.

Jane and Rose maintained an air of calm. Rose, in case of any possible interference at the door, someone asking what was her business, was prepared to say she was offering her services as a cleaning woman for four dollars an hour. If anyone accepted, Rose gave a false name and made a date which she never kept. This had happened only once. It was Rose who kept track of the houses they had robbed, and of the one house where someone had come to the door to answer her knock, even though no one had answered the telephone in that house just five minutes before. After they had robbed a certain neighborhood, sometimes three houses in one hour, they never went back to it. In Rose's car, they had gone as far as a hundred and fifty miles from their base, which was Jane's apartment in Red Cliff, New Jersey. If they had to separate for any reason, they had a roadside café picked out or a drugstore somewhere, as a meeting place, the one who was carless (Jane) having to make her way there by taxi or bus or on foot. This had happened also only once so far in their two months of operations, one time when Rose had been perhaps unnecessarily anxious and had driven off. Today their rendezvous was the bar-and-steakhouse where they had just been to ring the Ponsonby house.

Now Jane, with Eddie under her lightweight woolen coat, walked up the rather imposing front path of the Ponsonby mansion. Such goodies in there Jane could scarcely imagine. They'd certainly be more than she could carry away in the reticule she called her tapestry bag. Jane rang, waited, then knocked with the brass knocker, not at all expecting anyone to answer, but she had to go through the motions in case a neighbor was watching. Finally Jane went round by the driveway to the back door, with Eddie still clinging to her under her coat. She knocked again. Everything was as quiet as could be, including the garage with its one closed window over the closed doors.

"Eddie, it's the chimney again," Jane whispered. "Chimney, understand? Now you go right up! See it?" She pointed. Great elm trees sheltered her from view from any side. There seemed to be at least four chimneys projecting from the roof. "Chimney and then the door! Right, Eddie? Good boy!" She released Eddie on to a drainpipe which went up one corner of the house.

Eddie managed well, slipping a few inches here and there, but he had no trouble in getting a hold on the somewhat rough exterior brick. Suddenly he was up, for a second silhouetted against the sky, leaping, and then he vanished.

Jane saw him jump to a chimney pot, peer down, hesitate, then run to another. She was afraid to call encouragement. Were the chimneys stopped up? Well, wait and see. No use worrying yet. Jane stepped back to see better, did not see Eddie, and made her way to the front door again. She expected to hear Eddie sliding bolts, but she heard nothing at all. She rang halfheartedly, for appearance's sake.

Silence. Had Eddie got stuck in a chimney?

A passerby on the sidewalk glanced at Jane and went on, a man of about thirty, carrying a package. A car went by. Rose, in the car, was out of sight around the corner. Eddie might be stuck, Jane supposed, might have been put out of commission by soot. And the minutes were passing. Should she play it safe and leave? On the other hand, Eddie was damned useful, and there were a good two more months of summer to operate in.

Jane went to the back of the house again. She looked up at the roof, but saw no sign of Eddie. Birds cheeped. A car shifted gears in the distance. Jane went to the kitchen window at the back, and at once the monkey leapt on to the long aluminium drainboard. He was black with soot, even the top of his head was dark gray, and he rubbed his eyes with his knuckles. He tapped on a pane and hopped from one foot to the other, wanting her to open a window.

Why hadn't they trained him for windows? Well, they'd have to get on to that. Just a matter of unscrewing—even from here, Jane could see the mechanism. "Door!" said Jane, pointing towards the kitchen door, because any door would have done, but Eddie had the habit of going to front doors.

Eddie sprang down, and Jane heard him pulling bolts.

But the door did not open. Jane tried it.

Jane heard his "Chi-chi-chi!" which meant he was annoyed or frustrated. The bolts were stiff, Jane supposed, or it was a mortise lock, requiring a key from inside to open. And some bolts took strength beyond Eddie's. Jane felt suddenly panicky. Ten or twelve minutes had passed, she thought. Rose would be worried. Maybe Rose had already gone off to the roadside steakhouse. Jane wanted to go back to Rose and the car. The alternative was breaking a window, and she was afraid to make that much noise and still get away with Eddie on foot.

Again making an effort to appear unhurried, Jane went down the driveway to the sidewalk. Around the corner, Jane saw with relief that Rose was still waiting in the car.

"Well," said Jane, "Eddie can't get a door open and I'm scared. Let's take off."

"Oh? Where is he? He's still *in*?"

"In the kitchen in back." Jane was whispering through the car's open window. She opened the door on her side.

"But we can't just leave him there," Rose said. "Did you see anybody—watching you?"

Jane got in and closed the door. "No, but let's get going."

Rose was thinking the police might connect a monkey with the robberies they'd done. How could anyone explain a monkey in a closed house? Of course, anyone who found Eddie might not at once telephone the police, might just give him to the S.P.C.A. or a zoo. Or mightn't Eddie break a window and escape—and then what? Rose realized she wasn't thinking logically, but it seemed to her that they ought to get Eddie out. "Can't we break a back window?" Rose's hand was already on the door handle.

"No, don't!" Jane made a negative gesture, but Rose was already gone. Jane sat rigid. She'd get the blame if someone saw Rose breaking in. Rose would talk, Jane thought. And Jane had the police record.

Rose was forcing herself to walk slowly past a young man and a girl who were arm in arm, talking and laughing. The Ponsonby house. It was so grand, it had a name: Five Owls. Rose went into the driveway, still calm but not wanting to go through the motions of ringing the front doorbell, because she did not want to waste the time.

Eddie was in the kitchen, squatting on a table (she saw him through a side window), shaking something that looked like a sugar bowl upside down, and she had a brief impression of something broken, like a platter, on the yellow linoleum floor. Eddie must be desperate. By the time Rose came round the corner of the house, Eddie was on the drainboard just behind the back windows. Rose made an effort to raise a window and gave it up. She extricated a cuff of her white trousers from a rosebush. Almost at her feet, she found a rock the size of her fist, and tapped it once against a rectangular pane. She struck again at some jagged pieces of glass at the edges, but Eddie was already through, chattering with joy.

Rose gathered him quickly under her jacket, and walked into the driveway. She could feel Eddie trembling, maybe with relief. When Rose reached the corner, she saw that the car had gone. *Her* car. She'd have to find a taxi. Or walk to the roadhouse. No, that was too far. A taxi. And she'd left her handbag with her money in the car. Christ! She pressed Eddie's body reassuringly, and walked on, looking for some promising intersection where a taxi might be cruising. Where was Jane? Back at her own apartment? At the roadside place? What was the taxi driver going to say if she had no money to pay him? Rose couldn't tell the driver to go to the house of one of her friends, because she didn't want any of her friends to know about Eddie, about Jane, about what she'd been doing for the last weeks.

She had no luck spotting a taxi. But she did come to a shopping center—supermarket, dry cleaning shop, drugstore, all that—and she had some coins in her jacket pocket so she went into the drugstore. With Eddie holding on under her jacket, Rose looked up a taxi company and dialed. The shopping center was called Miracle Buy. She gave that name.

In about five minutes, a taxi arrived. Rose had been standing on a little cement island in the parking area, keeping a lookout for the taxi, because taxis weren't always painted in bright colors in neighborhoods like this.

"Can you drive to Red Cliff, please? Corner of Jefferson Avenue and Mulhouse."

They were off. Seventeen miles at least, Rose supposed. She didn't think Jane would have driven to the steakhouse, or have been able to find it. Jane wasn't a good driver. But she could have found her way home, and probably had. Rose had a key to Jane's apartment, but that was in her handbag too.

The taxi reached Jefferson and Mulhouse.

"Can you wait one minute? I want to speak to a friend, then I'll be back."

"How soon?" asked the driver, looking around at Rose. His eyes moved over her, and Rose could see that he thought she had no pocket-book, therefore no money. "What you got there, a *monkey*?"

Eddie had stuck an arm, then his head out of Rose's jacket before she could push him back. "Friend's pet," Rose said. "I'm delivering him. Then I'll be down and pay you." Rose got out.

Rose didn't see her own car. There were lots of cars parked at the curbs. She rang Jane's bell, one of four bells in the small apartment build-ing. She rang again, three short rings, one long, which was her ring by agreement with Jane, and to Rose's great relief, the release button sounded. Rose climbed the stairs, and knocked on a door on the third floor.

"It's Rose!" she said.

Jane opened the door, looking a bit frightened, and Rose went in.

"Here's Eddie. Take him. I need some money for the taxi. Give me twenty or thirty—or hand me my bag."

"Anything happen? Anybody following you?"

"No. Where's some money? You brought my bag up?"

Eddie had scampered on to the sofa, and was sitting on his haunches, scratching his sooty head.

Rose went down with her handbag, and paid the driver. He said the fare was twenty-seven, though he had no meter, and Rose gave him three tens. "Thanks very much!" Rose said with a smile.

"Right!" He drove off.

Rose didn't want to go back to Jane's, but she felt she had to say some-thing. Make a speech and end it, she thought, and now was as good a time as any, and thank God, the taxi driver hadn't said anything more about Eddie. Rose gave her special ring again.

"What happened with the silverware?" Rose asked.

"Tommy just took it. I called him right away—I'm sorry I got scared back there, Rosey dear, but I *did*. Breaking a window is nuts!"

Rose was relieved that Tommy had come and gone. He was a skinny, red-haired man with a stutter, inefficient looking, but so far he'd never made a mistake that Rose knew of. "Don't forget to give Eddie a bath, will you?" Rose said.

"You always like to do that. Go ahead—Don't you want a coffee? It's easy."

"I'm leaving." Rose hadn't sat down. "I'm sorry, Jane, but I think I'd better pull out. You said yourself—I did the wrong thing today, breaking a window."

Jane looked at Rose, braced her hands on her hips, and glanced at Eddie on the sofa.

Eddie was nervously examining the nails of his nearly hairless left hand.

"If something happened," Jane said, "it's better if you tell me. I'm the one who has to face it."

"Nothing *happened*. I just want to quit and—I don't want any share of today's, thanks. I'll—You left the keys in my car? Where is the car?"

"What happened with the taxi driver?"

"Nothing! I paid him and that was that."

"He saw Eddie?"

"Well, yes. I said he was a pet I was delivering. I'll be off, Jane.—Bye, Eddie." Rose felt compelled to cross the room and to touch Eddie's head.

Eddie glanced up sadly, as if he had understood every word, and began nibbling his nails.

Rose moved towards the door. "Don't forget to bathe him. He'll be happier."

"To *hell* with him!" said Jane.

Rose went down the stairs, as scared and shaky as she'd ever felt ringing somebody's doorbell, or waiting in the car while Jane did her job. She'd ring up Hank. Hank White his name was, living somewhere in Greenwich Village. She hoped she could dig up the number somehow, because she didn't think it was listed under his name, and she might have to ring other people to get it. He'd come, if it concerned Eddie. She realized she was worried about Eddie. And Hank was the only person she could tell this to, because Jane kept Eddie hidden from her friends, kept him in a locked closet when anyone came (even Tommy), and spanked him later if he'd chattered. Rose found her car finally. The keys were in the dashboard. She drove towards her home, which was an apartment in a town about eight miles away.

Jane washed her face and combed her curly, blonde-rinsed hair by way of pulling herself together, but it didn't help. She picked up a paperback book and flung it at Eddie in a backhanded gesture. It caught Eddie in the side.

"*Ik-ik!*" Eddie cried, and leapt a couple of inches into the air. He turned a puzzled face towards Jane, and braced himself to jump to one side or the other, in case Jane tried to strike him again.

"You'll damn well stay in your closet *tonight!*" said Jane, advancing. "Starting now!"

Eddie wriggled easily from her outstretched hands, and leapt to the frame of a picture over the sofa.

The picture fell, Eddie landed on the sofa again, and seized an icebag that had been lying there for some time. He hurled the icebag at Jane. It fell short. *"Chi-chi-chi-chi-chi!"* Eddie chattered without stopping, and his round eyes had gone wide and pink at the outer edges.

Jane was determined to catch him and stick him away. Suppose the cops for some reason suddenly knocked on the door? Or broke in? What kind of trail had that dumb Rose left behind? All Rose had to her credit was a nice face and a fast car. Jane picked up the end of the madras counterpane that covered the sofa, intending to throw it over Eddie and capture him, but Eddie leapt to the center of the room. Jane pulled the counterpane all the way off and advanced with it.

Eddie threw an ashtray at close range and hit Jane in the cheek with it. The ashtray fell and broke on the floor.

Jane got angrier.

Now Eddie was on the drainboard in the kitchenette, brandishing a paring knife, chattering and squeaking. he picked up half a lemon and threw it.

"You little *insect!*" Jane muttered, coming towards him with the counterpane. She had him cornered now.

Eddie dove straight for Jane, landed with four feet on her left arm, and bit her thumb. He had dropped the knife.

Jane cried out. Her thumb began to bleed, the blood oozed and dripped. She picked up a straight chair. She'd kill the little devil!

Eddie dodged the chair and at once attacked Jane's legs from behind, nipped into one calf and sprang away.

"Ow!" Jane yelled, more with surprise than pain. She hadn't even seen him go behind her. She looked at her injury and saw that he'd drawn blood again. She'd fix *him!* She closed the one open window so he couldn't escape, and went for the paring knife on the floor. She felt inspired to sink it into his neck.

Eddie jumped on to her bent back, on to the back of her head, and Jane toppled over. She hurt her elbow slightly, and before she could get up, Eddie had bitten her nose. Jane touched her nose to see if it was still all there.

And Eddie dived for the doorknob. He supported himself on one hind leg, and worked at the top bolt, turning the little knob. If he could turn the big knob at the same time, the door would open with a pull, but he had to abandon his effort when he heard Jane's steps close behind him. Eddie sprang down just as the knife point grated against the metal door.

"Chi-chi!"

Jane had dropped the knife. Eddie picked it up, ran up Jane's hip and shoulder and struck her in the cheek with the knife point. He used the knife as he had seen people do, sometimes with stabbing motions, sometimes sawing, and then suddenly he flung the knife away and leapt from Jane's shoulder to a bookcase, panting and chattering. Eddie smelled blood, and this frightened him. Nervously Eddie threw a book at Jane, which came nowhere near hitting her.

Jane was aware of blood running down her neck. Absurd that she couldn't catch the little beast! For an instant, she felt that she couldn't breathe, that she was going to faint, then she took a deep breath and gathered her strength.

Plock! A book hit Jane on the chest.

Well, well! One swat with a chair would do for Eddie!

Jane reached for the straight chair which had fallen on its side. When she had it in position to swing, Eddie was not on the bookcase. Jane felt his fast little feet going up her back, started to turn, and had a glimpse of Eddie with the counterpane in his hands, climbing over her head with it. Jane lost her balance and fell, stumbling against the chair that she was lowering.

Eddie skipped from one side of the hump on the floor to the other, pulling the thin cloth over his enemy. He seized the nearest object—a conch shell from the floor near the hall door—and took a grip with both hands. He came down with this on the woman's slightly moving head under the counterpane. Eddie slipped and rolled over, but he kept his fingers in the crease of the shell, and struck again with it. The *crack* was a satisfying sound to Eddie. *Crack! Crack!* He heard a dreary moan from the heap.

Then for no reason, as he had dropped the knife for no reason, Eddie dropped the conch shell on the carpet and gave it a nervous kick with a hind foot. He allowed himself a few chatters, and peered about as if to see if someone else were in the room with him.

He heard only the *tick-tick-tick* of the clock in the bedroom beyond the hall. He was aware of the blood smell again, and withdrew some distance from the counterpane. Eddie sighed, exhausted. He loped to the window, fiddled with it for an instant, and gave it up. It had to be raised, and it was heavy.

It was growing darker.

The telephone rang. There flitted across Eddie's mind the familiar image of Jane or someone picking up the telephone, talking into it. Once Eddie had been told or allowed to do this, and he had dropped the telephone, and people had laughed. Now Eddie felt fearful and hostile towards the telephone, towards the hump on the floor. He kept looking to see if the hump stirred. It did not. He was thirsty. Eddie leapt to the drainboard, looked around and felt for a glass of water or anything with liquid in it, which he always smelled before drinking, but he saw no such thing. Using both hands, he turned a tap and cupped one hand and drank. He made a perfunctory effort to turn the tap off, didn't quite succeed, and left it trickling.

The telephone stopped ringing.

Then Eddie opened the refrigerator—a little uncomfortably because he had been scolded and slapped for this—and seeing no fruit in the lighted interior, scooped a handful of cooked stringbeans from a bowl and started to nibble them, kicked the door shut with a hind foot, and loped off on three legs. He felt at once tired, flung the beans down, and jumped into a rocking chair to sleep.

When the doorbell rang, Eddie was curled in the seat of the rocking chair. He lifted his head. The room was quite dark.

Suddenly Eddie wanted to flee. The smell of blood was uglier. He could open the front door and go, he realized, unless the woman had put on the special lock which required a set of jingling keys to open. She kept the keys hidden. Eddie had succeeded only once with a key, somewhere for fun, with Jane and Rose. Keys were usually too stiff for him to turn.

Buzz-buzz.

It was the downstairs bell, different from the apartment door which gave a *ting*. Eddie was not interested in the bell, he simply wanted to escape now. He sprang to the doorknob again, and seized the smaller knob above with his left hand. It turned, but the door did not open. Eddie tried again, turning the doorknob also with his feet. Then he pushed the doorjamb, and the door swung towards him. Eddie leapt down and loped silently down the stairs, swinging himself out at the turnings by one of the balusters. Downstairs the door was easier—he thought—and he could also slip out when the next person came in.

Eddie jumped up to the round white knob, slipped, and then tried turning it while standing on his hind feet. The door opened.

"Eddie! *Ed*-die! *What* the—"

Eddie knew the voice. *"Chi-chi!"* Eddie jumped onto Hank's arm, flung himself against Hank's chest, chattering madly, and feeling that he had a long and desperate story to tell. *"Aieeee!"* Eddie was even inventing new words.

"What's goin' on, eh?" Hank said softly, coming in. "Where's Jane?" He glanced up the stairs. He closed the door, settled Eddie more securely inside his leather jacket, and climbed the stairs two at a time.

Jane's door was ajar and there was no light on.

"Jane?" he called, and knocked once. Then he went in. "Jane?— Where's the light here, Eddie boy?" Hank groped, and after a few seconds, found a light switch. He heard footsteps coming down from the next floor, and instinctively he closed the door. Something was wrong here. He looked around at Jane's living room in astonishment. He'd been here before, but only once. "What the hell happened?" he whispered to himself. The place was a shambles. A robbery, he thought. They'd dumped the stuff in the middle of the floor and intended to come back.

Hank moved towards the heap on the floor. He pulled the madras cover back slowly.

"Holy cow!—Holy *cow!*"

Eddie flattened himself against Hank's sweater and closed his eyes, terrified and wanting to hide.

"Jane?" Hank touched her shoulder, thinking maybe she'd fainted, or been knocked out. He tried to turn her over, and found that her body was a bit stiff and not at all warm. Her face, her neck were dark red with blood. Hank blinked and straightened up. "Anybody else here?" he called towards the next room, more boldly than he felt.

He knew there was no one else here. Slowly it dawned on him that Eddie had killed Jane with his little teeth, maybe with—Hank was looking at a kitchen knife a few feet away on the floor. Then he saw the cream-and-pink colored conch shell. "Get down, Eddie," he whispered. But Eddie wouldn't be dislodged from the sweater.

Hank picked up the knife, then the shell. He washed them both at the sink in the kitchenette, and saw a faint pinkness run off the shell. He turned the shell upside down, and shook the water out of it. He dried it thoroughly with a dishtowel. He did the same with the knife. Jane must have attacked Eddie. Hadn't Rose hinted as much? "We're gettin' out, Eddie! Yes, sir, yes, sir!"

Then Eddie heard the comforting sound of the zipper that closed Hank's jacket all the way up. They were going down the stairs now.

Hank had not forgotten to wipe the doorknobs when he left Jane's apartment, and he had made sure the door locked behind him in a normal way. Hank had thought to telephone the police at once, when he'd been in Jane's apartment, then had thought to telephone them later once he got

Eddie home safely. But he didn't. He wasn't even going to telephone Rose. Rose wouldn't want any part of it, and Hank knew she could be trusted to keep her mouth shut. The body would be found soon enough, was Hank's opinion, and he didn't want Eddie blamed for it. The police, if he'd rung, would have asked him what he knew about it, and they'd have found out somehow about Eddie, even if Hank had tried to hide him.

So Hank bided his time on Perry Street, Greenwich Village, where he shared an apartment with two young men, and two days later, he caught an item in a newspaper saying that Jane Garrity, aged forty-two, unemployed secretary, had been found dead in her apartment in Red Cliff, New Jersey, victim of an attack by an unknown assailant or assailants, maybe even children, because her wounds and blows had not been severe. The actual cause of death had been a heart attack.

The police would know Jane's record, Hank thought, and the company she kept. Let them worry about it. Hank reproached himself for having given Eddie to Rose, but she'd been fond of Eddie, and Hank had felt a bit guilty when he and Rose had broken up. But now that he had Eddie back, Hank was not going to part with him. Eddie showed no further interest in opening doors, because he was happy where he was. He had a small room to himself, with ropes to swing on, a basket bed, no door at all, and one of Hank's friends, a sculptor, constructed something like a tree for Eddie in the living room. Hank began writing a rather long epic poem about Eddie, whose life story was to be veiled, metamorphosed, allegorized. *The Conqueror Monkey.* Only Hank and Eddie knew the truth.

Hamsters vs. Websters

The circumstances under which Julian and Betty Webster and their ten-year-old son Laurence acquired a country house, a dog, and hamsters, were most sudden and unexpected for the family, and yet it all hung together.

One afternoon in his air-conditioned Philadelphia office Julian suffered a heart attack. He had pain, he sank to the floor, and he was whisked to a hospital. When he had recovered some five days later, his doctor gave him a serious talk. Julian would have to stop smoking, reduce his working hours to six or less per day, and a country atmosphere would be better for him than living in an apartment in Philadelphia. Julian was shocked. He was only thirty-seven, he pointed out.

"You don't realize how you've been driving yourself," the doctor replied calmly, smiling. "I've spoken with your wife. She's willing to make the change. She cares about your health, even if you don't."

Julian was of course won over. He loved Betty. He could see that the doctor's advice was reasonable. And Larry was hopping with joy. They were going to have a real country house with land, trees, space—a lot better than the silly paved playground of the big apartment building, which was all Larry could remember, since his family had moved there when he was five.

The Websters found a two-story white house with four gable windows and an acre and a half of land, seventeen miles from Philadelphia. Julian would not even have to drive to his office. His firm had changed his job from that of sales manager to sales consultant, which Julian realized was another way of saying traveling salesman. But his salary remained the same. Olympian Pool built swimming pools of all sizes, shapes and colors, heated and unheated, and also provided vacuum and filter-cleaning devices, purifiers, sprays and bubble-makers, and all kinds of diving boards. And Julian, he realized himself, made a good impression as salesman. His appointments were follow-ups of responses to mailed advertisements, so he was sure of being received. Julian was not high pressure. His manner was quiet and sincere, and he didn't mind disclosing difficulties and extra expenses from the start, if he saw that there were going to be any. Julian chewed his reddish-brown mustache, pondered, and expressed his opinion with the air of a man who was thinking out loud about his own problems.

Now, Julian got up at eight, strolled around his garden-in-progress, breakfasted on tea and a soft-boiled egg instead of coffee and cigarettes, looked at the newspaper and worked the crossword—all according to doctor's orders—before departing in his car around ten. He was due home around four, and that was the end of his day. Meanwhile, Betty measured windows for curtains, bought extra rugs, and happily took care of all the details that were necessary to make a new, bigger house a home. Larry had changed schools and was getting along well. It was the month of March. Larry wanted a dog. And there were rabbit warrens in an outhouse on the property. Couldn't he have rabbits?

"Rabbits breed so," said Julian. "What'll we do with them unless we sell them, and we don't want to start that. Let's get a dog, Larry."

The Websters went to a pet shop in their nearest town with the idea of inquiring about a kennel where they could buy a terrier or German shepherd puppy, but in the pet shop there were such splendid looking basset puppies, that Betty and Larry decided they had found what they wanted.

"Very healthy!" said the woman of the shop, fondling a floppy-eared, brown and white puppy in her arms.

That was obvious. The puppy grinned and slavered and wriggled in his loose hound's skin, which was so ready to fill out with the aid of Puppy-Spruce, Grow-Pup, dogbone-shaped biscuits and vitamins, all of which Julian bought in the shop.

"Look at these, Pop!" Larry said, pointing to some hamsters in a cage. "They're smaller than rabbits. They could live in the little *rooms* we've got."

Julian and Betty agreed to buy two hamsters. Only two, and they were so darling with their soft, clean fur, their innocent, inquisitive eyes, their twitching noses.

"All that space should be filled a little bit!" said Betty. She was as happy as Larry with the day's purchases.

Larry absorbed what the pet shop woman told him about hamsters. They should be kept warm at night, they ate cereals and grains of all kinds, and greenery such as carrots and turnips. They were nocturnal, and did not like direct sunlight. Larry installed his two in one of the cubicles in the rabbit warren. There were six such cubicles, three above, three below. He provided water and a pan of bread, plus a bowl of sweet corn from a tin he had found in the kitchen. He found an empty shoe box, which he filled with old rags, and this would be the hamsters' bedroom, he hoped. What to name them? Tom and Jerry? No, they were male and female. Jack and Jill? Too juvenile. Adam and Eve? Larry thought he would decide on names later. He could tell the male, because of a black patch between his ears.

Then there was the puppy. The puppy ate, peed, slept, and then awakened to play at two in the morning the first night. Everyone woke up, because the puppy had quit his box by the radiator and scratched at Larry's door.

"I *love* him!" said Larry, half asleep, rolling on the floor in pajamas with the puppy in his arms.

"Oh, Julian," said Betty, collapsing into her husband's arms. "What a wonderful day! Isn't this better than city life?"

Julian smiled, and kissed his wife on the forehead. It was better. Julian was happy. But he didn't want to make a speech about it. He'd had a tough time quitting cigarettes, and now he was putting on weight. If it wasn't one thing, it was another.

Larry, in his big room all his own, browsed in the *Encyclopaedia Britannica* on the subject of hamsters. He learned that they were of the order *Cricetus frumentarius,* belonging to the mouse-tribe *Muridae.* They made burrows some six feet deep which were vertical and sinuous. This burrow might have three or four chambers, in the deepest of which would be hidden the grain which the hamsters stored for the winter. Males and females and the young had separate rooms for sleeping. And when the young were only three weeks old, they were thrust from the parental burrow to fend for themselves. A female might have a dozen offspring at a time, and from twenty-five to fifty during her fertile eight months of the year. At six weeks, the female was ready for pregnancy. For four months of the year, or during winter, the hamsters hibernated, and fed upon the grain they had stored in their burrow. Among their enemies were owls and men who, at least in times past, had dug up their burrows in order to get at the grain the hamsters had stored.

"A dozen babies at a time!" said Larry to himself, astounded. A thought of selling them to his school chums crossed his mind, and just as quickly vanished. It was more pleasant to dream about a dozen tiny hamsters covering the floor of the three-foot by three-foot warren where his two now were. Probably they could fill all the six warrens before hibernation time.

Hardly six weeks had passed, when Larry looked into the barred front of the warren, and saw ten tiny hamsters suckling or trying to at the nether part of the female, whom Larry had named Gloria. Larry had just come home from school on the yellow bus. He let his book satchel fall to the ground, and he pressed his face close to the bars.

"Golly!—Gosh! Ten—no, *eleven!*" Larry went running to tell the news. "Hey, Mama!"

Betty was upstairs hemming a counterpane on the sewing machine. She came down to admire the hamster babies to please Larry. "Aren't they adorable! Like little white mice!"

The following morning, there were only nine in the warren, which Larry had carefully barricaded with newspaper to a height of eight inches behind the bars, so the little ones could not fall out. Where had the other two gone? Then he remembered, with a twinge of horror, that the *Encyclopaedia Britannica* had said that the mother hamster often ate inferior or sickly babies. Larry supposed that that was what had happened.

Julian came home at 4:30, and Larry dragged him out to show him the little ones.

"That's awfully quick. Isn't it?" said Julian. He was not much surprised, as hamsters were related to rabbits after all, but he wanted to say the right thing to his son. Julian's mind just then was on a swimming pool, and he strolled out with his briefcase still under his arm to take another look at his lawn.

Larry followed him, thinking that the lawn would offer an ample burrowing area for his hamsters and their offspring when winter rolled around—a long time away as yet. It would surely be better for the hamsters to hibernate in the ground than in straw in the brick warrens. They should have the right to store their grain supplies, as it said in the encyclopedia. The basset puppy had loped out to join Larry, and Larry scratched the top of the puppy's head while trying to pay attention to his father.

". . . or a nice pale blue pool, Larry my boy? What shape? Kidney shape? Boomerang? Clover?"

"Boomerang!" said Larry, pleased by the word at the moment.

Julian wanted to put in his order at once with his company. Olympian Pool was terribly busy in the spring and summer months, and far from getting priority as an employee, Julian knew he might have to wait a bit. Olympian boasted of being able to create a swimming pool in a week. Julian hoped he could get one while there was still some summer left.

Larry had brought a few of his chums to his house for milk and cookies after school, and to show them his hamsters. The little ones were now a
bigger attraction. A couple of the kids wanted to pick the little ones up,
which Larry permitted, after separating the mother. Larry picked the
mother up by the back of the neck, as his books advised.

"Your mother doesn't mind the babies," asked Eddie Carstairs, in a
guarded way.

"Why should she?" Larry said. "They're my pets. I take care of them."

Eddie glanced over his shoulder, as if to see if Larry's mother might be
coming. "I'll give you more if you want. My parents want me to get rid of
'em. But my father doesn't feel like drowning 'em, you see? Well—if you
want them—"

It was settled in a trice. The next afternoon, Eddie came on his bicycle
around 4 P.M. with a cardboard carton on the handlebars. He had ten baby
hamsters for Larry, of two different litters so they were not exactly the
same age, plus three adult hamsters, two of which had orange spots, which
Larry thought quite beautiful, since they introduced a new color to his
hamster warren. Eddie was furtive.

"You don't have to worry," Larry said. "My mother won't mind."

"You never know. Wait and see," said Eddie, and he declined politely to
come in for milk and apple pie.

Larry released two of the adult hamsters in the garden, and watched
with pleasure as they nosed their way about in their new freedom, sniffing
irises, nibbling grass, moving on. Mr. Johnson, the basset puppy, loped out
just then, and started to chase one of the hamsters who at once disappeared
into the lavender bushes, baffling Mr. Johnson. Larry laughed.

A couple of days later, Betty noticed the new babies in two more warrens. "Where'd they come from?"

Larry sensed a faint disapproval. "Oh, one of the kids in school. I said I
had room. And—well, you know I'm good at taking care of them."

"That you are.—All right, Larry, this once. But we don't want too
many, do we? All these are going to produce more, you know."

Larry nodded politely. His thoughts swam. His status had risen at
school because he could take on hamsters and knew a lot about them, and
on his own property he had the warrens that hamsters needed, not some
old crate or cardboard box. Another thought of Larry's was that he could
release adults or even young hamsters from the age of three weeks onward
whenever he wished in the garden. For the time being, he intended to be
an outlet for hamsters among his friends. At least four of his schoolmates
kept hamsters and had too many.

Three men arrived one afternoon with Larry's father to look over the lawn in regard to a swimming pool. Larry followed at a distance, keeping an eye on certain hamster burrow exits which he knew, and which he had concealed by discreet heaps of leaves and twigs. Some burrow outlets were obvious, however, and he had heard his father say, "Damned *moles!*" once to his mother. His father was supposed to jog twice around the lawn every morning, but did not always do it.

Now a workman in blue overalls and with a tape measure sank into a burrow up to his ankle, and laughed. "Moles'll help us out a little, don't you think, Julian? Looks like they've got it half dug already!"

"Ha-ha!" said Julian, to be friendly. He was talking to another workman about the boomerang shape, telling him at which point he wanted the outer arc of it. "And don't forget with the excess soil, my wife and I want to create a kind of hill—a rock garden eventually, you know. Over there." He pointed to a spot between him and a pear tree. "I know it's on the blueprint, George, but it's so much clearer when you can see the land in front of your eyes."

That was in late May. Larry now had a second litter from his original hamsters. The remaining single hamster was a female, and she soon had a litter by the original male, whom Larry had named Pirate, because of the black patch on his head. Larry thought if he held down his warren population to about twenty—three adults and a dozen or more little ones—his parents wouldn't complain. Since the hamsters were nocturnal, no one ever saw the garden hamsters in daytime, not even Larry. But he knew they were making burrows and doing all right, because he could see the burrow exits in various places in the lawn and garden, and could see that the grass seed, the corn kernels, also the peanuts that he put out in the afternoon were gone by the next day. Larry now had a bicycle, didn't have to take the school bus, and he spent much of his three dollars a week allowance on hamster food bought after school at the village grocery, which had a pet food section.

All that stored away! Or maybe eaten at once, Larry thought, because surely it was early to start saving for winter. He knew the garden was full of three-week-olds. Larry was tempted to demand twenty-five cents for every hamster he took on from his school chums and ten cents for a baby, to help pay for food, but he resisted. Larry in his fantasy imagined himself the protector of hamsters, the friend who gave them a happier life than the one they had known before, when they lived in cramped boxes.

"Hamster Heaven!" Larry said to himself as July rolled around. It was vacation time. Two litters had just been born in the warren. And maybe more were being born underground? Larry believed so. He imagined the burrows according to the encyclopedia's description: six feet deep and winding. How fascinating to know that the very ground he stood on was being used by families and their offspring as shelter and storage place, safe bedrooms—*home!* And no one could tell it from looking at the ground. What a good thing his father had stopped jogging, Larry thought, because even Larry sank in now and then if he stepped on a burrow entrance unawares. His father, being heavier, would sink in more, and might set about getting rid of the hamsters—even if his father still thought they were moles. Larry congratulated himself that his rather furtive feeding of the garden hamsters was paying off.

However, this same fact caused Larry to tell a lie, which weighed a bit on his conscience. It happened thus:

His mother remarked in the kitchen one afternoon, "There aren't so many as I thought there'd be by this time. To tell you the truth, I'm glad, Larry. So much easier—"

"I've given a few away to kids at school," Larry said, interrupting in his haste, and feeling awful at once.

"Oh, *I* see. I thought something was a little out of the ordinary about them." Betty laughed. "I was reading about them, and it seems they fight moles—destroy them. It might be a good idea if we put a couple in the garden. What do you think, Larry? Can you bear to part with a pair or two?"

Larry's slightly freckled face almost split with his smile. "I think the hamsters would like that."

After that, in a matter of ten days, things happened with lightning speed, or so it seemed to Larry. For a while, he was lying on his bed in his room, reading books propped on a pillow in lovely sunlight. His hamsters in the warren were plump and happy. Larry's father was looking forward to the last week in July and the first two weeks in August for his vacation, and Larry had learned that they were going to stay home this summer, because there was a river to fish in not far away, and a little gardening would be good exercise for Julian, his doctor had said. All was bliss, until the swimming pool men arrived in the last week in July.

They came early, around 7 A.M. Larry awakened at the noise of their two big trucks, and watched everything from his window. They were driving a bulldozer on to the lawn! Larry heard his father and mother talking in the hall, then Julian went downstairs and trotted on to the lawn. Larry saw it happen: his father's left foot sank suddenly, and he fell in a twisted way.

Then Julian gave a moan of pain.

One of the workmen took Julian gently by the shoulders. Julian was seated on the grass. Betty ran out. Julian was not getting up. Betty ran back to the house.

Then a doctor arrived. Julian was lying on the downstairs sofa, grimacing with pain, pale in the face.

"Do you think it's broken?" Betty asked the doctor.

"I don't think so, but we'd better take an X-ray. I've got some crutches in the car. I'll get them, and if your husband can just manage to get to my car . . ."

The bulldozer was already humming, groaning, stabbing at the lawn. Larry was more worried about his hamster burrows than about his father.

Julian was back in less than two hours, on crutches, his left foot thickly bandaged and with a metal bar underneath it to walk on when his ankle became better. And he was in a furious temper.

"That lawn is honeycombed!" Julian said to Betty and also Larry, who was in the kitchen having a second breakfast of milk and doughnuts. "The workmen say they're hamsters, not moles!"

"Well, the digging, darling—the excavation will at least scare some of them off," Betty said soothingly.

Julian focused his glare on his son. "It's quite plain, Larry, you've been putting your hamsters right in the garden. You didn't tell us. Therefore you *lied*. You didn't—"

"But I didn't *lie*," Larry interrupted in panic, because "lie" was his father's most awful word. "No one asked me about the—the—" Larry was on his feet, trembling.

"You led your mother to think, which is the same as lying, that the two you released in the garden recently were the only two. This is patently untrue, since the lawn is full of holes and tunnels and God knows *what*!"

"Darling, don't get excited," Betty said, fearing another heart attack. "There are ways—even if there are a lot of holes and things. Exterminators."

"You're damned right!" said Julian. "And I'm going to call them up now!" He went off on his crutches in the direction of the telephone.

"Julian, *I'll* call them," Betty said. "Have a rest. You're probably still in pain."

Julian wouldn't be dissuaded. Larry watched, breathing shallowly. He'd never seen his father quite so angry. *Exterminators*. That meant deadly poison, probably. Maybe men stood out there with clubs and hit the hamsters as they ran from their burrows. Larry wet his lips. Should he try to scare a few out now, and catch them, put them back in the warrens where it was safe? How many burrows with little ones were the pool men killing this very minute?

Larry looked out of the kitchen window. The bulldozer had already made a beginning on one wing of the boomerang shape, and was working now on the second wing, as if marking the land out. But not a hamster was in sight. Larry looked everywhere, even at the edges of the garden. He imagined his hamsters cringing far below in the earth, wondering what was causing all the reverberations. But they'd be only six feet below, and the pool would definitely be twelve feet deep in some places.

"Goddamn the whole batch of 'em!" Julian said in a voice like thunder, and crashed the telephone down.

Larry held his breath and listened.

"Darling, one said he could come possibly tomorrow. Call that one back," said Betty.

Larry escaped out of the kitchen door, intending to watch the workmen, and to try to save some hamsters if he could. For this reason, he detoured and went to the toolhouse for an empty carton. When Larry reached the excavation, he was just in time to see the big toothed scoop rise with a load of earth, swing and dump it exactly on a spot where Larry knew there was a hamster exit. Larry seethed with helpless fury. He wanted to cry out and stop them. Fortunately the hamsters always had a second exit, Larry reminded himself.

His sense of reassurance was brief. When he looked into the hole the bulldozer was digging, he saw part of a burrow exposed as cleanly as if someone had taken a knife and cut downward, as in the encyclopedia diagram. And there at the bottom were three or four little ones—visible, barely four feet under, wriggling! Where were the hamster parents?

"Stop!" Larry yelled in a shrill voice, waving his arms at the man up in the orange bulldozer. "There're animals *alive* there!"

The bulldozer man might not have heard him. The great jaw swung again and struck at a point lower than the baby hamsters' chamber.

"What's the matter, sonny?" asked the workman who had walked up beside Larry. "There're plenty more of those, I can tell you!"

"But these are pets!" Larry said.

The man shook his head. "Your father's plenty fed up with 'em, you know. Lawn's full of 'em! Just look. Now don't cry, kid! If we kill a few, you've got a hundred more around here!" He turned away before Larry could straighten up and assure the man he was not crying.

The rest of the day was a shambles. Julian was again on the telephone during the time the workmen stopped for lunch. Larry went out with his empty cardboard box to try to rescue a few hamsters, adults or babies, and didn't find a single one. Betty made a simple lunch, and Julian was still too upset to eat more than a bite. He was talking about getting at the hamsters himself, sticking burning brands down their holes, the way the farmers used to do with mole holes in Massachusetts where he'd been brought up.

"But Julian, the exterminators—" Betty glanced at her son. "They'll probably be able to come in a few days. Friday, they said. You mustn't get excited over nothing. It's bad for you."

"I'm damned well going to have a cigarette!" Julian said, and got up, dropped a crutch, picked it up, and made his way to the telephone table, where there were always cigarettes in a box.

Betty had cut her smoking down to five a day, which she smoked when Julian wasn't with her. Now she sighed, and glanced at Larry, who looked down at his plate.

His father, Larry thought, was mainly furious because he hadn't been able to smoke for the last several months, because the doctor had made him work shorter hours—little things like that. How could anyone get so angry just over hamsters? It was absurd. Larry said, "Excuse me," and left the table.

He went upstairs and wept on his bed. He knew it wouldn't last long, and it felt good to weep and get it over with. He was feeling a bit sleepy, when the sound of the bulldozer jolted him alert. They were at it again. His hamsters! Larry ran downstairs, with an idea of again trying, with his cardboard box, to save any refugee hamsters. He almost bumped into Julian who was coming in the kitchen door.

"Betty, you wouldn't believe it!" said Julian to his wife who was at the sink. "There's not a square foot of that damned lawn that isn't undermined! Larry—Larry, you take the cake for destroying property! Your *own* property!"

"Julian, please!" Betty said.

"I can't understand why you hadn't noticed it!" Julian said to her. "I can poke one of these crutches—*any* place and it sinks!"

"Well, I don't go around poking crutches!" Betty came back, but she was really wondering if she could get one of her tranquilizers (ancient pills, she hadn't taken one in at least two years) down Julian, or should she simply ring the doctor, their family doctor? Suppose he had another heart attack? "Darling, would you take one of my Libriums?"

"No!" said Julian. "I haven't time!" He turned on his crutches and went out again.

Larry went timidly out, drifted towards his hamster warrens, and felt a warm, happy relief at seeing Pirate and Gloria munching away at their bowl of wheat grain, and seven or eight young hamsters asleep in the hay.

"Hey there, Larry!" called his father. "Gather some firewood, would you? Twigs! From anywhere!"

Larry took a deep breath, hating it, hating his father. His father was going to try to smoke the hamsters out. Larry obeyed with leaden feet, picking up twigs from under hedges and rose bushes, until after five minutes or so Julian yelled at him to move a little faster. Larry's mother had come out, and Larry heard her vaguely protesting, and then she too was recruited for his father's awful work. Betty took stakes from the toolhouse, stakes that had been destined for tomato plants, Larry knew.

As Larry advanced towards the barbecue grill on the terrace, he caught sight of something that made him freeze, then smile. A pair of hamsters stood on their hind legs in the laurel, chattering as if talking to each other, and in an anxious way.

"Larry, take that stuff to the grill!" Julian called, and Larry moved.

When Larry looked again, the hamsters were not there. Had he imagined them? No. He had *seen* them.

Kar-*rumph!* The bulldozer bit out another hunk.

Betty joined Larry at the grill, poured a bit of paraffin on the charcoal, and struck a match. Larry dutifully added his twigs.

"Hand me the stakes, dear," Betty said.

Larry did so. "He's not going to stab them with the stakes, is he?" asked Larry, suddenly near tears. He wanted to fight his father with his fists. If he'd only been able to tackle his father man to man in a fight, he wouldn't be about to cry now, like a coward.

"Oh no, dear," said his mother in her artificially soft voice, which always meant some crisis was at hand. "He's just going to smoke them out. Then you can catch them and put them back in the warren."

Larry didn't believe a word of it. "And what about the little ones? All underneath? Without their parents?"

Betty only sighed.

Grimly, Larry watched his father poking with the tip of one of his crutches at the ground. He knew his father had found a hamster hole, and was trying to make it bigger, so a burning brand would go down there.

"Take these to your father, dear," said Betty, handing Larry two burning sticks at least three feet long. "Never mind if they go out. Hold them away from you."

Larry trudged across the lawn with them.

"Ha!" laughed one of the workmen. "You'll need more than that!"

Larry pretended not to hear. He handed Julian the stakes without looking into his face.

"Thanks, my boy," Julian said, and stuck a smoking stick at once into a hole four inches in diameter. The stake all but disappeared and showed just a few inches above the ground. "Ah, there we are!" Julian said in a tone of satisfaction. "Take this. Follow me."

Larry took back one stake, whose flame had gone out, but whose smoke made Larry close his eyes for an instant. His father had found two holes, the next just a yard or so away. The second stake went into this one.

"Splendid! More sticks, Larry!"

Larry walked back towards the terrace. The boomerang hole was now pretty deep, already looking like a boomerang shape, and Larry kept clear of it. He could not bring himself to glance at it, lest he see more destroyed hamster homes. But the two hamsters he had seen above ground cheered him greatly: maybe they'd all have time to escape before they were overcome by asphyxiation. Larry carried more stakes to his father, six, eight, maybe twelve. The sun was sinking. The bulldozer pulled back and dropped its toothy scoop as if intending to rest for the night.

"Hamsters, come out!" Larry said aloud. "It'll be dark soon! *Night!*" There must be some escape holes left, he thought.

The big rectangular lawn smoked from a dozen spots, but Larry was delighted to see that two or three stakes showed no smoke at ground level. He had relit several for his father. The puppy, Mr. Johnson, had retreated to the house, not liking the smoke.

Julian was smiling broadly as he came on crutches towards the terrace fire, which Betty still tended. The workmen had departed. "That'll give 'em something to think about!" he said, as he surveyed his land. "Larry, go and collect the sticks that've gone out, would you, boy?"

"I'll do it, Julian," Betty said. "Go in and rest, dear. I'm sure you shouldn't be hobbling around with your ankle. The doctor would have a fit if he knew."

"Ha-ha," said Julian.

Larry avoided looking at his father. His father's grin seemed insane under the circumstances. Larry stood at a corner of the terrace, straining his eyes to see if any hamsters had come to ground level. But their babies!

They were born blind, and some of the poor little things wouldn't even be able to see where to go to escape.

Betty came back with three stakes that had completely gone out, and stuck them on the charcoal.

"A little more paraffin!" Julian said. "I think we're getting somewhere!"

"It's not good for the roses, all this heat and smoke, Julian," Betty said.

Julian poured the paraffin himself, dropped the tin, and both he and Betty had to jump back as the flames leapt briefly. There hadn't been much in the tin. Julian laughed again. Betty became more nervous, and a little angry.

"These'll surely be enough, Julian," she said. "Let's let this be the end of it. Larry and I can take them out. It's almost too dark to see."

"I'll put on the terrace light," said Julian, and hobbled into the house and did so, but the lighted terrace only made the lawn seem darker. Julian found a flashlight. It was difficult for him to hold the flashlight and his crutches too, but it was his idea to hold the flashlight for Betty and Larry so they could find the hamster holes which still needed smoking stakes put into them.

The three of them went out to do this. Larry set his teeth trying to hold his anger and his tears back. He could hardly breathe. Partly it was because of the smoke, and partly because he was holding his breath. He saw a hamster, an adult that he didn't recognize, look at him with terrified eyes, then flee into some bushes. Larry, in a burst of rage, flung his burning sticks flat down on the lawn. The tips broke off, their flames went out.

"What're you doing there, Larry?" yelled his father. "Pick those up!"

"No!" Larry said.

"It's because of *you* we're in this mess!" Julian shouted, moving towards Larry. "You do as I say or you'll get the worst whipping of your life!"

"Julian, *please,* darling!" Betty said. "We're finished now! Let's go in the house!"

"Will you pick up—" Julian toppled. One crutch had sunk deep.

Larry was quite near him, but stepped back in the darkness and dodged a smoking stick that stuck up from the grass.

"Oh, Lord!" Betty cried, and ran—in a curve because of the pool excavation—towards Julian whose white ankle bandage was the most visible part of him in the darkness. She got a nasty whiff of smoke from somewhere, and coughed.

Larry heard the shriek of a fire engine siren, or maybe it was a police car. Under the cover of dark now, Larry removed every projecting stick he could see, and dropped them on the lawn. The rather dry grass was smoldering in some spots. Larry held his breath in smoky areas, and breathed only where it was a bit clearer. He saw that Julian was on his feet again. His father was yelling at him.

Larry didn't care. Now there were fire bells, rapid *clangs*. Good! A coal got into one of Larry's sneakers, and he had to remove his sneaker, knock it out, untie the lace and pull it on again.

Now the firemen were coming around the side of the house! With a hose! Larry could see them in the light of the terrace. Two or three firemen were getting the hose in position.

Hooray! Larry thought, but he didn't want the hamsters to be drowned either. He'd tell the firemen not to turn too much water on, he thought, and trotted towards the terrace.

Betty screamed from the lawn. "The hamsters! They're *biting!*" Three or four were attacking her ankles.

Julian stabbed at a hamster with his crutch tip. "*Damn* them!" They were all around him and Betty. He lunged again, lost his balance and fell. One rushed at his face and nipped. Another sank its incisors into his forearm. Julian struggled up again, despite the fact that a hamster clung to his wrist. "Betty!—*Tell the firemen*—"

At this point a spew of water like a battering ram caught Julian in the abdomen, and suddenly he was flat on his back with his breath knocked out. At once a half-dozen hamsters were attacking him.

"Julian, where are you?" Betty called. She debated trying to find Julian versus going to speak to the firemen—who must be thinking the whole lawn was on fire! She decided to run to the firemen. "Careful!" she yelled at them. "Be careful, my husband's on the lawn!"

"What?" came a man's voice from behind the horizontal torrent.

Betty got closer and shouted, nearly breathless. "It's not a fire! We're trying to smoke out some hamsters!"

"Smoke out *what?*"

"*Hamsters!* Cut the hose off! It isn't necessary!"

Larry watched, standing in the dark near the terrace. The water from the hose had created more smoke.

The great canvas hose abated slowly, as if reluctant, and became limp.

"What's going on, ma'am? That's an awful lot of smoke!" said a huge fireman wearing a black rubber coat and a splendid red helmet.

In the few seconds of silence, they all heard Julian scream, a pained scream yet an exhausted one, as if it were not his first.

A dozen or more hamsters, crazed by smoke, shocked by the bursts of hose water, were attacking Julian as if he were the cause of their woes. Julian fended some off with his hands and fists and one crutch, which he wielded clumsily, holding it in the middle. He had wrenched his bad ankle again, the pain was awful, and he'd given up trying to stand up. His main task was to get the hamsters' teeth out of his own flesh, out of his calves, his forearm which braced him in a half-recumbent position on the smoking grass.

"Help!" Julian cried. "Help *me!*"

And a fireman was coming, thank God! The fireman had a flashlight.

"Hey, what the hell is this?" the fireman said, kicking off a couple of hamsters with a thick boot.

Larry trotted towards the glow of the fireman's flashlight. Now Larry could see plenty of hamsters, scores of them, and his heart gave a jump as if he beheld a myriad fighters on his side. They were alive! They were lively and well! Larry stopped short. The fireman had dropped his father, having lifted him a little from the ground. What was happening?

The fireman had loosened his grip when a hamster bit him severely in the hand. The little beasts were running up his boots, falling, coming back. "Hey, Pete! Give us a hand! Bring an *axe!*" the fireman yelled towards the terrace. Then he began to stomp about, trying to protect the man on the ground from the hamsters that were coming from all sides. The fireman uttered some round Irish curses. Nobody was going to believe this story when he told it!

"Get them off—off!" Julian murmured with one hand over his face. He had been bitten in the nose.

Larry observed it all from the darkness. And he realized he didn't care. He didn't care what happened to his father! It was a little like watching something on the TV screen. Yes, he *did* care. He wanted the hamsters to win. He wanted his father to get defeated, to lose, and he wouldn't have cared if his father fell into the pool pit—but he was a fair distance away from it. The hamsters had a right to their land, their homes, had a right to protect their offspring. Larry trotted in place and punched his fists in the air like a silent cheering squad. Then he found his voice. "Come on, *hamsters!*" Larry yelled, and it crossed his mind to release Pirate and Gloria so they could join in—and yet they weren't even needed, there were so many hamsters!

Now a second fireman was trotting out with an axe. The two firemen got Julian up by putting one of Julian's arms around each of their necks. Julian's head sagged forward.

As the trio came into the terrace light, Larry saw hamsters at their feet flee back into the darkness of the lawn. His father's pale trousers, his shirt, were all splotched with blood.

And Larry's mother's face was absolutely white. An instant after Larry noticed this, his mother sank to the terrace tiles. She had fainted. One of the firemen picked her up and carried her into the living room, which was brightly lit now, because the firemen had turned on all the lights.

"We've got to get this one to the hospital," said the biggest fireman. "He's losing blood."

There was a pool of blood on the red tiles under Julian's half-supported feet.

Larry hovered and chewed a fingernail.

"We'll take him in the wagon."

"Think that's best?"

"Anything we can do for him now?"

"He's bleeding from too many places!"

"Put him on the wagon! The stretcher, Pete!"

"No time for that! Carry him and get going!"

Betty came to as Julian was being borne towards the driveway where the fire trucks were. A few neighbors stood there, and now they asked questions, questions about the fire. And what had happened to Julian?

"Hamsters!" said one of the firemen. "Hamsters in the lawn!"

The neighbors were amazed.

Betty wanted to go with Julian to the hospital, but one of the firemen advised her not to. A couple of the women neighbors stayed with her.

Julian's jugular vein had been pierced in two places, and he had lost a lot of blood by the time he arrived at the hospital. The doctors applied tourniquets and stitched. Transfusions were given. The process was slow. In came the blood and out it flowed. Julian died within an hour.

Betty, under sedation that night, was not notified until the following morning. With the resources of an adult, Betty mentally gave herself two days to recover from the shock, knowing all the while that she would sell the house and move somewhere else. Larry, realizing factually what had happened, did not take it in at once emotionally, his father's demise. He knew his mother would never want to see another hamster, so he set about releasing those he could capture into territory where they might have a chance of survival. He made three or four expeditions on his bicycle, carrying his cardboard box loaded with adults and baby hamsters. There was a wood not far away with plenty of trees, underbrush, and not a house for half a mile.

So, his father was dead, Larry realized, finally. Dead because of hamsters which had simply bitten him. But in a way hadn't his father asked for it? Couldn't they have taken the time to save the hamsters in the boomerang area, and still gone on with the swimming pool construction? Much as Larry loved his father, and knew he should love his father—who had been a pretty good father as fathers went, Larry realized—Larry was still somehow on the side of the hamsters. Because of his mother's feelings, Larry knew he had to part with Pirate and Gloria too. These with a few babies were the last to go one morning on Larry's bicycle in the cardboard box. Once more Larry fought against tears as he released this pair that he loved the best. But he did hold back the tears, and he felt he was at last becoming a man.

Harry: A Ferret

Harry, a ferret of uncertain age, perhaps one or two, was the prize possession of Roland Lemoinnier, a boy of fifteen. There was no doubt Roland was fifteen. He was pleased to tell anyone, because he considered fifteen a great step forward over fourteen. To be fourteen was to be a child, but to be fifteen was to enter manhood. Roland took pleasure in his new deep voice, and looked into the mirror every morning before brushing his teeth to see if more hair had sprouted where a mustache might have been or under his sideburns. He shaved elaborately with his own razor, but only once a week, because seeing the hair on his face gave him more pleasure than shaving.

Roland's new adulthood had got him into trouble in Paris, at least in his mother's opinion. He had begun going out with boys and girls several years older than he, and the police had hauled him in among six other young people, all around eighteen, to caution them about possession of marijuana. Being tall, Roland could pass for eighteen and often did. His mother had been so shocked by the police episode, she had acted on the advice of her mother, with whom in this case she was in complete accord, and moved to her house in the country near Orléans. Roland's father and mother had been divorced since he was five. With Roland and his mother went the two servants Brigitte, maid and cook, and Antoine, the elderly chauffeur and factotum who had been with the family since before Roland was born. Brigitte and Antoine were not married to each other, and both were single. Antoine was so aged as to be a joke to Roland, something left over from another century and mysteriously still alive, frowning disapproval on Roland's blue jeans at the lunch table and his bare feet on the carpets and the waxed floors of La Source. It was summer, and

Roland was free of the Lycée Lamartine, eight kilometers away, where he had gone for most of the preceding term after their move from Paris.

In fact Roland had been bored with country life in general until the day in late June when he had accompanied his mother to a nursery to buy plants for the garden. The nurseryman, a friendly old fellow with a sense of humor, had a ferret which he told Roland he had captured on the weekend while out hunting rabbits. Roland had been fascinated by the caged ferret which could hunch itself into a very short length as if its body were made like an accordion, then flash into its hole in the straw, looking three times that length. The ferret was black, light brown and cream, and to Roland looked part rat, part squirrel, and exceedingly mischievous.

"Careful! He bites!" the nurseryman said, when Roland put his finger against the wire of the cage.

The ferret had bitten Roland with a needle-like tooth, but Roland hid his bleeding finger in a handkerchief in his pocket. "Would you sell him? With the cage too?"

"Why? Do you hunt rabbits?" the nurseryman asked, smiling.

"A hundred new francs. A hundred and fifty," Roland said. He had that much in his pocket.

Roland's mother was bending over camellias yards away.

"Well—"

"You'll have to tell me what he eats."

"A little grass, of course. And blood," he added, bending close to Roland. "Give him some raw meat now and then, because he's got the taste for it now. And mind you don't let him loose in the house, because you'll never catch him. Hay to keep him warm, like this. He made that tunnel himself."

The ferret had darted into the little tunnel in the straw and turned around so that only his lively face peered out with low-set, mouse-like ears and black eyes that slanted downward at the outer corners, making him look thoughtful and a bit melancholic. Roland had the feeling the ferret was listening to the conversation and hoping he would be able to go away with Roland.

Roland pulled out a hundred note and a fifty. "How about it—with the cage?"

The nurseryman glanced over his shoulder, as if Roland's mother might interfere. "If he bites, stick an onion at him. He won't bite you after he bites into an onion."

Margaret Lemoinnier was surprised and annoyed that Roland had bought a ferret. "You'll have to keep the cage in the garden. You mustn't take it in the house."

Antoine said nothing, but his pink-white face took on a more sour expression than usual. He put lots of newspaper on the back seat of the Jaguar so that the cage would not touch the leather upholstery.

At home, Roland got an onion from the kitchen and went out on the lawn behind the house where he had set the cage. He opened the door of the cage slightly, onion at the ready, but the ferret, after hesitating an instant, darted through the door into freedom. He made for the woods at one side of the estate and disappeared. Roland warned himself to keep cool. He brought the cage, its door open, to the edge of the woods, then ran into the house via the back door. On a wooden board in the kitchen lay just what he wanted, a large raw steak. Roland cut off a piece and hurried back to the woods.

Slowly Roland entered the woods, intending to make a circle and drive the ferret back towards his cage. A ferret could probably climb a tree too. Roland had seen his sharp claws when the ferret had stood up in his cage at the nursery. The ferret had tiny pink-palmed hands that were rather like human hands, with miniature pads at the end of the fingers, and a freely moving thumb. Then Roland's heart gave a leap as he saw the ferret just a few yards away from him, sitting upright in the grasses, sniffing. The breeze blew towards the ferret, and Roland realized that he had smelled blood. Roland stooped and extended the raw meat.

Cautiously, rearing himself, then advancing a little, the ferret approached, eyes darting everywhere as if guarding against possible enemies. Roland was startled at the suddenness with which the ferret seized the meat in his teeth and jerked it away. The ferret chewed with bolting movements of head and neck, the brown and black hair on his back standing on end as he telescoped his lithe body. The steak was all gone, and the ferret looked at Roland, little pink tongue licking his face appreciatively.

Roland's impulse was to run back to the kitchen for more. But he thought it best to move slowly so the ferret would not become alarmed. "Wait! Or come with me," he said softly, because he wanted the ferret back in the cage. It would be dark soon, and Roland didn't want to lose him.

The ferret followed to the edge of the lawn and waited. Roland went to the kitchen and cut some more meat, then gently poured from the paper below the steak a tablespoon of blood into a saucer. He carried this out. The ferret was still in the same place, one paw raised, gazing expectantly. The ferret approached the saucer, where the meat was also, but he chose the blood first, and lapped it up like a kitten lapping milk. Roland smiled. Then the ferret looked at Roland, licked his face again, seized the meat in his teeth and carried it in an uncertain route on to the grass, then seeing his cage, he made a straight line for it.

Roland was very pleased. The onion, still in Roland's pocket, might not be necessary. And the ferret was safely back in his cage on his own initiative. Roland closed the cage door. "I think I'll call you Harry. How do you like that name? *Harry.*" Roland was studying English, and he knew that Harry was informal for Henry, and there was also an English word "hairy" pronounced the same way, so the name seemed appropriate. "Come up and see *my* room." Roland picked up the cage.

In the house, Roland encountered Antoine who was coming down the stairway.

"M. Roland, your mother said she did not want the animal in the house," said Antoine.

Roland drew himself up a little. He was no longer a child to be told what to do by a servant. "Yes, Antoine. But I'll speak to my mother on the subject," Roland said in his deepest voice.

Roland put the cage in the middle of the floor in his room, and went to the telephone in the hall. He dialed the number of his best friend, Stefan, in Paris, had to speak with Stefan's mother first, then Stefan came on.

"I have a new friend," Roland said, putting on a voice with a foreign accent. "He has claws and drinks blood. Guess what he is?"

"A—a vampire?" said Stefan.

"You are warm.—My mother's coming and I can't talk long," Roland said quickly. "He's a *ferret.* His name is Harry. Bloodthirsty! A killer! Maybe I can bring him to Paris! Bye-bye, Stefan!"

Mme. Lemoinnier had come up the stairs and was walking towards Roland down the hall. "Roland, Antoine says you have brought that animal into the house. I said you could keep it only if it stays in the garden."

"But—the nurseryman told me to watch out that he doesn't get cold. It's cold at night, Mama."

His mother went a few steps into Roland's room. Roland followed her.

"Look! He's gone to sleep in his burrow. He's perfectly clean, Mama. He'll stay in his cage. What's the matter with that?"

"You'll probably take him out. I know you, Roland."

"But I promise, I won't." Roland didn't mean that promise, and knew his mother knew it.

A minute later, Roland was reluctantly carrying Harry, now out of sight in the hay, down the stairway and into the garden. Harry was probably sleeping like a log, Roland thought, remembering what the nurseryman had said about ferrets falling asleep, often close to their victims for warmth, after they had drunk the blood of their prey. The primitiveness of it excited Roland. When his mother had gone back into the house (she had been watching him from the kitchen door), Roland opened the cage and lifted some of the hay, exposing Harry who raised his head drowsily. Roland smiled.

"Come on, you can sleep up in my room. Then we'll have some fun tonight," Roland whispered.

Roland picked Harry up and put the hay back in place. Harry lay limp and innocent in Roland's hand. Roland opened a button of his shirt, stuck Harry in and fastened the button. He closed the cage door and latched it.

Up in his room, Roland got his empty suitcase from a wardrobe top, put a couple of his sweaters into it, and put Harry in, propping the suitcase lid open a little with the sleeve of one sweater. Then Roland got a clean ashtray from the hall table, filled it with water from the bathroom tap and put it in the suitcase.

Roland then flopped on his bed, lit one of the cigarettes which he kept hidden in a bookshelf, and opened a James Bond which he had already read two or three times. He was thinking of things he might teach Harry. Harry should learn to travel around in a jacket pocket, certainly, and come out on command. He should also have a collar and lead, and the collar, or maybe a harness, would have to be custom-made because Harry was so small. Roland imagined commissioning a leather craftsman in Paris and paying a good price for it. Fine! It would be amusing in Paris—even in Orléans—if Harry could emerge from his pocket on his lead and eat meat from Roland's plate in a restaurant, for instance.

At dinner, Roland and his mother and a man friend of hers, who was an antique dealer of the neighborhood and very boring, were interrupted by Brigitte, who whispered to Mme. Lemoinnier:

"Madame, I beg to excuse myself, but Antoine has just been bitten. He is quite upset."

"Bitten?" said Mme. Lemoinnier.

"He says it is the ferret—in M. Roland's room."

Roland controlled his smile. Antoine had gone in to turn the bed down, and Harry had attacked.

"A *ferret*?" said the antique dealer.

Roland's mother looked at him. "Will you excuse yourself, Roland,

and put the animal back in the garden?" She was angry and would have said more if they had been alone.

"Excuse me, please," Roland said. He went into the hall and saw Antoine's tall figure in the little lavatory by the front door. Antoine stooped to hold a wet towel against his ankle. Blood, Roland thought, fascinated to think that Harry had drawn blood from that old creature Antoine, who in fact looked as if he hadn't any blood in him.

Roland ran up the stairs two at a time, and found his room in disorder. Antoine had obviously abandoned the bed-turning-down midway, an armchair was askew where Antoine must have dragged it looking for Harry, or maybe trying to protect himself. But the bed in disorder meant more to Roland than an explosion: Antoine would not have left a bed in that state unless he was ready for extreme unction. Roland looked around for Harry.

"Harry?—Where are you?" He looked up at the long curtains, which Harry would certainly be able to climb, in the wardrobe, under the bed.

The door of his room had been closed. Evidently Antoine had wanted to guard against Harry escaping. Then Roland looked at the folds in the bedcovers where nothing, however, twitched.

"Harry?"

Roland lifted the top sheet. Then he saw the counterpane move. Harry was between counterpane and blanket, and he sat up and regarded Roland with a desperate anxiety. Roland noticed another beautiful thing about Harry: his whole torso was beige and soft looking, from his little black chin down to the counterpane on which he stood, and a fine line of brown fur perhaps caused by the fur pressing together down the center of his body, gave the effect of a stripe, turned Harry into a bifurcated piece of beige fluff, quite concealing where his hind legs began and ended. Harry's dainty hands sought either side of the counterpane's folds, not to keep his balance which he had perfectly, but nervously, as the hands of a highly strung person might do. And perhaps Harry was asking, "Who was that giant who tried to shoo me, scare me, catch me?" But as Roland looked at Harry, Harry's face seemed to lose some of its terror. Harry lowered himself and advanced a little. Now he might be saying, "I'm delighted to see you! What's happening?"

Roland extended a hand without thinking, and Harry went up his arm and down his shirtfront—the collar of his shirt was open—and nestled with scratchy little claws against Roland's waist. Roland found his eyes full of tears which he could not explain. Was it pride because Harry had come to him? Or anger because Harry had to stay in the garden tonight? Tears, explained or not, had a poetic value, Roland thought. They signified importance of some kind.

Roland took Harry out of his shirt and put him on a curtain. Harry ran up the yellow curtain to the ceiling, Roland took the bottom of the curtain in his hands, and Harry ran down the slope. Roland laughed, lowered the curtain, and Harry ran up again. Harry seemed to enjoy it. Roland caught Harry at the bottom of the curtain and stuck him into the suitcase. "I'll be back in a minute!" This time Roland fixed the lid down with a straight chair turned sideways.

Roland intended to go back to the dining room until the meal was over, then ask Brigitte for some meat before he took Harry to the garden. But it seemed the meal was over. The dining room was empty. The antique dealer sat in the drawing room where the coffee tray already stood on the table, and Roland heard his mother's voice and Antoine's voice from the room opposite the drawing room. Its door was not quite closed.

". . . disobeyed me," Antoine was saying in his shaky old man's voice. "And *you,* madame!"

"Now you must not take it so seriously, my dear Antoine," Roland's mother said. "I am sure Roland will keep the animal in the garden . . ."

Roland made himself move away. Gentlemen did not eavesdrop. But it irked him that Antoine had said, "M. Roland disobeyed me." Since when did Antoine think he controlled him? Roland hesitated at the doorway of the drawing room, where the antique dealer sat smoking and gazing into space, his white trousered legs crossed. Roland wanted coffee, but it was not worth walking into that boredom for, he thought. Roland went through the dining room into the kitchen.

"Brigitte, may I have some meat for the ferret? Preferably raw," Roland said.

"M. Roland, Antoine is very upset, you know? A ferret is a *bête sauvage.* You must realize that."

Roland said courteously, "I know, Brigitte. I am sorry Antoine was bitten. I am going to take the ferret to the garden. In his cage. Now."

Brigitte shook her head and produced some veal from the refrigerator and cut a morsel grudgingly.

It wasn't bloody but it was raw. Roland flew up the stairs to his room, gently lifted the suitcase lid, whereupon Harry stood upright like a jack-in-the-box. Harry took Roland's offering with both front paws and his teeth, chewing it and turning it so he could get at the edges.

Roland extended his hand fearlessly, saying, "You've got to sleep in the garden tonight, sorry."

Harry flitted through the gap above Roland's shirt cuff, went up to his shoulder and down to his waist. Roland cradled him in his shirt, and went down the stairs like a soldier, the cage in his other hand.

It was dark, but Roland could see by the light from the kitchen window. He stuck Harry into the cage and closed the door with its pin latch which dropped through a loop. Harry had a tin mug of water which still held enough. "See you tomorrow, Harry my friend!"

Harry stood up on his hind legs, resting a pink palm lightly against the wire, black nose sniffing the last of Roland, who looked back at Harry as he walked across the lawn.

The next morning, a Sunday, Roland was brought tea by Brigitte at eight o'clock, a ritual that Roland had started a few weeks earlier. It made Roland feel more grown-up to fancy that he couldn't awaken properly without someone handing him a cup of something hot in bed.

Then Roland pulled on blue jeans, tennis shoes and an old shirt, and went down to see Harry.

The cage was gone. Or at least it was not in the same place. Roland looked in the corners of the garden, behind the poplar trees on the right, then next to the house. He went into the kitchen, where Brigitte was preparing his mother's breakfast tray.

"Someone's moved the ferret's cage, Brigitte. Do you know where it is?"

Brigitte bent over the tray. "Antoine took it, M. Roland. I don't know where."

"But—did he take the car?"

"I don't know, M. Roland."

Roland went out and looked in the garage. The car was there. Roland stood and turned in a circle, looking. Could Antoine have put the cage in the toolhouse? Roland opened the toolhouse door. There was nothing there but the lawnmower and garden tools. The woods. Antoine had probably been told, by his mother, to take Harry to the woods and turn him loose. Frowning, Roland started off at a trot.

He pulled up when some brambles caught at his shirt and tore it. Old Antoine wouldn't have gone too far in these woods, Roland thought. There weren't any real paths.

Roland heard a groan. Or had he imagined it? He was not sure where the sound had come from, but he plunged on the way he had been going. Now he heard a crackling of branches and another groan. It was unmistakably a groan from Antoine. Roland advanced.

He saw a splotch of dark through the trees. Antoine wore dark trousers, often a dark green cotton jacket. Roland stood still. The darkish splotch was pulling itself up only thirty feet away. But there were so many leaves in between! Roland saw a golden light streak from the left towards the vague form which was Antoine, heard Antoine's rather shrill cry—feeble, almost like the cry of a baby.

Roland went closer, a little frightened. Now he could see Antoine's head and face, and blood flowed from one of Antoine's eyes. Then Roland saw Harry make a flying leap at Antoine's thigh, saw Antoine's hand slap uselessly against his leg, because Harry was already at Antoine's throat. Or face. Antoine staggered back and fell.

He ought to go and help, Roland thought, grab a stick and fend Harry off. But Roland was spellbound and couldn't move. He saw Antoine try a swinging backhand blow at Harry, but the branch Antoine held struck a tree and shattered. Antoine stumbled again.

In a way it serves Antoine right, Roland was thinking.

Antoine got up clumsily and flung something—probably a rock—at Harry. Roland could see blood down the front of Antoine's white shirt. And Harry was fighting like a mysterious little bullet that came again and again at Antoine from different directions. It looked as if Antoine was trying to flee now. He was stumbling through the underbrush to the left. Roland saw Harry leap for Antoine's left hand and apparently cling there with his teeth. Or had it been a streak of sunlight? Roland lost sight of Antoine, because he fell again.

Roland gasped. He had not been breathing for several seconds, and his heart was pounding as if he had been fighting too. Now Roland forced himself to walk towards the place where he thought Antoine lay. Everything was silent except for Roland's footfalls on the leaves and twigs. Roland saw the black, white and green of Antoine's clothes, then Antoine's face streaked with blood. Antoine was lying on his back. Both his eyes were bleeding.

And Harry was at Antoine's throat!

Harry's head was out of sight under Antoine's chin, but his body and tail trailed down Antoine's chest—as a fur piece might do from someone's neck.

"*Harry!*" Roland's voice cracked.

Harry might not have heard.

Roland picked up a stick. "Harry, get away!" he said through his teeth.

Harry leapt to the other side of Antoine's throat and bit again.

"Antoine?" Roland went forward, raising the stick.

Harry lifted his head and backed on to Antoine's green lapel. His stomach was visibly larger. He was full of blood, Roland realized. Antoine didn't move. Seeing Roland, Harry advanced a little, nearly stood up on his hind legs, came down again and, staggering with the weight of his stomach, stepped down on to the leaves beside Antoine's outflung arm, lay down and lowered his head as if to sleep. Harry was in a patch of sun.

Roland felt considerably less afraid, now that Harry was still, but he feared now that Antoine might be dead, and the possible fact of death frightened him. He called to Antoine again. The blood was drying and darkening in the eye sockets. His eyes seemed to be gone, just as Roland had thought, or at least nearly entirely eaten out. The blood everywhere, on Antoine's clothing, down his face, was dark red and crusty now, and no more seemed to be coming, which was a sign that the heart had stopped beating, Roland thought. Before Roland realized what he was doing, he had stooped very close to the sleeping Harry and was holding Antoine's wrist to feel for a pulse. Roland tried for several seconds. Then he snatched his hand from the wrist in horror, and stood up.

Antoine must have died from a heart attack, Roland thought, not just from Harry. But he realized that Harry was going to be taken away, even hunted down and killed, if anybody found out about Antoine. Roland looked behind him, in the direction of La Source, then back at Antoine. The thing to do was hide Antoine. Roland felt a revulsion against Antoine, mainly because he was dead, he realized. But for Harry he felt love and a desire to protect. Harry after all had been defending himself, and Antoine had been a giant kidnapper, and possibly a killer too.

It was still only a little past 9:30, Roland saw by his watch.

Roland began to trot back through the woods, leaping the bad patches of underbrush. At the edge of La Source's lawn he stopped, because Brigitte was just then tossing a pan of water on to some flowers by the back steps. When she had gone inside the house again, Roland went to the toolhouse, took the fork and spade, and carried these into the woods.

He dug close beside where Antoine lay, which seemed as good a place as any to try to dig a grave. His exertions sobered him, and took away some of his panic. Harry continued to sleep on the other side of Antoine from where Roland was digging. Roland worked like one possessed, and his energy seemed to increase as he labored. He realized he was in terror of Antoine's body: what had been the living fossil, so familiar in the household in Paris and here, was now a corpse. Roland also half expected Antoine to rise up and reproach him, threaten him in some way, as ghosts or corpses did in stories that Roland had read.

Roland began to tire and worked more slowly, but with the same determination. The job had to be done by midday, he told himself, or his mother and Brigitte would be searching for Antoine by the lunch hour. Roland tried to think of what he would say.

The grave was deep enough. Roland set his teeth and pulled at Antoine's green jacket and the side of his trousers, and rolled him in. Antoine fell face downwards. Harry, ruffled by Antoine's arm, stood on four legs looking sleepy still. Roland shoveled the earth in, panting. He trod on the soil to make it sink, and there was still extra soil which he had to scatter, so it would not catch the eye of anyone looking in the woods. Then with the fork he pulled branches and leaves over the grave so it looked like the rest of the forest floor.

Then numb with fatigue, he picked Harry up. Harry was very heavy— as heavy as a pistol, Roland thought. Harry's eyes were closed again, but he was not quite limp in sleep. His neck supported his head, and as Roland lifted him to his own eye level, Harry opened his eyes and looked at Roland. Harry would never bite him, Roland felt sure, because he had always brought meat to him. In a way, he had brought Antoine to Harry. Roland trudged back with Harry towards the house, saw the cage in the woods and started to pick it up, then decided to leave it for the moment. Roland put Harry down beside a sun-warm rock not far from the lawn.

Roland put the fork and spade back in the toolhouse. He washed his hands as best he could at the cold water tap by the toolhouse, then thinking Brigitte might be in the kitchen, he entered the house by the front door. He went upstairs and washed more thoroughly and changed his shirt. He put on his transistor radio for company. He felt odd, not exactly frightened any longer, but as if he would do everything clumsily—drop or bump into things, trip on the stairs—though he had done none of these things.

His mother knocked on the door. He knew her knock.

"Come in, Mama."

"Where have you been, Roland?"

Roland was lying on his bed, the radio beside him. He turned the radio down. "In the woods. I took a walk."

"Did you see Antoine? He's supposed to fetch Marie and Paul for lunch."

Roland remembered. People were coming for lunch. "I saw Antoine in the woods. He said he was taking the day off, going to Orléans or something like that."

"Really?—He was letting the ferret loose, wasn't he?"

"Yes, Mama. He'd already let the ferret loose. I saw the cage in the woods."

His mother looked troubled. "I'm sorry, Roland, but it was not an appropriate pet, you know. And poor old Antoine—we've got to think of him. He's terrified of ferrets, and I think he's right to be."

"I know, Mama. It doesn't matter."

"That's a good boy. But Antoine, just to go off like that—He'll go to a film in Orléans and come back this evening probably. He didn't take the car, did he?"

"He said he was taking the Orléans bus.—He was very annoyed with me. Said he might be gone a couple of days."

"That's nonsense. But I'd better hop off now for Marie and Paul. You see what trouble you caused with that animal, Roland!" His mother gave him a quick smile and went out.

Roland managed to save some meat from dinner, and took it out around 10:30 P.M., when Brigitte had gone to bed and his mother was in her room for the night. Roland sat on the rock where he had left Harry earlier that day, and after seven or eight minutes, Harry arrived. Roland smiled, almost laughed.

"Meat, Harry!" Roland said in a whisper, though he was a good distance from the house.

Harry, slender once more, accepted the underdone lamb, though not with his usual eagerness, having eaten so much that day. Roland stroked Harry's head for the first time. Roland imagined coming to the woods in the daytime, training Harry to stay in his pocket, teaching him certain commands. Harry didn't need a cage.

After two days, Mme. Lemoinnier sent a telegram to Antoine's sister who lived in Paris, asking her please to telephone. The sister telephoned, and said she hadn't heard a word from Antoine.

It was curious, Mme. Lemoinnier thought, that Antoine had just walked off like that, leaving all his clothes, even his coat and raincoat. She thought she should notify the police.

The police came and asked questions. Roland said he had last seen Antoine walking towards the Orléans road where he intended to catch the bus that passed at 11 A.M. Antoine was old, Mme. Lemoinnier said, a little eccentric, stubborn. He had left his savings bank passbook behind, and the police were going to ask the bank to communicate if Antoine came to make a withdrawal or to get another passbook. The police went over the ground that Roland showed them. They found the empty cage, its door open, which Antoine had carried into the woods. The Orléans road was to the right, the opposite direction from where Antoine was buried. The police walked all the way to the Orléans road. They seemed to believe Roland's story.

Every night that Roland could go out unobserved, he fed Harry, and usually once during the day too. The few nights Harry did not turn up, Roland supposed he was hunting rabbits or moles. Harry was wild, yet not wild, tame, yet not reliably tame, Roland knew. Roland also realized that he didn't dare think too much about what Harry had done. Roland preferred to think that Antoine had died from a heart attack. Or—if Roland ever thought of Harry as a murderer, he put it in the same realm of fantasy as the murders in the books he read, real yet not real. It was not true that he was guilty, or Harry either.

Roland liked best to imagine Harry as his secret weapon, better than a gun. Secret because no one knew about him, though Roland intended to tell Stefan. Roland had fantasies of using Harry to kill a certain mathematics professor whom he detested in his lycée. Roland was in the habit of writing letters to Stefan, and he wrote Stefan the story of Harry killing Antoine, in fiction form. "You may not believe this story, Stefan," Roland wrote at the end, "but I swear it is true. If you care to check with the police, you will find that *Antoine has disappeared*!"

Stefan wrote back: "I don't believe a word of your ferret story, obviously inspired by Antoine walking out, and who wouldn't if they had to wait on *you?* However it is mildly amusing. Got any more stories?"

Goat Ride

Billy the goat was the main attraction at Playland Amusement Park, and Billy himself was the most amused—not the children or their parents who fished out endless quarters and dimes, after having paid the one-dollar-fifty admission for themselves and seventy-five cents per child. Hank Hudson's Playland wasn't cheap, but it was the only place of amusement for kids in or around the town.

Screams and cheers went up when Billy, pulling his gold and white cart, made his entry every evening around seven. Any president of the United States would have been heartened by such a roar from his adherents, and it put fire into Billy too. All sinew and coarse white hair, brushed to perfection by Mickie, Billy started on the gallop, dashed past a white rail fence against which children and adults pressed themselves out of his way and at the same time urged him on with "Hurrahs!" and "Oooooohs!" of admiration. The run was to take a little froth off Billy's energy, as well as to alert the crowd that Billy was ready for business. Back at the start of the Goat Ride, Billy skidded to a halt on polished hooves, hardly breathing faster but snorting for effect. The ride cost twenty-five cents for adult or child, and Billy's cart could take four kids, or two adults, plus Mickie who drove. Mickie, a redheaded boy whom Billy quite liked, rode in front on a bench.

"Gee up!" Mickie would say, slapping the reins on Billy's back, and off Billy would go, head down at first till he got the cart going, then head up and trotting, looking from side to side for mischief or handouts of ice cream and caramel popcorn which he was ever ready to pause for. Mickie wielded a little whip, more for show than service, and the whip didn't hurt Billy at all. Billy understood when Hank yelled at Mickie that Hank wanted them to get on with the ride in order to take on the next batch of customers. The Goat Ride had a course round the shooting gallery, through the crowd between the merry-go-round and the ice cream and popcorn stands, round the stand where people threw balls at prizes, making a big figure eight which Billy covered twice. If Mickie's whip didn't work, Hank would come over and give Billy a kick in the rump to tear him away from a popcorn or peanut bag. Billy would kick back, but his hooves hit the cart rather than Hank. Still it was seldom that Billy could call himself tired, even at the end of a hard weekend. And if the next day was a day when the park was closed, and he was tied to his stake with nothing to butt, no crowds to cheer him, Billy would dig his horns into the grass he had already cropped. He had a crooked left horn which could tear into the ground, giving Billy satisfaction.

One Sunday, Hank Hudson and another man approached the post at the start of the Goat Ride, and Hank held his hands out palms down, a signal to Mickie to stop everything. The man had a little girl with him who was hopping up and down with excitement. Hank was talking, and slapped Billy's shoulder, but the little girl didn't dare touch Billy until her father took one of his horns in his hand. Ordinarily Billy would have jerked his head, because people loved to laugh and turn loose before they were thrown off their balance. But Billy was curious now, and continued chewing the remains of a crunchy ice cream cone, while his gray-blue eyes with their horizontal pupils gazed blandly at the little girl who was now stroking his forelock. The four kids in Billy's cart clamored to get started.

Hank was taking lots of paper money from the man. Hank kept his back to the main part of the crowd, and he counted the money carefully. Hank Hudson was a tall man with a big stomach and a broad but flat behind which once or twice Billy had butted. He wore a Western hat, cowboy boots, and buff-colored trousers whose belt sloped down in front under his paunch. He had a wet pink mouth with two rabbit-like front teeth, and small blue eyes. Now his wife Blanche joined the group and watched. She was plump with reddish-brown hair. Billy never paid much attention to her. When Hank had pocketed the money, he told Mickie to get on with the ride, and Billy started off. Billy did his usual twelve or fifteen rides that evening, but at closing time he was not led back to his stable.

Mickie unhitched Billy near the entrance gate, and Billy was tugged towards a pick-up whose back hatch was open.

"Go on, git in theah, Billy!" Hank shouted, giving Billy a kick to show he meant business.

Mickie was pulling from the front. "Come on, Billy! Bye-bye, Billy boy!"

Billy clattered up the board they had put as a ramp, and the hatch was banged shut. The car started off, and there was a long bumpy ride, but Billy kept his balance easily. He looked around in the darkness at whizzing trees, a few houses that he could see whenever there was a streetlight. Finally the car stopped in a driveway beside a big house, and Billy was untied and pulled—he had to jump—down to the ground. A young woman came out of the house and patted Billy, smiling. Then Billy was led—he let himself be led mainly because he was curious—towards a lean-to against the garage. Here was a pan of water, and the woman brought another pan of a vegetable and lettuce mish-mash that tasted quite good.

Billy would have liked a gallop, just to see how big the place was and to sample some of the greenery, but the man had tied him up. The man spoke kindly, patted his neck, and went into the house, where the lights soon went out.

The next morning, the man drove off in his car, and then the woman and the little girl came out. Billy was taken for a sedate walk on a rope. Billy pranced and leapt, full of energy but content to stay on the rope until he realized that the woman was taking him back to the lean-to. Billy dashed forward, head down, felt the rope leave the woman's hands, and then he galloped and rammed his horns, not too hard, against the trunk of a small tree.

The little girl shrieked with pleasure.

Billy's rope caught under a white iron bench, and he made circles around the bench until there was no more rope left, then butted the bench, knocked it over, and tossed his head. He liked making his bells ring, and he looked gaily at the woman and the little girl who were running towards him.

The woman picked up his rope. She seemed to be a little afraid of him. Then much to Billy's annoyance, she tied the end of the rope to a nearby stone statue. The statue, which looked like a small fat boy eating something, stood by a little rock pond. Billy was alone. He looked all around him, ate some grass which was delicious but already cut rather short. He was bored. There was no one in sight now, nothing moving except an occasional bird, and one squirrel which stared at him for a moment, then disappeared. Billy tugged at his rope, but the rope held. He knew he could chew through the rope, but the task struck him as distasteful, so he made a good run from the statue and was jerked back and thrown to the ground. Billy was on his legs at once, prancing higher than ever as he assessed the problem.

Billy took another run and this time put his back into it, chin whiskers brushing the ground. A solid weight struck his chest—he was wearing his harness—and behind him he heard a *crack!* then a *plop!* as the statue fell into the water. Billy galloped on, delayed hardly at all as his plunging legs hauled the statue over the brim of the pond. Billy went on through hedges, over stone paths where the statue gave out more *cracks!* and became ever lighter behind him. He found some flowers and paused to refresh himself. At this point, he heard running feet, and turned his head to see the woman of the house plus a boy of about Mickie's age coming towards him.

The woman seemed very upset. The boy untied the rope from the remnant of statue, and Billy was tugged firmly back towards the lean-to. Then the woman handed the boy a big iron spike which the boy banged into the ground with a hammer. Billy's rope was then tied to the spike.

The boy smiled and said, "There you go, Billy!"

They went away.

A day or so passed, and Billy became more bored. He chewed through part of his rope, then abandoned the project, knowing he would only be tied up again if he were walking around free. Billy was well fed, but he would have preferred Playland Amusement Park with its noise and people, pulling his cart with four passengers plus Mickie, to being tied to a stick doing nothing. Once the man put the little girl astride Billy's back, but the man held the rope so short, it was no fun for Billy. Billy shied at something, the little girl slid off—and that seemed to be the end of his giving her rides.

One afternoon a rather large black dog came loping on to the lawn, saw Billy and started barking and nipping at him. This infuriated Billy, because the dog seemed to be laughing at him. Billy lowered his head and bounded forward, determined to pull up the iron stake, but the rope broke, which was even better. Now the dog was on the run, and Billy bore down at full speed. The dog went round the corner of the greenhouse. Billy cut the corner close, and there was a shattering of glass as one of his horns hit a pane. Blind with rage, Billy attacked the greenhouse for no reason—except that it made a satisfying sound.

Crash!—*Bang!*—*Clatter-tinkle!* and again *Crash!*

The dog nipped at Billy's heels, yapping, and Billy kicked and missed.

The goat charged the dog, his hooves thundering on the lawn. The dog, a streak of black, disappeared off the property and headed down a street. Billy went after him, but stopped after a few yards, feeling that he had routed his enemy. Billy upturned the nearest hedge for the hell of it, gave a snort and shook himself so his bells jingled like a full orchestra. Then he trotted up the street with his head high, in the general direction of his own lawn. But some flowers by a gate attracted him. There was a scream from one of the houses. Billy moved off at once.

More shouts and yells.

Then a policeman's whistle. Billy was rudely taken in hand by the policeman who jerked him by horn and harness, and then whacked him on the haunch with his nightstick. In retaliation, Billy rammed the policeman in the belly and had the pleasure of seeing the man roll on the ground in agony. Then four or five boys jumped on Billy and threw him onto his side. Much noise, yelling and dragging—and Billy was back on the lawn where the iron stick was, and the broken greenhouse. Billy stood foursquare, breathing hard, glaring at everyone.

That evening, the man of the house loaded Billy on to the pick-up, and tied him so securely he could not lie down. Billy recognized from afar the cheerful cymbal clashes and the booms of the merry-go-round's music. They were back at Playland!

Mickie ran up smiling. "Hey, Billy! Back again!"

Hank wasn't smiling. He stood talking solemnly with the man, pulling his underlip and shaking his head. The man looked sad too, as he went away back to his car. That very evening Billy was harnessed to his cart and made nearly a dozen rounds before closing time. There was much laughter from Mickie and Hank as they put Billy into his stable that night and fed him. Billy was already quite full of hot dogs and popcorn.

"*Billy!* . . . There's *Billy* back!" The yells from the crowd echoed in Billy's ears as he fell asleep in his old straw bed. *Some* people in the world liked him.

Billy slipped into his old routine, which wasn't at all bad, he thought. At least it wasn't boring. In the daytime, five days a week, he could wander over the deserted grounds where there wasn't much grass but a good many remnants of hot dog buns and discarded peanut bags with a few peanuts generally in them. All was as usual. So Billy was surprised one busy evening to be unhitched from his cart by Mickie and dragged by Hank towards an automobile with a box at the back of it big enough for a horse.

Billy knew what was happening. Hank was pushing him off somewhere else. Billy braced his legs and had to be lifted on to the ramp by Hank and another man in a Western hat similar to Hank's, while a third man pulled his horns from inside the box. Billy gave a twist of his body, landed on his feet, and at once bounded into freedom.

Freedom! But where was he to go? The place was fenced in except for the car entrance, and this Billy made for. Two men tried to block him, but jumped aside like scared rabbits as Billy hurtled towards them. Billy rammed the side of a car, not having seen it in the semi-darkness, and knocked himself nearly out. A cry went up from the car occupants. Two huge men fell on Billy and held him down. Then three men carried him back towards the car with the horse box. This time his feet were tied together, and Hank himself jerked Billy's legs from under him, and Billy fell on his side. Billy kicked to no avail. He hated Hank at that moment. He had never liked Hank, and now Billy's hostility was like an explosion in him. Once more Billy witnessed from his horizontal position Hank receiving lots of paper money from the man who owned the horse box. Hank shoved the money deep in a pocket of his baggy trousers. Then they closed the box door.

This time it was a longer ride, far out into the country, Billy could tell from the smell of fresh-cut hay and damp earth. There was also the smell of horses. The men untied Billy's feet and put him in a stable where there was straw and a bucket of water. Billy gave a mighty kick—*tat-tat!*—against the side of his stable, just to show everyone, and himself, that there was plenty of fight in him yet. Then Billy blew his breath out and shook himself, jingling all his bells, and leapt in place from hind feet to front feet again and again.

The men laughed and departed.

The next day, Billy was tied to a wooden stake in the center of a broad field of grass. Now he had a chain, not a rope. Billy was indifferent to the horses, though he attempted to charge one which had whinnied and looked scared. The horse broke away from the man's hold on his rein, but stopped in a docile fashion, and the man caught him again. Billy thought the morning quite boring, but the grass was thick, and he ate. A saddle fit for a child was put on Billy, but there wasn't a child in sight. There were three men on the place, it seemed. One man mounted a horse and led Billy, trotting, around a circular area that was fenced in. When the horse trotted, Billy galloped. The man seemed pleased.

This went on for a few days, along with more complicated routines for the horses. They walked and strutted, knelt, and galloped sideways to music from a record player which one of the men operated outside the fence. They tried to get Billy to do something with a ribbon to which a piece of metal was attached. Billy didn't understand what they wanted, and started eating the ribbon, whereupon they snatched it out of his mouth. The man kicked him in the haunch to make him pay attention, and tried again. Billy wasn't trying very hard.

A couple of days later they all went off with the horses to a place with the biggest crowd Billy had ever seen. These people were mostly sitting down in a great circle with a clear space in the middle. Billy wore his saddle. One of the men got on a horse and led Billy—amid a lot of other men and women on horses—twice round the arena in a big parade. Music and cheers. Then Billy was led to the sidelines, and the man stood beside him on foot. They were near a gap in the wall, which was a good thing, because they had to use it when a wild horse, bucking and kicking, came very near them and threw his rider off. Now Billy and the man were in a kind of pen with no top, people leaned over the edge above them, and someone dropped what looked like a sizzling hot dog on Billy's back. The man brushed it off Billy and was trying to stamp on it when it exploded with a terrible *Bang!*

Billy bolted forward and was in the middle of the arena suddenly. A roar of delight went up from the crowd. A man in a clown's costume spread his arms to stop Billy, or deflect him. Billy aimed himself straight at the clown who jumped nimbly into an ashcan, and Billy's horns hit the ashcan with a *Clang!* and sent it rolling yards away with the clown in it. The people yelled with glee, and Billy's blood tingled. Then a big man who looked purposeful came running for Billy, grabbed his horns as Billy attacked, and Billy and the man both fell to the ground. But Billy's hind feet were free, and he kicked with all his might. The man gave a scream and released him, and Billy trotted away triumphant.

Bang!

Someone had fired a gun. Billy hardly noticed. It was all part of the fun. Billy looked around for more targets, started for a man on horseback, but was distracted by two men on foot who were running towards him from different directions. Billy didn't know which to aim at, decided on the closer, and picked up speed. He whammed the man at hip height, but an instant later a rope hissed around Billy's neck.

Billy charged the rope-thrower, but still a third man threw himself at Billy and caught him round the body. Billy twisted, fighting with his crooked left horn, and got the man in the arm, but the man held on.

Someone else banged Billy in the head, stunning him. Billy was dimly aware of being carried off, amid the continuing cheers of the spectators.

Ka-plop!

Billy was dumped into one of the horse boxes. The man who mainly took care of him was tying up his legs now. His arm was bleeding, and he was muttering in an unpleasant way.

When they all got home to the ranch that night, the man took a whip to Billy. Billy was tied in one of the stables. The man kept shouting at him. It was a long strong whip and it hurt—a little. Another man watched. Billy butted the side of the stable in wrath, and on the rebound aimed himself at the man with the whip. The man jumped back, and was closing the stable door when Billy's horns banged into it. Then the man went away. It was a long time before Billy calmed down, before he began to feel the stings of the whip on his haunches and his back. He hated everybody that night.

In the morning, all three men escorted Billy to one of the horse boxes, though when Billy saw the horse box, he went along readily. Billy was willing to go anywhere that was somewhere else.

Once more, it was a longish ride. Then Billy heard the peculiar rattle under the wheels that cars made going over the metal roller bridge in front of Playland Amusement Park. They stopped, and Billy heard Hank's voice. Billy was let out. Billy was rather pleased. But Hank didn't seem pleased. Hank was frowning and looking at the ground, and at Billy. Then the men went away in their car, and when they were gone, Hank said something to Billy and laughed. He grabbed Billy's harness with one hand and steered him on to the grassier part of the park where cars and people never went. But Billy was too disturbed to eat. His back hurt worse, and his head throbbed, maybe from the blow he'd got in the arena.

Where was Mickie? Billy looked around. Maybe it was one of the days when Mickie didn't come.

As dusk fell, Billy was sure it was one of the evenings when no one came to Playland Amusement Park, not even Mickie. Then Hank put the usual lights on, or most of them, and hitched Billy to his cart. This was strange, Billy thought. Hank never took a ride all by himself.

"Come along, Billy, ni-ice Billy," Hank was saying in a soothing tone.

But Billy sensed fear in him. Hank's weight made the cart creak as if he were several people.

"Gee up, Billy. Easy does it," Hank said, and slapped the reins as Mickie always did.

Billy started off. It felt good to put some of his anger into pulling the cart. Billy's trot became a gallop.

"Ho theah, Billy!"

Hank's command made Billy run all the faster. He hit a tree, and knocked a wheel off the cart. Hank yelled for him to stop. Then Hank bounced out of the cart, and Billy made a curve and stopped, looking back. Hank was sitting on the ground, and Billy charged. Hank had just about got to his feet when Billy struck, and knocked him down.

"Ho theah, Billy," Hank was saying, more softly now, as if he were still guiding Billy by the reins. Hank wobbled towards Billy, pressing a hand to one of his knees, the other hand to his head.

Then Billy saw Hank evidently change his mind, and veer towards the popcorn stand for protection, and Billy charged again. Hank trotted away as best he could, but Billy whammed into Hank's broad, highly buttable backside. *Whoof!* Hank fairly doubled backward, and fell in a heap on the ground.

Billy trotted in a circle, oblivious of the half-a-cart behind him. Hank lifted a blood-stained face. Billy lowered his head and attacked the mass which was now about his own height. One curved horn, one crooked horn hit God knew where, and Hank rolled over backward. Billy gave an uppercut, pulled his horns out, backed a little, and came at Hank again.

Thuck! Hank's body seemed to be growing softer.

Billy struck again, backed a little, then footed it daintily over Hank's body, cart wreck and all. Dark blood ran into the grassless, much-trodden earth. The next thing Billy knew, he was yards away, trotting with his head up. The cart behind him seemed to weigh nothing at all. Was it even there? But Billy heard a bush—which he had leapt—crackle behind him, and felt the cart bump against the corner of a booth.

Then Hank's wife appeared. *"Billy! . . ."* She was yelling excitedly.

Billy trembled with leftover fury, and was on the brink of butting her, but he only snorted and shook himself.

"Hank! Where are you?" She hurried away.

The sound of "Hank!" made Billy jump, and he started off at a run, made a swipe at the gatepost by the car entrance, and knocked off the other wheel of the cart.

Hank's wife was still screaming somewhere.

Billy dashed down the road, took the first dirt road that he came to, and kept on into the darkness, into the country. A car slowed, and a man said something to Billy, but Billy ran on.

Finally Billy trotted, then walked. Here were fields and a patch of woods. In the woods, Billy lay down and slept. When he woke up, it was dawn, and he was thirsty, more thirsty than hungry. He came to a farmhouse, where there was a water trough behind a fence. Billy couldn't easily get to it, so he trotted on, sensing that there was water somewhere near. He found a brook in a sloping place. Then he ate some of the rich grass there. One shaft of his cart remained attached to his harness, which was annoying, but more important was that he was free. He could go in any direction he chose, and from what he could see there was grass and water everywhere.

Adventure beckoned.

So Billy took another dirt road and pushed on. Only two cars went by all morning, and each time Billy trotted faster, and nobody got out to bother him.

Then Billy caught a scent and slowed down, lifted his nose and sniffed again. Then he went in the direction of the scent. Very soon he saw another goat in a field, a black and white goat. For the moment, Billy felt more curious than friendly. He walked towards the goat, came to an opening in the rail fence, and entered the field, dragging the one gold and white shaft behind him. Billy saw that the other goat was tethered. She lifted her head—the goat was a female, Billy now realized—looked at him with mild surprise and went on chewing what she had in her mouth. Behind her was a long low white house, and near it clothes fluttered on a line. There was a barn, and Billy heard the "Moo" of a cow from somewhere.

A woman came out of the house and threw a pan of something on the ground, saw Billy, and dropped the pan in astonishment. Then she approached Billy cautiously. Billy stood his ground, chewing some excellent clover which he had just wrenched up. The woman made a shooing motion with her apron, but as if she didn't really mean it. She drew nearer, looking very hard at Billy. Then she laughed—a nice laugh. Billy was an expert on laughs, and he liked this woman's laugh at once, because it was easy and happy.

"Tommy!" the woman called to the house. "Georgette! Come out and see what's here!"

In a minute, two small children came out of the house and screamed with surprise, a little like the children at Playland.

They offered Billy water. The woman finally got up courage and unbuckled the shaft from the goat harness. Billy was still chewing clover. He knew the thing to do was not to look aggressive, and in fact he felt not in the least like butting any of them. When the woman and the children called him towards the barn, he followed. But nobody tried to tie him up. The woman seemed to be inviting Billy to do what *he* wanted to do, which was a nice relief. She would have let him walk away, Billy thought, back down the road again. Billy liked it here. Later, a man arrived, and looked at Billy. The man took off his hat and scratched his head, then he laughed too. When the sun went down, the woman untied the other goat, and led her towards the barn outside which Billy was walking about, looking things over. There were pigs, a water trough, and chickens and ducks behind a fence.

"Billy!" said the man, and laughed again when Billy recognized his name and looked at him. He gave Billy's harness a shake, as if he admired it. But he took it off and put it away somewhere.

The barn was clean and had straw in it. The man put a leather collar on Billy, patted him and talked to him. The other goat, which they called Lucy, was tied up near Billy, and the woman milked her into a small pail.

Billy opened his mouth and said "A-a-a-a!"

It made everybody laugh. Billy jumped back and forth from front feet to hind feet. The memory of Hank, of the smell of his blood, was fast fading, like a bad spell of temper that had happened longer ago than yesterday, although he knew he had given Hank more butts than he had ever given anyone or anything.

In the morning when the woman came into the barn, she looked surprised and really happy to see that Billy was still there. She said something friendly to him. Evidently he wasn't going to be tied up ever, Billy thought as he trotted into the meadow with Lucy. Now that was fair play!

Little Tales of Misogyny

The Hand

A young man asked a father for his daughter's hand, and received it in a box—her left hand.

Father: "You asked for her hand and you have it. But it is my opinion that you wanted other things and took them."

Young man: "Whatever do you mean?"

Father: "Whatever do you think I mean? You cannot deny that I am more honorable than you, because you took something from my family without asking, whereas when you asked for my daughter's hand, I gave it."

Actually, the young man had not done anything dishonorable. The father was merely suspicious and had a dirty mind. The father could legally make the young man responsible for his daughter's upkeep and soak him financially. The young man could not deny that he had the daughter's hand—even though in desperation he had now buried it, after kissing it. But it was becoming two weeks old.

The young man wanted to see the daughter, and made an effort, but was quite blocked by besieging tradesmen. The daughter was signing checks with her right hand. Far from bleeding to death, she was going ahead at full speed.

The young man announced in newspapers that she had quit his bed and board. But he had to prove that she had ever enjoyed them. It was not yet "a marriage" on paper, or in the church. Yet there was no doubt that he had her hand, and had signed a receipt for it when the package had been delivered.

"Her hand in *what*?" the young man demanded of the police, in despair and down to his last penny. "Her hand is buried in my garden."

"You are a criminal to boot? Not merely disorganized in your way of life, but a psychopath? Did you by chance cut off your wife's hand?"

"I did not, and she is not even my wife!"

"He has her hand, and yet she is not his wife!" scoffed the men of the law. "What shall we do with him? He is unreasonable, maybe even insane."

"Lock him up in an asylum. He is also broke, so it will have to be a State Institution."

So the young man was locked up, and once a month the girl whose hand he had received came to look at him through the wire barrier, like a dutiful wife. And like most wives, she had nothing to say. But she smiled prettily. His job provided a small pension now, which she was getting. Her stump was concealed in a muff.

Because the young man became too disgusted with her to look at her, he was placed in a more disagreeable ward, deprived of books and company, and he went really insane.

When he became insane, all that had happened to him, the asking for and receiving his beloved's hand, became intelligible to him. He realized what a horrible mistake, crime even, he had been guilty of in demanding such a barbaric thing as a girl's hand.

He spoke to his captors, saying that now he understood his mistake.

"What mistake? To ask for a girl's hand? So did I, when I married."

The young man, feeling now he was insane beyond repair, since he could make contact with nothing, refused to eat for many days, and at last lay on his bed with his face to the wall, and died.

Oona,
the Jolly Cave Woman

S he was a bit hairy, one front tooth missing, but her sex appeal was apparent at a distance of two hundred yards or more, like an odor, which perhaps it was. She was round, round-bellied, round-shouldered, round-hipped, and always smiling, always jolly. That was why men liked her. She had always something cooking in a pot on a fire. She was simple-minded and never lost her temper. She had been clubbed over the head so many times, her brain was addled. It was not necessary to club Oona to have her, but that was the custom, and Oona barely troubled to dodge to protect herself.

Oona was constantly pregnant and had never experienced the onset of puberty, her father having had at her since she was five, and after him, her brothers. Her first child was born when she was seven. Even in late pregnancy she was interfered with, and men waited impatiently the half hour or so it took her to give birth before they fell on her again.

Oddly, she kept the birthrate of the tribe more or less steady, and if anything tended to decrease the population, since men neglected their own wives because of thinking of her, or occasionally were killed in fighting over her.

Oona was at last killed by a jealous woman whose husband had not touched her in many months. This man was the first to fall in love. His name was Vipo. His men-friends had laughed at him for not taking some other woman, or his own wife, in the times when Oona was not available. Vipo had lost an eye in fighting his rivals. He was only a middle-sized man. He had always brought Oona the choicest things he had killed. He worked long and hard to make an ornament out of flint, so he became the first artist of his tribe. All the others used flint only for arrowheads or knives. He had given the ornament to Oona to hang around her neck by a string of leather.

When Vipo's wife slew Oona out of jealousy, Vipo slew his wife in hatred and wrath. Then he sang a loud and tragic song. He continued to sing like a madman, as tears ran down his hairy cheeks. The tribe considered killing him, because he was mad and different from everyone else, and they were afraid. Vipo drew images of Oona in the wet sand by the sea, then pictures of her on the flat stones on the mountains near by, pictures that could be seen from a distance. He made a statue of Oona out of wood, then one of stone. Sometimes he slept with these. Out of the clumsy syllables of his language, he made a sentence which evoked Oona whenever he uttered it. He was not the only one who learned and uttered this sentence, or who had known Oona.

Vipo was slain by a jealous woman whose man had not touched her for months. Her man had purchased one of Vipo's statues of Oona for a great price—a vast piece of leather made of several bison hides. Vipo made a beautiful watertight house of it, and had enough left over for clothing for himself. He created more sentences about Oona. Some men had admired him, others had hated him, and all the women had hated him because he had looked at them as if he did not see them. Many men were sad when Vipo was dead.

But in general people were relieved when Vipo was gone. He had been a strange one, disturbing some people's sleep at night.

The Coquette

There was once a coquette who had a suitor whom she couldn't get rid of. He took her promises and avowals seriously, and would not leave. He even believed her hints. This annoyed her, because it got in the way of new temporary acquaintances, their presents, flattery, flowers, dinners and so forth.

Finally Yvonne insulted and lied to her suitor Bertrand, and gave him literally nothing—which was a minus compared to the nothing she was giving her other men-friends. Still Bertrand would not cease his attentions, because he considered her behavior normal and feminine, an excess of modesty. She even gave him a lecture, and for once in her life she told the truth. Unaccustomed as he was to the truth, expecting falsehood from a pretty woman, he took her words as turnabouts, and continued to dance attendance.

Yvonne attempted to poison him by means of arsenic in cups of chocolate at her house, but he recovered and thought this a greater and more charming proof of her fear of losing her virginity with him, though she had already lost her virginity at the age of ten, when she had told her mother that she was raped. Yvonne had thus sent a thirty-year-old man to prison. She had been trying for two weeks to seduce him, saying she was fifteen, and mad about him. It had given her pleasure to ruin his career and to make his wife unhappy and ashamed, and their eight-year-old daughter bewildered.

Other men gave Bertrand advice. "We have all had it," they said, "maybe even been to bed with her once or twice. You haven't even had that. And she's worthless!" But Bertrand thought he was different in Yvonne's eyes, and though he realized he had pertinacity beyond the common order, he felt this a virtue.

Yvonne incited a new suitor to kill Bertrand. She won the new suitor's allegiance by promising to marry him, if he eliminated Bertrand. To Bertrand, she said the same thing about the other man. The new suitor challenged Bertrand to a duel, missed the first shot, and then began talking with his intended victim. (Bertrand's gun had refused to fire at all.) They discovered that each had been given promises of marriage. Meanwhile both men had given her expensive presents and had lent her money during small crises over the past months.

They were resentful, but could not come up with an idea for scotching her. So they decided to kill her. The new suitor went to her and told her he had killed the stupid and persistent Bertrand. Then Bertrand knocked on the door. The two men pretended to fight each other. In reality, they pushed Yvonne between them and killed her with various blows about the head. Their story was that she tried to interfere and was accidentally struck.

Since the judge of the town had himself suffered and been laughed at by the townsfolk because of Yvonne's coquetry with him, he was secretly pleased by her death, and let the two men off without ado. He was also wise enough to know that the two men could not have killed her if they had not been infatuated with her—a state that inspired his pity, since he had become sixty years old.

Only Yvonne's maid, who had always been well paid and tipped, attended her funeral. Even Yvonne's family detested her.

The Female Novelist

S he has total recall. It is all sex. She is on her third marriage now, having dropped three children on the way, but none by her present husband. Her cry is: "Listen to my past! It is more important than my present. Let me tell you what an absolute swine my last husband (or lover) was."

Her past is like an undigested, perhaps indigestible meal which sits upon her stomach. One wishes she could simply vomit and forget it.

She writes reams about how many times she, or her woman rival, jumped into bed with her husband. And how she paced the floor, sleepless—virtuously denying herself the consolation of a drink—while her husband spent the night with the other woman, flagrantly, etc., and to hell with what friends and neighbors thought. Since the friends and neighbors were either incapable of thinking or were uninterested in the situation, it doesn't matter what they thought. One might say that this is the time for a novelist's invention, for creating thought and public opinion where there is none, but the female novelist doesn't bother inventing. It is all stark as a jockstrap.

After three women friends have seen and praised the manuscript, saying it is "just like life," and the male and female characters' names have been changed four times, much to the detriment of the manuscript's appearance, and after one man-friend (a prospective lover) has read the first page and returned the manuscript saying he has read it all and adores it—the manuscript goes off to a publisher. There is a quick, courteous rejection.

She begins to be more cautious, secures entrées via writer acquaintances, vague, hedged-about recommendations obtained at the expense of winy lunches and dinners.

Rejection after rejection, nonetheless.

"I *know* my story is important!" she says to her husband.

"So is the life of the mouse here, to him—or maybe her," he replies. He is a patient man, but nearly at the end of his nerves with all this.

"What mouse?"

"I talk to a mouse nearly every morning when I'm in the bathtub. I think his or her problem is food. They're a pair. Either one or the other comes out of the hole—there's a hole in the corner of the bathroom—then I get them something from the refrigerator."

"You're wandering. What's that got to do with my manuscript?"

"Just that mice are concerned with a more important subject—food. Not with whether your ex-husband was unfaithful to you, or whether you suffered from it, even in a setting as beautiful as Capri or Rapallo. Which gives me an idea."

"What?" she asks, somewhat anxiously.

Her husband smiles for the first time in several months. He experiences a few seconds of peace. There is not the clicking of the typewriter in the house. His wife is actually looking at him, waiting to hear what he has to say. "You figure that one out. You're the one with imagination. I won't be in for dinner."

Then he leaves the flat, taking his address book and—optimistically—a pair of pajamas and a toothbrush.

She goes and stares at the typewriter, thinking that perhaps here is another novel, just from this evening, and should she scrap the novel she has fussed over for so long and start this new one? Maybe tonight? Now? Who is he going to sleep with?

The Dancer

They danced marvelously together, swooping back and forth across the floor to the erotic rhythms of the tango, sometimes the waltz. At the age of twenty and twenty-two respectively, Claudette and Rodolphe became lovers. They wanted to marry, but their employer thought they were more titillating to the customers if they were not married. So they remained single.

The nightclub where they worked was called The Rendez-vous, and was known amongst a certain jaded, middle-aged male clientele as a sure cure for impotence. Just come and watch Claudette and Rodolphe dance, everyone said. Journalists, trying to spice their columns, described their act as sado-masochistic, because Rodolphe often appeared to be choking Claudette to death. He would seize her throat and advance, bending her backward, or he would retreat—it didn't matter—keeping her throat in the grip of his hands, sometimes shaking her neck so that her hair tossed wildly. The audience would gasp, sigh, and watch with fascination. The drumrolls of the three-man band would grow louder and more insistent.

Claudette stopped sleeping with Rodolphe, because she thought deprivation would whet his appetite. It was easy for Claudette to excite Rodolphe when dancing with him, then to abandon him with a flounce as she made her exit to the applause, sometimes the laughter, of the spectators. Little did they know that Rodolphe was really being abandoned.

Claudette was whimsical, with no real plans, but she took up with a paunchy man called Charles, good-natured, generous and rich. She even slept with him. Charles applauded loudly when Claudette and Rodolphe danced together, Rodolphe with his hands about Claudette's graceful white neck, and she bending backward. Charles could afford to laugh. He was going to bed with her later.

Since their earnings were bound together, Rodolphe put it up to Claudette: stop seeing Charles, or he would not perform with her. Or at least he would not perform with his hands about her throat as if he were going to throttle her in an excess of passion, which was what the customers came for. Rodolphe meant it, so Claudette promised not to sleep with Charles again. She kept her promise, Charles drifted away and was seen at The Rendez-vous seldom, and then sadly moping, and finally he stopped coming at all. But Rodolphe gradually realized that Claudette was taking on two or three other men. She began sleeping with these, and business went up more than it had with the rich Charles, who after all was only one man, with one group of friends whom he could bring to The Rendez-vous.

Rodolphe asked Claudette to drop all three. She promised. But either they or their messengers with notes and flowers still hung around the dressing room every evening.

Rodolphe, who had not spent a night with Claudette in five months now, yet whose body was pressed against hers every night before the eyes of two hundred people—Rodolphe danced a splendid tango one evening. He pressed himself against her as usual, and she bent backward.

"More! More!" cried the audience, mostly men, as Rodolphe's hands tightened about her throat.

Claudette always pretended to suffer, to love Rodolphe and to suffer at the hands of his passion in the dance. This time she did not rise when he released her. Nor did he assist her, as he usually did. He had strangled her, too tightly for her to cry out. Rodolphe walked off the little stage, and left Claudette for other people to pick up.

The Invalid, or,
the Bedridden

She had suffered a fall while on a skiing holiday at Chamonix with her boyfriend some ten years ago. The injury had something to do with her back. The doctors couldn't find anything, nobody could see anything wrong with her back, but still it hurt, she said. Actually, she was not sure she would get her man unless she pretended an injury, and one acquired when she had been with him. Philippe, however, was quite in love with her, and she need not have worried so much. Still, hooking Philippe very firmly, plus ensuring a life of leisure—not to say flat on her back in bed, or however she chose to lie comfortably, for the rest of her life—was no small gain. It was a big one. How many other women could capture a man for life, give him nothing at all, not even bother to cook his meals, and still be supported in rather fine style?

Some days she got up, mainly out of boredom. She was sometimes up when the sun was shining, but not always. When the sun was not shining, or when there was a threat of rain, Christine felt terrible and kept to her bed. Then her husband Philippe had to go downstairs with the shopping net and come back and cook. All Christine talked about was "how I feel." Visitors and friends were treated to a long account of injections, pills, pains in the back which had kept her from sleeping last Wednesday night, and the possibility of rain tomorrow, because of the way she felt.

But she was always feeling rather well when August came, because she and Philippe went to Cannes then. Things might be bad at the very start of August, however, causing Philippe to engage an ambulance to Orly, then a special accommodation on an aeroplane to Nice. In Cannes she found herself able to go to the beach every morning at 11 A.M., swimming for a few minutes with the aid of water wings, and to eat a good lunch. But at the end of August, back in Paris, she suffered a relapse from all the excitement, rich food, and general physical strain, and once more had to take to bed, her tan included. She would sometimes expose tanned legs for visitors, sigh with memories of Cannes, then cover up again with sheets and blanket. September heralded, indeed, the onset of grim winter. Philippe couldn't sleep with her now—though for God's sake he felt he had earned better treatment, having worked his fingers to the bone to pay her doctors', radiologists' and pharmacies' bills beyond reckoning. He would have to face another solitary winter, and not even in the same room with her, but in the next room.

"To think I brought all this upon her," Philippe said to one of his friends, "by taking her to Chamonix."

"But why is she always feeling quite well in August?" replied the friend. "You think she is an invalid? Think again, really, old man."

Philippe did begin to think, because other friends had said the same thing. It took him years to think, many years of Augusts in Cannes (at an expense which knocked out the savings of a whole eleven months) and many winters sleeping mainly in the "spare bedroom," and not with the woman he loved and desired.

So the eleventh August in Cannes, Philippe summoned all his courage. He swam out behind Christine with a pin in his fingers. He stuck a pin in her water wings and made two punctures, one in each white wing. He and Christine were not far out, just slightly over their heads in water. Philippe was not in the best of form. Not only was he losing his hair, of no importance in a swimming situation, but he had developed a belly, which might not, he thought, have come if he had been able to make love to Christine all the past decade. But Philippe tried and succeeded in pushing Christine under, and at the same time had some difficulty in keeping himself afloat. His confused motions, seen by a few people finally, appeared to be those of a man trying to save someone who was drowning. And this of course was what he told the police and everyone. Christine, despite sufficient buoyant fat, sank like a piece of lead.

Christine was absolutely no loss to Philippe except for burial fees. He soon lost his paunch, and much to his own surprise found himself suddenly well-to-do, instead of having to turn every penny. His friends congratulated him, but politely, and in the abstract. They couldn't exactly say, "Thank God, you're rid of that bitch," but they said the next thing to it. In about six months, he met quite a nice girl who loved to cook, was full of energy, and she also liked to go to bed with him. The hair on Philippe's head even began to grow back.

The Artist

At the time Jane got married, one would have thought there was nothing unusual about her. She was plump, pretty and practical: she could give artificial respiration at the drop of a hat or pull someone out of a faint or a nosebleed. She was a dentist's assistant, and as cool as they come in the face of crisis or pain. But she had enthusiasm for the arts. What arts? All of them. She began, in the first year of her married life, with painting. This occupied all her Saturdays, or enough of Saturdays to prevent adequate shopping for the weekend, but her husband Bob did the shopping. He also paid for the framing of muddy, run-together oil portraits of their friends, and the sittings of the friends took up time on the weekends too. Jane at last faced the fact she could not stop her colors from running together, and decided to abandon painting for the dance.

The dance, in a black leotard, did not much improve her robust figure, only her appetite. Special shoes followed. She was studying ballet. She had discovered an institution called The School of Arts. In this five-story edifice they taught the piano, violin and other instruments, music composition, novel writing, poetry, sculpture, the dance and painting.

"You see, Bob, life can and should be made more beautiful," Jane said with her big smile. "And everyone wants to contribute, if he or she can, just a little bit to the beauty and poetry of the world."

Meanwhile, Bob emptied the garbage and made sure they were not out of potatoes. Jane's ballet did not progress beyond a certain point, and she dropped it and took up singing.

"I really think life is beautiful enough as it is," Bob said. "Anyway I'm pretty happy." That was during Jane's singing period, which had caused them to crowd the already small living room with an upright piano.

For some reason, Jane stopped her singing lessons and began to study sculpture and wood carving. This made the living room a mess of dropped bits of clay and wood chips which the vacuum could not always pick up. Jane was too tired for anything after her day's work in the dentist's office, and standing on her feet over wood or clay until midnight.

Bob came to hate The School of Arts. He had seen it a few times, when he had gone to fetch Jane at 11 P.M. or so. (The neighborhood was dangerous to walk in.) It seemed to Bob that the students were all a lot of misguided hopefuls, and the teachers a lot of mediocrities. It seemed a madhouse of misplaced effort. And how many homes, children and husbands were being troubled now, because the women of the households—the students were mainly women—were not at home performing a few essential tasks? It seemed to Bob that there was no inspiration in The School of Arts, only a desire to imitate people who had been inspired, like Chopin, Beethoven and Bach, whose works he could hear being mangled as he sat on a bench in the lobby, awaiting his wife. People called artists mad, but these students seemed incapable of the same kind of madness. The students did appear insane, in a certain sense of the word, but not in the right way, somehow. Considering the time The School of Arts deprived him of his wife, Bob was ready to blow the whole building to bits.

He had not long to wait, but he did not blow the building up himself. Someone—it was later proven to have been an instructor—put a bomb under The School of Arts, set to go off at 4 P.M. It was New Year's Eve, and despite the fact it was a semi-holiday, the students of all the arts were practising diligently. The police and some newspapers had been forewarned of the bomb. The trouble was, nobody found it, and also most people did not believe that any bomb would go off. Because of the seediness of the neighborhood, the school had been subjected to scares and threats before. But the bomb went off, evidently from the depths of the basement, and a pretty good-sized one it was.

Bob happened to be there, because he was to have fetched Jane at 5 P.M. He had heard about the bomb rumor, but did not know whether to believe it or not. With some caution, however, or a premonition, he was waiting across the street instead of in the lobby.

One piano went through the roof, a bit separated from the student who was still seated on the stool, fingering nothing. A dancer at last made a few complete revolutions without her feet touching the ground, because she was a quarter of a mile high, and her toes were even pointing skyward. An art student was flung through a wall, his brush poised, ready to make the master stroke as he floated horizontally towards a true oblivion. One instructor, who had taken refuge as often as possible in the toilets of The School of Arts, was blown up in proximity to some of the plumbing.

Then came Jane, flying through the air with a mallet in one hand, a chisel in the other, and her expression was rapt. Was she stunned, still concentrating on her work, or even dead? Bob could not tell about Jane. The flying particles subsided with a gentle, diminishing clatter, and a rise of gray dust. There were a few seconds of silence, during which Bob stood still. Then he turned and walked homeward. Other schools of art, he knew, would arise. Oddly, this thought crossed his mind before he realized that his wife was gone forever.

The
Middle-Class Housewife

Pamela Thorpe considered Women's Lib one of those silly protest movements that journalists liked to write about to fill their pages. Women's Lib claimed to want "independence" for women, whereas Pamela believed that women had the upper hand over men anyway. So what was all the fuss about?

The reason this question arose at all was because Pamela's daughter Barbara came home in June after graduating from university, and told her mother that there was going to be a Women's Lib rally in their neighborhood. Barbara had organized it with her college chum Fran, whose family Pamela knew. Of course Pamela went to the rally—in the local church—mainly to amuse herself and to hear what the younger generation had to say.

Colored balloons and paper streamers hung from the rafters and the sills of stained glass windows. Pamela was surprised to see young Connie Haines, mother of two small children, preaching away like a convert.

"Working women need *free state nurseries!*" shouted Connie, and her last words were almost obliterated by applause. "And *alimony*—the legalized soaking of divorced husbands—must *go!*"

Cheers! Women got to their feet clapping and shouting.

State nurseries! Pamela envisaged streams of working women (they only thought they wanted to work) abandoning their homes at 8 A.M., parking their tots somewhere, bringing home paychecks at the end of the week to houses where the next meal wasn't even on the stove. Many women were now raising their hands to be given the floor, so Pamela raised her hand, too. There was a lot she wanted to say.

"*Men* are not against us!" one woman cried out from a pew. "It is *women* who hold us back, selfish, cowardly women who think they'll be losing something by demanding equal pay for equal work! . . ."

"My *husband,*" Connie began, because she suddenly had the floor again, and was speaking in an even louder voice, "is about to take his final exams to become a doctor, and we're worried because we can hardly make ends meet. I've got to stay home and look after the two kids. If we hired a baby-sitter, it would cancel out my earnings if I took a job! *That's* why I'm in favor of free state nurseries! I'm not too lazy to take a job!"

More applause and cheering.

Now Pamela got to her feet. "State nurseries!" she said, and she had to be heard, because her voice overrode all the others. "You younger people—I'm forty-two—seem not to realize that a woman's place is in the home, to make a home, that you'll be breeding a generation of delinquents if a generation of state nursery–raised children—"

A general uproar silenced Pamela for a moment.

"That has not been proven!" a girl's voice yelled.

"And abolition of alimony! Maybe you're against that, too?" someone else demanded. It was her daughter Barbara.

The faces had become a blur. Pamela recognized some of them, neighbors since years, but in a way she couldn't recognize them in their new roles of attackers, enemies. "As for alimony," Pamela resumed, still on her feet, "it is a husband's *job* to support the family, is it not?"

"Even when a wife has walked out?" asked someone.

"Do you know some women are getting away with murder, and it's giving women a bad name?"

"Every divorce case should be examined *separately!*" cried another voice.

"Women will be victimized!" Pamela shot back. "The abolition of alimony has been called a licence for Casanovas, and that it is! It will destroy a woman's—*meal ticket!*"

Chaos! Now the fat was in the fire. It had perhaps been an unfortunate choice of phrase—meal ticket—but at any rate, the whole congregation, or mob, was on its feet.

Pamela's adrenaline rose to meet it. She realized also that she had to protect herself, because the atmosphere had suddenly turned nasty and hostile. But she was not alone: at least four women, all neighbors and all somewhat middle-aged like Pamela, were on her side, and Pamela saw that the armies were ranging themselves in groups, or knots. Voices rose still higher. Hymnals began to fly.

Splot!

"Reactionaries!"

"... home-breakers!"

"I suppose you're anti-abortion, too!"

An egg hit Pamela between the eyes. She wiped her face with a paper tissue. Where had the egg come from? But of course many of the women had their shopping bags with them.

Tomatoes arced like red bombs through the air. Apples also. The din resembled a loud cackling of hens or of some other kind of bird, much disturbed, within a confined space. The sides were not lined up. Groups fought among one another at close range.

Whop! That had been a tin of something walloped over a woman's head in retaliation for—so the attacker averred—a worse offense. Umbrellas, at least three or four, were being brought into play now.

"Listen to what I'm *saying!*"

"You *bitch!*"

"Stop the *fighting!*"

"Everybody sit down! Where's the chairwoman?"

Some women were leaving, Pamela saw, making a crush at the front doors. Then to her own surprise, she found she had a sturdy faldstool in her hands and was about to hurl it. How many had she thrown already? Pamela dropped the stool (on her own toes) and ducked just in time to avoid being hit by a cabbage.

But it was a two-pound tin of baked beans that did for Pamela, catching her smack in her right temple. She died within a few seconds, and her assailant was never identified.

The Fully Licensed Whore, or, the Wife

Sarah had always played the field as an amateur, and at twenty she got married, which made her licensed. To top it, the marriage was in a church in full view of family, friends and neighbors, maybe even God as witness, for certainly He was invited. She was all in white, though hardly a virgin, being two months pregnant and not by the man she was marrying, whose name was Sylvester. Now she could become a professional, with protection of the law, approval of society, blessing of the clergy, and financial support guaranteed by her husband.

Sarah lost no time. It was first the gas meter reader, to limber herself up, then the window cleaner, whose job took a varying number of hours, depending on how dirty she told Sylvester the windows had been. Sylvester sometimes had to pay for eight hours' work plus a bit of overtime. Sometimes the window cleaner was there when Sylvester left for work, and still there when he came home in the evening. But these were small fry, and Sarah progressed to their lawyer, which had the advantage of "no fee" for any services performed for the Sylvester Dillon family, now three.

Sylvester was proud of baby son Edmund, and flushed with pleasure at what friends said about Edmund's resemblance to himself. The friends were not lying, only saying what they thought they should say, and what they would have said to any father. After Edmund's birth, Sarah ceased sexual relations with Sylvester (not that they'd ever had much) saying, "One's enough, don't you think?" She could also say, "I'm tired," or "It's too hot." In plain fact, poor Sylvester was good only for his money—he wasn't wealthy but quite comfortably off—and because he was reasonably intelligent and presentable, not aggressive enough to be a nuisance and—Well, that was about all it took to satisfy Sarah. She had a vague idea that she needed a protector and escort. It somehow carried more weight to write "Mrs." at the foot of letters.

She enjoyed three or four years of twiddling about with the lawyer, then their doctor, then a couple of maverick husbands in their social circle, plus a few two-week sprees with the father of Edmund. These men visited the house mainly during the afternoons Monday to Friday. Sarah was most cautious and insisted—her house front being visible to several neighbors— that her lovers ring her when they were already in the vicinity, so she could tell them if the coast was clear enough for them to nip in. One-thirty P.M. was the safest time, when most people were eating lunch. After all, Sarah's bed and board was at stake, and Sylvester was becoming restless, though as yet not at all suspicious.

Sylvester in the fourth year of marriage made a slight fuss. His own advances to his secretary and also to the girl who worked behind the counter in his office supplies shop had been gently but firmly rejected, and his ego was at a low ebb.

"Can't we try again?" was Sylvester's theme.

Sarah counterattacked like a dozen battalions whose guns had been primed for years to fire. One would have thought she was the one to whom injustice had been done. "Haven't I created a lovely home for you? Aren't I a good hostess—the *best* according to all our friends, isn't that true? Have I ever neglected Edmund? Have I ever failed to have a hot meal waiting for you when you come home?"

I wish you would forget the hot meal now and then and think of something else, Sylvester wanted to say, but was too well brought up to get the words out.

"Furthermore I have taste," Sarah added as a final volley. "Our furniture is not only good, it's well cared for. I don't know what more you can expect from me."

The furniture was so well polished, the house looked like a museum. Sylvester was often shy about dirtying ashtrays. He would have liked more disorder and a little more warmth. How could he say this?

"Now come and eat something," Sarah said more sweetly, extending a hand in a burst of contact unprecedented for Sylvester in the past many years. A thought had just crossed her mind, a plan.

Sylvester took her hand gladly, and smiled. He ate second helpings of everything that she pressed upon him. The dinner was as usual good, because Sarah was an excellent and meticulous cook. Sylvester was hoping for a happy end to the evening also, but in this he was disappointed.

Sarah's idea was to kill Sylvester with good food, with kindness in a sense, with wifely *duty*. She was going to cook more and more elaborately. Sylvester already had a paunch, the doctor had cautioned him about overeating, not enough exercise and all that rot, but Sarah knew enough about weight control to know that it was what you ate that counted, not how much exercise you took. And Sylvester loved to eat. The stage was set, she felt, and what had she to lose?

She began to use richer fats, goose fat, olive oil, and to make macaroni cheese, to butter sandwiches more thickly, to push milk-drinking as a splendid source of calcium for Sylvester's falling hair. He put on twenty pounds in three months. His tailor had to alter all his suits, then make new suits for him.

"Tennis, darling," Sarah said with concern. "What you need is a bit of exercise." She was hoping he'd have a heart attack. He now weighed nearly 225 pounds, and he was not a tall man. He was already breathing hard at the slightest exertion.

Tennis didn't do it. Sylvester was wise enough, or heavy enough, just to stand there on the court and let the ball come to him, and if the ball didn't come to him, he wasn't going to run after it to hit it. So one warm Saturday, when Sarah had accompanied him to the courts as usual, she pretended to faint. She mumbled that she wanted to be taken to the car to go home. Sylvester struggled, panting, as Sarah was no lightweight herself. Unfortunately for Sarah's plans, two chaps came running from the club bar to give assistance, and Sarah was loaded easily into the Jag.

Once at home, with the front door closed, Sarah swooned again, and mumbled in a frantic but waning voice that she had to be taken upstairs to bed. It was their bed, a big double one, and two flights up. Sylvester heaved her into his arms, thinking that he did not present a romantic picture trudging up step by step, gasping and stumbling as he carried his beloved towards bed. At last he had to maneuver her on to one shoulder, and even then he fell on his own face upon reaching the landing on the second floor. Wheezing mightily, he rolled out from under her limp figure, and tried again, this time simply dragging her along the carpeted hall and into the bedroom. He was tempted to let her lie there until he got his own breath back (she wasn't stirring), but he could anticipate her recrimination if she woke up in the next seconds and found he had left her flat on the floor.

Sylvester bent to the task again, put all his will power into it, for certainly he had no physical strength left. His legs ached, his back was killing him, and it amazed him that he could get this burden (over 150 pounds) on to the double bed. "Whoosh-sh!" Sylvester said, and went reeling back, intending to collapse in an armchair, but the armchair had rollers and retreated several inches, causing him to land on the floor with a house-shaking thump. A terrible pain had struck his chest. He pressed a fist against his breast and bared his teeth in agony.

Sarah watched. She lay on the bed. She did nothing. She waited and waited. She almost fell asleep. Sylvester was moaning, calling for help. How lucky, Sarah thought, that Edmund was parked out with a baby-sitter this afternoon, instead of a baby-sitter being in the house. After some fifteen minutes, Sylvester was still. Sarah did fall asleep finally. When she got up, she found that Sylvester was quite dead and becoming cool. Then she telephoned the family doctor.

All went well for Sarah. People said that just weeks before, they'd been amazed at how *well* Sylvester looked, rosy cheeks and all that. Sarah got a tidy sum from the insurance company, her widow's pension, and gushes of sympathy from people who assured her she had given Sylvester the best of herself, had made a lovely home for him, had given him a son, had in short devoted herself utterly to him and made his somewhat short life as happy as a man's life could possibly have been. No one said, "What a perfect murder!" which was Sarah's private opinion, and now she could chuckle over it. Now she could become the Merry Widow. By exacting small favors from her lovers—casually of course—it was going to be easy to live in even better style than when Sylvester had been alive. And she could still write "Mrs." at the foot of letters.

The Breeder

To Elaine, marriage meant children. Marriage meant a lot of other things too, of course, such as creating a home, being a morale-booster to her husband, jolly companion, all that. But most of all children—that was what marriage was for, what it was all about.

Elaine, when she married Douglas, set about becoming the creature of her imagination, and within four months she had succeeded quite well. Their home sparkled with cleanliness and charm, their parties were successes, and Douglas received a small promotion in his firm, Athens Insurance Inc. Only one thing was missing, Elaine was not yet pregnant. A consultation with her doctor soon set this problem to rights, something having been askew, but after another three months, she still had not conceived. Could it be Douglas's fault? Reluctantly, somewhat shyly, Douglas visited the doctor and was pronounced fit. What could be wrong? Closer tests were made, and it was discovered that the fertilized egg (indeed at least one egg had been fertilized) had traveled upward instead of downward, in apparent defiance of gravity, and instead of developing somewhere had simply vanished.

"She should get out of bed and stand on her head!" said a wag of Douglas's office, after a couple of drinks one lunchtime.

Douglas chuckled politely. But maybe there was something to it. Hadn't the doctor said something along these lines? Douglas suggested the headstand to Elaine that evening.

Around midnight, Elaine jumped out of bed and stood on her head, feet against the wall. Her face became bright pink. Douglas was alarmed, but Elaine stuck it out like a Spartan, collapsing finally after nearly ten minutes in a rosy heap on the floor.

Their first child, Edward, was thus born. Edward started the ball rolling, and slightly less than a year later came twins, two girls. The parents of Elaine and Douglas were delighted. To become grandparents was as great a joy for them as it had been to become parents, and both sets of grandparents threw parties. Douglas and Elaine were only children, so the grandparents rejoiced that their lines would be continued. Elaine no longer had to stand on her head. And ten months later, a second son was born, Peter. Then came Philip, then Madeleine.

This made six small children in the household, and Elaine and Douglas had to move to a slightly larger apartment with one more room in it. They moved hastily, not realizing that their landlord was rather against children (they'd lied and told him they had four), especially little ones who howled in the night. Within six months, they were asked to leave—it being obvious then that Elaine was due to have another child soon. By now, Douglas was feeling the pinch, but his parents gave him $2,000 and Elaine's parents came up with $3,000, and Douglas made a down payment on a house fifteen minutes' drive from his office.

"I'm glad we've got a house, darling," he said to Elaine. "But I'm afraid we've got to watch our pennies if we keep up the mortgage payments. I think—at least for a while—we ought not to have any more children. Seven, after all—" Little Thomas had arrived.

Elaine had said before that it would be up to her, not him, to do the family planning. "I understand, Douglas. You're perfectly right."

Alas, Elaine disclosed one overcast winter day that she was pregnant again. "I can't account for it. I'm on the pill, you know that."

Douglas had certainly assumed that. He was speechless for a few moments. How were they going to manage? He could already see that Elaine was pregnant, though he'd been trying to convince himself for days that he was only imagining it, because of his anxiety. Already their parents were handing out fifty- and one-hundred-dollar presents on birthdays— with nine birthdays in the family, birthdays came along pretty frequently— and he knew they couldn't contribute a bit more. It was amazing how much shoes alone could cost for seven little ones.

Still, when Douglas saw the beatific, contented smile on Elaine's face as she lay against her pillows in the hospital, a baby boy in one arm and a baby girl in the other, Douglas could not find it in himself to regret these births, which made nine.

But they'd been married just a little more than seven years. If this kept up—

One woman in their social circle remarked at a party, "Oh, Elaine gets pregnant every time Doug *looks* at her!"

Douglas was not amused by the implied tribute to his virility.

"Then they ought to make love with the lights out!" replied the office wag. "Ha-ha-ha! Easy to see the only reason is, Douglas is *looking* at her!"

"Don't even glance at Elaine tonight, Doug!" someone else yelled, and there were gales of laughter.

Elaine smiled prettily. She imagined, nay, she was sure, that women envied her. Women with only one child, or no children, were just dried up beanbags in Elaine's opinion. Green beanbags.

Things went from bad to worse, from Douglas's point of view. There *was* an interval of a whole six months when Elaine was on the pill and did not become pregnant, but then suddenly she was.

"I can't understand it," she said to Douglas and to her doctor too. Elaine really couldn't understand it, because she had forgotten that she had forgotten to remember the pill—a phenomenon that her doctor had encountered before.

The doctor made no comment. His lips were ethically sealed.

As if in revenge for Elaine's absenting herself from fecundity for a while, for her trying to put a lid on nature's cornucopia, nature hurled quintuplets at her. Douglas could not even face the hospital, and took to his bed for forty-eight hours. Then he had an idea: he would ring up some newspapers, ask them a fee for interviews and also for any photographs they might take of the quints. He made painful efforts in this direction, such exploitation being against his grain. But the newspapers didn't bite. Lots of people had quintuplets these days, they said. Sextuplets might interest them, but quints no. They'd take a photograph, but they wouldn't pay anything. The photograph only brought literature from family planning organizations and unpleasant or downright insulting letters from individual citizens telling Douglas and Elaine how much they were contributing to pollution. The newspapers had mentioned that their children now numbered fourteen after about eight years of marriage.

Since it seemed the pill was not working, Douglas proposed that he do something about himself. Elaine was dead against it.

"Why, things just wouldn't be the same!" she cried.

"Darling, everything would be the same. Only—"

Elaine interrupted. They got nowhere.

They had to move again. The house was big enough for two adults and fourteen children, but the added expense of the quints made the mortgage payments impossible. So Douglas and Elaine and Edward, Susan and Sarah, Peter, Thomas, Philip and Madeleine, the twins Ursula and Paul, and the quints Louise, Pamela, Helen, Samantha and Brigid moved to a tenement in the city—tenement being a legal term for any structure housing more than two families, but in common parlance a tenement was a slum, which this was. Now they were surrounded by families with nearly as many children as they had. Douglas, who sometimes took papers home from the office, stuffed his ears with cotton wool and thought he would go mad. "No danger of going mad, if I *think* I'm going mad," he told himself, and tried to cheer up. Elaine, after all, was on the pill again.

But she became pregnant again. By now, the grandparents were no longer so delighted. It was plain that the number of offspring had lowered Douglas's and Elaine's standard of living—the last thing the grandparents wished. Douglas lived in a smoldering resentment against fate, and with a desperate hope that something—something unknown and perhaps impossible might happen, as he watched Elaine growing stouter day by day. Might this be quints again? Even sextuplets? Dreadful thought. What was the matter with the pill? Was Elaine some exception to the laws of chemistry? Douglas turned over in his mind their doctor's ambiguous reply to his question on this point. The doctor had been so vague, Douglas had forgotten not only the doctor's words, but even the sense of what he'd said. Who could think in all the noise, anyway? Diaper-clad midgets played tiny xylophones and tootled on a variety of horns and whistles. Edward and Peter squabbled over who was going to mount the rocking horse. All the girls burst into tears over nothing, hoping to gain their mother's attention and allegiance to their causes. Philip was prone to colic. All the quints were teething simultaneously.

This time it was triplets. Unbelievable! Three rooms of their flat now had nothing but cribs in them, plus a single bed in each, in which at least two children slept. If their ages only varied more, Douglas thought, it would somehow be more tolerable, but most of them were still crawling around on the floor, and to open the apartment door was to believe that one had come upon a day nursery by mistake. But no. All these seventeen were his own doing. The new triplets swung in an ingenious suspended playpen, there being absolutely no room on the floor for them. They were fed, and their nappies changed, through bars of the pen, which made Douglas think of a zoo.

Weekends were hell. Their friends simply did not accept invitations any longer. Who could blame them? Elaine had to ask guests to be very quiet, and even so, something always woke one of the little ones by 9 P.M.

and then the whole lot started yowling, even the seven- and eight-year-olds who wanted to join the party. So their social life became nil, which was just as well, because they hadn't the money for entertaining.

"But I do feel fulfilled, dear," Elaine said, laying a soothing hand upon Douglas's brow, as he sat poring over office papers one Sunday afternoon.

Douglas, perspiring from nerves, was working in a tiny corner of what they called their living room. Elaine was half-dressed, her usual state, because in the act of dressing, some child always interrupted her, demanding something, and also Elaine was still nursing the last arrivals. Suddenly something snapped in Douglas, and he got up and walked out to the nearest telephone. He and Elaine had no telephone, and they had had to sell their car also.

Douglas rang a clinic and inquired about vasectomy. He was told there was a waiting list of four months, if he wanted the operation free of charge. Douglas said yes, and gave his name. Meanwhile, chastity was the order of the day. No hardship. Good God! Seventeen now! Douglas hung his head in the office. Even the jokes had worn thin. He felt that people pitied him, and that they avoided the subject of children. Only Elaine was happy. She seemed to be in another world. She'd even begun to talk like the kids. Douglas counted the days till the operation. He was not going to say anything to Elaine about it, just have it. He rang up a week before the date to confirm it, and was told he would have to wait another three months, because the person who had fixed his appointment must have made a mistake.

Douglas banged the telephone down. It wasn't abstinence that was the problem, just goddamned fate, just the nuisance of waiting another three months. He had an insane fear that Elaine would become pregnant again on her own.

It happened that the first thing he saw when he entered the apartment that afternoon was little Ursula waddling around in her rubber panties, diligently pushing a miniature pram in which sat a tiny replica of herself.

"*Look at it!*" Douglas yelled at no one. "Motherhood already and she can hardly *walk!*" He snatched the doll out of the toy pram and hurled it through a window.

"Doug! What's come over you?" Elaine rushed towards him with one breast bared, baby Charles clamped to it like a lamprey.

Douglas pushed a foot through the side of a crib, then seized the rocking horse and smashed it against a wall. He kicked a doll's house into the air and when it fell, demolished it with a stomp.

"*Maa-aa—maa-aa!*"

"Daa–aaddy!"

"Ooooo–ooo!"

"Boo-hooo-oo-oo-hoo-oo!" from a half dozen throats.

Now the household was in an uproar with at least fifteen kids scream-ing, plus Elaine. Toys were Douglas's targets. Balls of all sizes went through the windowpanes, followed by plastic horns and little pianos, cars and tele-phones, then teddy bears, rattles, guns, rubber swords and peashooters, teething rings and jigsaw puzzles. He squeezed two formula bottles and laughed with lunatic glee as the milk spurted from the rubber teats. Elaine's expression changed from surprise to horror. She leaned out of a broken window and screamed.

Douglas had to be dragged away from an Erector set construction which he was smashing with the heavy base of a roly-poly clown. An intern gave him a punch in the neck which knocked him out. The next thing Douglas knew, he was in a padded cell somewhere. He demanded a vasectomy. They gave him a needle instead. When he woke up, he again yelled for a vasectomy. His wish was granted the same day.

He felt better then, calmer. He was just sane enough, however, to real-ize that his mind, so to speak, was "gone." He was aware that he didn't want to go back to work, didn't want to do anything. He didn't want to see any of his old friends, all of whom he felt he had lost, anyway. He didn't partic-ularly want to go on living. Dimly, he remembered that he was a laughing stock for having begotten seventeen children in not nearly so many years. Or was it nineteen? Or twenty-eight? He'd lost count.

Elaine came to see him. Was she pregnant again? No. Impossible. It was just that he was so used to seeing her pregnant. She seemed remote. She was fulfilled, Douglas remembered.

"Stand on your head again. Reverse things," Douglas said with a fool-ish smile.

"He's mad," Elaine said hopelessly to the intern, and calmly turned away.

The
Mobile Bed-Object

There are lots of girls like Mildred, homeless, yet never without a roof—most of the time the ceiling of a hotel room, sometimes that of bachelor digs, of a yacht's cabin if they're lucky, a tent, or a caravan. Such girls are bed-objects, the kind of thing one acquires like a hot water bottle, a traveling iron, an electric shoe-shiner, any little luxury of life. It is an advantage to them if they can cook a bit, but they certainly don't have to talk, in any language. Also they are interchangeable, like unblocked currency or international postal reply coupons. Their value can go up or down, depending on their age and the man currently in possession.

Mildred considered it not a bad life, and if interviewed would have said in her earnest way, "It's *interesting*." Mildred never laughed, and smiled only when she thought she should be polite. She was five feet seven, blondish, rather slender, with a pleasant blank face and large blue eyes which she held wide open. She slunk rather than walked, her shoulders hunched, hips thrust a bit forward—the way the best models walked, she had read somewhere. This gave her a languid, pacific air. Ambulant, she looked as if she were walking in her sleep. She was a little more lively in bed, and this fact traveled by word of mouth, or among men who might not speak the same tongue, by nods or small smiles. Mildred knew her job, and it must be said for her that she applied herself diligently to it.

She had floundered around in school till fourteen, when everyone including her parents had deemed it senseless for her to continue. She would marry early, her parents thought. Instead, Mildred ran away from home, or rather was taken away by a car salesman when she was barely fifteen. Under the salesman's direction, she wrote reassuring letters home, saying she had a job in a nearby town as a waitress and was living in a flat with two other girls.

By the time she was eighteen, Mildred had been to Capri, Mexico City, Paris, even Japan, and to Brazil several times, where men usually dumped her, since they were often on the run from something. She had been a second prize, as it were, for one American President-elect the night of his victory. She had been lent for two days to a sheik in London, who had rewarded her with a rather kinky gold goblet which she had subsequently lost—not that she liked the goblet, but it must have been worth a fortune, and she often thought of its loss with regret. If she ever wished to change her man, she would simply visit an expensive bar in Rio or anywhere, on her own, and pick up another man who would be pleased to add her to his expense account, and back she would go to America or Germany or Sweden. Mildred couldn't have cared less what country she was in.

Once she was forgotten at a restaurant table, as a cigarette lighter might be left behind. Mildred noticed, but Herb didn't for some thirty minutes which were mildly worrying for Mildred, though Mildred never got really distressed about anything. She did turn to the man sitting next to her—it was a business lunch, four men, four girls—and she said, "I thought Herb had just gone to the loo—"

"What?" The heavyset man next to her was an American. "Oh. He'll be back. We had some unpleasant business to talk over today, you know. Herb's upset." The American smiled understandingly. He had his girlfriend by his side, one he'd picked up last night. The girls hadn't opened their mouths, except to eat.

Herb came back and got Mildred, and they went to their hotel room, Herb in utmost gloom, because he'd come out badly in the business deal. Mildred's embraces that afternoon failed to lift Herb's spirits or his ego, and that evening Mildred was traded in. Her new guardian was Stanley, about thirty-five, pudgy, like Herb. The trade took place at cocktail time, while Mildred sipped her usual Alexander through a straw. Herb got Stanley's girl, a dumb blonde with artificially curled hair. The blondness was artificial too, though a good job, Mildred observed, make-up and hair-do being matters Mildred was an expert in. Mildred returned to the hotel briefly to pack her suitcase, then she spent the evening and night with Stanley. He hardly talked to her, but he smiled a lot, and made a lot of telephone calls. This was in Des Moines.

With Stanley, Mildred went to Chicago, where Stanley had a small flat of his own, plus a wife in a house somewhere, he said. Mildred wasn't worried about the wife. Only once in her life had she had to deal with a difficult wife who crashed into a flat. Mildred had brandished a carving knife, and the wife had fled. Usually a wife just looked dumbfounded, then sneered and walked off, obviously intending to avenge herself on her husband. Stanley was away all day and didn't give her much money, which was annoying. Mildred wasn't going to stay long with Stanley, if she could help it. She'd started a savings account in a bank somewhere once, but she'd lost her passbook and forgotten the name of the town where the bank was.

But before Mildred could make a wise move away from Stanley, she found herself given away. This was a shock. An economist would have drawn a conclusion about currency that was given away, and so did Mildred. She realized that Stanley came out a bit better in the deal he had made with the man called Louis, to whom he gave Mildred, but still—

And she was only twenty-three. But Mildred knew that was the danger age, and that she'd better play her cards carefully from now on. Eighteen was the peak, and she was five years past it, and what had she to show for it? A diamond bracelet that men eyed with greed, and that she'd twice had to get out of hock with the aid of some new bastard. A mink coat— same story. A suitcase with a couple of good-looking dresses. What did she want? Well, she wanted to continue the same life but with a sense of greater security. What would she do if her back was really to the wall? If she, kicked out maybe, not even given away, had to go to a bar and even then couldn't pick up more than a one-night stand? Well, she had some addresses of past men-friends, and she could always write them and threaten to put them in her memoirs, which she could say a publisher was paying her to write. But Mildred had talked with girls twenty-five and older who'd threatened memoirs, if they weren't pensioned off for life, and she'd heard of only one who had succeeded. More often, the girls said, it was a laugh they got, or a "Go ahead and write it" rather than any money.

So Mildred made the best of it for a few days with fat old Louis. He had a nice tabby cat, of which Mildred grew fond, but the most boring thing was that his apartment was a one-room kitchenette and dreary. Louis was good-natured but tightfisted. Also it was embarrassing for Mildred to be sneaked out when she and Louis went out for dinner (not usually, because Louis expected her to cook and to do a little cleaning too), and when Louis had people in to talk business, to be asked to hide in the kitchenette and not to make a sound. Louis sold pianos wholesale. Mildred rehearsed the speech she was going to make soon: "I hope you realize you haven't any hold over me, Louis . . . I'm a girl who's not used to working, not even in bed . . ."

But before she had a chance to make her speech, which would mainly have been a demand for more money, because she knew Louis had plenty tucked away, she was given away to a young salesman one night. Louis simply said, after they'd all finished dinner in a roadside café, "Dave, why don't you take Mildred to your place for a nightcap? I've got to turn in early." With a wink.

Dave beamed. He was nice looking, but he lived in a caravan, good God! Mildred had no intention of becoming a *gypsy*, taking sponge baths, enduring portable loos. She was used to grand hotels with room service day and night. Dave might be young and ardent, but Mildred didn't give a damn about that. Men said women were all alike, but in her opinion it was even truer that men were all alike. All they wanted was one thing. Women at least wanted fur coats, good perfume, a holiday in the Bahamas, a cruise somewhere, jewelry—in fact, quite a number of things.

One evening when she was with Dave at a business dinner (he was a piano distributor and order-taker, though Mildred never saw a piano around the caravan), Mildred made the acquaintance of a Mr. Zupp, called Sam, who had invited Dave to dine in a fancy restaurant. Inspired by three Alexanders, Mildred flirted madly with Sam, who was not unresponsive under the table, and Mildred simply announced that she was going home with Sam. Dave's mouth fell open, and he started to make a fuss, but Sam—an older, more self-assured man—most diplomatically implied that he would make a scene if it came to a fistfight, so Dave backed down.

This was a big improvement. Sam and Mildred flew at once to Paris, then to Hamburg. Mildred got new clothes. The hotel rooms were great. Mildred never knew from one day to the next what town they would be in. Now here was a man whose memoirs would be worth something, if she could only find out what he did. But when he spoke on the telephone, it was either in code, or in Yiddish, or Russian, or Arabic. Mildred had never heard such baffling languages in her life, and she was never able to find out just what he was selling. People had to sell something, didn't they? Or buy something, and if they bought something, there had to be a source of money, didn't there? So what was even the source of money? Something told Mildred that it would soon be time for her to retire. Sam Zupp seemed to have been sent by Providence. She worked on him, trying to be subtle.

"I wouldn't mind settling down," she said.

"I'm not the marrying kind," he retorted with a smile.

That wasn't what she meant. She meant a nest egg, and then he could say good-bye, if he wanted to. But wouldn't it take a few nest eggs to make a big nest egg? Would she have to go through all this again with future Sam Zupps? Mildred's mind staggered with the effort to see so far into the future, but there seemed no doubt that she should take advantage of Mr. Zupp, at least, while she had him. These ideas, or plans, frail as damaged spider webs, were swept away by the events of the days after the above conversation.

Sam Zupp was suddenly on the run. For a few days, it was airplanes with separate seats, because he and Mildred were not supposed to be traveling together. Once police sirens were behind them, as Sam's hired driver zoomed and careered over an Alpine road, bound for Geneva. Or maybe Zurich. Mildred was in her element, ministering to Sam with handkerchiefs moistened in eau de cologne, producing a *sandwich de jambon* out of her handbag in case he was hungry, or a flask of brandy if he felt his heart fluttering. Mildred fancied herself one of the heroines she had seen in films—good films—about men and their girlfriends fleeing from the awful and so unfairly well-armed police.

Her daydreams of glamour were brief. It must have been in Holland— Mildred didn't know where she was half the time—when the chauffeur-driven car suddenly screeched to a halt, just like in the films, and Mildred was bundled by both chauffeur and Sam into a mummy-like casing of stiff, heavy tarpaulin, and then ropes were tied around her. She was dumped into a canal and drowned.

No one ever heard of Mildred. No one ever found her. If she had been found, there would have been no immediate means of identification, because Sam had her passport, and her handbag was in the car. She had been thrown away, as one might throw away a cricket lighter when it is used up, like a paperback one has read and which has become excess baggage. Mildred's absence was never taken seriously by anyone. The score or so people who knew and remembered her, themselves scattered about the world, simply thought she was living in some other country or city. One day, they supposed, she'd turn up again in some bar, in some hotel lobby. Soon they forgot her.

The
Perfect Little Lady

Theadora, or Thea as she was called, was the perfect little lady born. Everyone said that who had seen her from her first months of life, when she was being wheeled about in her white satin-lined pram. She slept when she should have slept. Then she woke and smiled at strangers. She almost never wet her diapers. She was the easiest child in the world to toilet train, and she learned to speak remarkably early. Next came reading when she was hardly two. And always she showed good manners. At three, she began to curtsy on being introduced to people. Her mother taught her this, of course, but Thea took to etiquette like a duck to water.

"Thank you, I had a lovely time," she was saying glibly at four, dropping a farewell curtsy, on departing from children's parties. She would return home with her little starched dress as neat and clean as when she had put it on. She took great care of her hair and nails. She was never dirty, and she watched other children running and playing, making mud pies, falling and skinning their knees, and she thought them utterly silly. Thea was an only child. Other mothers, more harassed than Thea's mother, with two or three offspring to look after, praised Thea's obedience and neatness, and Thea loved this. Thea basked also in the praise she got from her own mother. Thea and her mother adored each other.

Among Thea's contemporaries, the gang age began at eight or nine or ten, if the word gang could be used for the informal group that roved the neighborhood on roller skates and bicycles. It was a proper middle-class neighborhood. But if a child didn't join in the "crazy poker" game in the garage of one of their parents, or go on aimless follow-my-leader bicycle rides through the residential streets, that child was nowhere. Thea was nowhere, as far as this gang went. "I couldn't care less, because I don't want to be one of *them,* anyway," Thea said to her mother and father.

"Thea cheats at games. That's why we don't want her," said a ten-year-old boy in one of Thea's father's history classes.

Thea's father Ted taught in a local grade school. He had long suspected the truth, but had kept his mouth shut and hoped for the best. Thea was a mystery to Ted. How could he, such an ordinary, plodding fellow, have begotten a full-blown woman?

"Little girls are born women," said Thea's mother Margot. "But little boys are not born men. They have to learn to be men. Little girls have already a woman's character."

"But this isn't character," Ted said. "It's scheming. Character takes time to be formed. Like a tree."

Margot smiled tolerantly, and Ted had the feeling he was talking like someone from the Stone Age, while his wife and daughter lived in the jet age.

Thea's main objective in life seemed to be to make her contemporaries feel awful. She'd told a lie about another little girl, in regard to a little boy, and the little girl had wept and nearly had a nervous breakdown. Ted couldn't remember the details, though he'd been able to follow the story when he had heard it first, summarized by Margot. Thea had managed to blame the other little girl for the whole thing. Machiavelli couldn't have done better.

"She's simply not a ruffian," said Margot. "Anyway, she's got Craig to play with, so she's not alone."

Craig was ten and lived three houses away. What Ted did not realize for a while was that Craig was ostracized too, and for the same reason. One afternoon, Ted observed one of the boys of the neighborhood make a rude gesture, in ominous silence, as he passed Craig on the pavement.

"Scum!" Craig replied promptly. Then he trotted, in case the other boy gave chase, but the other boy simply turned and said:

"And you're a *shit,* like Thea!"

It was not the first time that Ted had heard such language from the local kids, but he certainly didn't hear it often, and he was impressed.

"But what do they do—all alone, Thea and Craig?" Ted asked his wife.

"Oh, they take walks. I dunno," said Margot. "I suppose Craig has a slight crush on her."

Ted had thought of that. Thea had a candy-box prettiness that would assure her of boyfriends by the time she reached her early teens, and of course Thea was starting earlier than that. Ted had no fear of misbehavior on Thea's part, because she was the teasing type, and basically prim.

What Thea and Craig were then engaged in was observing the construction of a dugout, tunnel and two fireplaces in a vacant lot about a mile away. Thea and Craig would go there on their bicycles, conceal themselves in the bushes nearby, and spy and giggle. A dozen or so of the gang were working like navvies, hauling out buckets of earth, gathering firewood, preparing roasted potatoes with salt and butter, which was the high point of all this slavery, around 6 P.M. Thea and Craig intended to wait until the excavation and embellishments were completed, and then they meant to smash the whole thing.

Meanwhile, Thea and Craig came up with what they called "a new ballgame," this being their code word for a nasty scheme. They sent a typewritten announcement to the biggest blabble-mouth of the school, Veronica, saying that a girl called Jennifer was having a surprise birthday party on a certain date, and please tell everyone, but don't tell Jennifer. The letter was presumably from Jennifer's mother. Then Thea and Craig hid in the hedges and watched their schoolmates turn up at Jennifer's, some dressed in their best, nearly all bearing gifts, as Jennifer grew more and more embarrassed on the doorstep, saying she didn't know anything about a party. Since Jennifer's family was well-to-do, all the kids had expected a big evening.

When the tunnel and dugout, fireplaces and candle niches were all completed, Thea and Craig in their respective homes pretended bellyaches one day, and did not go to school. By prearrangement, they sneaked out and met at 11 A.M. with their bicycles. They went to the dugout and jumped in unison on the tunnel top until it caved in. Then they broke the chimney tops, and scattered the carefully gathered firewood. They even found the potatoes and salt reserve, and flung that into the woods. Then they cycled home.

Two days later, on Thursday which was a school day, Craig was found at 5 P.M. behind some elm trees on the lawn of the Knobel house, stabbed to death through the throat and heart. He had ugly wounds also about the head, as if he had been hit repeatedly by rough stones. Measurements of the knife wounds showed that at least seven different knives had been used.

Ted was profoundly shocked. By then he had heard of the destroyed tunnel and fireplaces. Everyone knew that Thea and Craig had been absent from school on the Tuesday that the tunnel had been ruined. Everyone knew that Thea and Craig were constantly together. Ted feared for his daughter's life. The police could not lay the blame for Craig's death on any member of the gang, neither could they charge an entire group with murder or manslaughter. The inquiry was concluded with a warning to all parents of the children in the school.

"Just because Craig and I were absent from school on the same day doesn't mean that we went together to break up a stupid old tunnel," said Thea to a friend of her mother's, a mother of one of the gang members. Thea could lie like an accomplished crook. It was difficult for an adult to challenge her.

So Thea's gang age, such as it was, ended with Craig's death. Then came boyfriends and teasing, opportunities for intrigues and betrayals, and a constant stream, ever changing, of young men aged sixteen to twenty, some of whom lasted only five days with Thea.

We take leave of Thea as she sits primping, aged fifteen, in front of her looking-glass. She is especially happy this evening, because her nearest rival, a girl named Elizabeth, has just been in a car accident and had her nose and jaw broken, plus an eye damaged, so she will never look quite the same again. The summer is coming up, with all those dinner dances on terraces and swimming pool parties. There is even a rumor that Elizabeth may have to acquire a lower denture, so many of her teeth got broken, but the eye damage must be the most telling. Thea, however, will escape every catastrophe. There is a divinity that protects perfect little ladies like Thea.

The Silent Mother-in-Law

This mother-in-law, Edna, has heard all the jokes about mothers-in-law, and she has no intention of being the butt of such jests, or falling into any of the traps with which her path is so amply sprinkled. First of all, she lives with her daughter and son-in-law, so she's got to be doubly or triply careful. She would never dream of criticizing anything. The young people could come home dead drunk, and Edna would never comment. They could smoke pot (in fact they do sometimes), they could fight and throw crockery at each other, and Edna wouldn't open her mouth. She's heard enough about mothers-in-law intruding, and she keeps a buttoned lip. In fact, the oddest thing about Edna is her silence. She does say, "Yes, thank you" to a second cup of coffee, and "Good night, sleep well," but that's about it.

The second outstanding thing about Edna is her thriftiness. Little does she suspect that it gives Laura and Brian a pain in the neck, because they are also trying to make the best of it, trying to be polite, and would never dream of saying that her thriftiness gives them a pain in the neck. For one thing, thrift obviously gives Edna so much pleasure. She exhibits a huge ball of saved string as other mothers-in-law might show a quilt they had made. She puts every last orange pip into a plastic bag destined for the compost heap. It would cost Laura and Brian about three hundred dollars a month to set Edna up in a flat by herself. Edna has some money which she contributes to their household, but if she lived alone, Laura and Brian would have to contribute more than she costs them now, so they let well enough alone.

Edna is fifty-six, rather lean and wiry, with short curly hair of mixed gray and black. Due to her habit of scurrying about doing things, she has a humped posture and gait. She is never idle, and seldom sits. When she does sit, it is usually because someone has asked her to, then she flings herself into a chair, and folds her hands with an attentive expression. She nearly always has something useful stewing on the stove, like apple sauce. Or she has started to clean the oven with some chemical product, which means Laura can't use the oven for at least the next hour.

Laura and Brian have no children as yet, because they are foresighted people, and in the back of their minds they are trying to think how to install Edna somewhere graciously and comfortably, even at their own expense, and after that they'll think of raising a family. All this causes a strain. Their house is a two-story affair in a suburb, twenty-five minutes' drive from the city where Brian works as an electronic engineer. He has good hopes for advancement, and is studying in his spare time at home. Edna takes a swat at the garden and lawn mowing, so Brian hasn't too much to do on weekends. But he has a feeling Edna is listening through the walls. Edna's room is next to their bedroom. There is an attic, which is unheated. In the attic, which Brian and Laura would gladly make habitable, Edna is collecting jam jars, cartons, wooden crates, old Christmas boxes and wrapping paper, and other things which might come in handy one day. Brian can't get a foot in the door now without knocking something down. He wants to have a look at the attic to see how difficult it might be to insulate and all that. The attic has become Edna's property, somehow.

"If she'd only *say* something—even now and then," Brian said one day to Laura. "It's like living with a robot."

Laura knew. She had assumed a chatty, extra pleasant manner with her mother in hopes of drawing her out. "I'll just put this here—mm-m—and the ashtray can just as well go here," Laura would say as she pottered about the house.

Edna would nod and smile a tense approval, and say nothing, though she would be hovering to help.

The atmosphere was driving Brian round the bend. He frequently muttered curses. One night when he and Laura were at a party in the neighborhood, an idea struck Brian. He told Laura his plan, and she agreed. She'd had a few drinks, and Brian told her to have another.

Laura and Brian drove home after the party, undressed in their car, walked up to the front door and pushed the bell. A long wait. They giggled. It was after 2 A.M., and Edna was in bed. Edna at last arrived and opened the door.

"Howdy doody, Edna!" said Brian, waltzing in.

"Evening, mama," said Laura.

Flustered and horrified, Edna blinked, but soon recovered enough to laugh and smile politely.

"Well, aren't you surprised? *Say* something!" Brian cried, but not being as drunk then as Laura, he seized a sofa pillow and held it so as to cover his nakedness, hating himself as he did so, for it was rather as if he had lost his guts.

Laura was executing a solo ballet, quite uninhibited.

Edna had vanished into the kitchen. Brian pursued her and saw that she was making instant coffee.

"Listen, Edna!" he shouted. "You might at least *talk* to us, no? It's simple, isn't it? Please, for the love of God, say something to us!" He was still clutching the pillow against himself, but he gesticulated with a fist of his other hand.

"It's true, mama!" Laura said from the doorway. Her eyes were full of tears. She was hysterical with conviction. "*Speak* to us!"

"I think it is disgraceful, if you want me to say something," said Edna, the longest sentence she had uttered in years. "Drunk and naked besides! I am ashamed of you both! Laura, take a raincoat from the downstairs hall, take anything! And *you*—my *son-in-law!*" Edna was shrieking.

The kettle water seethed. Edna fled past Brian and scurried upstairs to her room.

Neither Brian nor Laura remembered much of the hours after that. If they hoped they had broken Edna's silence permanently, they soon found they were wrong. Edna was just as silent as ever the next morning, Sunday, though she did smile a little—almost as if nothing had happened.

Brian went to work on Monday as usual, and when he came home, Laura told him that Edna had been unusually busy all day. She had also been silent.

"I think she's ashamed of herself," Laura said. "She wouldn't even have lunch with me."

Brian gathered that Edna had been busy stacking firewood, cleaning the barbecue pit, peeling green apples, sewing, polishing brass, searching through a large garbage bin—for God knew what.

"What is she doing now?" Brian asked with a prickle of alarm.

At the same moment, he knew. Edna was in the attic. There was an occasional creak of floor wood from way upstairs, a *clunk* as she set down a carton of glass jars or some such.

"We should leave her alone for a bit," said Brian, feeling he was being manly and sensible.

Laura agreed.

They didn't see Edna at dinner. They went to bed. Edna seemed to work through the night, judging from the noises on the stairs and in the attic. Around dawn, a terrible crash occurred, against which Brian had once warned Laura: the attic floor was made of laths, after all, just nailed to rafters. Edna fell through the floor along with jam jars, crates, raspberry preserves, rocking chairs, an old sofa, a trunk and a sewing machine. Crash, bang, tinkle!

Brian and Laura, who had been cringing in their bed, sprang up at once to rescue Edna from the debacle, but they knew before they touched her that all was up. Poor Edna was dead. Perhaps she had not died from the fall, even, but she was dead. Thus was the rather noisy end of Brian's silent mother-in-law.

The Prude

Sharon would never, and had never, thought of herself as a prude. She considered herself simply respectable. Her mother had always said, "Be pure in every way," and when Sharon reached adolescence, her mother had emphasized the importance of being a virgin until marriage. "What else has a woman to offer a man?" was her mother's rhetorical dictum. So Sharon practiced this, and as it happened, or maybe by inevitable destiny, her husband Matthew was a virgin until marriage also. Matthew had been a hard-working law student when Sharon met him.

Now Matthew was a hard-working lawyer, and he and Sharon had three daughters, Gwen, Penny and Sybille, ranging in age from twenty down to sixteen. Sharon had always said to her women friends, "I'll get them to the altar as virgins, if it's the last thing I do." Some of the women-friends thought Sharon was old-fashioned, others thought her hopes vain in the times in which they lived. But no one had the courage to say to Sharon that she was misplacing her energies, or even that she might be doomed to disappointment. After all, Sharon's and Matthew's attitudes were their own business, and their daughters were indeed models of young womanhood. They were polite, attractive, and doing well in their studies.

"You know, virgins are a bore," said Gwen's boyfriend to Sharon, though in a respectful tone. Toby was a bright, industrious young man, studying to become a doctor. He was twenty-three, and attended the same university as Gwen, fifty miles away. Toby had brought along two cuttings from *women's* magazines, which he thought would impress Gwen's mother (whom he rightly supposed was the origin of Gwen's scruples). He also had a newspaper cutting on the same subject written by a man-sociologist. The authors of these statements held responsible positions in business and the professions, they weren't just beatniks, Toby pointed out. "You see, there's no reason for a girl to be unpleasantly shocked when she's married. She ought to learn something, and so should the young man. Otherwise if both are virgins, it can be an awkward and even embarrassing experience for both."

Sharon was shocked into a long silence of more than a minute. Her first impulse was to ask Toby to leave the house. She laid the cuttings to one side, on a wine table, as if the very paper they were printed on were filthy. It was plain to Sharon that all Toby wanted was *that*, whereas until now he had spoken of marriage to Gwen. He'd even spoken to Matthew, and though the engagement had not been announced in the newspapers, Sharon and her husband considered it official. The marriage was to take place next June, after Gwen's graduation. Sharon managed a small smile. "I daresay after you've—taken advantage of my daughter, you won't be interested in marrying her, will you?"

Toby leaned forward and wanted to get to his feet, but didn't. "I'm sure you think that, but it's far from the truth. If anyone won't want to get married, it might be Gwen—but that's her perfect right, to know what she's marrying. It could be that she won't like me. It's best to find out first, isn't it?"

No, Sharon thought. Marry and be stuck with it, make the best of it, was her credo. It was a *lowering of standards* . . . The right words failed her, though she was sure she was right. "I think Gwen is perhaps not the right girl for you," Sharon said finally.

Toby's face fell. He nodded, with a stunned look. "Very well. I won't argue. I'm sorry I argued." He took back his cuttings carefully.

Gwen had stayed discreetly in the garden during this interview. At dinner, she sulked. It was summer holidays, and all three daughters were at home. The Matter was not mentioned. Toby did not come again to the house during the two weeks that remained of the holidays, but Sharon assumed that Gwen was seeing him. When Christmas holidays came, and Gwen arrived home from university, she announced to her mother that she had lost her virginity to Toby. Gwen looked radiant, though she held back her happiness as best she could, not wanting to be rudely rebellious.

Sharon turned pale and almost fainted.

"But we *are* going to be married, in just six months, Mother," Gwen said. "Now it's surer than ever. We know we like each other."

Sharon told Matthew. Matthew turned grim, not knowing what to say to Gwen, therefore keeping silent.

The more serious event was that Gwen told her sisters, who had quizzed her about their parents' change of mood until Gwen did tell them. After all, thought Gwen, one sister was eighteen and the other sixteen— both old enough to be married, if they'd wished to be. Gwen's two younger sisters were enthralled, but Gwen refused to answer their questions. For Penny and Sybille, this lent an even greater mystique to Gwen's experience.

They also decided to do the same thing, because goodness knew their respective boyfriends had been besieging them with the same request. The awful blows fell upon Matthew and Sharon that season of Christmas. Penny, then the baby Sybille, came home at 2 A.M. instead of the curfew hour of midnight on two successive weekends. Penny held out against the questions of her parents, but Sybille fairly blurted to her mother that she had said "Yes," as she put it, to Frank, aged eighteen.

"You *two*," said Sharon to her daughters Penny and Sybille, "will not bring either Peter or Frank to this house again! Do you hear me?"

Then Sharon collapsed. This was the evening of the day Sybille had broken her news. The doctor was summoned. Sharon had to be given a sedative. Matthew, who in the doctor's presence had almost struck Sybille in his anger, was persuaded by the family doctor to have a sedative injection also. But unlike Sharon, Matthew was not knocked out.

"You girls will not leave the house until you have my permission to do so!" Matthew fulminated, before he staggered up the stairs to his bedroom, which was separate from his wife's.

"They have all, all given away the only thing that they have to offer a husband," said Sharon to Matthew, and she called her blonde daughters into her bedroom to say the same thing to them.

The daughters hung their heads and appeared chastened, but inwardly they were not, and outside their mother's bedroom, the middle sister Penny said to her older sister, in the presence of the young Sybille, "Isn't the whole world on our side?"

All three daughters were happy with first love.

"Yes," said Gwen, with conviction.

Meanwhile Sharon, still abed, murmured to Matthew who visited her. "All our efforts wasted. The Grand Tour of Europe—" They'd taken their daughters two years ago to Florence, Paris, Venice. "The private French lessons, the piano lessons—*civilization*—"

The doctor had to come again with sedatives, though he advised Sharon to try to walk around a bit.

Then the real blow fell. Sybille found the courage to ask her father if her boyfriend Frank could move into the house. Frank's parents were in agreement, if Matthew was. Matthew could not believe his ears. And meanwhile Frank would continue to go to junior college in town, Sybille said.

"What on earth would the neighbors *think*?" said her father. "Hasn't that ever crossed your mind?"

"Estelle's got *her* boyfriend living in the house!" replied Sybille, before fleeing her father's study. She meant the Thompsons down the street. But what was the use with such fuddy-duddies? It was enough to make anybody leave home. Her father had probably never heard of The Pill.

"I feel like throwing a bucket of water on them," said Sharon from her bed, meaning the boyfriends of all her daughters. She was remembering the times she had thrown buckets of water at besieging tomcats, but it had not protected their female Siamese cat whose bastard son was even now a member of the household.

Matthew was trying his best to hold the home together. "There is one good thing," he said. "None of our daughters is pregnant. And Gwen's wedding is going to take place." He was mindful of Estelle Thompson's family down the road, with the boyfriend living in the household. Matthew couldn't tell his wife this, it would kill her. It had made a serious breach in his own wall. But wouldn't it be better to yield a little than to be completely vanquished?

"It is not the same," replied Sharon, dismally turning her face away. "Gwen is no longer pure."

Realizing that moving Frank into the house would deeply wound her parents, Sybille moved in with Frank. This shattered Matthew, his hands trembled, and he did not go to his office for a couple of days. He was ashamed even to be seen on the street. What were the neighbors thinking?

Really, the neighbors were no longer shocked by such things, and some thought it made for stability among the young.

Penny, the middle daughter, was sharing a small flat with Peter, in their college town now, and both were doing better in their studies. This was in January and February.

In January also, Sharon heard of her baby Sybille's having moved into Frank's household. The char told her. Matthew could never have told his wife such a thing. Sharon was still in bed. She had of course missed Sybille some ten days ago, and Matthew had said Sybille had taken a suitcase and was staying with Sharon's sister in town, and still going to school. But the char said with a merry laugh, out of the blue:

"I hear Sybille's moved into her boyfriend's house. Isn't she the grown-up young lady now!" The char had assumed that Sharon knew.

Sharon, doped on sedatives, thought the char was making a cruel joke. "It's no time for laughter—or funny stories, Mabel."

"But it's *true!*" said Mabel. Then she realized that Sharon hadn't known.

"Get out of my house!" Sharon cried with all the energy she had left.

"Sorry, madam," said Mabel, and went out of the room.

Sharon got with difficulty out of bed, intending to go downstairs and speak with Matthew who was again home. At the top of the stairs, Sharon lost her grip on the banister and fell the whole length—thirty-five dreadful steps, which though carpeted, bruised her horribly. Matthew found her at the bottom a few seconds later, and at once summoned the doctor.

"She is illustrating the fall of her house," said the doctor, who was a bit of a psychiatrist and thought himself wise.

"But how badly is she injured?" Matthew asked.

Nothing was broken, but now Sharon had to stay in bed. She became weaker and weaker. So did Matthew, as if by contagion. He stopped working. Fortunately, he could afford it. He and Sharon aged rapidly in the next months. Their daughters flourished. Gwen produced a baby boy a few months after her marriage. Sybille won a scholarship because of her good work in chemistry. Penny, unmarried, still lived with Peter, and both were doing well too. They were reading sociology and studying Eastern languages with a view to doing fieldwork. They all sensed a purpose in life.

For Sharon, life had lost its purpose, because her main purpose had failed. To her, her daughters were tramps, whores in masquerade, and still, Penny and Sybille (but not Gwen), taking money from home. Matthew was caught in the crossfire. He could see that his daughters were doing well, yet he was like his wife: he did not approve. After all, he had kept his chastity until marriage. Why couldn't everyone else, especially his own daughters? He went to see an analyst, whose words seemed to split Matthew further, instead of putting him back together again. Then there was his daughter Gwen implying in her letters that *his* attitude was a trifle vulgar. Matthew wanted to commit suicide, but didn't, because he had always considered suicide a coward's act. He died in his sleep aged seventy.

Sharon lingered on to an incredible old age, ninety-nine. She had long ago forbidden her daughters the house. She now had four great-grandchildren, and had never seen either grandchildren or great-grandchildren. In senility, Sharon reverted to the past, and her dying words were, "I'll get them to the altar as virgins . . . to the altar . . ." She had to be tied in bed. It was better than falling down the stairs again.

The Victim

It started when plump, blonde little Catherine was four or five years old: her parents noticed that she got hurt, fell, or did something disastrous far more often than did her contemporaries. Why was Cathy's nose so often bleeding, her knees scraped? Why did she so often wail for mama's sympathy? Why had she broken her arm twice before she was eight? Why, indeed? Especially since Cathy was not the outdoor type. She much preferred to play indoors. For instance, she liked dressing up in her mother's clothes, when her mother was out of the house. Cathy put on long dresses, high heels, and make-up which she applied at her mother's dressing table. Two such efforts had, both times, caused Cathy to catch her wobbly shoes in her skirts and fall down the stairs. She had been en route to see herself in the long looking-glass in the living room. This had been the cause of one of the arm breaks.

Now Cathy was eleven, and had long ago stopped trying on her mother's clothes. She had her own platform boots which made her five inches taller, her own dressing table with lipsticks, pancake make-up, hair curlers, curling irons, hair rinses, artificial eyelashes, even a wig on a pedestal. The wig had cost Cathy three months' allowance, and even so her parents had chipped in twenty dollars to buy it.

"I don't know why she wants to look like a grown-up woman aged thirty," said Vic, Cathy's father. "She's got plenty of time for that."

"Oh, it's normal at her age," said her mother, Ruby, though Ruby knew it wasn't quite normal.

Cathy complained about boys pestering her. "They just won't let me alone!" she said to her parents one evening, not for the first time. "Look at these bruises!" Cathy pushed up a colorful nylon blouse to show a couple of bruises on her ribs. She tottered a little in her white platform boots, topped incongruously by yellow knee-length stockings, which would have been more appropriate for a scoutmaster.

"Kee-rist!" said Vic, who was then drying dishes. "Look at these, Ruby! You didn't just fall down somewhere, did you, Cathy?"

At the sink, Ruby was not much impressed by the blue-brown bruises. She had seen compound fractures.

"The boys just grab me and squeeze me!" Cathy whined.

Vic almost threw the plate he was drying, but finally put it gently on top of a stack in the cupboard. "What do you expect, Cathy, if you wear phony long eyelashes to school at nine in the morning? You know, Ruby, it's her own fault."

But Vic couldn't make Ruby agree. Ruby kept saying it was normal at her age, or some such. Cathy would have turned him off, Vic thought, if he'd been a boy of thirteen or fourteen. But he had to admit that Cathy looked like fair game, a pushover to any stupid adolescent boy. He tried to explain this to Ruby, and get her to exert some control.

Ruby said, "You know, Vic darling, you're being the overprotective father. It's quite a common syndrome, and I don't want to reproach you. But you must relax about Cathy or you'll make things worse."

Cathy had round blue eyes, and long lashes by nature. Her Cupid's bow mouth tended to turn up at the corners in a sweet and willing smile. In school, she was rather good at biology, at drawing spirogyra, the circulatory systems of frogs, and cross sections of carrots as seen under a microscope. Miss Reynolds, her biology teacher, liked her, lent her pamphlets and quarterlies, which Cathy read and returned.

Then in summer vacation, when Cathy was almost twelve, she began hitchhiking, for no reason. The children of the neighborhood went to a lake ten miles away, where there was swimming, fishing and canoeing.

"Cathy, don't hitchhike. It's dangerous. There's a bus twice a day, going and coming," said Vic.

But there she went, hitchhiking, like a lemming rushing to its fate, Vic thought. One of her boyfriends called Joey, aged fifteen and with a car, could have driven her, but Cathy preferred to thumb rides from truck drivers. Thus she was raped for the first time.

Cathy made a big scene at the lake, burst into tears when she arrived on foot, and said, "I've just been raped!"

Bill Owens, the caretaker, at once asked Cathy to describe the man, and the kind of truck he'd been driving.

"He was redheaded," said Cathy tearfully. "Maybe twenty-eight. He was big and strong."

Bill Owens drove Cathy in his car to the nearest hospital. Cathy was photographed by journalists, and given ice cream sodas. She told her story to journalists and the doctors.

Cathy stayed home, pampered, for three days. The mysterious red-headed rapist was never found, although the doctors confirmed that she had been raped. Then Cathy went back to school, dressed to the nines, or the hilt again—platform shoes, pancake make-up, nail polish, scent, cleavage. She acquired more bruises. The telephone in her house kept ringing: the boys wanted to ask her out. Half the time Cathy sneaked out, half the time she stood the boys up with promises, causing the boys to hang around outside the house, in cars or on foot. Vic was disgusted. But what could he do?

Ruby kept saying, "It's natural. Cathy's just popular!"

Christmas holidays came, and the family went to Mexico. They had wanted to go to Europe, but Europe was too expensive. They drove to Juarez, crossed the border, and made their way to Guadalajara on their way to Mexico City. The Mexicans, men and women alike, stared at Cathy. She was obviously still a child, yet made up like a grown woman. Vic realized why the Mexicans stared, but Ruby seemed not to.

"Creepy people, these Mexicans," said Ruby.

Vic sighed. It might have been during one of these sighs that Cathy was whisked away. Vic and Ruby had been walking along a narrow pavement, Cathy behind them, on the way to their hotel, and when they turned round, Cathy wasn't there.

"Didn't she say she was going to buy an ice cream cone?" asked Ruby, ready to run to the next street corner to see if there wasn't an ice cream vendor there.

"I didn't hear her say that," said Vic. He looked frantically in all directions. There was nothing but men in business suits, a few peasants in sombreros and white trousers—mostly carrying bundles of some kind—and respectable looking Mexican women doing their shopping. Where was a policeman? For the next half hour, Vic and Ruby made their problem known to a couple of Mexican policemen who listened carefully and took down a description of their daughter Cathy. Vic even produced a photograph from his wallet.

"Only twelve? Really?" said one of the policemen.

Vic handed the photograph over to him and never saw it again.

Cathy returned to their hotel towards midnight. She was tired and dirty, but she made her way to the door of her parents' room. She told her parents she had been raped. Meanwhile the manager of the hotel had rung seconds before to say:

"Your daughter has returned! She went straight up in the elevator, didn't speak to us!"

Cathy said to her parents, "He was a nice looking man, and he spoke English. He wanted me to look at a monkey he said he had in his car. *I* didn't think there was anything wrong about him."

"A *monkey*?" said Vic.

"But there wasn't any monkey," Cathy said, "and we drove off." Then she began to cry.

Vic and Ruby were dismayed at the prospect of trying to find a nice looking man who spoke English, of trying to deal with Mexican courts if they did find him. They packed up and took Cathy back to America, hoping for the best, meaning that Cathy wasn't pregnant. She wasn't. They took Cathy to their doctor.

"It's all those cosmetics she puts on," said the doctor. "They make her look older."

Vic knew.

A real drama, however, took place the following year. Their next-door neighbors had a young doctor visiting them for a month that summer. His name was Norman, and he was a nephew of the woman of the house, Marian. Cathy told Norman she wanted to become a nurse, and Norman lent her books, and spent hours with her, talking about medicine and the nursing profession. Then one afternoon, Cathy ran into her house in tears and told her mother that Norman had been seducing her for weeks, and that he wanted her to run away with him, and had threatened to kidnap her if she didn't.

Ruby was shocked—and yet somehow *not* shocked, but more embarrassed. Ruby might have chosen to confine Cathy to the house, to say nothing about the story, but Cathy had already told Marian.

Marian arrived just two minutes after Cathy. "I don't know what to say! It's dreadful! I can't believe it of Norman, but it must be true. He's fled the house. He packed his suitcase in a flash, but he's left a few things behind."

This time, Cathy did not cease her tears, but kept them flowing for days. She told stories of Norman forcing her to do things she couldn't bring herself to describe. Word got around in the neighborhood. Norman was not in his apartment in Chicago, Marian said, because she had tried to ring him and there was no answer. A police hunt was mounted—though who initiated it, no one knew. Vic hadn't, nor Ruby, Marian nor her husband.

Norman was at last found holed up in a hotel hundreds of miles away. He had registered under his own name. A charge was made by police in the name of a government committee for the protection of minors. A trial began in Cathy's town. Cathy enjoyed every minute of it. She went to court daily, whether she had to testify or not, primly dressed, without make-up or artificial eyelashes, but she could not straighten her perma-nented hair, whose ultra-blondeness was starting to grow out, showing darker hair at the roots. When on the stand, she pretended she could not force the awful facts from her lips, so the prosecuting lawyer had to suggest them, and Cathy murmured "Yes," which she was often asked to say louder, so the court could hear. People shook their heads, hissed Norman, and by the end of the trial were in a mood to lynch him. All Norman and his lawyer were able to do was deny the charges, because there had been no witnesses. Norman was sentenced to six years for molesting, and plot-ting to abduct across a state border, a minor.

For a while Cathy enjoyed the role of martyr. But she couldn't keep it up more than a few weeks, because it wasn't gay enough. Her legion of boyfriends retreated a little distance, though they still asked her out. As time went on, when Cathy complained about rape, her parents paid not much attention. After all, Cathy had been on The Pill for years now.

Cathy's plans had changed, and she no longer wanted to become a nurse. She was going to be an air hostess. She was sixteen, but could easily pass for twenty or more, if she chose, so she told the airline she was eigh-teen, and went through their six-week training course in how to turn on the charm, serve drinks and meals graciously to all, soothe the nervous, administer first aid, and carry out emergency exit procedures if necessary. Cathy was a natural at all this. Flying to Rome, Beirut, Teheran, Paris, and having dates all along the way with fascinating men was just her cup of tea. Frequently the air hostesses were supposed to stay overnight in foreign cities, where their hotels were paid for. So life was a breeze. Cathy had money galore, and a collection of the weirdest presents, especially from gentlemen of the Middle East, such as a gold toothbrush and a portable narghile (also of gold) suitable for smoking pot. She had suffered a broken nose, thanks to the insane chauffeur of an Italian millionaire on the cliff-hanging road between Positano and Amalfi. But the nose had been set well, and did not mar her prettiness in the least. To her credit, Cathy sent money regularly to her parents, and she herself had a skyrocketing account in a New York savings bank.

Then the checks to her parents abruptly stopped. The airlines got in touch with Vic and Ruby. Where was Cathy? Vic and Ruby had no idea. She might be anywhere in the world—the Philippines, Hong Kong, even Australia for all they knew. Would the airline please inform them, her parents asked, as soon as they learned anything?

The trail went to Tangiers and ended. Cathy had told another stewardess, it seemed, that she had a big date in Tangiers with a man who was going to pick her up at the airport. Cathy evidently kept that date, and was never heard of again.

The Evangelist

God came late to Diana Redfern—but He came. Diana was forty-two when, walking down her rain-drenched street where droplets fell from the elms, due to a rain which had recently stopped, she experienced a change—a revelation. This revelation involved her mind, body, and also her soul. She realized the presence of nature, and of an all-powerful God streaming through her. At the same moment, the sun which had been forcing its way through the clouds, flooded over her face and body and the whole street, which was called Elm Street.

Diana stood still, her arms outspread, and heedless of what people might think, let her empty shopping bag drop, and knelt on the pavement. Then she arose, and her step became lighter, her chores were done without effort. Suddenly the dinner was ready, her husband Ben and daughter Prunella, aged fourteen, seated at the candlelit table with shrimp cocktails before them.

"Now we shall pray," said Diana, to the surprise of husband and daughter.

They dropped their little shrimp forks, and bowed their heads. There had been something commanding in Diana's voice.

"God is *here*," Diana said in conclusion.

No one could deny that, or deny Diana. Ben gave his daughter a puzzled glance, which was returned by Prunella, then they began eating.

Diana became at once a lay preacher. She started with Tuesday and Thursday afternoon teas at her house, to which she invited neighbors. The neighbors were mostly women, but a few retired men were able to come too. "Are you aware of the constant presence of God?" she would ask. "It is only unlucky people, who have never made acquaintance with God, who could possibly doubt man's immortality, and his eternal life after death."

The neighbors were silent, first because of trying to think of something to reply (the atmosphere was conversational), and then because they really were quite impressed, and preferred to let Diana do the talking. Attendance at her tea parties grew.

Diana began corresponding with elderly people, prisoners, and unwed mothers, whose names she got from her local church. The preacher there was the Reverend Martin Cousins. He approved of Diana's work, and spoke of her from the pulpit as "one among us who is inspired by God."

In the attic which Diana had partly cleared out and now used as her study, she knelt on a small, low stool at dawn every morning for nearly two hours. On Sunday mornings, too early to interfere with churchgoing at 11, she preached from streetcorners, while standing on a formica chair brought from her kitchen. "I ask not a penny from you. God is not interested in Caesar's coin. I ask that ye give yourselves to God—and kneel." She would hold out her arms, close her eyes, and she inspired quite a few people to kneel. Some people wrote their names and addresses in her big ledger. These people she later wrote to, with the objective of sustaining their faith.

Diana now wore a flowing white robe and sandals, even in the worst weather. She never caught a cold. Diana's eyelids had always been pinkish, as if she needed sleep, but she slept rather a lot, or she had in the past. Now she slept no more than four hours a night in the attic, where she wrote long after midnight. Her lids became pinker, making her eyes appear blue. When she fixed her gaze upon a stranger, he or she was apt to be afraid to move until she had delivered her message, which seemed a personal message: "Only be *aware*—and thou shalt conquer!"

It was hard for Ben to grasp what Diana wanted to achieve. She did not want any helpers, though she worked hard enough to exhaust three or four people. Her behavior caused some embarrassment to Ben, who was manager of a jewelry and watch repair shop in the town of Pawnuk, Minnesota. Pawnuk was a new suburb composed of affluent WASPs who had fled from a nearby metropolis.

"Best to take it easy and be tolerant," thought Ben. "Diana's all on the good side, anyway."

Prunella was somehow frightened of her mother, and stepped aside whenever Diana wanted to pass her in a room or a hall. Even Ben addressed his wife in a deferential manner now, and he sometimes stut-

tered. Diana was not often at home, however. She had begun making airplane trips to Philadelphia, New York and Boston, the cities most in need
of saving, she said. If she had not an auditorium laid on—she was in touch
by letter and telephone with various Chambers of Commerce which
could arrange these things for her—Diana would walk right into churches
and synagogues and take over. In her white robe and sandals whatever the
weather, and with her flowing blonde hair, she made a striking figure as she
strode down the aisle and mounted the pulpit or took the rostrum. Who
could, or dared to, throw her out? She was preaching The Word.

"Brothers—brethren—sisters! Ye must sweep out the cobwebs of the
past! Forget the old phrases learnt by heart! Think of yourselves as newborn—as of this hour! Today is your true birthday!"

Though some preachers and rabbis were annoyed, not one ever tried
to stop her. All the congregations, like the neighbors Diana addressed on
the pavements of her town, kept silent and listened. Within six months,
the fame of Diana Redfern had spread all over America. The few who
scoffed—and they were very few—kept their criticism mild. Most
annoyed were the people of the meat industry, for Diana preached vegetar-
ianism, and her converts were beginning to make a dent in the profits of
Chicago's slaughterhouses.

Diana planned a World Tour of Human Resurrection. Money flowed
to her, or fell like manna—money from strangers, Frenchmen, Germans,
Canadians, people who had only read about her and never seen her. So the
expenses of a world tour presented no problem. Some of the money, in
fact, Diana sent back to the donors. She was certainly not greedy, but it was
soon evident that she could not cope with all her letter writing (more
important), if she sent back all the contributions, so she deposited them in
a special bank account.

A part-time housekeeper was now preparing the meals for Diana's
household, vegetarian, of course. Often the house resembled a hostel for
young and old, because strangers rang the doorbell, stayed to talk, and Ben
had ceased to be surprised by families with three or more children intending to sleep on the two sofas in the living room and in the spare bedrooms.

"All, *all* is possible," said Diana to Ben.

Yes, thought Ben. But never had he imagined that his marriage would
come to this—Diana isolated from him, sleeping on a bed of nails, more or
less, in the attic, while strangers occupied his house. He sensed that events
were spiraling to a climax with Diana's round-the-world tour, and that like
biblical events they would be beyond his control. Diana would become

something like a living saint, perhaps, and more famous than any saint alive had ever been.

The morning of her departure on the world tour, Diana stood on the sill of her attic window, raised her arms to the rising sun, and stepped out, convinced that she could fly or at least float. She fell on to a round, white-painted iron table and the red bricks of the patio. Thus poor Diana met her earthly end.

The Perfectionist

Margot Fleming's father, whom Margot had greatly admired, had often said to her, "Anything worth doing is worth doing well." Margot believed that anything worth doing well was worth doing perfectly.

The Flemings' house and garden were at all times in perfect order. Margot did all the gardening, though they could have afforded a gardener. Even their Airedale, Rugger, slept only where he was supposed to sleep (on a carpet in front of the fireplace), and never jumped on people to greet them, only wagged his tail. The Flemings' only child, Rosamund, aged fourteen, had perfect manners, and her only fault was that she was inclined to asthma.

If, in putting away a fork in the silverware drawer, Margot noticed an incipient tarnish, she would get out the silver polish and clean the fork, and this would lead, whatever the hour of day or night, to her cleaning the rest of the silverware so it would all look equally nice. Then Margot would be inspired to tackle the tea service, and then the cover for the meat platter, and then there were the silver frames of photographs in the living room, and the silver stamp box on the telephone table, and it might be dawn before Margot was finished. However, there was a housemaid, named Dolly, who came three times a week to do the major cleaning.

Margot seldom dared to prepare a meal for her own family, and never for guests. This, despite a kitchen equipped with every modern convenience, including a walk-in deep freezer, three blending machines, an electric tin-opener and an electric knife-sharpener, a huge stove with two glass-doored ovens in it, and cabinets around the walls full of pressure cookers, colanders, and pots and pans of all sizes. The Flemings almost never ate at home, because Margot was afraid her cooking would not be good enough. Something—maybe the soup, maybe the salad—might not be just right, Margot thought, so she ducked the whole business. The Flemings might ask their friends for drinks before dinner, but then they would all get into their cars and drive eight miles to the city for dinner at a restaurant, then perhaps drive back to the Flemings' for coffee and brandy.

Margot was a bit of a hypochondriac. She got up early every morning (if she was not still up after polishing silver or waxing furniture) to do her Yoga exercises, which were followed by a half hour of meditation. Then Margot weighed herself. If she had lost or gained a fraction of a pound overnight, she would try to remedy this by the way she ate that day. Then she drank the juice of one lemon unsweetened. Twice a year she went for two weeks to a spa, and felt that she got rid of small aches and pains which had started in the preceding six months. At the spa, her diet was even simpler, and her slender face became a little more anxious, though she made an effort to maintain an intelligently pleasant expression, as this was part of the general perfection that she hoped to achieve.

"The So-and-sos are very informal," her husband Harold would say sometimes. "We don't have to give them a banquet, but it would be nice if we could ask them for dinner here." No luck. Margot would say something like:

"I just don't think I can cope with it. A restaurant is so much simpler, Harold dear."

Margot's expression would have become so pained, Harold could never bring himself to argue further. But he often thought, "All that big kitchen, and we can't even ask our friends for an omelet!"

Thus it came as a staggering surprise to Harold when Margot announced one day in October, with the solemnity of a Crusader praying before battle: "Harold, we're going to have a dinner party *here*."

The occasion was a double-barreled one: Harold's birthday was nine days off and fell on a Saturday. And he had just been promoted to vice-president of his bank with a rise in salary. That was enough to warrant a party, and Harold felt he owed it to his colleagues, but still—was Margot capable? "There might be twenty people at least," Harold said. "Even I'd been thinking of a restaurant this time."

But Margot plainly felt it was something she ought to do, to be a perfect wife. She sent out the invitations. She spent two days planning the menu with the aid of *Larousse Gastronomique,* typed it with two carbons, and made a shopping list with two carbons also in case she mislaid one or two of them. This left seven days before the party. She decided that the living room curtains looked faded, so she cruised the city in a taxi looking for the right material, then for just the right gold braid for the edges and the bottom. She made the new curtains herself. She hired an upholsterer to recover the sofa and four armchairs, and paid him extra for a rushed job. The already clean windows were washed again by Margot and Dolly, the already clean dinner service (for twenty-four people) washed again also. Margot was up all night the two nights preceding the birthday-promotion party, and of course she was busy during the days, too. She and Dolly made a trial batch of the complicated pudding that was to be the dessert, found it a success, and threw it away.

The big evening came, and twenty-two people arrived between 7:30 and 8 P.M. in a series of private cars and taxis. Margot and a hired butler and Dolly drifted about with trays of drinks and hot canapés and cheese dips. The dining table had been let out to its greatest length—a handsome field of white linen now, silver candelabra, and three vases of red carnations.

And all went well. The women praised the appearance of the table, praised the soup. The men pronounced the claret excellent. The president of Harold's bank proposed a toast to Margot. Then Margot began to feel ill. She had a second coffee, and accepted a second brandy which she didn't want, but one of Harold's senior colleagues had offered it. Then she ducked into her bedroom and took a benzedrine. She was not in the habit of taking pick-up pills, and had these only because she had recently begged her doctor for them "Just in case," and had been given them because she had promised not to abuse them. Ten minutes later, Margot felt up in the air, almost flying, and she became alarmed. She went back to her bedroom and took a mild sleeping pill. She drank another brandy, which someone pressed upon her. Harold proposed another toast, to his bank, and this was followed a few minutes later by a generally proposed toast to Harold, because it was his birthday. Margot dutifully partook of all these toasts. In the last moments of the party, Margot felt she was walking in her sleep, as if she were a ghost, or someone else. When the door closed after the last guest, she collapsed on the floor.

A doctor was summoned. Margot was rushed to hospital, and her stomach pumped. She was unconscious for many hours. "Nothing to worry about, really," the doctor said to Harold. "It's exhaustion plus the fact that her nerves are upset by pills. It's just a matter of flushing out her system." Water was being piped slowly down her throat. Margot regained consciousness, and at once experienced an agony of shame. She was sure she had done something *wrong* at the party, but just what she couldn't remember.

"Margot my dear, you did beautifully!" Harold said. "Everyone said what a superb evening it was!"

But Margot was convinced she had passed out, and that their guests had thought she was drunk. Harold showed Margot appreciative notes he had received from several of their guests, but Margot interpreted them as polite merely.

Once home from the hospital, Margot took to knitting. She had always knitted a little. Now she undertook a vast enterprise: to knit coverlets for every bed in the house (eight counting the twin beds in the two guest rooms). Margot neglected her Yoga meditation, but not her exercises, as she knitted and knitted from 6 A.M. until nearly 2 A.M., hardly pausing to eat.

The doctor told Harold to consult a psychiatrist. The psychiatrist had a chat with Margot, then said to Harold, "We must let her continue knitting, otherwise she may become worse. When she has got all the coverlets done, perhaps we can talk to her."

But Harold suspected that the doctor was only trying to make *him* feel better. Things were worse than ever. Margot stopped Dolly from preparing dinner, saying that Dolly's cooking wasn't good enough. The three Flemings made hurried trips to restaurants, then went back home so Margot could resume her knitting.

Knit, knit, knit. And what will Margot think of to do next?

Slowly, Slowly in the Wind

The Man
Who Wrote Books
in His Head

E. Taylor Cheever wrote books in his head, never on paper. By the time he died aged sixty-two, he had written fourteen novels and created one hundred and twenty-seven characters, all of whom he, at least, remembered distinctly.

It came about like this: Cheever wrote a novel when he was twenty-three called *The Eternal Challenge* which was rejected by four London publishers. Cheever, then a sub-editor on a Brighton newspaper, showed his manuscript to three or four journalist and critic friends, all of whom said, in quite as brusque a tone it seemed to Cheever as the London publishers' letters, "Characters don't come through . . . dialogue artificial . . . theme is unclear . . . Since you ask me to be frank, may I say I don't think this has a hope of being published even if you work it over . . . Better forget this one and write another . . ." Cheever had spent all his spare time for two years on the novel, and had come near losing the girl he intended to marry, Louise Welldon, because he gave her so little attention. However he did marry Louise just a few weeks after the deluge of negative reports on his novel. It was a far cry from the note of triumph on which he had intended to claim his bride and embark upon marriage.

Cheever had a small private income, and Louise had more. Cheever didn't need a job. He had imagined quitting his newspaper job (on the strength of having his first novel published), writing more novels and book reviews and maybe a column on books for the Brighton newspaper, climbing up from there to the *Times* and *Guardian*. He tried to get in as book critic on the Brighton *Beacon,* but they wouldn't take him on any permanent basis. Besides, Louise wanted to live in London.

They bought a town house in Cheyne Walk and decorated it with furniture and rugs given them by their families. Meanwhile Cheever was thinking about another novel, which he intended to get exactly right before he put a word on paper. So secretive was he, that he did not tell Louise the title or theme or discuss any of the characters with her, though Cheever did get his characters clearly in mind—their backgrounds, motivations, tastes, and appearance down to the color of their eyes. His next book would be definite as to theme, his characters fleshed out, his dialogue spare and telling.

He sat for hours in his study in the Cheyne Walk house, indeed went up after breakfast and stayed until lunchtime, then went back until tea or dinnertime like any other working writer, but at his desk he made hardly a note except an occasional "1877 + 53" and "1939–83," things like that to determine the age or birth year of certain characters. He liked to hum softly to himself while he pondered. His book, which he called *The Spoiler of the Game* (no one else in the world knew the title), took him fourteen months to think out and write in his mind. By that time, Everett Junior had been born. Cheever knew so well where he was going with the book that the whole first page was etched in his mind as if he saw it printed. He knew there would be twelve chapters, and he knew what was in them. He committed whole sequences of dialogue to memory, and could recall them at will. Cheever thought he could type the book out in less than a month. He had a new typewriter, a present from Louise on his last birthday.

"I *am* ready—finally," Cheever said one morning with an unaccustomed air of cheer.

"Oh, splendid, darling!" said Louise. Tactfully she never asked him how his work was going, because she sensed that he didn't like that.

While Cheever was looking over the *Times* and filling his first pipe before going up to work, Louise went out in the garden and cut three yellow roses, which she put into a vase and took up to his room. Then she silently withdrew.

Cheever's study was attractive and comfortable with a generous desk, good lighting, books of reference and dictionaries to hand, a green leather sofa he could take catnaps on if he chose, and a view of the garden. Cheever noticed the roses on the small roller table beside his desk and smiled appreciatively. *Page One, Chapter One,* Cheever thought. The book was to be dedicated to Louise. *To my wife Louise.* Simple and clear. *It was on a gray morning in December that Leonard . . .*

He procrastinated, and lit another pipe. He had put a sheet of paper in the typewriter, but this was the title page, and as yet he had written nothing. Suddenly, at 10:15 A.M., he was aware of boredom—oppressive, para-lyzing boredom. He knew the book, it was in his mind entirely, and in fact why write it?

The thought of hammering away at the keys for the next many weeks, putting words he already knew onto two hundred and ninety-two pages (so Cheever estimated) dismayed him. He fell onto the green sofa and slept until eleven. He awakened refreshed and with a changed outlook: the book was done, after all, not only done but polished. Why not go on to something else?

An idea for a novel about an orphan in quest of his parents had been in Cheever's mind for nearly four months. He began to think about a novel around it. He sat all day at his desk, humming, staring at the slips of paper, almost all blank, while he rapped the eraser end of a yellow pencil. He was creating.

By the time he had thought out and finished the orphan novel, a long one, his son was five years old.

"I can *write* my books later," Cheever said to Louise. "The important thing is to think them out."

Louise was disappointed, but hid her feelings. "Your father is a *writer,*" she said to Everett Junior. "A novelist. Novelists don't have to go to work like other people. They can work at home."

Little Everett was in a day nursery school, and the children had asked him what his father did. By the time Everett was twelve, he understood the situation and found it highly risible, especially when his mother told him his father had written six books. Invisible books. This was when Louise began to change her attitude to Cheever from one of tolerance and laissez-faire to one of respect and admiration. Mainly, consciously, she did this to set an example for Everett. She was conventional enough to believe that if a son lost respect for his father, the son's character and even the household would fall apart.

When Everett was fifteen, he was not amused by his father's work any longer, but ashamed and embarrassed by it when his friends came to visit.

"Novels? . . . Any good? . . . Can I see one?" asked Ronnie Phelps, another fifteen-year-old and a hero of Everett's. That Everett had been able to bring Ronnie home for the Christmas hols was a stupendous coup, and Everett was anxious that everything should go right.

"He's very shy about them," Everett replied. "Keeps 'em in his room, you know."

"Seven novels. Funny I never heard of him. Who's his publisher?"

Everett found himself under such a strain, Ronnie became ill at ease too, and after only three days went down to his family in Kent. Everett refused to eat, almost, and kept to his room where his mother twice found him weeping.

Cheever knew nothing of this. Louise shielded him from every domestic upset, every interruption. But since the holidays stretched ahead nearly a month and Everett was in such a bad state, she gently suggested to Cheever that they take a cruise somewhere, maybe to the Canaries.

At first, Cheever was startled by the idea. He didn't like vacations, didn't need them, he often said. But after twenty-four hours, he decided that a cruise was a good idea. "I can still work," he said.

On the boat, Cheever sat for hours in his deck chair, sometimes with pencil, sometimes not, working on his eighth novel. He never made a note in twelve days, however. Louise, next to him in her chair, could tell when he sighed and closed his eyes that he was taking a breather. Towards the end of the day, he often appeared to be holding a book in his hands and to be thumbing through it, and she knew he was browsing in his past work which he knew by heart.

"Ha-ha," Cheever would laugh softly, when a passage amused him. He would turn to another place, appear to be reading, then murmur, "Um-m. Not bad, not bad."

Everett, whose chair was on the other side of his mother's, would tear himself up grimly and stalk away when his father gave these contented grunts. The cruise was not an entire success for Everett, there being no people his own age except one girl, and Everett announced to his parents and the friendly deck steward that he had no desire whatever to meet her.

But things went better when Everett got to Oxford. At least his attitude towards his father became once more one of amusement. His father had made him quite popular at Oxford, Everett declared. "It's not everyone who's got a living limerick for a father!" he said to his mother. "Shall I recite one I—"

"Please, Everett," said his mother with a coldness that took the grin at once from Everett's face.

In his late fifties, Cheever showed signs of the heart disease which was to kill him. He wrote on as steadily as ever in his head, but his doctor counseled him to cut down on his hours of work, and to nap twice in the day. Louise had explained to the doctor (a new doctor to them, a heart specialist) what kind of work Cheever did.

"He is thinking out a novel," Louise said. "That can be just as tiring as writing one, of course."

"Of course," the doctor agreed.

When the end came for Cheever, Everett was thirty-eight and had two teenaged children of his own. Everett had become a zoologist. Everett and his mother and five or six relatives assembled in the hospital room where Cheever lay under an oxygen tent. Cheever was murmuring something, and Louise bent close to hear.

". . . ashes unto ashes," Cheever was saying. "Stand back! . . . No photographs allowed . . . 'Next to Tennyson?' " This last in a soft high voice. ". . . monument to human imagination . . ."

Everett was also listening. Now his father seemed to be delivering a prepared speech of some kind. A *eulogy,* Everett thought.

". . . tiny corner revered by a grateful people . . . Clunk! . . . Careful!"

Everett suddenly bent forward in a spasm of laughter. "He's burying himself in *Westminster Abbey!*"

"Everett!" said his mother. "Silence!"

"Ha-ha-ha!" Everett's tension exploded in guffaws, and he staggered out of the room and collapsed on a bench in the hall, pressing his lips together in a hopeless effort to control himself. What made it funnier was that the others in the room, except for his mother, didn't understand the situation. They knew his father wrote books in his head, but they didn't appreciate the Poets' Corner bit at all!

After a few moments, Everett sobered himself and walked back into the room. His father was humming, as he had often done while he worked. Was he still working? Everett watched his mother lean low to listen. Was he mistaken, or was it a ghost of *Land of Hope and Glory* that Everett heard coming from the oxygen tent?

It was over. It seemed to Everett, as they filed out of the room, that they should go now to his parents' house for the funeral meats, but no— the funeral had not really taken place yet. His father's powers were truly extraordinary.

Some eight years later, Louise lay dying of pneumonia which had followed flu. Everett was with her in the bedroom of the Cheyne Walk house. His mother was talking about his father, about his never having received the fame and respect due him.

"—until the last," said Louise. "He is buried in Poets' Corner, Everett—mustn't forget that . . ."

"Yes," said Everett, somehow impressed, almost believing it.

"Never room for the wives there, of course—otherwise I could join him," she whispered.

And Everett forbore to tell her she *was* going to join him in the family plot outside Brighton. Or was that true? Could they not find another niche in Poets' Corner? *Brighton,* Everett said to himself as reality started to crumble. *Brighton,* Everett recovered himself. "I'm not so sure," he said. "Maybe it can be arranged, Mummy. We'll see."

She closed her eyes, and a soft smile settled on her lips, the same smile of contentment that Everett had seen on his father's face when he had lain under the oxygen tent.

The Network

The telephone—two Princess telephones, one yellow, one mauve—
rang in Fran's small apartment every half hour or so. It rang so often,
because Fran now and indeed since about a year was unofficial Mother
Superior of the Network.

The Network consisted of a group of friends in New York who mutu-
ally bolstered one another's morale by telephoning, by giving constant
assurance of friendship and solidarity against the sea of enemies, the non-
friends, the potential thieves, rapists and diddlers. Of course they saw one
another frequently too, and many had the house keys of others, so they
could do favours such as dog walking, cat feeding, plant watering. The
important thing was that they could trust each other. The Network could
and had swung a life insurance policy in favor of one of them, against a lot
of odds. One of their group could repair hi-fi and television sets. Another
was a doctor.

Fran was nothing distinguished, a secretary-accountant, but hers had
always been a shoulder to cry on, she was generous with her time, and
besides all that, just now she wasn't working, which meant she had more
time than ever. Ten months ago she'd had a gall bladder operation, and this
had at once been followed by an intestinal adhesion calling for another
operation, then her old spinal column trouble (out-of-line disks) had acted
up, involving now a back brace which she didn't always wear. Fran was
fifty-eight, and not so spry any more at best. She was unmarried and had
worked for seventeen years for Consolidated Edison in the subscription
(actually the bill-collecting) department. Con Ed were treating her nicely
as to disability payments, and they had a good hospitalization plan. Con Ed
were keeping her job open for her, and Fran could have gone back to work

now, for the past two months even, but she had come to love her leisure. And she loved to be able to answer the telephone when it rang.

"Hello?—Oh, Freddie! How are *you*?" Fran would sit hunched, murmuring softly, as if afraid of being overheard by someone, cradling the lightweight telephone as if it were a little furry animal or perhaps the hand of the friend she was speaking to. "Yeah, I'm all right. You're really all right?"

"Oh, yeah. And you too?" Somehow all the Network had fallen into Fran's habit of doubly verifying that their members were all right. Freddie was a commercial artist with a studio and apartment on West 34th Street.

"Yeah, I'm okay. Say, did you hear those police sirens last night?—No, not fire, police," Fran said.

"What time?"

"Around two in the morning. Boy, they really were after someone last night! Musta been six cars zooming down Seventh. You didn't hear them?" Freddie hadn't and the subject was dropped. Fran murmured on, "Gee, it looks like rain today, and I've gotta go out and do a little shopping . . ."

When they hung up, Fran went on murmuring to herself. "Now where was I? The sweater. Had one rinse, needs one more . . . Garbage has to go to the incinerator . . ." She rinsed the sweater in the bathroom basin, squeezed it, and had just hung it on an inflated rubber hanger on the shower rail, when the telephone rang. Fran lifted the phone in the dressing room, an area between bathroom and dining area, learned that it was Marj (a forty-five-year-old woman who had a very well-paying job at Macy's as buyer) and murmured, "Oh, Marj, hi. Listen, I'm on the dressing room phone, so hang on and I'll take it in the living room."

Fran laid the phone down on the dressing table, and went into the living room, limping and stooping a bit as was her habit since her troubles. Though she was alone now, the habit stuck, she realized, and so much the better, because Con Ed were sending their insurance agent twice a month to snoop and ask how soon she thought she could go back to work. "Hello, Marj, how are you?"

The next telephone call was from a mail order sporting goods store, of which Fran had vaguely heard, on East 42nd Street, offering Fran a job starting Monday in their accounting department at two hundred and ten dollars a week take-home excluding their pensions and hospitalization plans.

Fran experienced a slight shock. How had this place got her name? She wasn't looking for a job. "Thank you. Thank you very much," Fran said gently, "but I'm going back with Con Ed as soon as I'm well enough."

"I believe we're offering you a better salary. Perhaps you could think about it," the smooth female voice went on. "We've filled our quotas, and we'd like a person like you."

Fran's sense of being flattered vanished quickly. Was Con Ed *not* holding her job? Had Con Ed phoned this company to get themselves off the hook of the disability money, which was nearly as much as her Con Ed salary? "Thank you again," Fran said, "but I think I'd prefer to stay with Con Ed. They've been so nice to me."

"Well, if that's your opinion . . ."

When they hung up Fran had a few minutes of uneasiness. She didn't dare phone Con Ed to ask them directly what was cooking. She recollected, thinking hard, the atmosphere of the last visit of the insurance inspector. Unfortunately, she'd forgotten her appointment with him at 4:30 P.M. at her apartment, and the inspector had had to wait nearly an hour for her, and she'd come into her building looking pretty lively in the company of Connie, one of her friends who worked as waitress at night and so had days off sometimes. They'd been to an afternoon film. On seeing the inspector standing in the big lobby (no furniture in the lobby downstairs, because it had all been stolen, even though it had been chained to the wall), Fran had put on a limp and a stoop. She'd told him she thought she was making progress, but she still wasn't capable of an eight-hour-a-day job, five days a week. She'd had to sign her name in a book he had, proving that he had seen her. He was a black, though a nice enough type. He could have been a lot worse, making snide remarks, but this one was polite.

Fran also remembered that that same day she'd run into Harvey Cohen who lived in her building, and Harvey had told her the inspector had accosted him in the hall and asked him what he knew about Miss Covak's state of health. Harvey said he'd "laid it on thick," stating that Miss Covak was still limping, made it to the delicatessen now and then because she had to, living alone, but she didn't look like someone who was ready for a job yet. Good old Harvey, Fran thought. Jews knew how to do things. They were clever. Fran had thanked Harvey profoundly, meaning it.

But now? What the hell had happened? She'd call up Jane Brixton about it. Jane had a head on her shoulders, was more than ten years older than Fran (in fact was a retired schoolteacher), and Fran was always soothed after talking with Jane. Jane lived in a wonderful floor-through apartment on West 11th Street, full of antique furniture.

"Ha, ha," Jane laughed softly, after hearing Fran's story. Fran had told it in such detail, she had even put in the woman's remark that the sporting goods company had filled its quota, and Jane said, "That means they've hired all the blacks they need to and they'd be delighted to stick in a white while they can." Jane spoke with a slightly southern accent, though she was from Pennsylvania.

Fran had been pretty sure the woman's remark had meant that.

"If you don't feel like going to work yet, don't," Jane said. "Life's—"

"As all of us said once, if you remember, I'm only taking money that I've put *in* all these years. Same goes for hospitalization. Say, Jane, I don't suppose you could sign a paper or something saying you gave me a couple of massage treatments for the spine?"

"Well—I'm not qualified, as you know. So I don't see how a paper would count."

"That's true." It had seemed to Fran that one more paper about her physical troubles might add that much more weight to her argument that she wasn't fit for work. "Coming to Marj's party Saturday? I hope so."

"Of course. By the way, my nephew's in town, staying with me. He's my nephew's son, actually, but I call him my nephew. I'm bringing him."

"Your nephew! How old is he? What's his name?"

"Greg Kaspars. He's about twenty-two. From Allentown. Thinks he might work in New York as a furniture designer. Anyway he wants to try his luck."

"How exciting! Nice boy?"

Jane laughed like an elderly aunt. "I think so. Judge for yourself."

They signed off, and Fran sighed, imagining being twenty-two, trying her luck in the great world of New York. She watched a little television on her not very good set. It was an old set, not so big a screen as most these days, but Fran didn't feel like spending the money to buy a new one. The only sharply focused program was awful, some quiz show. All rigged, of course. How could any adult get so excited about winning fifty bucks or even a refrigerator? Fran switched off and went to bed, after lifting off the sofa pillows and its cover and pulling out the heavy metal contraption which unfolded, revealing bedsheets and blankets all ready to crawl into, the pillows being in a semi-circular cavity with an upholstered top which made a decorative projection, even a seat, at one end of the sofa when it was a sofa. She lay thumbing through her latest *National Geographic,* looking at the pictures only because the telephone was still ringing now and then, interrupting her train of thought if she attempted to read an article. Fran's older brother, who was a vet in San Francisco, sent her regularly a subscription to the *National Geographic* as a birthday present.

Fran turned the light out and had just fallen asleep, when the telephone rang. She reached for it in the dark, not in the least annoyed at being awakened.

It was one of the Network called Verie (for Vera), and she announced that she was down in the dumps, really depressed. "I lost my billfold today."

"*What?* How?"

"I was checking out at the supermarket, put it on the counter after I'd paid and got my change—because I was loading my paper bags, y'know—and when I looked again, it was gone. I think the guy behind me—Oh, I don't know."

Fran asked questions fast. No, Verie hadn't seen anyone running away, it hadn't been on the floor, couldn't have fallen behind the counter (unless the checkout girl took it), but it *could* have been the guy just behind her who was one of those people (white) Verie just couldn't describe, because he didn't look especially honest or dishonest, but anyway she'd lost at least seventy dollars. Fran overflowed with sympathy.

"It's good to talk about it, though, y'know?" Fran said gently in the dark." It's the most important thing in life, communication . . . Yeah . . . Yeah . . . It's all that counts, communication. Isn't it true?"

"And the fact that you have friends," Verie put in, sounding a little weepy.

Fran's heart was touched even more deeply, and she murmured, "Verie, I know it's late, but want to come down? You could stay the night. Bed's big enough. If it'd make you feel—"

"Thanks, I better not. Work tomorrow. Make some more dough."

"You're coming to Marj's party, I hope."

"Oh, sure. Saturday."

"Oh! I talked with Jane. She's bringing her *nephew.* Or the son of her nephew." Fran told Verie everything she knew about him.

It was lovely, Saturday evening, to see all the familiar faces at Marj's. Freddie, Richard, Verie, Helen, Mackie (a big cheerful fellow who was manager of a record shop on Madison and could fix anything electronic) and his wife, Elaine, an equally friendly person with slightly crossed eyes, great to exchange embraces and how-are-yous with people in the flesh. But what made the party special for Fran was the presence of somebody new and young, Jane's nephew. Rather formally, Fran made her way, limping a little, to the end of the bar table where Jane stood talking with a young man in corduroys and a turtleneck sweater. He had dark wavy hair and a faintly amused smile, which Fran thought was probably defensive.

"Hello, Fran. This is Greg," Jane said. "Fran Covak, Greg, one of our gang."

"Howdy do, Fran." Greg stuck out a hand.

"How're you, Greg? So nice to meet a relative of Jane's! How're you liking New York?" Fran asked.

"I been here before."

"Oh, I'm sure you have! But I hear you're thinking about working here." Fran's mind was suddenly racing over people she knew who might be of help to Greg. Richard, who was a designer but more for theater. Marj, who might know someone in Macy's furniture department who might put Greg onto someone who—

"Fran! How's my girl!" Jeremy's arm encircled Fran's trouser-suited waist, and he slapped her playfully on the behind. Jeremy was about fifty-five with a shock of white hair.

"Jeremy! You're looking marvelous!" Fran said. "Love that crazy purple shirt!"

"How's the spine?" Jeremy asked.

"Better, thanks. Takes time. Have you met Greg yet? Jane's nephew."

Jeremy hadn't, and Fran introduced them. "What're your job plans, Greg?" Fran asked.

"I don't want to talk about work tonight," Greg replied, smiling and evasive.

"It's just that I was thinking," Fran went on to Jane in her earnest, clear way, though she spoke as gently as she spoke into her telephone, "among all the people we know, we'll certainly be able to do something for Greg. Give him the right ontrays, y'know? Jane says you're a furniture designer, Greg."

"Yeah, well. If you want me to go into my life story, I've been working for a cabinetmaker more than a year now. All handmade stuff, so naturally I designed a few things while I was there. Cabinets to certain specifications."

Fran glanced at his hands and said, "Bet you're strong. Isn't he a nice boy, Jeremy?"

Jeremy nodded and tossed back his scotch on the rocks.

Jane said, "Don't worry about Greg. I'll talk to Marj maybe in the course of the evening."

Fran brightened. "That's just what I'd been thinking! Someone at Macy's—"

"I don't want to work at Macy's," Greg said pleasantly but firmly. "I'm rather the independent type."

Fran gave him a motherly smile. "We don't mean for you to *work* at Macy's. Leave it to us."

There was a little music and dancing around eleven, but not so much noise that the neighbors might complain. Marj lived on the fourteenth floor (really the thirteenth) of a rather swank apartment house in the East Forties with round-the-clock doormen. Fran had only a 4 P.M. till midnight doorman, which meant it wasn't one hundred percent safe for her to arrive home after midnight, when she would have to use her downstairs key to get into her building. Thinking of this reminded her of Susie, whom she hadn't seen since her awful experience in the East Village about three weeks ago.

Fran found Susie, a tall, good-looking woman of about thirty-four, sitting on a double bed in an adjoining room, talking with Richard and Verie. Fran had first to say a few words to Verie, of course, about her billfold.

"I'd rather forget it," Verie said. "Part of the game. And the game's a rat race. We're surrounded by rats."

"Hear, hear!" said Richard. "But not everybody's a rat. There's always *us*!"

"That's right!" said Fran, feeling mellow now because she seldom drank alcohol, and what she had drunk was warming the cockles. "I was saying to Verie the other night, the most important thing in life is to communicate with people you love. Isn't it true?"

"True," said Richard.

"Y'know, when Verie called me up about her billfold—" Fran realized no one was listening, so she addressed Susie directly. "Susie, darling, are *you* recovering? Y'know, I haven't seen you since that thing in the East Village, but I heard about it." Of all the Network, Susie perhaps telephoned the least, and Fran hadn't even been treated to a firsthand account. It was Verie and Jeremy who'd filled Fran in.

"Oh, I'm all right," Susie said. "They thought my nose was broken, but it wasn't. Just this shaved spot on my head, and you can hardly see it now because it's growing out." Susie tipped her well-groomed head towards Fran so that Fran could see the shaved spot, nearly concealed, it was true, by billows of reddish-brown hair.

A pang went through Fran. "How many stitches?"

"Eight, I think," Susie said, smiling.

Susie and a friend, whom Susie had driven home in her, Susie's, car, had been attacked by a tall black as soon as Susie's friend had pulled out her front door key. They'd been trapped then between the outside door and the main locked door, the black had taken their money, wristwatches and rings ("Luckily the rings came off," Fran remembered Jeremy report-ing Susie as having said, "because some of them cut your fingers off if they can't get the rings off, and this fellow had a knife"), and then the black had told them both to get down on the floor for raping purposes, but meanwhile Susie, who was pretty tall, had been putting up a hell of a fight and wasn't about to get down on the floor. The other girl screamed, some-one who lived in the building finally heard them, and yelled back that he was going to call the police, whereupon the black ("maybe thinking the jig was up," Jeremy had said) pulled out some heavy instrument and whammed Susie over the head with it. Blood had spurted all over the walls and ceiling, and this was what had necessitated the stitches. Fran was thrilled that one of *them* had put up a real fight, unarmed, against the bar-barians.

"Something I'd rather forget," Susie said to Fran's wondering face. "I'm going to judo classes now, though. After all, we've got to live here."

"But nobody has to live in the *East Village,*" Fran said. "They've got everything there, y'know, blacks, Puerto Ricans, spicks, just name it. You don't see anybody *home* there late at night!"

By this time the big baked ham, the roast beef and potato salad on the buffet table had been well explored. Fran felt mellower than ever, sitting on a bed in one of Marj's two bedrooms (what elegance!) with several of the Network. They were talking about New York, what kept them here, besides the money. Richard was from Omaha, Jeremy from Boston. Fran had been born on Seventh Avenue and 53rd Street. "Before all those high buildings went up," Fran said. She considered her birthplace (now an office building) the heart of the city, though of course there could be other hearts of the city, if one thought about it: West 11th Street, Gramercy Park, even Yorkville. New York was exciting and dangerous, always changing—for the worse and for the better. Even Europe had to admit that New York was the art center of the world now. It was just too bad that the high welfare pay-ments attracted the worst of America, not always black or Puerto Rican by any means, just people who wanted to sponge. America's intentions were good. Just look at the Constitution that could stand up to anything, even Nixon, and come out winning. There was no doubt that America had *started out* right . . .

When Fran woke up the next morning, she didn't remember much about getting home, except she was sure that good old Susie had driven her home in her Cadillac (Susie was a model and made good money) and Fran thought Verie had been in the car too. Fran found in a pocket of her suit jacket, which she had not hung up last night, only put on the back of a chair, a note. "Fran dear, will call Carl at Tricolor in regard to Greg, so don't worry. Have told Jane. Love, Richard."

Wasn't that nice of Richard! "I knew he'd come up with something," Fran said softly to herself, smiling.

The telephone rang. Fran moved towards it, still in pajamas, and noticed by the clock on the coffee table that it was twenty past nine. "H'lo?" Fran murmured.

"Hi, dear, it's Jane. Greg can bring the pot roast up around eleven. All right?"

"Oh sure, I'll be here. Thanks, Jane." Fran vaguely remembered the promise of a pot roast. People were still giving her things to eat, as they had in her worst days when she'd been too incapacitated for shopping. "I thought Greg was awfully nice. He's really got character."

"He's seeing a friend of Richard's later this morning."

"Tricolor. I know. I'll keep my fingers crossed."

"Marj wants him to meet someone too. Nothing to do with Macy's proper, as I understand it," Jane said.

They talked for another few minutes, going over the party, and when she had hung up, Fran made some instant coffee and orange juice from a frozen tin. She folded her bed away, got dressed, all the while murmuring to herself such things as, "Did I take those arthritis pills yet? No, must do that . . . Tidy up a little. No, I suppose the place doesn't look bad . . ." And of course the telephone rang two or three times, delaying all these activities, so the next thing she knew there was a ring from downstairs, and Fran saw it was five past eleven.

Fran assumed it was Greg and pushed the release button. She hadn't a speaker through which she could talk to downstairs. When her apartment doorbell rang, Fran peeked through the round hole in the door and saw that it was Greg.

"Greg?"

"It's me," Greg said.

Fran opened the door.

Greg was carrying a heavy red casserole with a lid. "Jane said she wanted to leave it in this so you'd get all the juice."

"Just lovely, Greg. Thank you!" Fran said, taking it. "Your aunt Jane makes the most wonderful pot roasts, marinates them overnight, you know?" Fran deposited the casserole in her narrow kitchen. "Sit down, Greg. Would you like a cup of coffee?"

"No, thanks. I have a date in a few minutes." Greg wandered around the living room, looking at everything, wringing his hands.

"I wish you luck today, Greg. I offered to put you up, you know. I told Jane. Sounds ridiculous because she's got a bigger place. But if ever you're in this neck of the woods, I have a friend nearby I could stay with overnight. You could stay here. No trouble at all."

"I wish all of you wouldn't treat me like a kid," Greg said. "I'm going to take a furnished room. I like to be on my own."

"I understand. It's *normal*." But Fran didn't really understand. Separating himself from his *friends* like that? "I don't consider you a child, honestly!"

"It's enough to smother anybody. I hope you don't think I'm rude, saying that. It's like a clique—I mean the group last night."

Fran's polite, self-protective smile spread. She almost said, *All right, try it on your own,* but controlled herself for which she felt rather well-behaved and superior. "I know. You're a big boy."

"Not even a boy. I'm grown up." Greg nodded by way of affirmation or farewell, and went to the door. "Bye-bye, Fran, and I hope the roast is good."

"Luck, Greg!" she called after him, and heard him taking the stairs down. Six flights, there were.

Two days passed. Fran rang Jane to ask how Greg was doing.

Jane chuckled. "Not too well. He moved out—"

"Yes, he told me he was going to." Fran had of course telephoned Jane to say how good the pot roast was, but she hadn't mentioned Greg's saying he was going to move.

"Well, he got rolled the same night, night before last."

"Rolled?" Fran was horrified. "Was he hurt?"

"No, luckily. It was—"

"Where'd it happen?"

"Around Twenty-third and Third around one A.M. Greg said. He'd just come out of one of those bars that serve breakfast. I know he wasn't tight, because he hardly drinks even beer. Well, as he was walking to where his room is—"

"Where is his room?"

"Somewhere on East Nineteenth. Two fellows jumped on him and pulled his jacket up over his head, you know, sat him down the way they do elderly people on the sidewalk, and took what money he had. Fortunately he had only about twelve dollars on him, he said." Jane laughed softly again.

But Fran was pained deep within herself, as if the humiliating, sordid event had happened to a member of her own family. "The best thing is, if it teaches him a lesson. He can't walk the streets alone that late at night, even if he is young and strong."

"He said he fought back. He's got bruised ribs for his pains. But the worst is, he refused to see the man Marj wanted him to meet, another buyer who knows all kinds of cabinetmakers. Greg could've got some well-paying—finishing jobs at least."

It was unbelievable to Fran. "He's headed for failure," Fran announced solemnly.

Fran telephoned Jeremy to tell him about Greg. Jeremy was as surprised as Fran that Greg hadn't followed up Marj's introduction.

"Boy's got a lot to learn," Jeremy said. "Good thing he had just a few dollars on him this time. Maybe it won't happen again, if he's careful."

Fran assured Jeremy that that was what she'd told Jane. Fran's heart, unfulfilled by maternity, was suffering the most awful perturbations since Jane's news.

"I know a couple of painters in SoHo," Jeremy said. "I'm going to try there, ask if they need any cabinet work done. You know where I can reach Greg if I come up with something?"

"No, but I'm sure Jane'll know. He's somewhere on East Nineteenth Street."

A few minutes later, when they had hung up, Fran went out and walked a couple of blocks in order to deposit her disability check at her bank and to pick up a few things at the delicatessen supermarket downstairs, and when she got back, the telephone was ringing. She just made it before it logically should have stopped ringing, she thought, and found that it was Richard.

"The Tricolor people didn't have anything for Greg," Richard said. "I'm sorry about that, but I'll think of something else. How's he doing? Have you heard?"

Fran filled him in. She lit a cigarette and spoke long into the yellow telephone by the sofa, expressing her philosophy of no stone unturned, of not trying to be bigger than you really were. "I don't mean Greg's swellheaded. He's just so immature . . ." What she meant was that he *had* to come under their collective wing, that they mustn't let him escape, or rather fly away, to certain doom. "Maybe you should talk to him, Richard, man to man, you know? Maybe he'd listen, more than he listens to Jane."

On Friday, when Fran's cleaning woman came to do two hours in the apartment, Fran made a date to return Jane's iron casserole. Fran loved

Jane's apartment on West 11th. Jane had nice, knobby furniture always shining with polish, lots of books, and a real fireplace. Jane had made tea, and said something about spiking the second cup with vodka if they felt so inclined. When Fran asked how Greg was, Jane lifted a finger to her lips.

"Sh-h, he's in there," Jane whispered, pointing towards a bedroom door.

"Is he all right?"

"He's a little shook up. I don't think he wants to see anybody," Jane said with a quiet smile. Jane explained that just last night when Greg had gone back to his place after a late movie, he had found that his room had been broken into and everything stolen, his portable typewriter, his clothes, shoes, everything.

"How awful!" Fran whispered, leaning forward.

"I think what hurt him the most is losing his stud box with his father's cufflinks. My nephew—Greg's father—died two years ago, you know. And a ring or something that his girl friend in Allentown gave him. Greg's having a bad day."

"Oh, I can understand—"

"It's a shame, because I'd suggested that he leave anything valuable here with me, you know. This house has never had a robbery, knock wood." Jane did so.

"Does he—What does he want to do now?"

"He'll try again, I know. He's bloodied but unbowed."

"We've just got to help him."

Jane said nothing, but Fran could see that she was thinking too. Jane went and got the vodka bottle.

"I think the sun's sufficiently over the yardarm," Jane said.

How nice it was, Fran thought, to have friends like Jane.

The telephone rang. It was near the fireplace, and Fran could hear Jeremy's slightly husky voice asking Jane if she knew how he could reach Greg.

"He's here, but I think he's asleep. He's had a tough day. Can I take a message?"

Then Jeremy talked, Jane took a pencil, and she smiled. "Thanks so much, Jeremy. That does sound—rather ideal. I'll tell him as soon as he wakes up." When she had hung up, she said to Fran, "Jeremy found out that Paul Ridley in SoHo needs a lot of shelves put up right away—along a whole wall. You know how big those studios are down there. Sounds like Greg's dish."

"Good old Jeremy!"

"And Ridley—he's tops now. I bet it'll lead to other things—freelance. That's the way Greg wants to work."

"Let's hope he doesn't turn it down just because it came from *us*," Fran murmured.

"Ha! Maybe he's learned something. All the young have to learn." Jane swept her long, straight, graying hair back from her face and picked up her vodka.

Fran felt suddenly—civilized. That was the only word she could find for it. And strong. And solid. All because of people like Jane, all because of *communicating*. Fran went home in a glow. She took the bus up Eighth. The subway rattled just below the pavement outside her apartment building, a subway entrance was right there, but Fran never took the subway anymore. Buses were cleaner and safer, and often she bought "day excursions" as she and her friends called them, a ticket for three rides for seventy cents instead of a dollar ten, if you used it from 10 A.M. to 4 P.M., not in the rush hours. And one day a week the Museum of Modern Art was free, all you had to do was make a contribution, pay what you felt like, or pay nothing. Fran forced herself to wait two days before she telephoned Jane to ask how Greg had made out.

"My dear, it couldn't be better," Jane said in her drawling way. "He's got work lined up for the next six weeks and he's happy as a clam. He likes the informality down there. And I think the SoHo people like him too."

Fran smiled. "Tell him—Jane, you gotta give him my congratulations, would you? I don't care if he doesn't want my congratulations, tell him anyway." Fran laughed with joy.

The happy news about Greg even made Fran feel unworried and quite confident about the visit from the black Columbia Fire Insurance inspector due tomorrow morning at eleven. He worked for Columbia Fire, but Con Ed apparently employed Columbia Fire. Greg's success had given Fran a big charge of self-assurance.

Fran put on her limp the next morning, and admitted the black inspector to her clean and tidy apartment, even gave him a cup of coffee.

"Takes time," Fran said, "but the doctor says I'm doing as well as can be expected. Believe me, I'll tell Con Ed when I feel up to working again. It's not much fun doing nothing day after day." Work with the system, Fran was thinking. Don't try to buck it, let it work for you. All the money she was getting she'd put *in* in the past, so why not use it now, because how did she know she'd even be alive by the time—

"Okay, Miss Covak, could you sign this please? Then I'll be on my way—Glad you're feeling better."

What a relief—to be alone again! The phone rang. Verie. She told Verie about Greg. Then Fran cleared out and tidied her chest of drawers, which she'd meant to do for months. At 6 P.M. her doorbell rang, and Fran saw through the peephole that it was Buddy, her doorman, in visored cap and shirtsleeves as usual.

"Flowers, Miss Covak."

Fran opened the door. "Flowers?"

"Tha's right. Just delivered downstairs. Thought I'd bring 'em up. Got a birthday?"

"No." Fran was fussing around in the pockets of her coats in the front closet, looking for fifty cents to give Buddy. She found two quarters. "Thank you, Buddy. Aren't they pretty?" She could see pink blossoms through the green tissue.

"Bye now," said Buddy.

With the flowers was a small envelope with a note in it. Fran saw it was signed by Greg before she read the message. It said: "Sorry I was a little abrupt. Sure appreciate your kindness. Also of your friends. Best, Greg."

Fran hastened to get the long-stemmed gladioli into the tallest vase she had, set them on her glass-topped coffee table in front of the sofa, then made for the telephone to call Jeremy.

Fran said, "Jeremy! I think Greg's one of *us* now . . . Yeah, isn't it great?"

The Pond

Elinor Sievert stood looking down at the pond. She was half thinking, half dreaming, or imagining. Was it safe? For Chris? The agent had said it was four feet deep. It was certainly full of weeds, its surface nearly covered with algae or whatever they called the little oval green things that floated. Well, four feet was enough to drown a four-year-old. She must warn Chris.

She lifted her head and walked back towards the white, two-story house. She had just rented the house, and had been here only since yesterday. She hadn't entirely unpacked. Hadn't the agent said something about draining the pond, that it wouldn't be too difficult or expensive? Was there a spring under it? Elinor hoped not, because she'd taken the house for six months.

It was two in the afternoon, and Chris was having his nap. There were more kitchen cartons to unpack, also the record player in its neat, taped carton. Elinor fished the record player out, connected it, and chose an LP of New Orleans jazz to pick her up. She hoisted another load of dishes up to the long drainboard.

The doorbell rang.

Elinor was confronted by the smiling face of a woman about her own age.

"Hello. I'm Jane Caldwell—one of your neighbors. I just wanted to say hello and welcome. We're friends with Jimmy Adams, the agent, and he told us you'd moved in here."

"Yes. My name's Elinor Sievert. Won't you come in?" Elinor held the door wider. "I'm not quite unpacked as yet—but at least we could have a cup of coffee in the kitchen."

Within a few minutes, they were sitting on opposite sides of the wooden table, cups of instant coffee before them. Jane said she had two children, a boy and a girl, the girl just starting school, and that her husband was an architect and worked in Hartford.

"What brought you to Luddington?" Jane asked.

"I needed a change—from New York. I'm a freelance journalist, so I thought I'd try a few months in the country. At least I call this the country, compared to New York."

"I can understand that. I heard about your husband," Jane said on a more serious note. "I'm sorry. Especially since you have a small son. I want you to know we're a friendly batch around here, and at the same time we'll let you alone, if that's what you want. But consider Ed and me neighbors, and if you need something, just call on us."

"Thank you," Elinor said. She remembered that she'd told Adams that her husband had recently died, because Adams had asked if her husband would be living with her. Now Jane was ready to go, not having finished her coffee.

"I know you've got things to do, so I don't want to take any more of your time," said Jane. She had rosy cheeks, chestnut hair. "I'll give you Ed's business card, but it's got our home number on it too. If you want to ask any kind of question, just call us. We've been here six years—Where's your little boy?"

"He's—"

As if on cue, Chris called, "Mommy!" from the top of the stairs.

Elinor jumped up. "Come down, Chris! Meet a nice new neighbor!"

Chris came down the stairs a bit timidly, holding on to the banister.

Jane stood beside Elinor at the foot of the staircase. "Hello, Chris. My name's Jane. How are you?"

Chris's blue eyes examined her seriously. "Hello."

Elinor smiled. "I think he just woke up and doesn't know where he is. Say 'How do you do,' Chris."

"How do you do," said Chris.

"Hope you'll like it here, Chris," Jane said. "I want you to meet my boy Bill. He's just your age. Bye-bye, Elinor. Bye, Chris!" Jane went out the front door.

Elinor gave Chris his glass of milk and his treat—today a bowl of apple sauce. Elinor was against chocolate cupcakes every afternoon, though Chris at the moment thought they were the greatest things ever invented. "Wasn't she nice? Jane?" Elinor said, finishing her coffee.

"Who is she?"

"One of our new neighbors." Elinor continued her unpacking. Her article-in-progress was about self-help with legal problems. She would need to go to the Hartford library, which had a newspaper department, for more research. Hartford was only a half hour away. Elinor had bought a good secondhand car. Maybe Jane would know a girl who could baby-sit now and then. "Isn't it nicer here than in New York?"

Chris lifted his blond head. "I want to go outside."

"But of course! It's so sunny, you won't need a sweater. We've got a garden, Chris! We can plant—radishes, for instance." She remembered planting radishes in her grandmother's garden when she was small, remembered the joy of pulling up the fat red and white edible roots. "Come on, Chris." She took his hand.

Chris's slight frown went away, and he gripped his mother's hand.

Elinor looked at the garden with different eyes, Chris's eyes. Plainly no one had tended it for months. There were big prickly weeds between the jonquils that were beginning to open, and the peonies hadn't been cut last year. But there was an apple tree big enough for Chris to climb in.

"Our garden," Elinor said. "Nice and sloppy. All yours to play in, Chris, and the summer's just beginning."

"How big is this?" Chris asked. He had broken away and was stooped by the pond.

Elinor knew he meant how deep was it. "I don't know. Not very deep. But don't go wading. It's not like the seashore with sand. It's all muddy there." Elinor spoke quickly. Anxiety had struck her like a physical pain. Was she still reliving the impact of Cliff's plane against the mountainside—that mountain in Yugoslavia that she'd never see? She'd seen two or three newspaper photographs of it, blotchy black and white chaos, indicating, so the print underneath said, the wreckage of the airliner on which there had been no survivors of one hundred and seven passengers plus eight crewmen and stewardesses. No survivors. And Cliff among them. Elinor had always thought air crashes happened to strangers, never to anyone you knew, never even to a friend of a friend. Suddenly it had been Cliff, on an ordinary flight from Ankara. He'd been to Ankara at least seven times before.

"Is that a snake? Look, Mommy!" Chris yelled, leaning forward as he spoke. One foot sank, his arms shot forward for balance, and suddenly he was in water up to his hips. "Ugh! Ha-ha!" He rolled sideways on the muddy edge, and squirmed backward up to the level of the lawn before his mother could reach him.

Elinor set him on his feet. "Chris, I told you not to try wading! Now you'll need a bath. You see?"

"No, I won't!" Chris yelled, laughing, and ran off across the grass, bare legs and sandals flying, as if the muddy damp on his shorts had given him a special charge.

Elinor had to smile. Such energy! She looked down at the pond. The brown and black mud swirled, stirring long tentacles of vines, making the algae undulate. It was a good seven feet in diameter, the pond. A vine had clung to Chris's ankle as she'd pulled him up. Nasty! The vines were even growing out onto the grass to a length of three feet or more.

Before 5 P.M., Elinor rang the rental agent. She asked if it would be all right with the house-owner if she had the pond drained. Price wasn't of much concern to her, but she didn't tell Mr. Adams that.

"It might seep up again," said Mr. Adams. "The land's pretty low. Especially when it rains and—"

"I really don't mind trying it. It might help," Elinor said. "You know how it is with a small child. I have the feeling it isn't quite safe."

Mr. Adams said he would telephone a company tomorrow morning. "Even this afternoon, if I can reach them."

Mr. Adams telephoned back in ten minutes and told Elinor that the workmen would arrive the next morning, probably quite early.

The workmen came at 8 A.M. After speaking with the two men, Elinor took Chris with her in the car to the library in Hartford. She deposited Chris in the children's book section, and told the woman in charge there that she would be back in an hour for Chris, and in case he got restless, she would be in the newspaper archives.

When she and Chris got back home, the pond was empty but muddy. If anything, it looked worse, uglier. It was a crater of wet mud laced with green vines, some as thick as a cigarette. The depression in the garden was hardly four feet deep. But how deep was the mud?

"I'm sorry," said Chris, gazing down.

Elinor laughed. "Sorry?—The pond's not the only thing to play with. Look at the trees we've got! What about the seeds we bought? What do you say we clear a patch and plant some carrots and radishes—now."

Elinor changed into blue jeans. The clearing of weeds and the planting took longer than she had thought it would, nearly two hours. She worked with a fork and a trowel, both a bit rusty, which she'd found in the toolshed behind the house. Chris drew a bucket of water from the outside faucet and lugged it over, but while she and Chris were putting the seeds carefully in, one inch deep, a roll of thunder crossed the heavens. The sun had vanished. Within seconds, rain was pelting down, big drops that made them run for the house.

"Isn't that wonderful? Look!" Elinor held Chris up so he could see out of a kitchen window. "We don't need to water our seeds. Nature's doing it for us."

"Who's nature?"

Elinor smiled, tired now. "Nature rules everything. Nature knows best. The garden's going to look fresh and new tomorrow."

The following morning, the garden did look rejuvenated, the grass greener, the scraggly rose bushes more erect. The sun was shining again. And Elinor had her first letter. It was from Cliff's mother in Evanston. It said:

Dearest Elinor,

We both hope you are feeling more cheerful in your Connecticut house. Do drop us a line or telephone us when you find the time, but we know you are busy getting settled, not to mention getting back to your own work. We send you all good wishes for success with your next articles, and you must keep us posted.

The Polaroid shots of Chris in his bath are a joy to us! You mustn't say he looks more like Cliff than you. He looks like both of you . . .

The letter lifted Elinor's spirits. She went out to see if the carrot and radish seeds had been beaten to the surface by the rain—in which case she meant to push them down again if she could see them—but the first thing that caught her eye was Chris, stooped again by the pond and poking at something with a stick. And the second thing she noticed was that the pond was full again. Almost as high as ever! Well, naturally, because of the hard rain. Or was it natural? It had to be. Maybe there was a spring below. Anyway, she thought, why should she pay for the draining if it didn't stay drained? She'd have to ring the company today. Miller Brothers, it was called.

"Chris? What're you up to?"

"Frog!" he yelled back. "I *think* I saw a frog."

"Well, don't try to catch it!" Damn the weeds! They were back in full force, as if the brief draining had done them good. Elinor went to the toolshed. She thought she remembered seeing a pair of hedge clippers on the cement floor there.

Elinor found the clippers, rusted, and though she was eager to attack the vines, she forced herself to go to the kitchen first and put a couple of drops of salad oil on the center screw of the clippers. Then she went out and started on the long, grapevine-like stems. The clippers were dull, but better than nothing, faster than scissors.

"What're you doing that for?" Chris asked.

"They're nasty *things,*" Elinor said. "Clogging the pond. We don't want a messy pond, do we?" *Whack-whack!* Elinor's espadrilles sank into the wet bank. What on earth did the owners, or the former tenants, use the pond for? Goldfish? Ducks?

A carp, Elinor thought suddenly. If the pond was going to stay a pond, then a carp was the thing to clean it, nibble at some of the vegetation. She'd buy one.

"If you ever fall in, Chris—"

"What?" Chris, still stooped, on the other side of the pond now, flung his stick away.

"For goodness' sake, don't fall in, but if you do—" Elinor forced herself to go on "—grab hold of these vines. You see? They're strong and growing from the edges. Pull yourself out by them." Actually, the vines seemed to be growing from underwater as well, and pulling at those might send Chris into the pond.

Chris grinned, sideways. "That's not deep. Not even deep as I am."

Elinor said nothing.

The rest of that morning she worked on her law article, then telephoned Miller Brothers.

"Well, the ground's a little low there, ma'am. Not to mention the old cesspool's nearby and it still gets the drain from the kitchen sink, even though the toilets've been put on the mains. We know that house. Pond'll get it too if you've got a washing machine in the kitchen."

Elinor hadn't. "You mean, draining it is hopeless."

"That's about the size of it."

Elinor tried to force her anger down. "Then I don't know why you agreed to do it."

"Because you seemed set on it, ma'am."

They hung up a few seconds later. What was she going to do about the bill when they presented it? She'd perhaps make them knock it down a bit. But she felt the situation was inconclusive. Elinor hated that.

While Chris was taking his nap, Elinor made a quick trip to Hartford, found a fish shop, and brought back a carp in a red plastic bucket which she had taken with her in the car. The fish flopped about in a vigorous way, and Elinor drove slowly, so the bucket wouldn't tip over. She went at once to the pond, and poured the fish in.

It was a fat, silvery carp. Its tail flicked the surface as it dove, then it rose and dove again, apparently happy in wider seas. Elinor smiled. The carp would surely eat some of the vines, the algae. She'd give it bread too. Carps could eat anything. Cliff had used to say there was nothing like carp to keep a pond or a lake clean. Above all, Elinor liked the idea that there was something *alive* in the pond besides vines. She started to walk back to the house, and found that a vine had encircled her left ankle. When she tried to kick her foot free, the vine tightened. She stooped and unwound it. That was one she hadn't whacked this morning. Or had it grown ten inches since this morning? Impossible. But now as she looked down at the pond and at its border, she couldn't see that she had accomplished much, even though she'd fished out quite a heap. The heap was a few feet away on the grass, in case she doubted it. Elinor blinked. She had the feeling that if she watched the pond closely, she'd be able to see the tentacles growing. She didn't like that idea.

Should she tell Chris about the carp? Elinor didn't want him trying to find it, poking into the water. On the other hand, if she didn't mention it, maybe he'd see it and have some crazy idea of catching it. Better to tell him, she decided.

So when Chris woke up, Elinor told him about the fish.

"You can toss some bread to him," Elinor said. "But don't try to catch him, because he likes the pond. He's going to help us keep it clean."

"You don't want ever to catch him?" Chris asked, with milk all over his upper lip.

He was thinking of Cliff, Elinor knew. Cliff had loved fishing. "We don't catch this one, Chris. He's our friend."

Elinor worked. She had set up her typewriter in a front corner room upstairs which had light from two windows. The article was coming along nicely. She had a lot of original material from newspaper clippings. The theme was alerting the public to free legal advice from small claims offices which most people didn't know existed. Lots of people let sums like $250 go by the board, because they thought it wasn't worth the trouble of a court fight. Elinor worked until 6:30. Dinner was simple tonight, macaroni and cheese with bacon, one of Chris's favorite dishes. With the dinner in the oven, Elinor took a quick bath and put on blue slacks and a fresh blouse. She paused to look at the photograph of Cliff on the dressing table—a photograph in a silver frame which had been a present from

Cliff's parents one Christmas. It was an ordinary black and white enlargement, Cliff sitting on the bank of a stream, propped against a tree, an old straw hat tipped back on his head. That had been taken somewhere outside Evanston, on one of their summer trips to visit his parents. Cliff held a straw or a blade of grass lazily between his lips. His denim shirt was open at the neck. No one, looking at the hillbilly image, would imagine that Cliff had had to dress up in white tie a couple of times a month in Paris, Rome, London or Ankara. Cliff had been in the diplomatic service, assistant or deputy to American statesmen, gifted in languages, gifted in tact. He'd known how to use a pistol also, and once a month in New York he'd gone to a certain armory for practice. What had he done exactly? Elinor knew only sketchy anecdotes that Cliff had told her. He had done enough, however, to be paid a good salary, to be paid to keep silent, even to her. It had crossed her mind that his plane was wrecked to kill him, but she was sure that was absurd. Cliff hadn't been that important. His death had been an accident, not due to the weather but to a mechanical failure in the plane.

What would Cliff think of the pond? Elinor smiled wryly. Would he have it filled in with stones, turn it into a rock garden? Would he fill it in with earth? Would he pay no attention at all to the pond? Just call it "nature?"

Two days later, when Elinor was typing a final draft of her article, she stopped at noon and went out into the garden for some fresh air. She'd brought the kitchen scissors, and she cut two red roses and one white rose to put on the table at lunch. Then the pond caught her eye, a blaze of chartreuse in the sunlight.

"Good Lord!" she whispered.

The vines! The weeds! They were all over the surface. And they were again climbing onto the land. Well, this was one thing she could and would see about: she'd find an exterminator. She didn't care what poison they put down in the pond, if they could clear it. And of course she'd rescue the carp first, keep him in a bucket till the pond was safe again.

An exterminator was something Jane Caldwell might know about.

Elinor telephoned Jane before she started lunch. "This *pond,*" Elinor began and stopped, because she had so much to say about it. "I had it drained a few days ago, and now it's filled up again . . . No, that's not really the problem. I've given up the draining, it's the unbelievable vines. The way they grow! I wonder if you know a weed-killing company? I think it'll take professional—I mean, I don't think I can just toss some liquid poison in and get anywhere. You'll have to see this pond to believe it. It's like a jungle!"

"I know just the right people," Jane said. "They're called 'Weed-Killer,' so it's easy to remember. You've got a phone book there?"

Elinor had. Jane said Weed-Killer was very obliging and wouldn't make her wait a week before they turned up.

"How about you and Chris coming over for tea this afternoon?" Jane asked. "I just made a coconut cake."

"Love to. Thank you." Elinor felt cheered.

She made lunch for herself and Chris, and told him they were invited to tea at the house of their neighbor Jane, and that he'd meet a boy called Bill. After lunch, Elinor looked up Weed-Killer in the telephone book and rang them.

"It's a lot of weeds in a pond," Elinor said. "Can you deal with that?"

The man assured her they were experts at weeds in ponds, and promised to come the following morning. Elinor wanted to work for an hour or so until it was time to go to Jane's, but she felt compelled to catch the carp now, or to try to. If she failed, she'd tell the men about it tomorrow, and probably they'd have a net on a long handle and could catch it. Elinor took her vegetable sieve which had a handle some ten inches long, and also some pieces of bread.

Not seeing the carp, Elinor tossed the bread onto the surface. Some pieces floated, others sank and were trapped among the vines. Elinor circled the pond, her sieve ready. She had half filled the plastic bucket and it sat on the bank.

Suddenly she saw the fish. It was horizontal and motionless, a couple of inches under the surface. It was dead, she realized, and kept from the surface only by the vines that held it under. Dead from what? The water didn't look dirty, in fact was rather clear. What could kill a carp? Cliff had always said—

Elinor's eyes were full of tears. Tears for the carp? Nonsense. Tears of frustration, maybe. She stooped and tried to reach the carp with the sieve. The sieve was a foot short, and she wasn't going to muddy her tennis shoes by wading in. Not now. Best to work a bit this afternoon, and let the workmen lift it out tomorrow.

"What're you doing, Mommy?" Chris came trotting towards her.

"Nothing. I'm going to work a little now. I thought you were watching TV."

"It's no good. Where's the fish?"

Elinor took his wrist, swung him around. "The fish is fine. Now come back and we'll try the TV again." Elinor tried to think of something else that might amuse him. It wasn't one of his napping days, obviously. "Tell you what, Chris, you choose one of your toys to take to Bill. Make him a present. All right?"

"One of *my* toys?"

Elinor smiled. Chris was generous by nature and she meant to nurture this trait. "Yes, one of yours. Even one you like—like your paratrooper. Or one of your books. You choose it. Bill's going to be your friend, and you want to start out right, don't you?"

"Yes." And Chris seemed to be pondering already, going over his store of goodies in his room upstairs.

Elinor locked the back door with its bolt, which was on a level with her eyes. She didn't want Chris going into the garden, maybe seeing the carp. "I'll be in my room, and I'll see you at four. You might put on a clean pair of jeans at four—if you remember to."

Elinor worked, and quite well. It was pleasant to have a tea date to look forward to. Soon, she thought, she'd ask Jane and her husband for drinks. She didn't want people to think she was a melancholy widow. It had been three months since Cliff's death. Elinor thought she'd got over the worst of her grief in those first two weeks, the weeks of shock. Had she really? For the past six weeks she'd been able to work. That was something. Cliff's insurance plus his pension made her financially comfortable, but she needed to work to be happy.

When she glanced at her watch, it was ten to four. "Chrissy!" Elinor called to her half-open door. "Changed your jeans?"

She pushed open Chris's door across the hall. He was not in his room, and there were more toys and books on the floor than usual, indicating that Chris had been trying to select something to give Bill. Elinor went downstairs where the TV was still murmuring, but Chris wasn't in the living room. Nor was he in the kitchen. She saw that the back door was still bolted. Chris wasn't on the front lawn either. Of course he could have gone to the garden via the front door. Elinor unbolted the kitchen door and went out.

"Chris?" She glanced everywhere, then focused on the pond. She had seen a light-colored patch in its center. *"Chris!"* She ran.

He was face down, feet out of sight, blond head nearly submerged. Elinor plunged in, up to her knees, her thighs, seized Chris's legs and pulled him out, slipped, sat down in the water and got soaked as high as her breasts. She struggled to her feet, holding Chris by the waist. Shouldn't she try to let the water run out of his mouth? Elinor was panting.

She turned Chris onto his stomach, gently lifted his small body by the waist, hoping water would run from his nose and mouth, but she was too frantic to look. He was limp, soft in a way that frightened her. She pressed his rib cage, released it, raised him a little again. One had to do artificial respiration methodically, counting, she remembered. She did this. *Fifteen . . . sixteen . . .* Someone should be telephoning for a doctor. She couldn't do two things at once.

"*Help!*" she yelled. "Help me, *please!*" Could the people next door hear? The house was twenty yards away, and was anybody home?

She turned Chris over and pressed her mouth to his cool lips. She blew in, then released his ribs, trying to catch a gasp from him, a cough that would mean life again. He remained limp. She turned him on his stomach and resumed the artificial respiration. It was now or never, she knew. Senseless to waste time carrying him into the house for warmth. He could've been lying in the pond for an hour—in which case, she knew it was hopeless.

Elinor picked her son up and carried him towards the house. She went into the kitchen. There was a sagging sofa against the wall, and she put him there.

Then she telephoned Jane Caldwell, whose number was on the card by the telephone where Elinor had left it days ago. Since Elinor didn't know a doctor in the vicinity, it made as much sense to call Jane as to search for a doctor's name.

"Hello, *Jane!*" Elinor said, her voice rising wildly. "I think Chris's drowned!—Yes! *Yes!* Can you get a doctor? Right away?" Suddenly the line was dead. Elinor hung up and went at once to Chris, started the rib-pressing again, Chris prone on the sofa with his face turned to one side. The activity soothed her a little.

The doorbell rang, and at the same time Elinor heard the latch of the door being opened. Then Jane called:

"Elinor?"

"In the kitchen!"

The doctor had dark hair and spectacles. He lifted Chris a little, felt for a pulse. "How long—how long was he . . ."

"I don't know. I was working upstairs. It was the pond in the garden."

The rest was confused to Elinor. She barely realized when the needle went into her own arm, though this was the most definite sensation she had for several minutes. Jane made tea. Elinor had a cup in front of her. When she looked at the sofa, Chris was not there.

"Where is he?" Elinor asked.

Jane gripped Elinor's hand. She sat opposite Elinor. "The doctor took Chris to the hospital. Chris is in good hands, you can be sure of that. This doctor delivered Bill. He's our doctor."

But from Jane's tone, Elinor knew it was all useless, and that Jane knew this too. Elinor's eyes drifted from Jane's face. She noticed a book lying on the cane bottom of the chair beside her. Chris had chosen his dotted numbers book to give to Bill, a book that Chris rather liked. He wasn't half through doing the drawings. Chris could count and he was doing quite well at reading too. *I wasn't doing so well at his age, I think,* Cliff had said not long ago.

Elinor began to weep.

"That's good. That's good for you," Jane said. "I'll stay here with you. Pretty soon we'll hear from the hospital. Maybe you want to lie down, Elinor?—I've got to make a phone call."

The sedative was taking effect. Elinor sat in a daze on the sofa, her head back against a pillow. The telephone rang and Jane took it. The hospital, Elinor supposed. She watched Jane's face, and knew. Elinor nodded her head, trying to spare Jane any words, but Jane said:

"They tried. I'm sure they did everything possible."

Jane said she would stay the night. She said she had arranged for Ed to pick up Bill at a house where she'd left him.

In the morning, Weed-Killer came, and Jane asked Elinor if she still wanted the job done.

"I thought you might've decided to move," Jane said.

Had she said that? Possibly. "But I do want it done."

The two Weed-Killer men got to work.

Jane made another telephone call, then told Elinor that a friend of hers called Millie was coming over at noon. When Millie arrived, Jane prepared a lunch of bacon and eggs for the three of them. Millie had blonde curly hair, blue eyes, and was very cheerful and sympathetic.

"I went by the doctor's," Millie said, "and his nurse gave me these pills for you. They're slightly sedative. He thinks they'd be good for you. Two a day, one before lunch, one before bedtime. So have one now."

They hadn't started lunch. Elinor took one. The workmen were just departing, and one man stuck his head in the door to say with a smile:

"All finished, ma'am. You shouldn't have any trouble any more."

During lunch, Elinor said, "I've got to see about the funeral."

"We'll help you. Don't think about it now," Jane said. "Try to eat a little."

Elinor ate a little, then slept on the sofa in the kitchen. She hadn't wanted to go up to her own bed. When she woke up, Millie was sitting in the wicker armchair, reading a book.

"Feeling better? Want some tea?"

"In a minute. You're awfully kind. I do thank you very much." She stood up. "I want to see the pond." She saw Millie's look of uneasiness. "They killed those vines today. I'd like to see what it looks like."

Millie went out with her. Elinor looked down at the pond and had the satisfaction of seeing that no vines lay on the surface, that some pieces of them had sunk like drowned things. Around the edge of the pond were stubs of vines already turning yellow and brownish, wilting. Before her eyes, one cropped tentacle curled sideways and down, as if in the throes of death. A primitive joy went through her, a sense of vengeance, of a wrong righted.

"It's a nasty pond," Elinor said to Millie. "It killed a carp. Can you imagine? I've never heard of a carp being—"

"I know. They must've been growing like blazes! But they're certainly finished now." Millie held out her hand for Elinor to take. "Don't think about it now."

Millie wanted to go back to the house. Elinor did not take her hand, but she came with Millie. "I'm feeling better. You mustn't give up all your time to me. It's very nice of you, since you don't even know me. But I've got to face my problems alone."

Millie made some polite reply.

Elinor really was feeling better. She'd have to go through the funeral next, Chris's funeral, but she sensed in herself a backbone, morale—whatever it was called. After the service for Chris—surely it would be simple—she'd invite her new neighbors, few as they might be, to her house for coffee or drinks or both. Food too. Elinor realized that her spirits had picked up because the pool was vanquished. She'd have it filled in with stones, with the agent's and also the owner's permission of course. Why should she retreat from the house? With stones showing just above the water, it would look every bit as pretty, maybe prettier, and it wouldn't be dangerous for the next child who came to live here.

The service for Chris was at a small local church. The preacher conducted a short, nondenominational ceremony. And afterwards, around noon, Elinor did have eight or ten people to the house for coffee, drinks and sandwiches. The strangers seemed to enjoy it. Elinor even heard a few laughs among the group which gladdened her heart. She hadn't as yet, rung up any of her New York friends to tell them about Chris. Elinor realized that some people might think that "strange" of her, but she felt that it would only sadden her friends to tell them, that it would look like a plea for sympathy. Better the strangers here who knew no grief, because they didn't know her or Chris.

"You must be sure and get enough rest in the next days," said a kindly, middle-aged woman whose husband stood solemnly beside her. "We all think you've been awfully brave . . ."

Elinor gave Jane the dotted numbers book to take to Bill.

That night Elinor did sleep more than twelve hours and awoke feeling better and calmer. Now she began to write the letters that she had to, to Cliff's parents, to her own mother and father, and to three good friends in New York. She finished typing her article. The next morning, she walked to the post office and sent off her letters, and also her article to her agent in New York. She spent the rest of the day sorting out Chris's clothing, his books and toys, and she washed some of his clothes with a view to passing them on to Jane for Bill, providing Jane wouldn't think it unlucky. Elinor didn't think Jane would think that. Jane telephoned in the afternoon to ask how she was.

"Is anyone coming to see you? From New York? A friend, I mean?"

Elinor explained that she'd written to a few people, but she wasn't expecting anyone. "I'm really feeling all right, Jane. You mustn't worry."

By evening, Elinor had a neat carton of clothing ready to offer Jane, two more cartons of books and one of toys. If the clothes didn't fit Bill, then Jane might know a child they would fit. Elinor felt better for that. It was a lot better than collapsing in grief, she thought. Of course it was awful, a tragedy that didn't happen every day—losing a husband and a child in hardly more than three months. But Elinor was not going to succumb to it. She'd stay out the six months in the house here, come to terms with her loss, and emerge strong, someone able to give something to other people, not merely take.

She had two ideas for future articles. Which to do first? She decided to walk out into the garden, let her thoughts ramble. Maybe the radishes had come up? She'd have a look at the pond. Maybe it would be glassy smooth and clear. She must ask the Weed-Killer people when it would be safe to put in another carp—or two carps.

When she looked at the pond, she gave a short gasp. The vines had come *back*. They looked stronger than ever—not really longer, but more dense. Even as she watched, one tentacle, then a second actually moved, curved towards the land and seemed to grow an inch. That hadn't been due to the wind. The vines were growing visibly. Another green shoot poked its head above the water's surface. Elinor watched, fascinated, as if she beheld animate things, like snakes. Every inch or so along the vines a small green leaf sprouted, and Elinor was sure she could see some of these unfurling. The water looked clean, but she knew that was deceptive. The water was somehow poisonous. It had killed a carp. It had killed Chris. And she could still detect, she thought, the rather acid smell of the stuff the Weed-Killer men had put in.

There must be such a thing as digging the roots out, Elinor thought, even if Weed-Killer's stuff had failed. Elinor got the fork from the toolshed, and she took the clippers also. She thought of getting her rubber boots from the house, but was too eager to start to bother with them. She began by hacking all round the edge with the clippers. Some fresh vine ends cruised over the pond and jammed themselves amid other growing vines. The stems now seemed tough as plastic clotheslines, as if the herbicide had fortified them. Some had put down roots in the grass quite a distance from the pond. Elinor dropped the clippers and seized the fork. She had to dig deep to get at the roots, and when she finally pulled with her hands, the stems broke, leaving some roots still in the soil. Her right foot slipped, she went down on her left knee and struggled up again, both legs wet now. She was not going to be defeated.

As she sank the fork in, she saw Cliff's handsome, subtly smiling eyes in the photograph in the bedroom, Cliff with the blade of grass or hay between his lips, and he seemed to be nodding ever so slightly, approving. Her arms began to ache, her hands grew tired. She lost her right shoe in dragging her foot out of the water yet again, and she didn't bother trying to recover it. Then she slipped again, and sat down, water up to her waist now. Tired, angry, she still worked with the fork, trying to prize roots loose, and the water churned with a muddy fury. She might even be doing the damned roots good, she thought. Aerating them or something. Were they invincible? Why should they be? The sun poured down, overheating her, bringing nourishment to the green, Elinor knew.

Nature knows. That was Cliff's voice in her ears. Cliff sounded happy and at ease.

Elinor was half blinded by tears. Or was it sweat? *Chun-nk* went her fork. In a moment, when her arms gave out, she'd cross to the other side of the pond and attack that. She'd got some out. She'd make Weed-Killer come again, maybe pour kerosene on the pond and light it.

She got up on cramped legs and stumbled around to the other side. The sun warmed her shoulders though her feet were cold. In those few seconds that she walked, her thoughts and her attitude changed, though she was not at once aware of this. It was neither victory nor defeat that she felt. She sank the fork in again, again slipped and recovered. Again roots slid between the tines of the fork, and were not removed. A tentacle thicker than most moved towards her and circled her right ankle. She kicked, and the vine tightened, and she fell forward.

She went face down into the water, but the water seemed soft. She struggled a little, turned to breathe, and a vine tickled her neck. She saw Cliff nodding again, smiling his kindly, knowing, almost imperceptible smile. It was nature. It was Cliff. It was Chris. A vine crept around her arm—loose or attached to the earth she neither knew nor cared. She breathed in, and much of what she took in was water. *All things come from water,* Cliff had said once. Little Chris smiled at her with both corners of his mouth upturned. She saw him stooped by the pond, reaching for the dead carp which floated out of range of his twig. Then Chris lifted his face again and smiled.

Something You
Have to Live With

"Don't forget to lock all the doors," Stan said. "Someone might think
because the car's gone, nobody's home."

"All the doors? You mean two. You haven't asked me anything—
aesthetic, such as how the place looks now."

Stan laughed. "I suppose the pictures are all hung and the books are in
the shelves."

"Well, not quite, but your shirts and sweaters—and the kitchen. It
looks—I'm happy, Stan. So is Cassie. She's walking around the place
purring. See you tomorrow morning then. Around eleven, you said?"

"Around eleven. I'll bring stuff for lunch, don't worry."

"Love to your mom. I'm glad she's better."

"Thanks, darling." Stan hung up.

Cassie, their ginger and white cat aged four, sat looking at Ginnie as if
she had never seen a telephone before. Purring again. Dazed by all the
space, Ginnie thought. Cassie began kneading the rug in an ecstasy of contentment, and Ginnie laughed.

Ginnie and Stan Brixton had bought a house in Connecticut after six
years of New York apartments. Their furniture had been here for a week
while they wound things up in New York, and yesterday had been the final
move of smaller things like silverware, some dishes, a few pictures, suitcases, kitchen items and the cat. Stan had taken their son Freddie this
morning to spend the night in New Hope, Pennsylvania, where Stan's
mother lived. His mother had had a second heart attack and was recuper-
ating at home. "Every time I see her, I think it may be the last. You don't
mind if I go, do you, Ginnie? It'll keep Freddie out of the way while you're
fiddling around." Ginnie hadn't minded.

Fiddling around was Stan's term for organizing and even cleaning. Ginnie thought she had done a good job since Stan and Freddie had taken off this morning. The lovely French blue and white vase which reminded Ginnie of Monet's paintings stood on the living room bookcase now, even bearing red roses from the garden. Ginnie had made headway in the kitchen, installing things the way she wanted them, the way they would remain. Cassie had her litter pan ("What a euphemism, litter ought to mean a bed," Stan said) in the downstairs john corner. They now had an upstairs bathroom also. The house was on a hill with no other houses around it for nearly a mile, not that they owned all the land around, but the land around was farmland. When she and Stan had seen the place in June, sheep and goats had been grazing not far away. They had both fallen in love with the house.

Stanley Brixton was a novelist and fiction critic, and Ginnie wrote articles and was now half through her second novel. Her first had been published but had had only modest success. You couldn't expect a smash hit with a first novel, Stan said, unless the publicity was extraordinary. Water under the bridge. Ginnie was more interested in her novel-in-progress. They had a mortgage on the house, and with her and Stan's freelance work they thought they could be independent of New York, at least independent of nine-to-five jobs. Stan had already published three books, adventure stories with a political slant. He was thirty-two and for three years had been overseas correspondent for a newspaper syndicate.

Ginnie picked up a piece of heavy twine from the living room rug, and realized that her back hurt a little from the day's exertions. She had thought of switching on the TV, but the news was just over, she saw from her watch, and it might be better to go straight to bed and get up earlyish in the morning.

"Cassie?"

Cassie replied with a courteous, sustained, "M–wah–h?"

"Hungry?" Cassie knew the word. "No, you've had enough. Do you know you're getting middle-aged spread? Come on. Going up to bed with me?" Ginnie went to the front door, which was already locked by its automatic lock, but she put the chain on also. Yawning, she turned out the downstairs lights and climbed the stairs. Cassie followed her.

Ginnie had a quick bath, second of the day, pulled on a nightgown, brushed her teeth and got into bed. She at once realized she was too tired to pick up one of the English weeklies, political and Stan's favorites, which she had dropped by the bed to look at. She put out the lamp. *Home.* She and Stan had spent one night here last weekend during the big move. This was the first night she had been alone in the house, which still had no name. *Something like White Elephant maybe,* Stan had said. *You think of something.* Ginnie tried to think, an activity which made her instantly sleepier.

She was awakened by a crunching sound, like that of car tires on gravel. She raised up a little in bed. Had she heard it? Their driveway hadn't any gravel to speak of, just unpaved earth. But—

Wasn't that a *click*? From somewhere. Front, back? Or had it been a twig falling on the roof?

She had locked the doors, hadn't she?

Ginnie suddenly realized that she had not locked the back door. For another minute, as Ginnie listened, everything was silent. What a bore to go downstairs again! But she thought she had better do it, so she could honestly tell Stan that she had. Ginnie found the lamp switch and got out of bed.

By now she was thinking that any noise she had heard had been imaginary, something out of a dream. But Cassie followed her in a brisk, anxious way, Ginnie noticed.

The glow from the staircase light enabled Ginnie to find her way to the kitchen, where she switched on the strong ceiling light. She went at once to the back door and turned the Yale bolt. Then she listened. All was silent. The big kitchen looked exactly the same with its half modern, half old-fashioned furnishings—electric stove, big white wooden cupboard with drawers below, shelves above, double sink, a huge new fridge.

Ginnie went back upstairs, Cassie still following. Cassie was short for Cassandra, a name Stan had given her when she had been a kitten, because she had looked gloomy, unshakably pessimistic. Ginnie was drifting off to sleep again, when she heard a bump downstairs, as if someone had staggered slightly. She switched on the bedside lamp again, and a thrust of fear went through her when she saw Cassie rigidly crouched on the bed with her eyes fixed on the open bedroom door.

Now there was another bump from downstairs, and the unmistakable rustle of a drawer being slid out, and it could be only the dining room drawer where the silver was.

She had locked someone in with her!

Her first thought was to reach for the telephone and get the police, but the telephone was downstairs in the living room.

Go down and face it and threaten him with something—or them, she told herself. Maybe it was an adolescent kid, just a local kid who'd be glad to get off unreported, if she scared him a little. Ginnie jumped out of bed, put on Stan's bathrobe, a sturdy blue flannel thing, and tied the belt firmly. She descended the stairs. By now she heard more noises.

"Who's *there*?" she shouted boldly.

"Hum-hum. Just me, lady," said a rather deep voice.

The living room lights, the dining room lights were full on.

In the dining room Ginnie was confronted by a stocking-hooded figure in what she thought of as motorcycle gear: black trousers, black boots, black plastic jacket. The stocking had slits cut in it for eyes. And the figure carried a dirty canvas bag like a railway mailbag, and plainly into this the silverware had already gone, because the dining room drawer gaped, empty. He must have been hiding in a corner of the dining room, Ginnie thought, when she had come down to lock the back door. The hooded figure shoved the drawer in carelessly, and it didn't quite close.

"Keep your mouth shut, and you won't get hurt. All right?" The voice sounded like that of a man of at least twenty-five.

Ginnie didn't see any gun or knife. "Just what do you think you're doing?"

"What does it look like I'm doing?" And the man got on with his business. The two candlesticks from the dining room table went into the bag. So did the silver table lighter.

Was there anyone else with him? Ginnie glanced towards the kitchen, but didn't see anyone, and no sound came from there. "I'm going to call the police," she said, and started for the living room telephone.

"Phone's cut, lady. You better keep quiet, because no one can hear you around here, even if you scream."

Was that true? Unfortunately it was true. Ginnie for a few seconds concentrated on memorizing the man's appearance: about five feet eight, medium build, maybe a bit slender, broad hands—but since the hands were in blue rubber gloves, were they broad?—rather big feet. Blond or brunette she couldn't tell, because of the stocking mask. Robbers like this usually bound and gagged people. Ginnie wanted to avoid that, if she could.

"If you're looking for money, there's not much in the house just now," Ginnie said, "except what's in my handbag upstairs, about thirty dollars. Go ahead and take it."

"I'll get around to it," he said laughing, prowling the living room now. He took the letter-opener from the coffee table, then Freddie's photograph from the piano, because the photograph was in a silver frame.

Ginnie thought of banging him on the head with—with what? She saw nothing heavy enough, portable, except one of the dining room chairs. And if she failed to knock him out with the first swat? Was the telephone really cut? She moved towards the telephone in the corner.

"Don't go near the door. Stay in sight!"

"Ma-wow-wow-*wow!*" This from Cassie, a high-pitched wail that to Ginnie meant Cassie was on the brink of throwing up, but now the situation was different. Cassie looked ready to attack the man.

"Go back, Cassie, take it easy," Ginnie said.

"I don't like cats," the hooded man said over his shoulder.

There was not much else he could take from the living room, Ginnie thought. The pictures on the walls were too big. And what burglar was interested in pictures, at least pictures like these which were a few oils done by their painter friends, two or three watercolors—Was this really happening? Was a stranger picking up her mother's old sewing basket, looking inside, banging it down again? Taking the French vase, tossing the water and roses towards the fireplace? The vase went into the sack.

"What's upstairs?" The ugly head turned towards her. "Let's go upstairs."

"There's *nothing* upstairs!" Ginnie shrieked. She darted towards the telephone, knowing it would be cut, but wanting to see it with her own eyes—cut—though her hand was outstretched to use it. She saw the abruptly stopped wire on the floor, cut some four feet from the telephone.

The hood chuckled. "Told you."

A red flashlight stuck out of the back pocket of his trousers. He was going into the hall now, ready to take the stairs. The staircase light was on, but he pulled the flashlight from his pocket.

"Nothing *up* there, I tell you!" Ginnie found herself following him like a ninnie, holding up the hem of Stan's dressing gown so she wouldn't trip on the stairs.

"Cosy little nook!" said the hood, entering the bedroom. "And what have we here? Anything of interest?"

The silver-backed brush and comb on the dresser were of interest, also the hand mirror, and these went into the bag, which was now dragging the floor.

"Aha! I like that thing!" He had spotted the heavy wooden box with brass corners which Stan used for cufflinks and handkerchiefs and a few white ties, but its size was apparently daunting the man in the hood, because he swayed in front of it and said, "Be back for that." He looked around for lighter objects, and in went Ginnie's black leather jewelry box, her Dunhill lighter from the bedside table. "Ought to be glad I'm not raping you. Haven't the time." The tone was jocular.

My God, Ginnie thought, you'd think Stan and I were rich! She had never considered herself and Stan rich, or thought that they had anything worth invading a house for. No doubt in New York they'd been lucky for six years—no robberies at all—because even a typewriter was valuable to a drug addict. No, they weren't rich, but he was taking all they had, all the *nice* things they'd tried over the years to accumulate. Ginnie watched him open her handbag, lift the dollar bills from her billfold. That was the least of it.

"If you think for one minute you're going to get away with this," Ginnie said. "In a small community like *this*? You haven't a prayer. If you don't leave those things here tonight, I'll report you so quick—"

"Oh, shut up, lady. Where's the other rooms here?"

Cassie snarled. She had followed them both up the stairs.

A black boot struck out sideways and caught the cat sharply in the ribs.

"Don't touch that cat!" Ginnie cried out.

Cassie sprang growling onto the man's boot top, at his knee.

Ginnie was astounded—and proud of Cassie—for a second.

"Pain in the ass!" said the hood, and with a gloved hand caught the cat by the loose skin on her back and flung her against a wall with a backhand swing. The cat dropped, panting, and the man stomped on her side and kicked her on the head.

"You *bastard*!" Ginnie screamed.

"So much for your stinking—yowlers!" said the beige hood, and kicked the cat once again. His voice had been husky with rage, and now he stalked with his flashlight into the hall, in quest of other rooms.

Dazed, stiff, Ginnie followed him.

The guest room had only a chest of drawers in it, empty, but the man slid out a couple of drawers anyway to have a look. Freddie's room had nothing but a bed and table. The hood wasted no time there.

From the hall, Ginnie looked into the bedroom at her cat. The cat twitched and was still. One foot had twitched. Ginnie stood rigid as a column of stone. She had just seen Cassie die, she realized.

"Back in a flash," said the hooded man, briskly descending the stairs with his sack which was now so heavy he had to carry it on one shoulder.

Ginnie moved at last, in jerks, like someone awakening from an anesthetic. Her body and mind seemed not to be connected. Her hand reached for the stair rail and missed it. She was no longer afraid at all, though she did not consciously realize this. She simply kept following the hooded figure, her enemy, and would have kept on, even if he had pointed a gun at her. By the time she reached the kitchen, he was out of sight. The kitchen door was open, and a cool breeze blew in. Ginnie continued across the kitchen, looked left into the driveway, and saw a flashlight's beam swing as the man heaved the bag into a car. She heard the hum of two male voices. So he had a pal waiting for him!

And here he came back.

With sudden swiftness, Ginnie picked up a kitchen stool which had a square formica top and chromium legs. As soon as the hooded figure stepped onto the threshold of the kitchen, Ginnie swung the stool and hit him full on the forehead with the edge of the stool's seat.

Momentum carried the man forward, but he stooped, staggering, and Ginnie cracked him again on the top of the head with all her strength. She held two legs of the stool in her hands. He fell with a great thump and clatter onto the linoleum floor. Another whack for good measure on the back of the stockinged head. She felt pleased and relieved to see blood coming through the beige material.

"Frankie?—You okay?—*Frankie!*"

The voice came from the car outside.

Poised now, not at all afraid, Ginnie stood braced for the next arrival. She held a leg of the stool in her right hand, and her left supported the seat. She awaited, barely two feet from the open door, the sound of boots in the driveway, another figure in the doorway.

Instead, she heard a car motor start, saw a glow of its lights through the door. The car was backing down the drive.

Finally Ginnie set the stool down. The house was silent again. The man on the floor was not moving. Was he dead?

I don't care. I simply don't give a damn, Ginnie said inside herself.

But she did care. What if he woke up? What if he needed a doctor, a hospital right away? And there was no telephone. The nearest house was nearly a mile away, the village a good mile. Ginnie would have to walk it with a flashlight. Of course if she encountered a car, a car might stop and ask what was the matter, and then she could tell someone to fetch a doctor or an ambulance. These thoughts went through Ginnie's head in seconds, and then she returned to the facts. The fact was, he *might* be dead. Killed by her.

So was Cassie dead. Ginnie turned towards the living room. Cassie's death was more real, more important than the body at her feet which only might be dead. Ginnie drew a glass of water for herself at the kitchen sink.

Everything was silent outside. Now Ginnie was calm enough to realize that the robber's chum had thought it best to make a getaway. He probably wasn't coming back, not even with reinforcements. After all, he had the loot in his car—silverware, her jewelry box, all the nice things.

Ginnie stared at the long black figure on her kitchen floor. He hadn't moved at all. The right hand lay under him, the left arm was outstretched, upward. The stockinged head was turned slightly towards her, one slit showing. She couldn't see what was going on behind that crazy slit.

"Are you *awake*?" Ginnie said, rather loudly.

She waited.

She knew she would have to face it. Best to feel the pulse in the wrist, she thought, and at once forced herself to do this. She pulled the rubber glove down a bit, and gripped a blondish-haired wrist which seemed to her of astonishing breadth, much wider than Stan's wrist, anyway. She couldn't feel any pulse. She altered the place where she had put her thumb, and tried again. There was no pulse.

So she had murdered someone. The fact did not sink in.

Two thoughts danced in her mind: she would have to remove Cassie, put a towel or something around her, and she was not going to be able to sleep or even remain in this house with a corpse lying on the kitchen floor.

Ginnie got a dishtowel, a folded clean one from a stack on a shelf, took a second one, went to the hall and climbed the stairs. Cassie was now bleeding. Rather, she had bled. The blood on the carpet looked dark. One of Cassie's eyes projected from the socket. Ginnie gathered her as gently as if she were still alive and only injured, gathered up some intestines which had been pushed out, and enfolded her in a towel, opened the second towel and put that around her too. Then she carried Cassie to the living room, hesitated, then laid the cat's body to one side of the fireplace on the floor. By accident, a red rose lay beside Cassie.

Tackle the blood now, she told herself. She got a plastic bowl from the kitchen, drew some cold water and took a sponge. Upstairs, she went to work on hands and knees, changing the water in the bathroom. The task was soothing, as she had known it would be.

Next job: clothes on and find the nearest telephone. Ginnie kept moving, barely aware of what she was doing, and suddenly she was standing in the kitchen in blue jeans, sneakers, sweater and jacket with her billfold in a pocket. Empty billfold, she remembered. She had her house keys in her left hand. For no good reason, she decided to leave the kitchen light on. The front door was still locked, she realized. She found she had the flashlight in a jacket pocket too, and supposed she had taken it from the front hall table when she came down the stairs.

She went out, locked the kitchen door from the outside with a key, and made her way to the road.

No moon at all. She walked with the aid of the flashlight along the left side of the road towards the village, shone the torch once on her watch and saw that it was twenty past one. By starlight, by a bit of flashlight, she saw one house far to the left in a field, quite dark and so far away, Ginnie thought she might do better to keep on.

She kept on. Dark road. Trudging. Did *everybody* go to bed early around here?

In the distance she saw two or three white streetlights, the lights of the village. Surely there'd be a car before the village.

There wasn't a car. Ginnie was still trudging as she entered the village proper, whose boundary was marked by a neat white sign on either side of the road saying EAST KINDALE.

My God, Ginnie thought. *Is this true? Is this what I'm doing, what I'm going to say?*

Not a light showed in any of the neat, mostly white houses. There was not even a light at the Connecticut Yankee Inn, the only functioning hostelry and bar in town, Stan had remarked once. Nevertheless, Ginnie marched up the steps and knocked on the door. Then with her flashlight, she saw a brass knocker on the white door, and availed herself of that.

Rap-rap-rap!

Minutes passed. *Be patient,* Ginnie told herself. *You're overwrought.*

But she felt compelled to rap again.

"Who's there?" a man's voice called.

"A neighbor! There's been an accident!"

Ginnie fairly collapsed against the figure who opened the door. It was a man in a plaid woolen bathrobe and pajamas. She might have collapsed also against a woman or a child.

Then she was sitting on a straight chair in a sort of living room. She had blurted out the story.

"We'll—we'll get the police right away, ma'am. Or an ambulance, as you say. But from what you say—" The man talking was in his sixties, and sleepy.

His wife, more efficient looking, had joined him to listen. She wore a dressing gown and pink slippers. "Police, Jake. Man sounds dead from what the lady says. Even if he isn't, the police'll know what to do."

"Hello, Ethel! That you?" the man said into the telephone. "Listen, we need the police right away. You know the old Hardwick place? . . . Tell 'em to go there . . . No, *not* on fire. Can't explain now. But somebody'll be there to open the door in—in about five minutes."

The woman pushed a glass of something into Ginnie's hand. Ginnie realized that her teeth were chattering. She was cold, though it wasn't cold outside. It was early September, she remembered.

"They're going to want to speak with you." The man who had been in the plaid robe was now in trousers and a belted sports jacket. "You'll have to tell them the time it happened and all that."

Ginnie realized. She thanked the woman and went with the man to his car. It was an ordinary four-door, and Ginnie noticed a discarded Cracker Jack box on the floor of the passenger's seat as she got in.

A police car was in the drive. Someone was knocking on the back door, and Ginnie saw that she'd left the kitchen light on.

"Hya, Jake! What's up?" called a second policeman, getting out of the black car in the driveway.

"Lady had a house robbery," the man with Ginnie explained. "She thinks—Well, you've got the keys, haven't you, Mrs. Brixton?"

"Oh yes, yes." Ginnie fumbled for them. She was gasping again, and reminded herself that it was a time to keep calm, to answer questions accurately. She opened the kitchen door.

A policeman stooped beside the prone figure. "Dead," he said.

"The—Mrs. Brixton said she hit him with the kitchen stool. That one, ma'am?" The man called Jake pointed to the yellow formica stool.

"Yes. He was coming *back,* you see. You see—" Ginnie choked and gave up, for the moment.

Jake cleared his throat and said, "Mrs. Brixton and her husband just moved in. Husband isn't here tonight. She'd left the kitchen door unlocked and two—well, one fellow came in, this one. He went out with a bag of stuff he'd taken, put it in a waiting car, then came back to get more, and that's when Mrs. Brixton hit him."

"Um-*hum,*" said the policeman, still stooped on his heels. "Can't touch the body till the detective gets here. Can I use your phone, Mrs. Brixton?"

"They cut the phone," Jake said. "That's why she had to walk to my place."

The other policeman went out to telephone from his car. The policeman who remained put on water for coffee (or had he said tea?), and chatted with Jake about tourists, about someone they both knew who had just got married—as if they had known each other for years. Ginnie was sitting on one of the dining room chairs. The policeman asked where the instant coffee was, if she had any, and Ginnie got up to show him the coffee jar which she had put on a cabinet shelf beside the stove.

"Terrible introduction to a new house," the policeman remarked, holding his steaming cup. "But we all sure hope—" Suddenly his words seemed to dry up. His eyes flickered and looked away from Ginnie's face.

A couple of men in plainclothes arrived. Photographs were taken of the dead man. Ginnie went over the house with one of the men, who made notes of the items Ginnie said were stolen. No, she hadn't seen the color of the car, much less the license plate. The body on the floor was wrapped and carried out on a stretcher. Ginnie had only a glimpse of that, from which the detective even tried to shield her. Ginnie was in the dining room then, reckoning up the missing silver.

"I didn't mean to kill him!" Ginnie cried out suddenly, interrupting the detective. "Not *kill* him, honestly!"

STAN ARRIVED VERY early, about 8 A.M., with Freddie, and went to the Inn to fetch Ginnie. Ginnie had spent the night there, and someone had telephoned Stan at the number Ginnie had given.

"She's had a shock," Jake said to Stan.

Stan looked bewildered. But at least he had heard what happened, and Ginnie didn't have to go over it.

"All the nice things we had," Ginnie said. "And the cat—"

"The police might get our stuff back, Ginnie. If not, we'll buy more. We're all safe, at least." Stan set his firm jaw, but he smiled. He glanced at Freddie who stood in the doorway, looking a little pale from lack of sleep. "Come on. We're going home."

He took Ginnie's hand. His hand felt warm, and she realized her own hands were cold again.

They tried to keep the identity of the dead man from her, Ginnie knew, but on the second day she happened to see it printed—on a folded newspaper which lay on the counter in the grocery store. There was a photograph of him too, a blondish fellow with curly hair and a rather defiant expression. *Frank Collins, 24, of Hartford . . .*

Stan felt that they ought to go on living in the house, gradually buy the "nice things" again that Ginnie kept talking about. Stan said she ought to get back to work on her novel.

"I don't want any nice things any more. Not again." That was true, but that was only part of it. The worst was that she had killed someone, stopped a life. She couldn't fully realize it, therefore couldn't believe it somehow, or understand it.

"At least we could get another cat."

"Not yet," she said.

People said to her (like Mrs. Durham, Gladys, who lived a mile or so out of East Kindale on the opposite side from the Brixtons), "You mustn't reproach yourself. You did it in defense of your house. Don't you think a lot of us wish we had the courage, if someone comes barging in intending to rob you . . ."

"I wouldn't hesitate—to do what you did!" That was from perky Georgia Hamilton, a young married woman with black curly hair, active in local politics, who lived in East Kindale proper. She came especially to call on Ginnie and to make acquaintance with her and Stan. "These hoodlums from miles away—Hartford!—they come to rob us, just because they think we still have some family silver and a few *nice* things . . ."

There was the phrase again, the *nice* things.

Stan came home one day with a pair of silver candlesticks for the dining room table. "Less than a hundred dollars, and we can afford them," Stan said.

To Ginnie they looked like bait for another robbery. They were pretty, yes. Georgian. Modern copy, but still beautiful. She could not take any aesthetic pleasure from them.

"Did you take a swat at your book this afternoon?" Stan asked cheerfully. He had been out of the house nearly three hours that afternoon. He had made sure the doors were locked, for Ginnie's sake, before he left. He had also bought a metal wheelbarrow for use in the garden, and it was still strapped to the roof of the car.

"No," Ginnie said. "But I suppose I'm making progress. I have to get back to a state of concentration, you know."

"Of course I know," Stan said. "I'm a writer too."

The police had never recovered the silverware, or Ginnie's leather box which had held her engagement ring (it had become too small and she hadn't got around to having it enlarged), and her grandmother's gold necklace and so forth. Stan told Ginnie they had checked all the known pals of the man who had invaded the house, but hadn't come up with anything.

The police thought the dead man might have struck up acquaintance with his chum very recently, possibly the same night as the robbery.

"Darling," Stan said, "do you think we should *move* from this house? I'm willing—if it'd make you feel—less—"

Ginnie shook her head. It wasn't the house. She didn't any longer (after two months) even think of the corpse on the floor when she went into the kitchen. It was something inside her. "No," Ginnie said.

"Well—I think you ought to talk to a psychiatrist. Just one visit even," Stan added, interrupting a protest from Ginnie. "It isn't enough for neighbors to say you did the natural thing. Maybe you need a professional to tell you." Stan chuckled. He was in tennis shoes and old clothes, and had had a good day at the typewriter.

Ginnie agreed, to please Stan.

The psychiatrist was in Hartford, a man recommended to Stan by a local medical doctor. Stan drove Ginnie there, and waited for her in the car. It was to be an hour's session, but Ginnie reappeared after about forty minutes.

"He gave me some pills to take," Ginnie said.

"Is *that* all?—But what did he say?"

"Oh." Ginnie shrugged. "The same as they all say, that—nobody blames me, the police didn't make a fuss, so what—" She shrugged again, glanced at Stan and saw the terrible disappointment in his face as he looked from her into the distance through the windshield.

Ginnie knew he was thinking again about "guilt" and abandoning it, abandoning the word again. She had said no, she didn't feel guilty, that wasn't the trouble, that would have been too simple. She felt disturbed, she had said many times, and she couldn't do anything about it.

"You really ought to write a book about it, a novel," Stan said—this for at least the fourth time.

"And how can I, if I can't come to terms with it myself, if I can't even analyze it first?" This Ginnie said for at least the third time and possibly the fourth. It was as if she had an unsolvable mystery within her. "You can't write a book just stammering around on paper."

Stan then started the car.

The pills were mild sedatives combined with some kind of mild picker-uppers. They didn't make change in Ginnie.

Two more months passed. Ginnie resisted buying any "nice things," so they had nothing but the nice candlesticks. They ate with stainless steel. Freddie pulled out of his period of tension and suppressed excitement (he knew quite well what had happened in the kitchen), and in Ginnie's eyes became quite normal again, whatever normal was. Ginnie got back to work on the book she had started before moving to the house. She didn't ever dream about the murder, or manslaughter, in fact she often thought it might be better if she did dream about it.

But among people—and it was a surprisingly friendly region, they had all the social life they could wish—she felt compelled to say sometimes, when there was a lull in the conversation:

"Did you know, by the way, I once killed a man?"

Everyone would look at her, except of course those who had heard her say this before, maybe three times before.

Stan would grow tense and blank-minded, having failed once more to spring in in time before Ginnie got launched. He was jittery at social gatherings, trying like a fencer to dart in with something, anything to say, before Ginnie made her big thrust. *It's just something they, he and Ginnie, had to live with,* Stan told himself.

And it probably would go on and on, even maybe when Freddie was twelve and even twenty. It had, in fact, half-ruined their marriage. But it was emphatically not worth divorcing for. He still loved Ginnie. She was still Ginnie after all. She was just somehow different. Even Ginnie had said that about herself.

"It's something I just have to live with," Stan murmured to himself.

"What?" It was Georgia Hamilton on his left, asking him what he had said. "Oh, I know, I know." She smiled understandingly. "But maybe it does her good."

Ginnie was in the middle of her story. At least she always made it short, and even managed to laugh in a couple of places.

Slowly, Slowly in the Wind

E dward (Skip) Skipperton spent most of his life in a thunderous rage. It was his nature. He had been full of temper as a boy, and as a man impatient with people's slowness or stupidity or inefficiency. Now Skipperton was fifty-two. His wife had left him two years ago, unable to stand his tantrums any longer. She had met a most tranquil university professor from Boston, had divorced Skipperton on the grounds of incompatibility, and married the professor. Skipperton had been determined to get custody of their daughter, Margaret, then fifteen, and with clever lawyers and on the grounds that his wife had deserted him for another man, Skipperton had succeeded. A few months after the divorce, Skipperton had a heart attack, a real stroke with hemi-paralysis from which he miraculously recovered in six months, but his doctors gave him warning.

"Skip, it's life or death. You quit smoking and drinking and right now, or you're a dead man before your next birthday." That was from his heart specialist.

"You owe it to Margaret," said his GP. "You ought to retire, Skip. You've plenty of money. You're in the wrong profession for your nature—granted you've made a success of it. But what's left of your life is more important, isn't it? Why not become a gentleman farmer, something like that?"

Skipperton was a management adviser. Behind the scenes of big business, Skipperton was well known. He worked freelance. Companies on the brink sent for him to reorganize, reform, throw out—anything Skip advised went. "I go in and kick the ass off 'em!" was the inelegant way Skip described his work when he was interviewed, which was not often, because he preferred a ghostly role.

Skipperton bought Coldstream Heights in Maine, a seven-acre farm with a modernized farmhouse, and hired a local man called Andy Humbert to live and work on the place. Skipperton also bought some of the machinery the former owner had to sell, but not all of it, because he didn't want to turn himself into a full-time farmer. The doctors had recommended a little exercise and no strain of any kind. They had known that Skip wouldn't and couldn't at once cut all his connections with the businesses he had helped in the past. He might have to make an occasional trip to Chicago or Dallas, but he was officially retired.

Margaret was transferred from her private school in New York to a Swiss boarding school. Skipperton knew and liked Switzerland, and had bank accounts there.

Skipperton did stop drinking and smoking. His doctors were amazed at his willpower—and yet it was just like Skip to stop overnight, like a soldier. Now Skip chewed his pipes, and went through a stem in a week. He went through two lower teeth, but got them capped in steel in Bangor. Skipperton and Andy kept a couple of goats to crop the grass, and one sow who was pregnant when Skip bought her, and who now had twelve piglets. Margaret wrote filial letters saying she liked Switzerland and that her French was improving no end. Skipperton now wore flannel shirts with no tie, low boots that laced, and woodsmen's jackets. His appetite had improved, and he had to admit he felt better.

The only thorn in his side—and Skipperton had to have one to feel normal—was the man who owned some adjacent land, one Peter Frosby, who wouldn't sell a stretch Skipperton offered to buy at three times the normal price. This land sloped down to a little river called the Coldstream, which in fact separated part of Skipperton's property from Frosby's to the north, and Skipperton didn't mind that. He was interested in the part of the river nearest him and in view from Coldstream Heights. Skipperton wanted to be able to fish a little, to be able to say he owned that part of the landscape and had riparian rights. But old Frosby didn't want anybody fishing in his stream, Skipperton had been told by the agents, even though Frosby's house was upstream and out of sight of Skipperton's.

The week after Peter Frosby's rejection, Skipperton invited Frosby to his house. "Just to get acquainted—as neighbors," Skipperton said on the telephone to Frosby. By now Skipperton had been living at Coldstream Heights for four months.

Skipperton had his best whiskey and brandy, cigars and cigarettes—all the things he couldn't enjoy himself—on hand when Frosby arrived in a dusty but new Cadillac, driven by a young man whom Frosby introduced as his son, Peter.

"The Frosbys don't sell their land," Frosby told Skipperton. "We've had the same land for nearly three hundred years, and the river's always been ours." Frosby, a skinny but strong-looking man with cold gray eyes puffed his cigar daintily and after ten minutes hadn't finished his first whiskey. "Can't see why you want it."

"A little fishing," Skipperton said, putting on a pleasant smile. "It's in view of my house. Just to be able to wade, maybe, in the summer." Skipperton looked at Peter Junior, who sat with folded arms beside and behind his father. Skipperton was backed only by shambly Andy, a good enough handyman, but not part of his dynasty. Skipperton would have given anything (except his life) to have been holding a straight whiskey in one hand and a good cigar in the other. "Well, I'm sorry," Skipperton said finally. "But I think you'll agree the price I offer isn't bad—twenty thousand cash for about two hundred yards of riparian rights. Doubt if you'll get it again—in your lifetime."

"Not interested in my lifetime," Frosby said with a faint smile. "I've got a son here."

The son was a handsome boy with dark hair and sturdy shoulders, taller than his father. His arms were still folded across his chest, as if to illustrate his father's negative attitude. He had unbent only briefly to light a cigarette which he had soon put out. Still, Peter Junior smiled as he and his father were leaving, and said:

"Nice job you've done with the Heights, Mr. Skipperton. Looks better than it did before."

"Thank you," Skip said, pleased. He had installed good leather-upholstered furniture, heavy floor-length curtains, and brass firedogs and tongs for the fireplace.

"Nice old-fashioned touches," Frosby commented in what seemed to Skipperton a balance between compliment and sneer. "We haven't seen a scarecrow around here in maybe—almost before my time, I think."

"I like old-fashioned things—like fishing," Skipperton said. "I'm trying to grow corn out there. Somebody told me the land was all right for corn. That's where a scarecrow belongs, isn't it? In a cornfield?" He put on as friendly a manner as he could, but his blood was boiling. A mule-stubborn Maine man, Frosby, sitting on several hundred acres that his more forceful ancestors had acquired for him.

Frosby Junior was peering at a photograph of Maggie, which stood in a silver frame on the hall table. She had been only thirteen or fourteen when the picture had been taken, but her slender face framed in long dark hair showed the clean-cut nose and brows, the subtle smile that would turn her into a beauty one day. Maggie was nearly eighteen now, and Skip's expectations were being confirmed.

"Pretty girl," said Frosby Junior, turning towards Skipperton, then glancing at his father, because they were all lingering in the hall.

Skipperton said nothing. The meeting had been a failure. Skipperton wasn't used to failures. He looked into Frosby's greenish-gray eyes and said, "I've one more idea. Suppose we make an arrangement that I rent the land for the duration of my life, and then it goes to you—or your son. I'll give you five thousand a year. Want to think it over?"

Frosby put on another frosty smile. "I think not, Mr. Skipperton. Thanks anyway."

"You might talk to your lawyer about it. No rush on my part."

Frosby now chuckled. "We know as much about law as the lawyers here. We know our boundaries anyway. Nice to meet you, Mr. Skipperton. Thank you for the whiskey and—good-bye."

No one shook hands. The Cadillac moved off.

"Damn the bastard," Skipperton muttered to Andy, but he smiled. Life was a game, after all. You won sometimes, you lost sometimes.

It was early May. The corn was in, and Skipperton had spotted three or four strong green shoots coming through the beige, well-turned earth. That pleased him, made him think of American Indians, the ancient Mayans. Corn! And he had a classic scarecrow that he and Andy had knocked together a couple of weeks ago. They had dressed the crossbars in an old jacket, and the two sticks—nailed to the upright—in brown trousers. Skip had found the old clothes in the attic. A straw hat jammed onto the top and secured with a nail completed the picture.

Skip went off to San Francisco for a five-day operation on an aeronautics firm which was crippled by a lawsuit, scared to death by unions and contract pull-outs. Skip left them with more redundancies, three vice-presidents fired, but he left them in better shape, and collected fifty thousand for his work.

By way of celebrating his achievement and the oncoming summer that would bring Maggie, Skip shot one of Frosby's hunting dogs which had swum the stream onto his property to retrieve a bird. Skipperton had been waiting patiently at his bedroom window upstairs, knowing a shoot was on from the sound of guns. Skip had his binoculars and a rifle of goodly range. Let Frosby complain! Trespassing was trespassing.

Skip was almost pleased when Frosby took him to court over the dog. Andy had buried the dog, on Skipperton's orders, but Skipperton readily admitted the shooting. And the judge ruled in Skipperton's favor.

Frosby went pale with anger. "It may be the law but it's not human. It's not fair."

And a lot of good it did Frosby to say that!

Skipperton's corn grew high as the scarecrow's hips, and higher. Skip spent a lot of time up in his bedroom, binoculars and loaded rifle at hand, in case anything else belonging to Frosby showed itself on his land.

"Don't hit me," Andy said with an uneasy laugh. "You're shooting on the edge of the cornfield there, and now and then I weed it, y'know."

"You think there's something wrong with my eyesight?" Skip replied.

A few days later Skip proved there was nothing wrong with his eyesight, when he plugged a gray cat stalking a bird or a mouse in the high grass this side of the stream. Skip did it with one shot. He wasn't even sure the cat belonged to Frosby.

This shot produced a call in person from Frosby Junior the following day.

"It's just to ask a question, Mr. Skipperton. My father and I heard a shot yesterday, and last night one of our cats didn't come back at night to eat, and not this morning either. Do you know anything about that?" Frosby Junior had declined to take a seat.

"I shot the cat. It was on my property," Skipperton said calmly.

"But the cat—What harm was the cat doing?" The young man looked steadily at Skipperton.

"The law is the law. Property is property."

Frosby Junior shook his head. "You're a hard man, Mr. Skipperton." Then he departed.

Peter Frosby served a summons again, and the same judge ruled that in accordance with old English law and also American law, a cat was a rover by nature, not subject to constraint as was a dog. He gave Skipperton the maximum fine of one hundred dollars, and a warning not to use his rifle so freely in future.

That annoyed Skipperton, though of course he could and did laugh at the smallness of the fine. If he could think of something else annoying, something really *telling,* old Frosby might relent and at least lease some of the stream, Skip thought.

But he forgot the feud when Margaret came. Skip fetched her at the airport in New York, and they drove up to Maine. She looked taller to Skip, more filled out, and there were roses in her cheeks. She was a beauty, all right!

"Got a surprise for you at home," Skip said.

"Um-m—a horse maybe? I told you I learned to jump this year, didn't I?"

Had she? Skip said, "Yes. Not a horse, no."

Skip's surprise was a red Toyota convertible. He had remembered at least that Maggie's school had taught her to drive. She was thrilled, and flung her arms around Skip's neck.

"You're a darling, Daddy! And you know, you're looking *very* fell!"

Margaret had been to Coldstream Heights for two weeks at Easter, but now the place looked more cared for. She and Skip had arrived around midnight, but Andy was still up watching television in his own little house on the grounds, and Maggie insisted on going over to greet him. Skip was gratified to see Andy's eyes widen at the sight of her.

Skip and Maggie tried the new car out the next day. They drove to a town some twenty miles away and had lunch. That afternoon, back at the house, Maggie asked if her father had a fishing rod, just a simple one, so she could try the stream. Skip of course had all kinds of rods, but he had to tell her she couldn't, and he explained why, and explained that he had even tried to rent part of the stream.

"Frosby's a real s.o.b.," Skip said. "Won't give an inch."

"Well, never mind, Daddy. There's lots else to do."

Maggie was the kind of girl who enjoyed taking walks, reading or fussing around in the house rearranging little things so that they looked prettier. She did these things while Skip was on the telephone sometimes for an hour or so with Dallas or Detroit.

Skipperton was a bit surprised one day when Maggie arrived in her Toyota around 7 P.M. with a catch of three trout on a string. She was barefoot, and the cuffs of her blue dungarees were damp. "Where'd you get those?" Skip asked, his first thought being that she'd taken one of his rods and fished the stream against his instructions.

"I met the boy who lives there," Maggie said. "We were both buying gas, and he introduced himself—said he'd seen my photograph in your house. Then we had a coffee in the diner there by the gas station—"

"The Frosby boy?"

"Yes. He's awfully nice, Daddy. Maybe it's only the father who's not nice. Anyway Pete said, 'Come on and fish with me this afternoon,' so I did. He said his father stocks the river farther up."

"I don't—Frankly, Maggie, I *don't* want you associating with the Frosbys!"

"There's only two." Maggie was puzzled. "I barely met his father. They've got quite a nice house, Daddy."

"I've had unpleasant dealings with old Frosby, I told you, Maggie. It just isn't fitting if you get chummy with the son. Do me this one favor this summer, Maggie doll." That was his name for her in the moments he wanted to feel close to her, wanted her to feel close to him.

The very next day, Maggie was gone from the house for nearly three hours, and Skip noticed it. She had said she wanted to go to the village to buy sneakers, and she was wearing the sneakers when she came home, but Skip wondered why it had taken her three hours to make a five-mile trip. With enormous effort, Skip refrained from asking a question. Then Saturday morning, Maggie said there was a dance in Keensport, and she was going.

"And I have a suspicion who you're going with," Skip said, his heart beginning to thump with adrenaline.

"I'm going alone, I swear it, Daddy. Girls don't have to be escorted any more. I could go in blue jeans, but I'm not. I've got some white slacks."

Skipperton realized that he could hardly forbid her to go to a dance. But he damn well knew the Frosby boy would be there, and would probably meet Maggie at the entrance. "I'll be glad when you go back to Switzerland."

Skip knew what was going to happen. He could see it a mile away. His daughter was "infatuated," and he could only hope that she got over it, that nothing happened before she had to go back to school (another whole month), because he didn't want to keep her prisoner in the house. He didn't want to look absurd in his own eyes, even in simpleminded Andy's eyes, by laying down the law to her.

Maggie got home evidently very late that night, and so quietly Skip hadn't wakened, though he had stayed up till 2 A.M. and meant to listen for her. At breakfast, Maggie looked fresh and radiant, rather to Skip's surprise.

"I suppose the Frosby boy was at the dance last night?"

Maggie, diving into bacon and eggs, said, "I don't know what you've got against him, Daddy—just because his father didn't want to sell land that's been in their family for ages!"

"I don't want you to fall in love with a country bumpkin! I've sent you to a good school. You've got background—or at least I intend to give you some!"

"Did you know Pete had three years at Harvard—and he's taking a correspondence course in electronic engineering?"

"Oh! I suppose he's learning computer programming? Easier than shorthand!"

Maggie stood up. "I'll be eighteen in another month, Daddy. I don't want to be told whom I can see and can't see."

Skip got up too and roared at her. *"They're not my kind of people or yours!"*

Maggie left the room.

In the next days, Skipperton fumed and went through two or three pipe stems. Andy noticed his unease, Skipperton knew, but Andy made no comment. Andy spent his nonworking hours alone, watching drivel on his television. Skip was rehearsing a speech to Maggie as he paced his land, glancing at the sow and piglets, at Andy's neat kitchen-garden, not seeing anything. Skip was groping for a lever, the kind of weapon he had always been able to find in business affairs that would force things his way. He couldn't send Maggie back to Switzerland, even though her school stayed open in summer for girls whose home was too far away to go back to. If he threatened not to send her back to school, he was afraid Maggie wouldn't mind. Skipperton maintained an apartment in New York, and had two servants who slept in, but he knew Maggie wouldn't agree to go there, and Skip didn't want to go to New York either. He was too interested in the immediate scene in which he sensed a battle coming.

Skipperton had arrived at nothing by the following Saturday, a week after the Keensport dance, and he was exhausted. That Saturday evening, Maggie said she was going to a party at the house of someone called Wilmers, whom she had met at the dance. Skip asked her for the address, and Maggie scribbled it on the hall telephone pad. Skip had reason to have asked for it, because by Sunday morning Maggie hadn't come home. Skip was up at seven, nervous as a cat and in a rage still at 9 A.M., which he thought a polite enough hour to telephone on Sunday morning, though it had cost him much to wait that long.

An adolescent boy's voice said that Maggie had been there, yes, but she had left pretty early.

"Was she alone?"

"No, she was with Pete Frosby."

"That's all I wanted to know," said Skip, feeling the blood rush to his face as if he were hemorrhaging. "*Oh!* Wait! Do you know where they went?"

"Sure don't."

"My daughter went in her car?"

"No, Pete's. Maggie's car's still here."

Skip thanked the boy and put the phone down shakily, but he was shaking only from energy that was surging through every nerve and muscle. He picked up the telephone and dialed the Frosby home.

Old Frosby answered.

Skipperton identified himself, and asked if his daughter was possibly there?

"No, she's not, Mr. Skipperton."

"Is your son there? I'd like—"

"No, he doesn't happen to be in just now."

"What do you mean? He was there and went out?"

"Mr. Skipperton, my son has his own ways, his own room, his own key—his own life. I'm not about—"

Skipperton put the telephone down suddenly. He had a bad nose-bleed, and it was dripping onto the table edge. He ran to get a wet towel.

Maggie was not home by Sunday evening or Monday morning, and Skipperton was reluctant to notify the police, appalled by the thought that her name might be linked with the Frosbys', if the police found her with the son somewhere. Tuesday morning, Skip was enlightened. He had a letter from Maggie, written from Boston. It said that she and Pete had run away to be married, and to avoid "unpleasant scenes."

> . . . Though you may think this is sudden, we do love each other and are sure of it. I did not really want to go back to school, Daddy. I will be in touch in about a week. Please don't try to find me. I have seen Mommie, but we are not staying with her. I was sorry to leave my nice new car, but the car is all right.
>
> Love always,
Maggie

For two days Skipperton didn't go out of the house, and hardly ate. He felt three-quarters dead. Andy was very worried about him, and finally persuaded Skipperton to ride to the village with him, because they needed to buy a few things. Skipperton went, sitting like an upright corpse in the passenger seat.

While Andy went to the drugstore and the butcher's, Skipperton sat in the car, his eyes glazed with his own thoughts. Then an approaching figure on the sidewalk made Skipperton's eyes focus. Old Frosby! Frosby walked with a springy tread for his age, Skip thought. He wore a new tweed suit, black felt hat, and he had a cigar in his hand. Skipperton hoped Frosby wouldn't see him in the car, but Frosby did.

Frosby didn't pause in his stride, just smiled his obnoxious, thin-lipped little smile and nodded briefly, as if to say—

Well, Skip *knew* what Frosby might have wanted to say, what he had said with that filthy smile. Skip's blood seethed, and Skip began to feel like his old self again. He was standing on the sidewalk, hands in his pockets and feet apart, when Andy reappeared.

"What's for dinner tonight, Andy? I've got an appetite!"

That evening, Skipperton persuaded Andy to take not only Saturday night off, but to stay overnight somewhere, if he wished. "Give you a couple of hundred bucks for a little spree, boy. You've earned it." Skip forced three hundred dollar bills into Andy's hand. "Take off Monday too, if you feel like it. I'll manage."

Andy left Saturday evening in the pick-up for Bangor.

Skip then telephoned old Frosby. Frosby answered, and Skipperton said, "Mr. Frosby, it's time we made a truce, under the circumstances. Don't you think so?"

Frosby sounded surprised, but he agreed to come Sunday morning around eleven for a talk. Frosby arrived in the same Cadillac, alone.

And Skipperton wasted no time. He let Frosby knock, opened the door for him, and as soon as Frosby was inside, Skip came down on his head with a rifle butt. He dragged Frosby to the hall to make sure the job was finished: the hall was uncarpeted, and Skip wanted no blood on the rugs. Vengeance was sweet to Skip, and he almost smiled. He removed Frosby's clothes, and wrapped his body in three or four burlap sacks which he had ready. Then he burnt Frosby's clothing in the fireplace, where he had a small fire already crackling. Frosby's wristwatch and wallet and two rings Skip put aside in a drawer to deal with later.

He had decided that broad daylight was the best time to carry out his idea, better than night when an oddly playing flashlight that he would have had to use might have caught someone's eye. So Skip put one arm around Frosby's body and dragged him up the field towards his scarecrow. It was a haul of more than half a mile. Skip had some rope and a knife in his back pockets. He cut down the old scarecrow, cut the strings that held the clothing to the cross, dressed Frosby in the old trousers and jacket, tied a burlap bag around his head and face, and jammed the hat on him. The hat wouldn't stay without being tied on, so Skip did this after punching holes in the brim of the hat with his knife point. Then Skip picked up his burlap bags and made his way back towards his house down the slope with many a backward look to admire his work, and many a smile. The scarecrow looked almost the same as before. He had solved a problem a lot of people thought difficult: what to do with the body. Furthermore, he could enjoy looking at it through his binoculars from his upstairs window.

Skip burnt the burlap bags in his fireplace, made sure that even the shoe soles had burnt to soft ash. When the ashes were cooler, he'd look for buttons and the belt buckle and remove them. He took a fork, went out beyond the pig run and buried the wallet (whose papers he had already burnt), the wristwatch and the rings about three feet deep. It was in a patch of stringy grass, unused for anything except the goats, not a place in which anyone would ever likely do any gardening.

Then Skip washed his face and hands, ate a thick slice of roast beef, and put his mind to the car. It was by now half past twelve. Skip didn't know if Frosby had a servant, someone expecting him for lunch or not, but it was safer to assume he had. Skip's aversion to Frosby had kept him from asking Maggie any questions about his household. Skip got into Frosby's car, now with a kitchen towel in his back pocket to wipe off fingerprints, and drove to some woods he knew from having driven past them many times. An unpaved lane went off the main road into these woods, and into this Skip turned. Thank God, nobody in sight, not a woodsman, not a picnicker. Skip stopped the car and got out, wiped the steering wheel, even the keys, the door, then walked back towards the road.

He was more than an hour getting home. He had found a long stick, the kind called a stave by the wayfarers of old, Skip thought, and he trudged along with the air of a nature-lover, a bird-watcher, for the benefit of the people in the few cars that passed him. He didn't glance at any of the cars. It was still Sunday dinnertime.

The local police telephoned that evening around seven, and asked if they could come by. Skipperton said of course.

He had removed the buttons and buckle from the fireplace ashes. A woman had telephoned around 1:30, saying she was calling from the Frosby residence (Skip assumed she was a servant) to ask if Mr. Frosby was there. Skipperton told her that Mr. Frosby had left his house a little after noon.

"Mr. Frosby intended to go straight home, do you think?" the plump policeman asked Skipperton. The policeman had some rank like sergeant, Skipperton supposed, and he was accompanied by a younger policeman.

"He didn't say anything about where he was going," Skipperton replied. "And I didn't notice which way his car went."

The policeman nodded, and Skip could see he was on the brink of saying something like, "I understand from Mr. Frosby's housekeeper that you and he weren't on the best of terms," but the cop didn't say anything, just looked around Skip's living room, glanced around his front and back yards in a puzzled way, then both policemen took their leave.

Skip was awakened around midnight by the ring of the telephone at his bedside. It was Maggie calling from Boston. She and Pete had heard about the disappearance of Pete's father.

"Daddy, they said he'd just been to see you this morning. What happened?"

"Nothing happened. I invited him for a friendly talk—and it was friendly. After all we're fathers-in-law now . . . Honey, how do I know where he went?"

Skipperton found it surprisingly easy to lie about Frosby. In a primitive way his emotions had judged, weighed the situation, and told Skip that he was right, that he had exacted a just revenge. Old Frosby might have exerted some control over his son, and he hadn't. It had cost Skip his daughter—because that was the way Skip saw it, Maggie was lost to him. He saw her as a provincial-to-be, mother-to-be of children whose narrow-mindedness, inherited from the Frosby clan, would surely out.

Andy arrived next morning, Monday. He had already heard the story in the village, and also the police had found Mr. Frosby's car not far away in the woods, Andy said. Skip feigned mild surprise on hearing of the car. Andy didn't ask any questions. And suppose he discovered the scarecrow? Skip thought a little money would keep Andy quiet. The corn was all picked up there, only a few inferior ears remained, destined for the pigs. Skipperton picked them himself Monday afternoon, while Andy tended the pigs and goats.

Skipperton's pleasure now was to survey the cornfield from his upstairs bedroom with his 10× binoculars. He loved to see the wind tossing the cornstalk tops around old Frosby's corpse, loved to think of him, shrinking, drying up like a mummy in the wind. Twisting slowly, slowly in the wind, as a Nixon aide used to put it about the president's enemies. Frosby wasn't twisting, but he was hanging, in plain view. No buzzards came. Skip had been a little afraid of buzzards. The only thing that bothered him, once, was seeing one afternoon some schoolboys walking along a road far to the right (under which road the Coldstream flowed), and pointing to the scarecrow. Bracing himself against the window jamb, arms held tightly at his sides so the binoculars would be as steady as possible, Skip saw a couple of the small boys laughing. And had one held his nose? Surely not! They were nearly a mile away from the scarecrow! Still, they had paused, one boy stamped his foot, another shook his head and laughed.

How Skip wished he could hear what they were saying! Ten days had passed since Frosby's death. Rumors were rife, that old Frosby had been murdered for his money by someone he'd picked up to give a lift to, that he had been kidnapped and that a ransom note might still arrive. But suppose one of the schoolkids said to his father—or anyone—that maybe the dead body of Frosby was inside the scarecrow? This was just the kind of thing Skip might have thought of when he had been a small boy. Skip was consequently more afraid of the schoolkids than of the police.

And the police did come back, with a plainclothes detective. They looked over Skipperton's house and land—maybe looking for a recently dug patch, Skip thought. If so, they found none. They looked at Skip's two rifles and took their caliber and serial numbers.

"Just routine, Mr. Skipperton," said the detective.

"I understand," said Skip.

That same evening Maggie telephoned and said she was at the Frosby house, and could she come over to see him?

"Why not? This is your house!" Skip replied.

"I never know what kind of mood you'll be in—or temper," Maggie said when she arrived.

"I'm in a pretty *good* mood, I think," Skipperton said. "And I hope you're happy, Maggie—since what's done is done."

Maggie was in her blue dungarees, sneakers, a familiar sweater. It was hard for Skip to realize that she was married. She sat with hands folded, looking down at the floor. Then she raised her eyes to him and said:

"Pete's very upset. We never would have stayed a week in Boston unless he'd been sure the police were doing all they could here. Was Mr. Frosby—depressed? Pete didn't think so."

Skip laughed. "No! Best of spirits. Pleased with the marriage and all that." Skip waited, but Maggie was silent. "You're going to live at the Frosby place?"

"Yes." Maggie stood up. "I'd like to collect a few things, Daddy. I brought a suitcase."

His daughter's coolness, her sadness, pained Skip. She had said something about visiting him often, not about his coming to see them—not that Skip would have gone.

"I KNOW WHAT's in that scarecrow," said Andy one day, and Skip turned, binoculars in hand, to see Andy standing in the doorway of his bedroom.

"Do you?—And what're you going to do about it?" Skip asked, braced for anything. He had squared his shoulders.

"Nothin'. Nothin'," Andy replied with a smile.

Skip didn't know how to take that. "I suppose you'd like some money, Andy? A little present—for keeping quiet?"

"No, sir," Andy said quietly, shaking his head. His wind-wrinkled face bore a faint smile. "I ain't that kind."

What was Skip to make of it? He was used to men who liked money, more and more of it. Andy was different, that was true. Well, so much the better, if he didn't want money, Skip thought. It was cheaper. He also felt he could trust Andy. It was strange.

The leaves began to fall in earnest. Halloween was coming, and Andy removed the driveway gate in advance, just lifted it off its hinges, telling Skip that the kids would steal it if they didn't. Andy knew the district. The kids didn't do much harm, but it was trick or treat at every house. Skip and Andy made sure they had lots of nickels and quarters on hand, corn candy, licorice sticks, even a couple of pumpkins in the window, faces cut in them by Andy, to show any comers that they were in the right spirit. Then on Halloween night, nobody knocked on Skip's door. There was a party at Coldstream, at the Frosbys', Skip knew because the wind was blowing his way and he could hear the music. He thought of his daughter dancing, having a good time. Maybe people were wearing masks, crazy costumes. There'd be pumpkin pie with whipped cream, guessing games, maybe a treasure hunt. Skip was lonely, for the first time in his life. *Lonely.* He badly wanted a scotch, but decided to keep his oath to himself, and having decided this, asked himself why? He put his hands flat down on his dresser top and gazed at his own face in the mirror. He saw creases running from the flanges of his nose down beside his mouth, wrinkles under his eyes. He tried to smile, and the smile looked phony. He turned away from the mirror.

At that instant, a spot of light caught his eyes. It was out the window, in the upward sloping field. A procession—so it seemed, maybe eight or ten figures—was walking up his field with flashlights or torches or both. Skip opened the window slightly. He was rigid with rage, and fear. They were on his land! They had no right! And they were kids, he realized. Even in the darkness, he could see by the procession's own torches that the figures were a lot shorter than adults' figures would be.

Skip whirled around, about to shout for Andy, and at once decided that he had better not. He ran downstairs and grabbed his own powerful flashlight. He didn't bother grabbing his jacket from a hook, though the night was crisp.

"Hey!" Skip yelled, when he had run several yards into the field. "Get off my property! What're you *doing* walking up there!"

The kids were singing some crazy, high-pitched song, nobody singing on key. It was just a wild treble chant. Skip recognized the word "scarecrow."

"We're going to burn the scarecrow . . ." something like that.

"Hey, there! Off my land!" Skip fell, banged a knee, and scrambled up again. The kids had heard him, Skip was pretty sure, but they weren't stopping. Never before had anyone disobeyed Skip—except of course Maggie. *"Off my land!"*

The kids moved on like a black caterpillar with an orange headlight and a couple of other lights in its body. Certainly the last couple of kids had heard Skip, because he had seen them turn, then run to catch up with the others. Skip stopped running. The caterpillar was closer to the scarecrow than he was, and he was not going to be able to get there first.

Even as he thought this, a whoop went up. A scream! Another scream of mingled terror and delight shattered their chant. Hysteria broke out. What surely was a little girl's throat gave a cry as shrill as a dog whistle. Their hands must have touched the corpse, maybe touched bone, Skip thought.

Skip made his way back towards his own house, his flashlight pointed at the ground. It was worse than the police, somehow. Every kid was going to tell his parents what he had found. Skip knew he had come to the end. He had seen businessmen, seen a lot of men come to the end. He had known men who had jumped out of windows, who had taken overdoses.

Skip went at once to his rifle. It was in the living room downstairs. He put the muzzle in his mouth and pulled the trigger.

When the kids streaked down the field, heading for the road a few seconds later, Skip was dead. The kids had heard the shot, and thought someone was trying to shoot at them.

Andy heard the shot. He had also seen the procession marching up the field and heard Skipperton shouting. He understood what had happened. He turned his television set off, and made his way rather slowly towards the main house. He would have to call the police. That was the right thing to do. Andy made up his mind to say to the police that he didn't know a thing about the corpse in the scarecrow's clothes. He had been away some of that weekend after all.

Those Awful Dawns

Eddie's face looked angry and blank also, as if he might be thinking of something else. He was staring at his two-year-old daughter Francy who sat in a wailing heap beside the double bed. Francy had tottered to the bed, struck it, and collapsed.

"*You* take care of her," Laura said. She was standing with the vacuum cleaner still in her hand. "I've got things to do!"

"You hit her, f'Christ's sake, so *you* take care of her!" Eddie was shaving at the kitchen sink.

Laura dropped the vacuum cleaner, started to go to Francy, whose cheek was bleeding, changed her mind and veered back to the vacuum cleaner and unplugged it, began to wrap the cord to put it away. The place could stay a mess tonight for all she cared.

The other three children, Georgie nearly six, Helen four, Stevie three, stared with wet, faintly smiling mouths.

"That's a cut, goddamnit!" Eddie put a towel under the baby's cheek. "Swear to God, that'll need stitches. Lookit it! How'd you do it?"

Laura was silent, at least as far as answering that question went. She felt exhausted. The boys—Eddie's pals—were coming tonight at nine to play poker, and she had to make at least twenty liverwurst and ham sandwiches for their midnight snack. Eddie had slept all day and was still only getting dressed at 7 P.M.

"You taking her to the hospital or what?" Eddie asked. His face was half covered with shaving cream.

"If I take her again, they'll think it's always *you* smacking her. Mostly it is, frankly."

"Don't give me that crap, not this time," Eddie said. "And 'they,' who the hell're 'they'? Shove 'em!"

Twenty minutes later, Laura was in the waiting hall of St. Vincent's Hospital on West 11th Street. She leaned back in the straight chair and half closed her eyes. There were seven other people waiting, and the nurse had told her it might be half an hour, but she would try to make it sooner because the baby was bleeding slightly. Laura had her story ready: the baby had fallen against the vacuum cleaner, must've hit the connecting part where there was a sliding knob. Since this was what Laura had hit her with; swinging it suddenly to one side because Francy had been pulling at it, Laura supposed that the same injury could be caused by Francy's falling against it. That made sense.

It was the third time they'd brought Francy to St. Vincent's, which was four blocks from where they lived on Hudson Street. Broken nose (Eddie's fault, Eddie's elbow), then another time a trickling of blood at the ear that wouldn't stop, then the third time, the one time they hadn't brought her on their own, was when Francy had had a broken arm. Neither Eddie nor Laura had known Francy had a broken arm. How could they have known? You couldn't see it. But around that time Francy had had a black eye, God knew how or why, and a social worker had turned up. A neighbor must have put the social worker on their tail, and Laura was ninety percent sure it was old Mrs. Covini on the ground floor, damn her ass. Mrs. Covini was one of those dumpy, black-dressed Italian mommas who lived surrounded by kids all their lives, nerves of steel, who hugged and kissed the kids all day as if they were gifts from heaven and very rare things on earth. The Mrs. Covinis didn't go out to work, Laura had always noticed. Laura worked as a waitress five nights a week at a downtown Sixth Avenue diner. That plus getting up at 6 A.M. to fix Eddie's bacon and eggs, pack his lunchbox, feed the kids who were already up, and cope with them all day was enough to make an ox tired, wasn't it? Anyway, Mrs. Covini's spying had brought this monster—she was five feet eleven if she was an inch—down on their necks three times. Her name, appropriately enough, was Mrs. Crabbe. "Four children are a lot to handle . . . Are you in the habit of using contraceptives, Mrs. Regan?" Oh, crap. Laura moved her head from side to side on the back of the straight chair and groaned, feeling exactly as she had felt in high school when confronted by a problem in algebra that bored her stiff. She and Eddie were practicing Catholics. She might have been willing to go on the Pill on her own, but Eddie wouldn't hear of it, and that was that. On her own, that was funny, because on her own she wouldn't have needed it. Anyway, that had shut old Crabbe up on the subject, and had given Laura a certain satisfaction. She and Eddie had some rights and independence left, at least.

"Next?" The nurse beckoned, smiling.

The young intern whistled. "How'd this happen?"

"A fall. Against the vacuum cleaner."

The smell of disinfectant. Stitches. Francy, who had been nearly asleep in the hall, had awakened at the anesthetizing needle and wailed through the whole thing. The intern gave Francy what he called a mild sedative in a candy-covered pill. He murmured something to a nurse.

"What're these bruises?" he asked Laura. "On her arms."

"Oh—just bumps. In the house. She bruises easily." He wasn't the same intern, was he, that Laura had seen three or four months ago?

"Can you wait just a minute?"

The nurse came back, and she and the intern looked at a card that the nurse had.

The nurse said to Laura, "I think one of our OPTs is visiting you now, Mrs. Regan?"

"Yes."

"Have you an appointment with her?"

"Yes, I think so. It's written down at home." Laura was lying.

MRS. CRABBE ARRIVED at 7:45 P.M. the following Monday without warning. Eddie had just got home and opened a can of beer. He was a construction worker, doing overtime nearly every day in the summer months when the light lasted. When he got home he always made for the sink, sponged himself with a towel, opened a can of beer, and sat down at the oilcloth-covered table in the kitchen.

Laura had already fed the kids at 6 P.M., and had been trying to steer them to bed when Mrs. Crabbe arrived. Eddie had cursed on seeing her come in the door.

"I'm sorry to intrude . . ." Like hell. "How have you been doing?"

Francy's face was still bandaged, and the bandage was damp and stained with egg. The hospital had said to leave the bandage on and not touch it. Eddie, Laura and Mrs. Crabbe sat at the kitchen table, and it turned into quite a lecture.

". . . You realize, don't you, that you both are using little Frances as an outlet for your bad temper. Some people might bang their fists against a wall or quarrel with each other, but you and your husband are apt to whack baby Frances. Isn't that true?" She smiled a phony, friendly smile, looking from one to the other of them.

Eddie scowled and mashed a book of matches in his fingers. Laura squirmed and was silent. Laura knew what the woman meant. Before Francy had been born, they had used to smack Stevie maybe a little too often. They damned well hadn't wanted a third baby, especially in an apartment the size of this one, just as the woman was saying now. And Francy was the fourth.

". . . but if you both can realize that Francy *is—here* . . ."

Laura was glad that she apparently wasn't going to bring up birth control again. Eddie looked about to explode, sipping his beer as if he was ashamed to have been caught with it, but as if he had a right to drink it if he wanted to, because it was his house.

". . . a larger apartment, maybe? Bigger rooms. That would ease the strain on your nerves a lot . . ."

Eddie was obliged to speak about the economic situation. "Yeah, I earn fine . . . Riveter-welder. Skilled. But we got expenses, y'know. I wouldn't wanta go looking for a bigger place. Not just now."

Mrs. Crabbe lifted her eyes and stared around her. Her black hair was neatly waved, almost like a wig. "That's a nice TV. You bought that?"

"Yeah, and we're still paying on it. That's *one* of the things," Eddie said.

Laura was tense. There was also Eddie's hundred-and-fifty-dollar wristwatch they were paying on, and luckily Eddie wasn't wearing it now (he was wearing his cheap one), because he didn't wear the good one to work.

"And the sofa and the armchairs, aren't they new . . . You bought them?"

"Yeah," Eddie said, hitching back in his chair. "This place is furnished, y'know, but you shoulda seen that—" He made a derisive gesture in the direction of the sofa.

Laura had to support Eddie here. "What they had here, it was an old red plastic thing. You couldn't even sit on it." It hurt your ass, Laura might have added.

"When we move to a bigger place, at least we've got those," Eddie said, nodding at the sofa and armchairs section.

The sofa and armchairs were covered with beige plush that had a floral pattern of pale pink and blue. Hardly three months in the house, and the kids had already spotted the seats with chocolate milk and orange juice. Laura found it impossible to keep the kids off the furniture. She was always yelling at them to play on the floor. But the point was the sofa and the armchairs weren't paid for yet, and that was what Mrs. Crabbe was getting at, not people's comfort or the way the house looked, oh no.

"Nearly paid up. Finished next month," Eddie said.

That wasn't true. It would be another four or five months, because they'd twice missed the payments, and the man at the 14th Street store had come near taking the things away.

Now there was a speech from the old bag about the cost of installment-plan buying. Always pay the whole sum, because if you couldn't do that, you couldn't afford whatever it was, see? Laura smoldered, as angry as Eddie, but the important thing with these meddlers was to appear to agree with everything they said. Then they might not come back.

". . . if this keeps up with little Frances, the law will have to step in and I'm sure you wouldn't want that. That would mean taking Frances to live somewhere else."

The idea was quite pleasant to Laura.

"Where? Take'er where?" Georgie asked. He was in pajama pants, standing near the table.

Mrs. Crabbe paid him no mind. She was ready to leave.

Eddie gave a curse when she was out the door, and went to get another beer. "*Goddamn invasion of privacy!*" He kicked the fridge door shut.

Laura burst out in a laugh. "That old sofa! Remember? *Jesus!*"

"Too bad it wasn't here, she coulda broke her behind on it."

That night around midnight, as Laura was carrying a heavy tray of four superburgers and four mugs of coffee, she remembered something that she had put out of her mind for five days. Incredible that she hadn't thought of it for five whole days. Now it was more than ever likely. Eddie would blow his stack.

The next morning on the dot of nine, Laura called up Dr. Weebler from the newspaper store downstairs. She said it was urgent, and got an appointment for 11:15. As Laura left for the doctor's, Mrs. Covini was in the hall, mopping the part of the white tiles directly in front of her door. Laura thought that was somehow bad luck, seeing Mrs. Covini now. She and Mrs. Covini didn't speak to each other any more.

"I can't give you an abortion just like that," Dr. Weebler said, shrugging and smiling his awful smile that seemed to say, "It's you holding the bag. I'm a doctor, a man." He said, "These things can be prevented. Abortions shouldn't be necessary."

I'll damn well go to another doctor, Laura thought with rising anger, but she kept a pleasant, polite expression on her face. "Look, Dr. Weebler, my husband and I are practicing Catholics, I told you that. At least my husband is and—you know. So these things happen. But I've already got four. Have a heart."

"Since when do practicing Catholics want abortions? No, Mrs. Regan, but I can refer you to another doctor."

And abortions were supposed to be easy lately in New York. "If I get the money together—How much is it?" Dr. Weebler was cheap, that was why they went to him.

"It's not a matter of money." The doctor was restless. He had other people waiting to see him.

Laura wasn't sure of herself, but she said, "You do abortions on other women, so why not me?"

"*Who?*—When there's a danger to a woman's health, that's different."

Laura didn't get anywhere, and that useless expedition cost her $7.50, payable on the spot, except that she did get another prescription for half-grain Nembutals out of him. That night she told Eddie. Better to tell him right away than postpone it, because postponing it was hell, she knew from experience, with the damned subject crossing her mind every half hour.

"Oh, *Chr-r-rist!*" Eddie said, and fell back on the sofa, mashing the hand of Stevie who was on the sofa and had stuck out a hand just as Eddie plopped.

Stevie let out a wail.

"Oh, shut up, that didn't kill you!" Eddie said to Stevie. "Well, now what. Now what?"

Now what. Laura was actually trying to think *now what.* What the hell ever was there to do except hope for a miscarriage, which never happened. Fall down the stairs, something like that, but she'd never had the guts to fall down the stairs. At least not so far. Stevie's wailing was like awful background music. Like in a horror film. "Oh, can it, Stevie!"

Then Francy started yelling. Laura hadn't fed her yet.

"I'm gonna get drunk," Eddie announced. "I suppose there's no booze."

He knew there wasn't. There never was any booze, it got drunk up too fast. Eddie was going to go out. "Don't you want to eat first?" Laura asked.

"Naw." He pulled on a sweater. "I just want to forget the whole damned thing. Just forget it for a *little* while."

Ten minutes later, after poking something at Francy (mashed potatoes, a nippled bottle because it made less mess than a cup) and leaving the other kids with a box of Fig Newtons, Laura did the same thing, but she went to a bar farther down Hudson where she knew he didn't go. Tonight was one of her two nights off from the diner, which was a piece of luck. She had two whiskey sours with a bottle of beer as accompaniment, and then a rather nice man started talking with her, and bought her two more whiskey sours. On the fourth, she was feeling quite wonderful, even rather decent and important sitting on the bar stool, glancing now and then at her reflection in the mirror behind the bottles. Wouldn't it be great to be starting over again? No marriage, no Eddie, no kids? Just something new, a clean slate.

"I asked you—are you married?"

"No," Laura said.

But apart from that, he talked about football. He had won a bet that day. Laura daydreamed. Yes, she'd once had a marriage, love and all that. She'd known Eddie would never make a lot of dough, but there was such a thing as living decently, wasn't there, and God knew her tastes weren't madly expensive, so what took all the money? The kids. There was the drain. Too bad Eddie was a Catholic, and when you marry a Catholic—

"Hey, you're not listening!"

Laura dreamed on with determination. Above all, she'd *had a dream* once, a dream of love and happiness and of making a nice home for Eddie and herself. Now the outsiders were even attacking her *inside her house.* Mrs. Crabbe. A lot Mrs. Crabbe knew about being waked up at five in the morning by a screaming kid, or being poked in the face by Stevie or Georgie when you'd been asleep only a couple of hours and your whole body ached. That was when she or Eddie was apt to swat them. In those awful dawns. Laura realized she was near tears, so she began to listen to the man who was still going on about football.

He wanted to walk her home, so she let him. She was so tipsy, she rather needed his arm. Then she said at the door that she lived with her mother, so she had to go up alone. He started getting fresh, but she gave him a shove and closed the front door, which locked. Laura hadn't quite reached the third floor when she heard feet on the stairs and thought the guy must've got in somehow, but it turned out to be Eddie.

"Well, how d'y'do?" said Eddie, feeling no pain.

The kids had got into the fridge. It was something they did about once a month. Eddie flung Georgie back and shut the fridge, then slipped on some spilled stringbeans and nearly fell.

"And lookit the *gas,* f'Christ's sake!" Eddie said.

Every burner was on, and as soon as Laura saw it, she smelled gas, gas everywhere. Eddie flipped all the burners shut and opened a window.

Georgie's wailing started all the others.

"Shut up, shut up!" Eddie yelled. "What the hell's the matter, are they hungry? Didn't you feed 'em?"

"Of course I fed 'em!" Laura said.

Eddie bumped into the door jamb, his feet slipped sideways in a funny slow motion collapse, and he sat down heavily on the floor. Four-year-old Helen laughed and clapped her hands. Stevie was giggling. Eddie cursed the entire household, and flung his sweater at the sofa, missing it. Laura lit a cigarette. She still had her whiskey sour buzz and she was enjoying it.

She heard the crash of a glass on the bathroom floor, and she merely raised her eyebrows and inhaled smoke. Got to tie Francy in her crib, Laura thought, and moved vaguely towards Francy to do it. Francy was sitting like a dirty rag doll in a corner. Her crib was in the bedroom, and so was the double bed in which the other three kids slept. Goddamn bedroom certainly was a bedroom, Laura thought. Beds were all you could see in there. She pulled Francy up by her tied-around bib, and Francy just then burped, sending a curdled mess over Laura's wrist.

"Ugh!" Laura dropped the child and shook her hand with disgust.

Francy's head had bumped the floor, and now she let out a scream. Laura ran water over her hand at the sink, shoving aside Eddie who was already stripped to the waist, shaving. Eddie shaved at night so that he could sleep a little longer in the morning.

"You're pissed," Eddie said.

"And so what?" Laura went back and shook Francy to make her hush. "For God's sake, shut up! What've *you* got to cry about?"

"Give 'er an aspirin. Take some yourself," Eddie said.

Laura told him what to do with himself. If Eddie came at her tonight, he could shove it. She'd go back to the bar. Sure. That place stayed open till three in the morning. Laura found herself pushing a pillow down on Francy's face to shut her up just for a minute, and Laura remembered what Mrs. Crabbe had said: Francy had become the target—Target? Outlet for both of them. Well, it was true, they did smack Francy more than the others, but Francy yelled more, too. Suiting action to the thought, Laura slapped Francy's face hard. That's what they did when people had hysterics, she thought. Francy did shut up, but for only a stunned couple of seconds, then yelled even louder.

The people below were thumping on their ceiling. Laura imagined them with a broom handle. Laura stamped three times on her floor in defiance.

"Listen, if you don't get that kid *quiet*—" Eddie said.

Laura stood at the closet undressing. She pulled on a nightgown, and pushed her feet into old brown loafers that served as house slippers. In the john, Eddie had broken the glass that they used when they brushed their teeth. Laura kicked some of the glass aside, too tired to sweep it up tonight. Aspirins. She took down a bottle and it slipped from her fingers before she got the top unscrewed. Crash, and pills all over the floor. Yellow pills. The Nembutals. That was a shame, but sweep it all up tomorrow. Save them, the pills. Laura took two aspirins.

Eddie was yelling, waving his arms, herding the kids towards the other double bed. Usually that was Laura's job, and she knew Eddie was doing it because he didn't want them roaming around the house all night, disturbing him.

"And if you don't stay in that bed, all of yuh, I'll *wham* yuh!"

Thump-thump-thump on the floor again.

Laura fell into bed, and awakened to the alarm clock. Eddie groaned and moved slowly, getting out of bed. Laura lay savoring the last few seconds of bed before she would hear the clunk that meant Eddie had put the kettle on. She did the rest, instant coffee, orange juice, bacon and eggs, instant hot cereal for the kids. She went over last night in her mind. How many whiskey sours? Five, maybe, and only one beer. With the aspirins, that shouldn't be so bad.

"Hey, what's with Georgie?" Eddie yelled. "Hey, what the hell's in the john?"

Laura crawled out of bed, remembering. "I'll sweep it up."

Georgie was lying on the floor in front of the john door, and Eddie was stooped beside him.

"Aren't those Nembutals?" Eddie said. "Georgie musta ate some! And lookit Helen!"

Helen was in the bathroom, lying on the floor beside the shower.

Eddie shook Helen, yelling at her to wake up. "Jesus, they're like in a coma!" He dragged Helen out by an arm, picked Georgie up and carried him to the sink. He held Georgie under his arm like a sack of flour, wet a dishtowel and sloshed it over Georgie's face and head. "You think we oughta get a doctor?—F'Christ's sake, move, will yuh? Hand me Helen."

Laura did. Then she pulled on a dress. She kept the loafers on. She must phone Weebler. No, St. Vincent's, it was closer. "Do you remember the number of St. Vincent's?"

"No," said Eddie. "What d'y'do to make kids vomit? Anybody vomit? Mustard, isn't it?"

"Yeah, I think so." Laura went out the door. She still felt tipsy, and almost tripped on the stairs. Good thing if she did, she thought, remembering she was pregnant, but of course it never worked until you were pretty far gone.

She hadn't a dime with her, but the newspaper store man said he would trust her, and gave her a dime from his pocket. He was just opening, because it was early. Laura looked up the number, then in the booth she found that she had forgotten half of it. She'd have to look it up again. The newspaper store man was watching her, because she had said it was an emergency and she had to call a hospital. Laura picked up the telephone and dialed the number as best she remembered it. Then she put the forefinger of her right hand on the hook (the man couldn't see the hook), because she knew it wasn't the right number, but because the man was watching her, she started speaking. The dime was returned in the chute and she left it.

"Yes, please. An emergency." She gave her name and address. "Sleeping pills. I suppose we'll need a stomach pump . . . Thank you. Good-bye."

Then she went back to the apartment.

"They're still out cold," Eddie said. "How many pills're gone, do you think? Take a look."

Stevie was yelling for his breakfast. Francy was crying because she was still tied in her crib.

Laura took a look on the bathroom tiles, but she couldn't guess at all how many pills were gone. Ten? Fifteen? They were sugar-coated, that's why the kids had liked them. She felt blank, scared, and exhausted. Eddie had put the kettle on, and they had instant coffee, standing up. Eddie said there wasn't any mustard in the house (Laura remembered she had used the last of it for all those ham sandwiches), and now he tried to get some coffee down Georgie's and Helen's throats, but none seemed to go down, and it only spilled on their fronts.

"Sweep up that crap so Stevie won't get any," Eddie said, nodding at the john. "What time're they coming? I gotta get going. That foreman's a shit, I told you, he don't want nobody late." He cursed, having picked up his lunchbox and found it empty, and he tossed the lunchbox with a clatter in the sink.

Still dazed, Laura fed Francy at the kitchen table (she had another black eye, where the hell did *that* come from?), started to feed cornflakes and milk to Stevie (he wouldn't eat hot cereal), then left it for Stevie to do, whereupon he turned the bowl over on the oilcloth table. Georgie and

Helen were still asleep on the double bed where Eddie had put them. *Well, after all St. Vincent's is coming,* Laura thought. But they weren't coming. She turned on the little battery radio to some dance music. Then she changed Francy's diaper. That was what Francy was howling about, her wet diaper. Laura had barely heard the howling this morning. Stevie had toddled over to Georgie and Helen and was poking them, trying to wake them up. In the john, Laura emptied the kids' pot down the toilet, washed the pot out, swept up the broken glass and the pills, and picked the pills out of the dustpan. She put the pills on a bare place on one of the glass shelves in the medicine cabinet.

At ten, Laura went down to the newspaper store, paid the man back, and had to look up the St. Vincent number again. This time she dialed it, got someone, told them what was the matter and asked why no one had come yet.

"You phoned at seven? That's funny. I was on. We'll send an ambulance right away."

Laura bought four quarts of milk and more baby food at the delicatessen, then went back upstairs. She felt a little less sleepy, but not much. Were Georgie and Helen still breathing? She absolutely didn't want to go and see. She heard the ambulance arriving. Laura was finishing her third cup of coffee. She glanced at herself in the mirror, but couldn't face that either. The more upset she looked, the better, maybe. Two men in white came up, and went at once to the two kids. They had stethoscopes. They murmured and exclaimed. One turned and asked:

"*Whad* they take?"

"Sleeping pills. They got into the Nembutals."

"This one's even cold. Didn't you notice that?"

He meant Georgie. One of the men wrapped the kids up in blankets from the bed, the other prepared a needle. He gave shots in the arm to both kids.

"No use telephoning us for another two three hours," one of them said.

The other said, "Never mind, she's in a state of shock. Better have some hot tea, lady, and lie down."

They hurried off. The ambulance whined towards St. Vincent's.

The whine was taken up by Francy, who was standing with her fat little legs apart, but no more apart than usual, while pee dripped from the lump of diaper between them. All the rubber pants were still dirty in the pan under the sink. It was a chore she should have done last night. Laura went over and smacked her on the cheek, just to shut her up for a minute, and Francy fell on the floor. Then Laura gave her a kick in the stomach, something she'd never done before. Francy lay there, silent for once.

Stevie stared wide-eyed and gaping, looking as if he didn't know whether to laugh or cry. Laura kicked her shoes off and went to get a beer. Naturally, there wasn't any. Laura combed her hair, then went down to the delicatessen. When she came back, Francy was sitting where she had lain before, and crying again. Change the diaper again? Stick a pair of dirty rubber pants on her? Laura opened a beer, drank some, then changed the diaper just to be doing something. Still with the beer beside her, she filled the sink with sudsy water and dumped the six pairs of rubber pants into it, and a couple of rinsed-out but filthy diapers as well.

The doorbell rang at noon, and it was Mrs. Crabbe, damn her eyes, just about as welcome as the cops.

This time Laura was insolent. She interrupted the old bitch every time she spoke. Mrs. Crabbe was asking how the children came to get at the sleeping pills? What time had they eaten them?

"I don't know why any human being has to put up with intrusions like this!" Laura yelled.

"Do you realize that your son is dead? He was bleeding internally from glass particles."

Laura let fly one of Eddie's favorite curses.

Then the old bag left the house, and Laura drank her beer, three cans of it. She was thirsty. When the bell rang again, she didn't answer it, but soon there was a knocking on the door. After a few minutes, Laura got so tired of it, she opened the door. It was old Crabbe again with two men in white, one carrying a satchel. Laura put up a fight, but they got a strait-jacket on her. They took her to another hospital, not St. Vincent's. Here two people held her while a third person gave her a needle. The needle nearly knocked her out, but not quite.

That was how, one month later, she got her abortion. The most blessed event that ever happened to her.

She had to stay in the place—Bellevue—all that time. When she told the shrinks she was really fed up with marriage, her marriage, they seemed to believe her and to understand, yet they admitted to her finally that all their treatment was designed to make her go back to that marriage. Meanwhile, the three kids—Helen had recovered—were in some kind of free nursery. Eddie had come to see her, but she didn't want to see him, and thank God they hadn't forced her to. Laura wanted a divorce, but she knew

Eddie would never say yes to a divorce. He thought people just didn't get divorced. Laura wanted to be free, independent, and alone. She didn't want to see the kids, either.

"I want to make a new life," she said to the psychiatrists, who had become as boring as Mrs. Crabbe.

The only way to get out of the place was to fool them, Laura realized, so she began to humor them, gradually. She would be allowed to go, they said, on condition that she went back to Eddie. But she wrung from a doctor a signed statement—she insisted on having it in writing—that she was to have no more children, which effectively meant that she had a right to take the Pill.

Eddie didn't like that, even if it was a doctor's orders. "That's not marriage," Eddie said.

Eddie had found a girlfriend while she was in Bellevue, and some nights he didn't come home, and went to work from wherever he was sleeping. Laura hired a detective for just one day, and discovered the woman's name and address. Then Laura sued for divorce on the grounds of adultery, no alimony asked, real Women's Lib. Eddie got the kids, which was fine with Laura because he wanted them more than she did. Laura got a full-time job in a department store, which was a bit tough, standing on her feet for so many hours, but all in all not so tough as what she had left. She was only twenty-five, and quite nice looking if she took the time to do her face and dress properly. There were good chances of advancement in her job, too.

"I feel peaceful now," Laura said to a new friend to whom she had told her past. "I feel different, as if I've lived a hundred years, and yet I'm still pretty young . . . Marriage? No, never again."

SHE WOKE UP and found it was all a dream. Well, not *all* a dream. The awakening was gradual, not a sudden awareness as in the morning when you open your eyes and see what's really in front of you. She'd been taking two kinds of pills on the doctor's orders. Now it seemed to her that the pills had been trick pills, to make the world seem rosy, to make her more cheerful—but really to get her to walk back into the same trap, like a doped sheep. She found herself standing at the sink on Hudson Street with a dishtowel in her hands. It was morning. 10:22 by the clock by the bed. But she *had* been to Bellevue, hadn't she? And Georgie had died, because now in the apartment there were only Stevie and Helen and Francy. It was

September, she saw by a newspaper that was lying on the kitchen table. And—where was it? The piece of paper the doctor had signed?

Where did she keep it, in her billfold? She looked and it wasn't there. She unzipped the pocket in her handbag. Not there either. But she'd had it. Hadn't she? For an instant, she wondered if she was pregnant, but there wasn't a sign of it at her waistline. Then she went as if drawn by a mysterious force, a hypnotist's force, to a bruised brown leather box where she kept necklaces and bracelets. In this box was a tarnished old silver cigarette case big enough for only four cigarettes, and inside this was a folded piece of crisp white paper. That was it. She had it.

She went into the bathroom and looked into the medicine cabinet. What did they look like? There was something called Ovral. That must be it, it sounded sort of eggy. Well, at least she was taking them, the bottle was half empty. And Eddie was annoyed. She remembered now. But he had to put up with it, that was all.

But she hadn't tracked down his girlfriend with a detective. She hadn't had the job in the department store. Funny, when it was all so clear, that job, selling bright scarves and hosiery, making up her face so she looked great, making new friends. Had Eddie had a girlfriend? Laura simply wasn't sure. Anyway, he had to put up with the Pill now, which was one small triumph for her. But it didn't quite make up for what she had to put up with. Francy was crying. Maybe it was time to feed her.

Laura stood in the kitchen, biting her underlip, thinking she had to feed Francy now—food always shut her up a little—and thinking she'd have to start thinking hard, now that she could think, now that she was fully awake. Good God, life couldn't just go on like this, could it? She'd doubtless lost the job at the diner, so she'd have to find another, because they couldn't make it on Eddie's pay alone. *Feed Francy.*

The doorbell rang. Laura hesitated briefly, then pushed the release button. She had no idea who it was.

Francy yelled.

"All *right!*" Laura snapped, and headed for the fridge.

A knock on the door.

Laura opened the door. It was Mrs. Crabbe.

Woodrow Wilson's Necktie

The façade of Madame Thibault's Waxwork Horrors glittered and throbbed with red and yellow lights, even in the daytime. Golden balls like knobs—the yellow lights—pulsated amid the red lights, attracting the eye, holding it.

Clive Wilkes loved the place, the inside and outside equally. Since he was a delivery boy for a grocery store, it was easy for him to say a certain delivery had taken him longer than might be expected—he'd had to wait for Mrs. So-and-so to get home, because the doorman had told him she was due any minute, or he'd had to go five blocks to find some change, because Mrs. Zilch had had only a fifty-dollar bill. At these spare moments, and Clive found one or two a week, he visited Madame Thibault's Waxwork Horrors.

Inside the establishment, you went through a dark passage to get in the mood, and then you were confronted by a bloody murder scene: a girl with long blonde hair was sticking a knife into the neck of an old man who sat at a kitchen table eating his dinner. His dinner was a couple of wax frankfurters and wax sauerkraut. Then came the Lindbergh kidnapping, with Hauptmann climbing down a ladder outside a nursery window. You could see the top of the ladder outside the window, and the top half of Hauptmann's figure, clutching the little boy. Also there was Marat in his bath with Charlotte nearby. And Christie with his stocking throttlings of women. Clive loved every tableau, and they never became stale. But he didn't look at them with the solemn, vaguely startled expression of the other people who looked at them. Clive was inclined to smile, even to laugh. They were amusing. Why not laugh? Farther on in the museum were the torture chambers—one old, one modern, purporting to show twentieth-century torture methods in Nazi Germany and in French Algeria. Madame Thibault—who Clive strongly suspected did not exist—kept up to date. There were the Kennedy assassinations, of course, the Tate massacre, and as like as not a murder that had happened just a month ago somewhere.

Clive's first definite ambition in regard to Madame Thibault's Wax-work Horrors was to spend a night there. This he did one night, providently taking along a cheese sandwich in his pocket. It was fairly easy to accomplish. Clive knew that three people worked in the museum proper, down in the bowels as he thought of it, though the museum was on street level, while another man, a plumpish middle-aged fellow in a nautical cap, sold tickets out in front at a booth. There were two men and a woman who worked in the bowels. The woman, also plump with curly brown hair and glasses and about forty, took the tickets at the end of the dark corridor, where the museum began. One of the men lectured constantly, though not more than half the people ever bothered to listen. "Here we see the fanatical expression of the true murderer, captured by the wax artistry of Madame Thibault . . . blah–blah–blah . . ." The other man had black hair and black-rimmed glasses, and he just drifted around, shooing away kids who wanted to climb into the tableaux, maybe watching for pickpockets, or maybe protecting women from unpleasant assaults in the semi-darkness of the place, Clive didn't know.

He only knew it was quite easy to slip into one of the dark corners or into a nook next to one of the Iron Molls—maybe even into one of the Iron Molls, but slender as he was, the spikes might poke him, Clive thought, so he ruled out this idea. He had observed that people were gently urged out around 9:15 P.M. as the museum closed at 9:30 P.M. And lingering as late as possible one evening, Clive had learned that there was a sort of cloak room for the staff behind a door in one back corner, from which he had also heard the sound of a toilet flushing.

So one night in November, Clive concealed himself in the shadows, which were abundant, and listened to the three people as they got ready to leave. The woman—whose name seemed to be Mildred—was lingering to take the money box from Fred, the ticket-seller, and to count it and deposit it somewhere in the cloak room. Clive was not interested in the money, at least not very interested. He was interested in spending a night in the place, to be able to say that he had.

"Night, Mildred! See you tomorrow!" called one of the men.

"Anything else to do? I'm leaving now," said Mildred. "Boy, am I tired! But I'm still going to watch Dragon Man tonight."

"Dragon Man," the other man repeated, uninterested.

Evidently the ticket-seller Fred left from the front of the building after handing in the money box, and in fact Clive recalled seeing him close up the front once, cutting the lights from inside the entrance door, locking it.

Clive stood in a nook by an Iron Moll. When he heard the back door shut, and the key turn in the lock, he waited for a moment in delicious silence, aloneness, and suspense, then ventured out. He went first on tiptoe to the room where they kept their coats, because he had never seen it. He had brought matches (also cigarettes, though smoking was not allowed, according to several signs), and with the aid of a match, he found the light switch. The room contained an old desk, four or five metal lockers, a tin wastebasket, an umbrella stand, and some books in a bookcase against a rather grimy wall that had once been white. Clive slid open a drawer or two, and found the well-worn wooden box which he had once seen the ticket-seller carrying in through the front door. The box was locked. He could walk out with the box, he thought, but in fact he didn't care to, and he considered this rather decent of himself. He gave the box a wipe with the side of his hand, not forgetting the bottom where his fingertips had touched. That was funny, he thought, wiping something he hadn't stolen.

Clive set about enjoying the night. He found the lights, and put them on, so that the booths with the gory tableaux were all illuminated. He was hungry, and took one bite of his sandwich and put it back in the paper napkin in his pocket. He sauntered slowly past the John F. Kennedy assassination—Robert, Jackie, doctors bending anxiously over the white table on which JFK lay, leaking an ocean of blood which covered the floor. This time Hauptmann's descent of the ladder made Clive giggle. Charles Lindbergh Jr.'s face looked so untroubled, one might have thought he was sitting on the floor of his nursery playing with blocks. Clive swung a leg over a metal bar and climbed into the Judd-Snyder fracas. It gave him a thrill to be standing right *with* them, inches from the throttling-from-behind which the lover was administering to the husband. Clive put a hand out and touched the red-paint blood that was beginning to come from the man's throat where the wire pressed. Clive also touched the cool cheekbones of the victim. The popping eyes were of glass, vaguely disgusting, and Clive did not touch those.

Two hours later, he was singing a church hymn, "Nearer My God to Thee" and "Jesus Wants Me for a Sunbeam." Clive didn't know all the words. He smoked.

By 2 A.M. he was bored, and tried to get out by both front door and back, but couldn't. No spare keys anywhere that he could find. He'd thought of having a hamburger at an all-night place between here and home. His incarceration didn't bother him, however, so he finished the now dry cheese sandwich, made use of the toilet, and slept for a bit on three straight chairs which he arranged in a row. It was so uncomfortable, he knew he would wake up in a while, which he did at 5 A.M. He washed his face, and went for another look at the wax exhibits. This time he took a souvenir—Woodrow Wilson's necktie.

As the hour of nine approached—Madame Thibault's Waxwork Horrors opened at 9:30 A.M.—Clive hid himself in an excellent spot, behind one of the tableaux whose backdrop was a black and gold Chinese screen. In front of the screen was a bed and in the bed lay a wax man with a handlebar mustache, who was supposed to be dead from poisoning by his wife.

The public began trickling in shortly after 9:30 A.M., and the taller, solemn man began mumbling his boring lecture. Clive had to wait till a few minutes past ten before he felt safe enough to mingle with the crowd and make his exit, with Woodrow Wilson's necktie rolled up in his pocket. He was a bit tired, but happy. Though on second thought, who would he tell about it? Joey Vrasky, that blond idiot who worked behind the counter at Simmons's Grocery? Hah! Why bother? Joey didn't deserve a good story. Clive was half an hour late for work.

"I'm sorry, Mr Simmons, I overslept," Clive said hastily, but he thought quite politely, as he came into the store. There was a delivery job awaiting him. Clive took his bicycle and put the box in front of the handlebars on a platform which had a curb, so a box would not fall off.

Clive lived with his mother, a thin, highly strung woman who was a saleswoman in a shop that sold stockings, girdles and underwear. Her husband had left her when Clive was five. She had no other children but Clive. Clive had quit high school a year before graduating, to his mother's regret, and for a year he had done nothing but lie around the house or stand on street corners with his chums. But Clive had never been very chummy with any of his friends, for which his mother was thankful, as she considered them a worthless lot. Clive had had the delivery job at Simmons's for nearly a year now, and his mother felt that he was settling down.

When Clive came home that evening at 6:30 P.M., he had a story ready for his mother. Last night he had run into his old friend Richie, who was in the army and home on leave, and they had sat up at Richie's talking so late, that Richie's parents had invited him to stay, and Clive had slept on the couch. His mother accepted this explanation. She made a supper of beans, bacon and eggs.

There was really no one to whom Clive felt like telling his exploit of the night. He couldn't have borne someone looking at him and saying, "Yeah? Well, so what?" because what he had done had taken a bit of planning, even a little daring. He put Woodrow Wilson's tie among his others that hung over a string on the inside of his closet door. It was a gray silk tie, conservative and expensive. Several times that day, Clive imagined the two men in the place, or maybe the woman named Mildred, glancing at Woodrow Wilson and exclaiming:

"Hey! What happened to Woodrow Wilson's tie, I wonder?"

Each time Clive thought of this, he had to duck his head to hide his smile.

After twenty-four hours, however, the exploit had begun to lose its charm and excitement. Clive's excitement arose only again—and it could arise every day and two or three times a day—when he cycled past the twinkling façade of Madame Thibault's Waxwork Horrors. His heart would give a leap, his blood would run a little faster, and he would think of all the motionless murders going on in there, and all the stupid faces of Mr. and Mrs. Johnny Q. Public gaping at them. But Clive didn't even buy another ticket—price sixty-five cents—to go in and look at Woodrow Wilson and see that his tie was missing and his collar button showing—his work.

Clive did get another idea one afternoon, a hilarious idea that would make the public sit up and take notice. Clive's ribs trembled with suppressed laughter as he pedaled towards Simmons's, having just delivered a carton of groceries.

When should he do it? Tonight? No, best to take a day or so to plan it. It would take brains. And silence. And sure movements—all the things Clive admired. He spent two days thinking about it. He went to his local snack bar and drank Coca-Cola and beer, and played the pinball machines with his pals. The pinball machines had pulsating lights, too—MORE THAN ONE CAN PLAY and IT's MORE FUN TO COMPETE—but Clive thought only of Madame Thibault's as he stared at the rolling, bouncing balls that mounted a score he cared nothing about. It was the same when he looked at the rainbow-colored jukebox whose blues, reds and yellows undulated, and when he went over to drop a few coins in it. He was thinking of what he was going to do in Madame Thibault's Waxwork Horrors.

On the second night, after a supper with his mother, Clive went to Madame Thibault's and bought a ticket. The old guy who sold tickets barely looked at people, he was so busy making change and tearing off tickets, which was just as well. Clive went in at 9 P.M.

He looked at the tableaux, though they were not so fascinating to him tonight as usual. Woodrow Wilson's tie was still missing, as if no one had noticed it, and Clive had a good chuckle over this, which he concealed behind his hand. Clive remembered that the solemn-faced pickpocket-watcher—the drifting snoop—had been the last to leave the night Clive had stayed, so Clive assumed he had the keys, and therefore he ought to be the last to be killed.

The woman was the first. Clive hid himself beside one of the Iron Molls again, while the crowd oozed out, and as Mildred walked past him, in her hat and coat, to leave via the back door, Clive stepped out and wrapped an arm around her throat from behind.

She made only a small "Ur-rk" sound.

Clive squeezed her throat with his hands, stopping her voice. At last she slumped, and Clive dragged her into a dark, recessed corner to the left of the cloakroom as one faced that room, and he knocked an empty cardboard box of some kind over, but it didn't make enough noise to attract the attention of the other two men.

"Mildred's gone?" one of the men said.

"She might be still in the office."

"No, she's not." This voice had already gone into the corridor where Clive crouched over Mildred, and had looked into the empty cloakroom where the light was still on. "She's left. Well, I'm calling it a day, too."

Clive stepped out then, and encircled this man's neck in the same manner. The job was more difficult, because the man struggled, but Clive's arm was thin and strong, he acted with swiftness, and he knocked the man's head against the nearest wall.

"What's going on?" The thump had brought the second man.

This time, Clive tried a punch to the man's jaw, but missed and hit his neck. However, this so stunned the man—the solemn fellow, the snoop—that a second blow was easy, and then Clive was able to take him by the shirtfront and bash his head against the wall which was harder than the wooden floor. Then Clive made sure all three were dead. The two men's heads were bleeding. The woman was bleeding slightly from the mouth. Clive reached for the keys in the second man's pockets. They were in his left trousers pocket and with them was a penknife. Clive took the knife also.

Then the taller man moved slightly. Alarmed, Clive opened the pearl-handled penknife and went to work with it. He plunged it into the man's throat three or four times.

Close call! Clive thought, and he checked again to make sure they were all dead now. They most certainly were, and that was most certainly real blood coming out, not the red paint of Madame Thibault's Waxwork Horrors. Clive switched on the lights for the tableaux, and went into the exhibition hall for the interesting task of choosing the right places for the corpses.

The woman belonged in Marat's bath, not much doubt about that, and Clive debated removing her clothing, but decided against it, simply because she would look much funnier sitting in a bath with a fur-trimmed coat and hat on than naked. The figure of Marat sent him off in laughter. He'd expected sticks for legs, and nothing between the legs, because you couldn't see any more of Marat than from the middle of his torso up, but Marat had no legs at all, and his wax body ended just below the waist in a fat stump which was planted on a wooden platform so it would not topple. This crazy item Clive carried into the cloakroom and set squarely in the middle of the desk, like a Buddha. He then carried Mildred—who weighed a good bit—onto the Marat scene and stuck her in the bath. Her hat fell off and he pushed it on again, a bit over one eye. Her bleeding mouth hung open.

God, it *was* funny!

Now for the men. Obviously, the one whose throat he had cut would look good in the place of the old man who was eating franks and sauerkraut, because the girl behind him was supposed to be stabbing him in the throat. This work took Clive some fifteen minutes. Since the wax figure of the old man was in a seated position, Clive stuck him on the toilet off the cloakroom. It was amusing to see the old man on the toilet, throat bleeding, a knife in one hand and a fork in the other, apparently waiting for something to eat. Clive lurched against the doorjamb laughing loudly, not even caring if someone heard him, because it was so ludicrous, it was worth getting caught for.

Next, the little snoop. Clive looked around him, and his eye fell on the Woodrow Wilson scene, which depicted the signing of the armistice in 1918. A wax figure—Woodrow Wilson—sat at a huge desk signing a paper, and that was the logical place for a man whose head was split open and bleeding. With some difficulty Clive got the pen out of Woodrow Wilson's fingers, laid it to one side on the desk, and carried the figure—they did not weigh very much—into the cloakroom where Clive seated him at the desk, rigid arms in attitude of writing, and Clive stuck a ballpoint pen into his right hand. Now for the last heave. Clive saw that his jacket was now quite spotted with blood, and he would have to get rid of it, but so far no blood was on his trousers.

Clive dragged the second man to the Woodrow Wilson tableau, heaved him up onto the platform, and rolled him towards the desk. His head was still leaking blood. Clive got him up onto the chair, but the head toppled forward onto the green-blottered desk, onto the phony blank pages, and the pen barely stood upright in the limp hand.

But it was done. Clive stood back and smiled. Then he listened. Clive sat down on a straight chair somewhere and rested for a few minutes, because his heart was beating fast, and he suddenly realized that every muscle in his body was tired. Ah, well, now he had the keys. He could get out, go home, have a good night's rest, because he wanted to be ready to enjoy tomorrow. Clive took a sweater from one of the male figures in a log cabin tableau. He had to pull the sweater down over the feet to get it off, because the arms would not bend, and it stretched the neck of the sweater but that couldn't be helped. Now the wax figure had a bib of a shirtfront, and naked arms and chest.

Clive wadded up his jacket and went everywhere with it, erasing fingerprints wherever he thought he had touched. He turned the lights off, and made his way carefully to the back door, which was not locked. Clive locked it behind him, and would have left the keys in a mailbox, if there had been one, but there was none, so he dropped the keys on the doorstep. In a wire rubbish basket, he found some newspapers, and he wrapped his jacket in them, and walked on with it until he found another wire rubbish basket, where he forced the bundle down among candy wrappers and beer cans.

"A new sweater?" his mother asked that night.

"Richie gave it to me—for luck."

Clive slept like the dead, too tired even to laugh again at the memory of the old man sitting on the toilet.

The next morning, Clive was standing across the street when the ticket-seller arrived just before 9:30 A.M. By 9:35 A.M., only three people had gone in (evidently Fred had a key to the front door, in case his colleagues were late), but Clive could not wait any longer, so he crossed the street and bought a ticket. Now the ticket-seller was doubling as ticket-taker, or telling people, "Just go on in. Everybody's late this morning." The ticket man stepped inside the door to put on some lights, then walked all the way into the place to put on the display lights, which worked from switches in the hall that led to the cloakroom. And the funny thing to

Clive, who was walking behind him, was that the ticket man didn't notice anything odd, didn't notice Mildred in hat and coat sitting in Marat's bathtub.

The customers so far were a man and woman, a boy of fourteen or so in sneakers, and a single man. They looked expressionlessly at Mildred in the tub, as if they thought it quite "normal," which could have sent Clive into paroxysms of mirth, except that his heart was thumping madly, and he was hardly breathing for suspense. Also, the man with his face in franks and sauerkraut brought no surprise either. Clive was a bit disappointed.

Two more people came in, a man and a woman.

Then at last by the Woodrow Wilson tableau, there was a reaction. One of the women clinging to a man's arm, asked:

"Was there someone shot when the armistice was signed?"

"I don't know. I don't *think* so," the man replied vaguely. "Yes-s—Let me think."

Clive's laughter pressed like an explosion in his chest, he spun on his heel to control himself, and he had the feeling he knew all about history, and that no one else did. By now, of course, the real blood had turned dark red. The green blotter was now dark red, and blood had run down the side of the desk.

A woman on the other side of the hall, where Mildred was, let out a scream.

A man laughed, but only briefly.

Suddenly everything happened. A woman shrieked, and at the same time, a man yelled, "My God, it's *real!*"

Clive saw a man climbing up to investigate the corpse with its face in the frankfurters.

"The blood's *real!* It's a dead *man!*"

Another man—one of the public—slumped to the floor. He had fainted!

The ticket-seller came bustling in. "What's the trouble?"

"Coupla corpses here! *Real* ones!"

Now the ticket-seller looked at Marat's bathtub and fairly jumped into the air with surprise. "Holy Christmas! Holy *cripes!*—Mildred!"

"And this one!"

"And the one here!"

"My God, got to—got to call the police!" said the ticket-seller Fred. "Could you all, please—just leave?"

One man and woman went out hurriedly. But the rest lingered, shocked, fascinated.

Fred had trotted into the cloakroom, where the telephone was, and Clive heard him yell something. He'd seen the man at the desk, of course, Woodrow Wilson, and Marat on the desk.

Clive thought it was time to drift out, so he did, sidling his way through four or five people who were peering in the door, coming in maybe because there was no ticket-seller.

That was good, Clive thought. That was all right. Not bad.

He had not intended to go to work that day, but suddenly he thought it wiser to check in and ask for the day off. Mr Simmons was of course as sour as ever when Clive said he was not feeling well, but as Clive held his stomach and appeared weak, there was little old Simmons could do. Clive left the store. He had brought with him all his ready cash, about twenty-three dollars.

Clive wanted to take a long bus ride somewhere. He realized that suspicion was likely to fall on him, if the ticket-seller remembered his coming to Madame Thibault's very often, or especially if he remembered his being there last night, but this had little to do with his desire to take a bus ride. His longing for a bus ride was simply, somehow, irresistible and purposeless. He bought a ticket westward for something over seven dollars, one way. This brought him, by about 7 P.M., to a good-sized town in Indiana, whose name Clive paid no attention to.

The bus spilled a few passengers, Clive included, at a terminal where there was a cafeteria and a bar. Clive by now was curious about the newspapers, and went at once to the newsstand near the street door of the cafeteria. And there it was:

TRIPLE MURDER IN WAXWORKS

MASS MURDER IN WAXWORKS MUSEUM

MYSTERY KILLER: THREE DEAD IN WAXWORKS MUSEUM

Clive liked the last headline best. He bought the three newspapers, and stood at the bar with a beer.

This morning at 9:30 A.M., ticket man Fred J. Keating and several of the public who had come to see Madame Thibault's Waxworks Horrors, a noted attraction of this city, were confronted by three genuine corpses among the displays. They were the bodies of Mrs. Mildred Veery, 41; George P. Hartley, 43; and Richard K. MacFadden, 37, all employed at the waxworks museum. The two men were killed by concussions to the head, and in the case of one also by stabbing, and the woman by strangulation. Police are searching for clues on the premises. The murders are believed to have taken place shortly before 10 P.M. last evening, when the three employees were about to leave the museum. The murderer or murderers may have been among the last patrons of the museum before closing time at 9:30 P.M. It is thought that he or they may have concealed themselves somewhere in the museum until the rest of the patrons had left . . .

Clive was pleased. He smiled as he sipped his beer. He hunched over the papers, as if he did not wish the rest of the world to share his pleasure, but this was not true. After a few minutes, Clive looked to right and left to see if anyone else among the men and a few women at the bar were reading the story also. Two men were reading newspapers, but Clive could not tell if they were reading about him necessarily, because their newspapers were folded. Clive lit a cigarette and went through all three newspapers to see if there was any clue about him. He found none at all. One paper said specifically that Fred J. Keating had not noticed any person or persons entering the museum last evening who looked suspicious.

. . . Because of the bizarre arrangement of the victims and of the displaced wax figures in the exhibitions, in whose places the victims were put, police are looking for a psychopathic killer. Residents of the area have been warned by radio and television to take special precautions on the street and to keep their homes locked . . .

Clive chuckled over that one. Psychopathic killer. He was sorry about the lack of detail, the lack of humor in the three write-ups. They might have said something about the old guy sitting on the toilet. Or the fellow signing the armistice with the back of his head bashed in. Those were strokes of genius. Why didn't they appreciate them?

When he had finished his beer, Clive walked out onto the sidewalk. It was now dark and the streetlights were on. He enjoyed looking around in the new town, looking into shop windows. But he was aiming for a hamburger place, and he went into the first one he came to. It was a diner made up to look like a crack train made of chromium. Clive ordered two hamburgers and a cup of coffee. Next to him were two Western-looking men in cowboy boots and rather soiled broad-brimmed hats. Was one a sheriff, Clive wondered? But they were talking, in a drawl, about acreage somewhere. Land. Money. They were hunched over hamburgers and coffee, one so close his elbow kept brushing Clive's. Clive was reading his newspapers all over again, and he had propped one against the napkin container in front of him.

One of the men asked for a napkin and disturbed Clive, but Clive smiled, and said in a friendly way:

"Did you read about the murders in the waxworks?"

The man looked blank, then said, "Saw the headlines."

"Someone killed the three people who worked in the place. Look." There was a photograph in one of the papers, but Clive didn't much like it, because it showed the corpses lined up on the floor. He would have preferred Mildred in the bathtub.

"Yeah," said the Westerner, edging away from Clive as if he didn't like him.

"The bodies were put into a few of the exhibitions. Like the wax figures. They say that, but they don't show a picture of it," said Clive.

"Yeah," said the Westerner, and went on with his hamburger.

Clive felt let down and somehow insulted. His face grew a little warm as he stared back at his newspapers. In fact, anger was growing very quickly inside him, making his heart go faster, as it did when he passed Madame Thibault's Waxwork Horrors, though now the sensation was not at all pleasant. Clive put on a smile, however, and turned again to the man on his left. "I mention it, because I did it. That's my work there." He pointed at the picture of the corpses.

"Listen, boy," said the Westerner, chewing, "you just keep to yourself tonight. Okay? We ain't botherin' you, and don't you go botherin' us." He laughed a little, and glanced at his companion.

His friend was staring at Clive, but looked away at once when Clive looked at him.

This was a double rebuff, and quite enough for Clive. Clive got his money out and paid for his unfinished food with a dollar bill and a fifty-cent piece. He left the change and walked to the sliding door exit.

"But y'know, maybe that kid ain't kiddin'," Clive heard one of the men say.

Clive turned and said, "*I* ain't kiddin'!" Then he went out into the night.

Clive slept at a YMCA. The next day, he half expected he would be picked up by any passing cop on the beat, but he wasn't, and he passed a few. He got a lift to another town, nearer his home town. The day's newspapers brought no mention of his name, and no clues. In another café that evening almost the identical conversation took place between Clive and a couple of fellows around his own age. They didn't believe him. It was stupid of them, Clive thought, and he wondered if they were pretending? Or lying?

Clive hitched his way to his hometown, and headed for the police station. He was curious to see what *they* would say. He imagined what his mother would say after he confessed. Probably the same thing she had said to her friends sometimes, or that she'd said to a policeman when he was sixteen and had stolen a car:

"Clive hasn't been the same boy since his father went away. I know he needs a man around the house, a man to look up to, imitate, y'know. That's what people tell me. Since fourteen, Clive's been asking me questions like, 'Who am I, anyway?' and 'Am I a person, mom?' " Clive could see and hear her already in the police station.

"I have an important confession to make," Clive said to a guard, or somebody, sitting at a desk at the front of the station.

The guard's attitude was rude and suspicious, Clive thought, but he was told to walk to an office, where he spoke with a police officer who had gray hair and a fat face. Clive told his story.

"Where do you go to school, Clive?"

"I don't. I'm eighteen." Clive told him about his job at Simmons's Grocery.

"Clive, you've got troubles, but they're not the ones you're talking about," said the officer.

Clive had to wait in a room, and nearly an hour later a psychiatrist was brought in. Then his mother. Clive became more and more impatient. They didn't believe him. They were saying he was a typical case of false confessing in order to attract attention to himself. His mother's repeated statements about his asking questions like "Am I a person?" only seemed to corroborate the psychiatrist and the police in their opinion.

Clive was to report somewhere twice a week for psychiatric therapy.

He fumed. He refused to go back to Simmons's Grocery, but found another delivery job, because he liked having a little money in his pocket, and he was fast on his bicycle and honest with the change.

"You haven't *found* the murderer, have you?" Clive said to the psychiatrist, associating him, Clive realized, with the police. "You're all the biggest bunch of jackasses I've ever seen in my life!"

The psychiatrist lost his temper, which was at least human.

"You'll never get anywhere talking to people like that, boy."

Clive said, "Some perfectly ordinary strangers in Indiana said, 'Maybe that kid ain't kiddin'.' They seem to have had more sense than *you!*"

The psychiatrist laughed.

Clive smoldered. One thing might have helped to prove his story, Woodrow Wilson's necktie, which still hung in his closet. But these bastards damned well didn't deserve to see that tie. Even as he ate his suppers with his mother, went to movies with her, and delivered groceries, he was planning. He'd do something more important next time: start a fire in the depths of a big building, plant a bomb somewhere, take a machine gun up to some penthouse and let 'em have it down on the street. Kill a hundred people at least. They'd have to come up in the building to get him. They'd know then. They'd treat him like somebody who existed.

One for the Islands

The voyage wasn't to be much longer.

Most people were bound for the mainland, which was not far at all now. Others were bound for the islands to the west, some of which were very far indeed.

Dan was bound for a certain island that he believed probably farther than any of the others the ship would touch at. He supposed that he would be about the last passenger to disembark.

On the sixth day of the smooth, uneventful voyage, he was in excellent spirits. He enjoyed the company of his fellow-passengers, had joined them a few times in the games that were always in progress on the top deck forward, but mostly he strolled the deck with his pipe in his mouth and a book under his arm, the pipe unlighted and the book forgotten, gazing serenely at the horizon and thinking of the island to which he was going. It would be the finest island of them all, Dan imagined. For some months now, he had devoted much of his time to imagining its terrain. There was no doubt, he decided finally, that he knew more about his island than any man alive, a fact which made him smile whenever he thought of it. No, no one would ever know a hundredth of what he knew about his island, though he had never seen it. But then, perhaps no one else had ever seen it, either.

Dan was happiest when strolling the deck, alone, letting his eyes drift from soft cloud to horizon, from sun to sea, thinking always that his island might come into view before the mainland. He would know its outline at once, he was sure of that. Strangely, it would be like a place he had always known, but secretly, telling no one. And there he would finally be alone.

It startled him sometimes, unpleasantly, too, suddenly to encounter, face to face, a passenger coming round a corner. He found it disturbing to bump into a hurrying steward in one of the twisting, turning corridors of D-deck, which being third class was more like a catacomb than the rest, and which was the deck where Dan had his cabin. Then there had been the time, the second day of the voyage, when for an instant he saw very close to his eyes the ridged floor of the corridor, with a cigarette butt between two ridges, a chewing-gum wrapper, and a few discarded matches. That had been unpleasant, too.

"Are you for the mainland?" asked Mrs. Gibson-Leyden, one of the first-class passengers, as they stood at the rail one evening.

Dan smiled a little and shook his head. "No, the islands," he said pleasantly, rather surprised that Mrs. Gibson-Leyden didn't know by now. But on the other hand, there had been little talk among the passengers as to where each was going. "You're for the mainland, I take it?" He spoke to be friendly knowing quite well that Mrs. Gibson-Leyden was for the mainland.

"Oh, yes," Mrs. Gibson-Leyden said. "My husband had some idea of going to an island, but I said, not for me!"

She laughed with an air of satisfaction, and Dan nodded. He liked Mrs. Gibson-Leyden because she was cheerful. It was more than could be said for most of the first-class passengers. Now he leaned his forearms on the rail and looked out at the wake of moonlight on the sea that shimmered like the back of a gigantic sea dragon with silver scales. Dan couldn't imagine that anyone would go to the mainland when there were islands in abundance, but then he had never been able to understand such things, and with a person like Mrs. Gibson-Leyden, there was no use in trying to discuss them and to understand. Dan drew gently on his empty pipe. He could smell a fragrance of lavender cologne from Mrs. Gibson-Leyden's direction. It reminded him of a girl he had once known, and he was amused now that he could feel drawn to Mrs. Gibson-Leyden, certainly old enough to have been his mother, because she wore a familiar scent.

"Well, I'm supposed to meet my husband back in the game room," Mrs. Gibson-Leyden said, moving away. "He went down to get a sweater."

Dan nodded, awkwardly now. Her departure made him feel abandoned, absurdly lonely, and immediately he reproached himself for not having made more of an effort at communication with her. He smiled, straightened, and peered into the darkness over his left shoulder, where the mainland would appear before dawn, then his island, later.

Two people, a man and a woman, walked slowly down the deck, side by side, their figures quite black in the darkness. Dan was conscious of their separateness from each other. Another isolated figure, short and fat, moved into the light of the windows in the superstructure: Dr. Eubanks, Dan recognized. Forward, Dan saw a group of people standing on deck and at the rails, all isolated, too. He had a vision of stewards and stewardesses below, eating their solitary meals at tiny tables in the corridors, hurrying about with towels, trays, menus. They were all alone, too. There was nobody who touched anybody, he thought, no man who held his wife's hand, no lovers whose lips met—at least he hadn't seen any so far on this voyage.

Dan straightened still taller. An overwhelming sense of aloneness, of his own isolation, had taken possession of him, and because his impulse was to shrink within himself, he unconsciously stood as tall as he could. But he could not look at the ship any longer, and turned back to the sea.

It seemed to him that only the moon spread its arms, laid its web protectively, lovingly, over the sea's body. He stared at the veils of moonlight as hard as he could, for as long as he could—which was perhaps twenty-five seconds—then went below to his cabin and to sleep.

He was awakened by the sound of running feet on the deck, and a murmur of excited voices.

The mainland, he thought at once, and threw off his bedcovers. He did want a good look at the mainland. Then as his head cleared of sleep, he realized that the excitement on deck must be about something else. There was more running now, a woman's wondering "Oh!" that was half a scream, half an exclamation of pleasure. Dan hurried into his clothes and ran out of his cabin.

His view from the A-deck companionway made him stop and draw in his breath. The ship was sailing *downward,* had been sailing downward on a long, broad path in the sea itself. Dan had never seen anything like it. No one else had either, apparently. No wonder everyone was so excited.

"When?" asked a man who was running after the hurrying captain. "Did you see it? What happened?"

The captain had no time to answer him.

"It's all right. This is right," said a petty officer, whose calm, serious face contrasted strangely with the wide-eyed alertness of everyone else.

"One doesn't notice it below," Dan said quickly to Mr. Steyne who was standing near him, and felt idiotic at once, because what did it matter whether one felt it below or not? The ship was sailing downward, the sea sloped downward at about a twenty degree angle with the horizon, and such a thing had never been heard of before, even in the Bible.

Dan ran to join the passengers who were crowding the forward deck. "When did it start? I mean, where?" Dan asked the person nearest him.

The person shrugged, though his face was as excited, as anxious as the rest.

Dan strained to see what the water looked like at the side of the swath, for the slope did not seem more than two miles broad. But whatever was happening, whether the swath ended in a sharp edge or sloped up to the main body of the sea, he could not make out, because a fine mist obscured the sea on either side. Now he noticed the golden light that lay on everything around them, the swath, the atmosphere, the horizon before them. The light was no stronger on one side than on the other, so it could not have been the sun. Dan couldn't find the sun, in fact. But the rest of the sky and the higher body of the sea behind them was bright as morning.

"Has anybody seen the mainland?" Dan asked, interrupting the babble around him.

"No," said a man.

"There's no mainland," said the same unruffled petty officer.

Dan had a sudden feeling of having been duped.

"This is right," the petty officer added laconically. He was winding a thin line around and round his arm, bracing it on palm and elbow.

"Right?" asked Dan.

"This is it," said the petty officer.

"That's right, this is it," a man at the rail confirmed, speaking over his shoulder.

"No islands, either?" asked Dan, alarmed.

"No," said the petty officer, not unkindly, but in an abrupt way that hurt Dan in his breast.

"Well—what's all this talk about the mainland?" Dan asked.

"Talk," said the petty officer, with a twinkle now.

"Isn't it won-derful!" said a woman's voice behind him, and Dan turned to see Mrs. Gibson-Leyden—Mrs. Gibson-Leyden who had been so eager for the mainland—gazing rapturously at the empty white and gold mist.

"Do you know about this? How much farther does it go?" asked Dan, but the petty officer was gone. Dan wished he could be as calm as everyone else—generally he was calmer—but how could he be calm about his vanished island? How could the rest just stand there at the rails, for the most part taking it all quite calmly, he could tell by the voices now and their casual postures.

Dan saw the petty officer again and ran after him. "What happens?" he asked. "What happens next?" His questions struck him as foolish, but they were as good as any.

"This is *it*," said the petty officer with a smile. "Good God, boy!"

Dan bit his lips.

"This is *it!*" repeated the petty officer. "What did you expect?"

Dan hesitated. "Land," he said in a voice that made it almost a question.

The petty officer laughed silently and shook his head. "You can get off any time you like."

Dan gave a startled look around him. It was true, people were getting off at the port rail, stepping over the side with their suitcases. "Onto what?" Dan asked, aghast.

The petty officer laughed again, and disdaining to answer him, walked slowly away with his coiled line.

Dan caught his arm. "Get off here? Why?"

"As good a place as any. Whatever spot strikes your fancy." The petty officer chuckled. "It's all alike."

"All sea?"

"There's no sea," said the petty officer. "But there's certainly no land."

And there went Mr. and Mrs. Gibson-Leyden now, off the starboard rail.

"Hey!" Dan called to them, but they didn't turn.

Dan watched them disappear quickly. He blinked his eyes. They had not been holding hands, but they had been near each other, they had been together.

Suddenly Dan realized that if he got off the boat as they had done, he could still be alone, if he wanted to be. It was strange, of course, to think of stepping out into space. But the instant he was able to conceive it, barely conceive it, it became right to do it. He could feel it filling him with a gradual but overpowering certainty, that he only reluctantly yielded to. This was right, as the petty officer had said. And this was as good a place as any.

Dan looked around him. The boat was really almost empty now. He might as well be last, he thought. He'd meant to be last. He'd go down and get his suitcase packed. What a nuisance! The mainland passengers, of course, had been packed since the afternoon before.

Dan turned impatiently on the companionway where he had once nearly fallen, and he climbed up again. He didn't want his suitcase after all. He didn't want anything with him.

He put a foot up on the starboard rail and stepped off. He walked several yards on an invisible ground that was softer than grass. It wasn't what he had thought it would be like, yet now that he was here, it wasn't strange, either. In fact there was even that sense of recognition that he had imagined he would feel when he set foot on his island. He turned for a last look at the ship that was still on its downward course. Then suddenly, he was impatient with himself. Why look at a ship, he asked himself, and abruptly turned and went on.

A Curious Suicide

Dr. Stephen McCullough had a first-class compartment to himself on the express from Paris to Geneva. He sat browsing in one of the medical quarterlies he had brought from America, but he was not concentrating. He was toying with the idea of murder. That was why he had taken the train instead of flying, to give himself time to think or perhaps merely dream.

He was a serious man of forty-five, a little overweight, with a prominent and spreading nose, a brown mustache, brown-rimmed glasses, a receding hairline. His eyebrows were tense with an inward anxiety, which his patients often thought a concern with their problems. Actually, he was unhappily married, and though he refused to quarrel with Lillian—that meant answer her back—there was discord between them. In Paris yesterday he had answered Lillian back, and on a ridiculous matter about whether he or she would take back to a shop on the Rue Royale an evening bag that Lillian had decided she did not want. He had been angry not because he had had to return the bag, but because he had agreed, in a weak moment fifteen minutes before, to visit Roger Fane in Geneva.

"Go and see him, Steve," Lillian had said yesterday morning. "You're so close to Geneva now, why not? Think of the pleasure it'd give Roger."

What pleasure? Why? But Dr. McCullough had rung Roger at the American Embassy in Geneva, and Roger had been very friendly, much too friendly, of course, and had said that he must come and stay a few days and that he had plenty of room to put him up. Dr. McCullough had agreed to spend one night. Then he was going to fly to Rome to join Lillian.

Dr. McCullough detested Roger Fane. It was the kind of hatred that time does nothing to diminish. Roger Fane, seventeen years ago, had married the woman Dr. McCullough loved. Margaret. Margaret had died a year ago in an automobile accident on an Alpine road. Roger Fane was smug, cautious, mightily pleased with himself and not very intelligent. Seventeen years ago, Roger Fane had told Margaret that he, Stephen McCullough, was having a secret affair with another girl. Nothing was further from the truth, but before Stephen could prove anything, Margaret had married Roger. Dr. McCullough had not expected the marriage to last, but it had, and finally Dr. McCullough had married Lillian whose face resembled Margaret's a little, but that was the only similarity. In the past seventeen years, Dr. McCullough had seen Roger and Margaret perhaps three times when they had come to New York on short trips. He had not seen Roger since Margaret's death.

Now as the train shot through the French countryside, Dr. McCullough reflected on the satisfaction that murdering Roger Fane might give him. He had never before thought of murdering anybody, but yesterday evening while he was taking a bath in the Paris hotel, after the telephone conversation with Roger, a thought had come to him in regard to murder: most murderers were caught because they left some clue, despite their efforts to erase all the clues. Many murderers wanted to be caught, the doctor realized, and unconsciously planted a clue that led the police straight to them. In the Leopold and Loeb case, one of them had dropped his glasses at the scene, for instance. But suppose a murderer deliberately left a dozen clues, practically down to his calling card? It seemed to Dr. McCullough that the very obviousness of it would throw suspicion off. Especially if the person were a man like himself, well thought of, a nonviolent type. Also, there'd be no motive that anyone could see, because Dr. McCullough had never even told Lillian that he had loved the woman Roger Fane had married. Of course, a few of his old friends knew it, but Dr. McCullough hadn't mentioned Margaret or Roger Fane in a decade.

He imagined Roger's apartment formal and gloomy, perhaps with a servant prowling about full time, a servant who slept in. A servant would complicate things. Let's say there wasn't a servant who slept in, that he and Roger would be having a nightcap in the living room or in Roger's study, and then just before saying good night, Dr. McCullough would pick up a heavy paperweight or a big vase and—Then he would calmly take his leave. Of course, the bed should be slept in, since he was supposed to stay the night, so perhaps the morning would be better for the crime than the evening. The essential thing was to leave quietly and at the time he was supposed to leave. But the doctor found himself unable to plot in much detail after all.

Roger Fane's street in Geneva looked just as Dr. McCullough had imagined it—a narrow, curving street that combined business establishments with old private dwellings—and it was not too well lighted when Dr. McCullough's taxi entered it at 9 P.M., yet in law-abiding Switzerland, the doctor supposed, dark streets held few dangers for anyone. The front door buzzed in response to his ring, and Dr. McCullough opened it. The door was heavy as a bank vault's door.

"Hullo!" Roger's voice called cheerily down the stairwell. "Come up! I'm on the third floor. Fourth to you, I suppose."

"Be right there!" Dr. McCullough said, shy about raising his voice in the presence of the closed doors on either side of the hall. He had telephoned Roger a few moments ago from the railway station, because Roger had said he would meet him. Roger had apologized and said he had been held up at a meeting at his office, and would Steve mind hopping a taxi and coming right over? Dr. McCullough suspected that Roger had not been held up at all, but simply hadn't wanted to show him the courtesy of being at the station.

"Well, well, Steve!" said Roger, pumping Dr. McCullough's hand. "It's great to see you again. Come in, come in. Is that thing heavy?" Roger made a pass at the doctor's suitcase, but the doctor caught it up first.

"Not at all. Good to see you again, Roger." He went into the apartment.

There were oriental rugs, ornate lamps that gave off dim light. It was even stuffier than Dr. McCullough had anticipated. Roger looked a trifle thinner. He was shorter than the doctor, and had sparse blond hair. His weak face perpetually smiled. Both had eaten dinner, so they drank scotch in the living room.

"So you're joining Lillian in Rome tomorrow," said Roger. "Sorry you won't be staying longer. I'd intended to drive you out to the country tomorrow evening to meet a friend of mine. A woman," Roger added with a smile.

"Oh? Too bad. Yes, I'll be off on the one o'clock plane tomorrow afternoon. I made the reservation from Paris." Dr. McCullough found himself speaking automatically. Strangely, he felt a little drunk, though he'd taken only a couple of sips of his scotch. It was because of the falsity of the situation, he thought, the falsity of his being here at all, of his pretending friendship or at least friendliness. Roger's smile irked him, so merry and yet so forced. Roger hadn't referred to Margaret, though Dr. McCullough had not seen him since she died. But then, neither had the doctor referred to her, even to give a word of condolence. And already, it seemed, Roger had another female interest. Roger was just over forty, still trim of figure and bright of eye. And Margaret, that jewel among women, was just something that had come his way, stayed a while, and departed, Dr. McCullough supposed. Roger looked not at all bereaved.

The doctor detested Roger fully as much as he had on the train, but the reality of Roger Fane was somewhat dismaying. If he killed him, he would have to touch him, feel the resistance of his flesh at any rate with the object he hit him with. And what was the servant situation? As if Roger read his mind, he said:

"I've a girl who comes in to clean every morning at ten and leaves at twelve. If you want her to do anything for you, wash and iron a shirt or something like that, don't hesitate. She's very fast, or can be if you ask her. Her name's Yvonne."

Then the telephone rang. Roger spoke in French. His face fell slightly as he agreed to do something that the other person was asking him to do. Roger said to the doctor:

"Of all irritating things. I've got to catch the seven o'clock plane to Zurich tomorrow. Some visiting fireman's being welcomed at a breakfast. So, old man, I suppose I'll be gone before you're out of bed."

"Oh!" Dr. McCullough found himself chuckling. "You think doctors aren't used to early calls? Of course I'll get up to tell you good-bye—see you off."

Roger's smile widened slightly. "Well, we'll see. I certainly won't wake you for it. Make yourself at home and I'll leave a note for Yvonne to prepare coffee and rolls. Or would you like a more substantial brunch around eleven?"

Dr. McCullough was not thinking about what Roger was saying. He had just noticed a rectangular marble pen and pencil holder on the desk where the telephone stood. He was looking at Roger's high and faintly pink forehead. "Oh, brunch," said the doctor vaguely. "No, no, for goodness' sake. They feed you enough on the plane." And then his thoughts leapt to Lillian and the quarrel yesterday in Paris. Hostility smoldered in him. Had Roger ever quarreled with Margaret? Dr. McCullough could not imagine Margaret being unfair, being mean. It was no wonder Roger's face looked relaxed and untroubled.

"A penny for your thoughts," said Roger, getting up to replenish his glass.

The doctor's glass was still half full.

"I suppose I'm a bit tired," said Dr. McCullough, and passed his hand across his forehead. When he lifted his head again, he saw a photograph of Margaret which he had not noticed before on the top of the highboy on his right. Margaret in her twenties, as she had looked when Roger married her, as she had looked when the doctor had so loved her. Dr. McCullough looked suddenly at Roger. His hatred returned in a wave that left him physically weak. "I suppose I'd better turn in," he said, setting his glass carefully on the little table in front of him, standing up. Roger had showed him his bedroom.

"Sure you wouldn't like a spot of brandy?" asked Roger. "You look all in." Roger smiled cockily, standing very straight.

The tide of the doctor's anger flowed back. He picked up the marble slab with one hand, and before Roger could step back, smashed him in the forehead with its base. It was a blow that would kill, the doctor knew. Roger fell and without even a last twitch lay still and limp. The doctor set the marble back where it had been, picked up the pen and pencil which had fallen, and replaced them in their holders, then wiped the marble with his handkerchief where his fingers had touched it and also the pen and pencil. Roger's forehead was bleeding slightly. He felt Roger's still-warm wrist and found no pulse. Then he went out the door and down the hall to his own room.

He awakened the next morning at 8:15, after a not very sound night's sleep. He showered in the bathroom between his room and Roger's bedroom, shaved, dressed and left the house at a quarter past nine. A hall went from his room past the kitchen to the flat's door; it had not been necessary to cross the living room, and even if he had glanced into the living room through the door he had not closed, Roger's body would have been out of sight to him. Dr. McCullough had not glanced in.

At 5:30 P.M. he was in Rome, riding in a taxi from the airport to the Hotel Majestic where Lillian awaited him. Lillian was out, however. The doctor had some coffee sent up, and it was then that he noticed his briefcase was missing. He had wanted to lie on the bed and drink coffee and read his medical quarterlies. Now he remembered distinctly: he had for some reason carried his briefcase into the living room last evening. This did not disturb him at all. It was exactly what he should have done on purpose if he had thought of it. His name and his New York address were written in the slot of the briefcase. And Dr. McCullough supposed that Roger had written his name in full in some engagement book along with the time of his arrival.

He found Lillian in good humor. She had bought a lot of things in the

Via Condotti. They had dinner and then took a carozza ride through the Villa Borghese, to the Piazza di Spagna and the Piazza del Populo. If there were anything in the papers about Roger, Dr. McCullough was ignorant of it. He bought only the Paris *Herald-Tribune,* which was a morning paper.

The news came the next morning as he and Lillian were breakfasting at Donay's in the Via Veneto. It was in the Paris *Herald-Tribune,* and there was a picture of Roger Fane on the front page, a serious official picture of him in a wing collar.

"Good Lord!" said Lillian. "Why—it happened the night you were there!"

Looking over her shoulder, Dr. McCullough pretended surprise. " '—died some time between eight P.M. and three A.M.,' " the doctor read. "I said good night to him about eleven, I think. Went into my room."

"You didn't *hear* anything?"

"No. My room was down a hall. I closed my door."

"And the next morning. You didn't—"

"I told you, Roger had to catch a seven o'clock plane. I assumed he was gone. I left the house around nine."

"And all the time he was in the living room!" Lillian said with a gasp. "Steve! Why, this is terrible!"

Was it, Dr. McCullough wondered. Was it so terrible for her? Her voice did not sound really concerned. He looked into her wide eyes. "It's certainly terrible—but I'm not responsible, God knows. Don't worry, Lillian."

The police were at the Hotel Majestic when they returned, waiting for Dr. McCullough in the lobby. They were both plainclothes Swiss police, and they spoke English. They interviewed Dr. McCullough at a table in a corner of the lobby. Lillian had, at Dr. McCullough's insistence, gone up to their room. Dr. McCullough had wondered why the police had not come for him hours earlier than this—it was so simple to check the passenger list of planes leaving Geneva—but he soon found out why. The maid Yvonne had not come to clean yesterday morning, so Roger Fane's body had not been discovered until 6 P.M. yesterday, when his office had become alarmed by his absence and sent someone around to his apartment to investigate.

"This is your briefcase, I think," said the slender blond officer with a smile, opening a large manila envelope he had been carrying under his arm.

"Yes, thank you very much. I realized today that I'd left it." The doctor took it and laid it on his lap.

The two Swiss watched him quietly.

"This is very shocking," Dr. McCullough said. "It's hard for me to realize." He was impatient for them to make their charge—if they were going to—and ask him to return to Geneva with them. They both seemed almost in awe of him.

"How well did you know Mr. Fane?" asked the other officer.

"Not too well. I've known him many years, but we were never close friends. I hadn't seen him in five years, I think." Dr. McCullough spoke steadily and in his usual tone.

"Mr. Fane was still fully dressed, so he had not gone to bed. You are sure you heard no disturbance that night?"

"I did not," the doctor answered for the second time. A silence. "Have you any clues as to who might have done it?"

"Oh, yes, yes," the blond man said matter of factly. "We suspect the brother of the maid Yvonne. He was drunk that night and hasn't an alibi for the time of the crime. He and his sister live together and that night he went off with his sister's batch of keys—among which were the keys to Mr. Fane's apartment. He didn't come back until nearly noon yesterday. Yvonne was worried about him, which is why she didn't go to Mr. Fane's apartment yesterday—that plus the fact she couldn't have got in. She tried to telephone at eight-thirty yesterday morning to say she wouldn't be coming, but she got no answer. We've questioned the brother Anton. He's a ne'er-do-well." The man shrugged.

Dr. McCullough remembered hearing the telephone ring at eight-thirty. "But—what was the motive?"

"Oh—resentment. Robbery maybe if he'd been sober enough to find anything to take. He's a case for a psychiatrist or an alcoholic ward. Mr. Fane knew him, so he might have let him into the apartment, or he could have walked in, since he had the keys. Yvonne said that Mr. Fane had been trying for months to get her to live apart from her brother. Her brother beats her and takes her money. Mr. Fane had spoken to the brother a couple of times, and it's on our record that Mr. Fane once had to call the police to get Anton out of the apartment when he came there looking for his sister. That incident happened at nine in the evening, an hour when his sister is never there. You see how off his head he is."

Dr. McCullough cleared his throat and asked, "Has Anton confessed to it?"

"Oh, the same as. Poor chap, I really don't think he knows what he's doing half the time. But at least in Switzerland there's no capital punishment. He'll have enough time to dry out in jail, all right." He glanced at his colleague and they both stood up. "Thank you very much, Dr. McCullough."

"You're very welcome," said the doctor. "Thank you for the briefcase."

Dr. McCullough went upstairs with his briefcase to his room.

"What did they say?" Lillian asked as he came in.

"They think the brother of the maid did it," said Dr. McCullough. "Fellow who's an alcoholic and who seems to have had it in for Roger. Some ne'er-do-well." Frowning, he went into the bathroom to wash his hands. He suddenly detested himself, detested Lillian's long sigh, an "Ah-h" of relief and joy.

"Thank God, thank God!" Lillian said. "Do you know what this would have meant if they'd—if they'd have accused *you*?" she asked in a softer voice, as if the walls had ears, and she came closer to the bathroom door.

"Certainly," Dr. McCullough said, and felt a burst of anger in his blood. "I'd have had a hell of a time proving I was innocent, since I was right there at the time."

"Exactly. You couldn't have proved you were innocent. Thank God for this Anton, whoever he is." Her small face glowed, her eyes twinkled. "A ne'er-do-well. Ha! He did us some good!" She laughed shrilly and turned on one heel.

"I don't see why you have to gloat," he said, drying his hands carefully. "It's a sad story."

"Sadder than if they'd blamed you? Don't be so—so altruistic, dear. Or rather, think of us. Husband kills old rival-in-love after—let's see— seventeen years, isn't it? And after eleven years of marriage to another woman. The torch still burns high. Do you think I'd like that?"

"Lillian, what're you talking about?" He came out of the bathroom scowling.

"You know exactly. You think I don't know you were in love with Margaret? *Still* are? You think I don't know you killed Roger?" Her gray eyes looked at him with a wild challenge. Her head was tipped to one side, her hands on her hips.

He felt tongue-tied, paralyzed. They stared at each other for perhaps fifteen seconds, while his mind moved tentatively over the abyss her words had just spread before him. He hadn't known that she still thought of Margaret. Of course she'd known about Margaret. But who had kept the story alive in her mind? Perhaps himself by his silence, the doctor realized. But the future was what mattered. Now she had something to hold over his head, something by which she could control him forever. "My dear, you are mistaken."

But Lillian with a toss of her head turned and walked away, and the doctor knew he had not won.

Absolutely nothing was said about the matter for the rest of the day. They lunched, spent a leisurely hour in the Vatican museum, but Dr. McCullough's mind was on other things than Michelangelo's paintings. He was going to go to Geneva and confess the thing, not for decency's sake or because his conscience bothered him, but because Lillian's attitude was insupportable. It was less supportable than a stretch in prison. He managed to get away long enough to make a telephone call at five P.M. There was a plane to Geneva at 7:20 P.M. At 6:15 P.M., he left their hotel room empty-handed and took a taxi to Ciampino airport. He had his passport and traveler's checks.

He arrived in Geneva before eleven that evening, and called the police. At first, they were not willing to tell him the whereabouts of the man accused of murdering Roger Fane, but Dr. McCullough gave his name and said he had some important information, and then the Swiss police told him where Anton Carpeau was being held. Dr. McCullough took a taxi to what seemed the outskirts of Geneva. It was a new white building, not at all like a prison.

Here he was greeted by one of the plainclothes officers who had come to see him, the blond one. "Dr. McCullough," he said with a faint smile. "You have some information, you say? I am afraid it is a little late."

"Oh?—Why?"

"Anton Carpeau has just killed himself—by bashing his head against the wall of his cell. Just twenty minutes ago." The man gave a hopeless shrug.

"Good God," Dr. McCullough said softly.

"But what was your information?"

The doctor hesitated. The words wouldn't come. And then he realized that it was cowardice and shame that kept him silent. He had never felt so worthless in his life, and he felt infinitely lower than the drunken ne'er-do-well who had killed himself. "I'd rather not. In this case—I mean—it's so all over, isn't it? It was something else against Anton, I thought—and what's the use now? It's bad enough—" The words stopped.

"Yes, I suppose so," said the Swiss.

"So—I'll say good night."

"Good night, Dr. McCullough."

Then the doctor walked on into the night, aimlessly. He felt a curious emptiness, a nothingness in himself that was not like any mood he had ever known. His plan for murder had succeeded, but it had dragged worse tragedies in its wake. Anton Carpeau. And *Lillian*. In a strange way, he had killed himself just as much as he had killed Roger Fane. He was now a dead man, a walking dead man.

Half an hour later, he stood on a formal bridge looking down at the black water of Lake Leman. He stared down a long while, and imagined his body toppling over and over, striking the water with not much of a splash, sinking. He stared hard at the blackness that looked so solid but would be so yielding, so willing to swallow him into death. But he hadn't even the courage or the despair as yet for suicide. One day, however, he would, he knew. One day when the planes of cowardice and courage met at the proper angle. And that day would be a surprise to him and to everyone else who knew him. Then his hands that gripped the stone parapet pushed him back, and the doctor walked on heavily. He would see about a hotel for tonight, and then tomorrow arrange to get back to Rome.

The Baby Spoon

Claude Lamm, Professor of English Literature and Poetry, had been on the faculty of Columbia University for ten years. Short and inclined to plumpness, with a bald spot in the middle of his close-cropped black hair, he did not look like a college professor, but rather like a small businessman hiding for some reason in the clothes he thought a college professor should wear—good tweed jackets with leather patches on the elbows, unpressed gray flannels and unshined shoes of any sort. He lived in one of the great dreary apartment buildings that clump east and south of Columbia University, a gloomy, ash-colored building with a shaky elevator and an ugly miscellany of smells old and new inside it. Claude Lamm rendered his sunless, five-room apartment still more somber by cramming it with sodden-looking sofas, with books and periodicals and photographs of classic edifices and landscapes about which he professed to be sentimental but actually was not.

Seven years ago he had married Margaret Cullen, one of those humdrum, colorless individuals who look as if they might be from anywhere except New York and turn out, incredibly, to be native New Yorkers. She was fifty, eight years older than Claude, with a plain, open countenance and an air of desperate inferiority. Claude had met her through another professor who knew Margaret's father, and had married her because of certain unconscious drives in himself towards the maternal. But under Margaret's matronly exterior lay a nature that was half childish, too, and peculiarly irritating to Claude. Apart from her cooking and sewing—she did neither well—and the uninspired routine that might be called the running of the house, she had no interests. Except for an occasional exchange of letters, which she bored Claude by reading aloud at the table, she had detached herself from her old friends.

Claude came home about five most afternoons, had some tea and planned his work and reading for the evening. At 6:15, he drank a martini without ice and read the evening paper in the living room, while Margaret prepared their early dinner. They dined on shoulder lamb chops or meat loaf, often on cheese and macaroni, which Margaret was fond of, and Margaret stirred her coffee with the silver baby spoon she had used the first evening Claude had met her, holding the spoon by the tip end of the handle in order to reach the bottom of the cup. After dinner, Claude retired to his study—a book-glutted cubicle with an old black leather couch in it, although he did not sleep here—to read and correct papers and to browse in his bookshelves for anything that piqued his aimless curiosity.

Every two weeks or so, he asked Professor Millikin, a Shakespeare scholar, or Assistant Professor George and his wife to come to dinner. Three or four times a year, the apartment was thrown open to about twelve students from his special readings classes, who came and ate Dundee cake and drank tea. Margaret would sit on a cushion on the floor, because there were never enough chairs, and of course one young man after another would offer his chair to her. "Oh, no, thank you!" Margaret would protest with a lisping coyness quite unlike her usual manner, "I'm perfectly comfortable here. Sitting on the floor makes me feel like a little girl again." She would look up at the young men as if she expected them to tell her she looked like a little girl, too, which to Claude's disgust the young men sometimes did. The little girl mood always came over Margaret in the company of men, and always made Claude sneer when he saw it. Claude sneered easily and uncontrollably, hiding it unconsciously in the act of putting his cigarette holder between his teeth, or rubbing the side of his nose with a forefinger. Claude had keen, suspicious brown eyes. No feature of his face was remarkable, but it was not a face one forgot either. It was the restlessness, the furtiveness in his face that one noticed first and remembered. At the teas, Margaret would use her baby spoon, too, which as likely as not would start a conversation. Then Claude would move out of hearing.

Claude did not like the way the young men looked at his wife—disappointedly, a little pityingly, always solemnly. Claude was ashamed of her before them. She should have been beautiful and gay, a nymph of the soul, a fair face that would accord with the love poems of Donne and Sidney. Well, she wasn't.

Claude's marriage to Margaret might have been comparable to a marriage to his housekeeper, if not for emotional entanglements that made him passionately hate her as well as passionately need her. He hated her childishness with a vicious, personal resentment. He hated almost as much her competent, maternal ministerings to him, her taking his clothes to the cleaners, for instance; which was all he tolerated her for, he knew, and why he had her now instead of his nymph. When he had been down with flu one winter and Margaret had waited on him hand and foot, he had sneered often at her retreating back, hating her, really hating her obsequious devotion to him. Claude had despised his mother and she, too, between periods of neglect and erratic ill-temper, had been capable of smothering affection and attention. But the nearest he came to expressing his hatred was when he announced casually, once a week or oftener:

"Winston's coming over for a while tonight."

"Oh," Margaret would reply with a tremor in her voice. "Well, I suppose he'd like some of the raisin cake later. Or maybe a sandwich of the meat loaf."

Winston loved to eat at Claude's house. Or rather, he was always hungry. Winston was a genuinely starving poet who lived in a genuine garret at the top of a brownstone house in the West Seventies. He had been a student of Claude's three years ago, a highly promising student whose brilliant, aggressive mind had so dominated his classmates that the classes had been hardly more than conversations between Claude and Winston. Claude was immensely fond of Winston and flattered by Winston's fondness for him. From the first, it had excited Claude in a strange and pleasant way to catch Winston's smile, Winston's wink even, the glint of mad humor in his eyes, in the midst of Winston's flurry of words in class. While at Columbia, Winston had published several poems in poetry magazines and literary magazines. He had written a poem called "The Booming Bittern," a mournful satire on an undergraduate's life and directionless rebellion, that Claude had thought might take the place in Winston's career that "Prufrock" had taken in Eliot's. The poem had been published in some quarterly but had attracted no important attention.

Claude had expected Winston to go far and do him credit. Winston had published only one small book of verse since leaving college. Something had happened to Winston's easy, original flow of thought. Something had happened to his self-confidence after leaving college, as if the wells of inspiration were drying up along with the sap and vitality of his twenty-four-year-old body. Winston was thin as a rail now. He had always been thin, but now he slouched, hung his head like a wronged and resentful man, and his eyes under the hard, straight brows looked anxious, hostile and unhappy. He clung to Claude with the persistence of a maltreated child clinging to the one human being who had ever given him kindness and encouragement. Winston was working now on a novel in the form of a long poem. He had submitted part of it to his publishers a year ago, and they had refused to give him an advance. But Claude liked it, and Winston's attitude was, the rest of the world be damned. Claude was keenly aware of Winston's emotional dependence upon him, and managed to hide his own dependence upon Winston in a superior, patronizing manner that he assumed with Winston. Claude's hostility to Margaret found some further release in the contempt that Winston openly showed for her intellect.

One evening, more than usually late in arriving, Winston slouched into the living room without a reply to Claude's greeting. He was a head and a half taller than Claude, even stooped, his dark brown hair untidy with wind and rain, his overcoat clutched about his splinter of a body by the hands that were rammed into his pockets. Slowly and without a glance at Margaret, Winston walked across the living room towards Claude's study.

Claude was a little annoyed. This was a mood he didn't know.

"Listen, old man, can you lend me some money?" Winston asked when they were alone in the study, then went on over Claude's surprised murmur, "You've no idea what it took for me to come here and ask you, but now it's done, anyway." He sighed heavily.

Claude had a sudden feeling it hadn't taken anything, and that the despondent mood was only playacting. "You know I've always let you have money if you needed it, Winston. Don't take it so seriously. Sit down." Claude sat down.

Winston did not move. His eyes had their usual fierceness, yet there was an impatient pleading in them, too, like the eyes of a child demanding something rightfully his own. "I mean a lot of money. Five hundred dollars. I need it to work on. Five hundred will see me through six weeks, and I can finish my book without any more interruptions."

Claude winced a little. He'd never see the money again if he lent it to Winston. Winston owed him about two hundred now. It occurred to Claude that Winston had not been so intense about anything since his university days. And it also came to him, swiftly and tragically, that Winston would never finish his book. Winston would always be stuck at the anxious, furious pitch he was now, which was contingent upon his not finishing the book.

"You've got to help me out this last time, Claude," Winston said in a begging tone.

"Let me think it over. I'll write you a note about it tomorrow. How's that, fellow?"

Claude got up and went to his desk for a cigarette. Suddenly he hated Winston for standing there begging for money. Like anybody else, Claude thought bitterly. His lip lifted as he set the cigarette holder between his teeth, and Winston saw it, he knew. Winston never missed anything. Why couldn't tonight have been like all the other evenings, Claude thought, Winston smoking his cigarettes, propping his feet on the corner of his desk, Winston laughing and making him laugh, Winston adoring him for all the jibes he threw at the teaching profession?

"You crumb," Winston's voice said steadily. "You fat, smug sonovabitch of a college professor. You stultifier and castrator of the intellect."

Claude stood where he was, half turned away from Winston. The words might have been a blunt ramrod that Winston had thrust through his skull and down to his feet. Winston had never spoken to him like that, and Claude literally did not know how to take it. Claude was not used to reacting to Winston as he reacted to other people. "I'll write you a note about it tomorrow. I'll just have to figure out how and when," he said shortly, with the dignity of a professor whose position, though not handsomely paid, commanded a certain respect.

"I'm sorry," Winston said, hanging his head.

"Winston, what's the matter with you?"

"I don't know." Winston covered his face with his hands.

Claude felt a swift sense of regret, of disappointment at Winston's weakness. He mustn't let Margaret know, he thought. "Sit down."

Winston sat down. He sipped the little glass of whiskey Claude poured from the bottle in his desk as if it were a medicine he desperately needed. Then he sprawled his scarecrow legs out in front of him and said something about a book Claude had lent him the last time he was here, a book of poetry criticism. Claude was grateful for the change of subject. Winston talked with his eyes sleepily half-shut, jerking his big head now and then for emphasis, but Claude could see the glint of interest, of affection, of some indefinable speculation about himself through the half closed lids, and could feel the focus of Winston's intense and personal interest like the life-bringing rays of a sun.

Later, they had coffee and sandwiches and cake in the living room with Margaret. Winston grew very animated and entertained them with a story of his quest for a hotel room in the town of Jalapa in Mexico, a story pulled like an unexpected toy from the hotchpotch of Winston's mind, and by Winston's words set in motion and given a life of its own. Claude felt proud of Winston. "See what I amuse myself with behind the door of my study, while you creep about in the dull prison of your own mind," Claude might have been saying aloud as he glanced at Margaret to see if she were appreciating Winston.

Claude did not write to Winston the next day. Claude felt he was in no more need of money than usual, and that Winston's crisis would pass if he and Winston didn't communicate for a while. Then on the second evening, Margaret told Claude that she had lost her baby spoon. She had looked the house over for it, she said.

"Maybe it fell behind the refrigerator," Claude suggested.

"I was hoping you'd help me move it."

A smile pulled at Claude's mouth as he seesawed the refrigerator away from the wall. He hoped she had lost the spoon. It was a silly thing to treasure at the age of fifty, sillier than her high school scrapbooks and the gilt baby shoe that had sat on her father's desk and that Margaret had so unbecomingly claimed after his death. Claude hoped she had swept the spoon into the garbage by accident and that it was out of the house forever.

"Nothing but dust," Claude said, looking down at the mess of fine, sticky gray dust on the floor and the refrigerator wires.

The refrigerator was only the beginning. Claude's cooperation inspired Margaret. That evening she turned the kitchen inside out, looked behind all the furniture in the living room, even looked in the bathroom medicine cabinet and the clothes hamper.

"It's just not in the house," she kept saying to Claude in a lost way. After another day of searching, she gave up.

Claude heard her telling the woman in the next apartment about it.

"You remember it, I suppose. I think I once showed it to you when we had coffee and cake here."

"Yes, I do remember. That's too bad," said the neighbor.

Margaret told the news-store man, too. It embarrassed Claude painfully as he stood there staring at the rows of candy bars and Margaret said hesitantly to the man she'd hardly dared to speak to before, "I did mean to pay our bill yesterday, but I've been a little distracted. I lost a very old keepsake—an old piece of silver I was very fond of. A baby spoon."

Then at the phrase "an old piece of silver," Claude realized. *Winston* had taken it. Winston might have thought it had some value, or he might have taken it out of malice. He could have palmed it that last night he was at the house. Claude smiled to himself.

Claude had known for years that Winston stole little things—a glass paperweight, an old cigarette lighter that didn't work, a photograph of Claude. Until now, Winston had chosen Claude's possessions. For sentimental reasons, Claude thought. Claude suspected that Winston had a vaguely homosexual attachment to him, and Claude had heard that homosexuals were apt to take something from someone they cared for. What then was more likely than that Winston would take an intimate possession or two from him, which he probably made a fetish of?

Three more days passed without the spoon's turning up, and without a word from Winston. Margaret wrote some letters in the evenings, and Claude knew she was saying in each and every one of them that she had lost her baby spoon and that it was unforgivably careless of her. It was like a confession of some terrible sin that she had to make to everyone. And more, she seemed to want to tell everyone, "Here I stand, bereft." She wanted to hear their words of comfort, their reassuring phrases about such things happening to everybody. Claude had seen her devouring the sympathy the delicatessen woman had offered her. And he saw her anxiety in the way she opened the letter from her sister in Staten Island. Margaret read the letter at the table, and though it didn't say anything about the baby spoon, it put Margaret in better spirits, as if her sister's not mentioning it were a guarantee of her absolution.

Leonard George and his wife Lydia came to dinner one evening, and Margaret told them about the spoon. Lydia, who was by no means stupid but very good at talking about nothing, went on and on about how disquieting the losses of keepsakes were at first, and how unimportant they seemed later. Margaret's face grew gradually less troubled until finally she was smiling. After dinner, she said on her own initiative, "Well, who wants to play some bridge?"

Margaret put on a little lipstick now when they sat down to dinner. It all happened in about ten days. The inevitable pardons she got from people after confessing the loss of her baby spoon seemed to be breaking the barriers between herself and the adult world. Claude began to think he might never see that horrible coyness again when young men came to semester teas. He really ought to thank Winston for it, he supposed. It amused him to think of grasping Winston's hand and thanking him for relieving the household of the accursed baby spoon. He would have to be careful how he did it, because Winston didn't know that he knew about his petty thieveries. But perhaps it was time Winston did. Claude still resented Winston's money-begging and that shocking moment of rudeness the last time he had visited. Yes, Winston wanted bringing into line. He would let Winston know he knew about the spoon, and he would also let him have three hundred dollars.

Winston hadn't yet called, so Claude wrote a note to him, inviting him to dinner Sunday night, and saying he was prepared to lend him three hundred dollars. "Come early so we can have a little talk first," Claude wrote.

Winston was smiling when he arrived, and he was wearing a clean white shirt. But the white collar only accented the grayness of his face, the shadows in his cheeks.

"Working hard?" Claude asked as they went into his study.

"You bet," Winston said. "I want to read you a couple of pages about the subway ride Jake takes." Jake was the main character in Winston's book.

Winston was about to begin reading, when Margaret arrived with a shaker of whiskey sours and a plate of canapés.

"By the way, Winston," Claude began when Margaret had left. "I want to thank you for a little service I think you rendered the last time you were here."

Winston looked at him. "What was that?"

"Did you see anything of a silver spoon, a little silver baby spoon?" Claude asked him with a smile.

Winston's eyes were suddenly wary. "No. No, I didn't."

Winston was guilty, and embarrassed, Claude saw. Claude laughed easily. "Didn't you take it, Winston? I'd be delighted if you did."

"Take it? No, I certainly didn't." Winston started towards the cocktail tray and stopped, frowning harder at Claude, his stooped figure rigid.

"Now look here—" Why had he begun it before Winston had had a couple of cocktails? Claude thought of Winston's hollow stomach and felt as if his words were dropping into it. "Look here, Winston, you know I'm terribly fond of you."

"What's this all about?" Winston demanded, and now his voice shook and he looked completely helpless to conceal his guilt. He half turned round and turned back again, as if guilt pinned his big shoes to the floor.

Claude tipped his head back and drank all his glass. He said with a smile, "You know I know you've taken a few things from me. It couldn't matter to me less. I'm glad you wanted to take them, in fact." He shrugged.

"What things? That's not true, Claude." Winston laid his sprawling hand over the conch shell on the bookcase. He stood upright now, and there was something even militant about his tall figure and the affronted stare he gave Claude.

"Winston, have a drink." Claude wished now that he hadn't begun it. He should have known Winston wouldn't be able to take it. Maybe he had destroyed their friendship—for nothing. Claude wondered if he should try to take it all back, pretend he had been joking. "Have a drink," he repeated.

"But you can't accuse me of being a thief!" Winston said in a horrified tone. And suddenly his body began trembling.

"No, no, you've got the whole thing wrong," Claude said. He walked slowly across the room to get a cigarette from the box on his desk.

"That's what you said, isn't it?" Winston's voice cracked.

"No, I didn't. Now let's sit down and have a drink and forget it." Claude spoke with elaborate casualness, but he knew it sounded patronizing just the same. Maybe Winston *hadn't* stolen the spoon: after all, it belonged to Margaret. Maybe Winston was reacting with guilt because he had taken other things, and he now knew that Claude realized it.

That was his last thought—that he had sounded false and patronizing, that the spoon might have disappeared by some means other than Winston—before the quick step behind him, the brief whir of something moving fast through the air, and the shattering impact at the back of his head caused his arms to fling up in a last empty, convulsive gesture.

Broken Glass

Andrew Cooperman felt in a cheerful mood on a certain Wednesday morning, because he had a date. He was to ring Kate Wynant's doorbell a little after ten, and they were going to shop at the supermarket together. They did this once a week, avoiding Saturday because of the crowds, and they shopped together, because these days you couldn't buy one pound or six of anything, you had to buy five pounds of onions or ten pounds of potatoes, as if one had an army at home to feed, and Andrew lived alone, as did Kate. Andrew's wife Sarah had died nearly six years ago, and Kate's husband Al, who had been a subway guard, had passed away with bronchitis and pneumonia the year before Sarah. The Coopermans and the Wynants had been good friends and neighbors for more than thirty years. The Wynants had no children, but Andrew and Sarah had one son who had lived in New Jersey with his wife and son until ten years ago, when the family had moved to Dallas. Eddie was a good boy—Andrew's son—but not much for writing letters, two a year were about it, and one of those around Christmas. Andrew admitted to himself that he felt lonely sometimes.

And he had to admit that it was absurd to feel elated at the prospect of a date with old Kate, who would very likely have a new tale of horror for him, something else "atrocious" or "inhuman" that had happened in their Brooklyn neighborhood. Kate was on her phone half the time, people calling her or she calling them. She knew everything that was happening. Well, the neighborhood had gone down, to put it mildly. People on welfare were moving in, along with the kids that went with them. The neighborhood had used to be one of the best, lots of privately owned houses, well kept with trees and bushes and polished brass door knockers to brighten the scene. Everybody knew everybody, helped with the snow shoveling, visited at one another's birthday parties, weddings. Now with more people, and the owners dying out, the houses had had to be broken up into apartments, you couldn't do anything about that. Andrew and Sarah had always lived in the apartment Andrew had now, but once they had known the owners, the Kneses, older than he and Sarah, and long dead now. Andrew knew the owner of his four-apartment house only by name, couldn't even remember what he looked like . . . Andrew's thoughts trailed off. He glanced at his watch—five past ten—and wondered if he had forgotten anything. Money and keys, always the essentials, plus his shopping list. Yes, he had them.

Next to Andrew's apartment door, pushed against it, stood a big pine crate full of books and old magazines. That was Kate's idea, to have not only three locks plus a bolt and chain on the door, but a heavy object or two against the door. Anybody could open locks these days, said Kate, and cut through a chain quick as a wink, but if they had to do all that plus push something heavy out of the way, it would give Andrew time to use his telephone. Kate could of course tell a story or two about a woman or man whose life had probably been saved and whose possessions certainly had by this precaution. Andrew tugged at his crate, got it just far enough away that he could open his locks and squeeze out himself. Then he relocked his door, turning his keys twice. At the end of his shopping list, he had a pleasant item to acquire, a rectangular piece of glass of which he had noted the measurements. Andrew was quite a good framer, and sometimes his neighbors, like the Vernons and the Schroeders, brought him photographs and drawings to frame, and of course he didn't charge anything except the cost of his materials. Occasional framing and his own watercolors occupied much of Andrew's time. He had two portfolios of his watercolors, mostly what one might call landscapes of local parks and houses. He showed them to Kate when she asked to see his latest efforts. Two or three were framed in his apartment. Andrew frequently went through his portfolios and threw out the ones he considered not so good. No use hanging on to everything, as a lot of old people did.

Andrew had remounted his favorite photograph of Sarah, had bought a frame secondhand and spruced it up—nice bird's-eye maple—and this evening he intended to fix the glass in the frame and seal the back with brown paper, and hang it in his living room. Andrew had used to be a typesetter for a Brooklyn newspaper, and he appreciated precision, the loose but reliable bang and flop and jangle of huge printing machines. Sometimes in dreams Andrew heard the machines, almost smelled their oil, though even when he had stopped working fifteen years ago, the presses had been modernized and much quieter.

"That you, Andrew?" Kate's voice shrilled down the stairs seconds after he had pushed the bell.

"Me, Kate!" he called back.

"Down in a minute!"

The door behind Andrew, the unlocked front door, suddenly burst open and two, no three children bumped past him. One of them had a key, and they went screaming in, one black and two white, Andrew noticed. There was another apartment besides Kate's on the first floor.

Kate opened the door, nearly as wide as the doorway herself, her pink-ish face framed in the black fur of her coat collar. Kate's chubby hands clutched one shopping bag of blue plastic, plus her carrier which rolled on two wheels but was now flat and collapsed. "What a morning! Did Ethel call you about the Schroeders?" she asked in an unusually upset whisper.

"No, she didn't." Ethel was a neighbor, another great telephone user. Andrew supposed that the Schroeders had suffered another house robbery.

Kate descended her front steps and got her breath back. She planted a hand on Andrew's jacket sleeve. "They were found this morning in their apartment—both dead from sleeping pills. They left a note. *Suicides!*"

"No!" said Andrew, shocked. "Why?"

"They said—" Kate looked around her as if any ears might be enemies "—they couldn't take another robbery. They were too unhappy to go on. They'd had three or four, you know—"

"That's sad news, sad." Andrew felt that he was not taking it in as yet.

"Two burglaries just in the last six months. Remember, Andy? And Herman's back killing him since that last rip-off—when was it? December? It was cold then, anyway, I remember."

"Yes." Herman Schroeder had been taking some sun on a bench a couple of streets away—against Kate's advice, Andrew remembered, because few people were around on cold days—and a couple of boys had taken Herman's money plus his wristwatch and his winter coat. It wasn't so much what they took as the shock of it, and the boys had sat Herman down on the pavement. The benches might as well be traps, for the elderly, anyway. Once they'd all gone to the little park there, played chess and checkers in summer, but no more. Andrew could remember Herman sit-ting with his white pipe in the sun there, reading his newspaper. Gone now. The Schroeders were a decent couple and had been neighbors for decades, like himself and Kate. It was sinking in. "Killed themselves." He and Kate were moving in the direction of the big avenue and the super-market.

"They couldn't afford to move anywhere else. I remember Minnie say-ing that to me—oh, a couple of years ago." Kate had already slowed her walk to spare her bad arches.

Across the street Andrew saw the reassuring figures of two policemen, burly fellows, swinging their sticks, and at the same time he noticed four Hispanic boys coming towards him and Kate on the sidewalk, yelping in Spanish, jostling one another, and one had the glazed look of someone drugged—or was Andrew mistaken? One boy shouted a dirty phrase in English, shoved another who bumped into Andrew, and Andrew caromed into Kate. Andrew righted himself, touched Kate's arm apologetically, but didn't bother saying "Sorry." It was as if he and she were observing a respectful silence for a few minutes in memory of Herman and Minnie Schroeder, even as they made their way to the supermarket.

Andrew said he had to buy a piece of glass, and stepped into the hard-ware store near the corner. He knew Kate would be content to follow him and look around at kitchen gadgets. Andrew read out his measurements, which the young man noted on a scrap of paper.

" 'Bout fifteen minutes," the young man said.

"I'll be a little longer. Going to the supermarket. Thank you." Andrew made his way towards Kate. The shop glittered with chromium toasters, grills, electric machines of all kinds.

In the supermarket they separated as usual, having established that Andrew would buy the staples, potatoes, coffee, bread and such like, while Kate got the meat and chose whatever fruit and vegetables looked good. Andrew was thinking about the Schroeders. Lots of times he and Kate had seen Minnie's small figure here, often in a dark purple coat, shopping alone on a midweek morning, and they had always paused a minute to chat and to ask how everybody was. Herman had never given up his walks, though of course he'd taken them only in daylight hours, but even so—"They prey on the elderly, because they know we can't run or hit back," Kate had said many a time. As Andrew reached for a cardboard box of a dozen eggs, he imagined Minnie and Herman—maybe lying fully clothed on a double bed—in the apartment where Andrew had been several times. *Dead.* Couldn't stand the strain any longer. Was it right to feel so pessimistic, so hopeless, Andrew wondered. Or was it fair to ask that? They must have been too tired to try any longer. Andrew supposed one had to understand and forgive that.

The fingers of the checkout girl flew over the adding machine with an amazing quickness. Andrew didn't bother peering to see if all the figures were correct, though he knew Kate did.

Kate had already checked out and was waiting this side of the glass front doors. They added some items from Andrew's sacks to the carrier. They still had a sack each to carry.

"Bought a nice coffee ring," Kate said. "We can have some at my place, if you'd like."

"That sounds nice," said Andrew. He and Kate each climbed the stairs twice at Kate's house (one flight up) in order to transport all the sacks, while they guarded their purchases in turn in the downstairs hall. You could never tell who might dash in the front door, with a key even, and dash out again with some loot. Kate was convinced some of the kids had passkeys. Kate made Nescafé and warmed the coffee ring in the oven. Then she said, as Andrew had thought she might:

"This coffee ring reminds me of dear Minnie's, only she made better herself. I'm going to miss them, Andy—"

By then they were seated at Kate's oval table in the living room, their groceries divided in the kitchen, but the bill not yet reckoned up.

Andrew nodded solemnly. "I hope I won't have to go like *that*."

"You've had only two house robberies, isn't that it? I've had four. What've I got left?" she asked rhetorically, rolling her head back so her eyes swept the walls, the sideboard on which a green vase stood (Andrew did remember a silver tray and teapot there years ago), the old secondhand television set where—was it four or even more years ago now?—Kate had had a big new set that she had been quite proud of. Andrew did not know what to say. She had been robbed, yes, but all in all maybe her apartment looked more like a home than his own. "It's harder on a man if the wife dies first than the other way around," Kate had said to him after Sarah died. That was perhaps true. Women were better at the little things, making a house look nice. At the same time Andrew warned himself (as he always had since Sarah's death) not to start feeling sorry for himself, because that was the beginning of the end, shameful even. Yet the idea, the *image* of the Schroeders appeared to Andrew more strongly as he sat there sipping Kate's coffee and eating the cinnamon-flavored cake. They had been about seventy-six, Andrew thought, both of them. Not really ancient, was it? Andrew would be eighty-one next month.

"How were they found?" Andrew asked.

"Who?"

"The Schroeders."

"Oh. I think a neighbor on the same floor knocked a few times, then told a super or somebody—because their super doesn't live in the house. I guess the neighbor just said she was worried, because she hadn't seen them in days. They'd been there about four days, Ethel said, because one of the interns said that to somebody."

In the kitchen Andrew reckoned up their bills as best he could, looking over the two sales slips and the divided wax paper–wrapped package of two loaves of bread, the pounds of potatoes. Kate liked him to do the figuring. He arrived at nearly eighteen dollars for Kate and a little more for himself, because he was vague about one item. He reloaded two sacks for himself.

"They're *inhuman*," Kate was saying, even the slightly frayed hem of her skirt twitching now with her anger or upsetness. "You saw that piece in *Time* a couple of months ago, remember, Andy?"

He did. Kate had passed on the magazine when she had finished it, as she often did. It had not been their Brooklyn neighborhood described in the one-and-a-half page article, but one much like it. It told of people barricading their doors at night, not daring to go out after nightfall to buy anything or to visit a friend. Roving bands of teenagers, ninety-seven percent black or Hispanic, *Time* said, made people captive in their own homes, followed people back from the bank on the days when government checks came in, in order to mug them inside their own doors.

"When civilized people like the Schroeders have to kill themselves to escape—" Kate was at a loss for words and sat down, banged her reddish wig squarely on top to make sure it was in place. "The police can't offer enough protection. How can they be everywhere? They can't!"

"But don't forget," Andrew began, happy to recall a cheerful detail, "in that same *Time* piece they showed a picture of a tall black girl escorting some old people—just like us—around their neighborhood to shop. Or maybe back from the bank, I forgot."

Kate nervously picked up a pecan from her plate and pushed it between her lips. "All right, one example, one photograph. All right if we had fifty decent young people like that around here who'd escort *all* of us . . ."

Andrew knew he had best take his leave. Kate could go on another half hour. "I thank you for the delicious coffee and cake, Kate."

"Call me tonight. I feel uneasy, Andy, don't know why. Just today especially."

He nodded. "What time?" he asked, as if making another date, and in a way it was. He liked to have things to look forward to, little duties.

"Just before eight. Five minutes to eight, all right? Because I want to watch something on TV at eight."

Andrew departed, and was all the way home, his sacks emptied and the things put away in his own kitchen, before he realized that he had forgotten to pick up the piece of glass. Now if that wasn't stupid! Sign of old age, he thought, and smiled at himself. Andrew put on his jacket again. Again he unlocked, then relocked his apartment door, thinking he had only himself to blame for this extra exertion. He walked towards the big avenue again with his rather short-stepped gait, right foot a bit slower than the other.

"Morning, Andy," said an elderly woman who had her white dog tied to her wheeled grocery carrier, now full.

"Morning—" Andrew replied, not recalling at once her name. *Helen,* of course, now that it was too late to say it. Helen *Vernon.*

Andrew entered the hardware shop and claimed his glass. Two dollars and eighty-eight cents. The glass was neatly wrapped in brown paper, Scotch-taped. Andrew started home with the glass under his arm. He looked forward to a happy evening of puttering in the little spare room which had used to be Sarah's sewing and ironing room and where Andrew had always had his workbench, which was a flush door on a trestle. The sun had come out brighter now. Andrew glanced up and saw a helicopter pulling a streamer with something written on it that he could not read. A twist of smoke rose from someone's back garden: twigs being burnt. The air promised spring.

He heard rather quick steps behind him, and instinctively moved to the right to let someone pass him on the street side, then got a forceful jolt against his left arm under which he carried the glass. Andrew was knocked to the right, knocked off his feet, and he heard the glass strike the sidewalk with a *clink,* and at the same time Andrew's right hip gave a crack.

Andrew saw blue-jeaned legs, heard gasping as his jacket was wrenched backward, as a button leapt under his nose, and his arms were suddenly pinned to his sides. Now his hat was off, and Andrew expected a blow on the head, but instead a black hand tore his wallet out of the inside pocket of his jacket. Andrew blinked, saw big sneakered feet, long legs in blue jeans, blue denim jacket above, loping away up the sidewalk, turning right at the next corner.

Seconds later, almost at once, a woman bent over him, having come from behind him. "I *saw* that!" she said.

She was trying to help him up, and Andrew got on his knees, hampered by the jacket which still bound his arms. The woman—her head wrapped in a blue scarf, her shopping bag on the sidewalk—held his arm out and pulled up his jacket collar so that the jacket was on his shoulders again. He took her extended hand, and then he was up, on his feet.

"I do thank you," Andrew said, "very much."

"You think you're all right?" She looked in her forties, anxious now, and hair curlers showed under the scarf.

Andrew was much relieved to find that he could stand on his legs without pain. He had feared a hip fracture. "I thank you," he repeated, and realized he was dazed.

"Those *animals*! If I could just see a cop—" She looked all around, gave it up for the moment. "I'll make sure you get home. Where do you live? Want a taxi?"

"No, no, very near."

They began to walk. The nice woman held his arm. She went on talking:

"... 'course you never see a cop when you need one ... one of the old people in my house just last week. Do they think they can take over this neighborhood? Hah! They'd better think *again* ... And what do they want, when you come down to it, recreation halls they've already got, unemployment pay, welfare, a *salary* if they just go to a training school! ... Public libraries! But do you see 'em in the library here? No, they'd rather spend their time robbing ... Do these apes think we didn't *work* for what little we've got? ... Got a son. He talks about us getting guns the way they do in San Francisco or is it Los Angeles? ... Lookit this, no cop yet!"

"Here's where I live," Andrew said when they came to a two-story red brick and creamy cement house.

The woman offered to help him up the stairs, but Andrew said he could make it alone.

"How much did you lose by the way?" she asked.

Andrew tried to think. "Not more than ten dollars. I don't—" He stopped and began again. "It's identification cards and such. I'll write for some more. Got the numbers—"

"If you tell me your name, I'll report this to the police. I saw that tall boy—"

"Oh, no, no. Thank you," said Andrew rather firmly, as if her reporting the matter might be somehow in his disfavor.

"Take care. Bye-bye," said the woman, and went off in the direction they had come from.

Andrew made his way upstairs, fished keys from his trousers pocket, entered, relocked his door, and slowly prepared a pot of tea. Tea was always the best after a shock. He had to admit he'd had a shock. Yes. Even though this was the second or third time, the last having been more than a year ago—But this one in broad daylight, high noon! Andrew put two spoonfuls of sugar in his tea, and sat down at the kitchen table. At least his groceries were here at home safe. And his hip was not hurting much, just a little pain like a bruise. Just suppose he'd broken his hip, couldn't walk for the next two or three months, dependent on Kate to buy his food? Now that would've been catastrophic! Andrew felt grateful to fate.

He made a peanut butter sandwich, could eat only half of it, and suddenly realized that he needed to lie down. He pushed off his shoes and lay down on the living room couch, pulled up the crocheted coverlet that Sarah had made. It seemed to Andrew that he'd hardly begun to doze off, when the telephone rang. Probably Kate.

And Kate it was, saying the funeral for the Schroeders was Saturday at 11 A.M., and would Andrew like to come, because there was a small bus that several of the neighbors intended to take to go to the cemetery.

"Why, yes—sure," Andrew said, feeling it was a neighborly duty to go, a sign of his respect that he would be glad to make.

"Fine, Andy. I'll ring your bell around ten-fifteen Saturday because you're on the way. How you feeling? There's a documentary on TV tonight that might interest you. Nine o'clock, if that isn't too late. Till ten but—We *could* meet half way and sort of walk each other, but I suppose it's silly to take a chance just for a TV program."

It was silly, was Andrew's opinion at the moment, though he said nothing.

"Still there, Andy?—Are you okay?"

"Well, since you ask," Andrew replied, "I just got mugged, sat down on the—"

"Why didn't you tell me right away? I knew something would happen today! Did they hurt you?"

"Just one boy. No, I'm all right, Kate."

"Which one was it? D'you get a look at him?"

"Oh, yes. Tall black fellow with a little red in his hair."

"Maybe I know the one you mean. Not sure though. You went out again, Andy?"

"Forgot that piece of glass. Had to go back for it."

They agreed that Andrew shouldn't go out again today after dark, because lightning did sometimes strike the same place twice.

Then Andrew went back to the living room couch which, sagging though it was, he had always loved to snooze on. He quickly became drowsy again, but his half-sleep was troubled. He felt melancholic too, because he did not want to go out again, and this evening he would not have the glass he needed to frame the photograph of Sarah. What would happen to all those glass shards on the sidewalk which he'd been too upset to pick up? Would some other kids pick them up, make use of them against the local people? Andrew squirmed on the couch. The boys mostly carried knives, easier to handle. The first time Andrew had been ripped off, the time they got his leather wallet (after that he used plastic wallets), a younger boy had stood in front of him with a knife at the level of Andrew's eyes as he sat on the pavement, while an older boy had lifted his wallet. From beyond his apartment door, Andrew heard the clicking of locks, the slide of a bolt. Mrs. Wilkie was going out.

Tomorrow he'd acquire another piece of glass, and tomorrow evening or even afternoon he'd have the pleasure of hanging the photograph, and of seeing Sarah's gently smiling face as she had looked at twenty-five or -six—when Eddie had been about two—wearing the summer dress that was cut low in front with ruffles, and the coral necklace Andrew had given her. Andrew felt old. When he thought of all those *years*! To feel old was mainly to feel tired, he supposed. Maybe it was inevitable, for everyone. He had been lucky in the sense of being healthier than most people, free of rheumatism and the usual complaints. What depressed him, he realized, was the prospect of the grave, of death soon. Death would be perhaps merely a moment, maybe quite painless, but it was also a mystery. Was it just like fainting? Andrew still found life interesting enough to want to go on living. Day after tomorrow, he'd attend the funeral of Herman and Minnie Schroeder, and in a few years from now, maybe very few years, other neighbors like Kate and Helen Vernon would be attending *his* funeral. People like Kate would mention him in the months that followed, say perhaps that they missed him, and then they would stop mentioning him, as people would the Schroeders finally. What was life all about? It seemed to Andrew that there ought to be something more to hang onto, more to represent a man, even the humblest, than a few sticks of furniture, a few dollars in the bank, some old books and photographs, when he died. *Dust unto dust,* Andrew thought and turned over on his side, whereupon his bruised hip began to hurt, but he lay still, too tired to change his position. Of course there was his son Eddie, and his son Andy, a grown-up man of twenty-eight now himself. But what Andrew was thinking about was something personal and individual to him: what was he worth, as a human being?

So Andrew did not go to Kate's that evening, but made a supper of macaroni and cheese (not frozen, it was cheaper to make it himself) and a green salad. After his supper, he pulled out a kitchen drawer and reached behind the plastic tray, which contained knives, forks, and spoons, for his spare money, lest he go out and be down on the street tomorrow before he realized that he hadn't money. Andrew took four singles, which left a fiver in the drawer, and put them into his trousers pocket. Then he wrote his letters of notice of stolen cards to his bank and to the Social Security office.

The next morning, a lovely sunny morning, Andrew went again to the hardware store and put in his order for a piece of glass measuring twenty-four by eighteen inches. Andrew had expected the young man to say, "Broke it?" or something like that, in which case Andrew would have smiled and said yes, but the young man was too busy to say anything but "Fifteen minutes."

Fifteen minutes could pass quickly for Andrew in a hardware shop, so he browsed among hammers and wrenches, potato-peelers, coffee-makers which kept the pot warm on a little platform after it was done, fancy hooks for bathroom walls, bags of peat and supercharged humus for the garden, charcoal broilers of various heights and diameters, and then the young man was standing by him with the glass all wrapped again, and looking the same as yesterday's package. Andrew again paid two dollars and eighty-eight cents to the girl cashier. Andrew thought he would frame the picture before lunch. The picture might inspire him to call up Kate and invite her to tea. Kate liked tea with dainty but substantial ham and mayonnaise sandwiches, for instance, followed by a cake. Andrew might shop for all that after lunch.

Andrew had entered the second block of his three-block walk home, when he saw the same black boy in the same blue denim jacket approaching him, hands in his back pockets, whistling, swinging his feet out like a sailor.

Andrew stiffened. Did the boy recognize him? But the boy wasn't even looking at him. Same reddish black kinky hair, over six feet tall, yes, same boy. What had he bought with the ten dollars, Andrew wondered, at the same time noticing that the unbuttoned denim jacket sparkled with what seemed to be bottle caps fixed up and down the front. Who was he going to rip off next, this noon or later? These thoughts or impressions flashed through Andrew's mind in seconds, and then the big, freckled eyes of the boy met Andrew's, sharp but empty of recognition, and his figure came on, sure that Andrew would step aside for him. His hands and arms swung free now, maybe ready to give Andrew a shock by spreading out, as if he intended to crash into Andrew.

Now Andrew's right hand clenched the bottom of his package more firmly, tilted a corner forward as if it were a lance, and Andrew did not step aside. He simply kept his course—as the boy's arms flew out to make him jump—braced his body for an impact, and saw the point of the package hit near the white buttons on the pale blue shirt.

"Ow!"

The jolt sent Andrew backward, but he kept his footing.

"Oooh," the boy groaned more gently, and folded his hands over his stomach. "Son of a *bitch*!" Blood oozed over his clasped fingers.

A man appeared on the sidewalk behind Andrew. A woman with a shopping carrier like Kate's had come from the opposite direction and hesitated with her mouth slightly open.

"He stab me!" the boy whined in falsetto. He was bent double, leaning against a fire hydrant.

The man, who carried a lot of cardboard sheets under one arm, looked more curious than concerned. "What happened? Another boy?" he asked Andrew.

"He *stab* me!"

Neither the man nor the woman paid any attention to that.

". . . find a doctor?" the woman was saying vaguely to the man.

"Better find one. Yeah. Maybe," said the man, and went on his way.

The woman made a sound like "Tschuh!" and took two drifting steps away, plainly wanting to quit the scene. "They *live* like that," she said to Andrew, flinging out one hand for emphasis. "They do it to us and once in a while *they* get it." She hurried off, but turned back to say, "If I see a policeman . . ." She went on.

The boy looked at Andrew, muttered something that sounded like a threat, and here came his chums, two or three of them, Andrew walked on towards his house. The padding of sneakers, of leaping feet crossed the street, and Andrew saw one of the figures dodge a passing car. A corner of Andrew's glass package hung limp. He had really given the boy a slash. Andrew thought of rapes in his neighborhood (not always reported in the newspapers, he and Kate had noticed), in which the girl had suffered a knife wound in the cheek lest she scream, plus the insult of rape. He realized that his heart was thumping with anger, with fear too. He had meant to strike back. Well, he had. Let the police come, let them accuse him, charge him. Maybe they would. Andrew thought they might.

It was not until he had set the glass package down and was tackling his apartment door's three locks that Andrew noticed the fingers of his right hand were bleeding on the inside. Part of the brown paper was sodden with blood. Andrew went into his apartment and locked his door from inside again, letting the blood fall on the brown package which he had laid flat on the floor. Then carefully, so as not to drip on the hall carpet, Andrew held his right wrist and got to the kitchen which was closer than the bathroom. He ran cold water over his hand. The cuts were not bad, he thought, wouldn't need stitches anyway, just a few Band-Aids. He pushed the crate of books and magazines back against the door.

By two o'clock that afternoon Andrew was feeling better, though around noon he had had some bad moments. One finger had refused to stop bleeding for quite a while, then Andrew had made some lunch, and had lain down on the living room couch, feeling weak. Just after two he put on his jacket and went out again to buy his piece of glass. This time the same young man—who knew Andrew slightly because of Andrew's purchases of glass for pictures in the past—did make a remark, smiling a little, and Andrew, not having caught every word of what he said, replied, "Yes—got a couple of pictures same size to do." Andrew again waited, and when he got the glass, proceeded to the main avenue, where there was a bakery between the subway entrance and the public library. Andrew wished he had brought his books, not yet due, but he had read them and might have changed them. At the bakery, he bought a three-layer chocolate cake with white icing plus some brown-edged cookies. Then he walked home the way he had come, his usual route, past the spot where he had encountered the boy today, though he did not glance to his left where he might have seen blood stains. Andrew did not look around him at all, though he imagined, he felt sure, that the tall boy's chums were going to be on the lookout for him. From now on, to go out of his house would be to take more of a risk than usual.

At home again, he was conscious of taking another small risk when he telephoned Kate before he had framed the photograph, because the photograph in its frame was part of his tea invitation. Kate was in and said she would love to come over around four.

Andrew got busy. He had wrapped a clean rag around his right hand, which made him a little clumsy, but he worked carefully. One sweep of blood, crescent-shaped, got on the brown paper that Andrew had neatly sealed on the back of the frame, but that couldn't be helped, because he hadn't wanted to spend time changing the bandage. He put in the screw eyes and attached the brass picture wire for hanging. Then Andrew did change the bandage, keeping the Band-Aids on, and with his left hand hammered the nail into the wall for the picture, and put the picture up.

Now that looked beautiful! He straightened the picture delicately with one finger. Sarah brightened his whole living room, made a tremendous change. She smiled out at him, her head slightly turned but her eyes direct, and he imagined he could hear her saying, "Andy." Andrew smiled back at her, and for several seconds felt young, felt as if he were breathing the crisp air that one breathed on hills in the country. Ah, well! Tea!

Andrew got out cups and saucers and plates, making sure he took ones that weren't nicked. Sugar and a little pitcher of milk. By the time he had things ready and had lit the gas under the kettle, his doorbell rang.

"Hello, Andy, and how're you feeling today?" Kate asked as she came in, puffing a little from the stairs.

For the moment, Andrew was keeping his right hand behind his back. "Well enough, thank you, Kate. And yourself?" He relocked the door.

"Oh-h—" Kate was unbuttoning her coat over her rather vast front, turning round as she usually did to survey the living room. She spotted the new picture on the wall. "Why, that's lovely, Andy!" She went closer. "Sarah's just lovely there! And that bird's-eye maple!"

Andrew had waxed the frame. He felt a glow of satisfaction. Kate chattered on, recalling when they were younger, when all four of them had shared Christmas and Thanksgiving dinners and once in a while had gone out to a nearby Polish restaurant (long closed) where couples of all ages had used to dance rather sedately between courses, having a grand time. But before he had poured the tea, Kate noticed his hand.

"Cut it framing the photograph," Andrew said. "Clumsy of me. It's not serious." If he told the truth, Kate would say something alarming— Andrew didn't know exactly what, but it would have to do with the gang's hitting back, maybe all the roving gangs and there were three, one Hispanic, one black, one sort of mixed with an odd white or two. Kate might insist that he stay in for the next days while she brought him whatever he might need.

"You're sure we shouldn't look at it again while I'm here?" Kate asked through a mouthful of chocolate cake. "I can do a neat bandage for you. You can't tie a bandage with one hand. Have you got antiseptic? Alcohol?"

"Oh, Kate!"

Then inquiries about his papers, if he had written for new cards. Andrew said he had. He heated more water.

Kate insisted, before she left, on changing his bandage and tying a clean one properly. "It's just silly to stay all night with that one damp already." She had washed up the tea things, so Andrew would not get his hand wetter.

So Andrew let her undo the bandage with the aid of scissors. When she saw that four fingers had been cut, she was amazed.

"Well, it didn't happen the way I told it," Andrew said. "I—This morning I saw this same tall fellow coming at me again—just to scare me out of his way as usual, I suppose, but I didn't step out of his way, I let him walk right into the glass—point." There it was plain, and as they stood by the kitchen sink, Andrew glanced at Kate's face for shock, understanding maybe, for sympathy too.

"And you hurt him? Cut him, I mean?"

"Yes, I did." Andrew said. "He came straight at me to scare me, you know, that's why *he* didn't get out of the way one bit. But what I was carrying wasn't exactly a sack of eggs! I saw his stomach bleeding." Andrew told her about the man and woman stopping, and said maybe they had found a doctor somewhere, but Andrew had walked on home. Andrew realized he was boasting a bit, like a small boy who had done something courageous. In fact, Andrew admitted to himself that he *hoped* he had given the boy a bad cut, and a wound like that in the stomach might be fatal, Andrew thought.

"I wonder that you got home alive! What about his pals?"

"He was by himself," Andrew said, avoiding Kate's eyes. He wasn't going to say that he thought a couple of the boy's pals had seen him. Anyway the injured boy was going to tell his chums.

Kate had more questions. How badly did he think the so-and-so was hurt? Andrew said he couldn't say. Andrew said he had just wanted to stand up for people's rights to walk on the sidewalk without having to jump aside like scared rabbits for neighborhood hoodlums.

But Kate's plump, creased face still looked uneasy, she talked about getting penicillin powder for his fingers, about being afraid to take the Band-Aids off to change them. She said she would ring him later tonight, around nine, to see how he felt. Then she left.

As Andrew had supposed, Kate had told him he had better not go out of the house for the next couple of days, that she would find out by telephone what he needed and bring it to him. Andrew hadn't remonstrated, but he didn't want to be a semi-invalid, dependent upon Kate.

The next morning, Andrew found a letter from his son Eddie in his mail box. That was nice. Andrew read most of it, standing in the area between the unlocked front door and the door into his house. Eddie was well and so was Betty, his wife, and they had rented a cottage on the coast in South Carolina for a month this summer, and would Andrew like to join them for a week or two in June? Andrew at once asked himself, did they really mean it, really want him? Of course there was time to think about it, to read Eddie's typewritten letter more carefully when he got home. Now Andrew needed, besides a little fresh air, a container of cottage cheese and a jar of mayonnaise. He intended to buy those at the delicatessen instead of the supermarket.

Andrew walked to the big avenue, made these purchases, and was on his way home, had greeted two neighbors on the way, when he heard running footsteps behind him. Andrew moved to the right to let whoever it was pass on the street side of the pavement, then he felt a violent blow against the back of his head, just above the neck. Andrew sagged at once as if paralyzed. He was on his knees on the sidewalk when the next blow came, something like a stocking swung over his left shoulder, catching him in the left temple with a crack like an earthquake, like dynamite, a gunshot even, then came the faint padding of sneakers running away. Andrew's vision—one side of his head resting against pavement now—became gray, and the humming in his head was louder than anything else. He had a desire to vomit, couldn't, was aware of shoes, trouser legs, a woman's ankles near him, of voices which seemed to come through a thick sea, of a pair of feet that drifted away. This was their vengeance, and what could he do about it now? He had absolutely expected it, and it had come. He knew he was dying, knew if people tried to move him, as they were trying now, that it would not change anything. One died in one place or another. He was aware that he sighed, aware of a resignation like a wave of peace washing over him. He was aware of justice, of the absence of anger, aware of the value of what he had done—and done all his life, and even yesterday when he had struck a small blow in the name of his neighborhood. Kate would tell the neighbors. Kate would go to his funeral. But all that was unimportant compared to the great event happening to him, the event of dying, of stopping. What mattered justice, revenge, movement of any kind? He then reached a point of being unable to think further, and was aware of a most wonderful sense of balance.

A loud exclamation or command from one of the people lifting him was unintelligible to Andrew, like another language.

Please Don't Shoot
the Trees

"We *were* on the subject of water conservation in summer!" a voice screamed. "Just in principle!"

"We never finished the *fish*!" cried another voice, even shriller.

"Who's the chair today?"

"And the *trees* . . ." That voice faded off.

Elsie Gifford smiled, sighed, but was sufficiently interested to rise a little in her chair and look behind her to identify, if possible, the ones who were crying out. She had come to listen today, not having any particular problem at the moment.

"Be damned to you all!"

Laughter! That had been a hell of a voice.

Elsie laughed too. This would be something to tell Jack about tonight—though Jack thought Citizens for Life a silly organization. Elsie and Jack, like most of the people at the meeting, lived in a protected residential area called Rainbow, far enough south of Los Angeles to be free of smog. Los Angeles, in fact, was now abandoned by industry and residents, yet poor people still lived there. "The better-off" were doing their own fighting back now, thrusting their protected areas farther into the cesspools of such cities as Los Angeles, Detroit and Philadelphia. Now it was the underprivileged, the poor, forced to move ever closer together in the cities, because they had nowhere else to go. Everything had become so tidy, nobody could even go camping any more, park a trailer anywhere, or even sleep in the woods.

"The *trees*!" the same voice was shrieking again, and she was being shouted down.

What was that tree rumor, anyway? Elsie leaned towards a woman on her left, whom she knew by sight but whose name she had forgotten. "What's the business about trees?"

But her last words were drowned out.

The back doors—rather the front doors some distance behind Elsie— had burst open. A chorus of voices screamed:

"The Forty-Niners are here!"

More laughter! Lots of groans. Boos, even.

"Get them *out!*"

But there was a patter of applause too.

Elsie smiled again, because she had been thinking that this was all the meeting needed—the Forty-Niners. They were a group of teenagers (average age nineteen, Elsie remembered) who used a covered wagon as their emblem, and aimed to make the West, chiefly California or the Golden Gate, as pure as it had been, presumably, back in 1849, the year of the Gold Rush. Jack laughed at them, because the men of the Gold Rush era had not been particularly pure in spirit, and hadn't used covered wagons to get to California, just ponies, stagecoaches and shoe leather. But this was 2049, so the kids had hitched onto the date.

Now the youngsters were streaming down the aisle, holding aloft a banner ten feet long—or three meters—fixed to two poles, with a brown covered wagon painted on it and the words: KEEP THE WEST GOLDEN!

"Halt nuclear tests! Halt nuclear *reactors!*"

"You can stop them! You *women!* And *men!*"

"Many of you are married to men making these nukes!"

"... which are shattering the foundations of your own houses!" Several girls' voices came out clearest.

The Forty-Niners were always well-rehearsed. They kept their numbers around two hundred. They were a self-styled elite.

"An earthquake is fore-*CAST!* An earthquake is fore-*CAST!*" chanted the Forty-Niners.

Some rather senior citizens had folded their arms, smiling indulgently, but with an air of surrender. The meeting was finished, as far as scheduled agenda went. The Forty-Niners always took from five to seven minutes to make their point, then departed, but so many people had to get home or to work (there were so many job shifts now), that the agenda could never be resumed.

"...ABOLISH *NUKES!*"

What would Jack shout back if he were here, Elsie wondered. Jack was a physicist, and considered nuclear energy the greatest boon to mankind ever invented, or discovered, by technologists. He would certainly remind

these kids that the Rainbow scientists had extinguished an awful holo-
caust, that had been melting a nuke, by means of chemicals that had been
right on hand, as demanded by law. Lots of people were leaving now, Elsie
saw. She got up too.

"Aren't they loudmouths!" This was from Jane Newcombe, a blondish
woman of Elsie's age, a neighbor.

Elsie smiled more broadly. "But they *mean* well," she replied, laying on
the tongue-in-cheek tolerance, playing it safe. "Can I give you a lift home,
Jane?"

"Thanks, I came in my own copter. How's everything?"

"Oh, as usual. Fine," Elsie said.

Elsie climbed into her battery-run copter and rose gently straight up.
At sedate speed, she turned south towards Rainbow and floated almost
noiselessly towards it. On either side little red and green lights of other
copters circulated like lazy butterflies, heading for labs, factories, or home.
To the west on her right lay the darkness of the Pacific, bordered by a thin
string of lights that marked radar stations, all laser-gun equipped, though
the lights from a height looked like a carelessly tossed diamond necklace,
or like something natural, anyway, due to the shoreline. She could also see
the great more-than-half-circle of purple and orange lights that marked
the eastern boundary of Rainbow and extended almost to the shore. Rainbow's two arcs of light were laser gadgets which could slice through anything metal, however thick, which might be flying towards Rainbow with
unfriendly intent. Elsie descended, approaching her home now. Her
copter, like most household copters, went only sixty kilometers per hour
maximum. Such helicopters (the two for the kids had a fifty MPH maximum) were considered patriotic and conservative, because they used minimum juice and made almost no noise. They suited Elsie perfectly, though
Jack sometimes griped about the low speed.

Elsie made a pass straight over their copter hangar whose roof had a
scanning device. A number was written under her copter, and the roof
automatically opened for her. She lowered the copter, and the automatic
radar took over, parking her. Jack wasn't home yet, but the boys were, she
saw from their two copters. Today had been a sports afternoon, and they
had stayed until 5 P.M. at school.

Since it was already past seven, Elsie decided on a pushbutton dinner.
Her U-Name-It machine held thirty-six dinners, and it was now more
than half empty. One ordered an entire cylinder, glass-fronted, refrigerated,
but with individual electronic heating devices to heat the section desired.
There were kosher cylinders, vegetarian, diabetic, low-calorie, but the Gif-

fords preferred the mixed, which offered four Chinese meals, four Mexican, Greek, Italian and so on.

"UNDER CONTROL," JACK Gifford said with a smile, when Elsie asked him about the earthquake rumors. "We know all about the San Andreas fault."

Elsie told him about the meeting, not that there was much to tell, because of the break-up by the Forty-Niners.

At the mention of the Forty-Niners, their son Richard, aged ten, left the table to get something, and now he was coming back with a yellow airplane made of a folded piece of paper. "They were dropping these today," Richard said.

"Oh yeah, yeah," his younger brother Charles put in. "Dropping by copter. Lots of 'em."

Elsie opened the paper airplane and read:

MESSAGE FROM THE FORTY-NINERS:

AN EARTHQUAKE

is predicted—though you'll never hear it
from the "Authorities"!

DO YOU CARE?

FIGHT NOW AGAINST NUKES AND UNDERGROUND
NUCLEAR EXPLOSIONS!

Y O U R EARTH IS TREMBLING!

TREE ROOTS ARE BEING DISTURBED!

TREES ARE DEVELOPING STRANGE DISEASES,
DYING!

DO YOU CARE? MARCH WITH US TO GOLDEN GATE
STATE CAPITOL

NEXT SATURDAY NOON!

ASSEMBLE FIRST 11 AM GOLDEN GATE TOWN HALL
(outside)

or send a donation to FORTY-NINERS
Box 435 Electron Blvd
South San. Fran. OR DO BOTH!

Jack glanced at the paper too. "Always asking for handouts, you can bet on that. The parents ought to keep those kids at home. South San Fran! That slum!"

Elsie remembered when she and Jack had got out in the streets in the late thirties, before they were married, protesting—what? Elsie had some fellow-feeling for the kids, even the Forty-Niners, who seemed so much more militant and well-organized than any groups she and Jack had known.

"But what is all this about an earthquake? Just not true?" Elsie asked.

Jack put down his plastic chopsticks—it was a Chinese dinner—and replied, "First of all, not true, because we know one's not due for years. Second, if it came, we'd have hours of warning, and we'd control it by counterbombing underground, which would simply drain off the strain. I explained all that to you."

Jack certainly had, and Elsie remembered. She looked at the faces of her two sons. The boys were listening with the neutral, vaguely amused smiles which Elsie had come to detest, smiles that said, "Nothing's going to surprise us, because we don't give a damn, see?" Elsie had seen the same smiles while they watched the most horrific television programs—and also when she had informed them, about a year ago, that their grandparents, her mother and father, had been killed in a helicopter collision over Santa Fe. Something had gone wrong with the radar in the other people's copter, it had later been found. Helicopter collisions were impossible if the radar was functioning, even if one copter tried to ram another. The know-it-all, what-the-hell smiles protected Richard and Charles. Four or five years ago, when she and Jack had had the more or less usual trouble with the boy's resistance to reading and short-interest-span syndrome, the psychiatrist had called them semi-autistic, but he had also let slip out apathetic, which Elsie preferred because it was more accurate, in her opinion. Good old Greek! She had managed to take a year of Greek in university in the last year it was being taught in America. Elsie forced her eyes, with a nervous jerk of her head, away from her sons, and said, "What?" because Jack was still talking.

"Well, hon, if you're not listening—"

"I was listening."

"We've freed Golden Gate—and America, the whole *world* from the fear of earthquakes. If the bastards on the other side of the world like Italy and Japan had the dough to buy our equipment . . ."

Yes, Jack. But Elsie didn't say it. When she and Jack had been twenty-one or so, they hadn't talked like this. There had still been a hope, an intention of sharing everything with everyone, at least that intention had prevailed among lots of people besides "rabels" of which she and Jack had been two—rabels being a combination of rebel and rabble. Now America itself was partitioned into four big "states" of which Golden Gate was the richest (all of California up to Canada), and they didn't share anything with the others. The whole Western Coast was one big fortress against Sino-Russia, Japan being a demilitarized colony of theirs, Sino-Russia. The great cities had become unsupervised prisons of the poor and the black, and New York and San Francisco were dirty words, as dirty as Detroit and Philadelphia had been to Elsie's grandmother.

"And the trees, Jack. Have you heard anything about diseases? They were talking tonight—not just the Forty-Niners—"

"Nothing from our Forestry Department, hon. You know these kids ride the same old conservation jazz about spoiling nature, all that crap. Times haven't changed. If our nukes or the testing were putting us in danger of *anything,* we'd stop 'em, wouldn't we? We've got battery power in reserve everywhere." Jack exuded confidence, reassurance. Even his cheeks were rosy with health. The scientists at Jack's lab played tennis or swam three times a week, in the lab's big gymnasium.

So Elsie felt better. Jack had degrees in seismology and oceanography as well as in physics. She had graduated from a liberal arts university, and felt her own diploma to be on a par with a degree in knitting.

The next morning—a fine, sunny October morning—Elsie decided to hop over to Rainbow Library some eight miles away. She had hardly sat down in her copter when she saw more yellow papers wafting down from the sky. She got out and picked one up from the graveled driveway.

TREES BLISTERS NOW . . .
DUE TO JIGGLED SAP!
ARE YOU INTERESTED?
PROTECT YOUR TREES! PROTECT EARTH!
PROTECT YOURSELF!
BAN NUKES AND NUKE TESTS!

The rest was a repetition of time and place of the Forty-Niners' next meeting. Jiggled sap? What were they talking about? The page was badly printed as usual. Elsie got back into her copter.

There wasn't any need for Elsie to go to Rainbow Library, because audio-video books could be ordered by telephone and delivered by helicopter. Every home in Rainbow had a pick-up and delivery tower, radar-locked. But Elsie enjoyed looking at the big lighted bulletin board that reeled off new titles available, enjoyed running into friends and having a chat and a coffee on the Library grounds. The building was a vast mauve construction in the shape of RL, but joined, as in an old cattle brand, legible from the air. Elsie returned a couple of cylinders and took out three, one contemporary novel, the complete works of T. S. Eliot including his essays, and a new offering which she was lucky to get—new Chinese and Russian poems. Elsie often played these while she pottered about the house or worked in the garden. One cylinder could be of eight hours' duration. The same cylinder could be attached to the television set, and one could see the reader, plus background scenes appropriate to whatever the text was. The advantage in Elsie's opinion was that the cylinders always had the complete text of the original. They were considered classics now, slow and old-fashioned.

"Thanks, Gwyn," Elsie said to the woman behind the desk, though Elsie had got her cylinders by pushbutton. "Quiet here this morning!" Elsie hadn't met anyone she knew, or knew well enough to want to have a coffee with.

"Yes," said Gwyn. She was a woman of about forty, a health-faddist, good at sports.

It was unusual for Gwyn to be so unsmiling, and Elsie said, "Anything the matter?"

Gwyn looked for a second embarrassed, then shook her head and said, "Oh, no. Everything's under control."

Elsie thought perhaps something had happened in Gwyn's family—a death. A parent, maybe, because Gwyn was not married. Elsie went out to her copter. She was only a little distance from it when a spot on a tree trunk, at eye level, caught her attention. A funny mushroom, Elsie supposed. It was a bulging white disk and its center was slightly pink. Like a woman's breast, she thought, and repressed a giggle. She turned to her copter, and saw another larger circle on a larger tree. Fungus. That was what the Forty-Niners must mean about the trees. It didn't seem a huge problem. Rainbow had successfully fought fungi before, and they'd certainly had some odd ones.

Still, Elsie felt disturbed, and when she got home switched on the television news and listened as she deposited her library cylinders in the audio-video. The news sounded positively soothing, as usual. Elsie was about to ring U-Name-It for a refill of mixed, when the news announcer broke into a colorful smile and said, "Now for a special announcement. Please do *not* touch your trees, for any purpose, till further notice. Those funny looking growths aren't dangerous but they *can* spread, and some kids are shooting them with air rifles or poking them for fun. The Forestry Department is already taking care of them, so don't you folks worry. Forestry will make a stop at *your* house in the next forty-eight hours. But don't let the kids touch 'em. Okay, folks?" A big grin.

Elsie didn't like the sound of that. This was the local Rainbow news. She telephoned Jack, something she rarely did in working hours.

"Oh, forget it, honey! What else've they got to talk about on the news?" Jack sounded as calm as ever.

But when Elsie was looking over the U-Name-It mixed, which had been installed around 3 P.M., she noticed that the refrigerator power had automatically switched over from nuke to battery. That meant an emergency of some kind.

Elsie went at once to the telephone and rang up Jane Newcombe.

"Haven't you heard?" Jane said. "It's probably because Jack's in top-secret and sworn to silence. The trees are shooting inflammable *sap*, Elsie! Something like phosphorus or napalm. Remember napalm?"

Elsie did. "What do you mean, shooting?"

"These mushroom things explode. In fact they're not fungus. More like a cancer. Gosh, everyone's known about it for at least—since early this morning. Kids aren't supposed to poke them, so tell your boys."

"But it's a tree disease, isn't it?"

"I dunno. What's the use of giving it a name? As you always say, Elsie, does it make things any better?" Jane tried to laugh. "If you have any on your trees, don't walk too close, dear, because they go off."

"Like guns?"

"Can't talk anymore, Tommy's just come in and I want to make sure he's briefed. Okay?"

When she had hung up, Elsie went out the rear door of the house, out a second door in the covered passage to the copter and car garage onto her driveway. She loved her poplars, the young oak, the palm trees, the two pineapple trees. Elsie tended the garden, pruned the roses, kept an eye on everything. Jack wasn't keen on gardening. She walked down the broad graveled drive to the iron gates, stood for a moment looking through the gates at the gently rolling land beyond, at the yellowish but fertile soil, at the varying green of trees and the fuzzy orange and yellow patch in the distance, a citrus orchard. Heavenly, she thought. And healthy. At least to the eye.

She began to walk back to her house. Now she caught sight of a small whitish circle on the slender trunk of the oak. A pang went through her, as if she had seen a wound on one of her own children. The white circle confronted her directly, like some kind of accusation. It was hardly three inches in diameter, smaller than the two she had seen at Rainbow Library, but unmistakably *what it was,* and she could also see a pinkness at the center.

A rifle or pistol shot made Elsie jump, her sandals rattled on the gravel, and she realized how tense she was. Their nearest neighbors, the Osbournes, sometimes shot clay pigeons. Hunting was forbidden in Rainbow. She heard two more shots, more distant, and from another direction.

The telephone was ringing. Elsie ran in and answered it eagerly.

"This is Helen Ludlow at Rainbow Academy," said a pleasant young voice. "Mrs Gifford? . . . This is just to say Richard's had a slight accident. No, not serious, I can assure you, but we're bringing him home and he may be a little late because we're—treating him. Someone will bring his copter, so he'll have it at home. His brother Charles is quite all right."

Elsie asked if it had anything to do with the trees, but the line went dead. Miss Ludlow taught history, if Elsie remembered correctly.

Now there were more gunshots, some very distant, barely audible. She went out on her driveway again to look at the spot on the oak. She imagined that it had grown larger in the last five minutes. Its outer edge was crinkled like water-soaked flesh, like something prepared to expand. It seemed to quiver as she approached. Or was she imagining?

She decided to telephone the Forestry Department.

The Forestry Department's line gave out a constant busy signal. Rainbow Hospital? She anticipated evasiveness there. The police? They would probably say it was the business of the Forestry Department. Elsie put on the television. She got a Mozart opera, on another channel a Spanish lesson, then a gymnastics class, a cooking lesson, finally came to her senses and pushed Channel 30 which gave out news twenty-four hours a day. The announcer was talking about the President's warm reception at a Far Eastern capital, as if anyone cared.

Elsie was aware of a growing panic.

She grabbed a jacket and went to her copter. At least from the copter she would be able to *see* what was happening.

The sporadic gunshots kept up.

Elsie headed in the same direction she had gone that morning, towards the center of Rainbow called the Forum, which held the Library, Rainbow Hospital, Town Hall and Symphony Hall. Now she noticed a more than usual number of cars on the roads, all moving towards the eastern borders of Rainbow. They looked like ladybirds—some of them did have polka-dot roofs—but small as they were, they held more than most copters could, if one was moving home. Each battery car took only two passengers, but behind there was ample room for suitcases, crates and whatnot. Elsie flew lower as she approached a grove of trees. She saw men with rifles. Some were laughing, bending backward, though she couldn't hear what they said.

"Hey! Not so close!" a man on the ground yelled at her, waving his arms.

"Vibes! Keep clear!" called another voice.

"And shut up yourself!" said the first man.

Elsie saw two trees then a third wilt rapidly, and collapse—in a matter of ten seconds! Figures scattered away on the run.

More guns went off.

Two white ambulances rushed at top speed (they went faster than ordinary cars, but were also on battery) towards the tree area. Elsie cut her forward power and hovered. She was now over another part of the park, over trees which bordered Symphony Hall.

"Go *away* please!" That was from a middle-aged man below who brandished a stick. "Vibrations!" He wore the dark green uniform of the Forestry Department.

Then Elsie saw a white jet come from nowhere and hit the man in the face. The man screamed and fell, head in his hands.

At once, without even thinking, Elsie lowered her copter. The man had fallen in a wide lane, and she had space to land. She got out and ran the short distance to where he lay. She could hear his groans now.

"Are you—" Elsie stopped in horror. The man's face was burning. Steam actually rose, and she could smell it—scorched flesh plus something aromatic, like resin. She pulled the man's hands down instinctively from his face, then saw that his palms were burning too. "Can you walk to the copter?" Elsie looked around wildly for help, because he showed no sign of getting up, and she was not sure she could get him to the copter to fly him to the hospital a half mile away. Was this what had happened to *Richard*?

She caught the man under his arms, began to drag him towards the copter, and realized that he had fainted. No, he was dead. His eyes, open, had turned upward and were pink-white except for a crescent of gray. *Was* he dead? She bent quickly to look for a pulse in his wrist.

"Get away this place is *dangerous!*" This came from a tall, booted figure in green, another Forestry Department man, young, furious, with a rifle in his hands.

"What's *happening?*"

"We're shooting the trees and there's no telling which way they'll go off! *Take off,* ma'am!"

Elsie cast a glance around her, saw several trees wilting, heard more gunshots, then ran towards her copter. She imagined that the ground shook under her feet, but she dismissed the idea. She had just seen a man die. Why shouldn't she imagine that the ground was shaking? As she started the copter, she saw a man fire his rifle at a tree and duck at the same time, as if dodging a live enemy, and Elsie saw the jet of white sap—or some-thing—spew like a lanced boil, except that no boil was like this. The jet had looked strong as a garden hose turned on full, like a deliberate act of retaliation by the tree.

The copter rose, and Elsie looked fixedly at the sight below. In the grove, five or six slender columns of smoke swayed in the gentle wind. The fires could get out of control, she thought. She saw a Forestry man with a rifle creeping stealthily among wilting, smoking trees, looking for another mark. A jet got him first at chest level, knocked him sideways, and Elsie saw him tearing his jacket off, saw smoke coming from the cloth of his uni-form, then she had to give her attention to the copter controls. She flew homeward at top speed.

The surface of their swimming pool rippled, heaved almost, as if there was a high wind, but there was hardly any wind. *Phone Jack again,* Elsie told herself. But when she picked up the telephone, she found herself dialing Jane Newcombe's number.

There was no answer, though Elsie let it ring ten times. Maybe Jane was shopping. But a stronger feeling possessed her: the Newcombes had fled. Their family of four might have been in four of the cars she had seen this morning on the roads going out of Rainbow.

She was about to try Channel 30 again, when the chimes sounded, indicating a copter wanting to land. This was a friendly signal, activated by a visitor pushing a button in his copter. It would be Richard coming home, and Charles.

A nervous young man in white got out of the big hospital copter in the driveway. The boys' two copters were landing in the hangar. Richard was with the young man, had a light bandage round his head, but he was on his feet, walking just as usual.

"Nothing at all, Mrs. Gifford. Just a little scorch mark. We just ban-daged him to make sure—antiseptics, y'know. You can take the bandage off tomorrow. Better if the air gets to it—probably."

"What happened?—Can't you tell me?" she added, because the young man was trotting back to his copter, and his colleague ran to join him from the hangar.

"We got work to do, ma'am! Your boy's okay!"

In fact both Richard and Charles had their usual smiles. Elsie found her voice and said, "Come in the house, for goodness' sake! What happened, Richard?"

"He poked a tree blister," Charles said, "with a baseball bat. It was game period, see? But we weren't supposed to touch the trees." Charles's calm smile showed a hint of enjoyment.

"I ducked but the kid behind me—" Richard finished the sentence with a brush of his palms. "He really got it right in the face. Dead. Honest it was like something on TV." He spoke with a certain earnestness, as Elsie had heard him speak on rare occasions about a TV show he had enjoyed.

"What boy?" Elsie asked.

"They're closing all the schools!" Charles said. "Closed since noon! This tree stuff's like liquid fire! You ought to see it, mom!"

Richard's mouth was still turned up at the corners.

"Does it hurt, Richard?" Elsie asked.

"It would, but they put stuff on it so it won't."

"The trees are jiggling the earth," Charles told her. "The sap is jiggling the roots, and one of the fellows said there's going to be the biggest earthquake anybody's ever seen." Despite his unwonted intensity, Charles's bland smile returned, and his lids fell halfway down, sleepily, over glazed eyes.

Elsie wondered if the kids had made up most of it. "Who told you that?"

"Look at that picture on the *wall!*" Richard said, laughing.

The heaviest picture in the living room had gone very askew. Now there was a crash of glass in the kitchen, and she went to see what had happened. A glass platter of oranges and apples had jiggled from a sideboard and fallen on the tile floor. All the glasses teetered on the edges of shelves, some tinkling together like a discordant carillon. She pushed the glasses back, knowing that the gesture was futile, absurd.

"Hey, Dad's here!" Charles yelled.

Jack had come into the living room, white-faced, but with his usual smile—almost his usual smile.

"Jack—" Elsie began.

"They call it a sap disturbance in the tree roots, hon," Jack said in a calm, deep voice. "We're trying to counteract it, so don't worry."

"Did you know we've been on battery power since—maybe this morning?" Elsie asked. She heard a faint, hollow *boom* just then, distant, and the house quivered just after the sound. That had been an underground explosion. A *scree-eech* behind her: the heavy-framed picture was falling, taking the hook from the wall.

"I know," Jack said. "I didn't bother telling you. Safety measure, battery power. We had only a week to analyze this tree sap syndrome—not long enough. It's weird. Anyway—we didn't want to alarm the public by talking about it."

"Well—am I the public?"

"Honey, we're doing all the necessary. Trust me, trust us. San Andreas isn't kicking up at all yet. Just the trees. Irregular pattern. So it's hard to counterbomb. We're busy!" Jack now looked at his sons as if suddenly aware of, or annoyed by, their presence. "Hey, Ritchie—"

"Yes," Elsie said. "He punctured a tree. He—" Suddenly Elsie realized that Jack was in a state of shock, a kind of trance. He hadn't noticed Richard's bandage until now—and now he looked at Richard with eyes as glazed as the boys' eyes. "Shouldn't we leave, Jack? Everyone's leaving, aren't they? The Newcombes have left!"

The question did not bring Jack out of his semi-trance, but he talked. They were bombing peripherally to drain the strain, he said, and why didn't they all have some instant coffee or chocolate milk instead of standing around in the living room? Another crash came from the kitchen, and Elsie paid no attention. She was hanging on her husband's words, trying to derive some comfort, even information, from them.

"Suppose the bombing just activates the sap—and San Andreas?"

The boys were now hopping about the living room, screaming with laughter, feeling furniture that was trembling and drifting.

"We just shoot 'em and they wilt, finished," Jack said. "We're in asbestos suits. This is an asbestos suit, see?" He pulled up a headgear from the back of his neck, and peered at Elsie through a transparent panel. "I should be out fighting with 'em. Got to go. But I came home to see how you were. First of all, let's take down anything that's going to fall upstairs. *I* don't want to leave our nice home, do you?"

They all climbed the stairs. All the pictures were cockeyed, and worse, a pipe had cracked in the bathroom, and water gushed, steaming, into the tub. Elsie staggered as the house shook violently under her.

Crack!

She and Jack and the kids looked up and got their faces full of sharp plastic fragments. A split at least two inches wide ran the length of the hall ceiling and disappeared over a bedroom door.

"They can't kill all the trees in half an hour!" Elsie said. "If you mean it's just the trees *doing* it—"

"It's nothing," Jack said, waving a hand which in the last seconds had been encased in an asbestos glove.

A *clunk* came from the bathroom. Elsie saw that the basin had tumbled from its pedestal. "Jack—you've been told to say it's nothing, I suppose!" Elsie was hoping only that he would tell the truth. Had they given him a pill?

The telephone rang.

Elsie ran down the stairs, rather surprised that the telephone was still working.

"Hello, *Elsie!*" said Jane. "You're still there? Aren't you leaving?"

Then came awful crackles on the line. "Where're you phoning from?"

"Eastern border of Golden Gate! Everyone's leaving! I'm so glad to get you because nearly all the lines are out! There's going to be an *earthquake!* Jack should know! Where is he?"

"He's here. He says they're trying to counterbomb it!"

"Elsie, dear, Golden Gate is . . ." *R-ZZZZ!*

The line went dead, really dead. What had she been about to say? Gone? Finished? At any instant Elsie thought the house would give a great heave and collapse—a death trap. *"Jack,"* Elsie yelled up the stairway.

Maybe he was still taking a look for things that might fall. She could hear the boys yelping with glee. Elsie lost patience, or couldn't think any more, and switched on the television. Channel 30 had no picture, just an excited voice saying, ". . . *not* try to fight the trees. We repeat the following important message: everyone is ordered to leave Golden Gate by copter if possible and at once. The roads are crowded—" A gasp betrayed the announcer's terror. "An earthquake of unusual proportions is believed imminent. We repeat, all . . ." Wails and squeaks silenced the voice, as if a giant hand had twisted up the station controls or throttled the announcer himself. There was a loud, dull thud from the empty screen—then nothing.

Elsie turned to see Jack standing just inside the living room doorway. He had heard it. His headgear was off now, and his face paler than before. Their sons flanked him, one bandaged, one not, but both had the jaded smiles, both were calm now though their sneakered feet were planted more apart than usual to keep their balance in the shaking house.

"All right, let's go," Jack said. "Let's get in the copters. No use trying to take stuff with us. We head east, okay, Elsie? East. Even if it's the desert. There'll be others. They'll bring food and stuff—from somewhere."

"All right, *yes,*" Elsie said. "But why didn't you *tell* me—days ago? You *knew.*"

"C'mon, hon, no time for arguing," Jack said. "You kids hop, y'hear me? Head straight east, don't try to find us, just land where you see people. We'll get together later. C'mon, Elsie, let's *go!*" Jack trotted out after the boys.

A corner of the house collapsed, crushing the television and the sofa. Elsie walked out of her house. In the noise of distant sirens, explosions, she could not hear the hum of the boys' two copters, but she saw them rise and point east.

Jack's copter was in the driveway. "Get in your bus, hon! I started 'er for you!" He was standing with one foot on the copter step.

A tree fired at him—one of the poplars. Elsie saw the white jet shoot straight against the side of his head and fling him to the ground. Jack screamed. Another white bulge trembled as Elsie approached Jack, and at once she tiptoed, and bent low. Could the trees *see,* with a kind of radar?

Jack was trying to say something, but his jaw, half of it, had already been burnt away. He was dying, and there was nothing she could do. For a few seconds, Elsie endured a paralysis, clenched her teeth and looked upward, as if she expected some saving power to come from the heavens. She saw only a score of copters heading east, all flying unusually high.

"You all right, ma'am? Got a copter?" cried a voice behind her.

Elsie spun around and saw not far above her a copter with a rope ladder dangling, and the covered wagon device of the Forty-Niners on the side of the machine. A teenaged boy peered down from the driver's seat, friendly, smiling, anxious. Elsie said, "Yes, thanks. I'm just taking off."

"Can you manage him?" the boy asked quickly.

"He's dead."

The boy nodded. "Better hurry, ma'am." He floated off.

There was a rumble from the north like a huge wind, and a sound of splitting—and this came closer. Underground explosions? Or the earthquake? To the north Elsie saw vast woods and orchards tip slightly to the left. Elsie moved nearer her gates.

A crack was coming towards her like a live thing. She could see fresh brown and yellow earth to a depth of one hundred feet in the widening gorge whose point advanced by leaps. The earth left of the gorge had all been lifted, but was now tilting to the left. The crack veered to the right of her property. She could still dash to her copter and make it, she realized—just. But she didn't want to make it. What she witnessed seemed heroic, and right. A quick, fleeting thought of Jack came to her: *He treated me just like the public, as if I were just—*

Elsie turned to face the oak tree, *her* beloved young oak, which now quivered, pointing its crinkled white breast at her, as if gathering itself for its fatal spit. Elsie did not take her eyes from its pink center. Seconds passed, but it did not shoot.

The roar now was like that of a surf, and Elsie knew it was the sound of Golden Gate falling into the Pacific Ocean. Her house and land would go with it. Elsie clung to her iron gates, which themselves had tilted. Behind her and to her right, the oak shot its fiery sap, and bushes on her left burst slowly into flame. Elsie was glad the oak had fired before it drowned.

It was right, Elsie felt, right to go like this, conquered by the trees and by nature. How kind of the Forty-Niners—she thought as the iron bars jerked in her hands, bloodying her palms—to take a look at Rainbow, a district she knew the Forty-Niners hated because so many nuclear workers lived in it, just to see if they could be of assistance.

Now the wind whistled in her ears, and she was falling at great speed. A land mass, big as a continent, it seemed, big as she could see, was dropping—slowly for land but fast for her—into the dark blue waters.

The Black House

Something
the Cat Dragged In

A few seconds of pondering silence in the Scrabble game was interrupted by a rustle of plastic at the cat door: Portland Bill was coming in again. Nobody paid any attention. Michael and Gladys Herbert were ahead, Gladys doing a bit better than her husband. The Herberts played Scrabble often and were quite sharp at it. Colonel Edward Phelps—a neighbor and a good friend—was limping along, and his American niece Phyllis, aged nineteen, had been doing well but had lost interest in the last ten minutes. It would soon be teatime. The Colonel was sleepy and looked it.

"Quack," said the Colonel thoughtfully, pushing a forefinger against his Kipling-style mustache. "Pity—I was thinking of earthquake."

"If you've got *quack,* Uncle Eddie," said Phyllis, "how could you get quake out of it?"

The cat made another more sustained noise at his door, and now with black tail and brindle hindquarters in the house, he moved backwards and pulled something through the plastic oval. What he had dragged in looked whitish and about six inches long.

"Caught another bird," said Michael, impatient for Eddie to make his move so he could make a brilliant move before somebody grabbed it.

"Looks like another goose foot," said Gladys, glancing. "Ugh."

The Colonel at last moved, adding a P to SUM. Michael moved, raising a gasp of admiration from Phyllis for his INI stuck onto GEM, the N of which gave him DAWN.

Portland Bill flipped his trophy into the air, and it fell on the carpet with a thud.

"Really *dead* pigeon that," remarked the Colonel who was nearest the cat, but whose eyesight was not the best. "Turnip," he said for Phyllis's benefit. "Swede. Or an oddly shaped carrot," he added, peering, then chuckled. "I've seen carrots take the most fantastic shapes. Saw one once . . ."

"This is white," said Phyllis, and got up to investigate, since Gladys had to play before her. Phyllis, in slacks and sweater, bent over with hands on her knees. "Good *Chr*—Oh! Uncle Eddie!" She stood up and clapped her hand over her mouth as if she had said something dreadful.

Michael Herbert had half risen from his chair. "What's the matter?"

"They're human *fingers!*" Phyllis said. "Look!"

They all looked, coming slowly, unbelievingly, from the card table. The cat looked, proudly, up at the faces of the four humans gazing down. Gladys drew in her breath.

The two fingers were dead white and puffy, there was not a sign of blood even at the base of the fingers, which included a couple of inches of what had been the hand. What made the object undeniably the third and fourth fingers of a human hand were the two nails, yellowish and short and looking small because of the swollen flesh.

"What should we do, Michael?" Gladys was practical, but liked to let her husband make decisions.

"That's been dead for two weeks at least," murmured the Colonel, who had had some war experiences.

"Could it have come from a hospital near here?" asked Phyllis.

"Hospital amputating like that?" replied her uncle with a chuckle.

"The nearest hospital is twenty miles from here," said Gladys.

"Mustn't let Edna see it." Michael glanced at his watch. "Of course I think we—"

"Maybe call the police?" asked Gladys.

"I was thinking of that. I—" Michael's hesitation was interrupted by Edna—their housekeeper-cook—bumping just then against a door in a remote corner of the big living room. The tea tray had arrived. The others discreetly moved toward the low table in front of the fireplace, while Michael Herbert stood with an air of casualness. The fingers were just behind his shoes. Michael pulled an unlit pipe from his jacket pocket, and fiddled with it, blowing into its stem. His hands shook a little. He shooed Portland Bill away with one foot.

Edna finally dispensed napkins and plates, and said, "Have a nice tea!" She was a local woman in her mid-fifties, a reliable soul, but with most of her mind on her own children and grandchildren—thank goodness under these circumstances, Michael thought. Edna arrived at half past seven in the morning on her bicycle and departed when she pleased, as long as there was something in the house for supper. The Herberts were not fussy.

Gladys was looking anxiously toward Michael. "Get a-*way*, Bill!"

"Got to do something with this meanwhile," Michael murmured. With determination he went to the basket of newspapers beside the fireplace, shook out a page of the *Times,* and returned to the fingers which Portland Bill was about to pick up. Michael beat the cat by grabbing the fingers through the newspaper. The others had not sat down. Michael made a gesture for them to do so, and closed the newspaper around the fingers, rolling and folding. "The thing to do, I should think," said Michael, "*is* to notify the police, because there might have been—foul play somewhere."

"Or might it have fallen," the Colonel began, shaking out his napkin, "out of an ambulance or some disposal unit—you know? Might've been an accident somewhere."

"Or should we just let well enough alone—and get rid of it," said Gladys. "I need some tea." She had poured, and proceeded to sip her cup.

No one had an answer to her suggestion. It was as if the three others were stunned, or hypnotized by one another's presence, vaguely expecting a response from another which did not come.

"Rid of it where? In the garbage?" asked Phyllis. "*Bury* it," she added, as if answering her own question.

"I don't think that would be right," said Michael.

"Michael, do have some tea," said his wife.

"Got to put this somewhere—overnight." Michael still held the little bundle. "Unless we ring the police now. It's already five and it's Sunday."

"In England do the police care whether it's Sunday or not?" asked Phyllis.

Michael started for the armoire near the front door, with an idea of putting the thing on top beside a couple of hat boxes, but he was followed by the cat, and Michael knew that the cat with enough inspiration could leap to the top.

"I've got just the thing, I think," said the Colonel, pleased by his own idea, but with an air of calm in case Edna made a second appearance. "Bought some house slippers just yesterday in the High Street and I've still got the box. I'll go and fetch it, if I may." He went off toward the stairs, then turned and said softly, "We'll tie a string around it. Keep it away from the cat." The Colonel climbed the stairs.

"Keep it in whose room?" asked Phyllis with a nervous giggle.

The Herberts did not answer. Michael, still on his feet, held the object in his right hand. Portland Bill sat with white forepaws neatly together, regarding Michael, waiting to see what Michael would do with it.

Colonel Phelps came down with his white cardboard shoe box. The little bundle went in easily, and Michael let the Colonel hold the box while he went to rinse his hands in the lavatory near the front door. When Michael returned, Portland Bill still hovered, and gave out a hopeful "Meow?"

"Let's put it in the sideboard cupboard for the moment," said Michael, and took the box from Eddie's hands. He felt that the box at least was comparatively clean, and he put it beside a stack of large and seldom-used dinner plates, then closed the cabinet door which had a key in it.

Phyllis bit into a Bath Oliver and said, "I noticed a crease in one finger. If there's a ring there, it might give us a clue."

Michael exchanged a glance with Eddie, who nodded slightly. They had all noticed the crease. Tacitly the men agreed to take care of this later.

"More tea, dear," said Gladys. She refilled Phyllis's cup.

"M'wow," said the cat in a disappointed tone. He was now seated facing the sideboard, looking over one shoulder.

Michael changed the subject: the progress of the Colonel's redecorating. The painting of the first-floor bedrooms was the main reason the Colonel and his niece were visiting the Herberts just now. But this was of no interest compared to Phyllis's question to Michael:

"Shouldn't you ask if anyone's missing in the neighborhood? Those fingers might be part of a *murder.*"

Gladys shook her head slightly and said nothing. Why did Americans always think in such violent terms? However, what could have severed a hand in such a manner? An explosion? An ax?

A lively scratching sound got Michael to his feet.

"Bill, do *stop* that!" Michael advanced on the cat and shooed him away. Bill had been trying to open the cabinet door.

Tea was over more quickly than usual. Michael stood by the sideboard while Edna cleared away.

"When're you going to look at the ring, Uncle Eddie?" Phyllis asked. She wore round-rimmed glasses and was rather myopic.

"I don't think Michael and I have quite decided what we should do, my dear," said her uncle.

"Let's go into the library, Phyllis," said Gladys. "You said you wanted to look at some photographs."

Phyllis had said that. There were photographs of Phyllis's mother and of the house where her mother had been born, in which Uncle Eddie now lived. Eddie was older than her mother by fifteen years. Now Phyllis wished she hadn't asked to see the photographs, because the men were going to do something with the *fingers,* and Phyllis would have liked to watch. After all, she was dissecting frogs and dogfish in zoology lab. But her mother had warned her before she left New York to mind her manners and not be "crude and insensitive," her mother's usual adjectives about Americans. Phyllis dutifully sat looking at photographs fifteen and twenty years old, at least.

"Let's take it out to the garage," Michael said to Eddie. "I've got a workbench there, you know."

The two men walked along a graveled path to the two-car garage at the back of which Michael had a workshop with saws and hammers, chisels and electric drills, plus a supply of wood and planks in case the house needed any repairs or he felt in the mood to make something. Michael was a freelance journalist and book critic, but he enjoyed manual labor. Here Michael felt better with the awful box, somehow. He could set it on his sturdy workbench as if he were a surgeon laying out a body, or a corpse.

"What the hell do you make of this?" asked Michael as he flipped the fingers out by holding one side of the newspaper. The fingers flopped onto the well-used wooden surface, this time palm side upward. The white flesh was jagged where it had been cut, and in the strong beam of the spotlight which shone from over the bench, they could see two bits of metacarpals, also jagged, projecting from the flesh. Michael turned the fingers over with the tip of a screwdriver. He twisted the screwdriver tip, and parted the flesh enough to see the glint of gold.

"Gold ring," said Eddie. "But he was a workman of some kind, don't you think? Look at those nails. Short and thick. Still some soil under them—dirty, anyway."

"I was thinking—if we report it to the police, shouldn't we leave it the way it is? Not try to look at the ring?"

"Are you going to report it to the police?" asked Eddie with a smile as he lit a cigar. "What'll you be in for then?"

"In for? I'll say the cat dragged it in. Why should I be in for anything? I'm curious about the ring. Might give us a clue."

Colonel Phelps glanced at the garage door, which Michael had closed but not locked. He too was curious about the ring. Eddie was thinking, if it had been a gentleman's hand, they might have turned it in to the police by now. "Many farmworkers around here still?" mused the Colonel. "I suppose so."

Michael shrugged, nervous. "What do you say about the ring?"

"Let's have a look." The Colonel puffed serenely, and looked at Michael's racks of tools.

"I know what we need." Michael reached for a Stanley knife which he ordinarily used for cutting cardboard, pushed the blade out with his thumb, and placed his fingers on the pudgy remainder of the palm. He made a cut above where the ring was, then below.

Eddie Phelps bent to watch. "No blood at all. Drained out. Just like the war days."

Nothing but a goose foot, Michael was telling himself in order not to faint. Michael repeated his cuts on the top surface of the finger. He felt like asking Eddie if he wanted to finish the job, but Michael thought that might be cowardly.

"Dear me," Eddie murmured unhelpfully.

Michael had to cut off some strips of flesh, then take a firm grip with both hands to get the wedding ring off. It most certainly was a wedding ring of plain gold, not very thick or broad, but suitable for a man to wear. Michael rinsed it at the cold water tap of the sink on his left. When he held it near the spotlight, initials were legible: *W.R.—M.T.*

Eddie peered. "Now *that's* a clue!"

Michael heard the cat scratching at the garage door, then a meow. Next Michael put the three pieces of flesh he had cut off into an old rag, wadded it up, and told Eddie he would be back in a minute. He opened the garage door, discouraged Bill with a *"Whisht!"* and stuck the rag into a dustbin which had a fastening that a cat could not open. Michael had thought he had a plan to propose to Eddie, but when he returned—Eddie was again examining the ring—Michael was too shaken to speak. He had meant to say something about making "discreet inquiries." Instead he said in a voice gone hollow:

"Let's call it a day—unless we think of something brilliant tonight. Let's leave the box here. The cat can't get in."

Michael didn't want the box even on his workbench. He put the ring in with the fingers, and set the box on top of some plastic jerricans which stood against a wall. His workshop was even ratproof, so far. Nothing was going to come in to chew at the box.

As Michael got into bed that night, Gladys said, "If we don't tell the police, we've simply got to bury it somewhere."

"Yes," said Michael vaguely. It seemed somehow a criminal act, burying a pair of human fingers. He had told Gladys about the ring. The initials hadn't rung any bell with her.

Colonel Edward Phelps went to sleep quite peacefully, having reminded himself that he had seen a lot worse in 1941.

Phyllis had quizzed her uncle and Michael about the ring at dinner. Maybe it would all be solved tomorrow and turn out to be—somehow—something quite simple and innocent. Anyway, it would make quite a story to tell her chums in college. And her mother! So this was the quiet English countryside!

The next day being Monday, with the post office open, Michael decided to pose a question to Mary Jeffrey, who doubled there as postal clerk and grocery salesgirl. Michael bought some stamps, then asked casually:

"By the way, Mary, is anybody missing lately—in this neighborhood?"

Mary, a bright-faced girl with dark curly hair, looked puzzled. "Missing how?"

"Disappeared," Michael said with a smile.

Mary shook her head. "Not that I know. Why do you ask?"

Michael had tried to prepare for this. "I read somewhere in a newspaper that people do sometimes—just disappear, even in small villages like this. Drift away, change their names or some such. Baffles everyone, where they go." Michael was drifting away himself. Not a good job, but the question was put.

He walked the quarter of a mile back home, wishing he had had the guts to ask Mary if anyone in the area had a bandaged left hand, or if she'd heard of any such accident. Mary had boyfriends who frequented the local pub. Mary this minute might know of a man with a bandaged hand, but Michael could not possibly tell Mary that the missing fingers were in his garage.

The matter of what to do with the fingers was put aside for that morning, as the Herberts had laid on a drive to Cambridge, followed by lunch at the house of a don who was a friend of the Herberts. Unthinkable to cancel that because of getting involved with the police, so the fingers did not come up that morning in conversation. They talked of anything else during the drive. Michael and Gladys and Eddie had decided, before taking off for Cambridge, that they should not discuss the fingers again in front of Phyllis, but let it blow over, if possible. Eddie and Phyllis were to leave on the afternoon of Wednesday, day after tomorrow, and by then the matter might be cleared up or in the hands of the police.

Gladys also had gently warned Phyllis not to bring up "the cat incident" at the don's house, so Phyllis did not. All went well and happily, and the Herberts and Eddie and Phyllis were back at the Herberts' house around four. Edna told Gladys she had just realized they were short of butter, and since she was watching a cake . . . Michael, in the living room with Eddie, heard this and volunteered to go to the grocery.

Michael bought the butter, a couple of packets of cigarettes, a box of toffee that looked nice, and was served by Mary in her usual modest and polite manner. He had been hoping for news from her. Michael had taken his change and was walking to the door, when Mary cried: "Oh, Mr. Herbert!"

Michael turned round.

"I heard of someone disappearing just this noon," Mary said, leaning toward Michael across the counter, smiling now. "Bill Reeves—lives on Mr. Dickenson's property, you know. He has a cottage there, works on the land—or did."

Michael didn't know Bill Reeves, but he certainly knew of the Dickenson property, which was vast, to the northwest of the village. Bill Reeves's initials fitted the W.R. on the ring. "Yes? He disappeared?"

"About two weeks ago, Mr. Vickers told me. Mr. Vickers has the petrol station near the Dickenson property, you know. He came in today, so I thought I'd ask him." She smiled again, as if she had done satisfactorily with Michael's little riddle.

Michael knew the petrol station and knew how Vickers looked, vaguely. "Interesting. Does Mr. Vickers know why he disappeared?"

"No. Mr. Vickers said it's a mystery. Bill Reeves's wife left the cottage too, a few days ago, but everyone knows she went to Manchester to stay with her sister there."

Michael nodded. "Well, well. Shows it can happen even here, eh? People disappearing." He smiled and went out of the shop.

The thing to do was ring up Tom Dickenson, Michael thought, and ask him what he knew. Michael didn't call him Tom, had met him only a couple of times at local political rallies and such. Dickenson was about thirty, married, had inherited, and now led the life of gentleman farmer, Michael thought. The family was in the wool industry, had factories up north, and had owned their land here for generations.

When he got home, Michael asked Eddie to come up to his study, and despite Phyllis's curiosity, did not invite her to join them. Michael told Eddie what Mary had said about the disappearance of a farmworker called Bill Reeves a couple of weeks ago. Eddie agreed that they might ring up Dickenson.

"The initials on the ring could be an accident," Eddie said. "The Dickenson place is fifteen miles from here, you say."

"Yes, but I still think I'll ring him." Michael looked up the number in the directory on his desk. There were two numbers. Michael tried the first.

A servant answered, or someone who sounded like a servant, inquired Michael's name, then said he would summon Mr. Dickenson. Michael waited a good minute. Eddie was waiting too. "Hello, Mr. Dickenson. I'm one of your neighbors, Michael Herbert . . . Yes, yes, I know we have— couple of times. Look, I have a question to ask which you might think odd, but—I understand you had a workman or tenant on your land called Bill Reeves?"

"Ye-es?" replied Tom Dickenson.

"And where is he now? I'm asking because I was told he disappeared a couple of weeks ago."

"Yes, that's true. Why do you ask?"

"Do you know where he went?"

"No idea," replied Dickenson. "Did you have any dealings with him?"

"No. Could you tell me what his wife's name is?"

"Marjorie."

That fitted the first initial. "Do you happen to know her maiden name?"

Tom Dickenson chuckled. "I'm afraid I don't."

Michael glanced at Eddie, who was watching him. "Do you know if Bill Reeves wore a wedding ring?"

"No. Never paid that much attention to him. Why?"

Why, indeed? Michael shifted. If he ended the conversation here, he would not have learned much. "Because—I've found something that just might be a clue in regard to Bill Reeves. I presume someone's looking for him, if no one knows his whereabouts."

"I'm not looking for him," Tom Dickenson replied in his easy manner. "I doubt if his wife is, either. She moved out a week ago. May I ask what you found?"

"I'd rather not say over the phone . . . I wonder if I could come to see you. Or perhaps you could come to my house."

After an instant of silence, Dickenson said, "Quite honestly, I'm not interested in Reeves. I don't think he left any debts, as far as I know, I'll say that for him. But I don't care what's happened to him, if I may speak frankly."

"I see. Sorry to've bothered you, Mr. Dickenson."

They hung up.

Michael turned to Eddie Phelps and said, "I think you got most of that. Dickenson's not interested."

"Can't expect Dickenson to be concerned about a disappeared farm-worker. Did I hear him say the wife's gone too?"

"Thought I told you. She went to Manchester to her sister's, Mary told me." Michael took a pipe from the rack on his desk and began to fill it. "Wife's name is Marjorie. Fits the initial on the ring."

"True," said the Colonel, "but there're lots of Marys and Margarets in the world."

"Dickenson didn't know her maiden name. Now look, Eddie, with no help from Dickenson, I'm thinking we ought to buzz the police and get this over with. I'm sure I can't bring myself to bury that—object. The thing would haunt me. I'd be thinking a dog would dig it up, even if it's just bones or in a *worse* state, and the police would have to start with somebody else besides me, and with a trail not so fresh to follow."

"You're still thinking of foul play?—I have a simpler idea," Eddie said with an air of calm and logic. "Gladys said there was a hospital twenty miles away, I presume in Colchester. We might ask if in the last two weeks or so there's been an accident involving the loss of third and fourth fingers of a man's left hand. They'd have his name. It looks like an accident and of the kind that doesn't happen every day."

Michael was on the brink of agreeing to this, at least before ringing the police, when the telephone rang. Michael took it, and found Gladys on the line downstairs with a man whose voice sounded like Dickenson's. "I'll take it, Gladys."

Tom Dickenson said hello to Michael. "I've—I thought if you really would like to see me—"

"I'd be very glad to."

"I'd prefer to speak with you alone, if that's possible."

Michael assured him it was, and Dickenson said he could come along in about twenty minutes. Michael put the telephone down with a feeling of relief, and said to Eddie, "He's coming over now and wants to talk with me alone. That *is* the best."

"Yes." Eddie got up from Michael's sofa, disappointed. "He'll be more open, if he has anything to say. Are you going to tell him about the fingers?" He peered at Michael sideways, bushy eyebrows raised.

"May not come to that. I'll see what he has to say first."

"He's going to ask you what you found."

Michael knew that. They went downstairs. Michael saw Phyllis in the back garden, banging a croquet ball all by herself, and heard Gladys's voice in the kitchen. Michael informed Gladys, out of Edna's hearing, of the imminent arrival of Tom Dickenson, and explained why: Mary's information that a certain Bill Reeves was missing, a worker on Dickenson's property. Gladys realized at once that the initials matched.

And here came Dickenson's car, a black Triumph convertible, rather in need of a wash. Michael went out to greet him. "Hellos," and "you remember mes." They vaguely remembered each other. Michael invited Dickenson into the house before Phyllis could drift over and compel an introduction.

Tom Dickenson was blond and tallish, now in leather jacket and corduroys and green rubber boots which he assured Michael were not muddy. He had just been working on his land, and hadn't taken the time to change.

"Let's go up," said Michael, leading the way to the stairs.

Michael offered Dickenson a comfortable armchair, and sat down on his old sofa. "You told me—Bill Reeves's wife went off too?"

Dickenson smiled a little, and his bluish-gray eyes gazed calmly at Michael. "His wife left, yes. But that was after Reeves vanished. Marjorie went to Manchester, I heard. She has a sister there. The Reeves weren't getting on so well. They're both about twenty-five—Reeves fond of his drink. I'll be glad to replace Reeves, frankly. Easily done."

Michael waited for more. It didn't come. Michael was wondering why Dickenson had been willing to come to see him about a farmworker he didn't much like?

"Why're you interested?" Dickenson asked. Then he broke out in a laugh which made him look younger and happier. "Is Reeves perhaps asking for a job with you—under another name?"

"Not at all." Michael smiled too. "I haven't anywhere to lodge a worker. No."

"But you said you found something?" Tom Dickenson's brows drew in a polite frown of inquiry.

Michael looked at the floor, then lifted his eyes and said, "I found two fingers of a man's left hand—with a wedding ring on one finger. The initials on the ring could stand for William Reeves. The other initials are M.T., which could be Marjorie somebody. That's why I thought I should ring you up."

Had Dickenson's face gone paler, or was Michael imagining? Dickenson's lips were slightly parted, his eyes uncertain. "Good lord, found it where?"

"Our cat dragged it in—believe it or not. Had to tell my wife, because the cat brought it into the living room in front of all of us." Somehow it was a tremendous relief for Michael to get the words out. "My old friend Eddie Phelps and his American niece are here now. They saw it." Michael stood up. Now he wanted a cigarette, got the box from his desk and offered it to Dickenson.

Dickenson said he had just stopped smoking, but he would like one.

"It was a bit shocking," Michael went on, "so I thought I'd make some inquiries in the neighborhood before I spoke to the police. I think inform-ing the police is the right thing to do. Don't you?"

Dickenson did not answer at once.

"I had to cut away some of the finger to get the ring off—with Eddie's assistance last night." Dickenson still said nothing, only drew on his ciga-rette, frowning. "I thought the ring might give a clue, which it does, though it might have nothing at all to do with this Bill Reeves. You don't seem to know if he wore a wedding ring, and you don't know Marjorie's maiden name."

"Oh, that one can find out." Dickenson's voice sounded different and more husky.

"Do you think we should do that? Or maybe you know where Reeves's parents live. Or Marjorie's parents? Maybe Reeves is at one or the other's place now."

"Not at his wife's parents', I'll bet," said Dickenson with a nervous smile. "She's fed up with him."

"Well—what do you think? I'll tell the police? . . . Would you like to see the ring?"

"No. I'll take your word."

"Then I'll get in touch with the police tomorrow—or this evening. I suppose the sooner the better." Michael noticed Dickenson glancing around the room as if he might see the fingers lying on a bookshelf.

The study door moved and Portland Bill walked in. Michael never quite closed his door, and Bill had an assured way with doors, rearing a lit-tle and giving them a push.

Dickenson blinked at the cat, then said to Michael in a firm voice, "I could stand a whiskey. May I?"

Michael went downstairs and brought back the bottle and two glasses in his hands. There had been no one in the living room. Michael poured. Then he shut the door of his study.

Dickenson took a good inch of his drink at the first gulp. "I may as well tell you now that I killed Reeves."

A tremor went over Michael's shoulders, yet he told himself that he had known this all along—or since Dickenson's telephone call to him, anyway. "Yes?" said Michael.

"Reeves had been . . . trying it on with my wife. I won't give it the dignity of calling it an affair. I blame my wife—flirting in a silly way with Reeves. He was just a lout, as far as I'm concerned. Handsome and stupid. His wife knew, and she hated him for it." Dickenson drew on the last of his cigarette, and Michael fetched the box again. Dickenson took one. "Reeves got ever more sure of himself. I wanted to sack him and send him away, but I couldn't because of his lease on the cottage, and I didn't want to bring the situation with my wife to light—with the law, I mean, as a reason."

"How long did this go on?"

Dickenson had to think. "Maybe about a month."

"And your wife—now?"

Tom Dickenson sighed, and rubbed his eyes. He sat hunched forward in his chair. "We'll patch it up. We've hardly been married a year."

"She knows you killed Reeves?"

Now Dickenson sat back, propped a green boot on one knee, and drummed the fingers of one hand on the arm of his chair. "I don't know. She may think I just sent him packing. She didn't ask any questions."

Michael could imagine, and he could also see that Dickenson would prefer that his wife never knew. Michael realized that he would have to make a decision: to turn Dickenson over to the police or not. Or would Dickenson even prefer to be turned in? Michael was listening to the confession of a man who had had a crime on his conscience for more than two weeks, bottled up inside himself, or so Michael assumed. And how had Dickenson killed him? "Does anyone else know?" Michael asked cautiously.

"Well—I can tell you about that. I suppose I must. Yes." Dickenson's voice was again hoarse, and his whiskey gone.

Michael got up and replenished Dickenson's glass.

Dickenson sipped now, and stared at the wall beside Michael.

Portland Bill sat at a little distance from Michael, concentrating on Dickenson as if he understood every word and was waiting for the next installment.

"I told Reeves to stop playing about with my wife or leave my property with his own wife, but he brought up the lease—and why didn't I speak to *my* wife. Arrogant, you know, so pleased with himself that the master's wife had deigned to look at him and—" Dickenson began again.

"Tuesdays and Fridays I go to London to take care of the company. A couple of times, Diane said she didn't feel like going to London or she had some other engagement. Reeves could always manage to find a little work close to the house on those days, I'm sure. And then—there was a second victim—like me."

"Victim? What do you mean?"

"Peter." Now Dickenson rolled his glass between his hands, the cigarette projected from his lips, and he stared at the wall beside Michael, and spoke as if he were narrating what he saw on a screen there. "We were trimming some hedgerows deep in the fields, cutting stakes too for new markings. Reeves and I. Axes and sledgehammers. Peter was driving in stakes quite a way from us. Peter's another hand like Reeves, been with me longer. I had the feeling Reeves might attack me—then say it was an accident or some such. It was afternoon, and he'd had a few pints at lunch. He had a hatchet. I didn't turn my back on Reeves, and my anger was somehow rising. He had a smirk on his face, and he swung his hatchet as if to catch me in the thigh, though he wasn't near enough to me. Then he turned his back on me—arrogantly—and I hit him in the head with the big hammer. I hit him a second time as he was falling, but that landed on his back. I didn't know Peter was so close to me, or I didn't think about that. Peter came running, with his ax. Peter said, 'Good! Damn the bastard!' or something like that, and—" Dickenson seemed stuck for words, and looked at the floor, then the cat.

"And then? . . . Reeves was dead."

"Yes. All this happened in seconds. Peter really finished it with a bash on Reeves's head with the ax. We were quite near some woods—my woods. Peter said, 'Let's bury the swine! Get *rid* of him!' Peter was in a cursing rage and I was out of my mind for a different reason, maybe shock, but Peter was saying that Reeves had been having it off with his wife too, or trying to, and that he knew about Reeves and Diane. Peter and I dug a grave in the woods, both of us working like madmen—hacking at tree roots and throwing up earth with our hands. At the last, just before we threw him in, Peter took the hatchet and said—something about Reeves's wedding ring, and he brought the hatchet down a couple of times on Reeves's hand."

Michael did not feel so well. He leaned over, mainly to lower his head, and stroked the cat's strong back. The cat still concentrated on Dickenson.

"Then—we buried it, both of us drenched in sweat by then. Peter said, 'You won't get a word out of me, sir. This bastard deserved what he got.' We trampled the grave and Peter spat on it. Peter's a man, I'll say that for him."

"A man . . . And you?"

"I dunno." Dickenson's eyes were serious when he next spoke. "That was one of the days Diane had a tea date at some women's club in our village. The same afternoon, I thought, my God, the fingers! Maybe they're just lying there on the ground, because I couldn't remember Peter or myself throwing them into the grave. So I went back. I found them. I could've dug another hole, except that I hadn't brought anything to dig with and I also didn't want . . . anything more of Reeves on my land. So I got into my car and drove, not caring where, not paying any attention to where I was, and when I saw some woods, I got out and flung the thing as far as I could."

Michael said, "Must've been within half a mile of this house. Portland Bill doesn't venture farther, I think. He's been doctored, poor old Bill." The cat looked up at his name. "You trust this Peter?"

"I do. I knew his father and so did my father. And if I were asked—I'm not sure I could say who struck the fatal blow, I or Peter. But to be correct, *I'd* take the responsibility, because I did strike two blows with the hammer. I can't claim self-defense, because Reeves hadn't attacked me."

Correct. An odd word, Michael thought. But Dickenson was the type who would want to be correct. "What do you propose to do now?"

"Propose? I?" Dickenson's sigh was almost a gasp. "I dunno. I've admitted it. In a way it's in your hands or—" He made a gesture to indicate the downstairs. "I'd like to spare Peter—keep him out of it—if I can. You understand, I think. I can talk to you. You're a man like myself."

Michael was not sure of that, but he had been trying to imagine himself in Dickenson's position, trying to see himself twenty years younger in the same circumstances. Reeves had been a swine—even to his own wife—unprincipled, and should a young man like Dickenson ruin his own life, or the best part of it, over a man like Reeves? "What about Reeves's wife?"

Dickenson shook his head and frowned. "I know she detested him. If he's absent without tidings, I'll wager she'll never make the least effort to find him. She's glad to be rid of him, I'm sure."

A silence began and grew. Portland Bill yawned, arched his back and stretched. Dickenson watched the cat as if he might say something: after all the cat had discovered the fingers. But the cat said nothing. Dickenson broke the silence awkwardly but in a polite tone:

"Where are the fingers—by the way?"

"In the back of my garage—which is locked. They're in a shoe box." Michael felt quite off balance. "Look, I have two guests in the house."

Tom Dickenson got to his feet quickly. "I know. Sorry."

"Nothing to be sorry about, but I've really got to *say* something to them because the Colonel—my old friend Eddie—knows I rang you up about the initials on the ring and that you were to call on us—me. He could've said something to the others."

"Of course. I understand."

"Could you stay here for a few minutes while I speak with the people downstairs? Feel free with the whiskey."

"Thank you." His eyes did not flinch.

Michael went downstairs. Phyllis was kneeling by the gramophone, about to put a record on. Eddie Phelps sat in a corner of the sofa reading a newspaper. "Where's Gladys?" Michael asked.

Gladys was deadheading roses. Michael called to her. She wore rubber boots like Dickenson, but hers were smaller and bright red. Michael looked to see if Edna was behind the kitchen door. Gladys said Edna had gone off to buy something at the grocery. Michael told Dickenson's story, trying to make it brief and clear. Phyllis's mouth fell open a couple of times. Eddie Phelps held his chin in a wise-looking fashion and said "Um-hm" now and then.

"I really don't feel like turning him in—or even speaking to the police," Michael ventured in a voice hardly above a whisper. No one had said anything after his narration, and Michael had waited several seconds. "I don't see why we can't just let it blow over. What's the harm?"

"What's the harm, yes," said Eddie Phelps, but it might have been a mindless echo for all the help it gave Michael.

"I've heard of stories like this—among primitive peoples," Phyllis said earnestly, as if to say she found Tom Dickenson's action quite justifiable.

Michael had of course included the resident worker Peter in his account. Had Dickenson's hammer blow been fatal, or the blow of Peter's ax? "The primitive ethic is not what I'm concerned with," Michael said, and at once felt confused. In regard to Tom Dickenson he was concerned with just the opposite of the primitive.

"But what else is it?" asked Phyllis.

"Yes, yes," said the Colonel, gazing at the ceiling.

"Really, Eddie," said Michael, "you're not being much of a help."

"I'd say nothing about it. Bury those fingers somewhere—with the ring. Or maybe the ring in a different place for safety. Yes." The Colonel was almost muttering, murmuring, but he did look at Michael.

"I'm not sure," said Gladys, frowning with thought.

"I agree with Uncle Eddie," Phyllis said, aware that Dickenson was upstairs awaiting his verdict. "Mr. Dickenson was provoked—*seriously*—and the man who got killed seems to have been a creep!"

"That's not the way the law looks at it," Michael said with a wry smile. "Lots of people are provoked seriously. And a human life is a human life."

"*We're* not the law," said Phyllis, as if they were something superior to the law just then.

Michael had been thinking just that: they were not the law, but they were acting as if they were. He was inclined to go along with Phyllis—and Eddie. "All right. I don't feel like reporting this, given all the circumstances."

But Gladys held out. She wasn't sure. Michael knew his wife well enough to believe that it was not going to be a bone of contention between them, if they were at variance—just now. So Michael said, "You're one against three, Glad. Do you seriously want to ruin a young man's life for a thing like this?"

"True, we've got to take a vote, as if we were a jury," said Eddie.

Gladys saw the point. She conceded. Less than a minute later, Michael climbed the stairs to his study, where the first draft of a book review curled in the roller of his typewriter, untouched since the day before yesterday. Fortunately he could still meet the deadline without killing himself.

"We don't want to report this to the police," Michael said.

Dickenson, on his feet, nodded solemnly as if receiving a verdict. He would have nodded in the same manner if he had been told the opposite, Michael thought.

"I'll get rid of the fingers," Michael mumbled, and bent to get some pipe tobacco.

"Surely that's my responsibility. Let me bury them somewhere—with the ring."

It really was Dickenson's responsibility, and Michael was glad to escape the task. "Right. Well—shall we go downstairs? Would you like to meet my wife and my friend Colonel—"

"No, thank you. Not just now," Dickenson interrupted. "Another time. But would you give them—my thanks?"

They went down some other stairs at the back of the hall, and out to the garage, whose key Michael had in his key case. Michael thought for a moment that the shoe box might have disappeared mysteriously as in a detective story, but it was exactly where he had left it, on top of the old jerricans. He gave it to Dickenson, and Dickenson departed in his dusty Triumph northward. Michael entered his house by the front door.

By now the others were having a drink. Michael felt suddenly relieved, and he smiled. "I think old Portland ought to have something special at the cocktail hour, don't you?" Michael said, mainly to Gladys.

Portland Bill was looking without much interest at a bowl of ice cubes. Only Phyllis said, *"Yes!"* with enthusiasm.

Michael went to the kitchen and spoke with Edna who was dusting flour onto a board. "Any more smoked salmon left from lunch?"

"One slice, sir," said Edna, as if it weren't worth serving to anyone, and she virtuously hadn't eaten it, though she might.

"Can I have it for old Bill? He adores it." When Michael came back into the living room with the pink slice on a saucer, Phyllis said:

"I bet Mr. Dickenson wrecks his car on the way home. That's often the way it is." She whispered suddenly, remembering her manners, "Because he feels *guilty.*"

Portland Bill bolted his salmon with brief but intense delight.

Tom Dickenson did not wreck his car.

Not One of Us

It wasn't merely that Edmund Quasthoff had stopped smoking and almost stopped drinking that made him different, slightly goody-goody and therefore vaguely unlikable. It was something else. What?

That was the subject of conversation at Lucienne Gauss's apartment in the East 80s one evening at the drinks hour, seven. Julian Markus, a lawyer, was there with his wife Frieda, also Peter Tomlin, a journalist aged twenty-eight and the youngest of the circle. The circle numbered seven or eight, the ones who knew Edmund well, meaning for most of them about eight years. The others present were Tom Strathmore, a sociologist, and Charles Forbes and his wife, Charles being an editor in a publishing house, and Anita Ketchum, librarian at a New York art museum. They gathered more often at Lucienne's apartment than at anyone else's, because Lucienne liked entertaining and, as a painter working on her own, her hours were flexible.

Lucienne was thirty-three, unmarried, and quite pretty with fluffy reddish hair, a smooth pale skin, and a delicate, intelligent mouth. She liked expensive clothes, she went to a good beauty parlor, and she had style. The rest of the group called her, behind her back, a lady, shy even among themselves at using the word (Tom the sociologist had), because it was an old-fashioned or snob word, perhaps.

Edmund Quasthoff, a tax accountant in a law firm, had been divorced a year ago, because his wife had run off with another man and had therefore asked for a divorce. Edmund was forty, quite tall, with brown hair, a quiet manner, and was neither handsome nor unattractive, but lacking in that spark which can make even a rather ugly person attractive. Lucienne and her group had said after the divorce, "No wonder. Edmund *is* sort of a bore."

On this evening at Lucienne's, someone said out of the blue, "Edmund didn't used to be such a bore—did he?"

"I'm afraid so. *Yes!*" Lucienne yelled from the kitchen, because at that moment she had turned on the water at the sink in order to push ice cubes out of a metal tray. She heard someone laugh. Lucienne went back to the living room with the ice bucket. They were expecting Edmund at any moment. Lucienne had suddenly realized that she wanted Edmund out of their circle, that she actively disliked him.

"Yes, what *is* it about Edmund?" asked Charles Forbes with a sly smile at Lucienne. Charles was pudgy, his shirt front strained at the buttons, a patch of leg often showed between sock and trousers cuff when he sat, but he was well loved by the group, because he was good-natured and bright, and could drink like a fish and never show it. "Maybe we're all jealous because he stopped smoking," Charles said, putting out his cigarette and reaching for another.

"I admit *I'm* jealous," said Peter Tomlin with a broad grin. "I know I should stop and I damned well can't. Tried to twice—in the last year."

Peter's details about his efforts were not interesting. Edmund was due with his new wife, and the others were talking while they could.

"Maybe it's his wife!" Anita Ketchum whispered excitedly, knowing this would get a laugh and encourage further comments. It did.

"Worse than the first by far!" Charles avowed.

"Yes, Lillian wasn't bad at all! I agree," said Lucienne, still on her feet and handing Peter the Vat 69 bottle, so he could top up his glass the way he liked it. "It's true Magda's no asset. That—" Lucienne had been about to say something quite unkind about the scared yet aloof expression which often showed on Magda's face.

"Ah, marriage on the rebound," Tom Strathmore said musingly.

"Certainly was, yes," said Frieda Markus. "Maybe we have to forgive that. You know they say men suffer more than women if their spouses walk out on them? Their egos suffer, they say—worse."

"Mine would suffer with *Magda,* matter of fact," Tom said.

Anita gave a laugh. "And what a name, Magda! Makes me think of a lightbulb or something."

The doorbell rang.

"Must be Edmund." Lucienne went to press the release button. She had asked Edmund and Magda to stay for dinner, but they were going to a play tonight. Only three were staying for dinner, the Markuses and Peter Tomlin.

"But he's changed his job, don't forget," Peter was saying as Lucienne came back into the room. "You can't say he has to be clammed up— secretive, I mean. It's not *that*." Like the others, Peter sought for a word, a phrase to describe the unlikability of Edmund Quasthoff.

"He's stuffy," said Anita Ketchum with a curl of distaste at her lips.

A few seconds of silence followed. The apartment doorbell was supposed to ring.

"Do you suppose he's happy?" Charles asked in a whisper.

This was enough to raise a clap of collective laughter. The thought of Edmund radiating happiness, even with a two-month-old marriage, was risible.

"But then he's probably never been happy," said Lucienne, just as the bell rang, and she turned to go to the door.

"Not late, I hope, Lucienne dear," said Edmund coming in, bending to kiss Lucienne's cheek, and by inches not touching it.

"No-o. I've got the time but you haven't. How are *you*, Magda?" Lucienne asked with deliberate enthusiasm, as if she really cared how Magda was.

"Very well, thank you, and you?" Magda was in brown again, a light and dark brown cotton dress with a brown satin scarf at her neck.

Both of them looked brown and dull, Lucienne thought as she led them into the living room. Greetings sounded friendly and warm.

"No, just tonic, please . . . Oh well, a smidgin of gin," Edmund said to Charles, who was doing the honors. "Lemon slice, yes, thanks." Edmund as usual gave an impression of sitting on the edge of his armchair seat.

Anita was dutifully making conversation with Magda on the sofa.

"And how're you liking your new job, Edmund?" Lucienne asked. Edmund had been with the accounting department of the United Nations for several years, but his present job was better paid and far less cloistered, Lucienne gathered, with business lunches nearly every day.

"O-oh," Edmund began, "different crowd, I'll say that." He tried to smile. Smiles from Edmund looked like efforts. "These boozy lunches . . ." Edmund shook his head. "I think they even resent the fact I don't smoke. They want you to be like them, you know?"

"Who's them?" asked Charles Forbes.

"Clients of the agency and a lot of the time *their* accountants," Edmund replied. "They all prefer to talk business at the lunch table instead of face to face in my office. 'S funny." Edmund rubbed a forefinger along the side of his arched nose. "I have to have one or two drinks with them—

my usual restaurant knows now to make them weak—otherwise our clients might think I'm the Infernal Revenue Department itself putting—honesty before expediency or some such." Edmund's face again cracked in a smile that did not last long.

Pity, Lucienne thought, and she almost said it. A strange word to think of, because pity she had not for Edmund. Lucienne exchanged a glance with Charles, then with Tom Strathmore, who was smirking.

"They call me up at all hours of the night too. California doesn't seem to realize the time dif—"

"Take your phone off the hook at night," Charles' wife Ellen put in.

"Oh, can't afford to," Edmund replied. "Sacred cows, these worried clients. Sometimes they ask me questions a pocket calculator could answer. But Babcock and Holt have to be polite, so I go on losing sleep . . . No, thanks, Peter," he said as Peter tried to pour more drink for him. Edmund also pushed gently aside a nearly full ashtray whose smell perhaps annoyed him.

Lucienne would ordinarily have emptied the ashtray, but now she didn't. And Magda? Magda was glancing at her watch as Lucienne looked at her, though she chatted now with Charles on her left. Twenty-eight she was, enviably young to be sure, but what a drip! A bad skin. Small wonder she hadn't been married before. She still kept her job, Edmund had said, something to do with computers. She knitted well, her parents were Mormons, though Magda wasn't. Really wasn't, Lucienne wondered?

A moment later, having declined even orange or tomato juice, Magda said gently to her husband, "Darling . . ." and tapped her wristwatch face.

Edmund put down his glass at once, and his old-fashioned brown shoes with wing tips rose from the floor a little before he hauled himself up. Edmund looked tired already, though it was hardly eight. "Ah, yes, the theater—Thank you, Lucienne. It's been a pleasure as usual."

"But such a short one!" said Lucienne.

When Edmund and Magda had left, there was a general "Whew!" and a few chuckles, which sounded not so much indulgent as bitterly amused.

"I really wouldn't like to be married to that," said Peter Tomlin, who was unmarried. "Frankly," he added. Peter had known Edmund since he, Peter, was twenty-two, having been introduced via Charles Forbes, at whose publishing house Peter had applied for a job without success. The older Charles had liked Peter, and had introduced him to a few of his friends, among them Lucienne and Edmund. Peter remembered his first good impression of Edmund Quasthoff—that of a serious and trustworthy man—but whatever virtue Peter had seen in Edmund was somehow gone now, as if that first impression had been a mistake on Peter's part. Edmund had not lived up to life, somehow. There was something cramped about him, and the crampedness seemed personified in Magda. Or was it that Edmund didn't really like *them?*

"Maybe he deserves Magda," Anita said, and the others laughed.

"Maybe he doesn't like us either," said Peter.

"Oh, but he does," Lucienne said. "Remember, Charles, how pleased he was when—we sort of accepted him—at that first dinner party I asked Edmund and Lillian to here at my place. One of my birthday dinners, I remember. Edmund and Lillian were beaming because they'd been admitted to our charmed circle." Lucienne's laugh was disparaging of their circle and also of Edmund.

"Yes, Edmund did try," said Charles.

"His clothes are so boring even," Anita said.

"True. Can't some of you men give him a hint? You, Julian." Lucienne glanced at Julian's crisp cotton suit. "You're always so dapper."

"Me?" Julian settled his jacket on his shoulders. "I frankly think men pay more attention to what women say. Why should I say anything to him?"

"Magda told me Edmund wants to buy a car," said Ellen.

"Does he drive?" Peter asked.

"May I, Lucienne?" Tom Strathmore reached for the scotch bottle which stood on a tray. "Maybe what Edmund needs is to get thoroughly soused one night. Then Magda might even leave him."

"Hey, we've just invited the Quasthoffs for dinner at our place Friday night," Charles announced. "Maybe Edmund *can* get soused. Who else wants to come?—Lucienne?"

Anticipating boredom, Lucienne hesitated. But it might not be boring. "Why not? Thank you, Charles—and Ellen."

Peter Tomlin couldn't make it because of a Friday night deadline. Anita said she would love to come. Tom Strathmore was free, but not the Markuses, because it was Julian's mother's birthday.

It was a memorable party in the Forbeses' big kitchen which served as dining room. Magda had not been to the penthouse apartment before. She politely looked at the Forbeses' rather good collection of framed drawings by contemporary artists, but seemed afraid to make a comment. Magda was on her best behavior, while the others as if by unspoken agreement were unusually informal and jolly. Part of this, Lucienne realized, was meant to shut Magda out of their happy old circle, and to mock her stiff decorum, though in fact everyone went out of his or her way to try and get Edmund and Magda to join in the fun. One form that this took, Lucienne observed, was Charles's pouring gin into Edmund's tonic glass with a rather free hand. At the table, Ellen did the same with the wine. It was especially good wine, a vintage Margaux that went superbly with the hot-oil-cooked steak morsels which they all dipped into a pot in the center of the round table. There was hot, buttery garlic bread, and paper napkins on which to wipe greasy fingers.

"Come on, you're not working tomorrow," Tom said genially, replenishing Edmund's wine glass.

"I—yam working tomorrow," Edmund replied, smiling. "Always do. Have to on Saturdays."

Magda was giving Edmund a fixed stare, which he missed, because his eyes were not straying her way.

After dinner, they adjourned to the long sun parlor which had a terrace beyond it. With the coffee those who wanted it had a choice of Drambuie, Bénédictine or brandy. Edmund had a sweet tooth, Lucienne knew, and she noticed that Charles had no difficulty in persuading Edmund to accept a snifter of Drambuie. Then they played darts.

"Darts're as far as I'll go toward exercising," said Charles, winding up. His first shot was a bull's-eye.

The others took their turns, and Ellen kept score.

Edmund wound up awkwardly, trying to look amusing, they all knew, though still making an effort to aim right. Edmund was anything but limber and coordinated. His first shot hit the wall three feet away from the board, and since it hit sideways, it pierced nothing and fell to the floor. So did Edmund, having twisted somehow on his left foot and lost his balance.

Cries of "Bravo!" and merry laughter.

Peter extended a hand and hauled Edmund up. "Hurt yourself?"

Edmund looked shocked and was not laughing when he stood up. He straightened his jacket. "I don't think—I have the definite feeling—" His eyes glanced about, but rather swimmily, while the others waited, listening. "I have the feeling I'm not exactly well liked here—so I—"

"Oh-h, Edmund!" said Lucienne.

"What're you talking about, Edmund?" asked Ellen.

A Drambuie was pressed into Edmund's hand, despite the fact that Magda tried gently to restrain the hand that offered it. Edmund was soothed, but not much. The darts game continued. Edmund was sober enough to realize that he shouldn't make an ass of himself by walking out at once in a huff, yet he was drunk enough to reveal his gut feeling, fuzzy as it might be to him just then, that the people around him were not his true friends any more, that they really didn't like him. Magda persuaded him to drink more coffee.

The Quasthoffs took their leave some fifteen minutes later.

There was an immediate sense of relief among all.

"She is the end, let's face it," said Anita, and flung a dart.

"Well, we got him soused," said Tom Strathmore. "So it's possible."

Somehow they had all tasted blood on seeing Edmund comically sprawled on the floor.

Lucienne that night, having had more to drink than usual, mainly in the form of two good brandies after dinner, telephoned Edmund at four in the morning with an idea of asking him how he was. She knew she was calling him also in order to disturb his sleep. After five rings, when Edmund answered in a sleepy voice, Lucienne found she could not say anything.

"Hello?—Hello? Qu-Quasthoff here . . ."

When she awakened in the morning, the world looked somehow different—sharper edged and more exciting. It was not the slight nervousness that might have been caused by a hangover. In fact Lucienne felt very well after her usual breakfast of orange juice, English tea and toast, and she painted well for two hours. She realized that she was busy detesting Edmund Quasthoff. Ludicrous, but there it was. And how many of her friends were feeling the same way about Edmund today?

The telephone rang just after noon, and it was Anita Ketchum. "I hope I'm not interrupting you in the middle of a masterstroke."

"No, no! What's up?"

"Well—Ellen called me this morning to tell me Edmund's birthday party is off."

"I didn't know any was on."

Anita explained. Magda last evening had invited Charles and Ellen to a birthday dinner party for Edmund at her and Edmund's apartment nine days from now, and had told Ellen she would invite "everybody" plus some friends of hers whom everybody might not have met yet, because it would be a stand-up buffet affair. Then this morning, without any explanation such as that Edmund or she were ill with a lingering ailment, Magda had said she had "decided against" a party, she was sorry.

"Maybe afraid of Edmund's getting pissed again," Lucienne said, but she knew that wasn't the whole answer.

"I'm sure she thinks we don't like her—or Edmund much—which unfortunately is true."

"What *can* we do?" asked Lucienne, feigning chagrin.

"Social outcasts, aren't we? Hah-hah. Got to sign off now, Lucienne, because someone's waiting."

The little contretemps of the canceled party seemed both hostile and silly to Lucienne, and the whole group got wind of it within a day or so, even though they all might not as yet have been invited.

"We can also invite and disinvite," chuckled Julian Markus on the telephone to Lucienne. "What a childish trick—with no excuse such as a business trip."

"No excuse, no. Well, I'll think of something funny, Julian dear."

"What do you mean?"

"A little smack back at them. Don't you think they deserve it?"

"Yes, my dear."

Lucienne's first idea was simple. She and Tom Strathmore would invite Edmund out for lunch on his birthday, and get him so drunk he would be in no condition to return to his office that afternoon. Tom was agreeable. And Edmund sounded grateful when Lucienne rang him up and extended the invitation, without mentioning Magda's name.

Lucienne booked a table at a rather expensive French restaurant in the East 60s. She and Tom and three dry martinis were waiting when Edmund arrived, smiling tentatively, but plainly glad to see his old friends again at a small table. They chatted amiably. Lucienne managed to pay some compliments in regard to Magda.

"She has a certain dignity," said Lucienne.

"I wish she weren't so *shy*," Edmund responded at once. "I try to pull her out of it."

Another round. Lucienne delayed the ordering by having to make a telephone call at a moment when Tom was able to order a third round to fill the time until Lucienne got back. Then they ordered their meal, with white wine to be followed by a red. On the first glass of white, Tom and Lucienne sang a soft chorus of "Happy Birthday to You" to Edmund as they lifted their glasses. Lucienne had rung Anita, who worked only three blocks away, and Anita joined them when the lunch ended just after three with a Drambuie for Edmund, though Lucienne and Tom abstained. Edmund kept murmuring something about a three o'clock appointment, which maybe would be all right for him to miss, because it really wasn't a top-level appointment. Anita and the others told him it would surely be excusable on his birthday.

"I've just got half an hour," Anita said as they went out of the restaurant together, Anita having partaken of nothing, "but I did want to see you on this special day, Edmund old thing. I insist on inviting you for a drink or a beer."

The others kissed Edmund's cheek and left, then Anita steered Edmund across the street into a corner bar with a fancy decor that tried to be an old Irish pub. Edmund fairly fell into his chair, having nearly slipped a moment before on sawdust. It was a wonder he was served, Anita thought, but hers was a sober presence, and they were served. From this bar, Anita rang Peter Tomlin and explained the situation, which Peter found funny, and Peter agreed to come and take over for a few minutes. Peter arrived. Edmund had a second beer, and insisted upon a coffee, which was ordered, but the combination seemed to make him sick. Anita had left minutes before. Peter waited patiently, prattling nonsense to Edmund, wondering if Edmund was going to throw up or slip under the table.

"Mag's got people coming at six," Edmund mumbled. "Gotta be home—little before—or else." He tried in vain to read his watch.

"Mag you call her? . . . Finish your beer, chum." Peter lifted his first glass of beer, which was nearly drained. "Bottoms up and many happy returns!"

They emptied their glasses.

Peter delivered Edmund to his apartment door at 6:25 and ran. A cocktail party was in swing *chez* Magda and Edmund, Peter could tell from the hum of voices behind the closed door. Edmund had been talking about his "boss" being present, and a couple of important clients. Peter smiled to himself as he rode down in the elevator. He went home, put in a good report to Lucienne, made himself some instant coffee, and got back to his typewriter. Comical, yes! Poor old Edmund! But it was Magda who amused Peter the more. Magda was the stuffy one, their real target, Peter thought.

Peter Tomlin was to change his opinion about that in less than a fortnight. He watched with some surprise and gathering alarm as the attack, led by Lucienne and to a lesser extent Anita, focused on Edmund. Ten days after the sousing of Edmund, Peter looked in one evening at the Markuses' apartment—just to return a couple of books he had borrowed—and found both smirking over Edmund's latest mishap. Edmund had lost his job at Babcock and Holt and was now in the Payne-Whitney for drying out.

"What?" Peter said. "I hadn't heard a word!"

"We just found out today," said Frieda. "Lucienne called me up. She said she tried to call Edmund at his office this morning, and they said he was absent on leave, but she insisted on finding out where he was—said it concerned an emergency in his family, you know how good she is at things like that. So they told her he was in the Payne-Whitney, and she phoned there and talked with Edmund personally. He also had an accident with his car, he said, but luckily he didn't hurt himself or anyone else."

"Holy cow," said Peter.

"He always had a fondness for the bottle, you know," Julian said, "and a thimble-belly to go with it. He really had to go on the wagon five or six years ago, wasn't it, Frieda? Maybe you didn't know Edmund then, Peter. Well, he did, but it didn't last long. Then it got worse when Lillian walked out. But now *this* job—"

Frieda Markus giggled. "This job!—Lucienne didn't help and you know it. She invited Edmund to her place a couple of times and plied him. Made him talk about his troubles with Mag."

Troubles. Peter felt a twinge of dislike for Edmund for talking about his "troubles" after only three months or so of marriage. Didn't everyone have troubles? Did people have to bore their friends with them? "Maybe he deserved it," Peter murmured.

"In a way, *yes*," Julian said forcefully, and reached for a cigarette. Julian's aggressive attitude implied that the anti-Edmund campaign wasn't over. "He's weak," Julian added.

Peter thanked Julian for the loan of the two books, and took his leave. Again he had work to do in the evening, so he couldn't linger for a drink. At home, Peter hesitated between calling Lucienne or Anita, decided on Lucienne, but she didn't answer, so he tried Anita. Anita was home and Lucienne was there. Both spoke with Peter, and both sounded merry. Peter asked Lucienne about Edmund.

"Oh, he'll be sprung in another week or so, he said. But he won't be quite the same man, I think, when he comes out."

"How do you mean that?"

"Well, he's lost his job and this story isn't going to make it easier for him to get another one. He's probably lost Magda too, because Edmund told me she'd leave him if they didn't move out of New York."

"So . . . maybe they will move," said Peter. "He told you he'd definitely lost his job?"

"Oh yes. They call it a leave of absence at his office, but Edmund admitted they're not taking him back." Lucienne gave a short, shrill laugh. "Just as well they do move out of New York. Magda hates *us*, you know. And frankly Edmund never was one of us—so in a way it's understandable."

Was it understandable, Peter wondered as he got down to his own work. There was something vicious about the whole thing, and he'd been vicious plying Edmund with beers that day. The curious thing was that Peter felt no compassion for Edmund.

One might have thought that the group would leave Edmund alone, at least, even make some effort to cheer him up (without drinks) when he got out of the Payne-Whitney, but it was just the opposite, Peter observed. Anita Ketchum invited Edmund for a quiet dinner at her apartment, and asked Peter to come too. She did not ply him with drink, though Edmund had at least three on his own. Edmund was morose, and Anita did not make his mood any better by talking against Magda. She fairly said that Edmund could and should do better than Magda, and that he ought to try as soon as possible. Peter had to concur here.

"She doesn't seem to make you very happy, Ed," Peter remarked in a man-to-man way, "and now I hear she wants you to move out of New York."

"That's true," Edmund said, "and I dunno where else I'd get a decent job."

They talked until late, getting nowhere, really. Peter left before Edmund did. Peter found that the memory of Edmund depressed him: a tall, hunched figure in limp clothes, looking at the floor as he strolled around Anita's living room with a glass in his hand.

Lucienne was home in bed reading when the telephone rang at one in the morning. It was Edmund, and he said he was going to get a divorce from Mag.

"She just walked out—just now," Edmund said in a happy but a bit drunk-sounding voice. "Said she was going to stay in a hotel tonight. I don't even know where."

Lucienne realized that he wanted a word of praise from her, or a congratulation. "Well, dear Edmund, it may be for the best. I hope it can all be settled smoothly. After all, you haven't been married long."

"No. I think I'm doing—I mean she's doing—the right thing," said Edmund heavily.

Lucienne assured him that she thought so too.

Now Edmund was going to look for another job. He didn't think Mag would make any difficulties, financial or otherwise, about the divorce. "She's a young woman w-who likes her privacy quite a bit. She's surprisingly . . . *independent,* y'know?" Edmund hiccuped.

Lucienne smiled, thinking any woman would want independence from Edmund. "We'll all be wishing you luck, Edmund. And let us know if you think we can pull strings anywhere."

Charles Forbes and Julian Markus went to Edmund's apartment one evening, to discuss business, Charles later said to Lucienne, as Charles had an idea of Edmund's becoming a freelance accountant, and in fact Charles' publishing house needed such a man now. They drank hardly anything, according to Charles, but they did stay up quite late. Edmund had been down in the dumps, and around midnight had lowered the scotch bottle by several inches.

That was on a Thursday night, and by Tuesday morning, Edmund was dead. The cleaning woman had come in with her key and found him asleep in bed, she thought, at nine in the morning. She hadn't realized until nearly noon, and then she had called the police. The police hadn't been able to find Magda, and notifying anybody had been much delayed, so it was Wednesday evening before any of the group knew: Peter Tomlin saw an item in his own newspaper, and telephoned Lucienne.

"A mixture of sleeping pills and alcohol, but they don't suspect suicide," Peter said.

Neither did Lucienne suspect suicide. "What an end," she said with a sigh. "Now what?" She was not at all shocked, but vaguely thinking about the others in their circle hearing the news, or reading it now.

"Well—funeral service tomorrow in a Long Island—um—funeral home, it says."

Peter and Lucienne agreed they should go.

The group of friends, Lucienne Gauss, Peter Tomlin, the Markuses, the Forbeses, Tom Strathmore, Anita Ketchum, were all there and formed at least a half of the small gathering. Maybe a few of Edmund's relatives had come, but the group wasn't sure: Edmund's family lived in the Chicago area, and no one had ever met any of them. Magda was there, dressed in gray with a thin black veil. She stood apart, and barely nodded to Lucienne and the others. It was a nondenominational service to which Lucienne paid no attention, and she doubted if her friends did—except to recognize the words as empty rote and close their ears to it. Afterwards, Lucienne and Charles said they didn't wish to follow the casket to the grave, and neither did the others.

Anita's mouth looked stony, though it was fixed in a pensive, very faint smile. Taxis waited, and they straggled towards them. Tom Strathmore walked with his head down. Charles Forbes looked up at the late summer sky. Charles walked between his wife, Ellen, and Lucienne, and suddenly he said to Lucienne:

"You know, I rang Edmund up a couple of times in the night—just to annoy him. I have to confess that. Ellen knows."

"Did you," said Lucienne calmly.

Tom, just behind them, had heard this. "I did worse," he said with a twitch of a smile. "I told Edmund he might lose his job if he started taking Magda out with him on his business lunches."

Ellen laughed. "Oh, that's not serious, Tom. That's——" But she didn't finish.

We killed him, Lucienne thought. Everybody was thinking that, and no one had the guts to say it. Anyone of them might have said, "We killed him, you know?" but no one did. "We'll miss him," Lucienne said finally, as if she meant it.

"Ye-es," someone replied with equal gravity.

They climbed into three taxis, promising to see each other soon.

The Terrors of
Basket-Weaving

Diane's terror began in an innocent and fortuitous way. She and her
husband, Reg, lived in Manhattan, but had a cottage on the Massachusetts coast near Truro where they spent most weekends. Diane was a
press relations officer in an agency called Retting. Reg was a lawyer. They
were both thirty-eight, childless by choice, and both earned good salaries.

They enjoyed walks along the beach, and usually they took walks
alone, not with each other. Diane liked to look for pretty stones, interesting shells, bottles of various sizes and colors, bits of wood rubbed smooth
by sand and wind. These items she took back to the unpainted gray cottage
they called "the shack," lived with them for a few weeks or months, then
Diane threw nearly all of them out, because she didn't want the shack to
become a magpie's nest. One Sunday morning she found a wicker basket
bleached nearly white and with its bottom stoved in, but its frame and sides
quite sturdy. This looked like an old-fashioned crib basket for a baby,
because one end of it rose higher than the other, the foot part tapered, and
it was just the size for a newborn or for a baby up to a few months. It was
the kind called a Moses basket, Diane thought.

Was the basket even American? It was amusing to think that it might
have fallen overboard or been thrown away, old and broken, from a passing
Italian tanker, or some foreign boat that might have had a woman and
child on board. Anyway, Diane decided to take it home, and she put it for
the nonce on a bench on the side porch of the shack, where colored stones
and pebbles and sea glass already lay. She might try to repair it, for fun,
because in its present condition it was useless. Reg was then shifting sand
with a snow shovel from one side of the wooden front steps, and was going
to plant more beach grass from the dunes, like a second line of troops,

between them and the sea to keep the sand in place. His industry, which Diane knew would go on another hour or so until lunchtime—and cold lobster and potato salad was already in the fridge—inspired her to try her hand at the basket now.

She had realized a few minutes before that the kind of slender twigs she needed stood already in a brass cylinder beside their small fireplace. Withes or withies—the words sounded nice in her head—might be more appropriate, but on the other hand the twigs would give more strength to the bottom of a basket which she might use to hold small potted plants, for instance. One would be able to move several pots into the sun all at once in a basket—if she could mend the basket.

Diane took the pruning shears, and cut five lengths of reddish-brown twigs—results of a neighbor's apple-tree pruning, she recalled—and then snipped nine shorter lengths for the crosspieces. She estimated she would need nine. A ball of twine sat handy on a shelf, and Diane at once got to work. She plucked out what was left of the broken pieces in the basket, and picked up one of her long twigs. The slightly pointed ends, an angle made by the shears, slipped easily between the sturdy withes that formed the bottom rim. She took up a second and a third. Diane then, before she attempted to tie the long pieces, wove the shorter lengths under and over the longer, at right angles. The twigs were just flexible enough to be manageable, and stiff enough to be strong. No piece projected too far. She had cut them just the right length, measuring only with her eye or thumb before snipping. Then the twine.

Over and under, around the twig ends at the rim and through the withes already decoratively twisted there, then a good solid knot. She was able to continue with the cord to the next twig in a couple of places, so she did not have to tie a knot at each crosspiece. Suddenly to her amazement the basket was repaired, and it looked splendid.

In her first glow of pride, Diane looked at her watch. Hardly fifteen minutes had passed since she had come into the house! How had she done it? She held the top end of the basket up, and pressed the palm of her right hand against the floor of the basket. It gave out firm-sounding squeaks. It had spring in it. And strength. She stared at the neatly twisted cord, at the correct over-and-under lengths, all about the diameter of pencils, and she wondered again how she had done it.

That was when the terror began to creep up on her, at first like a faint suspicion or surmise or question. Had she some relative or ancestor not so far in the past, who had been an excellent basket-weaver? Not that she knew of, and the idea made her smile with amusement. Grandmothers and great-grandmothers who could quilt and crochet didn't count. This was more primitive.

Yes, people had been weaving baskets thousands of years before Christ, and maybe even a million years ago, hadn't they? Baskets might have come before clay pots.

The answer to her question, how had she done it, might be that the ancient craft of basket-weaving had been carried on for so long by the human race that it had surfaced in her this Sunday morning in the late twentieth century. Diane found this thought rather frightening.

As she set the table for lunch, she upset a wine glass, but the glass was empty and it didn't break. Reg was still shoveling, but slowing up, nearly finished. It was still early for lunch, but Diane had wanted the table set, the salad dressing made in the wooden bowl, before she took a swat at the work she had brought with her. Finally she sat with a yellow pad and pencil, and opened the plastic-covered folder marked RETTING, plus her own name, DIANE CLARKE, in smaller letters at the bottom. She had to write three hundred words about a kitchen gadget that extracted air from plastic bags of apples, oranges, potatoes or whatever. After the air was extracted, the bags could be stored in the bottom of the fridge as usual, but the product kept much longer and took up less space because of the absence of air in the bag. She had seen the gadget work in the office, and she had a photograph of it now. It was a sixteen-inch-long tube which one fastened to the cold water tap in the kitchen. The water from the tap drained away, but its force moved a turbine in the tube, which created a vacuum after a hollow needle was stuck into the sealed bag. Diane understood the principle quite well, but she began to feel odd and disoriented.

It was odd to be sitting in a cottage built in a simple style more than a hundred years ago, to have just repaired a basket in the manner that people would have made or repaired a basket thousands of years ago, and to be trying to compose a sentence about a gadget whose existence depended upon modern plumbing, sealed packaging, transport by machinery of fruit and vegetables grown hundreds of miles (possibly thousands) from the places where they would be consumed. If this weren't so, people could simply carry fruit and vegetables home in a sack from the fields, or in baskets such as the one she had just mended.

Diane put down the pencil, picked up a ballpoint pen, lit a cigarette, and wrote the first words. "Need more space in your fridge? Tired of having to buy more lemons at the supermarket than you can use in the next month? Here is an inexpensive gadget that might interest you." It wasn't

particularly inexpensive, but no matter. Lots of people were going to pay
thousands of dollars for this gadget. She would be paid a sizable amount
also, meaning a certain fraction of her salary for writing about it. As she
worked on, she kept seeing a vision of her crib-shaped basket and thinking
that the basket—per se, as a thing to be used—was far more important
than the kitchen gadget. However, it was perfectly normal to consider a
basket more important or useful, she supposed, for the simple reason that a
basket was.

"Nice walk this morning?" Reg asked, relaxing with a pre-lunch glass
of cold white wine. He was standing in the low-ceilinged living room, in
shorts, an unbuttoned shirt, sandals. His face had browned further, and the
skin was pinkish over his cheekbones.

"Yes. Found a basket. Rather nice. Want to see it?"

"Sure."

She led the way to the side porch, and indicated the basket on the
wooden table. "The bottom was all broken—so I fixed it."

"*You* fixed it?" Reg was leaning over it with admiration. "Yeah, I can
see. Nice job, Di."

She felt a tremor, a little like shame. Or was it fear? She felt uncomfortable as Reg picked up the basket and looked at its underside. "Might be
nice to hold kindling—or magazines, maybe," she said. "We can always
throw it away when we get bored with it."

"Throw it away, no! It's sort of amusing—shaped like a baby's cradle or
something."

"That's what I thought—that it must have been made for a baby." She
drifted back into the living room, wishing now that Reg would stop
examining the basket.

"Didn't know you had such talents, Di. Girl Scout lore?"

Diane gave a laugh. Reg knew she'd never joined the Girl Scouts.
"Don't forget the Gartners are coming at seven-thirty."

"Um-m. Yes, thanks. I didn't forget.—What's for dinner? We've got
everything we need?"

Diane said they had. The Gartners were bringing raspberries from their
garden plus cream. Reg had meant he was willing to drive to town in case
they had to buy anything else.

The Gartners arrived just before eight, and Reg made dacquiris. There
was scotch for any who preferred it, and Olivia Gartner did. She was a
serious drinker and held it well. An investment counselor, she was, and her
husband Pete was a professor in the math department at Columbia.

Diane, after a swim around four o'clock, had collected some dry reeds from the dunes and among these had put a few long-stemmed blossoming weeds and wild flowers, blue and pink and orangy-yellow. She had laid all these in the crib-shaped basket which she had set on the floor near the fireplace.

"Isn't this pretty!" said Olivia during her second scotch, as if the drink had opened her eyes. She meant the floral arrangement, but Reg at once said:

"And look at the basket, Olivia! Diane found it on the beach today and *repaired* it." Reg lifted the basket as high as his head, so Olivia and Pete could admire its underside.

Olivia chuckled. "That's fantastic, Diane! Beautiful! How long did it take you?—It's a sweet basket."

"That's the funny thing," Diane began, eager to express herself. "It took me about twelve minutes!"

"Look how proud she is of it!" said Reg, smiling.

Pete was running his thumb over the apple twigs at the bottom, nodding his approval.

"Yes, it was almost terrifying," Diane went on.

"Terrifying?" Pete lifted his eyebrows.

"I'm not explaining myself very well." Diane had a polite smile on her face, though she was serious. "I felt as if I'd struck some hidden talent or knowledge—just suddenly. Everything I did, I felt sure of. I was amazed."

"Looks strong too," Pete said, and set the basket back where it had been.

Then they talked about something else. The cost of heating, if they used their cottages at all in the coming winter. Diane had hoped the basket conversation would continue a little longer. Another round of drinks, while Diane put their cold supper on the table. Bowls of jellied consommé with a slice of lemon to start with. They sat down. Diane felt unsatisfied. Or was it a sense of disturbance? Disturbance because of what? Just because they hadn't pursued the subject of the basket? Why should they have? It was merely a basket to them, mended the way anyone could have mended it. Or could just anyone have mended it that well? Diane happened to be sitting at the end of the table, so the basket was hardly four feet from her, behind her and to her right. She felt bothered somehow even by the basket's nearness. That was very odd. She must get to the bottom of it—that was funny, in view of the basket repair—but now wasn't the time, with three other people talking, and half her mind on seeing that her guests had a good meal.

While they were drinking coffee, Diane lit three candles and the oil lamp, and they listened to a record of Mozart *divertimenti*. They didn't listen, but it served as background music for their conversation. Diane listened to the music. It sounded skillful, even modern, and extremely civilized. Diane enjoyed her brandy. The brandy too seemed the epitome of human skill, care, knowledge. Not like a basket any child could put together. Perhaps a child in years couldn't, but a child as to progress in the evolution of the human race could weave a basket.

Was she possibly feeling her drinks? Diane pulled her long cotton skirt farther down over her knees. The subject was lobbies now, the impotence of any president, even Congress against them.

Monday morning early Diane and Reg flew back to New York by helicopter. Neither had to be at work before eleven. Diane had supposed that New York and work would put the disquieting thoughts re the basket out of her head, but that was not so. New York seemed to emphasize what she had felt up at the shack, even though the origin of her feelings had stayed at the shack. What were her feelings, anyway? Diane disliked vagueness, and was used to labeling her emotions jealousy, resentment, suspicion or whatever, even if the emotion was not always to her credit. But this?

What she felt was most certainly not guilt, though it was similarly troubling and unpleasant. Not envy either, not in the sense of desiring to master basketry so she could make a truly great basket, whatever that was. She'd always thought basket-weaving an occupation for the simpleminded, and it had become in fact a symbol of what psychiatrists advised disturbed people to take up. That was not it at all.

Diane felt that she had lost herself. Since repairing that basket, she wasn't any longer Diane Clarke, not completely, anyway. Neither was she anybody else, of course. It wasn't that she felt she had assumed the identity, even partially, of some remote ancestor. How remote, anyway? No. She felt rather that she was living with a great many people from the past, that they were in her brain or mind (Diane did not believe in a soul, and found the idea of a collective unconscious too vague to be of importance), and that people from human antecedents were bound up with her, influencing her, controlling her every bit as much as, up to now, she had been controlling herself. This thought was by no means comforting, but it was at least a partial explanation, maybe, for the disquietude that she was experiencing. It was not even an explanation, she realized, but rather a description of her feelings.

She wanted to say something to Reg about it and didn't, thinking that anything she tried to say along these lines would sound either silly or fuzzy. By now five days had passed since she had repaired the basket up at Truro, and they were going up to the shack again this weekend. The five working days at the office had passed as had a lot of other weeks for Diane. She had had a set-to with Jan Heyningen, the art director, on Wednesday, and had come near telling him what she thought of his stubbornness and bad taste, but she hadn't. She had merely smoldered. It had happened before. She and Reg had gone out to dinner at the apartment of some friends on Thursday. All as usual, outwardly.

The unusual was the schizoid atmosphere in her head. Was that it? Two personalities? Diane toyed with this possibility all Friday afternoon at the office while she read through new promotion-ready material. Was she simply imagining that several hundred prehistoric ancestors were somehow dwelling within her? No, frankly, she wasn't. That idea was even less credible than Jung's collective unconscious. And suddenly she rejected the simple schizo idea or explanation also. Schizophrenia was a catch-all, she had heard, for a lot of derangements that couldn't otherwise be diagnosed. She didn't feel schizoid, anyway, didn't feel like two people, or three, or more. She felt simply scared, mysteriously terrified. But only one thing in the least awkward happened that week: she had let one side of the lettuce-swinger slip out of her hand on the terrace, and lettuce flew everywhere, hung from the potted bamboo trees, was caught on rose thorns, lay fresh and clean on the red tile paving, and on the seat of the glider. Diane had laughed, even though there was no more lettuce in the house. She was tense, perhaps, therefore clumsy. A little accident like that could happen any time.

During the flight to the Cape, Diane had a happy thought: she'd use the basket not just for floral arrangements but for collecting more *objets trouvés* from the beach, or better yet for potatoes and onions in the kitchen. She'd treat it like any old basket. That would take the mystique out of it, the terror. To have felt terror was absurd.

So Saturday morning while Reg worked on the nonelectric type-writer which they kept at the shack, Diane went for a walk on the beach with the basket. She had put a piece of newspaper in the basket, and she collected a greater number than usual of colored pebbles, a few larger smooth rocks—one orange in color, making it almost a *trompe l'oeil* for a mango—plus an interesting piece of sea-worn wood that looked like a boomerang. Wouldn't that be odd, she thought, if it really were an ancient boomerang worn shorter, thinner, until only the curve remained unchanged? As she walked back to the shack, the basket emitted faint squeaks in unison with her tread. The basket was so heavy, she had to carry it in two hands, letting its side rest against her hip, but she was not at all afraid that the twigs of the bottom would give. *Her work.*

Stop it, she told herself.

When she began to empty the basket on the porch's wooden table, she realized she had gathered too many stones, so she dropped more than half of them, quickly choosing the less interesting, over the porch rail onto the sand. Finally she shook the newspaper of its sand, and started to put it back in the basket. Sunlight fell on the glossy reddish-brown apple twigs. Over and under, not every one secured by twine, because for some twigs it hadn't been necessary. New work, and yet—Diane felt the irrational fear creeping over her again, and she pressed the newspaper quickly into the basket, pressed it at the crib-shaped edges, so that all her work was hidden. Then she tossed it carelessly on the floor, could have transferred some potatoes from a brown paper bag into it but she wanted to get away from the basket now.

An hour or so later, when she and Reg were finishing lunch, Reg laughing and about to light a cigarette, Diane felt an inner jolt as if— What? She deliberately relaxed, and gave her attention, more of it, to what Reg was saying. But it was as if the sound had been switched off a TV set. She saw him, but she wasn't listening or hearing. She blinked and forced herself to listen. Reg was talking about renting a tractor to clear some of their sand away, about terracing, and maintaining their property with growing things. They'd drawn a simple plan weeks ago, Diane remembered. But again she was feeling not like herself, as if she had lost herself in millions of people as an individual might get lost in a huge crowd. No, that was too simple, she felt. She was still trying to find solace in words. Or was she even dodging something? If so, what?

"What?" Reg asked, leaning back in his chair now, relaxed.

"Nothing. Why?"

"You were lost in thought."

Diane might have replied that she had just had a better idea for a current project at Retting, might have replied several things, but she said suddenly, "I'm thinking of asking for a leave of absence. Maybe just a month. I think Retting would do it, and it'd do me good."

Reg looked puzzled. "You're feeling tired, you mean? Just lately?"

"No. I feel somehow upset. Turned around, I don't know. I thought maybe a month of just being away from the office . . ." But work was supposed to be good in such a situation as hers. Work kept people from dwelling on their problems. But she hadn't a problem, rather a state of mind.

"Oh . . . well," Reg said. "Heyningen getting on your nerves maybe."

Diane shifted. It would have been easy to say yes, that was it. She took a cigarette, and Reg lit it. "Thanks. You're going to laugh, Reg. But that basket bothers me." She looked at him, feeling ashamed, and curiously defensive.

"The one you found last weekend? You're worried a child might've drowned in it, lost at sea?" Reg smiled as if at a mild joke he'd just made.

"No, not at all. Nothing like that. I told you last weekend. It simply bothers me that I repaired it so easily. There. That's it. And you can say I'm cracked—I don't care."

"I do not—quite—understand what you mean."

"It made me feel somehow—prehistoric. And funny. Still does."

Reg shook his head. "I can sort of understand. Honestly. But—another way of looking at it, Di, is to realize that it's a very simple activity after all, mending or even making a basket. Not that I don't admire the neat job you did, but it's not like—sitting down and playing Beethoven's Emperor Concerto, for instance, if you've never had a piano lesson in your life."

"No." She'd never had a basket-making lesson in her life, she might have said. She was silent, wondering if she should put in her leave of absence request on Monday, as a gesture, a kind of appeasement to the uneasiness she felt? Emotions demanded gestures, she had read somewhere, in order to be exorcised. Did she really believe that?

"Really, Di, the leave of absence is one thing, but that basket—It's an interesting basket, sure, because it's not machine-made and you don't see that shape any more. I've seen you get excited about stones you find. I understand. They're beautiful. But to let yourself get upset about—"

"Stones are different," she interrupted. "I can admire them. I'm not upset about them. I told you I feel I'm not exactly myself—me—any longer. I feel lost in a strange way—*Identity*, I mean," she broke in again, when Reg started to speak.

"Oh, Di!" He got up. "What do you mean you told me that? You didn't."

"Well, I have now. I feel—as if a lot of other people were inside me besides myself. And I feel lost because of that. Do you understand?"

Reg hesitated. "I understand the words. But the feeling—no."

Even that was something. Diane felt grateful, and relieved that she had said this much to him.

"Go ahead with the leave of absence idea, darling. I didn't mean to be so abrupt."

Diane put her cigarette out. "I'll think about it." She got up to make coffee.

That afternoon, after tidying the kitchen, Diane put another newspaper in the basket, and unloaded the sack of potatoes into it, plus three or four onions—familiar and contemporary objects. Perishable too. She made herself not think about the basket or even about the leave of absence for the rest of the day. Around 7:30, she and Reg drove off to Truro, where there was a street party organized by an ecology group. Wine and beer and soft drinks, hot dogs and jukebox music. They encountered the Gartners and a few other neighbors. The wine was undrinkable, the atmosphere marvelous. Diane danced with a couple of merry strangers and was for a few hours happy.

A month's leave of absence, she thought as she stood under the shower that night, was absurd and unnecessary. Temporary aberration to have considered it. If the basket—a really simple object as Reg had said—annoyed her so much, the thing to do was to get rid of it, burn it.

Sunday morning Reg took the car and went to deliver his Black & Decker or some appliance of it to the Gartners, who lived eight miles away. As soon as he had left, Diane went to the side porch, replaced the potatoes and onions in the brown paper bag which she had saved as she saved most bags that arrived at the shack, and taking the basket with its newspaper and a book of matches, she walked out onto the sand in the direction of the ocean. She struck a match and lit the newspaper, and laid the basket over it. After a moment's hesitation, as if from shock, the basket gave a crack and began to burn. The drier sides burned more quickly than the newer apple twigs, of course. With a stick, Diane poked every last pale withe into the flames, until nothing remained except black ash and some yellow-glowing embers, and finally these went out in the bright sunshine and began to darken. Diane pushed sand with her feet over the ashes, until nothing was visible. She breathed deeply as she walked back to the shack, and realized that she had been holding her breath, or almost, the entire time of the burning.

She was not going to say anything to Reg about getting rid of the basket, and he was not apt to notice its absence, Diane knew.

Diane did mention, on Tuesday in New York, that she had changed her mind about asking for a leave of absence. The implication was that she felt better, but she didn't say that.

The basket was gone, she would never see it again, unless she deliberately tried to conjure it up in memory, and that she didn't want to do. She felt better with the thing out of the shack, destroyed. She knew that the burning had been an action on her part to get rid of a feeling within her, a primitive action, if she thought about it, because though the basket had been tangible, her thoughts were not tangible. And they proved damned hard to destroy.

Three weeks after the burning of the basket, her crazy idea of being a "walking human race" or some such lingered. She would continue to listen to Mozart and Bartók, they'd go to the shack most weekends, and she would continue to pretend that her life counted for something, that she was part of the stream or evolution of the human race, though she felt now that she had spurned that position or small function by burning the basket. For a week, she realized, she had grasped something, and then she had deliberately thrown it away. In fact, she was no happier now than during that week when the well-mended basket had been in her possession. But she was determined not to say anything more about it to Reg. He had been on the verge of impatience that Saturday before the Sunday when she had burned it. And in fact could she even put any more into words? No. So she had to stop thinking about it. Yes.

Under a
Dark Angel's
Eye

Now he was on the last leg of his journey, the bus stretch from the airport to Arlington Hills. There would be nobody to meet him at the bus terminal, and Lee didn't mind in the least. In fact he preferred it. He could walk with his small suitcase the four or five blocks to the Capitol Hotel (he assumed it was still functioning), check in, then telephone Winston Greeves to say he had arrived. Maybe they could even wind up the business with the lawyer today, because it would be only four in the afternoon by the time Lee would be phoning Winston. It was a matter of signing a paper in regard to the house where Lee Mandeville had been born. Lee owned it, and now he had to sell it, because he needed the money. He didn't care, he wasn't sentimental about the two-story white house with the green lawn in front. Or was he? Lee honestly didn't think so. He'd had some nasty, unpleasant hours in that house, as well as a few happy ones—a barefoot boyhood, tossing a football with chums from the neighborhood on the front lawn. He had lost Louise there, too.

Lee shifted in his seat, rested his cheek against his hand which was lightly closed in a fist, and stared out the window at the Indiana landscape that drifted past. He barely recognized a small town they were going through. How long had it been, nine, no ten years since he had been to Arlington Hills. Ten years ago he had come to visit his mother in the nursing home called the Hearthside, and she had either not recognized him or pretended not to, or had really thought he was someone else. At any rate she had managed to come out with "Don't come back!" just as he had been going out the door of her room. Winston who had accompanied Lee had chuckled and shaken his head, as if to say, "What can you do with the old folks—except put up with them?"

Yes, they lived on forever these days. Doctors didn't let old people die, not as long as there were pills, injections, kidney machines, new drugs, all costing dearly. That was why Lee had to sell the house. For twelve years, since his mother had entered the nursing home, the house had been rented to a couple whose two children were in their teens now. Lee had never charged them much rent, because they couldn't afford a high rent, and Lee valued their reliability. But Lee's mother was now costing between five and six hundred dollars a week, her savings had run out five years ago, and Lee had borne the burden ever since, though Medicare paid some of it. His mother Edna wasn't ill, but she did need certain pills, tranquilizers alternating with pick-ups, plus checkups and special vitamins. Lee paid little attention to his mother's health, because it stayed the same year after year. She was ambulant but crochety, and never wrote to Lee, because he didn't write to her. Even before the nursing home, she had cursed Lee out by letter for imaginary faults and deeds, so Lee had washed his hands of his mother, except to pay her bills. An offspring owed that to a parent, Lee believed, just as a parent owed to a child love, care, and as much education as the parent could afford. Children were expensive and time-consuming, but the parents certainly were repaid when they became elderly and imposed the same burdens on their children.

Lee Mandeville was fifty-five, unmarried, and had a modestly successful antique shop in Chicago. He dealt in old furniture, a few good carpets, old pictures and frames, brass and silver items and silverware also. He was by no means a big wheel in the antique business, but he was known and respected in Chicago and beyond. He was trim of figure, not balding, and without much gray in his hair. His face was clean shaven, with a crease in either cheek, and he had rather heavy eyebrows above friendly, thoughtful blue-gray eyes. He liked meeting strangers in his shop, summing them up, finding out whether they wanted to buy something because it would look nice somewhere in their house or because they really fell in love with an object.

As the bus rocked and lumbered into Arlington Hills, Lee tensed himself, already uneasy, and unhappy. Well, he did not intend to see his mother this trip. He didn't want to see her, and he didn't have to. She was so far gone mentally that Lee had had power of attorney for nearly ten years. Winston had at last obtained his mother's signature for that. She had held out for months, not for any logical reason but out of stubbornness, and because she enjoyed making difficulties for other people. Twenty minutes to four, Lee saw from a glance at his wristwatch. He stood up and hauled his suitcase down from the rack before the bus had quite stopped.

"Lee!—How *are* you, Lee?"

Lee was surprised by the voice, and it took him a second to spot Win in the little crowd waiting for debarkers. "Win! *Hello!* I didn't expect to see you here!" Lee's smile was broad. They patted each other on the shoulder. "How're things?"

"Oh—much the same," Win replied. "Nothing much changes around here. That's all the luggage you've got? . . . My car's over here, Lee—and Kate and I expect you to be *our guest.* All right?" Win already had Lee's suitcase in his hand. Win was in his early sixties with straight gray hair that looked always windblown. He wore navy blue trousers and a blue shirt with no tie. Win was head of an insurance company that he himself had founded, and the Mandevilles had insured their house and cars with Win for decades.

"It's kind of you, Win, but honestly, for one night—I can just as well stay at the old Capitol, you know." Lee didn't want to say that he preferred to go to a hotel.

"Won't hear of it. Kate's got your room all ready."

Win was walking toward his car, and Lee went with him. After all, Win had been helpful, very, with Edna, and Win seemed really pleased to have him. "You win, Win," Lee said, smiling, "and thank you. How's Kate? And Mort?" Mort was their son.

"Oh—the same." Win stuck Lee's lightweight suitcase onto the back seat of his car. "Mort's working now in Bloomington. Car salesman."

"Still married?" Lee recalled some awful trouble with Mort's wife— she'd run off with another man, abandoned their small child, and then, Lee thought, they had got back together again.

"No, they finally arranged a—a divorce," Win said, and started the car.

Lee didn't know whether to say "Good" or not, so he said nothing. Now his mother, Lee thought. That was the next question. He didn't care how his mother was. Instead, Lee said, "I was thinking we might wind this business up this afternoon, Win. It's just a matter of signing a paper, isn't it?" The house in Barrett Avenue was sold, to a young couple named Varick—Ralph and Phyllis, Lee remembered from the real estate agent's letter.

"Ye-es," said Win, and his heavy hands opened on the steering wheel for a couple of seconds, then closed tightly. "I suppose we could."

Lee gathered that Win hadn't made an appointment as yet. "It's still old Graham, isn't it? He knows us both so well—can't we just barge in?"

"Sure—okay, Lee."

Win Greeves steered the car into Main Street, and Lee glanced at storefronts, shop signs, seeing a lot of change since he had been here last, and for the worse aesthetically. Main Street looked more crowded, both with people and shops. Maybe Graham's old office hadn't changed. Douglas Graham was a lawyer and notary public. He had drawn up a power of attorney statement years ago, at Lee's request, so that Lee could sign checks for his mother's bills, and Winston Greeves's name had been added also in executor capacity, because Win was on the scene in Arlington Hills, and even visited his mother sometimes—though his mother didn't always recognize him, Win said—and in the last years as Edna's bank account had grown low, Lee sent five hundred dollars or a thousand to bolster it every month or so. Win sent Lee the bank statements for the account now in Lee's name, and an explanation of the bills.

"I don't need the Varicks, I suppose," Lee said. "To be present when I sign, I mean."

"I know Ralph Varick's already signed," said Win. "Fine couple, those two. You should meet them, Lee."

"Well—not really necessary. Give them my best wishes—if you ever see them." Lee didn't want to go near the old house, didn't want to see it. The nice family, the Youngs, who couldn't afford to buy the house, were still there for the rest of this month, but Lee didn't want to visit them even merely to say hello. He felt sorry for them. He forced himself to ask the unavoidable. "And I suppose my mother's just the same too?"

Win chuckled and shook his head. "She's—yes—that's about it."

Don't they *ever* kick the bucket, Lee thought bitterly, and nearly laughed at himself. And after he had banked the money for the house, how much longer, how many more years would his mother live, eating up five or six hundred dollars a week? Now she was eighty-six. Couldn't she go on till ninety and ninety-one? Why not? Lee remembered three grandparents out of four, plus one maternal uncle, who had all died in their nineties.

"Here we are," said Win, pulling in at the curb.

Lee fished for a coin, and dropped it in the meter before Win could insert his. Doug Graham had no secretary, and came out of the office himself in response to the bell they had rung on entering his waiting room.

"Well, Lee—and Win. How are you, Lee? You're looking well." Doug Graham gave Lee a warm handshake. Doug was heavier than he had been ten years ago, in his late sixties now, a big man in a baggy beige suit that showed no sign of a proper crease.

"Quite all right, Doug. And you?" Lee wished he could have said friendlier words, but they didn't come for some reason. Doug had done many a service for Lee and his mother over the years. Lee remembered with embarrassment that Doug had talked his mother out of making a will some twenty years ago, which would have cut Lee out as only offspring and nearest of kin, and bestowed all on a young black woman who cleaned the house and who had talked her way into Edna's affections.

Doug Graham quietly and calmly arranged the few papers on his desk, and pointed out where Lee was to sign. "After you've read the agreement, of course, Lee," said Doug with a smile.

Lee glanced through. It was a bill of sale for the Barrett Avenue house, pretty plain and simple. Lee signed. The deed was there too, with Lee's father's signature, also that of Lee's grandfather, but before that a name that was not of the family. Ralph David Varick was the last name. Lee did not have to sign this.

"Hope you're not too sentimental about it, Lee," said Doug in his slow, deep voice. "After all, you're not here much of late—in the last years. We've missed you."

Lee shook his head. "Not sentimental, no."

The pen was handed to Winston Greeves, who got up to sign the purchase paper as witness.

"Sorry it has to be, though," said Doug, "somehow. And sorry about your mother."

Again Lee felt a twinge of shame, because Doug knew, everyone knew, that his mother was not merely senile but quietly insane. "Well—these things happen. At least she's not in pain," Lee said awkwardly.

"That *is* true. . . . Thank you, Win. And that about winds it up, I think. . . . How long're you here for, Lee?"

Lee told him just till tomorrow, because he had to get back to his shop in Chicago. He asked what he owed Doug, and Doug said nothing at all, and again Lee felt shame, because Doug must know that he had sold the house because he couldn't otherwise meet expenses.

"We need a little drink on this," said Doug, pulling out a whiskey bottle from a lower drawer in his desk. "It's just about quitting time anyway, so we deserve it."

They each had small, neat drinks, standing up. But the atmosphere remained sad and a little strained, Lee felt.

Ten minutes later, they were at the Greeveses' house—bigger than the house Lee had just signed away, with a bigger lawn and more expensive trees. Kate Greeves welcomed Lee as if he were one of the family, pressing his hand in both hers, kissing his cheek.

"Lee, I'm so glad Win persuaded you to stay! Come, I'll show you your room, then we can relax." She took him upstairs.

There was a smell of baking and of warm cinnamon from the kitchen. His room was neat and clean, furnished with factory-made dressing table and chairs and bed, but Lee had seen worse. The Greeveses were doing their best to be nice to him.

"I'd love to take a little walk," Lee said when he went back downstairs. "Hardly six. Still a lot of daylight—"

"Oh, no! Stay and talk, Lee. Or I'll *drive* you around, if you'd like to see the old town." Win seemed willing.

But that idea didn't appeal to Lee. He wanted to stretch his legs on his own, but he knew Win would protest that he'd have to walk fifteen minutes to get out of Rosedale, the residential section, and so on and so on. Lee found himself sitting in the living room with a strong scotch in his hands. Kate brought in a bowl of hot buttered popcorn.

The telephone rang, and the Greeveses exchanged a look, then Win went to get it in the hall.

Lee picked up an old glass paperweight with a spread blue butterfly in it. The paperweight was the size of a cake of soap and very pretty. He was about to ask Kate where she had got it from, when Win's voice saying *"No!"* made Lee keep his silence.

"*No,* I said," Win said softly but in a tone of repressed wrath. "And don't phone again tonight. I mean what I *say.*" There was a click as Win put the telephone down. When he returned to the living room, his hands were shaking slightly. He reached for his glass. "Sorry about that," he said to Lee with a nervous smile.

Something to do with Mort, Lee supposed. Maybe Mort himself. Lee thought it best not to ask questions. Kate also looked tense. Mort must be at least forty now, Lee thought. He was a weak type, and Lee remembered one adolescent scrape after another—a wrecked car, Mort picked up by the police for drunkenness somewhere, Mort marrying a girl because she was pregnant, the same wife Mort had just divorced, Win had said. Such troubles seemed silly to Lee, because they were so avoidable—compared to a deranged mother who lingered on and on.

"Not coming over, is he?" Kate whispered to Win as she bent to offer Win the popcorn bowl.

Win shook his head slowly and grimly.

Lee had barely heard Kate speak. They talked of other things during dinner, and only a little bit about Lee's mother. Her health was all right, she took walks in the garden there, came down to the dining room for every meal. Once a month there was a "birthday party" for everyone whose birthday fell during that month. There was TV, not in every room, but in the communal hall downstairs.

"She still reads the Bible, I suppose," said Lee, smiling a little.

"Oh, I suppose. There's one in every room there, I know," Win replied, and glanced at his wife, who responded by asking Lee how his shop in Chicago was doing.

As Lee replied, he thought about his mother, grim-lipped and gruesome without her false teeth which she didn't always care to wear, reading her Bible. What did she get out of it? Certainly not the milk of human kindness, but of course that phrase was Shakespeare's. Or had Jesus said it first? The Old Testament was bloodthirsty, vengeful, even barbaric in places. His mother had always, or frequently enough, said to him, "Read your Bible, Lee," when he was depressed, discouraged, or when he had been "tempted" maybe to buy a nice looking secondhand car on the installment plan, when he had been seventeen or eighteen. How innocent, buying a car on the installment plan, compared to what his mother had done when he was twenty-two! He had been engaged to Louisa Watts, madly in love with her, in love in a way, however, that could have lasted, that would have resulted in a good marriage, Lee believed. His mother had told Louisa that Lee had girls everywhere, prostitute favorites too, that in his car he drove to other towns for his fun. And so on. And Louisa had been only nineteen. She had believed that, and she had been hurt. *Goddamn my mother,* Lee thought. And what had his mother gained by her lies? Keeping him at home, for herself? She hadn't. Louisa had married another man in less than a year, moved somewhere, maybe New York, and Lee had left home and gone to San Francisco for a while, worked as a longshoreman, gone to New Orleans and done the same. If Louisa only hadn't been married, he would have tried again with her, because she was the only girl in the world for him. Yes, he had met other girls, four or five. He had wanted to marry, but had never been able to convince himself (and maybe not the other girls either) that marriage would work. Then he had gone to Chicago when he had been nearly thirty.

"You don't like the pie, Lee?" asked Kate.

Lee realized that he had barely touched the hot apple pie, that he was squeezing his napkin in his left hand as if it were someone's neck. "I do like the pie," Lee said calmly, and proceeded to finish it.

That night, Lee slept badly. Thoughts turned in his head, yet when he tried to devote a few minutes to thinking something out, he got nowhere. It was a pleasure for him to get out of bed at dawn, dress quietly, and sneak down the stairs for a walk before anyone else was up. He hadn't bothered shaving. Lee was out of the Rosedale area in less than ten minutes. The air was sweet and clear, coolish for May. The town was awakening. There were milk trucks making deliveries, mailmen of course, and a few workmen boarding early buses.

"Lee?—It's Lee Mandeville, isn't it?"

Lee looked into the face of a young man in his twenties with brown wavy hair, in a tweed suit with shirt and tie. Vaguely Lee remembered the face, but couldn't have come up with the name if his life had depended on it.

"Charles Ritchie!" said the young man, laughing. "Remember? I used to deliver groceries for your mother!"

"Oh, *sure.* Charlie." Lee smiled, remembering a skinny twelve-year-old who sometimes drank a soda pop in their kitchen. "Hey, aren't you missing your bus, Charlie?"

"Doesn't matter," said the young man, barely glancing at the bus that was pulling away. "What brings you here, Lee?"

"Selling the house. You remember the old house?"

"I sure do!—I'm sorry you're selling. I had the idea you might move back some time—for retirement or something."

Lee smiled. "I need the money, frankly. My mother's still alive, you know, and that costs a little. Not that I begrudge it, of course." He saw Charlie's face grow suddenly earnest.

Frowning, Charlie said, "I don't understand. Mrs. Mandeville died fo— yes, about five years ago. Yes, I—I went to her funeral, Lee." His eyes stared into Lee's.

Lee realized that it was true. He realized that this was why Win had insisted upon Lee's spending the night with him, so he wouldn't run into citizens of the town who might tell him the truth.

"What's the matter, sir? I'm sorry I brought it up. But *you* said—"

Lee gently took his elbow from the young man's grip, and smiled. "Sorry. I suppose I looked about to faint! *Yes.*" Lee took a breath and made an effort to pull himself together. "Yes, of course she's dead. I don't know what I was talking about, Charlie."

"Oh, that's *okay,* Lee . . . You're really all right?"

"Sure I'm all right. And that's another bus coming, isn't it?"

Through a haze of pale yellow morning sunlight and pale green leaves, the bus approached. Lee moved away, waved good-bye, ignoring Charlie's parting words. Lee walked slowly for several minutes, not caring in what direction his steps took him.

Now Lee realized that the Hearthside people, the accountant there, or someone, must be in league with Win Greeves, because Lee had seen real bills from the Hearthside in the last five years. Lee felt himself physically weak, as if he were walking in mud instead of on a cement pavement. And what the hell was he going to do about it? Five years. And in dollars? Twenty or twenty-four thousand dollars a year times five were—Lee smiled wryly, and stopped trying to calculate. He looked up at a street marker, and saw that he stood on a corner at which Elmhurst intersected South Billingham. He took Elmhurst, which he thought led, eastward, back to Rosedale. All he really wanted from the Greeveses' house was his suitcase.

When Lee got back to the house, he found the door unlocked, and noticed an aroma of coffee and bacon. Win came at once down the hall.

"Lee! We were a little worried! Thought maybe you'd sleepwalked right out of the house!" Win was grinning.

"No, no, just taking a walk—as I wanted to do last night." Win was staring at him. Was he pale, Lee wondered. Probably. Lee realized that he could still be polite. That was easy. It was also safe and natural to him. "Hope I didn't hold you up, Win?" Lee looked at his wristwatch. "Ten of eight now."

"Not—one—bit!" Win assured him. "Come and have some breakfast."

Now the food really refused to go down, but Lee kept his polite manner, sipped coffee and poked at his scrambled eggs. He saw Win and Kate exchange glances again, glances that Win tried to avoid, though his eyes kept being drawn back to his wife's as if he were hypnotized.

"Did you—uh—have a nice walk, Lee?" Win asked.

"Very nice, thanks. I ran into—Charles Ritchie," Lee said carefully and with some respect, as if Charles had been lifted from a grocer's delivery boy to the status of one of the disciples bearing a message of truth. "He used to deliver groceries for my mother." Lee noticed that Win was not doing much better than he with his breakfast.

The tension grew a few degrees tighter, then Kate said:

"Win said you wanted to leave today, Lee. Can't you change your mind?"

That remark was so false, Lee suddenly blew up, inwardly. But outwardly he kept his cool, except that he tossed his napkin down. "Sorry, but

I can't. No." His voice was hollow and hoarse. Lee stood up. "If you'll excuse me." He left the table and went up to his room.

Just as he was closing his suitcase, Win came in. Now Win looked white in the face, and ten years older.

Lee felt almost sorry for him. "Yes, I heard about my mother. I think that's what's on your mind. Isn't it, Win?" Now Lee had his small suitcase in his hand, and he was ready to leave the room.

Win tiptoed to the door and closed it. His hand that he drew away from the doorknob was shaking, and he lifted it and his other hand and covered his face. "Lee, I want you to know I'm ashamed of myself."

Lee nodded once, impatiently, unseen by Win.

"Morton was in such trouble. That damned wife of his . . . She hasn't turned loose, there's no divorce, and it's a damned mess. The girl—I mean the wife's pregnant again and she's accusing Mort now, but I doubt if that's true, I really do. But she keeps asking for money and legally—"

"Who the hell cares?" Lee interrupted. He squeezed the suitcase handle, eager to leave, but Win blocked him like an ugly mountain. Win's eyes, wide and scared, met Lee's.

He reminded Lee of an animal, sure that it was going to be slaughtered in the next seconds, but in fact Lee had never seen an animal in such circumstances. "I suppose," Lee said, "the nursing home had some kind of understanding with you. I remember the bills, anyway—recent ones."

Win said miserably, "Yes, yes."

Now Lee recalled Doug Graham's words to him, when Lee had said that at least his mother wasn't in pain now, and Doug had replied that that was true. Doug knew that his mother was dead, but their conversation wouldn't have caused him to repeat that fact, and of course he had assumed Lee knew it. Lee made a start for the door.

"Lee!" Win nearly caught him by the sleeve, but he drew his hand back, as if he didn't dare touch Lee. "What're you going to do, Lee?"

"I don't know . . . I think I'm in a state of shock."

"I know I'm to blame. Just me. But if you only knew the straits I was in, *am* in. Blackmail—first from Mort's wife, blackmailing him, I mean, and now—"

Lee understood: Mort the son was now blackmailing his father about this business. How low could human beings sink? For some bizarre reason, Lee wanted to smile. "How did she die?" He asked in a courteous tone. "Stroke, I suppose?"

"Died in her sleep," Win murmured. "Hardly anybody came to the funeral. She'd made such enemies, y'know, with her sharp tongue . . . The man—"

"What man?" Lee asked, because Win had stopped.

"The man at the Hearthside. His name is Victor Malloway. He's—you could say he's every bit as guilty as I am. But he's the only one—else." Again Win looked pitiably at Lee. "What're you going to do, Lee?"

Lee took a breath. "Well—what, for instance?" Win did not reply to that question, and Lee opened the door. "Bye-bye, Win, and thanks."

Downstairs, Lee said the same thanks and good-bye to Kate. The words she said did not register on Lee. Something about taking him to the bus terminal, or calling a taxi. ". . . quite all right," Lee heard himself saying. "I'll make it by myself."

He was gone, free, alone, walking with the suitcase in the direction of town, of the bus terminal. He walked all the way at an easy and regular pace, arrived at the terminal around ten, and waited patiently for the bus to the bigger town with the airport. He still felt dazed, but thoughts came anyway. They were bitter, unhappy thoughts that flowed through his mind like a polluted stream. He detested his thoughts.

And even on the moving bus, his thoughts went on, memories of his mother's odious vanity when she had been younger, her henpecking of his father (dead in his late fifties of cancer), of his mother's unremitting dislike and criticism of every girl he had ever brought to the house. Also his mother's backbiting at her own friends and neighbors, even at the ones who tried to be friendly and kind to her. His mother had always found something "wrong" with them. And now, the truly awful thing, the terrifying fact that her life had wound up like a classic tragedy played rather behind the scenes instead of on a stage in view of lots of people. His mother had been finished off, as it were, by a few shabby crooks like Win Greeves and son, and the fellow called Victor—Mallory, was it? Indeed, they had been feeding like vultures on her rotting corpse for the past five years.

Lee did not relax until he had opened the front door of his antique shop, and surveyed the familiar interior of shining furniture, the warm glint of copper, the soft curves of polished cherrywood. He left the CLOSED sign hanging in the door, and relocked it from the inside. He must return to normal, he told himself, must carry on as usual and forget Arlington Hills, or he would become ill himself—polluted, like his river of ugly memories on the bus and on the plane. Lee bathed and shaved and by five in the afternoon removed his CLOSED sign. He had one visitor after that, a man who drifted around looking, and didn't buy anything, but that was no matter.

Only occasionally, in moments when he was tired, or disappointed about something that had gone wrong, did Lee think of the false friend Win, and wish him ill. *An eye for an eye, a tooth for a tooth,* the Bible said, the Old Testament part, anyway. But he really *didn't* want that, Lee told himself, otherwise he would be doing something now to bring Win Greeves to justice, to hit back at him. Lee could even sue him and win handily, recover expenses and then some by forcing the Greeveses to sell their handsome house in Rosedale. With that money, he could buy his own house back, his birthplace. But Lee realized that he didn't want the two-story white house where he had been born. His mother's spirit had spoiled that house, made it evil.

From Win Greeves there was silence, not a letter or a line from him of further explanation, or of an offer to repay part of what he had wrongly taken. Now and then, Lee did imagine Win worried, probably very anxious as he tried to guess what Lee might be doing about the situation. Nearly a month had passed since Lee's visit to Arlington Hills. Wouldn't Win and Kate and Mort be assuming that Lee Mandeville had taken a lawyer and that he was preparing his case against Winston Greeves and the man at the Hearthside?

Then Lee received, to his surprise, a letter from Arlington Hills addressed by typewriter and with Win's company's name, Eagle Insurance, and the spread eagle trademark in the upper left corner of the envelope. Lee turned the envelope over—no name on the back—and for a few seconds wondered what might be in it. An abject apology, maybe even a check, however small? Absurd! Or was Eagle Insurance sending him a last bill for his mother's house insurance? Lee laughed at this idea and opened the letter. It was a short typewritten note.

Dear Lee,

After all our troubles, there is one more. Mort died last Tuesday night, after running into a man and seriously injuring him (but not killing him, thank God) and then hitting a tree in his car himself. I can almost say it's a blessing, considering the trouble Mort has caused himself and us. I thought you might like to hear. We are all sad here.

Yours,
Win

Lee gave a sigh, a shrug. Well. What was he supposed to reply, or think, or care, about this? Was Win possibly expecting a letter of condolence from him? This piece of information, Lee thought, affected him not at all. Morton Greeves's life or death was simply nothing to Lee.

Later that day, when Lee was tugging off rubber boots and feeling a bit tired—he had been paint-stripping with a water hose in his back alley—he had a vision of Mort dead and bleeding, having hit a tree in his car, and thought, "Good!" *An eye for an eye . . .* For a few seconds he relished a vengeance achieved. Morton was Win's only son, only child. Worthless all his life, and now dead! Good! Now Lee had his money for the Arlington Hills house he had sold, and he could, if he wished, buy a property he had looked at in a suburb of Chicago, a pleasant house near the lake. He could have a little boat.

An image of his mother came to Lee as he undressed for bed that night, his mother in her big wicker rocking chair in the living room, reading her Bible, peering up at him grim-mouthed (though with her teeth), and asking him why he didn't read the Bible more often. The Bible! Had it made his mother any better, kinder to her fellow men? A lot of the Bible seemed to be anti-sex, too. His mother was, certainly. If sex was so bad, Lee thought, how had his mother ever conceived him, ever got married in the first place?

"No," Lee said aloud, and shook himself as if he were shaking something off. No, he wasn't going to entertain any thoughts of the Bible, or of vengeance, in regard to Win's family, or in regard to the man at the Hearthside whose name by now Lee had forgotten, except for the first name Victor. What kind of Victor was he, for instance? Lee smiled at the absurdity of his name, the vainglorious ring of it.

Lee had a few friends in the neighborhood, and one of them, Edward Newton, a man of Lee's age and owner of a nearby bookshop, dropped in on Lee one afternoon as he often did, to have a coffee in the back of the shop. Lee had told Edward and others of his friends that his mother had been ill when he visited Arlington Hills, and that she had died a few days after his visit. Now Edward had found a small item in the newspaper.

"Did you know him? I thought I'd show it to you, because I remember the name Hearthside, where your mother was." Edward pointed to an item three inches long in the newspaper he had brought.

SUICIDE OF NURSING HOME
SUPERINTENDENT, 61

The report said that Victor C. Malloway, superintendent of the Hearthside retirement and nursing home in Arlington Hills, Indiana, had killed himself by closing his car and piping in the exhaust from a running engine in his own garage at home. He left no note of explanation. He was survived by a wife, Mary, a son Philip and daughter Marion, and three grandchildren.

"No," Lee said. "No, I never met him, but I've heard his name, yes."

"I suppose it's a depressing atmosphere—old people, you know. And *they're* dying pretty frequently there, I'd suppose."

Lee agreed, and changed the subject.

Win was next, Lee supposed. What would happen to him, or what would he do to himself? Maybe nothing, after all. His own son was dead, and how much of that death might be called suicide, Lee wondered. Surely Mort had known from Win that the game was up, that no more money would be coming from Lee Mandeville. Surely too Win and Victor Malloway would have had a couple of desperate conversations. Lee still remembered Win's defeated and terrified face in that upstairs bedroom in Arlington Hills. Enough was enough, Lee thought. Win was a half-destroyed man now.

With some of his money, Lee invested in ten Turkish carpets whose quality and colors especially pleased him. He was sure he could sell five or six at a profit, and he put a sign in his window to the effect that an exceptional opportunity to buy quality Turkish carpets was now offered, inquire within. The ones he did not sell would go well in the house in the suburbs on which Lee had put a down payment. Lee felt increasingly happy. He gave a birthday party on his own birthday, invited ten friends out to a restaurant, then took them back to his apartment and turned on the lights in his shop. One of his friends played on a piano that Lee had in his shop section, and there was a lot of laughter, because the piano was slightly out of tune. Everyone sang and drank champagne and toasted Lee's health.

Lee began to furnish his new house, which was smaller than the Arlington Hills house of his family, but still had two stories and a lovely fruit garden around it. It was almost thirty miles from Lee's shop, so he did not drive there every day, but used the place mainly for weekends, though the distance was not so great that he couldn't drive in the evening to stay the night there, if he chose. Now and again he thought, with a shock, of his mother, and the fact that she had been dead nearly *six* years, not the eight or ten months that he had told all his friends. And he thought without a tweak of resentment of the hundred thousand dollars or so down the

drain, money which Win had pocketed and shared with Mort and the suicide Victor. The score had been evened. A score, yes, like the score in a
game that Lee was not interested in—a domino score, an anagram-game
score. Best to forget it. All deaths were sad. Lee had not lifted a finger, yet
Mort and Victor were dead. It had not been necessary to gouge out an eye.

Autumn came, and Lee was busy with weatherstripping in his house,
when he heard a news item that caught his attention. He had heard the
name Arlington Hills, but he had missed the first part. It was something
about the death of a man in his own house due to a bullet wound possibly
self-inflicted. Lee worked on, feeling vaguely troubled. Could Winston
Greeves have been the name the announcer had said? The news would be
repeated in an hour, unless something more important crowded out the
Arlington Hills bit. Lee continued measuring his insulating tape, cutting,
sticking down. He worked on his knees in blue jeans.

If this were Win Greeves, it was really too much, Lee thought. Enough
vengeance. More than enough. Well, there were lots of people in Arlington
Hills, and maybe it hadn't been Win. But Lee felt troubled, angry in a
strange way, and nervous. The minutes crept as Lee worked, and when 5
P.M. came, Lee listened carefully to the news report. It was the last item
before the weather: Winston Greeves, aged sixty-four, of Arlington Hills,
Indiana, had died from a bullet wound that might or might not have been
self-inflicted. His wife said that he had recently acquired a pistol for target
practice.

Lee had listened to the news standing, and suddenly his shoulders bent
and he lowered his head. He felt weak for a few seconds, then gradually his
strength returned, and with it the strange anger that he had known an hour
ago. It was too much. *My cup runneth over . . .* No, that wasn't it. Christ had
said that. Christ wouldn't have approved of *this.* Lee was about to cover his
face with his hands, when he remembered Win making the same gesture.
Lee took his hands down and straightened. He went down the stairs to his
living room.

To the left and right of his fireplace there were bookshelves set into the
wall. He reached firmly for a black leatherbound book. This was the Bible,
the same one his mother had used to read, with the top and bottom of its
spine all worn and showing brown where the black had worn off the
leather. Lee quickly found where the Old Testament left off and the New
Testament began, and he seized the thicker Old in his left hand and tore it
from the binding. He thrust it like something unclean away from him and
into the fireplace where there was no fire now, and he wiped his left hand

on the side of his blue jeans. The pages had all spilled apart, thin and dry. Lee struck a match.

He watched the pages burn, and become even more gossamery and quite black, and he knew he had accomplished nothing. This was not the only Old Testament in the world. He had made an angry gesture to satisfy only himself. And he felt not at all satisfied, or cleansed, or rid of anything.

A letter of condolence to Kate Greeves, Lee thought, was due. Yes, he would write it this evening. Why not now? Words came to his mind as he moved toward the table where he kept his paper and pens. A longhand letter, of course. Kate had lost her son and her husband in a span of only a few months.

> Dear Kate,
> By accident this afternoon I heard on my radio the sad news about Win. I can realize that it is an awful blow to receive so shortly after the death of Morton. I would like you to know that I send you my sincerest sympathies now and that I can appreciate your grief . . .

Lee wrote on smoothly and slowly. The curious thing was that he did feel sympathy for Kate. He bore her no grievance at all, though she was a partner to her husband in his deception. She was, somehow, a separate entity. This fact transcended guilt or the necessity to forgive. Lee signed his name. He meant every word of the letter.

I Despise Your Life

A hole is a hole is a hole, Ralph was thinking as he stared at the keyhole. The key was in his hand, ready to stick in, but still he hesitated. He could just as well ring the doorbell! He was expected.

Ralph turned and clumped in a circle in his cowboy boots, and faced the door again. It was his father's apartment after all, and he had the key. Ralph set his teeth, his lower lip curled forward, and he stuck the key in the lock and turned it.

There was a light in the living room, ahead and to the right.

"Hello, Dad?" Ralph called, and walked toward the living room. A battered leather handbag swung from a strap over his shoulder.

"Hi there, Ralph!" His father was on his feet, in gray flannels and sweater, house shoes, and with a pipe in his hand. He looked his son up and down.

Ralph, taller than his father, walked past him. Everything neat and orderly as usual, Ralph saw, two sofas, armchairs, one with a book on its arm where his father must just have been reading.

"And how's life?" asked his father. "You're looking . . . pretty well."

Was he? Ralph realized that his jeans were dirty, and recalled that he hadn't bothered shaving even yesterday. The left side of his short-cut, blondish hair was a dark pink, because someone had smeared a handful of dye into it suddenly, sometime last night or rather early this morning. Ralph knew his father wasn't going to mention the dye, but his father's face bore a faintly amused smile. Not nice, Ralph thought. Such people were the enemy. Mustn't forget that.

"Sit down, boy. What brings you here? . . . Like a beer?"

"Yeah, sure. Thanks." Ralph was at that moment feeling a little fuzzy in the head. He had been a lot sharper less than an hour ago, higher and sharper, when he had been smoking with Cassie, Ben and Georgie back at the dump. The *dump*. That was what had brought him here, and he'd better get down to it. Meanwhile a beer was what they called socially acceptable. Ralph took the cold can that his father extended.

"You probably don't want a glass."

Ralph didn't, and so what? He threw his head back a little, smiling, and sipped from the triangle in the can. Another hole, this triangle. "Life's full of holes, isn't it?"

Now his father grinned. "What do you mean by that? . . . Sit down somewhere, Ralph. You look tired. Had a late night?" His father took the armchair, put a bookmark in the book and laid the book on a side table.

"Well, yeah—practicing as usual. Always gets later than we think." Ralph lowered his lean figure to the sofa. "We're going—" Now where was he? He had meant to tell his father about the record they were going to cut next Sunday at a place in the Bronx. The Plastics, Ralph's group called itself. Cassie was great on the bass fiddle, unusual for a girl. Cassie was great all round. She was their mascot, their pet, and she even cooked. "There's a kitchen where we're living," Ralph said finally.

"Oh, I assumed that. It's a big apartment, isn't it?"

"Well, yeah, but it's a loft. One very big room, then a smaller room, kitchen and bath. And that's—I need a hundred dollars now to hold up my end of it. The rent. That is, till we cut this record Sunday in the Bronx. That's what we're rehearsing now."

His father nodded calmly. "Then the record will be marketed?"

"Naturally," said Ralph, aware that he lied, or that the "marketing" was at best dubious. "Ten songs. That's a big deal. We're calling it 'Night on the Tiles' by the Plastics."

His father fiddled with his pipe, poked at the tobacco with a nail-like gadget.

Well, Ralph thought with impatience as the silence went on. "It's not that I like to ask you—" But that wasn't true, he didn't mind a damn asking for a hundred. What was a hundred to his father? The price of a business lunch!

"This time it's no, Ralph. Sorry."

"What do you mean?" Ralph felt a small, polite smile grow on his face, a smile of feigned incredulity. "What's a hundred to you? We owe the rent there, we have to chip in, and we want this record cut. That's business and it's pretty important!"

"And the record before that and before that? Do these records *exist?*" Stephen Duncan went on over his son's protest, "You're twenty, Ralph, you're behaving like somebody *ten,* and you're asking me to keep on subsidizing it."

His father smiled, but he was hotting up. That seldom happened. Ralph said, "You're giving my mother a thousand a month and you don't even feel it."

"Would you like to ask your mother for a hundred?" Steve gave a laugh.

No, that was a stone wall. Ralph's mother had gone back to California, to her parents' hometown. His mother and dad had been divorced about a year now. His mother had wanted the divorce, and there'd been a pretty nasty story about "the other man," his mother's lover Bert, but their affair had broken up after the divorce, and that wasn't the point, as far as Ralph and his mother were concerned. His mother didn't like his lifestyle, had been surprisingly unsympathetic when Cornell had kicked him out for bad grades in the middle of his sophomore year, and when Ralph had taken up with some musicians in New York his mother had fairly stopped talking to him. Even his father had been more understanding then. And here was his father making tons of money with his tools plant in New Jersey, with his house and a boat in Long Island, and balking at a hundred dollars! Ralph felt like yelling to his father that he was a tightwad, forty-six years old and living in the past, but caution warned him to take it easy, that all might not be lost today. "It's an emergency, dad. Just these next two weeks—are really important and if we—"

"Oh, for God's sake, Ralph, how many times have you said that? Pull yourself together and get a job! Any kind of job. Work behind a counter! Better men than you have started that way."

This was the enemy coming out. Ralph's lower lip curled from his teeth, as it had when he had stuck the key in the keyhole, but he kept his tone low and polite. "That's pretty negative, what you're saying. That's really death and the destruction of life."

His father laughed and shook his head. "What've you had today? Acid? . . . You've had something. You talk about death and you can't even keep yourself in a healthy state. Who're you fooling, Ralph?"

"I haven't had anything today, but we were working late last night. Rehearsing. We do work. And we write our own music. *Ben* writes our music."

Again the superior-looking nod from his father. "You never showed any particular interest in music till a few months ago. Clarinet now. A fine instrument, Mozart wrote for it, and you use it for rubbish. Face it, Ralph. The Plastics! You're well named!" His father stood up, his lips a straight line of tension. "Sorry, Ralph, but I've got to leave the house in about ten minutes. Got to go to the Algonquin to meet a man who's just arrived from Chicago. Work, you know? . . . This music thing, Ralph—I see it all over, mediocre pop bands—"

"Rock," said Ralph.

"Rock, all right. The music phase might as well be part of a school curriculum. A year of guitar, clarinet or whatever. Third-rate music and then it's all dropped."

His father was trying, a little bit, to be friendly, Ralph could see. "All right, maybe it's a phase. But give me a hand with it for a while. Would that kill you?"

"It might kill you. You've lost weight even. I can imagine the junk food you kids eat."

Ralph got to his feet, staggering very slightly, but that was because of his boot heels. He was ready to leave, more than ready. "I frankly think your whole life is junk."

"I don't think you mean that . . . Take it easy, Ralph."

Ralph was on his way to the door. When he had opened it, he turned as if automatically, because he hadn't thought to, and said, "Bye, Dad."

Twenty minutes later, he was home at the dump on the edge of SoHo. Ralph had walked a little, walking off his disappointment, trying to, then had caught a bus downtown. And here he was, breathing again. Home! The tall white walls and the white ceiling way up there were like the wide open spaces! Cassie had the stereo up high and was dancing to it by herself, snapping her fingers gently. She gave Ralph barely a nod when she saw him, but Ralph didn't mind. He was smiling. Ben, raking his guitar along with the electronic music, yelled a "Hi!" In the bathroom, a fellow strange to Ralph stood in shorts washing his hair at the basin, and Georgie was sloshing around in the tub. Ralph wanted to use the toilet, and did. When Ralph went back into the living room, a fellow and a girl whom Ralph didn't know came out of the small bedroom in the corner. Now these two sat down on one of the two pushed-together double beds that served as a big sofa in the daytime. The two lit cigarettes, Cassie was smiling and yelling something at them—Ralph couldn't hear through the music—and Ralph saw that the two newcomers had dropped their coats in the corner by the trestle table, where all their guests dropped their coats. Was a party on for tonight? Hardly eight o'clock now. Early for arrivals.

Suddenly Ralph had an idea: they'd give a rent-raising party. Ralph wasn't the only one of the four who was short of rent money just now. They could charge five dollars for admission—or better make it three—and people could bring their own booze or wine or whatever.

Ralph approached Cassie and shouted his idea.

Cassie's blue-gray eyes lit up, she nodded, and went over to scream it at Ben.

All they had to do was notify the right people, maybe twenty or thirty, Ralph thought. These might bring along a few other people, but the fewer right people would furnish the money. It was Wednesday. They'd make the party for Saturday.

"Come at *nine!*" Cassie was shrieking into the telephone. "Tell Teddie and Marcia, will you? That'll save me a call."

The electronic tape had now come to the human voice bit, which always made Ralph think they were chanting:

> *You've had it now . . .*
> *You've had it now . . .*

Now how was that meant? That you were finished, or that you'd just had something good? Like Cassie. Cassie belonged to all three of them just now, Georgie the pianist, Ben the guitar man, and himself. That was good. No arguments, no silly jealousy anywhere. None of the crap that bothered dead people like his father.

"Dead *people!*" Ralph shouted, raising a booted foot, lifting a hand. His fingers struck the brim of his secondhand Stetson, and reminded him that he still had it on. "Saw my *dad* today!" Ralph yelled, taking his Stetson off with a flourish.

But nobody heard him. The fellow who had been washing his hair came out of the bathroom with a towel over his head, bumped into Cassie and went on, bumped into the double beds and plunged down. The pair of strangers had left.

Around midnight they ate frankfurters, boiled up by Cassie, in the kitchen. Mustard lay in a big plate on the kitchen table. The music continued. Cassie brought a stick of coke from the hiding place (which kept changing) in the little bedroom, and Georgie did the honors, scraping away with a razor blade at the white stick on a piece of flat but jagged-edged marble that he held on his leather-covered thighs. He lined up carefully and equitably fourteen rows of white powder, which they all sniffed in polite and leisurely turn. Five takers, twice taking, left four rows to spare.

Ralph gallantly offered his second helping to Cassie, who rewarded him with a smile and a kiss on the lips. He was sitting next to her then, on an edge of the double bed. All five sat on the edges, lounging inward toward the marble slab in the center.

Gotta wrangle oh-and-oh-and-oh . . .

Did anyone hear those words but Ralph?

The fellow who had washed his hair later got unceremoniously thrown down the stairs by Ben, who could sometimes lose his temper.

"*That's* not very nice!" Cassie yelled, as she danced around the living room, snapping her fingers in her easy way.

Ralph didn't ask what had happened. He thought Cassie had said earlier that the boy had brought the coke, and if so, he'd surely been paid for it. Hadn't he? And did it matter? No. The rent mattered. And they'd get that. Ralph kept his eyes on Cassie, though she was dancing with Georgie. Ben was on his guitar again. Ralph didn't want to dance, he wanted to sleep.

And later it was Ralph who was in the same bed with Cassie, in the little bedroom. He couldn't make it with her, and didn't really try. It was great just to hold a girl in your arms, as they said in the old songs.

The party idea had made progress by the next noon, when the four of them were having coffee and Danish in the kitchen.

"It'll be one giant disco," said Ben, "and we'll put the eats on the beds, so people can lounge on the floor there, pickin'."

"Surrealist *fruit* deco. I know what *I'll* do." Georgie, wide-eyed, his blond hair waxed into points, munched his pastry.

"Paper cups. Safer if stuff gets broken. Have we got money for paper cups?" This from Cassie.

"We got at least fifty jam jars," Ralph put in. "Now listen, we want this to pay off. You think we should make a very *selective* guest list? Like twenty we're sure can pay, so there won't be a mob that can't?"

"Na-ah," Ben said. "We stick up an invite in the Meetcha with price of admission loud and clear, see? No three buck-see, no entree . . . They'll come!"

Saturday was only two days off. They'd get hardly any sleep Saturday, Ralph realized, but the date in the Bronx wasn't till noon, nothing ever got started there till 3 P.M. and on pills they'd make it, and maybe do the record even better. They'd be doing only five songs Sunday, half the record.

That afternoon, Cassie made a poster on a big piece of cardboard to be tacked on a wall of the Meetcha Bar down the street.

ROOF RAISIN'
RENT RAISIN'
PARTY!
SAT. NITE 9 PM ONWARD
103 FROTT ST. (3rd FLOOR)
BRING YOUR RAISIN
ALL WELCOME (this ain't no church)
DISCO ELECTRONIC
ADMISSION $3.00
AND BRING YOUR OWN POWDER, JUICE, Etc.

The last line, Cassie conceded, was a halfway thing between saying no refreshments would be offered (untrue), and a suggestion that if people really had a preference as to drink and other things, they should bring their own so they'd be sure and get it. Cassie had been imbibing beer as she worked, and after an hour she was tired, but picked up at the boys' praise of her artwork. She had drawn a couple of nudes dancing, with real raisins glued on where the sex organs would have been. The nude figures were lanky and blue-colored.

"Really great!" Ben said. "Eye-*catching!*"

Cassie flopped on a bed on her back, smiling, and closed her eyes, her arms curled above her head. She looked lovely to Ralph, with her thighs bulging her jeans, shirt buttons straining over her breasts that were partly visible through the gaps.

Ralph was assigned to put the poster up, and went out with it, taking along also an old envelope in which Georgie had put six or more thumbtacks. For some reason (well, Ralph knew why), he was considered just a little more square than the others, more respectable even. Ralph didn't care much for that, and maybe it wouldn't last forever. So far he hadn't run up a bill with Ed Meecham, who owned the Meetcha, whereas the others had. Small bills, of course, because Ed didn't give credit higher than twenty dollars. Into this wooden-tabled, wooden-chaired establishment Ralph clumped in his cowboy boots with the poster in hand, and at once glanced around the walls, looking for a free and suitable place. The walls were already pretty much filled by art exhibition posters, announcements of sales of secondhand items, apartment-sharing opportunities, and cartoons of the patrons. Ralph greeted a couple of fellows hunched over beer or coffee at the tables, and made his way to Ed Meecham behind the bar at the back.

"Okay if I put this up, Ed?"

Ed, bald, with a mustache like a black and gray shaving brush, eyed the poster sharply as if examining it for porn—and maybe he was—then nodded consent. "If you find a spot, Ralph."

"Thanks, Ed." Ralph felt flattered because Ed had called him by name. Ed knew him, of course, but up to now hadn't called him anything. Funny how little things like that built up the ego, Ralph thought. That was what the group at the dump spent a lot of time talking about—ego—what you thought of *yourself*. It was important. Ralph's newfound confidence inspired him to tack, smoothly and with suitable speed, Cassie's poster over a small poster of graffiti which Ralph considered the clientele had laughed at long enough. Ralph waved good-bye and departed.

Back at the loft building, Ralph glanced at the mailbox before climbing the stairs. Two items. The box had a lock, but it had been broken. To Ralph's surprise, one envelope was addressed to him in his father's large yet angular hand with his genuine pen. His father didn't like ballpoints. Ralph climbed the stairs, reported his success with the poster-fixing, and went into the kitchen to look at his letter. Ben and Georgie were working with guitar and piano, talking also. They'd already had a practice session that day, and Ben wanted another, but there were still five minutes to read a letter, and maybe his father had even enclosed a check, Ralph thought as he picked open the envelope of sturdy white paper. No stamp on it. His father had delivered the letter. Ralph had noticed that at once downstairs, but now that fact—or something—made his fingers shake.

There was no check in the letter. It went, after the date which was Wednesday, yesterday:

Dear Ralph,

It is late in the evening but I feel inspired or compelled to write a few words to you by way of explaining my attitude, which I know you consider wrong, inhuman perhaps, or plain blind. So it may come as a relief to you to know that I've decided not to interfere or try to influence you from now on. Every human being has the right to make his own life. Birds must fly the nest. So did I when I left my parents exactly at your age, 20, and went to try my luck in Chicago and then in New York. You have the same right.

And I realize that what seems to me wrong or unwise may be for you—right. At any rate, you are a man and you should be able to and be allowed to stand on your own feet.

I think this may help clear the atmosphere and enable us to have a better relationship, because God knows it cannot be pleasant for a son to sense "parental disapproval" all the time, even if for the most part you shrug it off.

However if you're sick, you know very well I'm here to look after you. You are not alone in the world, Ralph, just free. And my good wishes and love are with you.

Your dad, ever,
Steve

P.S. I know that the absence of your mother from the household has not helped, hasn't made you any happier or stronger. I am bitterly and personally sorry about that, and I am no happier for it either. We should both (you and I) realize that we are not the only father and son in the world who have had to experience the same thing.

Ralph felt shocked, in a strange and profound way. His father had cut him off. That P.S.—Well, they'd been over that, lots of times, in few words every time, but lots of times. That divorce had been his *mother's* fault, that "other man" and all that. His father had never wanted a divorce, in spite of Bert who had disappeared as his father had thought he would. Ralph knew his mother had also been disappointed in him, Ralph. But the divorce remarks in the letter weren't what upset Ralph. It was his father's washing his hands of him. And such a polite way of saying it: You have the same right. Ralph was still under twenty-one. Wasn't he still a minor? Well, no, if you could vote at eighteen, Ralph recalled.

"Love *letters*—in—the—sand—" Georgie came into the kitchen singing. "Somebody let you down?"

Ralph tried to get the frown off his face. "Na-ah. Letter from my dad. No dough.—Mister No-Dough."

"Well, you knew that." Georgie poured himself some cold coffee from the pot on the stove, and upended a cellophane bag of potato chips into his mouth, a bag nearly empty. "Let's go again, Ralphie? Another half hour or so. 'Airport Bird' now." Georgie gestured towards the living room.

Ralph got his clarinet from its place under the foot of one of the double beds, where he had put it while he tacked the poster. He had to lift the bed to get it, rake the case out with his foot, but at least the instrument was always safe there, unstolen, unstepped on. The record-cutting would cost seventy-five dollars. They had a deal with Mike, the man in the Bronx. He distributed their records to cut-rate pop record shops which tried to push new groups, according to Mike. So far the Plastics hadn't had any revenue from that, but what they had created was *on record,* and there were two earlier records here at the dump. They practiced, Cassie included. It was after six, and the ceiling spotlights were on, three pink ones, a couple of blues, but mainly white ones. Someone had said such lights ran into big electricity bills, but the lights gave atmosphere, and after the music got going, who thought about an electricity bill? Ralph tried to play with especial care and exactitude, letting himself go only in the finale of "Fried Chicks," the song that would be number five, the last, on the record Sunday.

But Ralph's thoughts, most of his thoughts, were on his father and he couldn't shake them off. Amazing. He was upset. And ordinarily he would have said to his chums, "I'm uptight today, sort of thrown." But that evening he didn't say it, even in the break they took around nine in the kitchen, where Cassie was stirring up a tomato sauce for their spaghetti dinner. Ben lit a joint which they passed around. Georgie went out for lettuce and a bottle of Italian table wine, the kind that came in a big glass jug. No meat for the spaghetti sauce, Cassie announced, but it was going to taste good anyway. And his father thought they didn't eat properly, Ralph remembered.

Why not invite Steve to the party? If his father condescended to come, he could see that they ran a going household with clean walls, that they weren't a bunch of apes. Ralph knew his father thought they never knew what day of the week it was, that they lived off their parents—absolutely not true in the case of Georgie and Ben, who gave piano and guitar lessons—and that they never washed their clothes, whereas the tub had clothes soaking in it half the time, and Cassie was a great ironer.

"Hey, does anybody *mind,*" Ralph began loudly, but the hi-fi was on, Ben had just said something funny, so everyone was laughing. Everyone now included two new people, a boy and girl who must have arrived with Georgie when he came back with lettuce and wine. Ralph tried again. "Hey, Cass! I feel like inviting my *father* Saturday night. Okay?"

Cassie, smiling, shrugged a little as usual. It looked like the movement she made when she was dancing. *"Why not?"*

Ralph smiled in a glow of contentment, even pride. Would his own parents, for instance, have opened their doors as freely to *his* chums of the dump? Good God, no! Who, between the two of them, was more charitable, Christian, tolerant, all that crap?

"That *crap!*" Ralph yelled. "Let's get rid of it! Let's conquer it with *love!*" No one was listening, no one heard, but that didn't matter. He had got his message out. "Across and *out!*" Ralph shouted, and plunged toward the telephone. Twenty to ten, if his watch was correct. Ralph dialed his father's number.

No one answered the telephone. This disappointed Ralph.

Throughout the evening, Ralph tried his father's number at half-hour intervals. By midnight, everyone at the dump, including three more arrivals, knew whom he was trying to reach and why, and Ben had said he would invite his uncle for Saturday. Ben's parents lived somewhere upstate, but he had an uncle in Brooklyn. At a little past 1 A.M. Ralph's father answered the telephone, and Ralph proceeded to invite him for Saturday night, any time after 9 P.M.

"Oh? A party. Well—y-yes, Ralph, thanks," his father said. "I'm glad you did call, because I was a little worried after I dropped that letter."

His father sounded unusually serious, even sad. "Oh, that's—Thanks, Dad, I was glad to get it really." The words came out of nowhere, and didn't mean anything, Ralph realized, but his tone was polite.

After they had hung up, Ralph had a strange feeling that the conversation hadn't really taken place, that he had imagined it. But his father's voice had said that he would come. Yes. Definitely.

The next two days till Saturday were enhanced by the coming party, in the way Ralph recalled that the approach of Christmas had made the days preceding magical, different, prettier, when he had been little. Ben had the brilliant idea of making potato soup their main dish, cheap and easy, and they would have thin slices of frankfurter floating in it, and a big bunch of parsley in the kitchen to garnish each bowl or paper cup or even plate of this thick soup, which Cassie promised to create. Plenty of garlic was to go into the soup, which would have a ham hock base. And Cassie and Georgie had also been busy with the decor. From a friend down the street she had acquired yards of old film reels, and these looked festive, twisted and strung from corner to corner of the room, and tied together in the center with somebody's long red scarf.

"Don't nobody strike a match!" Cassie said the evening of the party. "You know what they say about flaming cellophane!"

The potato soup, in two huge cauldrons (one borrowed from a girl who was coming to the party), steamed discreetly over low gas flames, the parsley stood ready, and there was one measly six-pack of beer in the fridge, two jugs of the Italian table wine, and six sticks of Italian bread. People were supposed to bring their own drink, after all. A shoe box labeled ALMS sat on the trestle worktable near the door, and Georgie voiced his disapproval of its being *so* near the door, because someone could depart hastily and be down the stairs with the box before anyone knew what had happened. But the box stayed there, because people were not to be admitted without their three dollars, and Ben and Cassie agreed that it would be silly to open the door and go off somewhere like the little bedroom to stick three dollars into the shoe box.

Stereo boomed and throbbed, and people trickled in. Coats and jackets even shoes got tossed in a heap on the double bed in the little bedroom, and then on the floor in the corner by the trestle table. On the pushed-together double beds, Cassie had placed a folded bridge table plus the ironing board to provide surfaces for bowls of potato chips, pretzels, popcorn and olives.

Olives! Black and green olives. Ralph suddenly remembered that he had bought them. A touch of elegance. He had spent about ten dollars on them. Ralph, in a clean shirt, cleanish jeans, boots which he had given a wipe, felt nervous, as if he alone were giving the party. He kept watching the door, expecting his father, feeling relieved though a bit sweaty when each time the door opened strange kids, or faces he barely recognized, came in. It was nearly eleven. Had his father changed his mind?

> *You ain't forgotten* mee-ah . . .
> *You ain't forgotten mee-eee* . . .

sang the male voice on the blaring hi-fi.

Ralph tossed back a paper cupful of distasteful red wine. Why was he drinking the stuff? He preferred beer any time.

Even Ben's uncle was here. Ralph saw him standing at the foot of the beds, paper cup in hand, conspicuous because he wore a tweed jacket with a white scarf at the neck in contrast to the blue denim everywhere. Had Ralph met him before? Ralph made his way toward Ben's uncle, stepping aside from or forging through the hopping dancers.

"Hello!" Ralph yelled. "You're Ben's *uncle!*"

"Yes. Right!" said Ben's uncle with a smile. "Huey! That's my name!"

Ralph wasn't sure he'd heard it aright. Huey? Louie? *"Ralph!"* Ralph yelled, rocked back on his boot heels, and once more glanced at the door.

It was impossible to talk, and so what? For a few moments, Ralph and Huey shouted things at each other, then a fellow in black leather and a cowboy hat, stoned to the gills, came up, to Ralph's relief, and tried to start a conversation with Ben's uncle. Ralph found himself laughing. Then Ralph looked again at the door, and there was his father!

Ralph saw Steve smile at a girl—who was she? long blonde hair and a black dress—who was asking him for the three dollars' admission fee. His father stuck a bill into the ALMS box, probably a ten, a fiver anyway. Ralph swallowed with difficulty, felt cold sober for an instant, then plunged toward his father, crashing through dancers.

"Dad!" Ralph and his father shook hands, each unable to hear what the other was saying.

His father gestured toward his shirt and tie apologetically, and Ralph thought he said something about having had to spend the evening with a business colleague. Ralph escorted his father around the edge of the dancers toward the kitchen, where if there was not a beer, there was at least instant coffee. Vaguely yet persistently, like a deep conviction, Ralph felt that *the kitchen,* the mere existence of a kitchen, would prove to his father that this was a household. But the kitchen was jammed with people, as if half the party had taken refuge in this appendix of the establishment to stand still and upright, even if they were packed as tightly as people on a subway train at rush hour.

"My *dad!"* Ralph yelled on a note of pride. "Is there a *beer?"*

"Beer, hah!" said a fellow with a little brown bottle in his hand, waggling the bottle upside down to show it was empty.

"Up yours!" Ralph retorted unheard, and lunged forward and downward, unsettling at least two standing girls, but the girls didn't mind, only giggled. Ralph was acutely aware of his father, standing more or less in the doorway, and aware also of people's surprised expressions upon seeing an older man among them. But Ralph found what he was after, Ben's precious beer cache behind the fridge, tepid, but still one small beer. Only one had been left there, and Ralph told himself to replace it tomorrow, otherwise Ben would be annoyed. He found an opener and got the top off. The paper cups were already gone.

"A beer!" said Ralph, proudly handing his father the bottle.

Then they were both in the big living room again, not quite together, because the dancers, the yelling people, somehow kept them apart, though Ralph pushed toward his father, who was now near the two-bed buffet spread. Someone—probably Georgie—had created a phallic symbol made of a banana plus a couple of oranges, which looked like a cannon on wheels or a sexual organ, whichever way you wanted to take it, underlaid and surrounded by purple grapes. This eye-catching display occupied the center of the gray-covered ironing board, and Ralph saw his father turn his eyes from it.

> . . . *yeeowr a* wing-*ding-ding* . . .
> *yeeowr a* wing-*ding-ding* . . .

the electronic voices were saying, not exactly human voices, but Ralph inevitably thought of those words when he heard this particular tape. Worse was to come on this tape, if by worse one meant porn. Ralph was fixated by his father's eyes, his expression. His father's eyes were wary, almost frightened, and he looked around, blinking a couple of times, then abruptly turned his head as if to try to change his view. These people, to his father, were the enemy, Ralph realized.

Damn that particular pair of faggots, smooching not for the first time as they danced in slow rhythm to music that was fast. Of course a lot of boy and girl couples were doing the same thing, but that would be okay from his father's point of view. Ralph heard a collective *"Oooh!"* and laughter, and saw a flame run up one of the film twists and burn itself out in a top corner, as the red scarf in the center fell and the other twists of film got yanked by, lost among, the dancers.

Ralph found Cassie and dragged her over to meet his father, intending to present her as their *housemother*—at least this respectable and maybe slightly funny term stuck in his head. Ralph hadn't reached his father, when somebody fell on the floor just in front of him and Cassie, causing another couple to fall also. The couple got up, but the one who had fallen first did not. He was a stranger to Ralph, in black trousers, red vest, white shirt with cufflinks, skinny and unconscious. A fellow in jeans dragged him by the heels, yelling for clearance, toward the trestle table, where there was a little clear space. Ralph pushed on with Cassie in hand.

"My father *Steve! Cassie!*" Ralph yelled.

Steve nodded and said, "Good evening!" loudly, but Cassie might as well not have heard it.

Cassie was tired, very tired, her eyes rolled toward the ceiling. She wore a fresh white shirt with big starched collar and cuffs, neat black trousers and stiletto heels, and she was standing up straight, too, but Ralph knew she was exhausted, and she'd plainly had a snort of something.

"Cassie *cooks for us all!*" Ralph shouted to his father, supporting Cassie with a firm grip. *"She's tired from all the work today!"*

"Not tired!" Cassie said. "It's a rectangle! Not a square, a rectangle! Same as—"

While Cassie sought for a word, and Ralph's father tried to hear, Ralph shook Cassie's arm. It shook Cassie's whole body, but she kept her eyes fixed on the ceiling and continued:

". . . saw it yesterday too in the bathroom *basin*. It's everywhere! Where I was washing my *hair* this afternoon!—It's a dim-diminishing TV screen, I swear to God! And it's a *window!* A window, too, Ralphie. Y'know what I mean? Outlined in *silver!*"

"Yep," Ralph said curtly, grinding his teeth for an instant. Cassie was in a trance. What had she had? She'd call it her mantra in a minute, the vision she'd had, or was having. "Okay, Cassie, very *good!*" Laughing, Ralph shook Cassie's arm again.

"And it's *heaving,*" she assured Steve. "Going up and down in the basin, y'know?"

"The water, you mean," said Ralph. "It's going *down,* the water!"

"Up—*and* down!"

Smiling, Ralph steered Cassie back to the kitchen, away from his father, away and safe from the dancers who might bump her. Cassie, however, walked quite well on her own, she was just somewhere else now in her head. Ralph dragged deeply on a limp joint that someone extended, held the smoke in his lungs, swung around to go back to the living room, and banged his forehead against the door jamb.

> *Weedjie meenie you like mee-e . . .*
> *Weedjie weenie ooo-wee-ee mee-ee . . .*

Ralph saw his father and pushed toward him. At that instant, Ralph's energy gave out, maybe because he was thinking that his father had just nodded good-bye and was leaving. And Ralph had meant to introduce him to Ben and Georgie! Next to impossible in all this crowd!

Yes, Steve was gone. Over all the people, Ralph could just see the top of the tall door closing.

Well, that was that. Ralph's ears were now aching and ringing from the loud music, and he felt slightly deaf. He couldn't hear what someone was shouting at him, as he headed back for the kitchen. No, maybe there was more space in the little bedroom, and he could close the door on himself for a minute. But when Ralph pushed wider the slightly open door, he saw what looked like at least two fellows and a girl on the bed, wallowing and laughing. Ralph reeled back and closed the door.

Sometime later, Ralph awakened, jolted by a kick in his leg. A strange girl smiled down at him. Ralph was on the floor near the two pushed-together beds. The music still throbbed, and everything was the same as before. Ralph stood up, thought for a moment that the green-covered bed was rushing toward him with its now empty plates and bowls and its phallic display, but the bed stopped, and Ralph found himself quite upright. Ben was embracing Cassie tightly, swaying among the dancers.

So was Georgie embracing Cassie. She was a black and white–clad blonde-topped doll between them, and would have fallen without their support, Ralph could see. He felt superior (maybe that little nap or black-out had done him good), and he felt on a different and separate plane from the others.

"Better plane. Everything is planes," he murmured to himself. He wanted to say this to anyone near, but everyone looked quite occupied with other people. His *father*. Yes, for Christ's sake, his father had been *here*. Tonight. *This* party. And his father had left in not such a good mood. Ralph suddenly recalled his father's pale, shocked face as he had gone out the door. That hadn't been good.

Ralph felt like throwing up, surely due to the wine. Best to get to the bathroom, the toilet of course, and Ralph at once headed for the bathroom. The door was not locked, though a fellow and a girl were in there, leaning against the basin, and suddenly Ralph was angry and yelled for both of them to get out. He heard his own voice yelling, and kept on, until with startled faces they slowly made their way out, and then Ralph slid the bolt on the door. He did not have to throw up, though he recalled that this had been his intent.

"I am on a different plane," Ralph said aloud, in a calm voice. He felt quite well now. Purposeful. Full of energy. Serious. "A man of intent." He opened the medicine cabinet over the basin, and took down what he wanted, the communal safety razor. "A man of—intent."

The next several seconds represented a geographical trip to Ralph. He thought of a plane ride he had had with his family—mom and dad, yes—over the desert between Dallas–Fort Worth and Albuquerque. Purplish lake-like shapes down there, dried-up lakes or slightly filled ones, ravines twisting like snakes, dry maybe, down there. Little canyons. Beautiful colors, tan and green. And now red. Razor cut through the swollen rivers, and came out red. Now that was colorful! Amusing. Dangerous, maybe, but exciting. And absolutely painless. No pain at all.

Ralph woke up in a horizontal position, on his back, dry in the mouth. And when he tried to move his arms, he couldn't, and he thought for a moment that he was imprisoned somewhere. *Police,* maybe. Then he saw his hands except for fingers were heavily bandaged to halfway up his forearms, and they seemed to weigh a ton each. He could just move them by tugging backward. He was in a room with at least ten beds like his own, and there was a dim blue light over the door.

"Jesus, is this another *dream?*" Ralph said in a scared voice that cracked. He looked around again, wide-eyed.

Then he became aware of the smell: medicine, disinfectant. He was in a *hospital.* Definitely. What had happened? He tried to move his legs and was relieved to find that he could. Had there been a fight at the dump? Ralph couldn't remember any. *What* hospital was this? Where? Ralph felt groggy—they'd surely given him a sedative here—but he felt more angry than sleepy, and his anger grew as he looked around him, and found neither a lamp nor a button to press.

So he yelled. "*Hey!* . . . Where's anybody? . . . He-ey!"

A groan came from one of the beds in the room, an unintelligible voice from another. The door opened and a dimly white figure with a white cap came in noiselessly.

"Hey!" Ralph said, though more softly.

"You're to keep quiet, please," said the girl. She had a flashlight thin as a pencil.

"Where *is* this?"

She told him such-and-such hospital in some street on the East Side. And it was Sunday night, midnight, she replied in answer to his question.

The party had been Saturday night, Ralph was thinking. And today, yes, today they had been due in the Bronx. Where were his friends? "Got to call my friends," Ralph said to the nurse, twisting his neck under her fingers. She was trying to check his pulse, but Ralph had thought for a minute that she meant to throttle him.

"You can't call anyone at this hour. Two of your friends were here this afternoon. I had to tell them you were sleeping and couldn't be disturbed."

"Well—how long have I got to *be* here?"

"Probably two more days," the nurse whispered. "You lost a lot of blood. You were in a state of shock. You've had some transfusions—and you may need more. Now take this, please." She extended a glass of water in the hand that held the pencil flashlight between its fingers, and on her other palm lay a largish pink pill.

"What is—"

"Take it, please. You'll feel better."

Ralph gulped it down, wincing, and when he opened his eyes, the nurse was going out the door.

In the next seconds, things became a little clearer. He had cut his wrists. That he remembered now with a twinge of shame. Sort of stupid, maybe. It had caused a lot of trouble. Blood on the bathroom floor. All those people! And his father had come to the party! Yes, that was what had made Ralph so sad, disappointed, a little ashamed. But why *should* he feel ashamed? Ashamed of what? Ralph felt his heart beating faster, belligerently, defiantly. He and his chums had given a *party,* that was all.

The pill hit him like a zinging piece of music in his ears. Like electronic cymbals, with faint but deep drums in the background.

> *. . . and a zing-zing-zing . . .*
> *and a wing-ding-ding . . .*

and Ralph slept.

He got out Tuesday noonish. Ben and Cassie came to fetch him, and treated him to a taxi ride to the dump. The hospital had made a fuss about the bill which was over five hundred dollars, and Ralph had given them his father's name and address and telephone number. When they had telephoned his father (home number), his father hadn't been in, and it hadn't occurred to Ralph to give them his father's office number, which Ralph didn't know by heart, at least he hadn't at that moment. Ben and Cassie had beer at home, and Ben went out at once for pastrami sandwiches, which were available around the corner. Georgie was out giving a piano lesson. It was great to be home, and Cassie was an angel, sympathetic, gentle, making him put his feet up, removing his shoes for him and putting pillows behind his head.

"You weren't the only one, Ralphie dear," Cassie said. "Two fellows passed out and didn't wake up till Sunday *afternoon,* and we thought we'd never get them out. But we took in three hundred and sixty-two *dollars!* Can you imagine?"

That sounded good, but it was for the rent, not his hospital bill, and the hospital had given Ralph a piece of paper that looked like a prison sentence or an extremely nasty threat to say the least, and it had a deadline for payment which Ralph had forgotten, but it was a matter of days and he had to see his father.

Ralph's father answered the telephone at a few minutes before eight that evening. Ralph had slept and felt better, braced for coolness on the part of his father, braced for his father even to say, "To be honest, Ralph, I don't ever want to see you again. You're a grown man now, etc." Or "My eyes were opened at that party."

But to his surprise, his father sounded calm and gentle. Yes, Ralph could come over, even this evening, if he wanted to, but not after ten, please.

Ralph shaved and washed as best he could. His wrists were still bandaged, of course, but the bandages were lighter. Ralph chose a big loose plastic jacket, hoping that his father might not see the bandages.

"Good luck, Ralphie," Cassie said, kissing him on the cheek. "We're glad you're still with us, and we can cut that record any old time."

"Take it easy now," Ben said. "Don't collapse anywhere."

Their words reminded Ralph of the faint pink stains in the corners of their bathroom floor. That floor must have been a mess, and his chums hadn't got the stains entirely removed as yet. Ralph caught a bus, found a seat, and tried to breathe in a slow Zen way.

His father had a white bandage all across his nose and onto his cheeks in the form of adhesive tape. Steve nodded, holding the door open. "Come in, Ralph."

Ralph went in. "What happened?"

"Something very stupid.—Funny." In the living room now, his father looked at Ralph, smiling. Again he wore house shoes and had been reading a book. "Had a slight accident—on the way home from that party. Very stupid accident. I turned too close on a left turn—hit another car nearly head-on. Third Avenue. Completely my fault. And my nose hit the windshield. Broken nose." His father laughed. His shoulders moved, but the laugh was silent.

"I'm sorry. The police—" Ralph at once thought of a drunken-driving charge, but how could Steve have been drunk?

"Oh! Well, yes, they gave me a test for alcohol and found I was well under the limit. Plain carelessness on my part, I said . . . Like a beer, Ralph?" Without waiting for an answer, Steve went off to the kitchen to get one.

Ralph felt shocked. His father in a dumb accident like that! And sober! Ralph understood: his father had been totally shook up by that party, just by what he had seen there. Ralph took the beer can from his father. "Thanks dad."

"And that?" His father had caught sight of the bandage on Ralph's right wrist, and at once looked at the other wrist, whose bandage was not entirely concealed by the loose blue plastic sleeve.

"Yeah, well—little accident at my place too. Nothing serious." Ralph sipped from the hole in the can, and felt his face grow warm. If it wasn't serious, why else was he here? He was here because of a five-hundred-dollar hospital bill. Ralph found himself looking into his father's eyes, aware of his father's firm mouth. His father knew what those bandages were for.

"Night of the party?" Steve asked, reaching for his matches.

"Yes," said Ralph.

"They put you in a hospital, I suppose. I tried to phone you yesterday. Got some kind of silly answer there. Man's voice."

Ralph swallowed dryly, and sipped more beer. "Nobody told me about that."

"Couldn't be that you need money for the hospital bill."

"Yeah, that's exactly it. That's true, Dad . . . And they were pretty nasty at the hospital. Insistent, I mean." And the cut wrists, the hospital bill had been his own fault, Ralph realized. *Unnecessary.* Ralph's gaze dropped to the level of his father's white coat sweater, to its brown leather buttons. His father's broken nose had been an accident, too, hadn't it? Really unnecessary. "I was upset—" Ralph shrugged, still unable to look his father in the eyes. Hadn't his father been upset too? Didn't everybody get upset now and then?

"You'll get the money," said his father finally, in a rather tense voice, as if he were paying off a blackmailer whom he didn't quite dare to treat rudely.

Or so Ralph felt. Ralph felt this even more, when his father added:

"After all, you're still my son." He walked to the secretaire bookcase where he kept his checkbook. "How much is it, Ralph?"

"It's a little over five hundred."

"I'll write this for not over six hundred. You can fill out the rest." His father wrote the check without sitting down.

"Thanks . . . I'm sorry, dad," Ralph said as he took the check from his father's hand.

"Shall I say it's the last? I wish it were."

"I swear I'll—"

"I despise your life," his father interrupted, "to be perfectly truthful."

Now Ralph stared into his father's blue eyes as if hypnotized by them. The white bandage across his father's nose and face, which might have been funny if they had both been in a different mood, now made Ralph think of a gas mask, or some kind of battle gear, not funny at all. And Ralph felt defeated.

"I've tried to—appreciate your way of life, to understand it, anyway."

Ralph said nothing. He knew his father had tried. One of his wrists was pulsing, and he glanced at its bandage to see if any blood had come through. None had, so far. Ralph took an awkward step backward, as if to leave. "Yeah, I know . . . I'm sorry, Dad."

His father nodded, but it wasn't an affirmative nod, rather a hopeless, resigned and rather tired nod. "Don't come back again—if you can help it."

Ralph bit his underlip, wanting to speak, finding no words. He resented being treated like a bum, fairly told not to come back for a handout. Now he stood like a dolt, wordless, unable even to get his anger together, and he did feel anger. Yes. Ralph started to shout "Yes!" like a big affirmative, a big okay for himself, but his lips barely opened. Then he turned and strode towards the door, opened it and went out, and closed the door firmly but he didn't bang it.

The battle wasn't over, Ralph knew.

The Dream
of
the Emma C

The nineteen-year-old Sam, youngest of the crew, was at the wheel when he caught sight of a white fleck in the blue water, about half a mile ahead and a bit to port. A lone gull, he thought, bobbing on the summer sea, all by itself. The *Emma C* was headed north in Cape Cod Bay, and the Cape shore with its clusters of white houses marking the towns was quite visible on Sam's right. The mackerel haul had been miserable early this morning, and Captain Bif Haskins had decided they should try again at another spot before heading for home. The rest of the crew, four men plus Bif, were having a second breakfast of coffee and doughnuts in the galley now.

When Sam looked again at the white gull, it looked round, like a beach ball. It wasn't a gull. Sam had good eyesight, and he concentrated his gaze. It was a *swimmer!* And way out here, at least two miles from shore! Was the fellow maybe dead? Just floating?

"Hey!" Sam yelled, at the same time turning the wheel so the *Emma C* would be headed straight for the white dot. "Hey, Louie!—*Johnny!*"

A heavy tread clunked on the deck, then Chuck appeared at the port door of the wheelhouse. "What's up?"

"Somebody's floating out there. Look!"

Within seconds, all of them were looking. Bif got his binoculars from a little locker behind the wheel. The face under the white cap was pronounced that of a girl.

"A *girl*?"

The binoculars were passed around.

"I can see her *eyes!*"

"She's not moving. If she was dead, her eyes'd be open too!"

"Got a blue bathing suit on!" Chuck reported.

Sam grabbed a quick look through the glasses which he held with one hand. "She's an exhausted swimmer. Get a blanket ready!"

Louie, the stocky half-Portuguese, lowered the Jacob's ladder on Captain Bif's orders. The ladder trailed in the sea. Now they were quite close. The girl was simply floating, making no movement with her arms or legs, as if she were too tired for any effort. But her eyes were open, a little. Louie was first down the ladder. Sam had cut the motor. Behind Louie went Johnny, a tallish fellow a little older than Sam.

Louie groped, wet to his thighs, and caught the girl's right arm at the elbow. They all heard her groan slightly. She was definitely alive, but so spent that her head nodded forward as Louie lifted her by both her arms. And Johnny tugged at Louie. Willing hands caught the girl's hands, then her waist, her feet, and four pairs of hands lowered her gently onto the rough olive-green blanket that someone had spread on the deck.

She was pale, just a little pink on shoulders and arms, not very tall, with a full breast, a smallish waist from which sprang rounded hips like those of a mermaid, but this was no mermaid. She had small, graceful feet, and legs, and the rest.

"Tea! Hot tea!" said Captain Bif. "Then we'd better radio to shore."

"Coffee's quicker, Bif!" Chuck went off to get some.

Sam was pulling back her white cap, ever so gently so as not to tug at her hair. She was very blonde. Her lips were pale and bluish, her tongue bright pink, running its tip along the edge of her white teeth.

"Ain't she *pretty*!" someone whispered in a tone of awe.

"Coffee, ma'am?" Chuck held the thick white cup to her lips. He knelt, as did Louie who supported her with the blanket around her shoulders.

"Um-m," she murmured, and took a tiny sip.

"Where you from? . . . Are you cold? . . . How'd you get way out here?" The questions came fast.

The girl's blue eyes had barely opened. "A bet—"

"Where'd you think you were swimming to?"

"Stow it, all of you!" Sam said as if he were the captain. "She needs a bunk to rest in. She can have mine. Give me a hand, Louie?" Sam was ready to carry her in the blanket.

"*My* bunk!" Chuck said. "Mine's got a *sheet* since this morning."

Every bunk was offered—there were only four tucked away under the forward deck—but Chuck's with the sheet was agreed upon. Chuck beamed as if he had won a bride, and followed Louie and Sam as they carried the girl toward the cabin. Chuck glanced over his shoulder as if to say to the three remaining men, including the captain, "Keep your distance!"

The low-ceilinged cabin held two bunks on either side, one above the other. The crew sometimes snoozed in shifts, but they were almost never out all night. Once in a while, a man treated himself to a sheet from home to put between the blankets, and now Chuck happened to be sporting a sheet, which he considered a piece of luck. He carefully tucked the girl's feet in, and made sure her shoulders were covered, because her skin was cool.

"Like the sleepin' beauty," Chuck said softly. "Isn't she?"

"Oughtn't we to take that wet suit off, Chuck?" Sam asked.

Chuck frowned, thinking. "Um—yeah, but we oughta leave that to her—in a while. Don't you think so? . . . Are you gettin' warmer, miss?"

The girl's eyes were open again. Her lips parted slightly, but she said nothing.

Sam went off and returned with a corked wine bottle which he wrapped in a towel. "Hot water from the stove," he said to Chuck, and placed the bottle carefully at the girl's feet, inside the blanket but outside the sheet.

Louie had departed, summoned by Bif. Filip, a boy of twenty, ugly and timid, peered curiously down the hatch at the girl in the lower starboard bunk.

"Let's let her be for a while," Chuck said. Sam was standing near him, and Chuck poked him in the ribs with an elbow, so hard that Sam winced. "And no funny business, fella. Leave her alone."

Sam glowered at the older man. "Funny business from *me*?"

The *Emma C* chugged northward in Massachusetts Bay but more slowly than before, moved in an almost dreamy way, as if the girl's presence had cast a spell not only over the six men, but the engine. Captain Bif was at the wheel, nervously chewing a cigar that had gone out, gazing ahead of him at familiar water and at the fading Cape on his right. He had radioed Provincetown, giving a description of the girl, blonde and about twenty, saying she was too tired to speak now, but she did not seem to be injured and would probably be all right. Judging from what the Provincetown operator said, such a girl had not been reported missing as yet. Now where was he heading? They had the right to try their luck anywhere along here, closer to shore, and farther north, to lower their nets, make a sweep and fill the hold, or try to, before turning back for Wellfleet, their home port. But Bif realized he didn't give a damn if they caught any more fish today or not. Neither did the crew, he knew. Where was the girl from? What was her name? She certainly was beautiful! Fantastic to pull something like *that* out of the sea! It was like a tall story, a legend that was amusing to listen to, but not to be believed. He and his men would treat her right. It was a time for all of them to be gentlemen. "Gentlemen," Captain Bif murmured to himself, with a certain satisfaction. Yes, he'd see to that. "Hey, *Sam!*" Bif called loudly over his shoulder.

Sam, organizing nets on the after deck, dropped his work and went to the wheelhouse.

"Keep her steady—as she goes," said Bif.

"Yessir." Sam took over the wheel. After a minute or so, he slightly decreased their speed. Today was a special day. Sam didn't want to look at another dead or dying fish today. Sam had done two years of college, which had included six months on the training ship *Westward* that operated out of Woods Hole, Massachusetts, whereby he had gained credits in nautical and marine science. Sam intended to be an oceanographer. His job on the *Emma C* was a one-month hitch during summer vacation. On the *Westward,* Sam had cruised the Caribbean and the Florida coasts, they had seen phosphorescent jellyfish at night, lovely porpoise leaping in schools, but somehow nothing so strange, startling and beautiful as this calm girl that the sea had presented to them out of nowhere.

Chuck was standing by the cabin hatch as Bif approached with an air of intending to enter. "She's okay, Bif. Sleeping now."

"Good. Thought I'd have a shave—and I can be quiet about it. Tell Filip to bring me a pan of hot water, would you, Chuck?"

Bif usually didn't bother shaving on board. Chuck slid open the hatches a little, saw that the girl looked asleep, and touched his lips with a forefinger to indicate to Bif to be quiet. Then Chuck looked around for Filip and found him sweeping little dead fish on the after deck into a heap. He gave Bif's order, and admonished Filip to be quiet when he entered the cabin, because the girl was sleeping. On second thoughts, Chuck decided to take the pan from Filip himself when he brought it. Filip trotted off, smiling. True there was a mirror on the wall between the bunks, but couldn't Bif have shaved somewhere in the galley?

Then a voice yelled, "Damn you to *hell,* Filip!"

There was a thud, a tinny clatter, and Chuck saw Filip reel backward out of the galley and fall, and his head hit the bulwark. Louie stood over him with a clenched fist, then picked up the pan and went into the galley with it. Filip sat up, bleeding from his head. Blood rapidly soaked the back of his denim shirt.

Chuck took the boy's arm, and helped him to his feet.

From the port door of the wheelhouse, Sam glanced aft and realized what had happened. He had also heard some of the conversation. Both had wanted to take the hot water to Bif in the cabin. Smiling, Sam steered the boat a little to starboard, toward the open Atlantic. They were passing Race Point and the tip of Cape Cod to their starboard.

Louie brought the pan of hot water, and stared at the sleeping girl until Bif told him to leave. Then Chuck reported Filip's accident to Bif, and said that Filip's head would need stitches. Bif cursed gently.

"I'll see to it," Bif said, knowing he was the best man for stitching, because he'd done it many times before. "Make Filip lie down somewhere—not here—till I finish my shave."

Chuck made Filip lie down on the deck with his head out of the sun. He had a nearly three-inch gash. Captain Bif arrived with a half bottle of whiskey, a bottle of surgical spirits, and his kit of gauze, adhesive tape, needle and scissors. He gave Filip a slug of whiskey for morale, because the boy was almost weeping, and when no one was looking Bif took a snort himself. Bif was rather strict about drinking on board: a little wine or beer was permissible, but no hard stuff, whatever the weather.

Then the girl came awake, and there was a big to-do in the galley about what to give her to eat.

"Soup," said Johnny, as there was a lot of vegetable soup left over from yesterday's lunch, but someone remarked that Johnny had thrown some fish fillets into it, like a dummox, and the soup at present wouldn't be fit for a dog. "If you don't like my cooking—" Johnny began, balling a fist at Chuck who had called him a dummox. This was a standing joke or threat: nobody wanted to cook on the *Emma C,* so anyone who criticized the food was apt to be appointed cook on the spot.

Chuck had clenched his fists too. "I just *meant*—fishy soup, lousy soup is not *appropriate* for her! Scrambled eggs are more like it!" Then Chuck's right fist shot forward as if released by a spring, and hit Johnny in the solar plexus.

Johnny gasped, and a second later swung a right to Chuck's jaw. Chuck staggered back and tripped, which was a good thing, as he fell on deck instead of over the low bulwark into the sea. Chuck shook his head and got up, thrust off Bif, and hit Johnny again under his ribs with a left, followed by a right to the jaw that floored him. Both men were big and evenly matched. Johnny did not get up.

"You guys better *stop* this!" Bif said. "That's enough! Understand? I'm giving orders here . . . We've got frozen steaks, haven't we? You make her a steak, Chuck. You feel up to it?"

Chuck stood tall, though his lip was bleeding. "I feel fine, Cap'n!" He went to the galley, stepping over Johnny as if Johnny were no more than a coiled rope.

Filip winced as Bif stuck a bandage on his clumsily shaved head with adhesive tape. Filip knew he was low man on the totem pole on the *Emma C*, a kid not even tall enough to impress anybody. But Louie wasn't any taller, just heavier, and Filip vowed his vengeance.

Captain Bif ordered Louie to clean the galley floor with a bucket and rag on his hands and knees by way of punishment for his attack on Filip, and Louie started his work. Louie was curious about the girl. Had she taken off her wet bathing suit? What could he possibly do to serve her? So he said to Chuck, as Chuck added some home fried potatoes to the steak plate and set a glass of milk on the tray, "I'll be glad to take that in to her, Chuck—sir."

Chuck gave a laugh. "I bet you would, fella! I'll do it. Get on with your job here." Chuck dipped half a dishtowel into the pot of hot water on the stove, wiped his lip and his hands, and picked up the tray. "Gangway!" he said, stepping on deck. The cabin hatch was closed, and he tapped with his foot. "Hello, miss! Can I—" Chuck scowled off Johnny, who was on his feet now, but holding the left side of his jaw as if it hurt. Johnny was ready to open the sliding hatch doors.

"Um-m—what?" came from within, and at a nod from Chuck, Johnny slid back the hatches.

Chuck went down the steps with his tray.

The girl was sitting up with the sheet pulled nearly to her shoulders, and Chuck saw at once that she had removed her blue bathing suit. In fact it lay on the floor beside the bunk. "Excuse me, ma'am. A bite to eat. You feeling better?"

She smiled at him. "Yes, sure . . . I don't think I'm hurt."

Chuck looked at her, remembering her smooth, pale body, unblemished. "Not a scratch, far as I know. Can you manage this?" He was ready to set the tray on her thighs, then it occurred to him that the sheet would fall from her shoulders, and he had a brilliant idea. "Hold this for a minute!" He set the tray on her lap, then knelt and pulled out a drawer from the side of the bunk. In this he had at least one clean shirt besides woolen socks and various underpants and T-shirts. He found the red-and-white checked flannel shirt that he wanted. "This. It's warm. You want to keep warm."

The girl extended an arm, and Chuck handed the shirt to her and at once turned his back. This caused him to notice Johnny and also Bif looking down through the open hatch. "Well, don't stand there *gawking*!" Chuck shouted, and advanced to the foot of the steps, blocking their view. There was even Louie peeking between Bif and Johnny!

"Thought there might be something else she needs," Johnny said. "Ketchup?"

Too annoyed to reply, Chuck turned his back on them. The girl was buttoning his big shirt over her breasts, and then she picked up knife and fork. She poked a piece of steak into her mouth, and smiled at Chuck, chewing with an appetite.

"Salt, miss? Is that all right?" Chuck had salted the steak.

"It's fine. Good, really."

Chuck glanced up, and saw a single figure, Louie, slip away. Chuck reached up and slammed the hatch doors firmly. "Will you tell me your name?"

"Natalie."

Natalie. It made Chuck think of things that came from the sea, like pearls and pretty corals, pink and red. He realized that he didn't want to ask her where she lived. Wouldn't it be fantastic if she could stay always in his bunk here, smiling at him, and he could wait on her hand and foot? "You're getting some color back in your cheeks."

She nodded, and sipped from the glass of milk.

"Would it annoy you, Natalie, if I shaved here? It's the only mirror on board—and I really need a shave."

The girl said it wouldn't annoy her, and Chuck opened the hatch and yelled, "Galley!"

Filip with bandaged head was first to arrive.

"Pan of hot water for shavin', Filip. Can you manage that?"

Filip gazed past Chuck at the girl. "Sure. Right away." He went off.

Chuck got his razor from the drawer, and whetted it on the leather strap that hung by the mirror. Then he heard a yelp from on deck, the snarl of an angry voice, and Bif's roar of reprimand.

"God's *sake*!" Bif said.

"*He's* not tellin' me what to do! *That* son of a bitch!"

Chuck climbed partway up the steps, opened the hatch doors and looked out. Louie was lying on the port deck outside the galley. Bif was feeling his pulse, and Filip stood with feet apart and a belaying pin in his right hand.

Louie was dead. Chuck could tell that from the way Bif straightened up from the fallen figure, from the way he rubbed his chin. Chuck quietly shut the cabin hatches. Louie must have asked Filip to let him carry the hot water. Something like that. And Filip had got his own back at Louie for causing the cut on his head. There'd be a burial at sea now. Wouldn't there be?

The girl had closed her eyes again. She had long golden lashes. Was she maybe twenty? Or even younger? Her delicate hands and slender wrists rested outside the covers, beside the tray. She had eaten nearly all the steak.

Filip with shaking hands brought a pan of steaming water a minute later. Chuck took it through the hatch and asked no questions, set the pan on a step and closed the hatch doors at once.

At the helm of the *Emma C,* Sam Wicker had composed a poem. He had made three drafts of it, writing on the ruled scrap paper that lay on the shelf before the wheel, and it had taken him some time.

> *I watched for leaping fish*
> *And troubled waters, signaling*
> *Action and the lowering of nets,*
> *The whirl of winches, and flapping death.*
> *Instead there floated tranquil*
> *On the sea's blue face*
> *A lovelier prize.*
> *We hauled it up gently*
> *Like coral that might break,*
> *In awe-struck silence beheld you,*
> *A beautiful girl, alive and perfect,*
> *Born of the sea!*
> *Need we, need I search further?*
> *Our prize is here, and as she sleeps*
> *A paradisic peace prevails.*

And Sam had just copied out the last line, when Louie's dying scream rent the air. Sam had been about to yell out himself for relief at the wheel, and now he watched in blinking astonishment the scene on the port deck.

Louie was being covered with a tarpaulin. Had Filip done that? Sam knew about Filip's cracked head. "Johnny!" Sam called, and when Johnny swaggered up, frowning, Sam nodded toward the wheel. "Take over, would you? I've been here a long time."

Slowly, saying nothing, Johnny stepped into the wheelhouse.

The *Emma C* moved gently northeastward, at creeping speed. Ordinarily Captain Bif would have given orders who was to man the helm, or would have taken the wheel himself, but today was a different day indeed. Sam kept silent and watched. Chuck, with a puffy lip and jaw but freshly shaved, stood on the deck in earnest conversation with Bif. Filip leaned against the superstructure near them, and the patch on his head glared white in the sunshine. Filip was from the gutter, Sam thought. Like Louie. Louie had been a little better, with a family in Truro, but Filip was rather like a street urchin. Funny to think of Filip standing trial for murder or manslaughter, and this was what Captain Bif and Chuck were dealing with now.

". . . accident," Bif was saying. "Slipped and hit his head, you know? Sure enough he *did* die from a concussion—that blow with the belaying pin . . ." Then Bif saw Sam and beckoned to him.

They went into the galley, Bif opened a locker, and pulled out a full bottle of whiskey. They all had a neat drink. Sam grimaced, but finished his.

"You're to say nothing, Sam, understand?" said Bif. "Unless asked. And then you say Louie tripped in some rope and fell and hit his head."

"Are we heading back for Wellfleet tonight?" Sam asked.

"Tonight? . . . Tonight," Bif repeated dreamily, and poured another drink for himself, frowning.

Sam fingered his poem, which was folded in the back pocket of his dungarees. "The girl's all right?" he asked both Chuck and Bif.

Chuck looked challengingly at him. "Sure, she's fine. Why shouldn't she be?"

It was past three, and they'd all forgotten lunch. Sam shook his head at the offer of another drink, and went out on deck. He pulled his poem out, glanced at the open page, then made his way forward to the cabin and knocked so gently on the hatch doors, it might not have awakened the girl, if she had been asleep.

"Yes? Come in?" the girl's voice said.

Smiling with sudden relief, Sam slid open the doors. Sunlight slanted down just above the girl's head, lighting her blonde hair as if she wore a halo. Her lips and cheeks were pink now with a natural color. "I came to ask how you are—and if I can do anything for you."

"Thanks. I feel much better. I'm—"

"Well—what're *you* doing here?" Chuck seized Sam's arm from behind.

"Hey, cut it *out,* Chuck!"

"Better leave, Sammy boy." Chuck pushed past Sam and went down a couple of steps.

"I found this girl!" Sam said. "I've got a poem to give her."

"A poem!" Chuck smiled, and waved Sam back.

To Sam, Chuck looked insane. In defense, Sam made a fist of his right hand. "Really, Chuck, I don't know why—"

Chuck jumped on deck, and a blow in the left side of Sam's ribs cut his words off. Sam let go with his fist against Chuck's chest, barely shaking the heavier man. Then Chuck shoved Sam with a foot, and Sam fell on the deck.

The girl said something in a tone of protest, and Chuck interrupted with, "I don't want those apes coming in here!"

Sam got to his feet a little breathless, furious. Apes? What was on *Chuck's* mind? "If you try anything—with *that* girl—"

Chuck closed the hatch doors in Sam's face.

Trembling, Sam folded his poem and stuck it back in his pocket. He went to Captain Bif, who was still drinking in the galley, sitting at the table, and said in a voice so hoarse, it didn't sound like his own, "Chuck's up to something in the cabin, I think, sir. Maybe you'd better go see."

"Wh-at?" said Bif incredulously, not getting up.

"I can't do anything. He's *over* me." Sam meant Chuck had higher rank, was next below Bif.

Captain Bif went out, past Louie's wrapped body, and Sam stood on the deck, sneakered feet braced, watching. Bif knocked and shouted. The cabin was some four yards distant from Sam.

Chuck opened the hatch a little, and Bif said, "Are you all right there, Chuck?" and Chuck replied something that included ". . . protecting this girl . . ."

Sam's anger mounted. Was Chuck telling the truth? Chuck was a tough customer, nearly thirty, with a scar in one eyebrow and a naked woman tattooed on his right forearm. And could Chuck write a poem? Sam spat bitterly over the side, and looked again toward the cabin. Bif must have given Chuck some order, because Chuck was climbing the steps, coming on deck. Sam walked past Chuck without looking at him to the prow, pulled his ballpoint pen out, and wrote in a small hand above the poem:

I am the one who saw you in the water. I wrote this for you. With all my love, Sam

And bitter tears stung his eyes for a moment. Sam glanced around, and saw no one except Bif, who was steering. The cabin was close. Sam tapped quickly on the hatch door, and said, " 'Scuse me, miss! Can I hand you something?" He heard a soft reply that he did not understand, but there was no time to lose, so he opened the hatch doors, fairly slid down the steps, and extended his folded paper to the girl in the lower starboard bunk. "Take this, please!" He stuck it into her hand, and as he scrambled up the steps, he saw Chuck approaching on the port deck.

"Well, well! Peeping *Tom*!" Chuck said, and dashed for the cabin hatch as if to see if Sam had murdered the girl or done her some other damage.

Sam waited tensely to see if the swine Chuck was going to make the girl give up the poem.

"It's just a piece of paper!" Sam heard the girl say. "I want to read it!"

Sam drew a breath and smiled with satisfaction as if he had bashed Chuck to the deck! He walked slowly aft, feeling happy. And there was Johnny, lowering buckets over the side, rinsing. Johnny was apparently sprucing up their toilet facilities, such as they were. Sam wanted to laugh, but he only grinned, through nervously set teeth. Did the girl like his poem? Where were they heading? And why? Captain Bif at the wheel was still chewing his old unlit cigar. The captain had a wife in Wellfleet, Sam knew. What was Captain Bif thinking about now? Bif had told Sam that he had radioed P'town about the girl. And surely the girl would tell them her name and where she lived. Had she already told Chuck?

Suddenly hungry, Sam stepped into the galley, over the back of Filip who was scrubbing away slowly at the floor. Sam cut a hunk of the orange cheese they called rat cheese, and stood munching it. The old linoleum floor of the galley had never looked so clean. Blood had appeared in Filip's white bandage, and as Sam gazed at him, Filip slumped over in a faint and dropped his scrub brush. Sam stretched him out, and put a towel moistened with cold water over his forehead. Filip's face was pale.

"You'll be okay," Sam said. "You've done enough. The floor looks great."

In the cabin, Chuck had ascertained that the girl's family name was Anderson, and that she lived in Cambridge. Her father was a history professor. She had been on a camping trip with some friends, and she had taken a swim around nine that morning, intending to swim to a certain little cape or projection (Chuck thought he knew where she meant), but she had deliberately swum out farther to sea, aiming for somewhere else, and then she had become very tired.

"I had a quarrel—with someone. Then a kind of bet with someone else—a girl."

Chuck thought he understood. Maybe she had quarreled over a boy, some worthless kid. Chuck resented that possibility, and in fact did not wish to ask details. He didn't want to imagine her attracted to anyone. "You're much too . . ." He hesitated a long while. ". . . valuable to risk your life in a silly way like that."

The girl laughed a little, amused. "Can I get up? I'm feeling much better now."

"You can do anything you *wish*—Natalie." Chuck got up from where he had been sitting, on the opposite lower bunk, and again pulled out his clothes drawer. Dungarees. There was a pair, reasonably clean. "May I offer you these, ma'am?—I'll wait outside while you put them on." Chuck went up on deck.

At that moment, Captain Bif gave a shout—his customary *"Hey!"* which could mean anything. Chuck didn't respond; there were other men on board.

Sam left Filip and went to answer. The captain wanted to see Chuck. Sam, finding Chuck on deck by the cabin, told him this.

"Tell Bif he can come to see me," said Chuck.

Sam relayed this message to Bif.

With a look of annoyance, Bif motioned for Sam to take the wheel, which Sam did.

"Did you find out her name?" Bif asked Chuck.

"Yessir. Natalie Anderson."

"And where does she live?"

"Cambridge."

"Um—I'd better call shore now and tell 'em."

"She doesn't care, Bif. I mean—she's not in a hurry."

"No? You asked her?"

Chuck hadn't. He didn't reply.

Bif went to the wheelhouse. Sam was steering. Bif started to use the radio-telephone, and found it dead. "What's the matter here, Sam?"

"Sir?"

"Radio's out." Bif looked at the back of the radio. The aerial was in place. But someone had removed an essential part, Bif knew, and maybe had it in his pocket now, or had thrown it over the side. "Do you know who touched this?"

"No, sir," said Sam, strongly suspecting Johnny.

"Damn nuisance," Bif murmured, and went out, toward the cabin.

Chuck saw him and said, "She's putting on some clothes now, Bif."

Bif snorted. "Well, ask her if she's finished yet."

Chuck knocked. "Are you finished dressing, ma'am?" he called to the closed hatch doors.

"Yes, you can come down."

The girl stood barefoot in Chuck's big dungarees, which she had rolled at the cuffs. She held the waist up with one hand.

"Got a belt—somewhere," said Chuck, and started rummaging in his drawer again. "Try this, Natalie." He handed her a brown leather belt. "You might have to tie it."

"Radio's dead," Bif said to Chuck, who looked only mildly surprised and not much interested. "We radioed shore that we picked a girl up, miss—but not your name. Won't your family be worried?"

The girl smiled her easy smile, which lit up her blue eyes. "My family?—They just think I'm on a camping trip. As long as you said you picked a girl *up*—What's the worry?"

Bif nodded, thinking that it wouldn't be long before the Coast Guard sent out a boat looking for the *Emma C,* and they were still headed away from home.

Chuck watched with fascination as the girl threaded the long belt through the loops of his dungarees, and tied it loosely in a way that left both ends hanging to one side. He was hoping the girl would hold out, that she'd decide she never wanted to go back on shore, that she'd stay—at least a week with them, even longer. Chuck envisaged the *Emma C* putting in for fresh food and water at any old port, while Natalie stayed below in the cabin out of sight.

"I'm not in a hurry to get back," the girl said finally.

Chuck glowed with satisfaction. His very words to Bif!

"I'd love to see the rest of the ship," she added.

Bif nodded in a puzzled way. "All right—Natalie."

"SOCKS!" ONCE MORE the drawer, and Chuck produced heavy white socks with a red stripe in the cuff.

The girl slipped these on quickly. "Marvelous!"

They all went up on deck. The girl lifted her face to the sun and smiled, looked above her at a gliding gull, at the horizon. Johnny stared with parted lips as she approached him.

Sam saw her and gripped the wheel hard in astonishment. Now she was walking toward the prow. Sam stared at her, wondering if she had his poem in a pocket of those trousers, thinking what a splendid figurehead she would make for the *Emma C,* looking just like this, leaning forward with the wind blowing her blonde hair back! Except that she deserved a better ship. What had Bif been thinking about while he was steering? They were way north, leaving Massachusetts Bay and entering the Atlantic, to eastward. It would take them all night to get back to Wellfleet, even if they put about now.

The girl turned and leaned back against the prow. She looked directly at Sam, and his heart jumped.

Sam raised his right hand in something between a wave and a salute, and suddenly grinned back at her.

Johnny came into the wheelhouse, and Sam left the helm before Johnny could say anything, so Johnny had to take it. Sam went down to the girl. The sun was setting.

"You're feeling better?" Sam asked.

She nodded. "Oh, sure!"

Sam kept a distance from her, partly out of courtesy, partly so he could better see her whole figure. "Did you—I'm the—"

"What?"

"I'm the one who wrote that lousy poem . . . You read it?"

"I don't think it's lousy."

Sam sighed, aching.

"Can you show me around the ship?"

"Certainly can!"

They began to walk aft on the starboard deck. Sam at once got a whiff of fish from the hold. He thought of the mackerel lying on salted ice below their feet now. That catch might have to be chucked. And why hadn't somebody thought to put Louie in the hold?

"That's the galley," Sam said, gesturing. "Cleaner than usual today, I have to admit. I think that's in your honor." He saw Filip still lying on the worn, shiny linoleum.

"Somebody's sleeping there?" she asked.

"Y-yes, ma'am," Sam said, aware of footsteps behind him.

It was Chuck behind him, with a grin that was merely bared teeth. "Well, Sam?"

"So—Chuck." Sam kept his cool. "Would you like to join us on a tour of the ship?"

Chuck followed them like a heavy, ugly shadow. Sam glanced at the girl for comfort, for alliance, but she was looking straight ahead, her gaze a bit lifted, as if unaware of Chuck's attitude. Her feet in the big white socks made no sound on the deck, and Sam could almost believe she didn't exist, except that when he glanced at her, the mere corner of her eye jolted him into reality. Sam heard Bif give an order for Johnny to put about. The port and starboard lights had come on. Filip's blood was still on the deck, but the girl didn't look down.

Then on the port deck, she stopped suddenly. She had seen the tarpaulin-wrapped form of Louie. The rope circle was smaller at his ankles. It was unmistakably a human form. *"This?"* she said, looking with wide blue eyes at Sam, then at Chuck.

Chuck cleared his throat and said, "Sacks.—Extra burlap sacks for fish. Have to keep 'em dry."

Sam walked on slowly with the girl, wishing he had thought to say that.

Now they were at the cabin hatch, and Chuck stopped, but the girl did not want to go in. She said she felt quite well now, and wanted to stay out in the air. Captain Bif spoke to Sam and also to Filip, who was now sitting on a bench in the galley: they were to prepare supper, a good supper as they'd all more or less missed lunch. Then the captain produced some red wine. It was homemade by the local Portuguese, not notably good, but not mouth-puckering either.

Sam slipped out the starboard galley door, and went forward to the cabin. From the drawer he shared with Johnny, Sam dragged out an orange waterproof jacket with a cozy lining, and dashed up the steps again and closed the hatches. He presented the jacket to the girl. "Getting cooler," Sam said.

She put it on. "Thank you, Sam. Just what I needed!"

Sam smiled, and without a glance at the other men, returned to his cooking. It was getting dark now. The *Emma C*'s white steaming light atop the mast shed a lovely glow over the ship, nearly as pretty as moonlight. And a moon would be coming up, Sam knew, nearly full. Someone, probably Johnny, had switched on a transistor to guitar music. Ordinarily Captain Bif forbade transistors except for news, but Bif was in a good mood tonight. Sam heard laughter, and occasionally the girl's soft voice, because the others fell silent when she spoke.

"Hey, the catch is starting to *stink!*" Chuck yelled out, and the others laughed, even Natalie.

Then Sam heard the planks over the hold being tossed aside on deck. Mackerel and the occasional pilchard arced over the bulwarks, over the stern.

"Pity the gulls're all asleep!" someone said.

Sam put frozen broccoli on to boil, and sipped his red wine. He could hear the captain laughing—a rare thing, Sam thought, with a half-a-hold catch going overboard. When Sam called everyone to table, the moon was up, and he had a glimpse of the girl leaning gracefully against the super-structure with her stemmed glass of wine—the only stemmed glass on board—and it seemed to Sam that she looked directly at him for a couple of seconds.

Johnny had lashed the helm. There was no other vessel in sight, and the Cape lights lay far ahead, somewhere, as yet invisible. Four sat at the table, including Natalie, who had been provided with a pillow for the hard bench and another pillow to lean back against. Sam was happy to stand and serve, and Captain Bif, with new found sprightliness, remained on his feet also, and peered out from time to time to see if another boat might be in the neighborhood.

"Natalie . . . Natalie . . ." But no one wanted to know her last name. No one asked where she lived. There were only questions like, "What is your favourite color? . . . What size shoe do you wear?" Were some of these idiots going to try to buy shoes for her, Sam wondered. But he also took note of her size: seven, sometimes seven and a half. No one asked her address. And there was much hearty laughter, at nothing. They were eating lamb chops, the best fare the freezer had afforded this evening. Natalie said the meal was delicious. Sam had discovered a jar of mint jelly to go with the lamb chops. And then ice cream. And more wine.

Johnny was a bit drunk, and sang "Moon River," addressing Natalie, but in a comical way addressing Chuck also, the man he had fought with that day.

"*. . . wherever you're going*
I'm going—with you-u . . ."

Chuck smiled contemptuously and told him to shut up.

After supper, they went on deck in the moonlight, and the jettisoning of fish continued. The girl declined the offer of a cigarette from Johnny.

She and two or three fellows were on the starboard deck where the moon shone brightest. Would he ever forget her face, Sam thought, as she stood leaning against the superstructure, hands behind her, in his orange jacket? The curve of her cheek, pale like the round moon? Sam wished another poem would spring full-blown to his mind, so he could write it out and give it to her, now.

More guffaws as Johnny fell into the stinking hold! Johnny pronounced the hold empty, and Chuck and Bif pulled him out. Sam went into the galley to help Filip, who was clearing away. They began to wash dishes.

On deck, the girl yawned like a child, and seeing this Captain Bif and Chuck both informed her that she was sleepy, that she'd had a long hard day.

"You'll sleep by yourself in the cabin," Chuck said. "And I'll be your guard." Chuck was weaving on his feet, from drink and fatigue. He had bumped his swollen lip, the skin had split, and it was bleeding a little.

"And I'll kiss her good night," said Johnny, approaching with a wobbling attempt at a bow.

Natalie laughed, turned slightly from Johnny, and at that moment Chuck swung a fist that caught Johnny squarely in the chest. Johnny went straight backward over the bulwark into the sea, and Chuck's feet slid forward, and he landed on his rump on the deck.

"What the hell *next* on this *boat!*" Bif bawled. "Na-ow—where in God's name's a *rope?*"

Natalie saw a rope first, the length that trailed from the tied feet of Louie, lifted it, and Bif hurled it over the side.

"Man overboard!" Bif yelled. "Turn about!"

Sam heard this and raced to the wheel. Johnny caught the rope after a minute or so, and was hauled gasping and spitting over a bulwark. He lay on the deck, mumbling still about kissing Natalie good night. Louie's shoes had become exposed, and the girl saw beyond a doubt what the tarpaulin contained. Chuck took her hand firmly, and led her to the cabin. The cabin light was on. Chuck took a blanket from another bunk and added this to the blanket she had, and tucked her feet.

"You'll be safe as a—as a bug in a rug," he assured her. He pulled two other blankets from the other bunks, and went on deck with them. Here he announced that no one was sleeping in the cabin that night except Natalie.

Bif laughed, as if Chuck's giving such an order amused him.

But no one protested. Filip wanted a sweater, and Chuck entered the cabin with a torch, as quietly as possible, got a sweater and jackets and oil slickers for warmth, and tossed them out on deck. Then he sat on deck with his back against the low cabin. Filip curled up on the galley floor, and Bif against the superstructure out of the wind. Sam was to steer for an hour or so, then awaken Bif. Sam lashed the wheel, leaned tiredly against the back wall of the wheelhouse, and smoked a rare cigarette, dreaming.

And *was* it a dream, Sam thought. His head was still buzzing from wine. If so, they were all dreaming it. Or was it only he, dreaming about all of them?

The captain offered to take over around 4 A.M. and Sam wrapped himself in a blanket and collapsed, face to the superstructure. Chuck was sleeping with his head between his knees, determined to sit up beside the cabin.

Around 6:30, Sam made coffee. The Cape showed fuzzily on the port side, but Wellfleet was a couple of hours away. The *Emma C* was still not doing her full speed. No one mentioned lowering the nets, trying for another catch. They were going to give up the girl, deliver her, in a little while. Johnny sipped black coffee and didn't want anything to eat. He cast dreary glances at the shore. It seemed to Sam that everyone's eyes were sad that morning. Chuck had finally stretched out with his back against the cabin below the hatch doors, and as others awakened, so did Chuck.

Sam wanted to go to Bif and say, "Let's put in for food and fuel and take off again!" But he couldn't give such an order. Instead, he poured two mugs of coffee and brought them on a tray to Chuck. "One for Natalie," Sam said.

Chuck stood up, folded his blanket, and fortified himself with a swallow of coffee. Then he rapped on the cabin hatch.

Sam lingered, not trying to look into the cabin, but listening for the girl's voice. She said, "Good morning, Chuck. Where are we now?" Sam walked on toward the galley.

A few minutes later, a Coast Guard launch slid near enough to hail them. "*Emma C!*—What's the matter with your *radio?*"

"Conked out!" Johnny replied before anyone else could.

"You got the Anderson girl?"

This time Bif replied. "Yep . . . Didn't know her name when we radioed you."

The man with the bullhorn said: "Heading for Wellfleet?"

"Yep!" Bif replied. "All's well."

The *Emma C* plowed on. Towards ten o'clock they were rounding the sandy spit that protected Wellfleet Harbor, and the wharves came into view. The girl was on deck in Chuck's dungarees, socks and shirt, and some five men on the dock stared and smiled and commented.

"... swimming and we picked her up!" Bif replied curtly to a question.

"That the Anderson girl? ... Why didn't you radio?"

Bif didn't reply. He was going to ignore or stave off the queries. The girl was safe, wasn't she? Unhurt.

Sam had a secondhand car on shore. So had Chuck, who did not live in Wellfleet. Sam was about to ask Natalie if he could drive her anywhere, even to Cambridge, when he heard the wharf fellows saying, "... police ... Coast Guard ..." and someone ran off to the wharf telephone booth, no doubt to notify these groups.

"Didn't you have your radio on, Bif, you—"

Bif didn't answer. But on the wharf he spoke with a police officer who had driven up in a patrol car. Bif was talking about their casualty, Louie Galganes, whose body they had on board. He had died as a result of a fall on deck, a head concussion. The officer said he would have to see Louie's work papers.

"From the looks of your crew, you had a rough trip, Bif," a wharf man said.

Another twenty-four hours on the *Emma C*, Bif was thinking, and he might not have had any crew at all.

Chuck held Natalie's hand as she stepped from the rocking boat onto the wharf. Two other men on the wharf were ready to assist. Natalie staggered a little and recovered, smiling. Three fellows stared at her, then a policeman spoke to her and began writing in a notebook. Chuck stood near, attentive.

"Your family's been really worried, miss. We'll phone them again to say that you're really here." Seeing that his fellow officer was busy with the tarpaulin bundle on the *Emma C*'s port deck, the officer went to the patrol car and spoke over the radio telephone.

"Chuck, you've been very nice to me. Thank you." The girl looked shy, a little awkward. She pulled a sock up higher. "Captain Bif—" She waited until he had removed his unlighted cigar and thrown it down. "I want to say thanks to all of you for saving me ... And you for finding me, Sam, and for the poem."

Sam was biting the tip of his tongue, staring at her as if sheer concentration could create a miracle, that she'd stay, that he'd have the courage to—to do what? If he asked her for a date next Saturday night, would she say yes? "A p-pleasure," he said finally.

The police officers were ready to take her in their car. "Nothing else with you, miss?"

Natalie lifted her hand, in which she carried her rolled up blue swimsuit. "No." She turned to Chuck. "I can return your clothes, if I know where to reach you—if I see you again. You can find my address in the phone book under Anderson—Herbert."

Chuck squirmed as if in pain. "Oh, I don't mind. I mean, you can keep the clothes. I just want to keep you—for my dream."

"For your what?"

"For my dream. Like a dream. *My* dream."

Sam heard this, with the taste of blood in his mouth, and realized that the girl must have left his orange jacket in the cabin. He could have given her *that*. Now he'd never wear that jacket again, just keep it. And damn fool Chuck, not to see her again! And yet, maybe that was what they all wanted, just this fantastic experience, this dream. Sam looked intently at Natalie as she waved to the crew, then got into the police car. All the crew, Filip, Johnny, and Chuck and Bif were staring at the girl in the same way. Then Sam blinked, and took his eyes away from the departing black car.

A police car was an ugly object.

Old Folks
at Home

"**W**ell," Lois said finally, "let's do it." Her expression as she looked at her husband was serious, a little worried, but she spoke with conviction.

"Okay," said Herbert, tensely.

They were going to adopt an elderly couple to live with them. More than elderly, old probably. It was not a hasty decision on the part of the McIntyres. They had been thinking about it for several weeks. They had no children themselves, and didn't want any. Herbert was a strategy analyst at a government-sponsored institution called Bayswater, some four miles from where they lived, and Lois was an historian, specializing in European history of the seventeenth and eighteenth centuries. Thirty-three years old now, she had three books and a score of articles to her credit. She and Herbert could afford a pleasant two-story house in Connecticut with a glass-enclosed sunroom that was Herbert's workroom and also their main library, handsome grounds and a part-time gardener all year round to look after their lawn and trees, bushes and flowers. They knew people in the neighborhood, friends and acquaintances, who had children—young children and teenagers—and the McIntyres felt a little guilty about not fulfilling their duty in this department; and besides that, they had seen an old people's nursing home at first hand a few months ago, when Eustace Vickers, a retired inventor attached to Bayswater, had passed away. The McIntyres, along with a few of Herbert's colleagues, had paid a visit every few days to Eustace, who had been popular and active until his stroke.

One of the nurses at the home had told Lois and Herbert that lots of families in the region took in old people for a week at a time, especially in winter or at the Christmas season, to give them a change, "a taste of family life for a few days," and they came back much cheered and improved. "Some people are kind enough to adopt an old person—even a couple— to live with them in their homes," the nurse had said.

Lois remembered her shudder at the thought, then, with a twinge of guilt. Old people didn't live forever. She and Herbert might be in the same boat one day, objects of semi-charity, really, dependent on the whim of nurses for basic physical needs. And old people loved to be helpful around the house, if they possibly could be, the nurse had said.

"We'll have to go—and look," Herbert said to Lois, then broke out in a grin suddenly. "Something like shopping for an orphan child, eh?"

Lois laughed too. To laugh was a relief after the earnest conversation of the past minutes. "Are you joking? Orphanages give people the children the *orphanages* choose to give. What kind of a child do you think we'd rate, Herb? White? High I.Q.? Good health? I doubt it."

"I doubt it too. We don't go to church."

"And we don't vote, because we don't know which party to vote for."

"That's because you're an historian. And I'm a policy analyzer. Oh yes, and I don't sleep at regular hours and sometimes switch on foreign news at four in the morning. But—you really mean this, Lois?"

"I said I did."

So Lois rang up the Hilltop Home and asked to speak to the superintendent. She was not sure of his or her title. A man's voice came on, and Lois explained her and her husband's intentions in prepared words. "I was told such arrangements were made sometimes—for six months, for instance." These last words had come out of nowhere, as if by themselves.

The man on the telephone gave the shortest of laughs. "Well—yes, it would be possible—and a great help usually for all concerned. Would you and your husband like to come and see us, Mrs. McIntyre?"

Lois and Herbert drove to the Hilltop Home just before seven that evening. They were received by a young nurse in blue and white uniform, who sat with them in a waiting room for a few minutes and told them that the ambulant guests were having their dinner in the refectory, and that she had spoken to three or four couples about the McIntyres' offer, and two of the couples had been interested, and two hadn't.

"These senior citizens don't always know what's good for them," the nurse said, smiling. "How long did you and your husband plan on, Mrs. McIntyre?"

"Well—doesn't it depend on whether *they're* happy?" Lois asked.

The nurse pondered with a slight frown, and Lois felt that she wasn't thinking about her question, but was turning over a formularized response. "I asked because we usually consider these arrangements permanent, unless of course the single guest or the couple wishes to return to the Hilltop."

Lois felt a cold shock, and supposed that Herbert did too, and she did not look at him. "Has that happened? They want to come back?"

"Not often!" The nurse's laugh sounded merry and practiced.

They were introduced to Boris and Edith Basinsky by the nurse in blue and white. This was in the "TV room," which was a big long room with two television sets offering different programs. Boris Basinsky had Parkinson's disease, the nurse volunteered within Mr. Basinsky's hearing. His face was rather gray, but he smiled, and extended a shaking hand to Herbert, who shook it firmly. His wife, Edith, appeared older than he and rather thin, though her blue eyes looked at the McIntyres brightly. The TV noise conflicted with the words the McIntyres were trying to exchange with the Basinskys, such as, "We live nearby . . . we're thinking . . ." and the Basinskys' "Yes, Nurse Phyllis told us about you today. . . ."

Then the Forsters, Mamie and Albert. Mamie had broken her hip a year ago, but could walk now with a cane. Her husband was a tall and lanky type, rather deaf and wearing a hearing aid whose cord disappeared down the open collar of his shirt. His health was quite good, said Nurse Phyllis, except for a recent stroke which made it difficult for him to walk, but he did walk, with a cane also.

"The Forsters have one son, but he lives in California and—isn't in a good position to take them on. Same with the two or three grandchildren," said Nurse Phyllis. "Mamie loves to knit. And you know a lot about *gardening,* don't you, Mamie?"

Mamie's eyes drank in the McIntyres as she nodded.

Lois felt suddenly overwhelmed, somehow drowned by gray heads all around her, wrinkled faces tipped back in laughter at the events on the TV screen. She clutched Herbert's tweed jacket sleeve.

That night around midnight, they decided on the Forsters. Later, they were to ask themselves, had they decided on the Forsters because their name sounded more ordinary, more "Anglo-Saxon"? Mightn't the Basinskys have been an easier pair, even if the man had Parkinson's, which required the occasional enema, Nurse Phyllis had warned?

A few days later, on a Sunday, Mamie and Albert Forster were installed in the McIntyre house. In the preceding week, a middle-aged woman from the Hilltop Home had come to inspect the house and the room the

Forsters would have, and seemed genuinely pleased with the standard of comfort the McIntyres could offer. The Forsters took the room the McIntyres called their guest room, the prettier of the two extra rooms upstairs, with its two windows giving on the front lawn. It had a double bed, which the McIntyres thought the Forsters wouldn't object to, though they didn't consult the Forsters about it. Lois had cleared the guest room closet completely, and also the chest of drawers. She had brought an armchair from the other twin-bed spare room, which meant two comfortable armchairs for the Forsters. The bathroom was just across the hall, the main bathroom with a tub in it, though downstairs there was also a shower with basin and toilet. This move took place around 5 P.M. Lois's and Herbert's neighbors the Mitchells, who lived about a mile away, had asked them for drinks, which usually meant dinner, but Herbert had declined on Saturday on the telephone, and had explained why. Then Pete Mitchell had said, "I understand—but how about our dropping in on you tomorrow around seven? For half an hour?"

"Sure." Herbert had smiled, realizing that the Mitchells were simply curious about the elderly pair. Pete Mitchell was a history professor at a local college. The Mitchells and the McIntyres often got together to compare notes for their work.

And here they were, Pete and Ruth Mitchell, Pete standing in the living room with his scotch on the rocks, and Ruth with a Dubonnet and soda in an armchair, both smiling.

"Seriously," Pete said, "how long is this going to last? Did you have to sign anything?" Pete spoke softly, as if the Forsters, way upstairs and in a remote corner, might hear them.

"Well—paper of agreement—responsibility, yes. I read it over, no mention of—time limit for either of us, perpetuity or anything like that."

Ruth Mitchell laughed. "Perpetuity!"

"Where's Lois?" Pete asked.

"Oh, she's—" At that moment, Herbert saw her entering the living room, brushing her hair to one side with a hand, and it struck him that she looked tired. "Everything okay, darling?"

"Hel-lo, Ruth and Pete!" Lois said. "Yes, everything's all right. I was just helping them unpack, hanging things and putting stuff in the medicine cabinet in the bathroom. I'd forgotten to clear a shelf there."

"Lots of pills, I suppose," said Pete, his eyes still bright with curiosity. "But you said they were both ambulant at least."

"Oh sure," said Lois. "In fact I asked them to come down and join us.

They might like—Oh, there's some white wine in the fridge, isn't there, Herb? Tonic too."

"Can they get down the stairs all right?" asked Herbert, suddenly recalling their rather slow progress up the stairs. Herbert went off toward the stairway.

Lois followed him.

At that moment, Mamie Forster was descending the stairs one at a time, with a hand touching the wall, and her husband, also with his cane, was just behind her. As Herbert dashed up to lend an arm to Mamie, Albert caught his heel, lurched forward and bumped his wife who went tumbling toward Herbert. Albert regained his balance with his cane, Herbert seized Mamie's right arm, but this did not prevent her from swinging forward and striking Lois who had started up the stairs at a fast pace. It was Lois who fell backward, landing on the floor and bumping her head against the wall. Mamie cried out with pain.

"My arm!" she said.

But Herbert had her, she hadn't fallen, and he released her arm and looked to his wife. Lois was getting to her feet, rubbing her head, putting on a smile.

"I'm quite okay, Herb. Don't worry."

"Good idea—" Albert Forster was saying as he shuffled toward the living room.

"What?" Herbert hovered near Mamie, who was walking all right, but rubbing her arm.

"Good idea to put a *handrail* on those stairs!" Albert had a habit of shouting, perhaps because he did not move his lips much when he spoke, and therefore what he said was not clear.

Lois introduced Mamie and Albert Forster to Pete and Ruth, who got up from her armchair to offer it to one or the other of them. There were pleasant murmurs from the Mitchells, who hoped the Forsters would enjoy their new surroundings. The Mitchells' eyes surveyed both the Forsters, Mamie's round gray head with its quite thin hair all fluffed up and curled evidently by a professional hairdresser to make it seem more abundant, the pale pink apron that she wore over her cotton dress, her tan house slippers with limp red pompoms. Albert wore plaid house slippers, creaseless brown corduroy trousers, an old coat sweater over a flannel shirt. His expression was slightly frowning and aggressively inquisitive, as if consciously or unconsciously he had decided to hang on to an attitude of a more vigorous prime.

They wanted the television on. There was a program at 7:30 that they always watched at the Hilltop.

"You don't like television?" asked Mamie of Lois, who had just turned the set on. Mamie was seated now, still rubbing her right elbow.

"Oh, of course!" said Lois. "Why not?" she added gaily.

"We were—we were just wondering—since it's there, why isn't it *on*?" said Albert out of his slightly parted but hardly moving lips. If he had chewed tobacco, one would have thought that he was trying to hold some juice inside his lower lip.

As Lois thought this, Albert drooled a little saliva and caught it on the back of his hand. His pale blue eyes, now wide, had fixed on the television screen. Herbert came in with a tray that held a glass of white wine for Albert, tomato juice for Mamie, and a bowl of cashew nuts.

"Could you turn up the *sound*, Mis'r McIntyre?" asked Albert.

"This all right?" asked Herbert, having turned it up.

Albert first laughed at something on the screen—it was a sitcom and someone had slipped and fallen on a kitchen floor—and glanced at his wife to see if she was also amused. Smiling emptily, rubbing her elbow as if she had forgotten to stop, eyes on the screen, Mamie did not look at Albert. "More—*louder,* please, if y'don't mind," said Albert.

With a quick smile at Pete Mitchell, who was also smiling, Herbert put it up even louder, which precluded conversation. Herbert caught his wife's eye and jerked his head toward the sunroom. The four adjourned, bringing their drinks, grinning.

"Whew!" said Ruth.

Pete laughed loudly, as Herbert closed the door to the living room. "Another TV set next, Herb. For them up in their room."

Lois knew Pete was right. The Forsters could take the living room set, Lois was thinking. Herbert had a TV set here in his workroom. She was about to say something to this effect, when she heard, barely, a call from Mamie. The TV drama was over and its theme music boomed. Through the glass door, she saw Mamie looking at her, calling again. When Lois went into the living room, Mamie said:

"We're used to eating at seven. Even earlier. What time do you people eat supper?"

Lois nodded—it was a bore to try to shout over the blaring TV—raised a forefinger to indicate that she would be right on the job, and went off to the kitchen. She was going to broil lamb chops for dinner, but the Forsters were in too much of a hurry for that.

After a few minutes, Herbert went looking for Lois, and found her spooning scrambled eggs onto warmed plates on the stove. She had made toast, and there were also slices of cold boiled ham on a separate plate. This was to go on trays of the kind that stood up on the floor.

"Help me with one of these?" Lois asked.

"The Mitchells think we're nuts. They say it's going to get worse—a lot worse. And then what do we do?"

"Maybe it won't get *worse*," Lois said.

Herbert wanted to pause a moment before taking the tray in. "You think after we tuck them in bed we could go over to the Mitchells'? They've asked us for dinner. You think it's safe—to leave them?"

Lois hesitated, knowing Herbert knew it wasn't safe. "No."

THE LIVING ROOM television set was brought up to the Forsters' room. TV was the Forsters' main diversion or occupation, even their only one, from what Lois could see. It was on from morning till night, and Lois sometimes sneaked into their bedroom at eleven o'clock or later to switch it off, partly to save electricity, but mainly because the noise of it was maddening, and her and Herbert's bedroom was adjacent on the same side of the hall. Lois took a small flashlight into their bedroom to do this. The Forsters' teeth stood in two glasses on their night table, usually, though once Lois had seen a pair in a glass on the shelf in the bathroom, out of which she and Herbert had moved their toothbrushes, shampoos and shaving articles to the smaller bathroom downstairs. The teeth gave Lois an unpleasant shock, and so they did when she switched off the loud TV every night, even though she did not shine the light on them: she simply knew they were there, one pair, anyway, and maybe the second pair was in the big bathroom. She marveled that anyone could fall asleep with the TV's bursts of canned laughter, marveled also that the sudden silence never woke the Forsters up. Mamie and Albert had said they would be more comfortable in separate beds, so Lois and Herbert had made the exchange between the two upstairs rooms, and the Forsters now had the twin beds.

A handrail had been installed on the stairway, a slender black iron rail, rather pretty and Spanish-looking. But now the Forsters seldom came downstairs, and Lois served their meals to them on trays. They loved the TV, they said, because it was in color, and those at the Hilltop hadn't been. Lois took on the tray-carrying, thinking it was what was called women's work, though Herbert fetched and carried some of the time too.

"Certainly a bore," Herbert said, scowling one morning in his pajamas and dressing gown, about to take up the heavy tray of boiled eggs and teapot and toast. "But it's better than having them fall down the stairs and break a leg, isn't it?"

"Frankly, what's the difference if one of them did have a leg broken now?" Lois replied, and giggled nervously.

Lois's work suffered. She had to slow up on a long article she was writing for an historical quarterly, and the deadline made her anxious. She worked downstairs in a small study off the living room and on the other side of the living room from Herbert's workroom. Three or four times a day she was summoned by a shout from Mamie or Albert—they wanted more hot water for their tea (four o'clock ritual), because it was too strong, or Albert had mislaid his glasses, and could Lois find them, because Mamie couldn't. Sometimes Lois and Herbert had to be out of the house at the same time, Lois at the local library and Herbert at Bayswater. Lois had not the same joy as in former days on returning to her home: it wasn't a haven any longer that belonged to her and Herbert, because the Forsters were upstairs and might at any moment yell for something. Albert smoked an occasional cigar, not a big fat one, but a brand that smelled bitter and nasty to Lois, and she could smell it even downstairs when he lit up. He had burnt two holes in the brown and yellow cover on his bed, much to Lois's annoyance, as it was a handwoven blanket from Santa Fe. Lois had warned him and Mamie that letting ash drop could be dangerous. She hadn't been able to tell, from Albert's excuses, whether he had been asleep or merely careless.

Once, on returning from the library with some borrowed books and a folder of notes, Lois had been called upstairs by Mamie. Mamie was dressed, but lying on her bed, propped against pillows. The TV was not as loud as usual, and Albert appeared to be dozing on the other twin bed.

"Can't find my *teet!*" Mamie said petulantly, tears started to her eyes, and Lois saw from her downturned mouth, her little clamped jaw, that she was indeed toothless just now.

"Well—that should be easy." Lois went into the bathroom, but a glance revealed that no teeth or toothglass stood on the shelf above the basin. She even looked on the floor, then returned to the Forsters' bedroom and looked around. "Did you have them out—in bed?"

Mamie hadn't, and it was her lowers, not her uppers, and she was tired of looking. Lois looked under the bed, around the TV, the tops of the bookcases, the seats of the armchairs. Mamie assured Lois they were not in the pockets of her apron, but Lois felt the pockets anyway. Was old Albert playing a silly trick, playing at being asleep now? Lois realized that she didn't really know these old people.

"You didn't flush them down the toilet by accident?"

"No! And I'm tired of looking," said Mamie. "I'm tired!"

"Were you downstairs?"

"No!"

Lois sighed, and went downstairs. She needed a cup of strong coffee. While she was making this, she noticed that the lid was off the cake tin, that a good bit of the pound cake was gone. Lois didn't care about the cake, but it was a clue: the teeth might be downstairs. Lois knew that Mamie—maybe both of them—came downstairs sometimes when she and Herbert were out. The big square ashtray on the coffee table would be turned a little so that it looked like a diamond shape, which Lois detested, or Herbert's leather chair would be pulled out from his desk, instead of shoved close as he always left it, as if Mamie or Albert had tried the chair. Why couldn't the Forsters be equally mobile for their meals? Now with her coffee mug in hand, Lois looked over her kitchen—for teeth. She looked in her own study, where nothing seemed out of place, then went through the living room, then into Herbert's workroom. His chair was as he would have left it, but still she looked. They'll turn up, she thought, if they weren't somehow down the toilet. Finally, Lois sat down on the sofa with the rest of her coffee, and leaned back, trying to relax.

"My God!" she said, sitting up, setting the mug down on the coffee table. She had nearly spilled what was in the mug.

There were the teeth—lowers, Lois assumed—on the edge of the shelf of the coffee table that was otherwise filled with magazines. The denture looked shockingly narrow, like the lower jaw of a little rabbit. Lois took a breath. She would have to handle them. She went to the kitchen for a paper towel.

HERBERT LAUGHED LIKE a fool at the teeth story. They told it to their friends. They still had their friends, no change there. After two months, the McIntyres had had two or three rather noisy and late dinner parties at their house. With their TV going, the Forsters presumably heard nothing; at any rate, they didn't complain or make a remark, and the McIntyres' friends seemed to be able to forget there was an elderly pair upstairs, though everyone knew it. Lois did notice that she and Herbert couldn't or didn't

invite their New York friends for the weekend any longer, realizing that
their friends wouldn't want to share the upstairs bathroom or the Forsters'
TV racket. Christopher Forster, the son in California, had written the
McIntyres a letter in longhand. The letter read as if it had been prompted
by the Hilltop Home: it was courteous, expressed gratitude, and he hoped
that Mom and Dad were pleased with their new home.

> I would take them on but my wife and me haven't got too much
> extra space here, just one room as spare that our own children and
> families use when they visit us . . . Will try to get the grandchildren
> to write but the whole family is not much for writing . . .

The letterhead stated the name and address of a drycleaning shop of
which Christopher Forster was not the manager. Albert Forster, Lois
remembered, had been a salesman of some kind.

Albert started wetting the bed, and Lois acquired a rubber sheet. Albert
complained of backache from "the damp," so Lois offered him the double
bed in the spare room, while she aired the twin-bed mattress for a couple
of days. She telephoned the Hilltop Home to ask if there were pills that
Albert might take, and had he had this complaint before? They said no, and
asked if Albert was happy. Lois went to see the Hilltop Home doctor in
attendance, and got some pills from him, but he doubted the complete
efficacy of the pills, he said, if the subject was not even aware of his damp-
ness until he woke up in the morning.

The second teeth story was not so funny, though both Herbert and
Lois laughed at first. Mamie reported that she had dropped her teeth—
again the lowers—down the heating vent in the floor of the bathroom. The
teeth were not visible down there in the blackness, even when Herbert and
Lois shone a flashlight. All they saw was a little dark gray lint or dust.

"You're sure?" Herbert asked Mamie, who was watching them.

"Dropped 'em *bot'* but only one fell t'rough!" said Mamie.

"Damned grill's so narrow," Herbert said.

"So are her teeth," said Lois.

Herbert got the grill off with a screwdriver. He rolled up his sleeves,
poked gently at first in the fluffy dust, then with equal delicacy explored
more deeply with a bottlebrush, not wanting to send the denture falling all
the way down, if he could help it. At last he and Lois had to conclude that
the teeth must have fallen all the way down, and the heating tube, rather
square, curved about a yard down. Had the teeth fallen all the way into the

furnace below? Herbert went down alone to the cellar, and looked with a feeling of hopelessness at the big square, rivet-secured funnel that went off the furnace and branched into six tubes that brought the heat to various rooms. Which one even belonged to the upstairs bathroom? Was it worth it to tear the whole furnace apart? Certainly not. The furnace was working as usual, and maybe the teeth had burned up. Herbert went downstairs and undertook to explain the situation to Mamie.

"We'll see that you get another set, Mamie. Might even fit better. Didn't you say these hurt and that's why—" He paused at Mamie's tragic expression. Her eyes could get a crumpled look that touched him, or disturbed him, even though he thought Mamie was usually putting on an act.

However, between him and Lois, she was consoled. She could eat "easy things" while the dental work was done. Lois at once seized on the idea of taking Mamie back to the Hilltop Home, where they might well have a dentist in residence, or an office there where dentists could work, but if they had, the Hilltop Home denied it on the telephone to Lois. This left her and Herbert to take Mamie to their own dentist in Hartford, twenty-three miles away, and the trips seemed endless, though Mamie enjoyed the rides. There was a cast of lower gums to be made, and of the upper denture for the bite, and just when Herbert and Lois, who took turns, had thought that the job was done in pretty good time, came the "fittings."

"The lowers always present more difficulties than the uppers," Dr. Feldman told them regretfully. "And my client here is pretty fussy."

It was plain to the McIntyres that Mamie was putting on an act about the lowers hurting or not fitting, so she could be taken for rides back and forth. Every two weeks, Mamie wanted her hair cut and waved at a beauty salon in Hartford, which she thought better than the one in the town near where the McIntyres lived. Social Security and the pension sent on by the Hilltop helped more than fifty percent with the Forsters' expenses, but bills of the hairdresser and also the dentist the McIntyres paid. Ruth and Pete Mitchell commiserated with the McIntyres by telephone or in person (at the same time laughing their heads off), as if the McIntyres were being afflicted with the plagues of Job. In Herbert's opinion, they were. Herbert became red in the face with repressed wrath, with frustration from losing work time, but he couldn't countenance Lois losing more of her time than he did, so he did his half of hauling Mamie back and forth, and both the McIntyres took books to read in the dentist's waiting room. Twice they took Albert along, as he wanted to go, but once he peed in the waiting room before Herbert could point out the nearby toilet (Albert's deafness made him slow to understand what people were saying), so Lois and Herbert flatly refused to take him along again, saying sympathetically but really quite grimly that he shouldn't risk having to go to the toilet again in a hurry, if he happened to be in a public place. Albert snatched out his hearing aid while Lois was speaking about this. It was Albert's way of switching off.

That was in mid-May. The McIntyres had intended to fly out to Santa Barbara, where Herbert's parents had a house plus a guest house in the garden, and to rent a car there and drive up to Canada. Every other summer they visited the older McIntyres, and it had always been fun. Now that was impossible. It was impossible to think of Mamie and Albert running the house, difficult but maybe not impossible to engage the services of someone who would look after them and sleep in, full time. When they had taken on the Forsters, Lois was sure they had been more able to get about. Mamie had talked of working in the garden of the Hilltop Home, but Lois had not been able to interest Mamie in doing anything in their garden in April, even the lightest of work, such as sitting and watching. She said something to this effect to Herbert.

"I know, and it's going to get worse, not better," he replied.

"What do you mean exactly?"

"This bed-wetting—Kids'll grow out of it. Kids grow other teeth if them lose 'em." Herbert laughed madly for an instant. "But these two'll just get more decrepit." He pronounced the last word with bitter amusement and looked Lois in the eyes. "Have you noticed the way Albert bangs his cane now—instead of just tapping it? They're not *satisfied* with us. And they're in the saddle! We can't even have a vacation this summer—unless we can possibly shove 'em back in the Hilltop for a month or so. You think it's worth a try?"

"Yes!" Lois' heart gave a leap. "Maybe. What a good idea, Herb!"

"Let's have a drink on it!" They were standing in the kitchen, about to have their own dinner, the Forsters having been served earlier upstairs. Herbert made Lois a scotch, and replenished his own glass. "And speaking of shoving," he went on, pronouncing his words very clearly as he did when he had something to say that passionately interested him, "Dr. Feldman said today that there was absolutely nothing the matter with Mamie's lowers, no sign of gum irritation, and he could hardly pull 'em off her jaw himself, they fitted so well. Ha!—Ha-ha-ha-a!" Herbert fell about the kitchen laughing. He had lost three hours taking Mamie to the dentist that afternoon. "The goddamn last time—*today!* I was saving it to tell you." Herbert lifted his glass and drank.

When Lois rang the Hilltop the next morning, she was told that their accommodations were more than filled, some people were four in a room or booked for that, because so many other people were placing their elderly relatives in the Hilltop in order to be free for vacations themselves. Somehow Lois didn't believe the mechanical-sounding voice. But what could she do about it? She didn't believe that *so* many people lived with their parents or grandparents these days. Yet if they didn't, what did people do with them? Lois had a vision of a tribe shoving its elders off a cliff, and she shook her head to get the thought out, and stood up from the telephone. Lois did not tell Herbert.

Unfortunately, Herbert, who fetched the tray down at lunchtime, shouted to the Forsters that they would be going back to the Hilltop for two months that summer. He turned the TV down and repeated it with a big smile. "Another nice change of *scene*. You can see some of your old friends again—visit with them." He looked at both of them, and saw at once that the idea did not appeal.

Mamie exchanged a look with her husband. They were lying on their respective beds, shoes off, propped facing the TV screen. "No particular friends *there*," said Mamie.

In her sharp eyes Herbert saw a blood-chilling hostility. Mamie knew also that she wasn't going to be driven to the Hartford dentist or hairdresser again. Herbert did not mention this conversation to Lois. But Lois told Herbert during their lunch that the Hilltop Home had no room this summer. She hadn't wanted to disturb Herbert with the bad news while he had been working that morning.

"Well, that cooks it," Herbert said. "Damn, I'd like to get away this summer. Even for *two* weeks."

"Well, you can. I'll—"

Herbert shook his head bitterly, slowly. "We might do it in shifts? No, darling."

Then they heard Albert's cane—it made a different sound from Mamie's—tapping down the stairs. Then another cane. Both the Forsters were coming down. Most unusual. Lois and Herbert braced themselves as if for enemy attack.

"We don't want to go to the Hilltop this summer," said Mamie. "You—"

"No!" said Albert with a bang of his cane from his standing position.

"You agreed to let us *live* with you." Mamie had her squinty, pity-poor-me face on again, while Albert's eyes were suspicious, his lower lip twisted with inquiry.

"Well," said Lois with an embarrassed, retreating feeling that she hated, "the Hilltop is filled up, so you needn't worry. Everything's all right."

"But you *tried*," said Mamie.

"We're trying—to have a little *vacation*," said Herbert loudly for the deaf Albert's benefit, and he felt like socking the old bed-wetting bastard and knocking him down, old as he was. How dare that recipient of charity glare at him as if he were a crook, or someone who meant to do him harm?

"We don't understand," said Albert. "Are you trying—"

"You're staying *here*," Lois interrupted, forcing a huge smile to calm the atmosphere, if she could.

But Mamie began again, and Herbert was livid. They both spoke at once, Albert joined in, and in the Babel-like roar, Lois heard her husband assuring the Forsters grimly that they were *staying*, and heard the Forsters saying that the McIntyres had gone back on their word to them and the Hilltop. The phrase ". . . not *fair*" came again and again from the mouths of Mamie and Albert, until Herbert uttered a dreadful curse and turned his back. Then there was a sudden silence which fairly made Lois's ears ring, and thank God Albert decided to turn and leave the kitchen, but in the living room he paused, and Lois saw that he had begun to pee. *Is that deliberate?* Lois wondered as she rushed toward him to steer him toward the downstairs bathroom which was to the right of the kitchen door around a partition of bookshelves. She and Albert were on the way, but by the time they got there, Albert was finished, and the pale green carpet quite splotched between kitchen and the bathroom door which she had not even opened. She jerked her hand away from his coat-sweatered arm, disgusted that she had even touched him.

She went back to her husband, past Mamie. "My God," she said to Herbert.

Herbert stood like a fortress with feet apart, arms folded, eyebrows lowered. He said to his wife, "We'll make it." Then he sprang into action, grabbed a floor rag from a cupboard under the sink, wet it, and tackled the splotches on their carpet.

Albert was on his slow way upstairs, Mamie started to follow him, but paused to present her stricken face to Lois once more. Herbert was stooped and scrubbing, and didn't see it. Lois turned away and faced the stove. When Lois looked again, Mamie was creeping toward the stairs.

As Herbert rinsed and re-rinsed the floor cloth, a task he would not let Lois take over, he muttered plans. He would speak with the Hilltop Home in person, inform them that since he and Lois worked at home and needed a certain amount of solitude and silence, they could not and should not have to spend more money for a full-time servant to take meals upstairs, plus changing bed linen every day. When they had taken on the Forsters, they had both been continent and more able to look after themselves, as far as the McIntyres had known.

Herbert went to the Hilltop Home that afternoon around three, without having made an appointment. He was in an aggressive enough mood to insist on seeing the right person, and he had thought it best not to make an appointment. Finally, he was shown into the office of one Stephen Culwart, superintendent, a slender, balding man, who told him calmly that the Forsters could not be taken back into the Hilltop, because there was no room. Mr McIntyre could get in touch with the Forsters' son, of course, and another home might be found, but the problem was no longer the responsibility of the Hilltop Home. Herbert went away frustrated, and a bit tired, though he knew the tiredness was only mental and that he'd best shake it off.

Lois had been writing in her study off the living room, with her door closed, when she heard a crash of breaking glass. She went into the living room and found Mamie in a trembling state near the bookshelf partition outside the kitchen door. Mamie said she had been downstairs and had wanted to use the downstairs toilet, and had bumped the vase at the end of one of the bookshelves by accident. Mamie's manner was one of curiously mixed aggression and apology. Not for the first time, Mamie gave Lois the creeps.

"And I'd like to have some knitting," Mamie said quaveringly.

"Knitting?" Lois pressed the side of the pencil in her hand with her thumb, not hard enough to break it. She herself felt shattered at the sight of the blue and white glass shards near her feet. She had loved that Chinese vase, which had belonged to her mother—not a museum piece, perhaps, that vase, but still special and valuable. The point was, Mamie had done it on purpose. "What kind of knitting? You mean—wool for knitting?"

"Ye-es! Several colors. And *needles,*" Mamie said almost tearfully, like a pitiable pauper begging for alms.

Lois nodded. "Very well."

Mamie made her slow, waddling way toward the stairs. Gay music came from the TV set above, an afternoon serial's theme music.

Lois swept up the vase, which was too much in pieces—or she thought so now—to be mended. Nevertheless, she kept the pieces, in a plastic bag, and then Herbert came in and told her his lack of success.

"I think we'd better see a lawyer," Herbert said. "I don't know what else to do."

Lois tried to calm him with a cup of tea in the kitchen. They could get in touch with the son again, Lois said. A lawyer would be expensive and maybe not even successful. "But they know something's up," Lois said as she sipped her tea.

"How so? . . . What do you mean?"

"I feel it. In the atmosphere." Lois didn't tell him about the vase, and hoped that he would not soon notice it.

Lois wrote to Christopher Forster. Mamie knitted, and Albert peed. Lois and their once-a-week cleaning girl, Rita, a plump half–Puerto Rican girl who was cheerful and an angel, rinsed the sheets and hung them on the garden line. Mamie presented Lois with a round knitted doily which was rather pretty but of a dark purple color that Lois didn't care for, or was she simply all round turned off of Mamie? Lois praised Mamie for her work, said she loved the doily, and put it in the center of the coffee table. Mamie did not seem gratified by Lois's words, strangely, but put on her wrinkled frown. After that, Mamie began turning out messes of mixed colors, dropped stitches, in articles presumably meant to be more doilies, or teapot cozies, even socks. The madness of these items made Lois and Herbert more uneasy. Now it was mid-June. Christopher had replied that his house situation was more strained than ever, because his own four-year-old grandson was spending the summer with him and his wife, as his parents were probably going to get a divorce, so the last thing he could do just now was take on his father and Mamie. Herbert invested in an hour's consultation with a lawyer, who suggested that the McIntyres might take up the situation with Medicare, combined with cooperation from Christopher Forster, or Herbert might look for another rest home for the elderly, where the problem might be difficult for him, because he was not a blood relation, and would have to explain that he had taken on responsibility for the Forsters from the Hilltop Home.

Herbert and Lois's neighbors rallied round with moral support and invitations to break their monotony, but none offered to put the Forsters up for even a week. Lois mentioned this to Herbert, jokingly, and both of them smiled at the idea: that was too much to expect even from the best of friends, and the fact that such an offer had not been forthcoming from the Mitchells or their other good friends the Lowenhooks did not diminish the McIntyres' esteem for their friends. The fact was that the Forsters were, combined, a pain, a cross, albatrosses. And now the Forsters were waging a subtle war. Things got broken. Lois no long cared what happened to

Albert's mattress, or the carpet upstairs for that matter, as she had crossed them off. She did not suggest taking Albert's trousers to the cleaners, because she didn't care what their condition was. Let them stew in their own juice was a phrase that crossed her mind, but she never said it aloud. Lois was worried that Herbert might crack up. They had both reached the point, by early August, at which they could no longer laugh, even cynically.

"Let's rent a couple of studios—office rooms to work in, Lois," Herbert said one evening. "I've been looking around. There're two free in the same building on Barington Street in Hartford. Four hundred dollars a month—each. It's worth it, to me at least and I'm sure to you. You've really had the worst of it." Herbert's eyes were pinkish from fatigue, but he was able to smile.

Lois thought it a wonderful idea. Eight hundred dollars a month seemed not outrageous to pay for peace of mind, for the ability to concentrate. "I can make them a box lunch with thermoses . . ."

Herbert laughed, and tears of relief made his eyes shine. "And I'll be your chauffeur for our nine-to-five jobs. Think of it—*solitude*—in our own little cells!"

Lois and Herbert installed themselves the following Monday in the Hartford office rooms. They took typewriters, business files, letters, books, and Lois her manuscript-in-progress. When Lois had told Mamie about the move the weekend before, Mamie had asked who was going to serve their meals, and then Lois had explained that she would be here to serve their breakfast and dinner, and for lunch they'd have—a picnic, a surprise, with a thermos of hot soup, another of hot tea.

"Teatime . . ." Albert had begun vaguely, with an accusing eye fixed on Lois.

"Anyway, it's *done*," Lois had said, meaning it, because she and Herbert had signed a six-month agreement.

Mamie and Albert soured still more against the McIntyres. Albert's bed was wet every evening when the McIntyres came home between six and seven, and changing it was Lois's duty before preparing dinner. Herbert insisted on rinsing the sheet or sheets himself and hanging them either on the garden line or on the cellar line if it looked like rain.

"Moving out of your own house for those so-and-sos," Pete Mitchell said one evening when he and Ruth came for drinks. "That's a bit much, isn't it?"

"But we can work," Herbert replied. "It *is* better. Isn't it, Lois?"

"It really is. It's obvious," Lois said to the Mitchells, but she could see that they didn't believe her, that they thought she was merely trying hard. Lois was aware that she and Herbert had been to the Mitchells' house perhaps only once for dinner since the Forsters' arrival six months ago, because they, she and Herbert, felt too uneasy to leave the Forsters alone from eight in the evening till maybe after midnight. But wasn't that a little silly? After all, now the Forsters were alone in the house from before nine until around six in the evening. So Lois and Herbert accepted a dinner invitation, so often extended by the Mitchells, and the Mitchells were delighted. It was for next Saturday.

When the McIntyres returned from the Mitchells' the following Saturday night, or rather Sunday morning at nearly 1 A.M., all was well in their house. Only the living room light was on, as they had left it, the TV murmured in the Forsters' room as usual, and the Forsters' light was off. Herbert went into their room, switched off the TV, and tiptoed out with their dinner tray. He was feeling pleasantly mellow, as was Lois, because the Mitchells had given them a good dinner with wine, and the Lowenhooks had been there too.

Herbert and Lois had a nightcap in the kitchen while Lois washed up the Forsters' dinner dishes. They were making it, weren't they? In spite of the jokes tonight from the Lowenhooks. What had they said? *What if Mamie and Albert outlive you both?* Herbert and Lois managed to laugh heartily in their kitchen that night.

On Sunday, Mamie asked Lois where they had been last evening, though Lois had left the Mitchells' name and telephone number with the Forsters. The phone had rung "a dozen times," said Mamie, and she had not been able to answer it quickly enough before it stopped ringing, and neither had Albert been able to reach the phone in the McIntyres' bedroom in time, though he had tried when Mamie got tired of trying.

Lois didn't believe her. How could they hear a ring with their TV on so loud? "Funny it hasn't rung at all today."

One evening in the next week, when Lois and Herbert came home together from their offices, they found a large pot of dwarf rhododendrons upset on the living room floor, though the pot was not broken. No one could have knocked over such a big pot by merely bumping into it, and they both knew this but didn't say it. Herbert got to work with broom and scoop and righted the pot, leaving Lois to admire the new item in the living room, a vaguely hexagonal knitted thing—if it was a doily, it was pretty big, nearly a yard in diameter—which lay over one arm of the sofa. Its colors were turquoise, dark red, and white, and its surface undulated.

"Peace offering?" asked Herbert with a smirk.

It was on a Friday in early autumn, around seven, when the McIntyres drove home, that they saw smoke coming out of one of the Forsters' room windows. The window was open very little at the top, but the smoke looked thick and in earnest.

"F' God's sake!" said Herbert, jumping out of the car, then stopping, as if for a few seconds he didn't know what to do.

Lois had got out on the passenger side. Higher than the poplars the gray smoke rose, curling upward. Lois also felt curiously paralyzed. Then she thought of an unfinished article, the first four chapters of a book she was not working on now, but would soon, which were in the downstairs front room, below the Forsters' room, and a need for action took hold of her. She flung her handbag onto the front seat of the car. "Got to get our *things* out!"

Herbert knew what she meant by things. When he opened the front door, the smell of smoke made him step back, then he took a breath and plunged forward. He knew that leaving the door open, creating a draft, was the worst thing to do, but he didn't close the door. He ran to the right toward his workroom, then realized that Lois was in the house too, so he turned back and joined her in her study, flung open a window, and tossed outside to the grass the papers and folders and boxes that she handed to him. This was achieved in seconds, then they dashed across the living room to Herbert's workroom, which was comparatively free of smoke, though its door was open. Herbert opened a French window, and out onto the lawn went his boxes and files, his spare portable typewriter, reference books, current reading, and nearly half of a fourteen-volume encyclopaedia. Lois, helping him, finally paused for breath, her mouth wide open.

"And—upstairs!" she said, gasping. "Fire department? Not too late, is it?"

"Let the goddamn thing burn!"

"The Forsters—"

Herbert nodded quickly. He looked dazed. He glanced around in the sunroom to see if he had forgotten anything, then snatched his letter-opener from his desk and pocketed it, and slid open a drawer. "Traveler's checks," he murmured, and pocketed these too. "Don't forget the house is insured," Herbert said to Lois with a smile. "We'll make it. And it's *worth* it!"

"You don't think—upstairs—"

Herbert, after a nervous sigh, crossed the living room to the stairs.

Smoke was rolling down like a gray avalanche. He ran back to Lois, holding part of his unbuttoned jacket over his face. "Out! *Out,* darling!"

When they were both on the lawn, the window top of the Forsters' room broke through in flames that curled upward toward the roof. Without a word, Lois and Herbert gathered the items they had tossed onto the lawn. They stowed their possessions away rather neatly, in spite of their haste, on the back seat and in the boot of the car.

"*They* could've rung the fire department, don't you think?" Herbert said with a glance up at the flaming window.

Lois knew, and Herbert knew, that she had written FIRE DEPT. and the number on the upstairs telephone in her and Herbert's bedroom, in case anything did happen. But now the Forsters were certainly overcome by smoke. Or were they possibly *outdoors,* hidden in the dusk behind the hedges and the poplars, watching the house burn? Ready to join them—now? Lois hoped not. And she didn't think so. The Forsters were up there, already dead. "Where're we going?" she asked as Herbert turned the car onto the road, not in the Hartford direction. But she knew. "The Mitchells'?"

"Yes, sure. We'll telephone from there. The fire department. If some neighbor hasn't already done it. The Mitchells'll put us up for the night. Don't worry, darling." Herbert's hands were tense on the wheel, but he drove smoothly and carefully.

And what would the Mitchells say? *Good,* probably, Lois thought.

When in Rome

Isabella had soaped her face, her neck, and was beginning to relax in the spray of deliciously warm water on her body when suddenly—there he was again! An ugly grinning face peered at her not a meter from her own face, with one big fist gripping an iron bar, so he could raise himself to her level.

"Swine!" Isabella said between her teeth, ducking at the same time.

"Slut!" came his retort. "Ha, ha!"

This must have been the third intrusion by the same creep! Isabella, still stooped, got out of the shower and reached for the plastic bottle of yellow shampoo, shot some into a bowl which held a cake of soap (she removed the soap), let some hot shower water run into the bowl and agitated the water until the suds rose, thick and sweet-smelling. She set the bowl within easy reach on the rim of the tub, and climbed back under the shower, breathing harder with her fury.

Just let him try it again! Defiantly erect, she soaped her facecloth, washed her thighs. The square recessed window was just to the left of her head, and there was a square emptiness, stone-lined, between the blue-and-white tiled bathroom walls and the great iron bars, each as thick as her wrist, on the street side.

"Signora?" came the mocking voice again.

Isabella reached for the bowl. Now he had both hands on the bars, and his face was between them, unshaven, his black eyes intense, his loose mouth smiling. Isabella flung the suds, holding the bowl with fingers spread wide on its underside.

"Oof!" The head disappeared.

A direct hit! The suds had caught him between the eyes, and she thought she heard some of the suds hit the pavement. Isabella smiled and finished her shower.

She was not looking forward to the evening—dinner at home with the First Secretary of the Danish Embassy with his girlfriend; but she had had worse evenings in the past, and there were worse to come in Vienna in the last week of this month, May, when her husband Filippo had to attend some kind of human-rights-and-pollution conference that was going to last five days. Isabella didn't care for the Viennese—she considered the women bores with nothing on their minds but clothes, who was wearing what, and how much did it cost.

"I think I prefer the green silk tonight," Isabella said to her maid, Elisabetta, when she went into her bedroom, big bathtowel around her, and saw the new black dress laid out on her bed. "I changed my mind," Isabella added, because she remembered that she had chosen the black that afternoon. Hadn't she? Isabella felt a little vague.

"And which shoes, signora?"

Isabella told her.

A quarter to eight now. The guests—two men, Filippo had said, besides the Danish secretary, who was called Osterberg or Ottenberg, were not due until eight, which meant eight-thirty or later. Isabella wanted to go out on the street, to drink an espresso standing up at the bar, like any other ordinary Roman citizen, and she also wanted to see if the Peeping Tom was still hanging around. In fact, there were two of them, the second a weedy type of about thirty who wore a limp raincoat and dark glasses. He was a "feeler," the kind who pushed his hand against a woman's bottom. He had done it to Isabella once or twice while she was waiting for the porter to open the door. Isabella had to wait for the porter unless she chose to carry around a key as long as a man's foot for the big outside doors. The feeler looked a bit cleaner than her bathroom snoop, but he also seemed creepier and he never smiled.

"Going out for a cafè," Isabella said to Elisabetta.

"You prefer to go out?" Elisabetta said, meaning that she could make a cafè, if the signora wanted. Elisabetta was forty-odd, her hair in a neat bun. Her husband had died a year ago, and she was still in a state of semi-mourning.

Isabella flung a cape over her shoulders, barely nodded, and left. She crossed the cobbled court, whose stones slanted gently toward a center drain, and was met at the door by one of the three porters who kept a round-the-clock guard on the palazzo, which was occupied by six affluent tenants. This porter was Franco. He lifted the heavy crossbar and opened the big doors enough for her to pass through.

Isabella was out on the street. Freedom! She stood tall and breathed. An adolescent boy cycled past, whistling. An old woman in black waddled by slowly, burdened with a shopping bag that showed onions and spaghetti on top, carelessly wrapped in newspaper. Someone's radio blared jazz through an open window. The air promised a hot summer.

Isabella looked around, but didn't see either of her nuisances, and was aware of feeling slightly disappointed. However, there was the bar-cafè across the street and a bit to the right. Isabella entered, conscious that her fine clothes and well-groomed hair set her apart from the usual patrons here. She put on a warm smile for the young barman, who knew her by now.

"Signora! *Buona sera!* A fine day, no? What is your wish?"

"Un espress', per piacere."

Isabella realized that she was known in the neighborhood as the wife of a government official who was reasonably important for his age, which was still under forty, aware that she was considered rather rich, and pretty too. The latter, people could see. And what else, Isabella wondered as she sipped her espresso. She and Filippo had a fourteen-year-old daughter in school in Switzerland now. Susanna.

Isabella wrote to her faithfully once a week, as Susanna did to her. How was Susanna going to shape up? Would she even *like* her daughter by the time she was eighteen or twenty-two? Was Susanna going to lose her ·passion for horses and horseback riding (Isabella hoped so) and go for something more intellectual such as geology and anthropology, which she had shown an interest in last year? Or was she going to go the usual way— get married at twenty before she'd finished university, trade on her good looks and marry "the right kind of man" before she had found out what life was all about? What *was* life all about?

Isabella looked around her, as if to find out. Isabella had had two years of university in Milan, had come from a rather intellectual family, and didn't consider herself just another dumb wife. Filippo was good-looking and had a promising career ahead of him. But then Filippo's *father* was important in a government ministry, and had money. The only trouble was that the wife of a man in diplomatic service had to be a clotheshorse, had to keep her mouth shut when she would like to open it, had to be polite and gracious to people whom she detested or was bored by. There were times when Isabella wanted to kick it all, to go slumming, simply to laugh.

She tossed off the last of her coffee, left a five-hundred-lire note, and turned around, not yet leaving the security of the bar's counter. She surveyed the scene. Two tables were occupied by couples who might be lovers. A blind beggar with a white cane was on his way in.

And here came her dark-eyed Peeping Tom! Isabella was aware that her eyes lit up as if she beheld her lover walking in.

He grinned. He sauntered, swaggered slightly as he headed for the bar to a place at a little distance from her. He looked her up and down, like a man sizing up a pick-up before deciding yes or no.

Isabella lifted her head and walked out of the bar-cafè.

He followed. "You are beautiful, signora," he said. "I should know, don't you think so?"

"You can keep your filthy ideas to yourself!" Isabella replied as she crossed the street.

"My beautiful lady-love—the wife of my dreams!"

Isabella noticed that his eyes looked pink. Good! She pressed the bell for the porter. An approaching figure on her left caught her eye. The bottom-pincher, the gooser, the real oddball! Raincoat again, no glasses today, a faint smile. Isabella turned to face him, with her back to the big doors.

"Oh, how I would like to . . ." the feeler murmured as he passed her, so close she imagined she could feel the warmth of his breath against her cheek, and at the same time he slapped her hip with his left hand. He had a pockmark or two, and big cheekbones that stuck out gauntly. Disgusting type! And a disgusting phrase he had used!

From across the street, Peeping Tom was watching, Isabella saw; he was chuckling silently, rocking back on his heels.

Franco opened the doors. What if she told Filippo about those two? But of course she had, Isabella remembered, a month or so ago, yes. "How would *you* like it if a psychopath stared at you nearly every time you took a shower?" Isabella had said to Filippo, and he had broken out in one of his rare laughs. "If it were a *woman* maybe, yes, I might like it!" he said, then he had said that she shouldn't take it so seriously, that he would speak to the porters, or something like that.

Isabella had the feeling that she didn't really wake up until after the dinner party, when the coffee was served in the living room. The taste of the coffee reminded her of the bar that afternoon, of the dark-haired Peeping Tom with the pink eyes walking into the bar and having the nerve to speak to her *again!*

"We shall be in Vienna too, at the end of the month," said the girlfriend of the Danish First Secretary.

Isabella rather liked her. Her name was Gudrun. She looked healthy, honest, unsnobbish. But Isabella had nothing to say except, "Good. We shall be looking forward," one of the phrases that came out of her automatically after fifteen years of being the wife-of-a-government-employee. There were moments, hours, when she felt bored to the point of going insane. Like now. She felt on the brink of doing something shocking, such as standing up and screaming, or announcing that she wanted to go out for a walk (yes, and have another espresso in the same crummy bar), of shouting that she was bored with them *all,* even Filippo, slumped with legs crossed in an armchair now, wearing his neat, new dinner suit with a ruffled shirt, deep in conversation with the three other men. Filippo was long and lean like a fashion model, his black hair beginning to gray at the temples in a distinguished way. Women liked his looks, Isabella knew. His good looks, however, didn't make him a ball of fire as a lover. Did the women know that, Isabella wondered.

Before going to bed that night, Isabella had to check the shopping list with Luigi the cook for tomorrow's dinner party, because Luigi would be up early to buy fresh fish. Hadn't the signora suggested fish? And Luigi recommended young lamb instead of tournedos for the main course, if he dared say so.

Filippo paid her a compliment as he was undressing. "Osterberg thought you were charming."

They both slept in the same big bed, but it was so wide that Filippo could switch his reading-light on and read his papers and briefings till all hours, as he often did, without disturbing Isabella.

A couple of evenings later Isabella was showering just before 7 P.M. when the same dark-haired creep sprang up at her bathroom window, leering a "Hello, beautiful! Getting ready for me?"

Isabella was not in a mood for repartee. She got out of the shower.

"Ah, signora, such beauty should not be hidden! Don't try—"

"I've told the *police* about you!" Isabella yelled back at him, and switched off the bathroom light.

Isabella spoke to Filippo that evening as soon as he came in. "Something's got to be done—opaque glass put in the window—"

"You said that would make the bathroom look ugly."

"I don't care! It's revolting! I've told the porters—Giorgio, anyway. He doesn't do a damned thing, that's plain!—Filippo?"

"Yes, my dear. Come on, can't we talk about this later? I've got to change my shirt, at least, because we're due—already." He looked at his watch.

Isabella was dressed. "I want your tear-gas gun. You remember you showed it to me. Where is it?"

Filippo sighed. "Top drawer, left side of my desk."

Isabella went to the desk in Filippo's study. The tear-gas gun looked like a fountain pen, only a bit thicker. Isabella smiled as she placed her thumb on the firing end of it and imagined her counterattack.

"Be careful how you use that tear gas," Filippo said as they were leaving the house. "I don't want you to get into trouble with the police just because of a—"

"*Me* in trouble with the police! Whose side are you on?" Isabella laughed, and felt much better now that she was armed.

The next afternoon around five, Isabella went out, paid a visit to the pharmacy where she bought tissues and a bottle of new eau de cologne which the chemist suggested, and whose packaging amused her. Then she strolled toward the bar-cafè, keeping an eye out for her snoops as she went. She was bareheaded, had a bit of rouge on her lips, and she wore a new summer frock. She looked pretty and was aware of it. And across the street, walking past her very door now, went the raincoated creep in dark glasses again—and he didn't notice her. Isabella felt slightly disappointed. She went into the bar and ordered an espresso, lit a rare cigarette.

The barman chatted. "Wasn't it a nice day? And the signora is looking especially well today."

Isabella barely heard him, but she replied politely. When she opened her handbag to pay for her espresso, she touched the tear-gas gun, picked it up, dropped it, before reaching for her purse.

"*Grazie,* signora!"

She had tipped generously as usual.

Just as she turned to the door, the bathroom peeper—her special persecutor—entered, and had the audacity to smile broadly and nod, as if they were dear friends. Isabella lifted her head higher as if with disdain, and at the same time gave him an appraising glance, which just might have been mistaken for an invitation, Isabella knew. She had meant it that way. The creep hadn't quite the boldness to say anything to her inside the cafè, but he did follow her out of the door. Isabella avoided looking directly at him. Even his shoes were unshined. What could he do for a living, she wondered.

Isabella pretended, at her door, to be groping for her key. She picked up the tear-gas gun, pushed off its safety, and held it with her thumb against its top.

Then he said, with such mirth in his voice that he could hardly get the words out, "Bellissima signora, when are you going to let me—"

Isabella lifted the big fountain pen and pushed its firing button, maneuvering it so that its spray caught both his eyes at short range.

"Ow!—Ooh-h!" He coughed, then groaned, down on one knee now, with a hand across his eyes.

Even Isabella could smell the stuff, and blinked, her eyes watering. A man on the pavement had noticed the Peeping Tom struggling to get up, but was not running to help him, merely walking toward him. And now a porter opened the big wooden doors, and Isabella ducked into her own courtyard. "Thank you, Giorgio."

The next morning she and Filippo set out for Vienna. This excursion was one Isabella dreaded. Vienna would be dead after 11:30 at night—not even an interesting coffee house would be open. Awful! But the fact that she had fired a shot in self-defense—in attack—buoyed Isabella's morale.

And to crown her satisfaction she had the pleasure of seeing Peeping Tom in dark glasses as she and Filippo were getting into the chauffeured government car to be driven to the airport. The figure in dark glasses had stopped on the pavement some ten meters away to gaze at the luggage being put into the limousine by the liveried driver.

Isabella hoped his eyes were killing him. She had noted there was a box of four cartridges for the tear-gas gun in the same drawer. She intended to keep her gadget well charged. Surely the fellow wasn't going to come back for more! She might try it also on the feeler in the dirty raincoat. Yes, there was one who didn't mind approaching damned close!

"Why're you dawdling, Isabella? Forget something?" Filippo asked, holding the car door for her.

Isabella hadn't realized that she had been standing on the pavement, relishing the fact that the creep could see her about to get into the protective armor of the shiny car, about to go hundreds of kilometers away from him. "I'm ready," she said, and got in. She was not going to say to Filippo, "There's my Peeping Tom." She liked the idea of her secret war with him. Maybe his eyes were permanently damaged. She hoped so.

This minor coup made Vienna seem better. Isabella missed Elisabetta— some women whose husbands were in government service traveled with their maids, but Filippo was against this, just now. "Wait a couple of years till I get a promotion," Filippo had said. Years. Isabella didn't care for the word year or years. Could she stand it? At the stuffy dinner parties where the Austrians spoke bad French or worse Italian, Isabella carried her tear-gas gun in her handbag, even in her small evening bag at the big gala at the Staatsoper. *The Flying Dutchman*. Isabella sat with legs crossed, feet crossed also with tension, and dreamed of resuming her attack when she got back to Rome.

Then on the last evening Filippo had an "all-night meeting" with four men of the human rights committee, or whatever they called it. Isabella expected him back at the hotel about three in the morning at the latest, but he did not get back till 7:30, looking exhausted and even a bit drunk. His arrival had awakened her, though he had tried to come in quietly with his own key.

"Nothing at all," he said unnecessarily and a little vaguely. "Got to take a shower—then a little sleep. No appointment till—eleven this morning and it won't matter if I'm late." He ran the shower.

Then Isabella remembered the girl he had been talking to that evening, as he smoked a fine cigar—at least, Isabella had heard Filippo call it "a fine cigar"—a smiling, blonde Austrian girl, smiling in the special way women had when they wanted to say, "Anything you do is all right with me. I'm yours, you understand? At least for tonight."

Isabella sighed, turned over in bed, tried to sleep again, but she felt tense with rage, and knew she would not sleep before it was time for breakfast, time to get up. Damn it! She knew Filippo had been at the girl's apartment or in her hotel room, knew that if she took the trouble to sniff his shirt, even the shoulders of his dinner jacket, she would smell the girl's perfume—and the idea of doing that revolted her. Well, she herself had had two, no, three lovers during her married life with Filippo, but they had been so brief, those affairs! And so discreet! Not one servant had known.

Isabella also suspected Filippo of having a girlfriend in Rome, Sibilla, a rather gypsy-like brunette, and if Filippo was "discreet," it was because he was only lukewarm about her. This blonde tonight was more Filippo's type, Isabella knew. She heard Filippo hit the twin bed that was pushed close to her bed. He would sleep like a log, then get up in three hours looking amazingly fresh.

When Isabella and Filippo got back to Rome, Signor Sore-Eyes was on hand the very first evening, when Isabella stood under the shower about 7:30 in the evening. Now that was fidelity for you! Isabella ducked, giggling. Her giggle was audible.

And Sore-Eyes' response came instantly: "Ah, the lady of my heart is pleased! She laughs!" He had dropped to his feet, out of sight, but his voice came clearly through the stone recess. "Come, let me see more. *More!*" Hands grasped the bars; the grinning face appeared, black eyes shining and looking not at all damaged.

"Get lost!" she shouted, and stepped out of the shower and began to dry herself, standing near the wall, out of his view.

But the other nut, the feeler, seemed to have left the neighborhood. At least Isabella did not see him during three or four days after her return from Vienna. Nearly every day she had an espresso at the bar-café across the street, and sometimes twice a day she took taxis to the Via Veneto area, where a few of her friends lived, or to the Via Condotti for shopping. Shiny-Eyes remained faithful, however, not always in view when she came out of her big doors, but more often than not.

Isabella fancied—she liked to fancy—that he was in love with her, even though his silly remarks were intended either to make her laugh or, she had to admit it, to insult and shock her. It was this line of thinking, however, which caused Isabella to see the Peeping Tom as a rival, and which gave her an idea. What Filippo needed was a good jolt!

"Would you like to come for after-dinner coffee tonight?" Isabella murmured to Shiny-Eyes one day, interrupting his own stream of vulgarity, as she stood not yet pushing the bell of her house.

The man's mouth fell open, revealing more of his stained teeth.

"Ghiardini," she said, giving her last name. "Ten-thirty." She had pushed the bell by now and the doors were opening. "Wear some better clothes," she whispered.

That evening Isabella dressed with a little more interest in her appearance. She and Filippo had to go out first to a "buffet cocktail" at the Hotel Eliseo. Isabella was not even interested in what country was host to the affair. Then she and Filippo departed at 10:15 in their own government car, to be followed by two other groups of Americans, Italians, and a couple of Germans. Isabella and Filippo were earlier than the rest, and of course Luigi and Elisabetta already had the long bar-table well equipped with bottles, glasses, and ice, and platters of little sausages stuck with toothpicks. Why hadn't she told Shiny-Eyes eleven o'clock?

But Shiny-Eyes did the right thing, and arrived just after eleven. Isabella's heart gave a dip as he entered through the living room door, which had been opened by Luigi. The room was already crowded with guests, most of them standing up with drinks, chattering away, quite occupied, and giving Shiny-Eyes not a glance. Luigi was seeing to his drink. At least he was wearing a dark suit, a limp but white shirt, and a tie.

Isabella chatted with a large American and his wife. Isabella hated speaking English, but she could hold her own in it. Filippo, Isabella saw, had left his quartet of diplomats and was now concentrating on two pretty women; he was standing before them while they sat on the sofa, as if mesmerizing them by his tall elegant presence, his stream of bilge. The women were German, secretaries or girl friends. Isabella almost sneered.

Shiny-Eyes was nursing his scotch against the wall by the bar-table, and Isabella drifted over on the pretense of replenishing her champagne. She glanced at him, and he came closer. To Isabella he seemed the only vital person in the room. She had no intention of speaking to him, even of looking directly at him, and concentrated on pouring champagne from a small bottle.

"Good evening, signora," he said in English.

"Good evening. And what is your name?" she asked in Italian.

"Ugo."

Isabella turned gracefully on her heel and walked away. For the next minutes she was a dutiful hostess, circulating, chatting, making sure that everyone had what he or she wanted. People were relaxing, laughing more loudly. Even as she spoke to someone, Isabella looked in Ugo's direction and saw him in the act of pocketing a small Etruscan statue. Isabella drifted slowly but directly across the room toward Ugo.

"You put that back!" she said between her teeth, and left him.

Ugo put it back, flustered, but not seriously.

Filippo had caught the end of this, Isabella speaking to Ugo. Filippo rose to find a new drink, got it, and approached Isabella. "Who's the dark type over there? Do you know him?"

Isabella shrugged. "Someone's bodyguard, perhaps?"

The evening ended quietly, Ugo slipped out unnoticed even by Isabella. When Isabella turned back to the living room expecting to see Filippo, she found the room empty. "Filippo?" she called, thinking he might be in the bedroom.

Filippo had evidently gone out with some of the guests, and Isabella was sure he was going to see one of the blondes tonight. Isabella helped herself to a last champagne, something she rarely did. She was not satisfied with the evening after all.

When she awakened the next morning, at the knock of Elisabetta with the breakfast tray, Filippo was not beside her in bed. Elisabetta, of course, made no comment. While Isabella was still drinking cafè latte, Filippo arrived. All-night talk with the Americans, he explained, and now he had to change his clothes.

"Is the blonde in the blue dress American? I thought she and the other blonde were Germans," Isabella said.

Now the row was on. So what, was Filippo's attitude.

"What kind of life is it for *me?*" Isabella screamed. "Am I nothing but an *object?* Just some female figure in the house—always here, to say *buona sera*—and smile!"

"Where would I be without you? Every man in government service needs a wife," replied Filippo, using the last of his patience. "And you're a very good hostess, Isabella, really!"

Isabella roared like a lioness. "Hostess! I detest the word! And your girl friends—*in* this house—"

"Never!" Filippo replied proudly.

"Two of them! How many have you now?"

"Am I the only man in Rome with a mistress or two?" He had recovered his cool and intended to stand up for his rights. After all, he was supporting Isabella and in fine style, and their daughter, Susanna, too. "If you don't like it—" But Filippo stopped.

More than ever, that day, Isabella wanted to see Ugo. She went out around noon, and stopped for an americano at the little bar-cafè. This time she sat at a table. Ugo came in when she had nearly finished her drink. Faithful, he was. Or psychic. Maybe both. Without looking at him, she knew that he had seen her.

She left some money on the table and walked out. Ugo followed. She walked in an opposite direction from the palazzo across the street, knowing that he knew she expected him to follow her.

When they were safely around another corner, Isabella turned. "You did quite well last night, except for the attempted—"

"Ah, sorry, signora!" he interrupted, grinning.

"What are you by profession—if I dare to ask?"

"Journalist, sometimes. Photographer. You know, a freelance."

"Would you like to make some money?"

He wriggled, and grinned more widely. "To spend on you, signora, yes."

"Never mind the rubbish." He really was an untidy specimen, back in his old shoes again, dirty sweater under his jacket, and when had he last had a bath? Isabella looked around to see if anyone might be observing them. "Would you be interested in kidnapping a rich man?"

Ugo hesitated only two seconds. "Why not?" His black eyebrows had gone up. "Tell me. Who?"

"My husband. You will need a friend with a gun and a car."

Ugo indulged in another grin, but his attitude was attentive.

Isabella had thought out her plans that morning. She told Ugo that she and Filippo wanted to buy a house outside of Rome, and she had the names of a few real estate agents. She could make an appointment with one for Friday morning, for instance, at nine o'clock. Isabella said she would make herself "indisposed" that morning, so Filippo would have to go alone. But Ugo must be at the palazzo with a car a little before nine.

"I must make the hour the same, otherwise Filippo will suspect me," Isabella explained. "These agents are always a little late. You should be ten minutes early. I'll see that Filippo is ready."

Isabella continued, and walked slowly, since she felt it made them less conspicuous than if they stood still. If Ugo and his friend could camp out somewhere overnight with Filippo, until she had time to get a message from them and get the money from the government? If Ugo could communicate by telephone or entrust someone to deliver a written message? Either way was easy, Ugo said. He might have to hit Filippo on the head, Isabella said, but Ugo was not to hurt him seriously. Ugo understood.

After some haggling, a ransom sum was agreed for the kidnapping on Friday morning. Tomorrow was Thursday, and if Ugo had spoken to his friend and all was well, he was to give Isabella a nod, merely, tomorrow afternoon about five when she would go out for an espresso.

Isabella was so exhilarated she went that afternoon to see her friend Margherita, who lived off the Via Veneto. Margherita asked her if she had found a new lover. Isabella laughed.

"No, but I think Filippo has," Isabella replied.

Filippo also noticed, by Thursday afternoon, that she was in a merry mood. Filippo was home Thursday evening after their dinner out at a restaurant where they had been two at a table of twenty. Isabella took off her shoes and waltzed in the living room. Filippo was aware of his early date with the real estate agents, and cursed it. It was already after midnight.

The next morning Elisabetta awakened them with the breakfast tray at 8:30, and Isabella complained of a headache.

"No use in my going if you're not going," Filippo said.

"You can at least tell if the house is possible—or houses," she replied sleepily. "Don't let them down or they won't make a date with us again."

Filippo got dressed.

Isabella heard the faint ring of the street-door bell. Filippo went out.

By this time he was in the living room or the kitchen in quest of more coffee. It was two minutes to nine. Isabella at once got up, flung on a blouse, slacks and sandals, ready to meet the real estate agents who she supposed would be twenty minutes late, at least.

They were. Elisabetta announced them. Two gentlemen. The porter had let them into the court. All seemed to be going well, which was to say Filippo was not in view.

"But I thought my husband had already left with you!" She explained that her husband had left the house half an hour ago. "I'm afraid I must ask you to excuse me. I have a migraine today."

The agency men expressed disappointment, but left in good humor finally, because the Ghiardinis were potentially good clients, and Isabella promised to telephone them in the near future.

Isabella went out for a pre-lunch cinzano, and felt reassured by the absence of Ugo. She was about to answer a letter from Susanna which had come that morning when the telephone rang. It was Filippo's colleague Vincenzo, and where was Filippo? Filippo was supposed to have arrived at noon at Vincenzo's office for a talk before they went out to lunch with a man who Vincenzo said was "important."

"This morning was a little strange," Isabella said casually, with a smile in her voice, "because Filippo went off with some estate agents at nine, I thought, then—"

"Then?"

"Well, I don't know. I haven't heard from him since," Isabella replied, thinking she had said quite enough. "I don't know anything about his appointments today."

Isabella went out to mail her letter to Susanna around four. Susanna had fallen from her horse taking a low jump, in which the horse had fallen too. A miracle Susanna hadn't broken a bone! Susanna needed not only new riding breeches but a book of photographs of German cathedrals which the class was going to visit this summer, so Isabella had sent her a check on their Swiss bank. As soon as Isabella had got back home and closed her door, the telephone rang.

"Signora Ghiardini—" It sounded like Ugo speaking through a handkerchief. "We have your husband. Do not try to find out where he is. One hundred million lire we want. Do you understand?"

"*Where* is he?" Isabella demanded, putting on an act as if Elisabetta or someone else were listening; but no one was, unless Luigi had picked up the living room extension phone. It was Elisabetta's afternoon off.

"Get the money by tomorrow noon. Do not inform the police. This evening at seven a messenger will tell you where to deliver the money." Ugo hung up.

That sounded all right! Just what Isabella had expected. Now she had to get busy, especially with Caccia-Lunghi, Filippo's boss, higher than Vincenzo in the Bureau of Public Welfare and Environment. But first she went into her bathroom, where she was sure Ugo would not be peering in, washed her face and made herself up again to give herself confidence. She would soon be putting a lot of money into Ugo's pocket and the pocket of his friend—whoever was helping him.

Isabella now envisaged Ugo her slave for a long time to come. She would have the power of betraying him if he got out of hand, and if Ugo chose to betray *her,* she would simply deny it, and between the two of them she had no doubt which one the police would choose to believe: her.

"Vincenzo!" Isabella said in a hectic voice into the telephone (she had decided after all to ring Vincenzo first). "Filippo has been kidnapped! That's why he didn't turn up this morning! I've just had a message from the kidnappers. They're asking for a hundred million lire by tomorrow noon!"

She and Filippo, of course, had not that much money in the bank, she went on, and wasn't it the responsibility of the government, since Filippo was a government employee, an official?

Vincenzo sighed audibly. "The government has had enough of such things. You'd better try Filippo's father, Isabella."

"But he's so stubborn!—The kidnapper said something about throwing Filippo in a *river!*"

"They all say that. Try the father, my dear."

So Isabella did. It was nearly 6 P.M. before she could reach him, because he had been "in conference." Isabella first asked, "Has Filippo spoken to you today?" He had not. Then she explained that Filippo had been kidnapped, and that his captors wanted a hundred million lire by tomorrow noon.

"What? Kidnapped—and they want it from me? Why *me?*" the old man spluttered. "The government—Filippo's in the government!"

"I've asked Vincenzo Carda." Isabella told him about her rejection in a tearful voice, prolonging her story so that Filippo's predicament would have time to sink in.

"Va bene, va bene." Pietro Ghiardini sounded defeated. "I can contribute seventy-five million, not more. What a business! You'd think Italy . . ." He went on, though he sounded on the brink of a heart attack.

Isabella expressed gratitude, but she was disappointed. She would have to come up with the rest out of their bank account—unless of course she could make a deal with Ugo. Old Pietro promised that the money would be delivered by 10:30 the following morning.

If she and Filippo were due to go anywhere tonight, Isabella didn't give a damn, and she told Luigi to turn away people who might arrive at the door with the excuse that there was a crisis tonight—and they could interpret that as they wished, Isabella thought. Luigi was understanding, and most concerned, as was Elisabetta.

Ugo was prompt with another telephone call at seven, and though Isabella was alone in her bedroom, she played her part as though someone were listening, though no one could have been unless Luigi had picked up the living room telephone. Isabella's voice betrayed anxiety, anger, and fear of what might happen to her husband. Ugo spoke briefly. She was to meet him in a tiny square which Isabella had never heard of—she scribbled the name down—at noon tomorrow, with a hundred million lire in old bills in twenty-thousand and fifty-thousand denominations in a shopping bag or basket, and then Filippo would be released at once on the edge of Rome. Ugo did not say where.

"Come *alone*. Filippo is well," Ugo said. "Good-bye, signora."

Vincenzo telephoned just afterward. Isabella told Vincenzo what she had to do, said that Filippo's father had come up with seventy-five million and could the government provide the rest? Vincenzo said no, and wished Isabella and Filippo the best of luck.

And that was that. So early the next morning Isabella went to their bank and withdrew twenty-five million lire from their savings, which left so little that she had to sign a check on their Swiss bank for a transfer when she got home. At half past ten a chauffeur in uniform and puttees, with a bulge under his tunic that must have been a gun, arrived with a briefcase under each arm. Isabella took him into the bedroom for the transfer of money from the briefcases into the shopping bag—a black plastic bag belonging to Elisabetta. Isabella didn't feel like counting through all the soiled banknotes.

"You're sure it's exact?" she asked.

The calm and polite chauffeur said it was. He loaded the shopping bag for her, then took his leave with the briefcases.

Isabella ordered a taxi for 11:15, because she had no idea how long it might take her to get to the little square, especially if they ran into a traffic jam somewhere. Elisabetta was worried, and asked for the tenth time, "Can't I come with you—just sit in the taxi, signora?"

"They will think you are a man in disguise with a gun," Isabella replied, though she intended to get out of the taxi a couple of streets away from the square, and dismiss the taxi.

The taxi arrived. Isabella said she should be back before one o'clock. She had looked up the square on her map of Rome, and had the map with her in case the taxi driver was vague.

"What a place!" said the driver. "I don't know it at all. Evidently you don't either."

"The mother of an old servant of mine lives there. I'm taking her some clothing," Isabella said by way of explaining the bulging but not very heavy shopping bag.

The driver let her out. Isabella had said she was uncertain of the house number, but could find out by asking neighbors. Now she was on her own, with a fortune in her right hand.

There was the little square, and there was Ugo, five minutes early, like herself, reading a newspaper on a bench. Isabella entered the little square slowly. It had a few ill-tended trees, a ground of square stones laid like a pavement. One old woman sat knitting on the only sunlit bench. It was a working-class neighborhood, or one mainly of old people, it seemed. Ugo got up and walked toward her.

"Giorno, signora," he said casually, with a polite nod, as if greeting an old acquaintance, and by his own walking led her toward the street pavement. "You're all right?"

"Yes. And—"

"He's quite all right.—Thank you for this." He glanced at her shopping bag. "Soon as we see everything's in order, we'll let Filippo—loose." His smile was reassuring.

"Where are we—"

"Just here," Ugo interrupted, pushing her to the left, toward the street, and a parked car's door suddenly swung open beside her. The push had not been a hard one, only rude and sudden enough to fluster Isabella for a moment. The man in the driver's seat had turned half around and had a pistol pointed at her, held low on the back of the front seat.

"Just be quiet, Signora Isabella, and there will be no trouble at all—nobody hurt at all," the man with the gun said.

Ugo got in beside her in the back and slammed the door shut. The car started off.

It had not even occurred to Isabella to scream, she realized. She had a glimpse of a man with a briefcase under his arm, walking only two meters away on the pavement, his eyes straight ahead. They were soon out in the country. There were a few houses, but mostly it was fields and trees. The man driving the car wore a hat.

"Isn't it necessary that I *join* Filippo, Ugo?" she asked.

Ugo laughed, then asked the man driving to pull in at a roadside bar-restaurant. Here Ugo got out, saying he would be just a minute. He had looked into the shopping bag long enough to see that it contained money and was not partly stuffed with newspaper. The man driving turned around in his seat.

"The signora will please be quiet," he said. "Everything is all right." He had the horrible accent of a Milan tough, attempting to be soothing to an unpredictable woman who might go off in a scream louder than a police siren. In his nervousness he was chewing gum.

"Where are you taking me?"

Ugo was coming back.

Isabella soon found out. They pulled in at a farmhouse whose occupants had evidently recently left—there were clothes on the line, dishes in the sink—but the only people now in the house seemed to be Isabella, Ugo, and his driver chum whom Ugo called Eddie. Isabella looked at an ashtray, recognizing Filippo's Turkish cigarette stubs, noticed also the pack empty and uncrumpled on the floor.

"Filippo has been released, signora," Ugo said. "He has money for a taxi and soon you should be able to phone him at home.—Sit down. Would you like a coffee?"

"Take me back to Rome!" Isabella shouted. But she knew. They had kidnapped *her*. "If you think there is any *more* money coming, you are quite mistaken, Ugo—*and you!*" she added to the smiling driver, an old slob now helping himself to whiskey.

"There is always more money," Ugo said calmly.

"Swine!" Isabella said. "I should have known from the time you first stared into my bathroom! That's your real occupation, you creep!" A fear of assault crossed her mind, but only swiftly. Her rage was stronger just now. "After I tried to—to give you a break, turn a little money your way! *Look* at all that money!"

Eddie was now sitting on the floor counting it, like a child with an absorbing new toy or game, except that a big cigar stuck out of his mouth.

"Sit down, signora. All will be well when we telephone your husband."

Isabella sat down on a sagging sofa. There was mud on the heels of her shoes from the filthy courtyard she had just walked across. Ugo brought some warmed-over coffee. Isabella learned that still another chum of Ugo's had driven Filippo in another car and dropped him somewhere to make his own way home.

"He is quite all right, signora," Ugo assured her, bringing a plate of awful-looking sliced lamb and hunks of cheese. The other man was on his feet, and brought a basket of bread and a bottle of inferior wine. The men were hungry. Isabella took nothing, refusing even whiskey and wine. When the men had finished eating, Ugo sent Eddie off in the car to telephone Filippo from somewhere. The farmhouse had no telephone. How Isabella wished she had brought her tear-gas gun! But she had thought she would be among friends today.

Ugo sipped coffee, smoked a cigarette, and tried to assuage Isabella's anger. "By tonight, by tomorrow morning you will be back home, signora. No harm done! A room to yourself here! Even though the bed may not be as comfortable as the one you're used to."

Isabella refused to answer him, and bit her lip, thinking that she had got herself into an awful mess, had cost herself and Filippo twenty-five million lire, and might cost them another fifty million (or whatever she was worth) because Filippo's father might decide not to come up with the money to ransom her.

Eddie came back with an air of disappointment and reported in his disgusting slang that Signor Ghiardini had told him to go stuff himself.

"What?" Ugo jumped up from his chair. "We'll try again. We'll threaten—didn't you threaten—"

Eddie nodded. "He said . . ." Again the revolting phrase.

"We'll see how it goes tonight—around seven or so," said Ugo.

"How much are you asking?" Isabella was unable to repress the question any longer. Her voice had gone shrill.

"Fifty million, signora," replied Ugo.

"We simply haven't got it—not after *this*!" Isabella gestured toward the shopping bag, now in a corner of the room.

"Ha, ha," Ugo laughed softly. "The Ghiardinis haven't got another fifty million? Or the government? Or Papa Ghiardini?"

The other man announced that he was going to take a nap in the other room. Ugo turned on the radio to some pop music. Isabella remained seated on the uncomfortable sofa. She had declined to remove her coat. Ugo paced about, thinking, talking a little to himself, half drunk with the realization of all the money in the corner of the room. The gun lay on the center table near the radio. She looked at it with an idea of grabbing it and turning it on Ugo, but she knew she could probably not keep both men at bay if Eddie woke up.

When Eddie did wake up and returned to the room, Ugo announced that he was going to try to telephone Filippo, while Eddie kept watch on Isabella. "No funny business," said Ugo like an army officer, before going out.

It was just after six.

Eddie tried to engage her in a conversation about revolutionary tactics, about Ugo's having been a journalist once, a photographer also (Isabella could imagine what kind of photographer). Isabella was angry and bored, and hated herself for replying even slightly to Eddie's moronic ramblings. He was talking about making a down payment on a house with the money he had gained from Filippo's abduction. Ugo would also start leading a more decent life, which was what he deserved, said Eddie.

"He deserves to be behind bars for the protection of the *public!*" Isabella shot back.

The car had returned. Ugo entered with his slack mouth even slacker, a look of puzzlement on his brow. "Gotta let her go, he may have traced the call," Ugo said to Eddie, and snapped his fingers for action.

Eddie at once went for the shopping bag and carried it out to the car.

"Your husband says you can go to hell," said Ugo. "He will not pay one lira."

It suddenly sank into Isabella. She stood up, feeling scared, feeling naked somehow, even though she still wore her coat over her dress. "He is joking. He'll—" But somehow she knew Filippo wouldn't. "Where're you taking me now?"

Ugo laughed. He laughed heartily, rocking back as he always did, laughing at Isabella and also at himself. "So I have lost fifty million! A pity, eh? Big pity. But the joke is on *you!* Hah! Ha, ha, ha!—Come on, Signora Isabella, what've you got in your purse? Let's see." He took her purse rudely from her hands.

Isabella knew she had about twenty thousand in her billfold. This Ugo laid with a large gesture on the center table, then turned off the radio.

"Let's go," he said, indicating the door, smiling. Eddie had started the car. Ugo's happy mood seemed to be contagious. Eddie began laughing too at Ugo's comments. *The lady was worth nothing!* That was the idea. *La donna niente,* they sang.

"You won't get away with this for long, you piece of filth!" Isabella said to Ugo.

More laughter.

"Here! Fine!" yelled Ugo who was with Isabella in the back seat again, and Eddie pulled the car over to the edge of the road.

Where were they? Isabella had thought they were heading for Rome, but wasn't sure. Yes. She saw some high-rise apartment buildings. A truck went by, close, as she got out with Ugo, half pulled by him.

"Shoes, signora! Ha, ha!" He pushed her against the car and bent to take off her pumps. She kicked him, but he only laughed. She swung her handbag, catching him on the head with it, and nearly fell herself as he snatched off her second shoe. Ugo jumped, with the shoes in his hand, back into the car which roared off.

To be shoeless in silk stockings was a nasty shock. Isabella began walking—toward Rome. She could see lights coming on here and there in the twilight dimness. She'd hitch a ride to the next roadside bar and telephone for a taxi, she thought, pay the taxi when she got home. A large truck passed her by as if blind to her frantic waving. So did a car with a single man in it. Isabella was ready to hitch a lift with anyone!

She walked on, realizing that her stockings were now torn and open at the bottom, and when she stopped to pick something out of one foot, she saw blood. It was more than fifteen minutes later when Isabella made her painful way to a restaurant on the opposite side of the road, where she begged the use of the telephone.

Isabella did not at all like the smile of the young waiter who looked her up and down and was plainly surmising what must have happened to her: a boy friend had chucked her out of his car. Isabella telephoned a taxi company's number which the waiter provided. There would be at least ten minutes to wait, she was told, so she stood by the coat rack at the front of the place, feeling miserable and ashamed with her dirty feet and torn stockings. Passing waiters glanced at her. She had to explain to the proprietor—a stuffy type—that she was waiting for a taxi.

The taxi arrived, Isabella gave her address, and the driver looked dubious, so Isabella had to explain that her husband would pay the fare at the other end. She was almost in tears.

Isabella fell against the porter's bell, as if it were home, itself. Giorgio opened the doors. Filippo came across the court, scowling.

"The taxi—" Isabella said.

Filippo was reaching into a pocket. "As if I had anything left!"

Isabella took the last excruciating steps across the courtyard to the door out of which Elisabetta was now running to help her.

Elisabetta made tea for her. Isabella sat in the tub, soaking her feet, washing off the filth of Ugo and his ugly chum. She applied surgical spirits to the soles of her feet, then put on clean white woolen booties and a dressing gown. She cast one furious glance at the bathroom window, sure Ugo would never come back.

As soon as she came out of her bathroom, Filippo said, "I suppose you remember—tonight we have the Greek consul coming to dinner with his wife. And two other men. Six in all. I was going to receive them alone— make some excuse." His tone was icy.

Isabella did remember, but had somehow thought all that would be canceled. Nothing was canceled. She could see it now: life would go on as usual, not a single date would be canceled. They were poorer. That was all. Isabella rested in her bed, with some newspapers and magazines, then got up and began to dress. Filippo came in, not even knocking first.

"Wear the peach-colored dress tonight—not that one," he said. "The Greeks need cheering up."

Isabella began removing the dark blue dress she had put on.

"I know you arranged all this," Filippo continued. "They were ready to kill me, those hoodlums—or at least they acted like it. My father is furious! What stupid arrangements!—I can also make some arrangements. Wait and see!"

Isabella said nothing. And *her* future arrangements? Well, she might make some too. She gave Filippo a look. Then she gritted her teeth as she squeezed her swollen feet into "the right shoes" for the evening. When she got up, she had to walk with a limp.

Blow It

The two other young and unmarried men in the office considered Harry Rowe lucky, very. Harry had two pretty girls in love with him. Sometimes one girl or the other picked him up at his midtown Manhattan office, because Harry often had to stay a half hour or more after the usual quitting time at five or five-thirty, and one girl, Connie, could leave her office rather easily at five. The other girl, Lesley, was a fashion model with irregular hours, but she had been to his office a few times. That was how the firm of five men knew about Harry's girls. Otherwise Harry would have kept his mouth shut, not introduced them to—well, everybody, because someone would have been bound to blabble to one girl about the other girl. Harry did not mind, however, that Dick Hanson knew the situation. Dick was a thirty-five-year-old married man who could be trusted to be discreet, because he must have had experiences along the same lines, and even now had a girlfriend, Harry knew. Dick was a senior partner in the accounting firm of Raymond and Hanson.

Harry really didn't know which girl he preferred, and wanted to give himself time to consider, to choose. These days, Harry thought, lots of girls didn't care about marriage, didn't believe in it, especially at the age of twenty-three, as these girls were. But both Lesley and Connie were quite interested in marriage. They had not proposed to him, but he could tell. This further boosted Harry's ego, because he saw himself as a good catch. What man wouldn't, under such circumstances? That meant, he was earning well (true), and would go on to bigger and better, and also he wasn't bad looking, if he did say so himself (and he did), and he took the trouble to dress in a way that girls liked, always a clean shirt, not always a tie if the occasion didn't demand it, good shoes informal or not, far-out shirts sometimes, safari trousers or shorts maybe on the weekends when he loafed around with Lesley on Saturday and Connie on Sunday, for instance. Harry was a lawyer as well as a Certified Public Accountant.

Lesley Marker, a photographers' model, made even better money than Harry. She had dark brown, straight hair, shining brown eyes, and the loveliest complexion Harry had ever seen, not to mention a divine body, not even too thin, as a lot of models were, or so Harry had always heard. Lesley had a standing date with her parents and grandmother for Sunday lunch, so this ruled out Lesley for Sundays, but there was Friday night and Saturdays. There were of course seven nights in the week, and Lesley could spend the night at his apartment, or he at hers, if she did not have to get up very early. Lesley was always cheerful, it wasn't even an act with her. It was marvelous and refreshing to Harry. She had a sense of humor in bed. She was a delight.

Connie Jaeger was different, more mysterious, less open, and certainly she had more moods than Lesley. Harry had to be careful with Connie, subtle, understanding of her moods, which she did not always explain in words. She was an editor in a publishing house. Sometimes she wrote short stories, and showed them to Harry. Two or three she had sold to little magazines. Connie often gave Harry the impression that she was brooding, thinking of things she would not disclose to him. Yet she loved him or was in love with him, of that Harry was sure. Connie was more interesting than Lesley, Harry would have had to admit, if anyone asked him.

Harry had a walk-up apartment on Jane Street, on the fourth floor. It was an old house, but the plumbing worked, the kitchen and bath were nicely painted, and he had a terrace with a roof garden of sorts: the garden was some three yards square, its earth contained within a wooden frame, and the watering drained into a corner hole on the terrace. Harry had acquired deck chairs, metal chairs and a round table. He and Lesley or Connie could lunch or dine out here, and the girls could take naked sunbaths, if they wished, as in a certain corner no one could see them. Lesley did that more often than Connie, who had done it only once, and then not naked entirely. He had met both girls around the same time, about four months ago. Which did he like better? Or love more? Harry could not tell as yet, but he had realized weeks ago that his other girlfriends, two or three, had simply faded away. Harry hadn't rung them up for dates, didn't care to see them. He was in love with two girls at the same time, he supposed. He had heard of it before, and somehow never believed it was possible. He supposed also that Lesley and Connie might think he had other girlfriends, and for all Harry knew, both the girls might be going to bed with other men now and then too. But considering the time they both gave Harry, they hadn't a lot of time, or many nights, for other fellows.

Meanwhile Harry was careful to keep the girls apart, very good about changing his bedsheets, which were drip-dry and which he could hang on a line on his terrace. He was also careful to keep out of sight Lesley's shampoo and Connie's cologne. Twice he had found one of Connie's little crescent-shaped yellow combs in the bed when he changed it, had stuck them in a pocket of one of his raincoats and returned them the next time he saw Connie. He was not going to be tripped up by the usual, the cliché of a hairpin or something like that on the night table.

"I'd love to live in the country," Connie said one night around eleven, lying in his bed naked and smoking a cigarette, with the sheet pulled up to her waist. "Not too far from New York, of course."

"I too," said Harry. He meant it. He was in pajama pants, barefoot, slumped in an armchair with his hands behind his head. A vision of a country house, maybe in Connecticut, maybe Westchester if he could afford it, came into his eyes: white maybe, a bit of lawn, old trees. And with Connie. Yes, Connie. She wanted it. Lesley would always have to spend her nights in New York, Harry thought, because of having to get up so often at six and seven in the morning for the photographers. On the other hand, how long did a model's career last? Harry was ashamed of his thoughts. He and Connie had just spent a wonderful hour in bed. How dare he think of Lesley now! But he did think of Lesley, and he was thinking of her. Would he have to give up those enchanting brown eyes, that smile, that straight brown hair (always with an excellent cut, of course) that looked freshly washed every time he saw it? Yes, he would have to give it up, if he married Connie and slept in Connecticut every night.

"What're you thinking about?" Connie smiled, sleepy looking. Her full lips were lovely without rouge, as they were now.

"Us," said Harry. It was a Sunday night. He had been in the same bed with Lesley last night, and she had left this morning for her Sunday parental lunch.

"Let's do something about it," Connie said in her soft but very definite voice, and put out her cigarette. She held the sheet against her breasts, but one breast was exposed.

Harry stared at the one breast, stupidly. What was he going to do? Stall both girls indefinitely? Enjoy them both and not get married? How long could that go on until one or the other got fed up? Two more months?

One month? Some girls moved fast, others hung on. Connie was the patient type, but too intelligent to waste a lot of time. Lesley would fly even sooner, Harry believed, if she thought he was being evasive on the subject of marriage. Lesley would leave him with a smile and without a scene. In that way, the two girls were the same: neither was going to wait forever. Why couldn't a man have two wives?

Lesley, on the following Tuesday evening, brought him flowers, in a pot. "A Japanese something or other. Geranium, I think they said. Anyway the studio would just've thrown it away."

They both went out on the terrace and chose a spot for the new orange-colored plant. Harry had a climbing rose, a large pot of parsley from which he took sprigs when he needed them. He pinched off some now. Harry had bought halibut steaks for their dinner. Lesley was fond of fish. After dinner they watched a television program as they lay on Harry's bed, holding hands. The program became boring, lovemaking more interesting. *Lesley.* Lesley was the girl he wanted, Harry thought. Why should he doubt it? Why debate? She was every bit as pretty as Connie. And Lesley was more cheerful, better balanced. Wouldn't Connie's moods get in the way sometimes, make things difficult—because Harry didn't know how to pull Connie out of them, her silences sometimes, as if she were brooding on something far away, or maybe deep inside her, but she would never enlighten him, therefore he never knew what to say or do.

Around midnight Harry and Lesley went out to a disco three streets away, a modest place as discos went, where the music didn't break your eardrums. Harry had a beer, Lesley a tonic without the gin.

"It's almost as if we're married," Lesley said in a moment when the music was not so loud. She smiled her fresh smile, the corners of her lips went up like a child's. "You're the kind of man I could live with. There are very few."

"Easygoing, eh? No demands," Harry replied in a mocking tone, but his heart was thumping with pride. A couple of fellows at the table on their right were looking at Lesley with envy, even though they had their girls with them.

Harry put Lesley into a taxi a few minutes later. She had to be up by 7:30, and her make-up kit was at her apartment. As he walked back to Jane Street, Harry found himself thinking of Connie. Connie *was* as beautiful as Lesley, if one wanted to think about beauty. Connie didn't earn her living by it, as it happened, as Lesley did. Connie had admirers too, whom she brushed off like gnats, because she preferred him. Harry had seen this.

Could he really abandon *Connie*? It was unthinkable! Was he drunk? On two gin-and-tonics before dinner and one beer? Two beers counting the one with dinner? Of course he wasn't drunk. He just couldn't come to a decision. Twenty past midnight now. He was tired. That was logical. People couldn't think after a sixteen-hour day. Could they? Think tomorrow, Harry told himself.

When he got home, the telephone was ringing. Harry ran for it. "Hello?"

"Hello, darling. I just wanted to say good night," Connie said in a quiet, sleepy voice. She always sounded young on the telephone, like a child of twelve sometimes.

"Thanks, my love. You all right?"

"Sure. Reading a manuscript—which is putting me to sleep." Here she sounded as if she were stretching in bed. "Where were you?"

"Out buying cigarettes and milk."

"When do we see each other? Friday? I forgot."

"Friday. Sure." Was she deliberately avoiding Saturday, Lesley's night? Had Connie done this before? Harry couldn't remember. "Come to my place Friday? I'll be home by six-thirty anyway."

The next day, Wednesday, Dick Hanson buzzed Harry's office around ten and said, "Got a little news that might interest you, Harry. Can I come in for a minute?"

"I would be honored," said Harry.

Dick came in smiling, with a couple of photographs in his hand, a manila envelope, a couple of typewritten pages. "House for sale in my neck of the woods," said Dick, after closing Harry's door. "We know the owners, their name is Buck. Anyway, look. See if it interests you."

Harry looked at the two photographs of a Westchester house—white, with a lawn, with grown-up trees, and it looked to him like his dream house, the one that came into his head when he was with Connie or Lesley. Dick explained that the Bucks didn't want to put it with an agent if they could avoid it, that they wanted to sell it quickly at a fair price, because Nelson Buck's company was transferring him to California on short notice, and they had to buy a house in California.

"Ninety thousand dollars," Dick said, "and I can tell you it'd go for a hundred and fifty thousand via an agent. It's five miles from where we live. Think about it, Harry, before it's too late—meaning in the next two or three days. I could see that you get good mortgage terms, because I know the town bank people . . . What do you think?"

Harry had been speechless for several seconds. Could he? Dare he?

Dick Hanson's reddish brown eyes looked down affectionately at Harry, eagerly. Harry had the feeling he stood on the edge of a swimming pool or a diving board, hesitating.

"Handsome, isn't it? Helen and I know the house well, because we're good friends with the Bucks. This is on the up and up. And . . . well, the general impression is that you're going to get married soon. I hope I'm not jumping the gun by saying that." Dick looked as if he were doing anything but talking out of turn, as if Harry were already due for congratulations. "Which girl is it going to be—you lucky swine," Dick drawled with good humor. "You look like the cat—who just swallowed the bird."

Harry was thinking, *I dunno which girl.* But he kept a smug silence, as if he did know.

"You're interested?" Dick asked.

"Sure I'm interested," Harry replied. He held a photograph in each hand.

"Think it over for a couple of days. Take the photos. I brought the envelope. Show them—you know." Dick meant to one of the girls, Harry knew. "It'd be great to be neighbors, Harry. I mean that. We could have fun up there—besides a little useful business on weekends, maybe."

Around three, Dick sent a memo in a sealed envelope to Harry with more information on mortgage terms, and Dick added that Harry couldn't go wrong on this house purchase, even if he didn't intend to get married in the immediate future. An 1850s house in superb condition, three bedrooms, two baths, and the value could only go up.

That afternoon Harry seized ten or fifteen minutes, did some figuring on his computer, and also in his own head with pencil and paper. He could swing the Westchester house, all right. But he wouldn't want to move there alone. Could Lesley live there with him and still commute? At very early hours sometimes? She might not consider a country house worth it. Could Connie? Yes, more easily. She didn't have to get to work till nine-thirty or even ten. But a man didn't choose a wife for her ease of commuting. That was absurd.

Harry's thoughts drifted back to a perfect weekend (Sunday noon till Monday morning), when he and Connie had painted his kitchen bright orange. Wonderful! Connie in already paint-spattered jeans, on the ladder, alternating with him on the ladder—drinking beer, laughing, making love. God! He could see Connie more easily in the Westchester house than Lesley.

By five o'clock, Harry had come to at least one decision. He would take a look at the house, and right away, if possible. He rang Dick's office, caught Dick in the middle of a talk with Raymond, but Harry was able to say, "I'd love to *see* the house. Can I maybe drive up with you this evening?"

"Absolutely! Stay overnight with us? See it in the morning too?—I'll give Helen a blast. She'll be pleased, Harry."

So at 6 P.M. Harry walked with Dick to his garage, and got into Dick's car. It was a pleasant drive of less than forty minutes, Dick in cheerful mood, and not trying to query Harry again about which girl it might be. Dick talked about the easy driving, the easy route he was taking. Harry was thinking that he would have to acquire a car too. But that would still be within his financial possibilities. His parents in Florida would give him a car as a wedding present, Harry was sure, if he dropped a hint. No problem there.

"You seem to have pre-marital tension," Dick remarked.

"No. Ha-ha." Harry supposed he had been silent for several minutes.

They went to the Bucks' house first, because it was on the way, and because Dick wanted Harry to see the place and sleep on it. Dick said he had not bothered telephoning Julie Buck, because he knew the Bucks so well, and Julie was quite informal.

Julie welcomed them with a smile on the white front porch.

Harry and Dick went into a large hall which had a polished wooden staircase, carpeted, three handsome rooms going off the hall, one being the library. Julie said she was packing up the books, and there were cartons of books on the floor, some of the shelves empty. The Bucks' ten-year-old son, in blue jeans with holes in the knees, followed them around, tossing his football in his hands and eyeing Harry with curiosity.

"Very good apple trees. You'll have to give the apples away to the neighbors, they're so many," Julie said as they gazed from a second-story window.

The lawn sloped beautifully downward from the back of the house. Julie said something about a brook in the hollow beyond, which marked property boundary. The upstairs bedrooms were square and generous, the two baths not the last word in modernity but somehow just right for the country. The upstairs hall had a window front and back of the house. Harry was sold, though he didn't at once say so.

"I like it. But I've got to think, you know," Harry said. "A couple of days, Dick said I had."

"Oh, of course. You ought to look at some other houses too," said Julie. "Of course we love this one. And we'd like to think of a friend of the Hansons taking it over."

Julie insisted on giving them a scotch before they left. Dick and Harry drank theirs standing up in the living room, which had a fireplace. The scotch was neat and tasted lovely. Wouldn't it be great to be master of such a house, Harry was thinking. And which girl would be mistress? He had a vision of Lesley walking through the door from the hall, bearing a tray of something, smiling her divine smile. And almost immediately he saw Connie strolling through, blonde, calm and gentle, lifting her blue eyes to meet his.

Good Christ!

That night, after roast beef, cheese and wine at the Hansons', Harry hoped he would have a dream that might enlighten him about Connie and Lesley. Connie or Lesley. He did not dream at all, or if he did, he did not remember any dream. He awakened to blue-flowered wallpaper, maple furniture, sunlight streaming into his room, and thought, *this* was the kind of life he wanted. Fresh air, no city grit.

Dick and Harry departed at 8:30 with well-wishes from Helen, who hoped as much as Dick that Harry would opt for the Bucks' house. In the early morning, Harry fell more deeply in love with the white house which could, with a word and a check, be his. One solution was, Harry thought, to speak to both girls and ask them straight out if they would like such a house, in such a location, and—either Lesley or Connie might say no. Maybe for different reasons. Lesley might find it impossible with her present work. Connie might prefer a house in Long Island. Harry hated feeling vague, but what else could he do? How else could he feel?

When Harry tried to get down to it, asking the question, in the next days, he found that he couldn't. He spent one night at Connie's manuscript-and-book-cluttered apartment, and couldn't get the question out. That was Thursday night. Was he really hanging onto Lesley, therefore, because he preferred Lesley? But the same thing happened with Lesley during a hasty Friday lunch. Harry was rather obliged to give an answer to Dick that day. The Bucks were leaving Tuesday, and Monday was the date for putting the house on the market, before their departure for California. Harry had considered looking at other houses in the area, but the low price of the Bucks' house made the effort appear absurd. From a glance at newspaper ads, Harry saw that the Bucks' property was a bargain, with its acreage. Harry pulled himself together at the end of the lunch with Lesley, and said:

"I've seen a house—"

Lesley looked at him over her coffee cup. "Yes? What house?"

"House for sale, Westchester. In the area where Dick Hanson lives. You know, Dick in my office. You've met him."

They went on from there. Harry told her about spending the night at Dick's, that the house was a bargain and about thirty-five minutes from Manhattan, a railway station two miles away, a bus also.

Lesley looked dubious, or hesitant. She was concerned about the commuting angle. They didn't even mention marriage, maybe because Lesley took that for granted, Harry thought.

"The problem is, it's such a bargain, they want an answer now, or it'll be put with an agent Monday at a higher price. The house."

Lesley said she'd love to see the place, anyway, since Harry seemed to like it so much, and maybe they could go up tomorrow? Saturday? Harry said he was sure he could arrange that, either through Dick or the Bucks who would probably not mind at all picking them up at the railway station or the bus stop. That afternoon, Harry spoke with Dick Hanson about a Saturday afternoon appointment with the Bucks. Dick said he would ring Norman Buck at his New York office and fix it. By 4:30 that afternoon, Harry had a date with Norman, who would meet the train that left from Grand Central and got in at Gresham, Westchester, at 3:30.

Harry had a date that evening with Connie, who was to come to his apartment. Harry did some shopping in his neighborhood, having decided to speak to Connie at home and not in a restaurant. He was so nervous, a bottle of red wine slipped from his hands and broke on the kitchen floor, before Connie arrived. Fortunately he had another bottle in his rack, and it was so warm Connie might prefer beer, but the wine had been a good one.

He had come to a desperate but at the same time not very clear conclusion that afternoon just before leaving the office: he would invite *both* girls to see the Westchester house. He could at least see which girl liked the house better. Maybe there would be a scene, maybe there wouldn't be. Maybe they'd both say no. At least it would clear the atmosphere. Harry had not been able to concentrate during the afternoon, and had scraped through the minimum of work that he should have done. He had reasoned: if he showed the house to the girls one at a time, what then? Suppose both Lesley and Connie liked the house equally? Would he have come to any decision about Connie or Lesley even then? No. He somehow had to confront both of them, and himself, with the Westchester house at the same time. Since the girls had never met, this presented a different problem: introduce them at Grand Central, and they would all ride up on the same train? This seemed unthinkable.

Harry poured himself a straight scotch, not a big one, and lifted it with a shaking hand. There were times when a person needed steadying, he thought, and this was one of them. Harry remembered that he had said after lunch with Lesley today that he would ring her back about a time to meet tomorrow to go up to Westchester. He hadn't rung Lesley, however. Why not? Well, for one thing, more than half the time he didn't know where to ring her, because of her hopping around at her work. Should he try her at her apartment now? As Harry frowned at his telephone, it rang.

It was Lesley.

Harry smiled. "I was just about to call *you.*"

"Did you make any arrangement about tomorrow?"

Harry said he had, and stammered out something about the train from Grand Central at 3 P.M. or a couple of minutes before. Lesley asked him why he was so nervous.

"I dunno," Harry said, and Lesley laughed.

"If you've got it all arranged with the Bucks, don't change anything, but I can't make it by three, I know," Lesley said. "Werner—you know, Werner Ludwig, he needs me at two tomorrow, and I know he'll need an hour anyway, but the good thing is, he lives near that town you mentioned."

"Gresham?"

"That's it, and he said he'd be glad to take me up with him in his car. I think he even knows the Bucks' house. So I could be there by four, I should think."

Suddenly that problem was solved, for Harry. Or postponed, he thought, the girls' meeting. At least they wouldn't be meeting in Grand Central.

They hung up, and the doorbell rang. Connie had his key (so did Lesley), but Connie always buzzed when she knew he was home.

Harry's nerves did not improve during the evening. He was cheerful, even made Connie laugh once, but he felt that his hands were shaking. When he looked at his hands, they were not shaking.

"Jitters already, and you haven't even signed anything?" Connie asked. "You don't have to take *this* house. It's the first one you've looked at up there, isn't it? Nobody buys the first thing they see." Connie spoke in her serious, logical way.

He was no good in bed that night. Connie thought it funny, but not as funny as Lesley would have. Connie had brought two manuscripts. They slept late on Saturday morning (Harry had at last fallen asleep after hours of trying to, and trying to be motionless so as not to disturb Connie), and she read one of the manuscripts after their brunch, until it was time to leave for Grand Central. They took a taxi to the station. Connie read the second manuscript, absorbed and silent, during the short ride, and was not even half through the script when they got to Gresham, doing as usual her careful job, Harry was sure.

Dick Hanson met them, not Nelson Buck as Harry had expected.

"Welcome, Harry!" Dick said, all smiles. "So it's—" He looked at Connie.

"Connie Jaeger," Harry said. "You've met her, I think. I know."

Dick and Connie exchanged "Hellos" and they got into Dick's car, Harry in the back seat, and off they went into the countryside. Twenty to four. Would Lesley be there ahead of time? Would it be any worse than her coming five minutes *after* they got to the Bucks'? No. Should he mention now that he was expecting someone else? Harry tried rehearsing the first sentence, and realized that he couldn't have got the first words out. Maybe Lesley wouldn't be able to make it, after all. Maybe Werner had had a puncture, was going to be delayed? And what then?

"There's the house," said Dick as he made a turn in the road.

"Oh. Very lovely," said Connie, quietly and politely.

Connie never went overboard about anything, Harry reminded himself, with a little comfort.

Harry saw a car in front of the Bucks' house on the curving graveled driveway. Then Harry saw Lesley come out the front door, onto the porch, with Julie Buck.

"Well, well, they've got visitors," said Dick, pulling his handbrake.

"My friend Lesley," Harry mumbled. Did he black out for the next seconds? He opened the car door for Connie.

Much chatter, introductions.

"Connie—this is Lesley—Marker. Connie Jaeger," Harry said.

"How do you do?" the girls said simultaneously, looking each other in the eyes, as if each was trying to memorize the other's face. Their smiles were polite and minimal.

Dick shuffled, brushed his hands together for no reason, and said, "Well, shall we all go in and look around? May we, Julie?"

"Su-ure! That's what we're here for!" said Julie cheerfully, not digging a whit of the situation, Harry realized.

Harry felt that he walked into purgatory, into hell, into another life, or maybe death. The girls were stiff as pokers, didn't even look at him as they all walked from room to room. Julie gave them a guided tour, mentioning defects and assets, and as on many a guided tour, Harry felt, some of the tourists were not listening. He caught the girls sizing each other up with lightning glances, which were followed by an ignoring of each other. Dick Hanson wore a puzzled frown, even when he looked at Harry.

"What's going on?" Dick whispered to Harry, when he could.

Harry shrugged. It was more like a twitch, though he tried for a desperate couple of seconds to say something intelligent or normal to Dick. He couldn't. The situation was bizarre, the rooms, the house suddenly meaningless, their parading back down the stairs as useless as some rehearsal in a play in which no one had any interest.

"*Thank* you, Mrs. Buck," Lesley was saying with careful politeness in the downstairs hall.

Lesley's friend, who had brought her, had evidently departed, because his car was gone, Harry saw. Connie looked at him with her quiet, knowing smile. Her smile was not friendly, but rather amused.

"Harry, if you—"

"I'm afraid it's off," Harry said, interrupting Dick. "Off, yes."

Dick still looked puzzled. So did both the Bucks, maybe Julie Buck less so.

The end, Harry thought. *Ruin, finish.* He tried to stand up straighter but mentally he was on the floor, crawling along like a worm.

"Maybe you'd like to talk a little—by yourselves," said Nelson Buck to Harry and the girls, gesturing toward the library on his right, which now had more cartons on the floor and fewer books on the shelves. His gesture, his glance had included Harry and the two girls.

Did Nelson Buck think he maintained a harem, Harry wondered.

"No," said Lesley, coolly. "Not your fault, Mr. Buck. It's a lovely house. Really. Thank you too, Mrs. Buck. I think I must be on my way, because of an appointment in New York tonight. Maybe I can phone for a taxi?"

"Oh, I can take you to the station!" said Nelson.

"Or I can," said Dick. "No problem."

It was agreed that Dick would take Lesley, now. Harry walked out with them to Dick's car. Dick went ahead of them, and opened his car door.

Lesley said to Harry, "What was the idea, Harry? That we'd *both* commute?" She laughed aloud, and in it Harry heard a little bitterness but also a real amusement. "I knew you had a friend, but *this*—It's a bit much, isn't it? Bye-bye, Harry."

"*How* did you know?" Harry asked.

Lesley had got into the front seat. "Easy," she said in her easy voice.

"Not coming, Harry?" Dick asked.

"No. I'll stay here with Connie. Bye-bye, Lesley."

Harry turned back to the house as they drove off. Stay here with Connie? What was *she* going to say? Harry walked back into the hall.

Connie and Julie and Nelson Buck were conversing pleasantly in the big hall, Connie with her hand on the newel post, one trousered leg and sneakered foot extended. Her face was smiling, her eyes steady as she looked at Harry. The Bucks faded away, Julie to the rear of the house somewhere, Nelson into the living room on Harry's right.

"I'll be going too," said Connie, not changing her stance. "I hope you'll be happy with Lesley."

"*Lesley?*" said Harry in a tone of astonishment. It had simply come out of him. He had nothing to say afterward.

Connie gave a silent laugh, shrugged her shoulders. "Nice to meet her finally. I knew she existed."

Were Harry's cheeks warm because of shame? He was not sure. "How?"

"Lots of little things. The dishes were always stacked differently when I turned up on Sundays. Different from Wednesdays maybe. Little things." Slowly she got a cigarette from her canvas jacket pocket, having put her briefcase with her manuscripts in it on the floor between her feet.

Harry sprang to light the cigarette for her, but Connie swung herself slightly, out of his reach, and had the cigarette lit. He had lost her, Harry knew. "I'm sorry, Connie."

"Are you? I don't know. You couldn't have got your *dates* mixed," she said, not like a question, not quite like a statement either, something in between. Connie's serious, straight blue eyes, her shake of her head seemed to penetrate Harry's body from his head down to his feet. Connie was finished, had said good-bye to him, inside. "My taxi's there," Connie said, looking past Harry through the open front door. She went down the hall to find Julie.

Then Connie went out to the taxi, talked to the Bucks for an instant through the open taxi window, before the taxi moved off.

The Bucks came into the house, both looking puzzled, Julie barely managing a faint smile, absurd below her frown.

"Well," Nelson said, a little heavily.

The moment was relieved by Dick's car crunching up the driveway. Both the Bucks turned to it as if it were a lifesaver. How soon could he take off, Harry was thinking. Thank God for Dick! Dick could whisk him off. Unthinkable that Harry would have taken the same train as one of the girls, or both of them.

"Harry, old boy," Dick said, then added, as Nelson had and in the same tone, "Well!"

"Maybe you two would like a word by yourselves," said Nelson to Dick and Harry.

"I should be leaving," Harry said. "I thank you both—for your time."

A few more polite phrases, then Harry was in Dick's car, rolling away.

"Harry, what in the name of God," Dick began in the gruff tone of a senior brother, a man of the world who had made some mistakes in life but learned a little from them.

"I think I did it deliberately," Harry said. The words came out before his brain had formed them, or so he felt. "I couldn't make up my mind. I had to—get rid of them both. I love them *both*."

"Rubbish! Well, it isn't rubbish, I don't mean that. Something— could've been arranged . . . But my God, Harry, to bring them both like that! I had the feeling they hadn't met before."

"They hadn't."

"Come to our place and have a drink. Won't hurt you."

"No, thanks," Harry said. He knew they were heading for Dick's house. "I'd better get to the station, if you don't mind."

Harry insisted, over Dick's protests. Dick wanted to put him up for the night, have a talk with him. Dick knew the next train, and it would not be the train the girls would have taken. There were quite a few trains, Dick said, and probably the girls had taken different ones, and anyway there was plenty of room on the trains, so they needn't have ridden in the same car. On the way to the station, Dick began again his speech about there being a way to patch things up, to decide which girl he wanted, and then either drop the other girl or hang onto her in some way.

"They're both *lovely*," Dick said. "I can understand your problem! Believe me, Harry! But don't give up. You look like a guy who's just been through a war. Don't be silly. You can patch things up."

"Not with those girls. No," Harry said. "That's why I liked them so. They're different."

Dick shook his head in despair. They had arrived at the station. Harry bought his ticket. Then Harry and Dick shook hands with a hard grip that left Harry's hand tingling for a couple of minutes. Harry walked alone onto the platform and waited, then the train came and he rode back to

Grand Central. Deliberately. He knew he had done it deliberately. He had somehow wanted to do this, break it all up, but what did he have now? People said the world was full of girls, pretty girls. True maybe. But not many as interesting as Lesley and Connie.

During the next week the girls came, separately, and picked up their few belongings from Harry's Jane Street apartment, each leaving her key under his doormat.

The Kite

The voices of Walter's mother and father came in jerky murmurs down the hall to his room. What were they arguing about now? Walter wasn't listening. He thought of kicking his room door shut, and didn't. He could shut their words out of his ears quite well. Walter was on his knees on the floor, carefully notching a balsa wood strip which was nearly nine feet long. It would have been exactly nine feet long, but he had notched it too deeply, he thought, a few minutes ago, and had cut that little piece off and started again. This was the long center piece for the kite he was making. The crosspiece would be nearly six feet long, so only by turning the kite horizontally would he be able to get it out his room door.

"*I didn't say* that!" That was his mother's shrill voice in a tone of impatience.

A couple of times a week, his father went mumbling into the living room to sleep on the sofa there instead of in the bedroom with his mother. Now and then they mentioned Elsie, Walter's sister, but Walter had stopped listening even to that. Elsie had died two months ago in the hospital, because of pneumonia. Walter now noticed a smell of frying ham or bacon. He was hungry, but the menu for dinner didn't interest him. Maybe they would get through the meal without his father standing up and leaving the table, maybe even taking the car and going off. That didn't matter.

The work under his hands mattered, the big kite, and Walter was so far pleased. It was the biggest kite he had ever tried to make, and would it even fly? The tail would have to be pretty long. He might have to experiment with its length. In a corner of his room stood a six-foot tall roll of pinkish rice paper. Walter looked forward with pleasure and a little fear to cutting a single big piece for his kite. He had ordered the paper from a stationery-

and-book shop in town, and had waited a month for it, because it had come from San Francisco. He had paid the eight dollars for it from money saved out of his allowance, meaning from not going to Cooper's for ice cream sodas and hamburgers with Ricky and other neighborhood chums.

Walter stood up. Above his bed he had thumbtacked a purple kite to the wall. This kite had a hole in its paper, because a bird had flown through it as if on purpose, like a bomber. The bird had not been hurt, but the kite had fallen quickly, while Walter had wound in his string as fast as he could to save the kite before it got caught in a tree. He had saved the kite, what was left of it. He and Elsie had made the kite together, and Walter was fond of it.

"Wally-y? . . . Dinner!" his mother called from the kitchen.

"Coming, Mom!"

Walter was now brushing balsa wood chips, tiny ones, into a dustpan. His mother had taken away the carpet last year. The plain wooden floor was easier to sweep, easier to work on when he was gluing something. Walter dumped the chips into his wastebasket. He glanced up at a box kite— blue and yellow—which hung from his ceiling. Elsie had loved this kite. He thought she would admire the one he was making now. Suddenly Walter knew what he would put on his kite, simply his sister's name— Elsie—in graceful script letters.

"Wally?"

Walter walked down the hall to the kitchen. His mother and father sat already at the rectangular table which had X-shaped legs. His sister's chair, the fourth chair, had not been removed, and perhaps was there just to complete the picture of four, Walter thought, a chair on each side of the table, though the table was big enough for eight people to sit at. Walter barely glanced at his father, because his father was staring at him, and Walter expected a critical remark. His father had darker brown hair than Walter's, and the straight brows that Walter had inherited. Lately his father had an amused smile on his lips that Walter had learned was not to be counted on. His father Steve sold cars, new and used, and he liked to wear tweed suits. He had a couple of favorite tweed suits that he called lucky. Even now, in June, his father was wearing brown tweed trousers, though his tie was loosened and his shirt open at the neck. His mother's blonde hair looked fluffier than usual, meaning she had been to the beauty parlor that afternoon.

"Why so quiet, Wally?" asked his mother.

Walter was eating his rice and ham casserole. There was a plate of crisp green salad on his left. "*You're* not saying anything."

His father gave a soft laugh.

"What've you been doing this afternoon?" his mother asked.

Walter shrugged. She meant since he had got home from school at half past three. "Fooling around."

"As long as he hasn't been—you know." Steve reached for his mug of beer.

Walter felt a warmth in his face. His father meant had he been to the cemetery again. Well, Walter didn't go often, and in fact he hated the place. Maybe he'd gone there just twice on his own, and how had his parents even found out?

"I know Wally was home—all afternoon," his mother said gently.

"Caretaker there—he mentioned it, you know, Gladys?"

"All right, Steve, do you have to—"

Steve bit into garlic bread and looked at his son. "Caretaker there, Wally. So why do you jump the fence? . . . If you want to go in, just ring his doorbell across the road there. That's what he's for."

Walter pressed his lips together. He didn't want to visit his sister's grave in the company of an old caretaker, for God's sake! "So what if I did—once?" Walter retorted. "Frankly—I think it's *boring* there." Ugly and stupid, all those tombstones, Walter might have added.

"Then don't go," said his father, smiling more broadly now.

Walter looked in rage at his mother, not knowing what to reply now, not expecting that she could help him either.

"*Cuck*-oo!—*Cuck*-oo!—*Cuck*-oo!—"

"And I'm goddam sick of that *cuckoo* clock!" yelled his father, jumping up from the table at the same time. He lifted the clock from the wall and looked about to throw it on the floor, while the bird kept popping in and out, announcing seven.

"Ha-ha!—Ha-ha-*haa-aa*!" Walter laughed and tried to stifle it. He nearly choked on lettuce, and grabbed his milk glass and laughed into that.

"Don't break it, Steve!" cried his mother. "Wally, *stop* it!"

Walter did stop laughing, suddenly, but not because his mother had told him to. He finished his meal slowly. Now his father wasn't going to sit down again, and they were talking about the Beachcomber Inn, whether his father was going there tonight, and his mother was saying she didn't want to go, and asking Steve if he expected to meet anyone there. One person or several, Walter couldn't tell, and it didn't matter to Walter. But his mother was getting more angry, and now she was standing up also, leaving her baked apple untouched.

Steve said, "Is that the only place in this—"

"You know that's where you were for days and nights—*that* time!" said his mother, sounding out of breath.

Steve glanced at Walter, who lowered his eyes and pushed his half-eaten dessert away. Walter wanted to jump up and go, but sat for the next seconds as if paralyzed.

"That is . . . not . . . true," said his father. "But am I going out tonight? Yes!" He was pulling on a summer jacket that had been hanging over a chair.

Walter knew they were talking about the time his sister had caught fever. Elsie had had her tonsils out a week or so before, and everything had seemed all right, even though she was home from school and still eating mostly ice cream, and then she had become pink in the face. And his mother had been away just then, because *her* mother—Grandma Page— had been sick in Denver, something with her heart, and everybody had thought *she* might die, but she hadn't. Then when his mother had come home, Elsie was already in the hospital, and the doctor had said it was double pneumonia or at least a very bad case of pneumonia, which Walter thought nobody had to die from, but Elsie had died.

"Can't you finish your baked apple, Wally?" asked his mother.

"He's daydreaming again." Steve had a cigarette in his mouth. "Lives in a dream world. Bikes and kites." His father was about to go out of the back door to the garage.

"Can I leave now?" Walter stood up. "I mean—for my room?"

"Yes, Wally," said his mother. "That police program you like is on tonight. Want to watch it with me?"

"Not sure." Walter shook his head awkwardly, and left the kitchen.

A minute later, Walter heard the car rolling down the driveway. Walter crossed the hall from his room into the living room. Here there were bookshelves, the TV set, a sofa and armchairs. On top of one of the bookshelves stood two pictures of Elsie.

In the larger photograph, Elsie was holding the purple kite lightly between her palms, the kite that later the same day had been hit by a bird. Elsie was smiling, almost laughing, and the wind blew her hair back, blonder hair than Walter's. The second picture Walter liked less, because it had been taken last Christmas in a photographer's studio—he and Elsie in neat clothes sitting on a sofa. His father had taken the kite picture in the backyard just three months ago. And now Elsie was dead, "gone away," someone had said to him, as if he were a little kid they had to tell lies to, as if she would "come back" one day, if she only decided to. Dead was dead, and dead was to be limp and not breathing—like a couple of mice Walter had seen his father take out of traps under the sink. Things dead would never move or breathe again. They were hopeless and finished. Walter also didn't believe in ghosts, didn't imagine his sister walking around the house at night, trying to speak to him. Certainly not. Walter didn't even believe in a life after death, though the preacher had talked about something like that during the service for Elsie. Did a mouse have a life after death? Why should it have? How could it? Where was that life, for instance? Could anybody say? No. *That* was a dream world, Walter thought, and a lot sillier than his kites that his father called a dream world. You could touch kites, and they had to be correctly made, just like airplanes.

When he heard his mother's step, Walter slipped across the hall into his own room.

Within two or three minutes, Walter was ready to leave the house with a red and white kite some two feet in length, and a roll of string. It was still daylight, hardly eight o'clock.

"Wally?" His mother was in the living room and had turned on the TV. "Got your homework done?"

"Sure, Mom, this afternoon." That was true. Wally went reluctantly to the living room door, having dropped his kite out of sight in the hall. "I'm going out with my bike. Just for a few minutes."

His mother sat in an armchair, and she had pushed her shoes off. "That program you like's at nine, you know?"

"Oh, I can be back by then." Walter snatched up his kite and headed for the back door.

He took his bike from the garage, and installed the kite between two rags in one of the satchels behind the seat. Walter rolled down the driveway and turned right in the street, coasting downhill and standing on the pedals.

Walter's school friend Ricky was watering his front lawn. "Going up to Coop's?" Ricky meant the hamburger-and-ice-cream place.

"Naw, just cruisin' for a few minutes," Walter said over his shoulder. Walter had no extra money at the moment, and was not in the mood for Coop's with Ricky, anyway.

The boy rolled on, through the town's shopping center, then turned left, and began to pedal harder up a long slope. The wind was picking up, and blew against him as he went up the hill. Houses grew fewer, then there were more trees, and finally he saw the spiked iron fence of Greenhills, the cemetery where his sister was buried. Walter cycled around to the right, had to walk his bike across a grassy ditch, then he walked several yards more until he reached a sheltered spot concealed from the road by a big tree. He leaned his bike against the fence, poked his kite and string through the bars, and climbed the fence, bracing his sneakers against the bars. He eased himself over the spikes at the top, dropped to the ground, and picked up his kite and ran.

He ran for the pleasure of running, and also because he disliked the low forest of mainly white tombstones all around now. He felt not in the least afraid of them, or even respectful of them, they were simply ugly, like jagged rocks that could block or trip a person. Walter zigzagged through them, aiming for a rise in the land a bit to his left.

Walter came to Elsie's grave and slowed, breathing through his mouth. Her grave was not quite at the crest of the hill. Her stone was white, curved at the top because of the figure of an angel lying on its side with one wing slightly lifted. MARY ELIZABETH MCCREARY, the stone said, with her dates that Walter hardly glanced at. The dates did not span ten years. Something below about a LAMB GATHERED. What baloney! The grass over her grave had not grown together yet, and he could still see the squares cut by the gravediggers' spades. For an instant, he felt like saying, "Hi, Elsie! I'm going to try the red and white. Want to watch?" but instead, he set his teeth and pressed his lips together. Trying to talk to the dead was baloney, too. Walter stepped right onto her short grave and over it, and walked to the crest of the hill. Even here the ground was not free of gravestones, but at least they lay flat on the ground, as if the owners of the cemetery or whoever controlled it didn't want tombstones showing against the sky.

Walter dropped his roll of string, took the rubber band off the rag tail of the kite and shook it out. This was also a kite that Elsie had helped him make. She had liked to cut the paper, slowly and cautiously, after he had marked it out. This tail consisted of parts of an old white sheet Walter had taken from the rag bag, and he recalled that his mother had been annoyed, because she had wanted the sheet for window polishing. Walter took a run against the wind, and the kite leapt promisingly. He stood and eased the kite up with long tugs on the string. It was going! And Walter had not been optimistic, because the wind was nothing great today. He let out more string, and felt a thrill as the kite began to pull at his fingers like something alive up in the sky. An upward current sent it zooming, took the string from his hand, and Walter had to grab for it.

Smiling, Walter walked backward and tripped on a grave marker, rolled over and jumped to his feet again, the string still in his hand. "How about *that,* Elsie?" He meant the kite, way up now. The wind blew his hair over his forehead and eyes. A little ashamed because he had spoken out loud, he began to whistle. The tune was one he and Elsie had used to hum or whistle together, when they were sandpapering balsa strips, measuring and cutting. The music was by Tchaikovsky, and his parents had the record.

Walter stopped whistling abruptly, and pulled his kite in. The kite came reluctantly, then dived a few yards as if it gave up, and Walter wound it in faster, and ran to save it. It had not landed in trees. The kite was undamaged.

By the time Walter mounted his bicycle, it was nearly dark, and he put on his headlight. The cops program his mother had talked about would still be on, but Walter didn't feel like watching it. Now he was passing the Beachcomber Inn, and he supposed his father was there, having a beer, but Walter didn't glance at the cars parked in front of the place. His mother was accusing his father of seeing someone there, or meeting someone there. A girl, of course, or a woman. Walter did not like thinking about that. Was it his business? No. He also knew that his mother thought his father had been spending all his spare time at the Beachcomber, or somewhere with "that woman," when his sister had been coming down with fever, and so his father hadn't taken care of Elsie. All this had caused an awful atmosphere in the house, which was why Walter spent a lot of time in his own room, and didn't want to look at TV so much any more.

Walter put his bike in the garage against the wall—the car was still gone—cut his headlight, and took his kite and string. He went in quietly by the back door and down the hall to his room. His mother was in the living room with the TV on and didn't hear him, or, if she did, she didn't say anything. Walter closed his room door softly before he switched on his ceiling light. He folded the kite's tail, put a rubber band on it, and set the kite in a corner where two or three other kites stood. Then he moved his straight chair closer to his worktable so there would be more room on the floor, swept the floor again, and removed his sneakers. He felt inspired to measure his rice paper for the big kite. He walked barefoot to a corner of the room and fetched the roll, laid it on the floor and carefully rolled a length out. Rice paper was quite strong, Walter had read in lots of books about kites. This big kite of course had to be extra strong, because a lot of surface would be hit by the wind, and a strong wind would go right through tissue paper of this area, just as surely as the bird had gone through his smaller kite.

From his table Walter took his list of measurements, a metal tape measure, a ruler, and a piece of blue chalk. He measured and marked out with the chalk the right half of the kite. When he had cut the first long line from bottom tip to the right hand point, he felt a surge of pride, maybe of fear. Maybe such a big kite wouldn't even get off the ground, or not get far up, anyway. In that case, he would try to shrug off his disappointment, and he would be hoping that no one was watching at that moment. Meanwhile, Walter whistled cautiously to himself, cut the top line, then folded the triangle carefully down the center line which he had drawn with the blue chalk. He then traced the triangle on the left-hand side.

His mother had lowered or cut the TV and was on the telephone now. "Tomorrow night, *sure!*" came her high voice, then a laugh. "You'd better have it. Basted *and* sewn. I know it's right now. . . . What?"

She was probably talking to Nancy, her friend who did a lot of sewing. His mother did a lot of cutting—of cloth—for coats and dresses. It was a "pastime," she said, but she earned money from it. *Cutting is always the most important operation,* his mother said. Walter thought of that as he cut as surely as he could in the middle of his chalk lines. Besides making good kites, Walter would have liked to write a good poem, not the kind of silly poems his English composition teacher ordered the class to write now and then. "Tell about a walk in the woods . . . a rainstorm in summer . . ." No. Walter wanted to write something good about a kite flying in the air, for instance, about his thoughts, *himself,* being up there with the kite, his eyes too, able to look down at all the world, and able to look up at space. Walter had tried three or four times to write such a poem, but on reading his efforts the day after, had found them not as good as he had first thought, so he had thrown them all away. He always felt that he addressed his poems to his sister, but that was because he wanted her, would have wanted her to enjoy what he had written, and maybe to give him a word of praise for it.

A knock on his door startled him. Walter withdrew his scissors from the paper, rocked back on his heels and said, "Yep?"

His mother opened the door, smiling, glanced at the paper on the floor, then looked at him. "It's after ten, Wally."

"Tomorrow's Saturday."

"What're you making now?"

"Um-m—This is paper for a kite."

"*That* big! One kite?" She glanced from top to bottom of what he had cut, which did stretch almost from the far wall to the door where she stood. "You mean, you'll fold it."

"Yes," said Walter flatly. He felt his mother wasn't really interested, and was just making conversation with him. Her squarish face looked worried and tired tonight, though her lips continued to smile.

"Where'd you go this evening? Up to Cooper's?"

Walter started to say yes, then said, "No, just for a ride around. Nowhere."

"You start thinking about going to bed."

"Yep. I will, Mom."

Then she left him, and Walter finished his cutting and laid the long piece of paper, lightly folded in half, on top of his worktable, and put away in a corner what was left of the rice paper roll. He looked forward to tomorrow when he would tie the balsa strips and glue the paper, and even more to Sunday when he would try the kite, if there was a good wind.

Hours later, the popping sound of his father's car on the gravel awakened Walter, but he did not stir, only blinked his eyes sleepily. Tomorrow. The big kite. It wouldn't matter if his parents quarreled, if his mother and her yackety friends spent all evening over patterns in the living room—and in Elsie's room at the back opposite the kitchen, which his mother was lately turning into her workroom, even calling it that. Walter could shut all that out.

His father looked at the big kite and chuckled. "That'll never fly. You expect that to *fly*?"

This was just after lunch on Saturday. They were in the backyard.

Walter's face grew warm, and he felt flustered. "No, it's just for fun . . . For decor," he added, a word his mother used quite a lot.

His father nodded, pink-eyed, and drifted off with a can of beer in his hand. Then he said over his shoulder, "I think you're getting a little obsessed on the subject of kites, you know, Wally?—How's your schoolwork these days? Haven't you got final exams coming up?"

Walter, with one knee on the grass, straightened his back. "Yes . . . Why don't you ask Mom?"

His father walked on, toward the back door. Walter resented the school question as much as he did the kite remark. He was first in his class in math, without even trying very hard, and maybe second in English, behind Louise Wiley, who was nearly a genius, but anyway he had A's in both subjects. Walter returned to his gluing. When was the last time his father had looked at his report card, for that matter? Walter pushed his kite nearer the fence. He was working in a corner made by the bamboo fence, the most sheltered spot against the breeze. The grass was short and even, not as good as his room floor to work on, but the kite was too big to lie flat in his room now. Walter weighted the periphery of his kite with stones about the size of oranges which he had taken from a border and intended to put back. The breeze and the sunlight would hasten the glue setting, or so Walter liked to think. He wanted to forget his father's remarks, and enjoy the rest of the afternoon.

But there was something else disagreeable: they were going to Grandma McCreary's for tea. Walter's mother told him. Had Walter forgotten? she asked him. Yes, he had forgotten. This Grandma was called Edna, and Walter liked her less than his Grandma Page, who was called Daisy, the one who had nearly died from a heart attack. Walter had to change into better clothes and put on shoes. Edna lived about fifteen miles away in a house right on the coast with a view of the ocean. They got there around four.

"You've grown another inch, Wally!" said Edna, fussing around the tea tray.

Walter hadn't, not since he had seen Edna a month ago, anyway. He was worried about his kite. He had had to take it very carefully into his room and lean it against his worktable. Walter was worried that the glue hadn't set enough, and that something might go wrong, the paper be unusable, and he hadn't enough paper left over for a second effort. These thoughts, and the general uncomfortableness of his grandmother's living room—magazines lying everywhere, and no place to put anything—caused Walter to drop his plate off his pressed-together knees, and a blob of vanilla ice cream fell on the carpet with the slice of marble cake on top of it now instead of underneath.

His mother groaned. "Wally—you're so clumsy—sometimes."

"I *am* sorry," Walter said.

His father gave a soft chuckle. He had taken a glass and poured a couple of inches of scotch into it from the bar cart a few minutes before.

Walter was diligent with the sponge, and tackled the spot a second time. It was more fun to be doing something than to sit.

"You're a helpful boy though, Wally. *Thank* you," said Edna. "That's really good enough!" Edna took the saucepan and sponge from him. She had pink-polished fingernails and smelled of a sweet perfume Walter didn't like. Walter knew her very blonde hair was dyed.

". . . misses his sister," Walter heard his mother murmuring, hissing, as she and Edna walked into the kitchen.

Walter shoved his hands into his pockets and turned his back on his father, went over and stared at a bookcase. He declined another helping of ice cream and cake. The sooner they could leave, the better. But then they had to file out and admire Edna's rose bed, all freshly turned with black, wet-looking earth and yellow, red and pink roses all starting to bloom. Then there were more mumblings, and his mother said something about kites, while his father went into the living room for another drink.

It was after six when they got home. Walter went at once, but not hurriedly so as not to cause any more remarks, to check on the kite. He saw two small gaps between paper and wood, touched them with some of his brown-colored glue, and held them with his fingers for several minutes, standing on his straight chair to reach the spots.

From the living room Walter heard a low, grim hum, the tone that meant his parents were quarreling again. "I didn't *say* that!" This time it was his father saying the words.

When Walter thought the glue was reasonably firm, he got down from the chair, changed back into jeans and sneakers, and started making the kite's tail. He hoped an eight-foot length might do. It was the weight not the length that mattered. He had bought two great rolls of nylon cord, light and strong, each of three hundred yards' length. This purchase had been wildly optimistic, he realized, but even now he was inspired to tie the end of the first roll—which he found loose in its center hollow—to the start of the second roll. He could take them both on his bike, one in each satchel. The kite he would have to carry with one hand as he cycled. Walter cut four strands and tied these to the four wooden pieces (already notched for this purpose) at the back of his kite, joined the four ends, and tied this to the starting end of the first roll of nylon. He then uncoiled what he estimated as two hundred yards of cord, and fixed a stout eight-inch long stick in the cord, tying it with an extra piece of nylon. This was for him to hang on to, if the kite was very far up, and a stick was also easier on his hands than holding plain cord. He added two more such sticks at intervals, then decided that was enough.

The evening promised rain. Clouds and a gusty wind. But tomorrow who knew? He gazed at his kite—it was upright now, its point nearly touching the ceiling though it slanted against his table—and he bit his underlip. The long strips of balsa looked clean and beautiful. Should he turn the kite around now and write ELSIE on it with watercolor paint? No, it might be bad luck to do it so soon, like boasting. Walter's heart was beating faster than usual, and he looked away from the kite.

But the next morning, Sunday, inspired by the brilliant sunlight and the strong and steady wind, Walter wrote ELSIE in blue watercolor on the leading side of his kite. It had rained during the night. The wind came from the south mainly, Walter saw. He set out on his bike around ten o'clock. His father was not yet up. Walter and his mother had breakfasted together, his mother looking a bit sleepy, because Louise and another friend had come over after dinner, and they had stayed up late.

"Wow, *that's* a monster!" Ricky was again on his front lawn, tossing a Frisbee around.

Just at that moment, Walter had to get off his bike and take a better grip on the kite. He had made a loose but reliable noose or sling out of ordinary string by which to hold the kite while he cycled, but the bottom point of the kite was still apt to touch the ground, and the least breeze made his bike wobble. Walter said nothing at first to Ricky, and was a little embarrassed as he tried to tighten the string without hurting the kite.

Ricky was coming over to look. A car passed between them, then Ricky came nearer. "You're not gonna try to *fly* that. It'll bust!"

"And so what?" Walter replied. "But why should it bust?"

"Not strong enough, I bet. Even if it gets up, wind's gonna tear it. You think you know all about kites!" Ricky smiled with a superior air. His voice was changing, and lately he was trying to treat Walter as if he were a much smaller kid, or so Walter felt.

"My problem, anyway," said Walter, and got back on his bike. "See you, Ricky!"

"Hey, Wally, where're you going?" Ricky wanted to join him.

"Haven't decided yet. Maybe nowhere!" Walter was on his way, coasting precariously down toward the shopping center.

He knew he would soon have to start walking, and walk all the rest of the way with his big kite, because it caught so much wind, he could not control his bike. There were only two heights within reasonable distance, Greenhills, where Walter didn't want to go, and the hill beyond Cooper's, which Walter headed for. He walked his bike along the very edge of the road, holding his kite on the right side of his bike, so he could see passing cars and keep clear of them. One car driver laughed at him and made some remark that Walter didn't catch. At last he arrived at the base of the hill he wanted. The footpath faded into grass, and Walter lowered his head and trudged the rest of the way, still holding his kite close to his bike, and leaning his weight against the push of the wind.

At the top of the hill, Walter laid his bike on the grass, and sat down with the kite flat on the grass beside him. He held his right wrist in his left

hand, and gazed between his knees at the splendid view below: lots of little white houses, green lawns, winding gray streets, and way over to the left
the blueness that was the Pacific, disappearing in a haze at the horizon. An
airliner was coming in from the north, still rather high because it was going
to land south of here in Los Angeles, but it was heading into the wind
already. The wind was from the south, as it had been earlier that morning.
Walter got to his feet.

"Hoo-o!—Hoo-o!" the wind said in his ears. It sounded warm and
friendly, nicer than a human voice.

He shook out his string, and took a position from which he could run
a few yards to launch the kite, but he did not need to. The kite rose at once
toward the north. The tail flipped around wildly at first, the nose of the kite
pointed right at him as the kite flew flat in the wind, then the tail pulled it
upright, and the cord ran through his hand.

He held the cord with both hands, and let it slip for nearly a minute.
The kite was a flyer! He had hardly to coax it at all!

"Yee-hoo-oo!" Walter yelled into the wind. No one was near him to
hear, to stare, to heckle—or even to admire his kite. Walter leaned his
whole weight back against the kite's pull. Now the pinkish diamond-
shaped kite looked happy, waggling a little in the blue emptiness, and
climbing ever higher. Walter let out more cord, until he felt the first
wooden stick jump into his hands, and he held on to it.

This was fun! He could tug slowly and hard, then feel the kite pull
against him even harder, lifting him forward, off the ground for several feet
until his weight and his efforts with the stick got him back to earth. He
was just about a match for the kite. That was an exciting thought.

A dog barked in the distance, down where the town was. The kite
looked smaller now, like an ordinary kite, because it was so high. Walter
pulled at the cord with all his strength, leaning back until his body nearly
touched the ground. Then the kite pulled him up slowly and gently and
lifted him off his feet. Walter moved his feet, thinking to find ground under
them, then the kite gave another playful and powerful tug, like a beckoning, and Walter was flying.

He glanced behind him, and saw the roll of cord dancing around on
the ground, unwinding itself, and the second roll near it, as yet motionless.
Then the nylon twisted, the stick turned, and Walter saw the trees on the
hill diminishing under him, and a valley below that he had been unaware
of before, with a thin railroad track snaking through it. Walter held his
breath for a few seconds, not knowing whether to be afraid or not. His

arms, bent at the elbows, supported him quite comfortably on the stick tied in the nylon. Below him he saw another stick he had tied in the cord, and he tried for this with his feet, missing a couple of times, then he had it.

Now he was twisting again, and he could see to the southwest the town where he lived, the round white dot of Cooper's hamburger-and-ice-cream place on a green rise. *The town where he lived!* That was funny to think about while he floated high up in the air like a bird, like a kite himself.

"Hey, looka tha . . . !" The rest of the faraway voice was unintelligible to Walter.

Walter looked down and saw two figures, both men or both in trousers anyway, pointing up at him.

"Wha' you . . . *doing?*" one of them yelled.

Walter was silent, as if he couldn't reply. He didn't reply, because he didn't want to. He looked up, and pulled comfortably now at the pink kite, sending it a bit higher, he thought, straight up. Walter attempted to steer it more to the right, the east, but that didn't work with this length of cord. The kite seemed to have its own ideas where to go. Walter saw one of the men on the ground running now, looking like an insect, maybe an ant, moving up the gray thread of street. Walter felt in a more beautiful atmosphere. The nylon cord hummed musically now and then in the wind. Elsie would have loved a flight like this. Walter wasn't dumb enough to think Elsie's "spirit" might be with him now, but her name *was* on the kite, he felt somehow near to her, and for a few seconds wondered if she could be aware that he was flying now, borne by a kite? Even the white clouds looked close, tumbling over themselves like somersaulting sheep.

And the ocean! Now as the cord twisted, Walter had a slow, sweeping view of its blueness. A long white ship was sailing southward—maybe to Acapulco! "Shall we go to Acapulco, Elsie?" Walter said out loud, and then laughed. He tugged southward, westward, but the kite wanted to go northeast. Walter saw rows of fruit trees, maybe orange trees, and a low rectangular building whose silvery roof reflected the sunlight. Cars moved like ladybirds in two directions on a road down there. Walter saw a cluster of people beside what looked like a roadside diner. Were they staring up at him? A couple of them seemed to be pointing at him.

". . . *kid,* not a man!" one of them said.

"Hey!—Can you get that thing *down?*"

Walter noticed that one man in the group had binoculars, and after staring up, passed the binoculars to another person. He floated over them and beyond, motionless with his hands on the stick and his sneakered feet on the stick below.

"Sure it's a *kid!* Not a dummy! Look!"

Over more fruit-tree fields, the kite soared in an updraft, northward. A bird like a small eagle zoomed close on Walter's right, as if curious about him, then with a tilt of its wings went up and away again.

He heard the hum of a motor, thought it might be from the plane he saw coming from the northeast, then realized the plane was much too far away to be audible. The sound was behind him, and Walter looked. There was a helicopter behind him, nearly a mile away, Walter estimated. Walter was higher. He looked up at his kite with pride. He could not be sure at this distance, but he thought that every inch of his paper must be holding to the wood, that the length of tail was just right. His work! Now was the time to compose a poem for his sister!

> *The wind sings in your magic paper!*
> *I made a bird that the birds love . . .*

"*Hey,* there!" The voice cut through the helicopter's rattle.

Walter was startled to see the helicopter above and just behind him. "Keep clear!" Walter yelled, frowning for emphasis, because he couldn't spare a hand to wave them back. He didn't want the copter blades snarling his cord, cutting it maybe. There were two men in the copter.

"How're you getting down? Can you get 'er *down?*"

"Sure!"

"You're sure?—How?" This man had goggles. They had opened the glass roof of their compartment and were hovering. The copter had something like SKY PATROL on its side. Maybe they were police.

"I'm okay! Just keep *clear!*" Walter suddenly felt afraid of them, as if they were enemies.

Now the boy saw more people on the ground, looking up. He was over another little community, where twenty or more people gawked up. Walter did not want to come down, didn't want to go back to his family, didn't particularly want to go back to his own room! The men in the copter were shouting something about pulling him in.

"Leave me alone, I'm *okay!*" Walter screamed in desperation, because he saw now that they were lengthening something like a long fishing rod, pulling out sections of it. Walter supposed it had a hook like a boathook at one end, and that they were going to make a try for the nylon cord. The cord trailed away, out of sight under Walter's feet.

"*. . . above!*" came one man's voice on the wind, and a second later the copter rose up, climbed to the height of his kite and maybe higher.

Walter was furious now. Were they going to attack his *kite?* Walter pulled defensively at his kite cord—which was so long, the pink kite scarcely bobbed. "Don't *touch* that, don't *touch* it!" Walter yelled with all his force, and he cursed the noisy chopping motor that had probably drowned out his words. "*Idiots!*" he screamed at them, blinded by his own tears now. He blinked and kept looking up. Yes, they were grappling with that long stick for the cord not far below the kite, or so it looked to him.

If the kite rose suddenly now, it would hit the blades and get chopped to bits. Couldn't the idiots know that? The long stick reached to the right of the copter, and slanted downward. Walter assumed it had a hook at the end—impossible to see, because the sun was directly in Walter's eyes now. Besides the copter's chopping noise, the people on the ground were yelling, laughing, shouting advice. Still, Walter screamed again:

"Keep away, *please!* Keep *awaa-aay!*"

The helicopter was still higher than the kite. The man had caught the cord, it seemed, and was trying to pull it toward him. Walter could see his tugs. The kite waggled crazily, as if it were as angry as Walter. Then there was a roar from the people below, and at the same time Walter saw his kite fold in half. The crosspiece had broken—from the idiot's tugging!

"*Stop* it!" For a couple of seconds his kite, folded and flat, was almost invisible, then the kite opened and spread, but in the wrong way, like a bird with broken wings. The kite flapped, leapt and leapt again and failed, as the beige stick drew the cord toward the copter.

Then Walter realized that he had pitched a bit forward and that he was dropping fast. He gripped his stick harder, terrified. Now the trees were zooming up, and ground also, faster and faster.

A shout, a groan like a big sigh came from the people below who were now quite close to Walter and in front of him on his right. Walter crashed into branches that punctured his body and tore off his shirt. He screamed in panic, "*Elsie!*" Upside down, he struck a heavy branch that cracked his skull, then he slid the last few yards to the ground, limp.

The Black House

An abandoned, three-story house stood black on the horizon of Canfield, a middle-sized town in upstate New York, whose industry was chiefly papermaking and leather processing, since the town had a river flowing through it. Houses and lawns in Canfield were neat and well-tended, people took a pride in keeping up their rose gardens and trimming their hedges, though none of the houses was a mansion. Canfield was composed of respectable middle-class Americans, many of whose families had been there two hundred years. Nearly everyone knew nearly everyone else, the atmosphere was friendly, people were neighborly, exchanging plants and trees from gardens, Christmas and birthday invitations, recipes and favors. They had cleaned up the river, which had used to carry yellowish refuse from the factories, at some expense and after some fighting against the government regulations that had demanded the cleaning, but now they were proud: the river looked rather clear again and certainly didn't smell sour or sulfurous when the wind blew, even though as yet there were no fish in it.

But the black house? Women chose to forget it, as if it were an eyesore they could do nothing about, but the men made jokes and told stories about it. First of all, the land was in dispute, said to be owned by a family now based in Ithaca, New York. But just who owned the land and the house? No one in Canfield really knew, though a couple of names were bandied about, Westbury and MacAllister, who were cousins, but nobody recalled ever seeing them or meeting them. The house had stood so, empty and neglected, before most of the people in Canfield had been born.

"Why doesn't somebody put a match to it?" a man would say, laughing over a scotch or a beer with his friends in the White Horse Tavern, a favorite gathering place.

"What harm's it doing anyone?" another would reply.

Another round of drinks—perhaps it would be "after church" at half-past noon on a Sunday—and Frank Keynes would relate a story of when he was fourteen with a crush on a girl in school, and he'd made a date with her to meet at nine o'clock at night at the foot of the hill to the black house, and she had stood him up. "But what do you know? Along came *another* girl who was quite willing to go up to the black house. *Quite* willing!"

The men would laugh. Was it true or not?

Ed Sanders, manager of the Guardian Paper Mills, might say, "The last time we heard that story, the *first* girl went up with you. Where are you, Frank? Whiskey's rotted your brain?"

And everyone would smile, while fantasies of boyhood, boastful tall tales, drifted through their minds like smoke, mingling together, trailing off. The men preferred to stand at the slightly curving mahogany bar. Their wives or girlfriends sat at the little tables, out of hearing, content to sip their own drinks and chatter until usually Kate Sanders, Ed's wife, would make the first move, come up to the bar and suggest that she and Ed get home for lunch, which would be ready, thanks to their automatic cooker, though she didn't have to say all this, because Ed knew it.

The youngest of the listeners was Timothy Porter, twenty-three, unmarried, a new employee of the leather factory, where he doubled as accountant and salesman. He had graduated from Cornell, tried his luck for a year in New York, and decided to return to his home town of Canfield, at least for a while. He was about six feet in height, with reddish blond hair, friendly but reserved. He rented a room in his uncle's house in town, his parents having moved away in the last years. Once he had brought an Ithaca girl to Canfield for the weekend, and they had both had a drink in the White Horse, but the girl had not visited him since. Timothy was alone one Sunday when he said, smiling, to the men at the bar:

"I remember when I was about ten, going to school here, we used to pretend that an ogre lived in the black house. Or a madman that even the police couldn't get out, and if we went very close to the house, he'd rush out and choke us to death. You know how kids are. Nothing but fantasies. But I remember aged ten it seemed very *real*." Tim smiled broadly and downed the rest of his beer.

"There *is* something funny about the house," Ed Sanders said dreamily, perched on a bar stool. "It *looks* haunted—you know? The way that roof and the chimney tilts at the top, as if it's about to fall down on some-body." Ed saw his wife approaching, and was sorry. He was having a good time, talking about the black house. It was like being in another world, like being a boy again, twelve years old perhaps, and not a thirty-nine-year-old man with a growing paunch, knowing all about life, and more than enough.

Sam Eadie, plump, blond and balding, bent close to Ed, having also seen Ed's wife, and whispered rapidly, "I still say, because it's true, I made love *for the first time* to a girl there—when I was fifteen." He straightened and put on a smile. "Good morning, Kate! Second good morning today! I think you've come to collect?"

You're not the only one who did, Ed Sanders thought, a bit resentfully and proudly, but he couldn't say it aloud, because his wife was present. Ed only frowned for a couple of seconds at his old friend Sam Eadie.

Timothy Porter went home to his uncle Roger Porter's house for his Sunday lunch. Uncle Roger had not been to church, but then neither had Timothy, who had been walking in the woods before joining the locals at the White Horse. At Uncle Roger's house, the Sunday meal, prepared yesterday by his uncle's part-time housekeeper Anna, was ready to serve: a pork and rice casserole which Roger had been warming in the oven. Roger, in shirtsleeves, gave the final touches, Timothy finished setting the table—wine glasses and his own napkin which Roger had forgotten—and then Roger put on a tweed jacket and they sat down.

"Nice morning?" asked Tim, serving himself after his uncle. He knew his uncle had been either pottering in the back garden or going over his law office briefs.

"Not bad. And yours?"

"Sure, fine. In the woods. Then I had a beer at the White Horse."

"Lots of people? . . . Well, Ed Sanders, I'm sure." Roger smiled. "Frank Keynes too."

Why don't you join them sometimes, Tim wanted to ask, but his uncle at fifty-five was older than most of the White Horse group, and a little sad after the death of Tim's Aunt Meg about three years ago. Roger had not yet got used to her absence, and Tim knew Roger was glad of his company in the house, though Roger was not the type to put it into words. "I was wondering," Tim began, "why—"

"Why what?"

"Why the conversation in the White Horse always turns to that house they call the black house. Here. You know, the old abandoned house on the hill."

Roger looked at his nephew and smiled, his fork poised near his lips. "Because it's been there a long time, perhaps. It's our castle." He chuckled, and ate.

"But they sound like a bunch of kids talking about it. I remember too, when I was little, all the kids used to pretend to be afraid of it. But these grown men talk as if it's . . . haunted or somehow dangerous even now. Granted they've all had a couple of drinks by the time they start talking about it. But this is the third or fourth time I've noticed." Tim suddenly laughed. "And these old guys brag about taking *girls* there! When they were teenagers, I mean. It's really a panic to listen to them!"

Roger chewed reflectively, and looked into a corner of the room. His thinning brown and gray hair was neatly parted, his forehead wrinkled with thought, but his lips still smiled. "Well—they dream. They make stories up, I'm sure. After all, there was that murder there five or six years ago. Adolescent boy—body found on the ground floor of the house. Throat cut. He'd been there three or four days. Awful story." Roger shook his head with distaste.

"And they never found out who did it?"

"They never found out. Not a boy from around here. He was from— oh, Connecticut, I think. Doesn't matter." Roger went on in a more cheerful tone, "I used to play in that house when I was eight and nine. I remember distinctly, I and a lot of kids, running up and down the stairways there, telling each other the stairs would fall down with us, that there was an idiot behind the doors—things like that. The place was abandoned even in my day. Imagine."

Tim tried to imagine forty-five years back. "Why didn't somebody take care of the house?"

"Because legally speaking no one's got the right to touch the property till the case is settled, and since the house isn't a fire hazard up there on the hill with no trees around it . . . Even the trees died, I think, from sheer neglect."

They talked of other things. Roger was a lawyer, the most highly esteemed in town. He had his own office, with a couple of secretaries and a younger partner who would finally take over. Roger and Meg had had no children. Tim asked his uncle about the progress of a difficult case he was working on, which he knew worried Roger, and Roger answered him. But Tim's mind kept returning to the black house, as if it held some kind of mystery unsolved.

"Do you think there were tramps sleeping there? When that boy you mentioned was murdered?"

For an instant, Roger didn't seem to know what Tim was talking about. "Oh! The black house! No. Not at that time. Well . . . there may be a tramp or two sleeping there sometimes. I don't know. No, Tim, if you want to know the truth—" Here his uncle lowered his voice as if someone might be able to hear him. "What I'm saying was not in the papers here or anywhere. The girl in the picture was pregnant by the boy who was killed. And she and the boy had made a date to meet again—in that house. As I recall, they often met there. The story is that her father was furious. And the boy—just a hoodlum—to tell the truth. The father left town afterward with his daughter."

Tim was stunned. Such violence hardly two miles from where he sat now! "Do you mean the father wasn't even suspected?"

Roger gave a laugh and touched his lips with his napkin. "I think he was. I think the judge let him off. Everyone was on the father's side—somehow. There's something evil about that house."

There was something evil about murder too. A pregnant daughter didn't warrant killing the boyfriend, in Tim's view, since it seemed not at all a case of rape. "I feel like going there again—taking a look. To that house, I mean. What is it but a lot of empty rooms?"

"Oh-h—why go?" Roger was serving the ice cream, but he paused to look at his nephew. "What'll you be accomplishing, going there?" He added as he sat down, "A floor might give way under you."

Tim laughed. "I'll test 'em with a foot first. I'm not afraid of the place."

Roger shook his head. "You'll be gaining nothing, Tim."

Why was Roger looking at him so sternly? Tim started on his ice cream.

The next day, Tim left Canfield Leather at exactly 5 P.M., quitting time, though he usually stayed a little later. He was eager to drive to the black house and have a look, before it became dark. The month was October. The house wasn't even black, he recalled, but a dark brown or red. It was only black at night, as any house would be without lights in it.

Tim drove his tomato-colored Chrysler up an unpaved road, whose bends he had quite forgotten. He stopped the car at a brambly spot where the lane ended, where there might have been gates to the estate in the very old days, before Tim's childhood. Now there was no sign of gates or fence. The old dark house seemed taller, seen close now, and somehow frowning down on him. Tim dropped his eyes from it, and watched the ground as he climbed the slope. It was still rather light, he could distinguish pebbles, blades of grass in the patchy and dried-out lawn on either side of the footpath that led to the front door. Had people even stolen the paving stones that surely must have been here once?

Some ten yards from the house, Tim stopped, and looked up. True enough, the house wasn't really black, but a dark brown. Stone front steps, with cement pillars at the foot. A paneled front door whose knocker had been removed or gouged out, leaving a hole in its place. There were two windows on either side of the door, of course with no glass in them. Was the door unlocked, able to be pushed open? Tim smiled a little, and walked to the right, intending to circle the house before he entered it.

He glanced at the sterile-looking ground for beer cans, sandwich papers, or any other sign of revelry, and found none. Tim lifted his eyes again to the windows of the second story, the third. Most of the windows were broken, open to the elements. Black inside. Was some face going to look out at him in a moment, some madman having heard his car motor, or his footsteps? Some white ghost?

Timothy laughed out loud. His laugh sounded deeper than his usual laugh, reassuring to him. Sure, it was an empty house, a classic, dark and all that. But why be afraid of it, unless you were a ten-year-old child? Tim walked more briskly around the other side of the house toward the front door. Off to the right of the front corner of the house, he did see a tossed away beer can, and he smiled at the sight.

He went up the front steps. Even the doorknob had been removed, he saw, but probably one could simply push the door open. Or if it was locked, the window to the right . . . No, that was too high from the ground to climb into easily, though it gaped wide, glassless. Tim looked at the door, and decided to put the fingers of his right hand into the gap where the doorknob had been, his left hand against the door, and push. He lifted his hands to do this, then hesitated, dropped his hands, and smiled at himself. As his uncle had said, why bother? What would he be proving? Nothing at all, and indeed he might break a leg with a first step onto a rotten floor.

Tim eased his shoulders, ran down the steps and turned and shouted up at the house: "Halloo-oo! . . . Anyone there? . . . Ha-ha!"

He trotted down the path toward his car, looked back, and gave the house a wave, as if he were waving good-bye to someone he saw at a window there, but there was nobody.

It was suddenly dark.

Tim had intended to say to his uncle Roger that he had visited the black house, walked around it, gone into it—and so what? But he felt ashamed, that evening, of not having entered the house after all, and there-

fore he said nothing about his visit there at dusk. Tim found himself thinking about, remembering a fair-haired little girl he had been in love with
when he was nine, and she about the same age, in school. *In love,* at that
age? What an absurdity! Yet the sensations, Tim realized, were much the
same at nine as at twenty and so on, when one was in love. The sensation
posed an unanswerable question: why is one certain person of such fantastic importance to me? Tim remembered his fantasies of asking the little girl
to meet him at the empty house, as Tim remembered his contemporaries
calling it. Had she ever? Of course she hadn't. What would her parents have
thought, if their little eight- or nine-year-old daughter had said, after supper, that she had a date with a boy at the black house, or the empty house,
maybe a mile from where she lived? Tim found himself smiling again. He
could see that it would be so easy to pretend she *had* come, that they had
kissed and embraced madly, and done nothing else, at that age. Yes, so easy
to invent, and to come to believe that what he had invented and told to
other people was true. That, of course, was exactly what the old boys at the
White Horse were doing every Sunday after church, and maybe a little bit
on Friday and Saturday nights too.

By the following Sunday, Tim's ideas had taken a different and more
realistic form. He felt calmer and more detached, as if he were seeing the
situation—even the black house itself—from a certain distance. So he was
quite cool and collected as he walked into the White Horse Tavern at
twenty past noon on Sunday. He wore his walking boots, twill trousers, an
anorak jacket of bright blue.

The boys were here, Ed Sanders, Frank Keynes, a couple of others
whose names Tim knew also, even one high school acquaintance, Steve,
whose last name Tim couldn't at once recollect, though it began with a C.
With a friendly nod at Ed, who had one leg over a stool, facing him, Tim
walked up to the bar near the group, not as if he intended to join them, but
not putting a distance between him and them either. Tim ordered a beer,
as usual.

Before a minute had passed, Frank Keynes, who was standing at the bar
with a Christmasy-looking old-fashioned in his hand, turned to Tim and
said, "Hiking again?—How *are* you, Tim?"

"Quite well, thank you, sir!" said Tim. In the mirror beyond the row of
bottles, he saw his own face, rosy-cheeked from his hike, and he felt pleased
with himself, happy to be twenty-three years old, and also—in the left
back corner of the room he could see reflected a pretty girl with short
brown hair who sat at a table. Tim had noticed her when he came in just

now, but in the mirror he could stare at her with pleasure, without her being aware of his staring. She was with two fellows, unfortunately. Tim lifted his beer and drank, and brought his thoughts back to what he intended to say to the men near him. The right moment came when he was on his second beer, and there was a lull in the conversation in which Tim had joined.

"By the way, I went to the black house Friday evening," Tim said.

Short silence.

Then Frank Keynes said, "Y'did? . . . Inside it?"

Tim quickly noticed that four men, even the younger Steve, were all attention, and he wished very much that he could say that he had been inside the house. "No, not inside. I mean, I went up and looked around, walked around the grounds there. I didn't see any signs of tramps—or people. Just one old beer can, I remember."

"What time of night was it?" asked a tallish man named Grant Dunn, who seldom spoke.

"Wasn't night. Just before six, I think."

Ed Sanders, flushed of face, lips slightly parted as if about to say something, exchanged a glance with Frank who was standing to Tim's right. Ed said nothing, but Frank cleared his throat and spoke.

"You didn't go *in*," Frank said.

"No, I just walked *around* the house." Tim looked Frank in the eyes and smiled, though he frowned at the same time. What was all the fuss about? Did one of these fellows *own* the house? What if one of them did? "I did go up to the door, but—I didn't open it, no. No doorknob even. Is the place locked?" Tim noticed that Sam Eadie had joined the circle, drink in hand.

"The place is not locked," Frank said steadily. He had gray-blue eyes which were now as cold as metal. He looked as if he were accusing Tim of trespassing, of having tried to break in.

Tim glanced to his left toward the tables where the women sat, and his eyes met briefly the eyes of one of the wives, whose wife, Tim wasn't sure.

Ed suddenly laughed. "Don't go there again, boy . . . What're you trying to prove, eh?" Ed looked at Frank and Grant as if for approval or support. "What would you be proving?" he repeated.

"I'm not trying to prove anything," Tim replied amiably. Ed's a little pissed again, Tim thought, and felt tolerant, and quite sure of himself by comparison. A beer and a half had not gone to Tim's head. Tim took his time, let the curiously hostile glances at him die away, and finally he said, "My Uncle Roger told me about an adolescent boy being killed there."

Tim had lowered his voice, as his uncle had done. He felt the coolness of perspiration on his forehead.

"True enough," said Frank Keynes. "You interested in that?"

"No. Not really," Tim replied. "I'm not a detective."

"Then—best to stay away, Tim," said Sam Eadie with a small smile, looking at Tim sharply for an instant. He turned to Frank as if for confirmation of what he had just said, winked at Frank, then said to everyone, "I'll be pushing off. My wife's getting impatient over there."

Frank and Ed smiled more broadly, almost chuckled, as they watched Sam's round figure in dark blue Sunday-best suit walk away toward a table of four women.

"Henpecked," one of the men said softly, and a couple of others laughed.

"You never went into the black house—when you were a kid, Tim?" Ed Sanders asked, now on a fresh scotch and ice.

"Yes, sure!" Tim said. "We all did. When we were around ten or eleven. Halloween, I remember, we'd take lighted pumpkins up and march around it. Sometimes we—"

Guffaws interrupted Tim's sentence. Men rocked back on their heels, those who were standing up.

Tim wondered what was so funny? The clap of laughter had made his ears ring.

"But not afterwards?" asked Frank Keynes. "Not when you were sixteen or so?"

Tim hadn't, that he could remember. "Around that time I was in—boarding school for one year. Out of town." That was true. He'd had to go to a crammer to pull his grades up enough to enter Cornell. Tim felt, and saw, the men looking at him as if he had disappointed them, missed something, failed another exam. Tim, vaguely uneasy, asked, "Is there some mystery about that boy who was killed there? . . . Maybe there's a local secret I don't know." Tim glanced at the barman, but he was quite busy over to Tim's left. "I don't mean to be prying into anything, if it *is* a secret."

Ed Sanders shook his head with an air of boredom, and finished his drink. "No."

"Naw," said Frank. "No secrets. Just the truth."

Now a man laughed, as if at Frank's remark. Tim looked behind him, to his left, because the man who had laughed was standing there. This man was a stranger to Tim, tall with neat black hair, wearing a cashmere sweater with a blue-and-yellow silk scarf, one of the group obviously. Tim glanced again quickly at the very pretty girl in the front corner, who was smiling, but not at him. Tim took no comfort from his glimpse of her. He suddenly thought of Linda, his last girl friend, who had stopped seeing him because she had met a fellow she liked better. Tim hadn't been much in love with Linda, just a little bit, but her telling him she wouldn't be coming to Canfield had hurt his ego. Tim wanted very much to meet a new girl, someone more exciting than the three or four girls he knew from college days, two of whom lived in New York.

"That story's as plain as day, sure . . ."

The jukebox had started up, not loudly, but the song happened to be a loud one, with horns and drums. Tim couldn't hear every word the men were saying. A wife came up, Ed's, and he disappeared.

"Good story!" Frank yelled into Tim's ear. "That story you mentioned. Dramatic, y'know? The girl was going to have a baby. Maybe she loved the boy. Must have—to've gone up to the black house again to meet him."

And her father had cut the boy's throat. Tim was not going to bring *that* up, not going to query the truth of it, because his uncle Roger had said it was supposed that the father had killed the boy. Two more wives came up to claim their husbands.

A few minutes later, Tim was walking to his uncle's house with a feeling of having been slighted, even laughed at by the men in the White Horse Tavern. He hadn't gone into the house, true enough, but he certainly hadn't been afraid of the black house. There'd be nothing there, that he could see, to be afraid of. What was all the drama about, which seemed to extend from Ed Sanders to the rather stuffy-looking guy in the cashmere and scarf today? Was the black house some kind of private club that the men didn't visit any longer? Why not go in and tell them he'd gone in, and join the club thereby?

Tim realized that he was angry, resentful, that he'd best cool down and not say a word about the White Horse conversation today to his uncle. Uncle Roger, Tim knew, had a touch of the same mystic reverence for the black house as Ed and Frank and the others.

So Tim kept his thoughts to himself all Sunday. But he did not change his mind about going into the black house, walking up the two flights of stairs, and he intended to do it one night that week. By Friday afternoon, Tim felt inspired, irresistibly inspired, to visit the black house that evening, though he had been thinking of Saturday night.

His uncle Roger on Friday evening was engrossed in a television play which had not interested Tim from the start. Roger took hardly any notice, when around ten o'clock Tim said he was going out for an hour. Tim drove his car to the north of Canfield, toward the black house, and he parked it in the same place as before, on the unpaved road, and got out.

Tim had brought a flashlight. Now it was really dark, utterly black all around him, until after a few seconds he could make out clumps of trees nearby, not belonging to the black house property, which were darker than the starless sky. Tim flicked on his flashlight, and began to climb the pebbly path.

He shone the light to right and left: nothing but empty and untended ground. And then he walked up the steps. Now with more assurance, he pushed against the door, and it opened with his second thrust. Timothy turned his flashlight beam around the front room, which seemed to be a large living room without any small front hall. Empty. The gray, neglected floorboards were each some five inches wide. Tim set his left foot beyond the threshold, and the floor supported him. In fact, he saw, at least at this point, no sign of missing boards or of decay in the wood. There was a hall to the right, or a wall which partly concealed a staircase. Tim walked softly toward this, stopped before he reached the wide doorway to the stairs, and shouted:

"Hello?" He waited. "Anyone here?" He smiled, as if to put on a friendly face to an unseen person.

No answer. Not even a rustle of someone stirring upstairs or anywhere else. He advanced.

The stairs creaked, the banister and steps were covered with very fine whitish dust. But they held his weight. On the second floor there was a worn-out rug in the hall, one corner folded under. And as far as Tim could yet see, this was the only sign of furnishings. Not even a broken chair stood in any of the four rooms on the second floor. The rooms were rather square. A swallow, two of them, took flight from a room's upper corner at his presence, and made their way with audible flutter out a window which had no glass. Tim laughed nervously, and turned around, shining his flashlight now toward the stairs to the next floor.

This banister was shaky. Tim didn't trust it, not that he needed it, and stepped carefully upward more on the wall side of the steps than the middle, as this stairway seemed more sagging. Up here, there were four more rooms, and one tiny one with no door, which Tim saw had once been a toilet, though the toilet bowl had been removed. He stood on one room's threshold and shone his light into its four corners. He saw faded rose-colored wallpaper with an indefinable pattern in it, three windows with half their glass gone, and absolutely nothing on the floor except the ubiquitous pale dust. Somehow he had expected an old blanket or carpet, even a burlap bag or two. Nothing! Just space. A fine place to invite a girl!

Tim gave a laugh. He felt both amused and disappointed.

"Hey!" he yelled, and imagined that he heard his voice echo.

He glanced behind him at the dark hall, the darker well of the stairway down, and for an instant he felt fear at the thought of two flights of stairs to descend to get out. He swallowed and stood taller. He took a breath of air that was surely fresh because the windows were open, but he could still smell the dust.

Graffiti! Surely there'd be graffiti, considering all that had presumably gone on here. Tim focused his light on the floorboards of the pink room, tested their strength as he had tested the strength of all the other floors he had stepped on, and then he walked toward the front wall of the room. He stopped close to the wall, and moved his light slowly over a wide surface of the sun-blanched wallpaper, looking for pencil marks, initials. He found nothing. He looked over the other three walls quickly, then went into the hall, and with the same caution entered a back room. This room's wallpaper had been stripped, for the most part, curls of it lay on the floor, and the patches that remained were of a dirty yellow color. Tim picked up a dry coil of paper, and out of curiosity straightened it. There was nothing on it.

Not a cap or a glove someone might have forgotten on the floor. "Not a sock!" Tim said out loud.

Courage flowed back into him. Well, he had seen the place. The floorboards held. There were no ghosts, and not a tramp or a hitchhiker was making use of the house as a pad, even though the winter was coming on.

Tim looked at the other two rooms upstairs, found them equally unrewarding, and then made his way downstairs. He felt like running downstairs, but he went down rather slowly. An old step could still give way, he supposed, and he didn't want a broken leg or ankle. On the ground floor, he turned and looked up at the dark tunnel of the stairwell.

"Ha-ha!" Tim laughed softly.

One look into the closed room back? This turned out to be the remains of a kitchen. A scarred white sink was still there, but no water taps projected from the wall. Four marks in the green and white linoleum showed where the legs of a stove had rested.

This was enough!

"Hal-loo-*oo!*" Tim shouted, and let his voice break, as he pulled open the front door. "Happy next Halloween!" he added.

Carefully, as if he were observing himself trying to do the right thing, Timothy closed the front door, using his fingers in the hole where the doorknob had been, trying to leave the door as he had found it.

It was good to be on solid ground again, to hear grit and pebbles under the soles of his tennis shoes.

On the familiar streets that he took driving homeward, he began to relax. Here he was, safe! Safe from what? There hadn't been one spookily creaking door in the black house, not a current of wind through a crack that could have suggested the moan of a ghost. He felt proud for having explored every room, and he realized that his pride was silly, juvenile. He had best forget his satisfaction and simply state to the men on Sunday that he had gone in and . . . looked the place over.

And what was the matter with telling them now? Tim saw by his watch that it wasn't yet midnight. Mightn't a couple of the fellows be at the White Horse? If no one was there, he'd drink a beer by himself. He turned right at the next corner.

The White Horse was indeed busy this Friday night. Tim had an impression of yellow lights everywhere, balls of yellow lights across the eaves, yellow light pouring through the door when it opened and a couple came out. Tim parked his car in the graveled forecourt, and entered the bar. The jukebox music which he had heard only faintly outside now sounded nearly as loud as that of a disco. Of course Friday night wasn't Sunday noon after church! And there were the fellows, the men, in their Sunday noon place at the back half of the bar, but in rather different clothes. Frank Keynes wore blue jeans and a turtleneck sweater. Ed Sanders was even in overalls with shoulder straps, as if he had been painting or working on his car, as maybe he had.

"Evening, Ed!" Tim shouted over the music, nodding and smiling. "Frank!"

"Timmy!" Frank replied. "Out on the town?"

Ed laughed, as if the town didn't offer much.

Tim shook his head, and when he caught the eye of the barman, he ordered a draft beer.

Then Tim saw Sam Eadie turn from the jukebox into which he had evidently dropped some coins, because he was stuffing a hand back into his baggy trousers. He had a drink in his hand. The tables were only half-filled, and these mostly with young fellows and their girls.

"Not walking in the woods this time of night, Tim?" asked Ed.

"Na-aw." Tim had his beer now, and sipped. "No, matter of fact I went up to the black house. Just now. Again." Tim smiled, and wiped a bit of froth from his lips with the back of his hand.

"You did?" asked Frank.

Tim saw that he had caught their attention at once, including that of Sam Eadie who had been close enough to hear.

"You went in?" asked Frank sharply, as if Tim's answer yes or no would be important.

Tim knew it was important, to them. "Yes. I had a flashlight. Went in all the rooms. Up to the third floor. No sign of tramps—or anything else." He had to talk loudly and clearly, because of the jukebox song which was something about *Golden . . . golden . . . hair and eyes . . . and paradise . . .*

The three stared at him, Frank frowning in a puzzled way. Frank looked a bit tight, pink-eyed. Maybe Frank didn't believe him.

"Just nothing. All quiet," Tim said with a shrug.

"What do you mean—nothing?" Frank asked.

"Oh, take it easy, Frank," said Sam Eadie, pulling cigarettes from a pocket. He brought the package to his lips.

"I just thought," Tim continued over the music, "you thought the place might be partly occupied. Not at all! Not even any interesting graffiti for all the—the—" Tim couldn't find the phrase for what he meant, which was taking or meeting girls there, making love to them on the barren floors, probably, unless the fellow or the girl had thought to bring a blanket. Tim shifted on his feet and laughed. "*Nothing* there! Empty!" He looked into the faces of the three men, expecting a smile in return, a nod of approval, because he'd gone all over the place at night.

Their expressions were a bit different, each man's, but in each was disappointment, a hint of disapproval, perhaps. Tim felt uncomfortable. Sam Eadie's face seemed to combine contempt with his disapproval. Ed's long face looked sad. Frank Keynes had a glint in his eye.

"Nothing?" Frank said. "You better step outside, boy!"

Ed suddenly laughed, though his frown remained.

Tim laughed too, knowing what Frank meant: a fight over the reputation, the charisma of the black house. What was he supposed to say, that he'd seen a lot of *memories* there? Ghosts or ghostly faces of pretty girls aged fifteen? In which room had that teenaged boy had his throat cut, Tim wondered suddenly.

The barman arrived at the tap of Sam's empty glass on the bar.

The jukebox song ended with a long drawn out *paradi-ise . . .*

"I said, step outside," Frank repeated, plucking at Tim's sleeve.

This little half-pissed middle-aged guy! Tim found himself following, walking beside the slightly wobbling Frank toward the door. Tim was still smiling, a little, because he felt like smiling. What had he done to antagonize them, or Frank in particular? Nothing at all.

Outside, as soon as Tim, who had walked ahead of Frank through the door, turned to speak with him, Frank hit him with his right fist in the jaw. Tim had not been prepared, and he staggered and fell to the gravel, but at once leapt up. Before he could get a word out, or his fists up, Frank hit him in the pit of his stomach. Then came a shove in his chest, and a loud crack at the back of his head.

"Frank, cut it out!" a voice shouted.

Tim, flat on his back, heard feet crunching on gravel, more voices.

"His head's bleeding!"

"O-kay, I didn't meant to—didn't mean to knock him *out!*"

Tim struggled to stay conscious, to get up, but he could not even move his arms.

"Just lay still, boy, we're getting a wet towel." It sounded like Sam Eadie, a stooped figure on Tim's right.

". . . doctor maybe? Or an ambulance?"

"Yeah . . . his head . . ."

Tim wanted to say, *It's a handsome house, a fantastic house. I can still see the ivory-painted moldings all covered with dust now, and the good floorboards that held my weight. I didn't mean to insult the black house, to make fun of the house.* But Tim could not get any of these words out, and worse, he heard himself moaning, and felt ashamed and afraid because he couldn't control the idiotic sounds coming from his throat.

". . . blood out of his mouth now! Look!"

A siren's scream rose and fell.

". . . that—house," Tim said, and warm blood ran over his chin.

Many more feet on gravel.

"Sh-h! Up!"

Tim's body was lifted suddenly in a sickening way, and he felt that he fainted, or maybe died. If he was dead, his thoughts, his dreams were worse than before. He saw the dark interior of a room in the black house, and Frank Keynes coming at him from a corner with a big stick like a club that he was gripping with both hands, about to take a swat at him, grinning. In a dark hall stood Ed with a faint smile, and behind him, just visible enough to be recognizable, stood Sam Eadie, hoisting his belt a little over his paunch, smiling also in an unfriendly way, as if he were about to witness something he would enjoy. *You have failed, Tim,* the men were saying. And *Nothing? Nothing?* in a scoffing way, as if Tim had sealed his doom by uttering that word in regard to the black house. Tim could see it all clearly now as he journeyed through space into hell, perhaps, into an afterlife of some kind that might go on forever.

Now he was moving through a ringing space. His ears rang, and he was jostled on the journey. Voices came through the ringing. He felt a touch on his shoulder.

"It's Ed," a voice said. "Look, Frank didn't mean to hit you so hard. He's too cracked up even to ride with us—now. He's—"

"If your name is Ed," said another deeper voice, "would you please keep quiet, because . . . doing you a favor letting you ride with us . . ."

Tim could not speak, but words came abundantly to his mind. He understood. That was all he wanted to say. The house was of great importance and he had treated it as if it were—nothing. He remembered Frank saying just a while ago, "Nothing—Nothing?" But to die for this mistake? Was it that serious? The words did not come. Tim moved his lips which were sticking together with blood. His eyelids seemed as heavy as his arms. They had given him a needle in his arm, a long time ago.

Now the two men in the ambulance with him argued, their voices came like gusts of angry wind, sometimes singly, sometimes together. And Tim saw the club in the grinning Sam Eadie's hands now. Sam meant to kill him.

Timothy Porter fell into a coma from which he did not awaken. His uncle Roger came to visit. Tim's lips remained parted, wiped free of blood which had ceased to flow, and a slender tube in one nostril furnished extra oxygen to him. His eyes were slightly open, but he no longer saw or heard anything. On the third day, he died.

Frank Keynes had to appear in the town court. He had already been to Roger Porter's house, made his apologies and expressed his grief and regret at having been responsible for the death of the young man. The town judge considered it a case of manslaughter. Frank Keynes was not imprisoned, but a fine was imposed, which Frank paid, and he was admonished not to drink any alcohol in any public place for six months, or his driving license would be taken away for two years. Chastened, Frank Keynes obeyed Judge Hewitt's orders, but he did still visit the White Horse, where he drank Coca-Cola or 7Up, both of which he disliked.

He felt that his old pals liked him less now, kept a funny distance from him, though Frank wasn't sure, because at the same time they tried to cheer him up, reminding him that he hadn't meant to cause any damage so serious, that it was a piece of bad luck that the boy had hit his head on something—the parking area curb that was made of stones as big as a man's head—when he fell.

Then came a Sunday in April when Frank could have a drink, according to the date of the calendar. Frank and his chums were gathered at the bar of the White Horse Tavern after church, as usual, while their wives sat around at the little tables. On his second scotch, which felt like four to Frank, because his wife Helen had been quite stern with him at home about not drinking, almost as if their home were "a public place," Frank said to Ed and Sam:

"Any one of us might have done it too. Don't you think so?"

Grant was standing nearby, and Frank included him in this question. Frank could see that Ed took a second to realize what Frank was talking about, then Ed glanced at Sam Eadie.

There was no answer from anybody, and Frank said, "Why don't you admit it? We were all—a little annoyed that night, same as me."

Ed leaned close to Frank, Ed in his Sunday suit, white shirt and silk tie. "You had better shut *up*, Frank," Ed said through clenched teeth.

He won't admit it. They won't admit it, Frank thought. *Cowards!* But he didn't dare say another word. As bad as they were with their wives, Frank thought, just as cowardly! And he admitted that he had to include himself here. Did they ever talk to their *wives* about what they'd all done in the black house when they were kids? No. Because the wives weren't the girls—mostly weren't, Frank was sure—that the fellows had been with in the black house. Frank understood, a little bit: they were like a club, maybe, and the club had rules. Certain things, facts, existed, but were not talked about. You could boast even, but not talk, somehow.

"Okay!" said Frank, feeling reproached but unbent. Not cowed by any means, no. He stood taller and finished his drink, glanced at Ed and Sam and Grant before he set his empty glass down on the bar. They had a certain respect for what he had done, Frank was sure. But like a lot of other things, facts, that respect was never going to be put into words by any of them.

Mermaids on the Golf Course

Mermaids
on the
Golf Course

Friday, fifteenth of June, was a big day for Kenneth W. Minderquist and family, meaning his wife, Julia, his granddaughter, Penny, aged six and the apple of his eye, and his mother-in-law, Becky Jackson, who was due to arrive with Penny.

The big house was in top-notch order, but Julia had double-checked the liquor supply and the menu—canapés, cold cuts, open-face sandwiches, celery, olives—a real buffet for the journalists and photographers who were due at eleven that morning. Last evening, a telegram had arrived from the President:

CONGRATULATIONS, KEN. HOPING TO LOOK IN FRIDAY MORNING IF I CAN. IF NOT, BEST WISHES ANYWAY. LOVE TO YOU AND FAMILY. TOM.

This had pleased Minderquist and made Julia, always a rather nervous hostess, check everything again. Their chauffeur-butler, Fritz, would be on hand, of course, a big help. Fritz had come with the house, as had the silverware and the heavy white napkins and the furniture and in fact the pictures on the walls.

Minderquist watched his wife with a cool and happy confidence. And he could honestly say that he felt as well now as he had three months ago, before the accident. Sometimes he thought he felt even better than before, more cheerful and lively. After all, he had had weeks of rest in the hospitals, despite all their tests for this and that and the other thing. Minderquist considered himself one of the most tested men in the world, mentally and physically.

The accident had happened on St. Patrick's Day in New York. Minderquist had been one of a couple of hundred people in a grandstand with the President, and after the parade was over, and everyone in the grandstand had climbed down and were dispersing themselves in limousines and taxis, gunshots had burst out—four of them, three quick ones and one following—and quite fortuitously Minderquist had been near the President when he had seen the President wince and stoop (he had been shot in the calf), and not even thinking what he was doing, Minderquist had hurled himself on to the President like a trained bodyguard, and both of them had fallen. The last shot had caught Minderquist in the left temple, put him into a coma for ten days, and kept him in two hospitals for nearly three months. It was widely believed that if not for Minderquist's intervention, the last bullet would have hit the President in the back (newspapers had printed diagrams of what might have happened with that last shot), perhaps severing the spinal cord or penetrating his liver or whatnot, and therefore Minderquist was credited with having saved the President's life. Minderquist had also suffered a couple of cracked ribs, because bodyguards had hurled themselves on *him* after he had covered the President.

To express his gratitude, the President had presented the Minderquists with "Sundocks," the handsome house in which they now lived. Julia and Fritz had been here a month. Minderquist had come out of the Arlington hospital, his second, ten days ago. The house was a two-story colonial, with broad and level lawns, on one of which Fritz had set up a croquet field, and there was also a swimming pool eighteen by ten yards wide. Somehow their green Pontiac had been exchanged for a dark blue Cadillac, which looked brand new to Minderquist. Fritz had driven Minderquist a couple of times in the Cadillac to a golf course nearby, where Minderquist had played with his old set of clubs, untouched in years. His doctors said mild sports were good for him. Minderquist thought he was in pretty good shape, but he had added a few inches to his waistline during the last weeks in the hospital.

Today, for the first time since he had emerged from the Arlington hospital, on which day there had been only a few photographers taking shots, Minderquist was to face the press. In the months before the seventeenth of March mishap, Minderquist had been in the public eye because of his closeness to the President in the capacity of economic advisor, though Minderquist held no official title. Minderquist had a Ph.D. in economics, and had been a director of a big electrical company in Kentucky, until six months ago when the President had proposed a retaining salary for him and offered him a room in the White House in which to work. One of the President's aides had heard Minderquist speak at Johns Hopkins University (Minderquist had been invited to give a lecture), and had introduced him to Tom, and things had gone on from there. *A man who talks simple and straight,* a newspaper heading had said of Minderquist earlier that year, and Minderquist was rather proud of that. He and the President didn't always see eye to eye. Minderquist presented his views calmly, with a take-it-or-leave-it attitude, because what he was saying was the truth, based on laws of economics of which the President knew not much. Minderquist had never lost his temper in Washington, D.C. It wasn't worth it.

Minderquist hoped that Florence Lee of the *Washington Angle* would be coming today. Florrie was a perky little blonde, very bright, and she wrote a column called "Personalities in Politics." Besides being witty, she had a grasp of what a man's or woman's job was all about.

"Hon-*ey*?" Julia's voice called. "It's after ten-thirty. How're you doing?"

"Fine! Coming!" Minderquist called back from the bedroom where he was checking his appearance in the mirror. He ran a comb through his brown and gray hair, and touched his tie. On Julia's advice, he wore black cotton slacks, a blue summer jacket, a pale blue shirt. Good colors for TV, but probably there would be none today, just journalists and a few cameras snapping. Julia was not as happy as he in Sundocks, Minderquist knew, and maybe in a few weeks they would move back to their Kentucky place, after he and Julia discussed the matter further. But now for the President's sake, for the sake of his future in Washington, which was interesting and remunerative, and for the pleasure of the media, the Minderquists had to look as if they appreciated their new mansion. Minderquist strode out of the bedroom.

"Penny and Becky aren't here yet?" he said to his wife who was in the living room. "Ah, maybe that's them!" Minderquist had heard car tires in the driveway.

Julia glanced out of a side window. "That's Mama's car.—Doesn't it look nice, Ken?" She gestured towards the long buffet table against a wall of the huge living room.

"Great! Beautiful! Like a wedding or something. Ha-ha!" Glasses stood in sparkling rows, bottles, silver ice buckets, plates of goodies. Minderquist was more interested in his granddaughter, and headed for the front door.

"Ken!" said his wife. "Don't overdo it today. Keep calm—you know? And careful with your language. No four-letter words."

"Sure, hon." Minderquist got to the front door before Fritz, and opened it. "Hel-lo, Penny!" He wanted to pick the little fair-haired child up and hug her, but Penny shrank back against Becky and buried her face shyly in her great-grandmother's skirt. Minderquist laughed. "Still afraid of me? 'S matter, Penny?"

"You scared her—coming at her so fast, Ken," said Becky, smiling. "How are you? You're looking mighty handsome today."

Chitchat between the women in the living room. Minderquist slowly followed the child—his only grandchild—towards the hall that led to the kitchen, but Penny darted down the hall as if running for her life, and Minderquist shook his head. His glimpse of the child's blue eyes lingered in his mind. She had used to leap into his arms, confident that he would catch her. Had he ever let her down, let her drop? No. It was since he had come out of the hospitals that Penny had decided to be "afraid" of him.

"Kenny? Ken?" said Julia.

But Minderquist addressed his mother-in-law. "Any news from Harriet and George, Becky?"

Harriet was the Minderquists' daughter, mother of Penny, and Harriet and her husband, George, had parked Penny at Sundocks, much to Minderquist's delight, while they took a three-week vacation in Florida. But Penny had started acting strangely towards Minderquist, crying real tears for no reason, having a hard time getting to bed or to sleep at night, so Becky, who lived twenty miles away in Virginia, had taken the child to her house a few days ago.

Minderquist never heard Becky's answer, if she made any, because the press was arriving. Two or three cars rolled up the drive. Julia summoned Fritz from the kitchen, then went to open the front door herself.

There were at least fifteen of them, maybe twenty, mostly men, but five or six were women. Minderquist's eyes sought Florrie Lee and found her! His morale rose with a leap. She brought him luck, put him at his ease. Not to mention that it was a pleasure to look at a pretty face! Minderquist looked at her until her eyes met his and she smiled.

"Hello, Ken," she said. "You're looking well. Glad to see you up and around again."

Minderquist seized her slightly extended hand and pressed it. "A pleasure to see *you,* Florrie."

Minderquist greeted a few other people politely, recognizing some of the faces, then steered those who wanted refreshments towards the buffet table, where Fritz in his white waistcoat was already busy taking orders. A couple of cameras flashed.

"Mr. Minderquist," said an earnest, lanky young man with a ballpoint pen and a notepad in one hand. "Can I have a couple of minutes with you later in private? Maybe in your study? I'm with the *Baltimore Herald*."

"Cain't promise you, son, but Ah'll try," Minderquist replied, putting on his genial southern drawl. "Meanwhile come over here and par-take."

Julia was pulling up chairs for those who wanted chairs, making sure that people had the drink or fruit juice that they wished. Her mother, Becky, who Minderquist thought looked very trim and well done-up today, was helping her. Becky managed a nursery in Virginia, not for children, Minderquist remembered he had said a few times to the media, when they asked him about family life, but for plants.

"Ah, tell 'em to shove it!" Minderquist said with a grin, in reply to a journalist's question, were the rumors true that he was going to retire. Minderquist was gratified by the ripple of laughter that this evoked, though he heard Julia say: "Such language, Ken!"

Minderquist had not sat down. "Where's Penny?" he asked his wife.

"Oh—" Julia gestured vaguely towards the kitchen.

"Going back to Washington again soon then, sir?" asked a voice from among the seated people. "Or maybe Kentucky? Lovely place you've got here."

"Bet yer ass—Washington!" Minderquist said firmly. "Julia, honey, isn't there a beer for me anywhere? Where's Fritz?" Minderquist looked for Fritz, and saw him heading for the kitchen with an ice bucket.

"Yes, Ken," Julia replied, and turned to the buffet table.

He wasn't supposed to drink anything alcoholic, because of some pills he still had to take, but he treated himself to a beer on rare occasions, such as his fifty-ninth birthday just after he had left the second hospital, and this was another rare occasion, meeting the press with his favorite female journalist, Florrie Lee, sitting just two yards away from where he stood. Minderquist ignored one boring question, as he saw Becky leading his granddaughter in from the kitchen hall, holding Penny by the hand. Penny hung back, squirming at the sight of so many people, and Minderquist's smile grew broader.

"Here comes the sweetest little granddaughter in the world!" Minderquist said, but maybe nobody heard him, because several of the photographers started clamoring for Minderquist to pose for a shot with Penny.

"Out by the pool!" someone suggested.

They all went out, Julia too. Minderquist placed his beer glass which someone, not Julia, had put into his hand a few seconds ago, by a big flow-

erpot on the blue-tiled border of the pool, frowned into the bright sunlight, and kept his smile. But Penny refused to take his hand, and evaded
like an eel his efforts to grasp her. Becky managed to catch Penny by the
shoulders, and they grouped themselves, Minderquist, Julia, Becky and
Penny, for several shots, until Penny ducked and escaped, running the
length of the pool's side, and everyone laughed.

Back in the living room, the questions continued.

"Any pains now, Mr. Minderquist?"

Minderquist was staring at Florrie, who he thought was giving him a
special smile today. "Na-ah," he answered. "If I get any pains—" He did get
headaches sometimes, but he didn't want to mention that. "Not to mention, no. I'm feeling fine, doing a little golfing—"

"When do the doctors say you can be back on the job?"

"I'm back at work now, you might say," Minderquist replied, smiling in
the direction of the question. "Yes. I get—you know—memos from the
President—make decisions." Where was Tom? Minderquist looked over his
shoulder, as if the President's car might be slipping up the driveway, or
more likely a helicopter would be landing on the big lawn out there, but
he had heard nothing. "Tom said he might look in. Don't know if he can
today. Does anybody know?"

Nobody answered.

"Don't you want to sit down, Ken?" Julia asked.

"No, I'm fine, thanks, hon."

"You swim on your own out in the pool?" asked a female voice from
somewhere.

"Sure, on my own," Minderquist said, though Fritz was always in the
pool with him when he swam. "Think I've got a lifeguard out there? Or a
mermaid to hold me up? Wish I had, I'd like that!" Minderquist guffawed,
as did a few of the journalists. Minderquist glanced at his wife just in time
to see her make a gesture which said, "Watch it," but Minderquist thought
he was doing pretty well. A few laughs never hurt. He knew he looked full
of energy, and the press always liked energy. "Ah really would like to ride
on a mermaid," he went on. "Now on the *golf* course—" Minderquist had
been going to indulge in a little fantasy about mermaids on the golf
course, but he noticed a murmur among the assembled, as if the journalists
were consulting one another. Mermaids who graced the links and flipped
their tails to send the balls to a more convenient position for the golfer,
Minderquist had been going to say, but suddenly three people put questions to him at once.

The questioners wanted to get back to the accident, the attempted assassination of the President.

"Just how you think of it now," a male voice said.

"Well, as I always said—it was a clear day. Peaceful, sunny. Fun. On that grandstand near the street. Till we climbed down." Minderquist glanced at Florrie Lee who was looking straight at him, and he blinked. "When I heard the shots—" Minderquist's mind went into a fog suddenly. Maybe he'd told the story too many times. Was that it? But the show had to go on. "I didn't know what the shots were, you know? Could've been firecrackers or a car backfiring. Then when I saw Tom bend forward, grabbing for his leg, I somehow knew. I was standing so near the President—there was only one thing to do, so I did it," Minderquist concluded with a chuckle, as if he had just related a funny story. He touched the dent in his left temple absently, as he watched the journalists scribbling, though some of them had tape recorders. He looked across the room at Julia, and saw her nod at him with a faint smile, meaning she thought he had said all that pretty well.

"You were talking about recreation, Mr. Minderquist," said another male voice. "You play golf now?"

"Sure do. Fritz drives me over. Quite a few mermaids on the golf course, I must say!" Minderquist was thinking of the pretty teenaged girl golfers in their shorts and halters, flitting about like butterflies. Just kids, but they were decorative. Not so attractive as Florrie Lee though, who Minderquist realized was not only more approachable than the teenagers (one of whom had declined his offer of a soft drink at the clubhouse last week), but seemed to be inviting an approach from him this morning. Never had he seen her look at him like this, fixedly and with a subtle smile from her front-line position among the media in their chairs.

Someone laughed softly. Minderquist saw the laughter, a young man with dark-rimmed glasses, who had turned to the man beside him and was whispering something.

"*Mermaids* on the golf course?" asked a woman, smiling.

"Yes. I mean all the pretty girls." Minderquist laughed. "Wish there *were* mermaids, all blonde with long hair and bare bosoms. Ha-ha! By the way, I know a mermaid joke." Minderquist tugged the sides of his jacket together, but he knew the jacket wouldn't button, and he didn't try. "You all know the one about the Swedish mermaid who spoke only Swedish and got picked up by some English fishermen? They thought she was saying—"

"Ken, *don't!*" came Julia's voice clearly from Minderquist's left. "Not that one."

More laughter from the assembled.

"Let's have it, Ken!" someone said.

And grinning, Minderquist would gladly have continued, but Julia was beside him, gripping his left arm, begging him to stop, but smiling also to put a good face on it. Minderquist folded his arms with husbandly resignation. "Okay, not that one, but it's one of my best. Anything to please the ladies."

"You and your wife play Scrabble, sir? I noticed a Scrabble set on the table over there," said a man.

The word "Scrabble" was like a small bomb exploding in Minderquist's mind or memory. He and Julia didn't play any more. The fact was, Minderquist couldn't concentrate or didn't want to. "Oh-h, sometimes," he said with a shrug.

Then Minderquist was aware of whispering again among a few people. He looked for Julia, and saw her taking someone's glass to replenish it. Yes, at least six heads, including even Florrie Lee's, were bent as people murmured, and Minderquist had the feeling they were picking at him, maybe saying he wasn't his old self, just trying to act as if he were. Maybe they even suspected that he was impotent now (how long would that last?), and could they know this from the doctors to whom he had spoken? But doctors weren't supposed to disclose information about their patients. *Steady improvement every day,* the newspapers had said during the coma days and after, during the days when the President had looked in to be photographed with him when he had been confined to his bed, and he was better and better up to this moment, in fact, if the newspapers took the trouble to print anything about him, and they did every couple of weeks . . . *sitting up in bed cracking jokes* . . . Sure, sometimes he felt like joking, and at other times he knew he was a changed man, made over into someone else almost, as changed as his abdomen, now bulging, or as his face, which looked bloated and sometimes a bit swimmy to him. Minderquist had heard about lobotomy, and suspected that this was what had happened to him with that bullet through his temple, but when he had asked his chief doctor, and the next doctor under him, both had emphatically denied it. "Phonys," Minderquist murmured with a quick frown.

"What? How's that, Mr. Minderquist?"

"Nothing." Minderquist shook his head at a plate of canapés that Fritz extended.

"Sit down for a while, Ken," said Julia who was beside him again.

"Going okay?" he whispered.

"Just fine," she whispered back. "Don't worry about anything. It's nearly over." She went away.

"Delicious liverwurst, Kenneth. Have one." It was Florrie Lee at his side now, holding a round plate with little round liverwurst canapés on it.

"Thank you, ma'am." Minderquist took one and shoved it into his mouth.

"You did well, Ken," Florrie said. "And you're looking well, too."

He was aware of her nearness, her scent that suggested a caress, and he wanted to seize her and carry her away somewhere. Impulsively, he took her free hand. "C'mon, let's go out in the sun," he said, nodding towards the wide open doors on the lawn and the swimming pool.

"Could we possibly see your study, Mr. Minderquist? Maybe take a picture there?"

Damn the lot of 'em, Minderquist thought, but he said, "Sure. Got a nice one here. It's this way." He led the way, smiling a small but real smile, because Florrie had given him a mischievous look, as if she knew he hated to turn loose of her hand. He glanced behind him and saw that Florrie was coming too, along with God knew how many others.

His study or office was book-lined, the books being all from the Kentucky house, and the square room looked orderly to say the least. His new desk had a green blotter, a letter-opener, a pen-and-pencil set, a brown leather folder (what was that for?), a heavy glass ashtray, and no papers at all on it. The wastebasket was empty. Minderquist obligingly leaned against his desk, hands gripping its edge.

Flash! Click! Click! Done!

"Thanks, Ken!"

"When do the doctors say you can go back to Washington, Ken?"

Minderquist kept his smile. "Well—ask the doctors. Maybe next week. I dunno why not."

Minderquist left his study as the others did, feeling relief because it was after twelve noon, the media would be thinking about lunch, and taking off. So was Minderquist thinking about lunch, and he meant to invite Florrie Lee out somewhere. Fritz could drive them anywhere. There were charming hostelries in the area, old taverns with cozy nooks and tables. And then? With Florrie, he wouldn't have any problems, he was sure.

" 'Bye, Mr. Minderquist. Many thanks!"

"Keep well, sir!"

Cars were taking off.

Minderquist's eyes met Florrie's once more as he poured himself a scotch on the rocks at the buffet table. He deserved this one drink. He took a sip, then set the glass down. Florrie had that come-hither look again: she liked him. Minderquist moved towards her, with the intention of bowing, and proposing that he and she have lunch together somewhere.

But Florrie turned quickly away.

Minderquist grabbed her hand. She undid his grasp with a twisting movement, and walked towards the big open doors, Minderquist behind her. "Florrie?"

"Take . . ." The rest of what Florrie said was lost.

But Florrie wasn't gone. In the sunshine, her light dress and her hair seemed all golden, like the sun itself. Minderquist followed her along the border of the pool, where Penny had run a few minutes ago.

"Ken, stop it!" Florrie called, laughing now, and she stepped behind a round table, which she plainly intended to circle if he came any closer.

Minderquist darted, choosing the left side of the table. "Florrie—just for *lunch!* I—"

"*Ken!*"

Had that been his wife's voice? Grinning, trotting, loping, Minderquist chased Florrie down the other side of the pool, the long side, Florrie turned the corner, her little high heels flying, Minderquist leapt the corner, and fell short. His foot struck the blue-tiled edge, and suddenly he was falling sideways, towards the water.

A thud of water in Minderquist's ears blocked yelps of laughter which for a few seconds he had heard. Minderquist gulped and inhaled water, then his head poked above the surface, barely. Hands reached for him from the edge of the pool.

"You okay, Ken?"

"Good diving there! Ha-ha!"

Minderquist struggled to get up to the rim of the pool. People pulled at his arms, his belt. Someone produced a towel. Where was Florrie? Even when Minderquist had wiped his eyes, he couldn't see her anywhere, and she was all that mattered.

"Didn't hurt yourself, did you, Mr. Minderquist?" asked a young man.

"No, no, Chris' sake!—What's happened to Florrie?"

"Ha-ha!"

More laughter. One man even bent double for an instant.

" 'Bye, Mr. Minderquist. We're taking off."

Minderquist strode towards the house, head high, wiping the back of his neck with the towel. He was still host in his house. He wanted to see if Florrie was all right. Minderquist looked around in the big living room, which was eerily empty. A car was pulling away down the driveway. Minderquist thought he heard his wife's voice from the direction of the hall across the living room.

"You will *not*," Julia said.

"But this is—This can be *funny*," said a man's voice. "It's harmless!"

Minderquist reached the threshold of his and his wife's bedroom, whose door was open. Julia stood with a revolver in her hand, the gun that Minderquist knew lived in the top drawer of the chest of drawers to Julia's left, and Julia was pointing it at a man whose back was to Minderquist.

"Drop that thing on the floor or I'll shoot it to pieces," Julia said in a shaking voice.

The man obediently pulled a strap over his head and let his camera sink to the carpet.

"Now get out," Julia said.

"I wouldn't mind having that camera back. I'm with the *Baltimore*—"

"What the hell's going on here?" Minderquist asked, walking into the room.

"I want those pictures. Simple as that," Julia said.

"Just pictures of you and Florrie by the pool, sir!" the young man said. "Nothing wrong. A little action!"

"Of Florrie? *I* want them!" Minderquist said.

The young man smiled. "I understand, sir. Well, y-you've sure got the pictures and the camera too. Unless you want me to get 'em developed for you."

"No!" Julia said.

"Why not? Might be quicker," said Minderquist.

"Empty that camera now." Julia pointed the gun at the young man.

Two men stood in the hall, gawking.

The photographer wound up the rest of his roll, opened the camera, and laid the roll on top of the chest of drawers.

"Thanks," Minderquist said, and put the roll into his jacket pocket, realized that the pocket was sopping wet, and pulled the roll out and held it in his hand.

" 'Bye, Mrs. Minderquist," said one of the men in the hall. "And thank you both."

" 'Bye, and thanks for coming," Julia said pleasantly, both hands behind her.

The photographer put his strap around his neck again. "Good-bye and good luck, Mr. Minderquist!" He stumbled a little getting out of the doorway.

"Let me have that roll, Ken," Julia said quietly.

"No, no, *I* want it," Minderquist said, knowing his wife would destroy the thing if she could, just because Florrie was on it.

"I'll shoot you if you don't." She leveled the gun at him.

Minderquist pressed his thumb against one flat end of the roll in his hand. He'd have pictures of Florrie of his own, maybe a couple of good ones that he could have blown up. "You go ahead," he replied.

Julia bent towards the chest of drawers, holding the gun in both hands as if it weighed a lot suddenly. She put the revolver back into the top drawer.

The Button

Roland Markow bent over his worktable in the corner of his and his wife's bedroom, and again tried to concentrate. Schultz had neglected to report his Time Deposit gains for the end of the year. Roland was now looking at Schultz's December totals, and all Schultz's papers were here, earnings and bills paid for the twelve months of the year, but did he have to go through all those to find Schultz's Time Deposits and God knew what else—a few stocks, Roland knew—himself? Schultz was a freelance commercial artist, considered himself efficient and orderly, Roland knew, but that was far from the truth.

"Goo-*wurr*-kah!" came the mindless voice again, loudly, though two doors were shut between the voice and Roland.

"Goo-woo-*woo*," said his wife's voice more softly, and with a smile in it.

Sickening, Roland thought. One would think Jane was encouraging the idiot! The *child,* Roland corrected himself, and bent again over Schultz's tax return.

It was a tough time of the year, late April, when Roland habitually took work home, as did his two colleagues. The Internal Revenue Service had its deadlines. *Fake it,* Roland thought in regard to Schultz's Time Deposit interest. He could estimate it in his head within a hundred dollars or so, but Roland Markow wasn't that kind of man. By nature he was meticulous and honest. He was convinced that his tax clients came out better in the long run if he turned in meticulous and honest income tax return forms for them. He couldn't phone Schultz and ask him to do it, because all Schultz's papers were here in twelve envelopes, each labeled with the name of the month. He'd have to go through them himself. And it was almost midnight.

"Goo-*wurr*-kah-*wurr-r*—kah!" screamed Bertie.

Roland could stand it no longer and leapt up, went to the door, crossed the little hall, and knocked perfunctorily before he opened the door to Bertie's room halfway.

Jane was on the floor on her knees, sitting on her heels, smiling as if she were having a glorious time. Her eyes behind the black, round-rimmed glasses looked positively merry, and her hands on her thighs were relaxed.

Bertie sat in a roundish heap before her, swimmy-eyed, thick tongue hanging out. The child had not even looked Roland's way when the door opened.

"How's the work going, dear?" Jane asked. "Do you know it's midnight?"

"I know, can't be helped. Does he have to keep saying this 'Guhwurka' all the time? What *is* this?"

Jane chuckled. "Nothing, dear. Just a game.—You're tired, I know. Sorry if we were loud."

We. A crazy anger rose in Roland. Their child was a mongoloid, daft, hopelessly brainless. Did she have to say "we"? Roland tried to smile, pushed his straight dark hair back from his forehead, and felt a film of sweat, to his surprise. "Okay. Just sounded like Gurkha to me. You know, those Indian soldiers. Didn't know what he was up to."

"G'wah-h," said Bertie, and collapsed sideways on to the carpet. He wasn't smiling. Though his slant eyes seemed to meet Roland's for an instant, Roland knew they did not. Epicanthal folds was the term for this minor aberration.

Roland knew all the terminology for children—organisms—who had Down's syndrome. He had of course read up on it years ago, when Bertie had been born. The complicated information stuck, like some religious rote he had learned in childhood, and Roland hated all this information, because they could do nothing about Bertie, so what good was knowing the details?

"You are tired, Rollie," said Jane. "Mightn't it be better to go to bed now and maybe get up an hour earlier?"

Roland shook his head wearily. "Dunno. I'll think about it." He wanted to say, "Make him shut *up*!" but Roland knew Jane got a pleasure out of playing with Bertie in the evenings, and God knew it didn't matter when Bertie got to sleep, because the longer he stayed up, the longer he might sleep and keep quiet the next morning. Bertie had his own room, this room, with a low bed, a couple of heavy chairs that he couldn't tip over (he was amazingly strong), a low and heavy wooden table whose corners had been rounded and sanded by Roland, soft rubber toys on the floor, so that if Bertie threw them against the window, the glass wouldn't break. Bertie had thin reddish hair, a small head that was flat on top and behind, a short flat nose, a mouth that was merely a pink hole, ever open, with his oversized tongue usually protruding. The tongue had ugly ridges down it. Bertie was always drooling, of course. The awful thing was that they were going to be stuck with him for the next ten or fifteen years, or however long he lived. Mongoloids often died of a heart condition in their teens or earlier, Roland had read, but their doctor, Dr. Reuben Blatt, had detected no weakness in Bertie's heart. Oh no, Roland thought bitterly, they weren't that lucky.

Roland pressed the ballpoint pen with the fingertips of his right hand, pressed it against his palm. The worst thing was that Jane had completely changed. He watched her now, bending forward, smiling and cooing at Bertie again, as if he weren't still in the room. Jane had gained weight, she wore sloppy espadrilles around the house all the time, even to go shopping, if the weather permitted. They'd lost nearly all their friends over the past four or five years, all except the Drummonds, Evy and Peter, who Roland felt kept on seeing them out of morbid curiosity about Bertie. They never failed to ask "to see Bertie for a few minutes," when they came for drinks or dinner, and they usually brought Bertie a little toy or some candy, to be sure, but their avid eyes as they looked at Bertie Roland could never forget. The Drummonds were fascinated by Bertie, as one might be fascinated by a horror film, something out of this world. And Roland always thought, out of this world, no, out of his own loins, as the Bible said, out of Jane's womb. Something had gone wrong, one chance in seven hundred, according to statistics, providing the mother wasn't over forty, which Jane had not been, she'd been twenty-seven. Well, they had hit that one in seven hundred. Roland remembered as vividly as if it had been yesterday or last week the expression on the obstetrician's face as he had come out of the labor ward. The obstetrician (whose name Roland had forgotten) had been frowning, with his lips slightly parted as if he were mustering the right words, as indeed he had been. He had known that the nurse had already given the anxiously waiting Roland a fuzzy and rather alarming announcement.

"Ah, yes—Mr. Markow?—Your child—It's a boy. He's not normal, I'm sorry to say. May as well tell you now."

Down's syndrome. Roland hadn't at once connected this with mongolism, a term he was familiar with, but seconds later, he had understood. Roland recollected his puzzlement at the news, a stronger feeling than his disappointment. And was his wife all right? Yes, and she hadn't seen the child.

Roland had seen the child an hour or so later, lying in a tiny metal box, one of thirty or so other metal boxes visible through a glass wall of the sterile and specially heated room where the newborns lay. No one had needed to point out his son to him: the miniature head with its flat top, the eyes that appeared slanted though they were closed when Roland had seen them first. Other babies stirred, clenched a little fist, opened their mouths to breathe, yawn. Bertie didn't stir. But he was alive. Oh yes, very much alive.

Roland had read up on mongoloids, and had learned that they were singularly still in the womb. "No, he's not kicking as yet!" Roland remembered Jane saying half a dozen times to well-meaning friends who had inquired during her pregnancy. "Maybe he's reading books already," Jane had sometimes added. (Jane was a great reader, and had been a scholarship student at Vassar, where she had majored in political science.) And how different Jane had looked then! Roland realized that he could hardly have recognized her as the same person, Jane five years ago and Jane now. Slender and graceful, with lovely ankles, straight brown hair cut short, an intelligent and pretty face with bright and friendly eyes. She still had the lovely ankles, but even her face had grown heavier, and she no longer moved with youthful lightness. She had concentrated herself, it seemed to Roland, upon Bertie. She had become a kind of monument, something mostly static, heavy, obsessed, concentrating on Bertie and on caring for him. No, she didn't want any more children, didn't want to take a second chance, she sometimes said cheerfully, though the chances were next to nil. Both Roland and Jane had had their blood cultures photographed for chromosome count. Usually the woman was "the carrier," but Jane was not deficient of one chromosome, and neither was he. By no means had she a chromosome missing, which might have meant that one of the forty-five she did have carried the "D/G translocation chromosome" which resulted in a mongoloid offspring in one in three cases. So if he and Jane did have another child, they would be back to the one-in-seven-hundred odds again.

It had more than once crossed Roland's mind to put Bertie down, as they said of dogs and cats who were hopelessly ill. Of course he'd never uttered this to Jane or to anyone, and now it was too late. He might have asked the doctor, just after Bertie's birth, with Jane's consent, of course. But now as Jane frequently reminded Roland, Bertie was a human being. Was he? Bertie's I.Q. was probably 50, Roland knew. That was the mongoloid average, though Bertie's I.Q. had never been tested.

"Rollie!" Smiling, Jane lay on her back now, propped on her elbows. "You do look exhausted, dear! How about a hot chocolate? Or coffee if you've really got to stay up?—Chocolate's better for you."

Roland mumbled something. He did have to work another hour at least, as there were two more returns to wind up after Schultz's. Roland stared at his son's—yes, his *son's*—toad-like body, on its back now: stubby legs, short arms with square and clumsy hands at their ends, hands that could do nothing, with thumbs like nubbins, mistakes, capable of holding nothing. What had he, Roland, done to deserve this? Bertie was of course wearing a diaper, rather an oversized diaper. At five, he looked indeed like an oversized baby. He had no neck. Roland was aware of a pat on his arm as his wife slipped past him on the way to the kitchen.

A few minutes later, Jane set a steaming mug of hot chocolate by his elbow. Roland was back at work. He had found Schultz's Time Deposit interest payments, which Schultz had duly noted in April and in October. Roland finished Schultz and reached for his next dossier, that of James P. Overland, manager of a restaurant in Long Island. Roland sipped the hot chocolate, thinking that it was soothing, pleasant, but *not* what he needed, as Jane had informed him. What he needed was a nice wife in bed, warm and loving, even sexy as Jane had used to be. What they both needed was a healthy son in the room across the hall, reading books now, maybe even sampling Robert Louis Stevenson by now, as both Roland and Jane had done at Bertie's age, a kid who'd try to hide the light after lights-out time to sneak a few more pages of adventure. Bertie would never read a corn flakes box.

Jane had said she would sleep on the sofa tonight, so he could work at his table in the bedroom. She couldn't sleep with a light on in the bedroom. She had often slept on the sofa before—they had a duvet which was simple to put on top of the sofa—and sometimes Roland slept there too, to spell Jane on the nights when Bertie appeared restless. Bertie sometimes woke up in the night and started walking around his room, butting his head against the door or one of his walls, and one or the other of them would have to go in and talk to him for a while, and usually change his diaper. The carpet would look a mess, Roland thought, except that its very dark blue color did not show the spots that must be on it. They had sedatives for Bertie from their doctor, but neither Roland nor Jane wanted Bertie to become addicted.

"Damn the bastard!" Roland muttered, meaning James P. Overland, whose face he scarcely remembered from the two interviews he had had with Overland months ago. Overland hadn't prepared his expenses and income nearly as well as the commercial artist Schultz, and Roland's colleague Greg MacGregor had dumped the mess on him! Of course Greg had his hands full now too, Roland thought, and was no doubt burning the midnight oil in his own apartment down on 23rd Street, but still—Greg was junior to Roland and should have done the tough work first. Roland's job was to do the finishing touches, to think of every legitimate loophole and tax break that the IRS permitted, and Roland knew them all by heart. "I'll settle Greg's hash tomorrow," Roland swore softly, though he knew he wouldn't. The matter wasn't that serious. He was just goddamned tired, angry, bitter.

"Guh—*wurrr-rr*-kah!"

Had he heard it, or was he imagining? What time was it?

Twenty past one! Roland got up, saw that the bedroom door was closed, then nervously opened the door a little. Jane was asleep on the sofa, he could just make out the paleness of the blue duvet and the darker spot which was Jane's head, and she hadn't wakened from Bertie's cry. She was getting used to it, Roland thought. And why not, he supposed. Before "Goo-*wurr*-kah" it had been "Aaaaagh!" as in the horror films or the comic strips. And before that?

Roland was back at his worktable. Before that? He was staring down at the next tax return after Overland (to whom he had written a note to be read to Overland by telephone tomorrow if a secretary could reach him), and actually pondering what Bertie had used to utter before "Aaaaagh!" Was he losing his mind? He squirmed in his chair, straightened up, then bent again over the nearly completed form, ballpoint pen poised as he moved down a list of items. It was not making any sense. He could read the words, the figures, but they had no meaning. Roland got up quickly.

Take a short walk, he told himself. Maybe give it up for tonight, as Jane had suggested, try it early tomorrow morning, but now a walk, or he wouldn't be able to sleep, he knew. He was wide awake and jumpy with nervous energy.

As he tiptoed through the dark living room towards the door, he heard a low, sleepy wail from Bertie's room. That was a mewing sort of cry that meant, usually, that Bertie needed his diaper changed. Roland couldn't face it. The mewing would eventually awaken Jane, he knew, and she could handle it. She wasn't going to a job tomorrow. Jane had given up her job with a U.N. research group when Bertie had been born, though she wouldn't have given it up, Roland found himself thinking for the hundredth time, if Bertie hadn't had Down's syndrome. She would have gone back to her job, as she had intended to do. But Jane had made an immediate decision: Bertie, her little darling, was going to be her full-time job.

It was a relief to get out into the cool air, the darkness. Roland lived on East 52nd Street, and he walked east. A pair of young lovers, arms around each other's waist, strolled slowly towards him, the girl tipped her head back and gave a soft laugh. The boy bent quickly and kissed her lips. They might have been in another world, Roland thought. They were in another world, compared to his. At least these kids were happy and healthy. Well, so had he and Jane been—just like them, Roland realized, just about six years ago! Incredible, it seemed now! What had they done to deserve this? Their fate? What? Nothing that Roland could think of. He was not religiously inclined, and he believed as little in prayer, or an afterworld, as he did in luck. A man made his own destiny. Roland Markow was the grandson of poor immigrants. Even his parents had had no university education. Roland had worked his way through CUNY, living at home.

Roland was walking downtown on First Avenue, walking quickly, hands in the pockets of his raincoat which he had grabbed out of the hall closet, though it wasn't raining. There were few people on the sidewalk, though the avenue had a stream of taxis and private cars flowing uptown in its wide, one-way artery. Now, out of a corner coffee shop, six or eight adolescents, all looking fourteen or fifteen years old, spilled on to the sidewalk, laughing and chattering, and one boy jumped twice, as if on a pogo stick, rather high in the air before a girl reached for his hand. More health, more youth! Bertie would never jump like that. Bertie would walk, could now in a way, but jump for joy to make a girl smile? Never!

Suddenly Roland burnt with anger. He stopped, pressed his lips together as if he were about to explode, looked behind him the way he had come, vaguely thinking of starting back, but really not caring how late it got. He was not in the least tired, though he was now south of 34th Street. He thought of throttling Bertie, of doing it with his own hands. Bertie wouldn't even struggle much, Roland knew, wouldn't realize what was happening, until it was too late. Roland turned and headed uptown, then crossed the avenue eastward at a red light. He didn't care if he roamed the rest of the night. It was better than lying sleepless at home, alone in that bed.

A rather plump man, shorter than Roland, was walking towards him on the sidewalk. He wore no hat, he had a mustache, and a slightly troubled air. The man gazed down at the sidewalk.

Suddenly Roland leapt for him. Roland was not even aware that he leapt with his hands outstretched for the man's throat. The suddenness of Roland's impact sent the man backwards, and Roland fell on top of him. Scrambling a little, grasping the man's throat ever harder, Roland tugged the man leftward, towards the shadow of the huge, dark apartment building on the left side of the sidewalk. Roland sank his thumbs. There was no sound from the man, whose tongue protruded, Roland could barely see, much like Bertie's. The man's thick brows rose, his eyes were wide— grayish eyes, Roland thought. With a heave, Roland moved the fallen figure three or four feet towards a patch of darkness on his left, which Roland imagined was a hole. Not that Roland was thinking, he was simply aware of a column or pit of darkness on his left, and he had a desire to push the man down it, to annihilate him. Panting finally, but with his hands still on the man's throat, Roland glanced at the darkness and saw that it was an alleyway, very narrow, between two buildings, and that part of the darkness was caused by black iron banisters, with steps of black iron that led downwards. Roland dragged the man just a little farther, until his head and shoulders hung over the steps, then Roland straightened, breathing through his mouth. The man's head was in darkness, only part of his trousered legs and black shod feet were visible. Roland bent and grabbed the lowest button of the man's gray plaid jacket and yanked it off. He pocketed this, then turned and walked back the way he had come, still breathing through parted lips. He paid no attention to two men who walked towards him, but he heard some words.

". . . told her to go to *hell!*—Y'know?" said one.

The other man chuckled. "No kidding!"

At First Avenue, Roland turned uptown. Roland's next thought, or rather the next thing that he was aware of, was that he stood in front of the mostly glass doors of his apartment building, for which he needed his key, but in his left side trousers pocket he had his keys, as always. He glanced behind him, vaguely thinking that the taxi that had brought him might just be pulling away. But he had walked. Of course, he had gone out for a walk. He remembered that perfectly. He felt pleasantly tired.

Roland took the elevator, then entered the apartment quietly. Jane was still asleep on the sofa, and she stirred as he crossed the living room, but did not wake up. Roland tiptoed as before. The lamp was still on, on his worktable. Roland undressed, washed quietly in the bathroom, and got into bed. He had killed a man. Roland could still feel the slight pain in his thumbs from the strain of his muscles there. That man was dead. One human being dead, in place of Bertie. That was the way he saw it, now. It was a kind of vengeance, or revenge, on his part. Wasn't it? What had he and Jane done to deserve Bertie? What had all the healthy, normal people walking around on the earth, what had *they* done to deserve their happy state? Nothing. They'd simply been born. Roland slept.

When Jane brought him a cup of coffee in bed at half past seven, Roland felt especially well. He thanked her with a smile.

"Thought I'd let you sleep this morning no matter what," Jane said cheerfully. "No tax returns are worth your *health,* Rollie dear." She was already dressed in one of her peasant skirts that concealed the bulk of her hips and thighs, a blue shirt which she had not bothered to tuck into the skirt top, her old pale blue espadrilles. "Now what for breakfast? Pancakes sound nice? Batter's all made, because Bertie likes them so much, you know. Or—bacon and eggs?"

Roland sipped his coffee. "Pancakes sound great. With bacon too, I hope."

"You bet, with bacon! Ten minutes." Jane went off to the kitchen.

Roland felt in good spirits the entire day. Jane remarked on it before he left the apartment that morning, and Greg at the office said: "Miracle man! Did you win on the horses or something? Did you see that pile of stuff on your desk?"

Roland had, and he had expected it. Greg had worked till two-thirty in the morning, he said, and he looked it. The telephones, four of them, rang all day, clients calling back after having had questions put to them by Roland or Greg by telephone or by letter. Roland did not feel so much cheerful as confident that day. He felt calm, really, and if he looked consequently cheerful, that was an accident. He could remind himself that the office had gone through last year's deadline, and the year's before that, in the same state of nerves and overwork, and they'd always made it, somehow.

Roland wore the same trousers, and the button was in the right-hand pocket. He pulled it out in a moment when he was alone in his office and looked at it in the light that came through his office window. It was grayish brown, with holes in which some gray thread remained. Roland pulled the thread out and dropped the bits into his wastebasket. Had he really throttled a man? The idea seemed impossible at ten past four that afternoon, as he stood in his pleasant office with its green carpet, pale green curtains and white walls lined with familiar books and files. The button could have come from anywhere, Roland was thinking. It could have fallen off one of his own jackets, he could have shoved it into his pocket with an idea of asking Jane to sew it on, when she found the time.

It did cross Roland's mind just after five o'clock (the office, including the two secretaries, was working till seven) to look at the *Post* tonight for the discovery of a body on—what street? A man of forty or so with mustache, named—Strangled. But Roland's mind just as quickly shied away from this idea. Why should he look in the newspapers? What had it got to do with him? There wouldn't be a clue, as they said in mystery novels. Sheer fantasy! All of it. A corpse lying on East 40th Street or 45th Street or wherever it had been? Not very likely.

In four days, the office work had greatly let up. Some clients were going to be a little late (their own fault for not having their data all together), and would have to pay small fines, but so be it. Fines weren't life or death. Roland ate better. Jane was pleased. Roland showed more patience with Bertie, and he could laugh with the child now and then. He sat on the floor and played with him for fifteen and twenty minutes at a time.

"That'll help him, you know, Rollie?" said Jane, watching them arrange a row of soft plastic blocks. Jane spoke as if Bertie couldn't understand a word, which was more or less true.

"Yep," said Roland. The row of blocks had a space between each block and the next and Roland began setting more blocks on these gaps with the objective of building a pyramid. "Why don't we ask the Jacksons over soon?" He looked up at Jane. "For dinner."

"Margie and Tom! I'd love to, Rollie!" Jane was beaming, and she brought her hands down on her thighs for emphasis. "I'll phone them tonight. It was always you who didn't want them, you know, Rollie. *They* didn't mind. I mean—about Bertie. Bertie was always locked up in his room, anyway!" Jane laughed, happy at the idea of inviting the Jacksons. "It was always you who thought Bertie bothered *them,* or they didn't like Bertie. Something like that."

Roland remembered. The Jacksons, like most people, were disgusted by Bertie, a little afraid of him for all Bertie's smallness, as normal people were always afraid of idiots, unpredictable things that might do them harm. Now Roland felt that he wouldn't mind that. He knew he would be able to laugh, make a joke, put the Jacksons at their ease about Bertie, if they went into Bertie's room "to visit with him" the night they came. They never asked to, but Jane usually proposed it.

The Jackson evening turned out well. Everyone was in a good mood, and Jane didn't suggest during the pre-dinner drinks time "saying hello to

Bertie," and the Jacksons hadn't brought a toy for him, as they had a few times in the past—a small plastic beach ball, something inane, for a baby. Jane had made an excellent Hungarian goulash.

Then around ten o'clock, Jane said brightly, "I'll bring Bertie out to join us for a few minutes. It'll do him good."

"Do that," said Margerie Jackson automatically, politely.

Roland saw Margerie glance at her husband who was standing with his small coffee by a bookcase. Roland had just poured brandies all round into the snifters on the coffee table. Bertie could easily sweep a couple of snifters off the low table with a swing of his hand, Roland was thinking, and he realized that he had grown stiff with apprehension or annoyance.

Bertie was carried in, in Jane's usual manner, held by the waist, face forward, and rather bumped along against her thighs as she walked. Bertie weighed a lot for a five-year-old, though he wasn't as tall as a normal child of that age.

"Aaaaagh-wah!" Bertie's small slant eyes looked the same as they might if he were in his own room, which was to say they showed no interest in or awareness of the change of scene to the living room or of the people in it.

"*There* you are!" Jane announced to Bertie, dumping him down on his diapered rump on the living room carpet.

Bertie wore the top of his pajama suit with its cuffs turned up a couple of times because his arms were so short.

Roland found himself frowning slightly, averting his eyes in a miserable way from the unsightly—or rather, frightening—flatness of Bertie's under-sized head, just as he had always done, but especially in the presence of other people, as if he wished to illustrate his sympathy with people who might be seeing Bertie for the first time. Then Margerie laughed at something Bertie had done. She had given Bertie one of the cheese stick canapés that were still on the coffee table, and he had crushed it into one ear.

Margerie glanced at Roland, still smiling, and Roland found himself smiling back, even grinning. Roland took a sip of his brandy. Bertie was a little clown, after all, and maybe he enjoyed these get-togethers in the living room. Bertie did seem to be smiling now. Occasionally he *did* smile. Little *monster!* But he'd killed a man in return, Roland thought, and stood a bit taller, feeling all his muscles tense. He, Roland, wasn't entirely helpless in the situation, wasn't just a puppet of fate to be pushed around by— *everything*—a victim of a wildly odd chance, doomed to eternal shame. Far from it.

Roland found himself joining in a great burst of laughter, not knowing what it was about, till he saw Bertie rolling on his back like a helpless beetle.

"Trying to stand on his *head*!" cried Jane. "Ha-ha! Did you see that, Rollie, dear?"

"Yes," said Roland. He topped up the brandies for those who wanted it.

When the Jacksons departed around eleven, Jane asked Roland if he didn't think it had been a successful evening, because she thought it had been. Jane stood proudly in the living room, and opened her arms, smiling.

"Yes, my love. It was." Roland put his arms around her waist, held her close for a moment, without passion, without any sexual pleasure whatsoever, but with the pleasure of companionship. His embrace was like saying, "Thanks for cooking the dinner and making it a nice evening."

Bertie was stowed away in his room, in his low bed, Roland was sure, though he hadn't accompanied Jane when she was trying to settle him for the night. Jane was doing things in the kitchen now. Roland went to a corner of the bedroom where he and Jane stacked old newspapers. Because of Roland's work, he kept newspapers a long while, in case he had to look for a new tax law, or bond issue, or any of a dozen such bits of news that he or his colleagues might not have cut out. What he was looking for was not old and was rather specific: an item about a man found dead on a sidewalk during the night of April 26–27. In about four minutes, Roland found an item not two inches long in a newspaper one day later than he had thought it might be. MAN FOUND STRANGLED was the little heading. Francisco Baltar, 46, said the report, had been found strangled on East 47th Street. Robbery had evidently been the motive. Mr. Baltar had been a consulting engineer of Vito, a Spanish agricultural firm, and had been in New York for a short stay on business. Police were questioning suspects, the item concluded.

Robbery, Roland thought with astonishment. Not the same man, surely, unless someone had robbed the corpse. Roland realized that this was pretty likely, in New York. A robber might suppose the man was drunk or drugged, and seize the opportunity to relieve him of wallet and wristwatch and whatever. The street fitted, Roland thought, and the date. And the man's age. But Spanish, with that brownish hair? Well, Roland had heard of blond Spaniards.

But they hadn't mentioned a missing button.

On the other hand, why should they mention a missing button in an item as short as this? As clues went, a grayish brown button was infinitesimal. For the police to find the button in Roland's right-hand pocket (he kept the button in that pocket no matter which trousers he wore) would be like finding a needle in a haystack. And noticing the absence of a button on the man's jacket, why should the police assume the murderer had taken it?

Nevertheless, the finding of the corpse—or *a* corpse—gave the button a greater significance. The button became more dangerous. Roland thought of putting it in Jane's little tin box which held an assortment of buttons, but when he opened the box and saw the hundred or more innocent buttons of all sizes there, Roland simply could not.

Throw it away, Roland thought. Down the garbage chute in the hall. Better yet and easier, straight into the big plastic bag in the kitchen. Who'd ever notice or find it? Roland realized that he wanted to keep the button.

And as the weeks went by, the button took on varying meanings to Roland. Sometimes it seemed a token of guilt, proof of what he had done, and he felt frightened. Or on days when Roland happened to be in a cheery mood, the button became a joke, a prop in a story that he had told to himself: that he had strangled a stranger and snatched a button off the stranger's jacket to prove it.

"Absurd," Roland murmured to himself one sunny day in his office as he stood by his window, turning the button over in his fingers, scrutinizing its grayish brown horn, its four empty holes. "Just a nutty fantasy!" Well, no need ever to *tell* anyone about it, he thought, and chuckled. He dropped the button into his right-hand pocket and returned to his desk.

He and Jane were going to a resort hotel in the Adirondacks for the last two weeks of June, Roland's vacation time, and of course they were taking Bertie with them. Bertie was walking better lately, but oddly this achievement came and went: he'd been walking better at three, for instance, than he was at the moment. One never knew. Jane had bought a suit of pale blue cotton—jacket and short trousers—and had patiently let out the waist by sewing in extra material, and had shortened the sleeves, "So he'll look nice at the dinner table at the St. Marcy Lodge," Jane said.

Roland had winced, then rapidly recovered. He had always hated taking Bertie out in public, even for walks in Central Park on Sundays, and the Lodge was going to be worse, he thought, because they'd be stuck with the same people, other guests, or under their eyes, for almost two weeks. He would have to pass through that period of curious and darting glances, unheard murmurs as people confirmed to one another, "Mongoloid idiot," then the period of studied eyes-averted-no-staring that such a group always progressed to.

The St. Marcy Lodge was a handsomely proportioned colonial mansion set on a vast lawn, backgrounded by thick forests of pine and fir. The lobby had a homey atmosphere, the brass items were polished, the carpet thick. There was croquet on the lawn, tennis courts, horses could be rented, and there was a golf course half a mile away to which a Lodge car could take guests at any hour of the day. The dining room had about twenty tables of varying sizes, so that couples or parties could dine alone if they preferred, or join larger tables. The manager had told the Markows that the guests were never assigned tables, but had freedom of choice.

Roland and Jane preferred to take a smaller table meant for four when the dinner hour came. A pillow was brought for Bertie by a pleasant waitress, who at once changed her mind and suggested a high chair. It was easy, she said, bustling off somewhere. Roland had not protested: a high chair was safer for Bertie, because the tray part pinned him in, whereas he could topple off a cushion before anyone could right him. Bertie wore his blue suit. His ridged tongue hung out, and his eyes, though open, showed no interest in his new surroundings, which he did not even turn his head to look at.

"Isn't it nice," Jane said, resting her chin on her folded fingers, "that the Lodge put that crib in the room this afternoon? Just the right thing for Bertie, isn't it?"

Roland nodded, and studied the menu. He was enduring those moments he had foreseen, when the eyes of several people in the dining room had fixed on Bertie, and for a few seconds it was worse as the waitress returned with the high chair. Roland sprang up to lift Bertie into it. *Slap!* The tray part was swung over Bertie's head to rest on the arms of the chair. Roland tugged Bertie's broad hands up and plopped them on the wooden tray where his food would be set, but the hands slid back and dropped again at Bertie's sides.

Jane wiped some drool from Bertie's chin with her napkin.

The food was delicious. The eyes around them now looked at other things. Jane had edged her chair closer to Bertie's, and she patiently fed him his mashed potatoes and tiny bits of tender roast beef. The lemon meringue pie arrived hot with beautifully browned egg white on top. Bertie brought his heavy little hand down on the right side of his plate, and his half-portion of lemon pie catapulted towards Roland. Roland caught it adroitly with his left hand and laughed, dumped it back on to Bertie's plate, and soaked an end of his napkin in his glass of water to wash the stickiness off his palm and fingers.

So did Jane laugh, as if they were alone at home.

They finished a bottle of wine between them.

As they were walking towards the stairway in the lobby, with an idea of getting Bertie to bed, because it was nearly ten, Roland heard voices behind him.

". . . a pity, you know? Young couple like that."

". . . could frighten other kids too. Did you notice that dog today, mom? That poodle?" This voice was young, female, with a giggle in it.

Roland remembered the dog, a black miniature poodle on a leash. The dog had stiffened and backed away from Bertie, growling, when Roland and Jane had been signing the register. Roland's hand reached into his right side pocket and squeezed the button, felt its reassuring reality, its hardness. He turned by the stairway to the two women behind him, one young and one older.

"Yes, Bertie," he said to them. "He's not much trouble, you know. Quite harmless. Sorry if he bothers you. He's quite a clown really. Gives us a lot of fun." Smiling, Roland nodded for emphasis.

Jane was smiling too. "Good evening," she said in a friendly tone to the two women.

Both the older and younger woman nodded with awkward politeness, plainly embarrassed that they had been overheard. " 'Evening," said the older.

Roland and Jane held Bertie by the hands in their usual manner, hoisting him up one step at a time, sometimes two steps. They performed this chore without thinking about it. Bertie sometimes moved his blunt little feet in their blunt shoes to touch a step, but mostly he dragged them, and his legs went limp. Roland's right hand was still in his trousers pocket.

A pretty girl moved at a faster pace up the stairs on Roland's right. His eyes were drawn to her. She had soft, light brown hair, a lovely profile which instantly vanished, but she glanced back at him at the landing, and their eyes met: bluish eyes, then she disappeared. Roland had been aware of a sudden attraction towards her, like a leap within him, the first such feeling he had had in years. Funny. He was not going to approach the girl, he knew. Maybe best if he avoided looking at her if he saw her again, as he probably would. Still, it was nice to know he was capable of such an emotion, even if the emotion had completely gone in regard to Jane. He squeezed the button harder than ever as they heaved Bertie up the last step to the floor level. He had killed a man in revenge for Bertie. He had superiority, in a sense, one-upmanship. He must never forget that. He could face the years ahead with that.

Where the Action Is

Here it was, some action finally—an armed holdup of a town bus—and Craig Rollins was in urgent need of a toilet! Nevertheless, Craig raised his camera once again and snapped, just as a scared-looking man was hopping down the steps of the halted bus. Then Craig ran, heading for Eats and Take-Away, where he knew there was a men's room by the telephones.

Craig was back in something under a minute, but by then the action seemed to be over. He hadn't heard any gunshots. A cop was blowing a whistle. An ambulance had pulled up, but Craig didn't see anybody who was wounded.

"Take it easy, folks!" yelled a cop whose face Craig knew. "We've got everything in hand!"

"*I* haven't! They got my *handbag*!" cried a woman's voice, shrill and clear.

A June sun boiled down. It was midmorning.

"There were *three* of 'em!" yelled a man in an assertive way. "You just got two here!"

Craig saw some shirtsleeved police hustling two young men towards a Black Maria. *Click!*

The passengers from the bus, thirty or more, milled about the street as if dazed, chatting with one another.

"Hi, Craig! Get anything good?" It was Tom Buckley, another free-lance photographer a couple of years older than Craig, and friendly, though Craig considered him competition.

Craig didn't want to ask if Tom had got a shot of the guy with the gun, because Craig had missed this shot, which might have been possible at exactly the time he had had to dash to a men's room. "Dunno till they come out!" Craig replied cheerfully. He moved closer to the police wagon, and took a picture of the two young men, who looked about twenty, as they were urged into the back of the wagon. Tom Buckley was also snapping. One or maybe even two of Tom's photos would make it in the afternoon edition of the *Evening Star*, Craig was thinking. Craig shot up the rest of his roll, aiming at any place—at a cop reassuring an elderly woman, at a girl rushing from a narrow passageway into Main Street where the bus was, and being greeted by a man and woman who might have been her parents.

Then Craig went home to develop his roll. He lived with his parents in the home where he had been born, a two-story frame house in a modest residential area. Craig had turned his bathroom—itself an adjunct to the house when he had been fifteen—into his darkroom. All his pictures looked dull as could be, worse than he had expected. No action in them, apart from a cluttered street scene of people looking bewildered. Still, Craig presented them at the office of Kyanduck's *Evening Star* about half past noon, imagining that Tom Buckley had got there a few minutes earlier and with better photos.

Ed Simmons bent his balding head over Craig's ten photographs. The big messy room held seven people at their desks, and there was the usual clatter of typewriters.

"Got there a little late," Craig murmured apologetically, not caring if Ed heard him or not.

"Hey! You got Lizzie Davis? With her *folks!*—Hey, Craig, this one is great!" Ed Simmons looked up at Craig through horn-rimmed glasses. "We'll use this one. Just the moment *after*—running out of that alley! Beautiful!"

"Didn't know her name," Craig said, and wondered why Ed was so excited.

Ed showed the photo to a man at another desk. Others gathered to look at the picture, which was of a girl of twenty or younger, with long dark hair, her white blouse partly pulled out of her skirt top, looking anxious as she rushed forward towards a man and woman approaching her from Main Street.

"This is the girl who was nearly raped. Or maybe she even was," Ed Simmons said to Craig. "Didn't you know that?"

Craig certainly hadn't heard. Raped by whom, he wondered, then the snatches of conversation that he heard enlightened him. The third holdup boy, who was still at large, had dragged Lizzie Davis off the bus and into an alley and threatened to stick a knife in her throat, or to rape her, unless she kept her mouth shut when the police came up the alley. The police hadn't come up that alley. In the picture, Lizzie's father, in a pale business suit and straw hat, was just about to touch his daughter's shoulder, while her mother on the right in the picture rushed towards the girl with both arms spread.

Now he saw, in the upside-down photo on Ed's desk, that the girl's eyes were squeezed shut with horror or fear, and her mouth open as if she were crying or gasping for breath.

"Was she raped?" Craig asked.

The reply he got was vague, the implication being that the girl wasn't telling. So Craig's photo appeared on page two of the Kyanduck *Evening Star* that day, and one by Tom Buckley of a local cop with two of the holdup boys on the front page. Both photographs had a two-column spread.

Craig pointed out the photo to his parents that night at the supper table. Craig didn't make it every day, or even every week, a photo in the *Evening Star* or the Kyanduck *Morning News.* His father knew Ernest Davis, the girl's father, who was an old customer at Dullop's Hardware, where Craig's father was manager.

Craig received thirty dollars for his picture, which was the going rate for local photographs, no matter what they were, and Craig mentioned this, with modest pride, to his girlfriend Constance O'Leary, who was called Clancy. Craig, twenty-two and ruggedly handsome, had three or four girlfriends, but Clancy was his current favorite. She had curly reddish blonde hair, a marvelous figure, a sense of humor, and she loved to dance.

"You're the greatest," Clancy said, at that moment diving into her first hamburger at the Plainsman Café, just outside of town, where the jukebox boomed.

Craig smiled, pleased, "Human interest. That's what Ed Simmons said my photo had."

And Craig didn't think any more about that picture of Lizzie Davis until ten days later, when on one of his visits to the *Evening Star* office with a batch of new photographs, Ed Simmons told Craig that the *New York Times* had telexed, wanting to use Craig's photograph in a series of articles about crime in America.

"You'd better be pleased, Craig."

"With a credit?" Craig was nearly speechless with surprise.

"Well, natch.—Now let's see what you've got here." Ed looked over Craig's offerings: three photos of the Kyanduck Boy Scouts' annual picnic at Kyanduck Park, and three of current weddings. Ed showed no visible interest. Tom Buckley had probably topped him on these events, Craig was thinking. "I'll look 'em over again. Thanks, Craig."

That was Ed's phrase when he wasn't going to buy anything.

Still, Craig's dazed smile at the news about the *New York Times* lingered on his face as he left the office. He'd never yet had a photo in the *New York Times!* What was so great about that picture?

Craig found out some five days later. His photograph was one of three in the first of a three-part series of articles in the *New York Times* called "Crime in America's Streets." His photograph had been cleverly cut to show it to better advantage, Craig noticed. The text beneath said:

A young woman in a small town in Wyoming rushes towards her parents, seconds after being held hostage under threat of rape by one of a three-man armed holdup team who robbed bus passengers in midmorning.

And there was his name in tiny letters at one side of the picture: Craig Rollins.

When Craig showed the article to his parents that evening, he saw real joy and surprise in their faces. Their son with his work in the *New York Times!*

"That girl Lizzie's a changed girl, you know, Mart?" Craig's father addressed his mother.

"Yes, I've heard," said his mother. "Edna Schwartz was talking about Lizzie just yesterday. Told me Lizzie's broken off her engagement. You know, she was supposed to get married in late June, Craig."

Craig hadn't known. "Was she really raped?" he asked, as if his parents might know the truth, as indeed they might, because his mother worked behind the counter of Odds and Ends, a shop that sold dry goods and buttons, and his mother chatted with nearly every woman of the town, and his father certainly saw a lot of people in the hardware store.

"She's saying so," his mother replied in a whisper. "At least she's hinting at it. And nobody knows if she broke off her engagement or her boyfriend did. What's his name, dear? Peter Walsh?"

"*Paul* Walsh," corrected his father. "You know, the Walshes up on Rockland Heights," his father added to Craig.

Craig didn't know the Walshes, but he knew Rockland Heights, a neighborhood famous for fine houses and the well-to-do minority of the populace of Kyanduck. Snobs, he thought, to break an engagement these days because a girl's virginity might have been lost. Like prehistoric times!

Craig looked with interest at the two following articles in the *New York Times,* which he was able to see daily at the office of the *Evening Star.* The series was about car thefts, robberies of apartments, muggings, plus the efforts of the police in big cities to control such crime, of course, but also about the danger of its increasing, now that unemployment was spreading among the under-twenty-fives. A couple of photographs Craig admired very much: one a night-shot of a teenager picking the lock of a Chinese laundry; another of a mugging in the South Bronx, in which an elderly man had been flung to the ground, his grocery bag spilled beside him, while a boy in shorts and sneakers was diving into the inside pocket of the man's jacket. Now these were damned good photographs! Why had they liked his so much, Craig wondered. Because Lizzie Davis's face was pretty? Or because she really had been raped?

"You know any more details about this Lizzie Davis thing?" Craig asked Clancy on one of their dates.

"What do you mean, details? I know she broke her engagement with the Walsh boy. And she *says* she was raped."

"That's what I mean," said Craig. "Amazing."

"What is?"

"That a guy running away from a holdup pushes a girl into an alley and rapes her—in maybe five minutes or less. I just don't believe it."

"Oh, you don't."

"No."

"Well, she says so. I heard through somebody—yes, Josie MacDougal, that a journalist came to Lizzie's house to interview her about it."

Craig frowned. "Journalist from here? Why didn't you tell me?"

"From Chicago, I think. And anyway, I only heard about it when it was all over. Couple of weeks ago, after the *New York Times* thing. Anyway, Lizzie doesn't go out much any more, so I've heard. Stays at home. She's like a psycho."

"Wha-at?" said Craig. "You mean she's gone nuts—at *home?*" At the same time, Craig was thinking that another photo or two of Lizzie Davis might be a good idea, salable.

"I don't mean *nuts,*" Clancy said, her freckled face sobering with thought for a moment. "Just that she's not interested in any kind of social life any more. She's become sort of a *reck*-loose."

That was a bit of a puzzle to Craig Rollins, but then he didn't understand girls completely and didn't really want to. He didn't believe Lizzie Davis had been raped, though she might well have been threatened with it. Maybe she was putting on an act, breaking her engagement with the Walsh fellow because she didn't really want to marry him.

The day after that evening, part of which Clancy had spent with him in his room at home, Craig received a letter that had been forwarded to him by the *Evening Star*. His "excellent photograph" of June 10, reprinted in the *New York Times,* had won the year's Pulitzer Prize for newspaper photography.

Craig, with lips parted in disbelief, looked at the letterhead again. It looked authentic with the committee's name, New York address and all that, but was somebody pulling his leg? The signature at the bottom was that of Jerome A. Weidmuller, Chairman of Selections Committee. The last paragraph expressed the pleasure and congratulations of the Committee, and stated that they would be in touch in regard to bestowing an award of a thousand dollars plus a citation.

Craig was afraid to mention the Pulitzer letter to his parents. It might be a joke.

But the next day, a man who said he was the secretary of Mr. Weidmuller telephoned Craig at home. He said he had got Craig's telephone number from the *Evening Star*'s office. Craig was cordially invited to a dinner to be given in New York in a few days, and he would receive an invitation by post. His return air fare would be paid, plus hotel expenses in New York for one or two nights, as he preferred. "Congratulations, Mr. Rollins," said the voice as it signed off.

If this was a joke, it was pretty convincing, Craig thought. A bit dazed, he crumpled up the wet photograph he had been developing in his darkroom, and went to the fridge for a beer to celebrate.

When an express letter arrived that same day at 6 P.M., Craig knew that the Pulitzer Prize affair was real. The air ticket was in the envelope, with the proviso that if he could not keep the date six days thence, he would notify the Committee and return the ticket. His hotel was booked, with dates, and the letter assured him that all expenses would be paid by the Committee.

"What was that?" asked his mother, who was preparing supper in the kitchen.

Craig had walked into the kitchen with the letter in his hand. "Well, Ma—I wasn't sure it was true till now. I won the Pulitzer for my photo of Lizzie Davis."

"The Pulitzer?" said his father. "The Pulitzer Prize? Didn't know there was one for photography."

Craig attended the dinner in New York. For a few seconds Craig was visible on the TV screen, his parents told him, among other Pulitzer Prize winners for the novel, journalism, drama and so on.

After that, Craig's telephone began to ring. The Kyanduck *Evening Star* passed on callers and messages to Craig. Journalists wanted to interview him. A boy of nineteen wrote to him care of the *Evening Star*, asking if he gave photography lessons. This letter made Craig smile, because he had never had any lessons himself, apart from a course in high school, a course he had dropped after a month, because the work had become too complicated. A university in California that Craig had never heard of wanted him to come and give a lecture, travel expenses paid, plus fee of three hundred dollars. A Philadelphia school of journalism invited him to make a speech of about forty-five minutes, and offered a fee of five hundred dollars. Craig intended to write both schools a polite letter of refusal, on the grounds that he had never made a speech in his life and that the idea terrified him. But after a good dinner at home, and mentioning these invitations to his parents, and his parents' saying in their old-fashioned way, "Sure you can, Craig, if you just put your mind to it. Be friendly! People just want to see you and meet you now," Craig decided to accept the California offer.

This affair went off amazingly well. One of the audience asked a question, after that, Craig went rolling along, talking in his own free style about hanging around the office of the Kyanduck *Evening Star* and the town police station, hoping for a good photogenic story to break, hoping even for a fire, though it wasn't maybe very nice to hope for a fire that might hurt people. And then—*this* had happened, the great day when the bus had been held up in his home town, a minor tragedy by world standards, but upsetting for some thirty or forty ordinary citizens, disastrous for the young girl called Lizzie Davis, who had intended to marry in a few days, but whose life had been shattered, maybe ruined, by *crime in the streets*. Craig hammered the crime angle, because the articles on crime in the streets had launched his photograph. Never in the speeches that followed, or in his maiden speech in California, did he say that he had given up on that famous day, that he had thought the action was over when he had taken that photograph. Never would he say, though he tried to make his speeches as amusing as possible, that he had missed the action, because he had had to run to a toilet at the crucial instant when the holdup man had been disarmed.

After four speeches, Craig had got the hang of it. And the fees were great. He began to insist on a thousand dollars plus expenses. He flew to Atlanta, Tucson, Houston and Chicago. Meanwhile, he had job offers. Would he care to join the staff of the *Philadelphia Monitor* at forty thousand dollars a year? Craig wrote a stalling, polite answer to this job offer. He sensed that the lecture circuit could dry up. A tiny town in Atlanta wanted him, but for a hundred dollars, and Craig had no intention of accepting that. He would take the highest salary offer, he thought, when he had exhausted the lecture invitations.

With the extra money from his speeches, Craig Rollins was a changed young man. He was able to buy more clothes, and discovered that he had a taste for quality in clothes and also in food. He acquired a new Japanese camera that could do more things than his old ones, which were second-hand anyway. He still had Clancy as his main girlfriend, but he had met a girl called Sue in Houston who seemed to like him a lot, and who had the money to fly to meet him sometimes in a town where he was making a speech. A pretty girl beside him enhanced his image, Craig had noticed.

Craig also went to a good barber now, his hair was not so short, and the barber fluffed it out in a style that Craig might have called sissy a few months ago, though no one could possibly have called Craig or his face sissy. He had the head and neck of a line-hitter, a tackle, which he had been on the high school football team and in his first year at Greeves College, Wyoming. Craig's grades would have got him kicked out of almost any college, he knew, but Greeves had been willing to keep him on, because of his football prowess. The coach had thought he might make All-American, but Craig had quit college after a month in sophomore year, out of sheer boredom with the scholastic part of it. Now, however, still in top physical form, Craig felt pleased with himself. He wrote to the *Monitor* saying that he had had a better offer from a California paper, but if the *Monitor* could raise their offer to fifty thousand dollars, Craig would accept, because he preferred the East Coast.

"Have you been to see Lizzie at all?" Clancy asked Craig.

"Lizzie—Davis? No, why should I?"

"Just thought it might be nice. She did bring you a lot of luck, and it seems she's so sad."

Craig knew Lizzie was sad, because a couple of newspapers had interviewed her. Kyanduck's *Evening Star* had, of course, in a discreet little piece with a picture of Lizzie in her family's house.

So Craig telephoned the Davis residence one day around 5 P.M. A woman answered, sounding as if she might be Lizzie's mother. Craig identified himself and asked if he could speak with Lizzie.

"Well, I don't know. I'll have to ask her. She's just back from a little trip. Hold on a minute.—*Lizzie?*"

While he waited, Craig reflected that he might, with Lizzie's agreement, take a few more pictures of her.

Lizzie came on, with a sad voice. But she agreed to see him, when Craig proposed to come over in half an hour and stay just a few minutes.

Craig got into his car and picked up a bouquet of flowers at a shop on the way. He wore his camera on a strap around his neck, as if—today, anyway—his camera were as much a part of his dress as his woolen muffler.

Lizzie opened the door for him. She still had long dark hair that hung in gentle waves to below her shoulders. "Oh, thank you. That's very sweet of you," she said, accepting his gladioli. "I'll get a vase for these. Sit down."

Craig sat down in the rather swank living room. The Davises had a lot more money than his family. Lizzie came back, and set the vase in the center of the coffee table between them.

Then she proceeded to tell him about her broken engagement, five months ago now, and how quiet her life had been since.

"In a way, I've lost my self-confidence—my self-respect. No use trying to gain it back," Lizzie said. "That was shattering—that day."

How had they got here so quickly, Craig wondered. Lizzie was talking to him as if he were interviewing her, though he hadn't asked her a single question.

"Just this afternoon—you won't believe it—I was being photographed in Cheyenne—for a perfume ad. I've become a photographer's model— maybe because I want to get the phobia of photographs out of my soul. Maybe I'm succeeding, I don't know."

Craig was wordless for a moment. "You mean—my picture embarrassed you so much? I'm sorry."

"Not the picture so much. What *happened*," Lizzie replied, lifting her round, dark eyes to his. "Well, it wasn't *your* fault, and the picture brought you a huge success, I know. It ruined my engagement, but—Well, in a way, I'm lucky too, because there's a market for a sad-dog face like mine. I can see that. The other day I even posed for an ad for men's clothing, you won't believe it, but I was supposed to be the girl with the knowing eyes—for clothing, that is—whose face would brighten up, if the fellow I liked just wore good-looking clothes, see? Very complicated, but it really came off. If I had the photo I'd show you, but the ad isn't even out yet."

Craig saw Lizzie's face brighten briefly, when she described the way the girl's face would brighten, if her boyfriend only wore good clothes. Then an instant later, Lizzie's glum expression was back, as if it were a garment she wore for the public. Craig moistened his lips. "And—your fiancé? I mean—I know you broke it off a few months back. I was thinking maybe you'd both get together again."

Lizzie's sadness deepened. "No. No, indeed. I felt as if—I'd never want to live with a man as long as I live. Still do feel that way."

But Lizzie was hardly nineteen as yet, Craig was thinking, though he kept silent. The funny idea came just then: he didn't believe Lizzie. What if she were faking this whole thing? Lying even about having been raped? What if she hadn't liked her boyfriend much anyway, and hadn't minded breaking off their engagement? "I'm sure your fiancé is sad too," Craig said solemnly.

"Oh, seems to be. That's true," Lizzie replied. "But I can't help that." She sighed.

"Would you mind if I took a couple of shots of you now?"

Lizzie lifted her eyes to his again. Her eyes were alert, wary, yet interested. "Whatever for?—Well, not while I'm in these shoes, I hope," she added with a quick smile. She was in house shoes, but otherwise very smartly dressed in a hand-knitted beige sweater and dark blue skirt, with a gold chain around her neck.

"Don't have to take the feet," Craig said, standing now, aiming his camera. He could sell three or four photos to New York and Philadelphia newspapers, he was sure, if he suggested that a staff writer write a few lines about her quiet life five months after the rape. *Click!* A rape that Craig was more and more sure never took place. *Click!—Click!* "Look a bit to your left.—That's good! Hold it!" *Click!*

Five minutes later, as he was taking his leave, Craig said, "I sure appreciate your letting me snap you again, Lizzie. And would you mind if I found a writer to do a little piece on you? N-not for the local paper," Craig hastened to add. "For the big papers east. Maybe west too. Might help your fashion model work, mightn't it?"

"That's true." She was plainly reflecting on this, blinking her sad eyes. "It's funny, you know, that *day* bringing you all that success and prizes and everything, and *me*—just ruining my life. Nearly."

Craig nodded. "That's a great angle for the writer." He smiled. " 'Bye, Lizzie. I'll be in touch soon."

"Let me see the photos first, would you? I want to make the choice."

That very evening, Craig telephoned Richard Prescott, a journalist of the *Monitor,* and gave him his ideas, which had developed a bit since he had seen Lizzie. He would be the puzzled, guilt-ridden, small town photographer who had contributed to, even caused the upset of a young woman's life.

"She really was raped?" asked Prescott. "I remember the story and your photo, of course, but I thought she'd just been scared. The boy they caught always denied it, you know."

Never mind, Craig started to say, but instead he replied, "She certainly implied she was. Girls never want to say it flat out, y'know. But you get my angle, that *I'm* the one upset now, because I—" Craig squeezed his eyes shut, thinking hard. "Because I captured in a split second that expression of a girl who's just been—assaulted. You know?"

"Assaulted. Yeah, might work fine."

"In fact, the article should be as much about me as her."

Prescott said he would get in touch soon, because he had another assignment on the West Coast, and might be able to squeeze Wyoming in.

Craig then rang up Tom Buckley, who agreed at once to take some pictures of Craig. Craig reminded Tom that Tom would get credit lines in some big newspapers, if he did the job. Tom was still friendly with Craig, and had never shown the least jealousy of Craig's success.

Tom Buckley came over the next morning to photograph Craig in his modest darkroom at home, and at his worktable, brooding over a print of the now famous "Crime in America's Streets" photo of Lizzie Davis. In this shot, Craig held the photograph at an angle at which it was recognizable, and in his other hand he held his head in the manner of a man with a terrible headache, or tortured by guilt. Tom chuckled a little as he snapped this one. "Good angle, yeah, your feeling sorry for the girl. She's doing fine, I heard, with her modeling work."

Craig straightened up. "But I do feel sorry for her. Sorry about her shame and all that stuff. She sure called her marriage off."

"She wasn't mad about that guy. And he wasn't about her. One of these things the parents were keen on, y'know?—Everybody in town knows that. You haven't been paying much attention to town gossip, Craig old boy. Too busy with your big-town newspapers lately." Tom smiled good-naturedly.

In a curious way, Craig realized that he had to hold on to his conviction that Lizzie Davis's life had been altered, ruined—or he couldn't make a success of the article-plus-photos that he had in mind. "You think she's a phony?" Craig asked in a soft, almost frightened voice.

"Phony?" Tom was putting away his camera. "Sure. Little bit. Not worth much thought, is it? All the public wants is a sensational photo—

someone killing themselves jumping off a building, somebody else getting shot. The hell with who's to blame for it, just give the public the action. The sex angle in your Lizzie picture gave it its kick, y'know? Who cares if she's telling the truth or not?—I don't believe for a minute she was raped."

That conversation gave Craig something to chew on after Tom Buckley had departed. Craig was sure Tom was right. Tom was a bright fellow. The public wanted pictures of buildings bombed high in the air, a wrecked car with a body in it, or bodies lying on pavements. *Action.* Even the story wasn't terribly important, if the picture was eye-catching. Now Craig struggled like a drowning person to hang on to the Lizzie story, that she *had* been raped and had broken her engagement because of the rape. Craig knew he would have to talk to Richard Prescott as if he believed what he was saying.

Craig did. He prepared himself as if he were an actor. He emoted. He struck his forehead a couple of times, grimaced, and a genuine tear came to support him, though Prescott had a tape recorder and not a camera, unfortunately.

"... and then the awful moment—moments—when I realized that in my last-minute shot that day, I'd caught the nineteen-year-old girl and her anxious parents at maybe the most dramatic moment of their lives." Craig was giving this monologue in his parents' living room, both his parents being out at their respective jobs. Prescott had a few questions jotted down in his notebook, but Craig was going along well enough on his own. "And just after that," Craig continued, "the terrific, unbelievable acclaim that my photo got! Reproduced in the *New York Times,* and then winning the Pulitzer Prize! It really didn't seem fair. It made me rethink my whole life. I thought about Fate, money, fame. I even thought about God," Craig said with earnestness, and a thrill passed over him. He believed, he knew now, that he was being sincere, and he wanted to look Prescott straight in the eyes. "I began to ask myself—"

Prescott at that moment stuck a cigarette in his mouth, reached for his lighter, and stared at the little black machine that was recording all this.

"—what I'd done to deserve all this, when the young girl—Well, she didn't get anything from it except suffering and shame. I began to ask myself if there was a God, and if so was he a just God? Did I have to do something in return for my good luck either to him or to—I mean— maybe to the human race? I began—"

"End of tape, sorry," Prescott interrupted. "In fact, this might be enough. You've talked through two tapes."

For a moment, Craig felt cut off, then glad it was over.

Prescott gave a laugh. "That bit about religion at the end. You thinking of writing a book, maybe? Might sell."

Craig didn't reply. He had decided in the last seconds that he didn't like Prescott. He had met Prescott only once before, in the *Monitor*'s office, knew he was highly thought of, but now Craig didn't like him.

However, the article that Prescott wrote which appeared ten days later in the *Monitor* was top-notch. Craig's words came out hardly changed, and they rang true, in Craig's opinion. In Tom Buckley's photos, Craig looked serious in one, agonized in the other. An excellent, if only one, picture of Lizzie Davis showed her seated in an armchair in her house, holding what the caption stated was a print of the photograph that had changed her life. Lizzie looked hopeful, modest and pretty, as she stared the camera straight in its eye.

The article brought Craig a few more invitations to lecture, one from a prestigious university in the east, which he accepted. He wrote to the *Monitor* saying that for the next few months he expected to be busy on his own, and so could not at once say yes to the staff photographer's job they had offered, even with the augmented salary to which they had agreed. Craig had higher aspirations: he was going to write a book about it all. When he thought of Fate's part in it, God's part, his brain seemed to expand and to take wings of fancy. He might call his book *Fate Took the Picture,* or maybe *The Lens and the Soul.* The word *conscience* in the title might be a bit heavy. Craig gave a few more talks, and managed easily to bring his religious thoughts and pangs of conscience into his text. "Life is not fair sometimes—and it troubles me," he would say to an awed or at least respectfully listening audience. "Here *I* am, lauded by so many, recipient of honors—whereas the poor girl victim, Lizzie, languishes . . ."

Craig's book, *Two Battles: The Story of a Photographer and a Girl,* appeared four months later, after a rushed printing. The book was ghosted by a bright twenty-two-year-old journalist from Houston named Phil Spark, who was not given credit on the title page. *Two Battles* sold about twenty thousand copies in its first six months, thanks to aggressive publicity by its New York publisher and to a good photo of Lizzie Davis on the back of the jacket. This meant that the sales more than covered Craig's advance, so Craig was going to have more money in his pocket due to royalties. He and Clancy got married, and moved into a house with a mortgage.

He had sent half a dozen copies of *Two Battles* to Lizzie Davis, of course, and in due time she had replied with a formal note of thanks for his having told "her story." But she showed no sign of wanting to see Craig again, and he didn't particularly want to see her again, either. She and Craig had met briefly with the ghostwriter to get some background in regard to Lizzie's schooldays in Kyanduck.

Craig appeared on a few religious programs on TV, which did his book a world of good, and he dutifully answered almost all his fan mail—though some of it was pretty stupid, from teenagers asking how they could start out "being a newspaper photographer." Still, contact with the public gave Craig the feeling that he was making new friends everywhere, that America was not merely a big playground, but a friendly and receptive one, which conflicted a bit with his playing the reflective and publicity-shy cameraman. Craig eased himself over this little bump in the road by convincing himself that he had discovered another métier: exploring God and his own conscience. This seemed to Craig an endless path to greater things. Craig decided to tour America with Clancy in his new compact station wagon, and to photograph poor families in Detroit and Boston, maybe some in Texas too; and fires, of course, in case he encountered any; rape and mugging victims the same; street urchins of wherever; sad-faced animals in zoos. He would make himself famous as the photographer compelled to photograph the seamier side of life.

He envisaged a book with a few lines under each photograph which would reflect his personal conflict in regard to God and justice. Craig Rollins was convinced of his own conviction, and that was what counted. Plus the belief, of course, that such a book would sell. Hadn't he proved by *Two Battles* that such a book would sell?

Chris's Last Party

Among the six or eight letters waiting for Simon Hatton in his hotel suite, he noticed a telegram and opened that first. The sender was Carl, a name that didn't ring a definite bell.

> CHRIS NEAR THE END! WE ARE ALL HERE EXCEPT YOU. ELEVEN
> OF US. PLEASE COME DONT HESITATE. KNOW YOU ARE WORKING
> BUT THIS IS IMPORTANT. PHONE 01-984-9322 AND CONFIRM.
> CHRIS WONT BUDGE WITHOUT YOU! YOUR OLD PAL CARL.

Carl Parker, of course, and not an old pal, rather an acquaintance, even a rival once. But Christopher Wells on the brink of dying? It seemed incredible, but the old boy was ninety at least—no, ninety-four. And it was emphysema, of course. Chris had been living with an oxygen gadget in his bedroom for the last decade, Simon knew, inhaling from it when he needed it, trying not to inhale the mild cigars the doctor had yielded to and the occasional cigarette that Chris had never totally abandoned. The telegram had come from Zurich. Chris had a chalet with generous grounds near Zurich, and Simon had been there once, the last time he'd seen Chris, perhaps four years ago. Chris had spent half the time in a wheelchair, and what must he be like now? But Simon could imagine: Chris would be throwing a party, keeping his butler busy with champagne, his cook with gourmet dishes at all hours. Chris loved his protégés, and he wouldn't die without saying good-bye to all of them in person, including Simon, the twelfth (what a coincidence) of the disciples.

Simon felt suddenly afraid, and it occurred to him that he could ring Zurich and say he ought not to come because as long as he didn't show up,

Chris might go on living, not to mention that Simon was giving eight performances a week now in *William* in New York.

Simon jumped at a knock on his door. "Yes? Come in." He knew it was his champagne arriving.

"Good evening, sir," said the white-jacketed waiter. He bore a tray with a quarter bottle of champagne and a few English biscuits of a nonsweet variety. "Am I too early, sir?"

"No, no, just right." Simon knew it was six or five past, but he glanced at his wristwatch anyway (it was four past six), then removed his overcoat and noticed that a drop of moisture fell from it. It was snowing today. His fair, rather crinkly hair was damp too.

Johnny took his coat before Simon realized it, and hung it in a wardrobe. "You'd like to be called as usual, sir, seven-twenty?"

"Y-yes." Seven-twenty for a curtain rise at eight-forty.

Simon always took a nap at this hour until the hotel switchboard awakened him, though he had his own travel clock's alarm set too. Yesterday being Monday, he'd had the day off and gone to Connecticut to visit friends. He'd been fetched late Sunday night after the show and driven up to Connecticut in his host's car with a driver. Now Simon felt tired, though it hadn't been a strenuous holiday. Was he starting to feel old at forty-nine? Awful age, forty-nine, because the next number was fifty. No longer middle-aged, that number, but elderly, definitely.

He slipped out of his shoes and walked back to the sitting-room table for the rest of his letters. He took off his jacket, trousers and shirt and got into bed. Two letters were fan mail, he saw from the strange names on the return addresses, and one letter had a red EXPRES-EIL-SENDUNG stamp on its front. He didn't recognize this hand either, but it was from Zurich. He opened this, bracing himself for further grim information about Chris. The letter was in longhand and signed Carl again.

Dec. 7, 19–

Dear Simon,

Chris took a turn for the worse about a week ago, and it really seems it is going to be the end. For one thing, he has summoned all his old what shall I call us—students?—to him. He wrote you to California, where he later realized you weren't, because of the N.Y. show. (Must congratulate you on *William,* by the way.) There are nine of us now at High-Ho, two due tomorrow, Freddy Detweiler and Richard Cook. Plenty of room here and you mustn't think it's a wake. Chris looks pretty well for a few hours a day when he's up entertaining us. The rest of the time he's in bed, but loves us to come in and talk with him round the clock!

So please come because for Chris there's something strange about your not being here. Use your understudy for a couple of days, but hurry, please.

Chris phoned me nearly a month ago and said he was sure he would die in December, end of year and a life and so on. So he said come on the first of December or as soon after as pos. and "I won't hold you up long." Isn't that typical of Chris? . . .

Yes, Simon understood, but his mind as he laid the letter aside and sank into his pillow was disturbed and undecided. He couldn't have found a word or words to describe how he felt. Shocked, and on guard too. It was as if Chris had given him a sharp poke in the ribs to remind Simon that Chris still existed. Chris hadn't always been kind or even fair. Or was that true? No, the kindness, the concern of Chris did outweigh the rest. Chris had been selfish, demanding of attention, but Simon couldn't honestly tell himself that Chris had ever been heartless, or had ever let him down. And he had told Simon that he would be a fine actor, if he did this and that, if he disciplined himself, if he studied the technique of so-and-so. Chris was a director, if he could be called anything, and had three or four famous productions to his credit, but he had always had money from his family, and he dabbled, didn't have to work all the time.

But it was the word of praise in the ears of twenty-year-old Simon Hatton that had inspired him, coming as it had from a man over sixty, who had troubled to come backstage to meet him, when he had been acting with a summer theater group in Stockbridge, Massachusetts. When Simon recalled this, his heart seemed to tumble. It was Christopher Wells's enthusiasm that had lighted his own fire. Could he ever have made it without Chris? Christopher Wells had been a silly, aging dandy, in a way, wearing odd clothes to attract eyes in New York or London restaurants and theaters. Chris had taken Simon on his first trip to Europe.

For a few seconds, Simon felt a mixture of resentment, pride, and independence. Then came the memory of his happiness in those first weeks with Chris. He had felt bewildered, flattered, and as if he were walking on air, different from being in love, because the feeling was so much bound up with his work, yet like it too. Chris had cracked the whip at him, as if he were a circus dog, Simon remembered quite well.

At this recollection, Simon got up and walked around his bedroom, deliberately relaxed his shoulders, and did not take a cigarette that he was tempted to take. He went back to his bed and lay face down and closed his eyes. In forty-five minutes he had to be ready for his taxi downstairs, and he must do his job tonight. He must entertain. The audience would be silent and sad at the end. It was a serious and sad play, *William*.

And he knew he would get a ticket to fly to Zurich, maybe not tonight but tomorrow, after he had arranged for his understudy Russell Johnson to take over for him.

Fantasy! *William* was fantasy, so was acting—all make-believe. After the others in the cast, Simon took one curtain bow, and not two. He was smiling, but a few women in the audience, and men too, pushed handkerchiefs against their lids. Simon closed his own wet eyes, and walked off with a straight back.

Simon took off for Zurich the next morning. He had spoken with his understudy, who had been visibly elated by the chance to replace him for a few days, as Simon had thought he might be. Simon had played well last night. He had recalled Chris's words: "It's a craft, it's not magic—but the audience helps to inspire you, of *course*. You could say the audience makes the magic." Simon could hear Chris's voice saying, under varying circumstances, "Of *course*," which was reassuring when you'd already resolved to do something, and reassuring also when Chris was proposing something like jumping off a cliff without a parachute. "Of *course*—you can make it. What's talent for? You've got it. It's like money in the bank. Use it, my boy." And there was a couplet from William Blake that Chris used to say:

> *If the Sun and Moon should doubt,*
> *They'd immediately go out.*

He felt strange, as if he were going to meet his own death. What nonsense! He was in good form, and at Chris's house there was not only fresh air but mineral water, paths to hike on, a tennis court that had been there when Chris bought the land, but which Chris had never used. It was going to be something, renewing old acquaintances such as Carl Parker, Peter de Molnay, some phony and some not, some maybe balding and plump. But all successful, like himself. Simon wasn't in close touch with any. At Christmas, he'd receive an unexpected card from one or two, just as he on some impulse would send a Christmas card to one or two. They all had one thing in common, Chris Wells, who had discovered or befriended or encouraged them all, touched them when they were young with a magic finger, like God giving life to Adam. The image of Michelangelo's ceiling fresco flashed for an instant into Simon's mind's eye, and he flinched at the triteness of it.

Simon had telephoned High-Ho and told someone, who had sounded like a servant, at what time he would be arriving in Zurich. He had expected Peter or Carl at the airport, but he saw no identifiable faces among the group of waiting people, and then a card with HATTON written on it caught his eye. It was held by a stranger, a sturdy, dark-haired man.

Simon nodded. "Hatton, yes. Good evening."

"Good evening, sir," said the man with a German accent. "Is this all your luggage?" The man took it from Simon's grasp. "The car is just this way, sir. Please."

The air was crisp, different. Simon sank into the back seat of a large car, and they moved off. "And how is—Mr. Wells?"

"Y-yes, sir. He is doing quite well. But he must rest much of the time."

Simon gave up asking anything more. They rolled on into darkness, and after an hour's drive Simon sensed the black mountains rising around them, hiding the glints of the stars, though the car did not seem to be climbing. Finally they drove between tall iron gates and tree-shaded house-lights came into view. Simon braced himself. A tall, slender figure came to meet the car.

"Simon! Is that you?"

This was Peter de Molnay, who opened the door before the driver could. Peter and Simon shook hands firmly—they had known each other very well indeed fifteen years or so ago, but it occurred to Simon that they might as well be strangers now, polite, with polite smiles.

"Chris is in bed now—but still awake," Peter said.

It was midnight, but the eleven guests or visitors were all up, spread between the spacious living room where a fire blazed and the arch-doored kitchen which was now fully lighted and where no doubt a chef was still working.

"Hello, Simon! Richard—Richard Cook. Remember?" Awkwardly, Richard drew back his hand and gave Simon an embrace with one arm. Richard had quite a belly and was bald on top, gray at the sides—but of course there were roles for just such types, and Simon knew Richard kept busy.

"Simon! Welcome!"

"Hey! There's *Simon!*—We knew you'd make it!" Carl Parker, blondish and slender still, the eternal juvenile, clasped Simon's hand.

Several people spoke to him at the same time. Questions. Was he tired? How long could he stay? The atmosphere was party-like. Simon felt not tired but nervous. He wanted to see Chris, and said so.

"Oh, he wants to see *you*, Simon! Go up!"

Simon followed the dark-haired man, who carried his suitcase up to his room.

"I hope this will be all right, sir. You have it to yourself. This room has not a private bath but . . ."

Simon half-listened as the man (whose name was Marcus, Simon had learned downstairs) explained that there was a bathroom three doors down the hall on the left. "May I see Chris—Mr. Wells?"

"Just a minute, sir." He went out.

Simon unlatched his suitcase lid, but did not open it. Then he stood at attention facing the door, as if Marcus would appear at any second with a military order, summoning him into Chris's presence. This was exactly what happened.

"You may come in now, sir."

Simon marched forward, turned left, and was escorted down the hall to a room on the right on whose door Marcus rapped gently.

"Yes, Marcus. Come in."

Simon heard the age in Chris's voice and felt a painful ache, though he realized he wasn't young either, and what would Chris think of him? Simon tripped on the threshold—not being used to raised thresholds—and laughed.

So did Chris. "Ha-ha! Splendid entrance! Bless you, Simon—for coming. Give us a kiss!—Um-m!"

Blinded with tears, Simon bent and kissed a half-pale, half-pink cheek. He was aware of a mountainous form under a white sheet and a pink blanket. The room was overheated. Simon stood back and blinked. "You're—"

"I'm looking bloody awful, don't say it, but I'll be up in a few minutes—and looking a bit better." Chris's thin blond hair was even thinner, and limp, the face beneath it broader and flabbier than Simon could have imagined. My God, thought Simon, this is really death! Was Chris taking cortisone too? His blue eyes, once so bright and quick, seemed to be faking a brightness by a deliberate tightening at the corners. "I've read your reviews, Simon—of *William,* I keep up, y'know. Must congratulate you. Where's your hand?"

Simon gave his right hand again. His hand was colder than Chris's just now. Simon glanced again at the shiny cylinder at the end of the bed, which suggested a fire extinguisher.

"All goes well, doesn't it, Simon? I'm proud of you. I saw your film
Barter—last year. You were excellent all the way through. Supporting
actor—who really carried the cast."

"Yes, well—" Simon had seldom heard such praise from Chris, not
even when he had been twenty-four, with his first good part in a Bernard
Shaw play. What was its name?

"Wash your hands and face, go and have a nice drink, and I'll be down
in five minutes. We've got a round-the-clock party going—going to see
me out. Ask August to come up, would you? He's maybe—near the
kitchen."

Simon watched Chris stirring under all the covers, perhaps trying to
get out of bed, and Simon felt tongue-tied about asking if Chris wanted
any help.

"Right away, Chris!" Simon made for the door.

Less than five minutes later, Simon was standing with a heavy glass of
scotch in his hand, his back to the fireplace, Peter and Richard on either
side of him, all chattering about nothing. Simon felt, yet of course something, because each knew something about the careers of the others, that
Peter had been working in Hollywood for a year or two, that Richard had
with difficulty, being American, played in a musical two years ago in London. Peter was in his mid-forties. In his twenties, nearly to the present,
Peter had danced and sung. Simon was aware that he had a place of honor
in the house, because he was the oldest, he reckoned, and had known Chris
probably before the others had.

The phone was ringing again. Nobody paid any attention, because a
servant was going to answer it.

A trio of men, one of whom Simon recognized as Jonathan Truman,
was attempting to sing in harmony in an armchaired corner of the living
room. They looked unshaven and rumpled. Simon glanced at his watch:
nearly 1 A.M. local time and nearly 8 P.M. in New York. His understudy
would be in his dressing room, making up before Simon's mirror, aging
himself, not trying to look younger, and perhaps nervously saying some
lines to himself. Simon drank all his glass.

Someone banged him on the back.

"Chris is here!"

"Chris is coming!" shouted Freddy Detweiler, spreading his arms at
the foot of the stairs.

Chris was wheeled down, step by step, by Marcus and August, a
blondish man whom Simon had indeed found in the kitchen. August
leaned back like a thin mast in a wind against the weight of the chair.

"*Chris!*" A scattered cheer went up, a patter of applause that seemed to Simon pitiable, as when an audience was scant. Simon had not joined in, he merely stared in wonder at the heavy man in a blue-and-white striped dressing gown with long-fingered hands gripping the arms of his chair, with the fixed pink and white smile on closed lips. Safely down with his charge, August went to the sideboard and poured champagne, while at least four figures fluttered around Simon like bees.

"Chris, what do you fancy? Carl on the piano? Me—standing on my head? Or my impersonation of an English tourist in Uganda?" This question came from Freddy, forty-five if he was a day, and could he still stand on his head? The question might have been unheard by Chris whose blue eyes were roving as usual, taking in essentials.

"What kind of music tonight, Chris?"

"Indian," said Chris absently, like a man doped or talking in his sleep. "*Simon* is here!" Chris announced, as if the others didn't know it.

Fortunately, only a couple of smiling faces troubled to turn to Simon for an instant, and Simon looked away. Simon squeezed his eyes shut, not near tears again, but something like it. He remembered the pleasure, the terror even, of meeting Christopher Wells at twenty. Well, maybe some of the others had met him when they were at that age too, or near enough. Otherwise why would they be here? Freddy was in a London show now, Simon knew, yet he was here. "Can I see you in New York? Do you ever come to New York?" Chris had asked that first night backstage in Stockbridge. Simon in those days had traveled everywhere by bus or by hitchhiking, his worldly goods in a duffel bag. Twenty-nine years ago, and Chris Wells had been even then sixty-five! Had Chris's age ever crossed Simon's mind then? Amazingly, it hadn't. "You'll go to school with me for a few weeks," Chris had said, meaning that Simon was to move into his Park Avenue apartment. That huge, rambling apartment with at least six big rooms looked as large in Simon's memory as if he had been a small child then. You must do this and you must not do that, Chris had said a dozen times a day, and though Chris had often had lunch or dinner with people in Manhattan (Simon sometimes accompanied him too), Chris had always set Simon some lines to learn out of Shakespeare, Pirandello, Shaw, Eugene O'Neill. Simon hadn't had to memorize them, but he had had to be able to read them, and Chris would play the other parts, male or female. He showed Simon how to get up from a chair without lurching, corrected his diction without insulting him (Simon was from Idaho), and Chris had paid all the bills, saying that he was taking Simon away from possible work then. And when Simon had been strangely in love with Chris, Simon had known that Chris knew it. Simon was not homosexual, and would not have known, at least not then, what to do with a man in bed. But it was not so simple as bed, what he had felt for Chris. It was more like hero worship, more like devotion and absolute confidence. Chris had once said, "Your work is more important than I am—than anybody. *People* come and go." Had Christopher meant girls then? Or friends? Even that bit of advice had sunk in. Simon had had at least four affairs, two of which he considered important, meaning that they had made him happy and that the ends of them had hurt, but he had never married, and though he had not willed it, or taken it on himself, he realized now that he had followed Chris's advice: keep yourself independent, your work is more important than personal relationships.

In the next couple of minutes, the drink took effect, the atmosphere, the realization that Russ Johnson was on the stage now, playing William in New York. There was music, a buffet banquet laid out on a table in a grotto of the garden, down some lighted stone steps from Chris's house. Simon remembered a summer lunch here the one time he had been to High-Ho. August was tending a brazier, grilling beef, and a few figures stood near the fire for warmth. The cheerful voices carried to the black curtain of fir trees all around: they were talking of former visits, telling old anecdotes, and Chris was among them, in his wheelchair. How much longer did he have to live, Simon wondered.

Simon glanced at several faces. Whom did he dare ask that question? Who would give him a straight answer, even a straight opinion? However, he was here, the last of the disciples that Chris had wanted. The rest was up to Chris. Was Chris going to die with a smile on his lips, like now, lifting a glass of champagne? Simon watched Chris tip his head back and laugh at a remark Peter had made, and Simon fancied he saw Chris's belly shake like jelly under the mohair coverlet that was pulled up to his waist. Death and decay—was indeed not funny. Simon went to the buffet table for some wine with which to finish his supper. He had decided not to ask anyone his opinion of when Chris might die.

Now it was nearly 3 A.M. At least four had drifted off to the house to retire. Detweiler was rather drunk.

"A toast to Simon!" Chris shouted. "One of my more brilliant children. Oh, you're all brilliant! To Simon!"

"Simon!" echoed a half-dozen voices and the name seemed to reach the mountains.

"And to those who never doubt," Chris added.

They chuckled and drank.

A few minutes later, Detweiler did attempt to stand on his head, and fell, got up to mocking laughs, rubbing the end of his spine, but he wasn't hurt. Plucky of him to have tried it, Simon thought, with no soft grass to land on here, just stone.

Simon turned towards the descending steps, and took a deep breath. He needed relief from the scene of Chris surrounded, oppressed even, by his former protégés. Somewhere ahead on the stone path another electric light glowed. Then Simon caught his heel on an uneven stone and plunged forward. He had not been walking fast, but he was going to land on his head, and he was aware that he did not put out his hands to protect himself. He was going to die, now. This was the great plunge, and it was like a dream, after all, painless yet final.

He woke up to a soft roar of voices that sounded like a sea, blinked his eyes and recognized the faces bending over him, smelled the wood smoke of Chris's fireplace. He was lying on one of Chris's long leather sofas in the living room.

"He's come to! He's okay!"

"Oh, good—good." That was Chris's tired and relieved voice in the background.

A man laughed. "Simon, you really took a header! We heard the plop!"

"But there's no bleeding! Not a scratch on him!"

"Take a sip of this hot tea."

"I'm going off to bed . . ."

Simon got up, and in a near daze said good night to Chris and walked up the stairs, even washed to some extent before he donned pajamas. He felt even stranger than when he had arrived, not drunk though he must be a little drunk, but as if he had left this world and entered another. He pinched his forearm hard through his pajama sleeve, and felt it.

He flopped into bed and at once fell asleep.

He had a very vivid dream of being about sixteen, on a bicycle, hampered by groceries which he was supposed to bring to his family's house. He knew the old way—in the dream it was along certain curving unpaved lanes, though in Simon's boyhood the streets near his home had been paved—but he kept getting lost. And Chris Wells was hovering somewhere above, like God, saying, "Come on, Simon, to the *left* here. You know the way. What's the matter with you?" And Simon awakened, unsuccessful in returning home.

What did that dream mean? Anxiety, insecurity. Even Chris had not been able to show him the way.

Simon lay on his back in the near darkness of his room, enjoying the slow coming of dawn at his windows which made black lumps of Chris's handsome furniture, of the high-backed chair on which Simon had put his jacket last night. The jacket looked like a bat hanging there. The house was silent, and only one bird's voice—it did not sound like a lark—cried once or twice beyond the windows.

And maybe Chris would be found dead this morning in his bed. Simon imagined August going in with a tea tray and finding him. Simon tensed, preparing himself for this, as if it were a truth to be announced in an hour or so.

Weren't some of the others thinking the same thing, since his own arrival last evening?

Simon showered and shaved in the bathroom down the hall, then dressed in old gray flannels, a shirt and heavy sweater. The bruise on his head throbbed a bit more painfully. It had awakened him last night, an ache and a rising lump that felt like the classic egg. He wasn't going to mention it to anyone, though it made some of his short hair stand straight out.

Simon went out the front door and retraced his steps of last evening, went past the old stone table that had held their supper, and was unable to identify exactly the spot where he had tripped. Wouldn't it be odd if he had died here a few hours ago, if the others had carried up his corpse instead of him merely unconscious? Simon looked quickly back at the big chalet, and heard a faint *ting* of metal striking metal, a sound from the kitchen. Two soft lights glowed behind curtains.

He ran back up the steps.

Detweiler was in the living room, on his feet, looking tired but nervously alert, dressed as was Simon in trousers and sweater. "Up already! 'Morning, Simon!"

"Good morning! And how's Chris?"

"Chris? Same, I suppose."

"Well—" Simon hesitated. "Is he really going to die? Is he on the brink, I mean? Carl's telegram to me—said so."

"Yes," said Freddy, looking Simon straight in the eye.

Was Freddy Detweiler still drunk? Simon strolled towards the fireplace where embers still burned, then turned. "Last night—I didn't have a chance and I didn't really want to ask what the doctors said. Do you know?"

"Oh, to hell with the doctor or doctors. They're amazed he's still alive. A piece of a lung he's got, as they said of old Keats, or maybe Keats said it about himself. The rest is water. But with Chris it's mental, whether and when he dies. You know that. I could use a weak scotch, how about you?"

"No, thanks." He watched as Detweiler poured an inch into a glass and added water from a Perrier bottle. "But now that we're all here—"

Just then, August came in with a tray. "Good morning, sir. Good morning. Your tea, sirs." He arranged teacups and toast plates on the low table near the fireplace.

"What?" asked Detweiler.

Simon saw in Detweiler's nervous eyes the same question that he had asked. When was Chris going to decide to die? "I meant," Simon began as he poured tea, "how long do you think this will go on?" He handed Detweiler his cup. "Sugar?"

"Today, tomorrow. Who knows?"

"You're going to stay—till the end?"

"Yes," said Detweiler with the same firmness as before, though now he looked whipped by fatigue. "But Richard has to go back to London today, I think. He's been here four days, and I—three or four."

Simon felt uneasy, and tried to take comfort from the tea. Chris would be incomplete again with Richard gone. Then what? "Won't it be—"

"We haven't had our presents yet," Detweiler interrupted on a suddenly cheerful note. "He's giving us all little presents. Maybe big ones, I don't know.—What were you going to say?"

"I—I started to say, isn't it impossible to imagine Chris gone? Not with us any more. He—Not that I wrote to him so often in the past—lately. But I always knew he was there. He always spoke on the phone at Christmas or around Christmas. Somehow we each found out where the other was."

"What're you trying to say?" asked Detweiler.

Simon frowned and glanced at the fire. August had added wood to it. "I suppose I'm asking, do you think Chris is going to die—or not?"

"Are you in a hurry?" Detweiler asked with a smile, and sipped his scotch.

Simon knew Detweiler wanted an angry reaction, but Simon didn't feel angry. "I love Chris—and I'm upset. Also I know he's going to die. So I'm sorry I asked you."

"You should be." Detweiler reached for the bottle again.

The telephone rang in the room. "Is a servant supposed to answer this?" Simon asked, but Detweiler showed only indifference, and Simon picked the telephone up. "Hello. Christopher Wells's residence."

"Simon, it's *you*. What luck! I know it's early for you but I had to tell you—all goes well. Russ did a good job, really made it last night. The *Times* this morning even had an item about him. Russ must've done some fast phoning before he went on or somebody else did it for him. He's happy as a fool. Probably thinks he's become Laurence Olivier overnight." It was the voice of Stew Davis, the director of *William*.

"I'm glad, Stew. That's a relief to know." Simon was glad, for the sake of *William* and for Russell Johnson, who was a serious and dedicated young man. Young, yes, not quite thirty, and William in the play was not quite forty, which Russ would be able to do well. William was not supposed to be nearly fifty, as was Simon Hatton.

"When're you coming back?—Any news?"

"I really can't say, Stew. Maybe in two days, three. As long as things are going so well there—Would you tell Russ I'm delighted? Is he with you now?"

Stew laughed richly. "I'm sure he's asleep, if he can get to sleep. But I'll tell him."

They exchanged good-byes, and Simon turned to Detweiler who was now drinking his tea. "Just found out my understudy made a big hit last night. Russell Johnson. Maybe you'll hear of him—very soon."

"But you're going back to the part."

"Oh—certainly. When I go back to New York. I—"

August came in again, slender and quiet, and bowed a little. "Excuse me, gentlemen, Mr. Wells is awake and would like to see you—and anyone else who is up," he added with a glance at the windows as if he might see a figure or two walking in the garden.

"Haven't seen anybody else," Detweiler said, instantly alert. "Let's go, Simon."

Simon saw something unusual in both August's and Detweiler's attitude. He followed them up the stairs to Chris's room whose door was ajar. Simon heard voices from inside. August knocked for them.

Chris lay propped up on pillows, but he turned, fairly rolled his heavy body towards the door as they entered. "Simon—and Freddy. Bless you, come in. Having a wake—very early one. Shocking hours for me, don't you think, but I didn't sleep a wink, I felt so happy. With all of you here. I don't know why—"

"Now take it easy, Chris dear," said Richard Cook who was in pajamas and a dark blue dressing gown under which his abdomen bulged. So was Carl Parker in pajamas, and stood at the foot of the bed. "Of course we're all here. Maybe just not all up yet."

"But we can start the presents. Like Christmas when we were all children, you know, and got up early to see what we had from Santa Claus—much to the annoyance of our parents, but I'm not annoyed one bit. August?" Chris's tired, reddish eyes wobbled uncontrollably as he leaned to his left to see August, if he could. August was there, but plainly Chris didn't see him for a few seconds. "August—no, first champagne for all of us, and then—you know. Call Marcus to help."

"Yes, sir." August hurried off.

Chris was not going to live the day out, Simon thought. He watched Richard Cook expertly unhitch the oxygen tank from the foot of the bed and bring it with its deathly-looking mask of limp rubber to Chris, who clamped the mask over his nose and mouth. Chris's eyes above the flabby gray mask showed a childlike fear, did not focus on anything, and their expression seemed to Simon that of a scared human being, acquainted with life for a very long while and yet now terrified of leaving it.

Then there was a glass of champagne in Simon's left hand, a small white tissue-wrapped package in the other. Someone had told him to sit in a chair, so Simon sat. Three or four others had come into the room, and all had champagne and were unwrapping, talking, laughing.

"Jonathan isn't up yet. Typical," said Chris.

Simon's present was Chris's silver cigarette case—for six cigarettes, Simon remembered from the first dinner he had ever had with Chris—which Simon had admired so much then. A slightly raised snake with tiny emerald eyes coiled its way across the lid of the case, smooth to the touch, yet dangerous looking. The corners of the case were rounded by Chris's fingers over the years, by being slipped in and out of jacket pockets.

"Thank you, Chris," Simon said, looking at the man on the bed, but Detweiler was bending over to kiss Chris's cheek just then, below the ugly mask. Detweiler had a wristwatch in his left hand.

Richard was holding up a gold chain with a medallion on it.

August made discreet but anxious signs. They were to leave. Mr. Wells needed repose.

But Chris was not having it. He removed his mask to call for more champagne, and coffee and tea and toast. "And we're not all here yet." Chris coughed. "August, where're my cheroots?"

August knelt and produced a box from a lower compartment of Chris's bed table.

Simon slipped away, went to his room and dropped the cigarette box and its tissue and its card in Chris's hand saying, "This wise little snake has seen a lot. Try and show him something new. My love always, Chris."

Simon went to the bathroom down the hall, splashed cold water on his face, dried himself on the corner of a towel probably not his own, and vowed not to have a drink today, not even a glass of wine. He still felt strange, and it was not jet lag or even like lack of sleep. Someone rapped gently on the door.

"One minute," said Simon with false cheer, and opened the door to a sleepy-looking Jonathan, barefoot and in pajamas.

"You're looking spruce," said Jonathan.

"Am I? Have a wash and go in and see Chris. The party's already launched."

"At eight o'clock in the *mo-orning,*" Jonathan moaned, shuffling in. "How much more of this can I stand? Can we stand?"

"Lots more." Simon closed the door on him.

That wasn't true. Was he going to go on pretending or not? Go on acting with false cheer or not? Detweiler had been acting last night, when he had tried to stand on his head. He hadn't been acting this morning, when he had said, "Yes," he was going to stay to the end.

Simon wondered if he could face the end? That was what the trouble was about. The truth was, that Simon felt he might become nothing, with Chris gone. Chris had picked him up from nowhere, when he had been (Simon knew) a rotten actor with barely a dream in his head. Chris had even given him his dream. Chris had made him able to achieve it. Chris had introduced him to the people who had helped him. So what was he, really? Now pushing fifty, and a twenty-nine-year-old had taken over his part with great success in New York. Who needed Simon Hatton any longer? *I'd better die before Chris.* The words came as soon as the thought.

Simon was suddenly frightened, yet resolved. Did any of the other fellows feel the same? Well, certainly not Richard with a wife and a couple of children. Not even Detweiler, probably, who was a realist. Jonathan? Somehow he looked the softest of the lot with his puzzled eyes. But why make a pact with Jonathan? Simon didn't need a pact with anyone.

He drifted towards the window, but looked away from the pine forest beyond the lawn to the writing table in the corner, cinquecento, scarred and much polished, and he stared at a brass letter-opener curved like a little scimitar with a single red stone in its haft. Kill himself with that? Absurd. Yet the letter-opener fascinated him, because it was beautiful. Then Simon realized that he had bought the letter-opener in Gibraltar, decades ago, and given it to Chris. Simon had been about twenty-two then, lithe and agile, running through the narrow cobbled streets of Gibraltar, up earlier than Chris as usual, bringing back the letter-opener in a brown paper bag from an unpretentious little shop, sneaking back into the hotel room where Chris still lay asleep. Chris's June birthday had been near.

Simon made an effort, picked up the letter-opener, ran his thumb along the edge as if it were a knife, then laid it down exactly where it had been.

Before noon, Simon had taken a walk around Chris's property, looking for a place, a gorge deep enough to throw himself down, fatally. But wouldn't it be a mess, his corpse on the estate, discovered perhaps by police dogs? Better to jump into the Limmat in Zurich. Better yet to take sleeping pills in an hotel, leaving money for disposal or shipping corpse back to America, or whatever they did.

Lunch was in Chris's big room, which really was big enough to hold them all. August had pulled back the curtains of its two big windows, sunlight poured in (Chris said he had cut down forty pines to obtain this low-slanting winter sunshine), and August had laid out meats and salads on a long wooden commode.

"This is bliss," announced Chris, beatifically smiling on all his twelve, and in danger of tipping the champagne glass which he held in his right hand. In his left was a long cigarette in a black and gold holder.

Simon's eyes were drawn to Chris, and then he had to look away. He held a glass of red wine, otherwise it would have been remarked that he had nothing to drink, but Simon had hardly sipped it. He went to Jonathan and asked softly, "Do you want to die too?"

Jonathan put a forkful of smoked salmon into his mouth. "No," he said, apparently amused.

Detweiler looked more awake, like a different person from earlier this morning. Carl Parker was standing beside him.

"Where's your plate, Simon?" said Detweiler. "Have you tried the potato salad? Divine."

"How's the bump on your head?" asked Carl, looking at Simon's head where the hair stood out. "You had a shock last night. Are you really feeling okay?"

"Yes, thanks. Do I look funny?—Did Freddy tell you my understudy in New York had a big success last night? The theater phoned me this morning."

"No. Well, that's a relief to you, I'm sure," said Carl with his mid-Atlantic accent. "Did you tell Chris?"

"N-not as yet." Jonathan and Richard were on either side of Chris's bed just then, Richard cutting something on Chris's plate, which lay on a big tray spanning his body. Chris would not be interested, Simon thought. It was rather a negative piece of information, nothing particularly to Simon's good.

"Simon, you must come and visit us, since you're working in New York," said Carl, fishing in his wallet for a card. "Us being me and Jennifer. My girlfriend," he added with a smile, as if he expected Simon not to believe him. "This is our L.A. place, but I'll write our present number on the back.—New Canaan. We've rented a house for a year."

Simon thanked him, and pocketed the card. The noise of conversation made it difficult to talk. "Do you think—How does Chris look to you today? You've been here longer than I have."

Carl looked at Simon as if he didn't understand. Or maybe Carl understood Simon to mean that he, Simon, was in a hurry to leave. Thinking of this, Simon said:

"I understand Richard's taking off today."

"Or maybe tonight. You're pressed, Simon?"

"I'm *not*," said Simon, realizing painfully that Carl had misunderstood. "No, it's just that I don't know how Chris usually looks, if this is an ordinary day—"

"You can't tell with Chris." Carl smiled serenely, indulgently, as if he had all the time in the world, and worse, as if it didn't matter if Chris died today, tomorrow or next week. Carl's eyes were bright with confidence, even happiness, because his life would keep on its same runners with Jennifer and his work, whatever it was just now.

Nor did Detweiler understand, looking at Simon levelly, almost challengingly, as if Simon had said something disrespectful in regard to Chris. It was more comforting to hear Richard's deep laugh from the direction of Chris's bed, but Simon knew the laugh was half-phony too.

No one loves Chris as I do, Simon thought. He felt bitter and miserable. He put on a pleasant face, said, "See you," and moved away towards Chris.

The white splotches on Chris's face looked whiter, and did Simon see a faint blueness at the lips or was he imagining? Chris's breathing was audible. His blue eyes, still alert and striving, swam in water or tears held within bounds by the pink lids. Simon clasped two fingers of the unnaturally plump hand that Chris extended, the left hand which held still another cigarette.

"Chris, I love the cigarette case," said Simon. "You know I always loved it. Just the right present for me. Thank you."

"Simon, what's the matter? You're not yourself." Chris's voice creaked like old furniture, old bones.

"Noth-*ing*," Simon replied, smiling.

A few seconds later, Simon was out of the room. Chris had called for music now, and was there enough champagne?

Simon ran down the garden steps. Wasn't there a gorge, a small waterfall somewhere down here to the right? He looked through trees and underbrush, then he found it—like a promise come true, but how small it was! Barely seven feet to jump down there and hit the rocks, then hardly enough water to drown a baby or a cat! Still if he smashed his skull, that would do. Simon rubbed his palms together, breathed deeply, and felt himself smiling. He was happy, in a quiet and important way. This scene had momentum, a tempo that didn't wish to be slowed or hastened. He looked at the stony, half-grassy ground under his desert boots: nothing to trip him or cause a bad takeoff. He prepared to run.

Then a crackle made him stop. It had come from his right, up the slope.

"Simon?—Hey, *Simon!* We're all looking for you!" It was Carl Parker loping towards him.

"Could you leave me alone? Would you?"

"What do you mean?—*Freddy!*" Carl called loudly up the slope. "Simon's here!"

"Coming," Detweiler's voice said, not far distant.

Carl clapped an arm around Simon's shoulder suddenly. "Come back," he said in a serious tone, swinging Simon towards the house.

Simon's strength exploded, he threw off Carl, and saw Detweiler approaching. Simon ran towards the little gorge, aware that Carl was just behind him. Carl grabbed his arm, Carl's hand slipped down and took a grip on Simon's left hand, swinging Simon around.

"What're you—"

Simon silenced him with a hard punch in the face. Now he had Freddy to deal with, and Freddy was trying to hold his arms. Simon kicked with his knee—ineffectively—got his right arm free and swung at Freddy's chin. Simon dashed again for the gorge.

He was aware of a sharp and long-drawn-out pain, on his head, against his ribs.

His next sensation came through his ears. He imagined that he heard a chorus, though the tune was not discernible. Simon knew he had just passed through a crisis. What kind of crisis? Death. He was dead. Vaguely he recalled that he had wished to die. Where? No matter. So there was a consciousness after death then, not pleasant or unpleasant, and very hazy now, but clarity would come, if he tried for it. Human voices. And what were they speaking? Maybe a strange language that he would have to learn. He imagined that his eyes saw something, and that the color was gray with some pink in it.

"Hello, Simon . . ."

"Simon . . ." said another voice.

"The *second* time . . ."

Simon could not move his arms. His feet also refused to move, or his knees to bend. He thought he was lying flat on his back. Shadow turned into images of human figures. A voice murmured in German. A thin man with a black mustache and white shirt bent over him, thrust a needle into Simon's left thigh or hip, but Simon felt nothing. It was Chris's house again. Or was it another world that merely looked like Chris's house?

"You're okay, Simon. You'll be all right." This was Carl bending over Simon.

Simon realized that he was again on the big leather sofa which was at least three yards long. "And Chris?"

The number of voices reached a crescendo, then died down.

"Go ahead!" a man's voice said in a tone of impatience.

"Chris died around one o'clock. Very peacefully. He—" This was Carl again, speaking softly. "Now it's nearly midnight. You've got to stay put for a while, Simon. Best not to move you tonight, the doctor said."

"Wh—" Simon was growing increasingly sleepy. He tried without success to form the word "Why?"

"Tell him!" said Detweiler's voice.

"You've got two broken arms, Simon, no doubt a few cracked ribs, and a very swollen ankle. Now do you understand why you can't move?" Jonathan spoke gently, then moved back from the sofa and became a shadow that disappeared among the others.

When Simon next woke up, it was different. Dawn was coming through the tall curtains that were not totally closed. And Detweiler—yes, it was Detweiler's form, propped on a similar big sofa some three yards away and parallel to the one Simon was lying on. A dim light from a standing lamp flowed down on Freddy, who had fallen asleep over his book. Freddy was in pajamas and bathrobe again.

And Chris was dead, Simon remembered, his body probably no longer in the house. They were all alone, Detweiler, Jonathan, Carl, and the others who had not left. And Simon was in a state in which he could not move, like someone dead, too. He gasped, but the sound did not awaken Detweiler. He was going to live. He was broken a bit, and he would remain broken, even when the bones mended.

An existence now with Chris gone. That was the fact. And Simon had to see himself in a different way, not exactly reborn—at his age—but as having died and come back to life. He felt he had really done this. Call himself fifty, yes. And give the *William* lead to Russell Johnson. Tell him today. And carry on in Chris's tradition. Chris wouldn't want to see him downcast. Chris wouldn't have wanted him to try to kill himself, and at exactly the same time that Chris himself had died, Simon realized. Chris would have said, "Absurd, Simon. For me? I'm not that important. The rest of your life is important."

Simon laughed a little, and pain hit his ribs on both sides. Simon kept on smiling.

A Clock Ticks
at Christmas

"**H**ave you got a spare franc, madame?"

That was how it began.

Michèle looked down over her armsful of boxes and plastic bags at a small boy in a loose tweed coat and tweed cap that hung over his ears. He had big dark eyes and an appealing smile. "Yes!" She managed to drop two francs which were still in her fingers after paying the taxi.

"*Merci,* madame!"

"And this," said Michèle, suddenly remembering that she had stuck a ten-franc note into her coat pocket a moment ago.

The boy's mouth fell open. "Oh, madame! *Merci!*"

One slippery shopping bag had fallen. The boy picked it up.

Michèle smiled, secured the bag handle with one finger, and pressed the door button with an elbow. The heavy door clicked open, and she stepped over a raised threshold. A shove of her shoulder closed the door, and she crossed the courtyard of her apartment house. Bamboo trees stood like slender sentinels on left and right, and laurels and ferns grew on either side of the cobbled path she took to Court E. Charles would be home, as it was nearly six. What would he say to all the packages, the more than three thousand francs she had spent today? Well, she had done most of their Christmas shopping, and one of the presents was for Charles to give his family—he could hardly complain about that—and the rest of the presents were for Charles himself and her parents, and only one thing was for her, a Hermés belt that she hadn't been able to resist.

"Father Christmas!" Charles said as Michèle came in. "Or Mother Christmas?"

She had let the packages fall to the floor in the hall. "Whew! Yes, a good day! A lot done, I mean. Really!"

"So it seems." Charles helped her to gather the boxes and bags.

Michèle had taken off her coat and slipped out of her shoes. They tossed the parcels on the big double bed in their bedroom, Michèle talking all the while. She told him about the pretty white tablecloth for his parents, and about the little boy downstairs who had asked her for a franc. "A franc—after all I bought today! Such a sweet little boy about ten years old. And so poor looking—his clothes. Just like the old stories about Christmas, I thought. You know? When someone with less asks for such a little bit." Michèle was smiling broadly, happily.

Charles nodded. Michèle's was a rich family. Charles Clement had worked his way up from apprentice mason at sixteen to become the head of his company, Athenas Construction, at twenty-eight. At thirty, he had met Michèle, the daughter of one of his clients, and married her. Sometimes Charles felt dazzled by his success in his work and in his marriage, because he adored Michèle and she was lovely. But he realized that he could more easily imagine himself as the small boy asking for a franc, which he would never have done, than he could imagine himself as Michèle's brother, for instance, dispensing largesse with her particular attitude, at once superior and kindly. He had seen that attitude before in Michèle.

"Only one franc?" Charles said finally, smiling.

Michèle laughed. "No, I gave him a ten-franc note. I had it loose in my pocket—and after all it's Christmas."

Charles chuckled. "That little boy will be back."

Michèle was facing her closet whose sliding doors she had opened. "What should I wear tonight? That light purple dress you like or—the yellow? The yellow one's newer."

Charles circled her waist with his arm. The row of dresses and blouses, long skirts, looked like a tangible rainbow: shimmering gold, velvety blue, beige and green, satin and silk. He could not even see the light purple in all of it, but he said, "The light purple, yes. Is that all right with you?"

"Of course, dear."

They were going out to dinner at the apartment of some friends. Charles went back into the living room and resumed his newspaper, while Michèle showered and changed her clothes. Charles wore his house slippers—the habit of an old man, he thought, though he was only thirty-two. At any rate, it was a habit he had had since his teens, when he had been living with his parents in the Clichy area. Half the time he had come home with his shoes and socks damp from standing in mud or water on a construction lot, and woolen house slippers had felt good. Otherwise Charles was dressed for the evening in a dark blue suit, a shirt with cuff links, a silk tie knotted but not yet tightened at the collar. Charles lit his pipe—Michèle would be a long while yet—and surveyed his handsome living room, thinking of Christmas. Its first sign was the dark green wreath some thirty centimeters in diameter, which Michèle must have bought that morning, and which leaned against the fruit bowl on the dining table. Michèle would put it on the knocker of the apartment door, he knew. The brass fixtures by the fireplace gleamed as usual, poker and tongs, polished by Geneviève, their *femme de ménage*. Four of the six or seven oil paintings on the walls were of Michèle's ancestors, two of them in white ruffled lace collars. Charles poured himself a small Glenfiddich whiskey, and sipped it straight. The best whiskey in the world, in his opinion. Yes, fate had been good to him. He had luxury and comfort, everywhere he looked. He stepped out of his clumsy house slippers and carried them into the bedroom, where he put on his shoes for the evening with the aid of a silver shoehorn. Michèle was still in the bathroom, humming, doing her make-up.

Two days later Michèle again encountered the small boy to whom she had given the ten-franc note. She was nearly at her house door before she saw him, because she had been concentrating on a white poodle that she had just bought. She had dismissed her taxi at the corner of the street, and was carefully leading the puppy on his new black and gold leash along the curb. The puppy did not know in which direction to go, unless Michèle tugged him. He turned in circles, scampered in the wrong direction until his collar checked him, then looked up smiling at Michèle and trotted after her. A man paused to look and admire.

"Not quite three months," Michèle replied to his question.

It was then that she noticed the small boy. He wore the same tweed coat with its collar turned up against the cold, and she realized that it was a man's suit jacket, much too big, with the cuffs rolled back and the buttons adjusted so it would fit more tightly around the child's body.

"*B'jour,* madame!" the boy said. "This is *your* dog?"

"Yes, I've just bought him," said Michèle.

"How much did he cost?"

Michèle laughed.

The boy whipped something out of his pocket. "I brought this for you."

It was a tiny bunch of holly with red berries. As Michèle took it with her free hand, she realized that it was plastic, that the berries were bent on their artificial stems, the tinsel cup crushed. "Thank—you," she said, amused. "Oh, and what do I owe you for this?"

"Nothing at all, madame!" He had an air of pride and looked her straight in the eyes, smiling. His nose was running.

She pressed the door button of her house. "Would you like to come up for a minute—play with the puppy?"

"*Oui, merci!*" he replied, pleased and surprised.

Michéle led the way across the court and into the lift. She unlocked her apartment door, and unfastened the puppy's leash. Then she handed the boy a paper tissue from her handbag, and he blew his nose. The boy and the puppy behaved in the same manner, Michéle thought, looking around, turning in circles, sniffing.

"What shall I name the puppy?" Michèle asked. "Any ideas? What's your name?"

"Paul, madame," the boy replied, and returned to gazing at the walls, the big sofa.

"Let's go in the kitchen. I'll give you—a Coca-Cola."

The boy and the puppy followed her. Michèle set down a bowl of water for the puppy, and took a bottle of Coca-Cola from the fridge.

The boy sipped his drink from a glass, while his eyes wandered over the big white kitchen, eyes that reminded Michèle of open windows, or of a camera's lens. "You give the puppy *biftek hâché*, madame?" asked the boy.

Michèle was spooning the red meat from the butcher's paper into a saucer. "Oh, today, yes. Maybe all the time, a little bit. Later he can eat from tins." The child's eyes had fixed on the meat she was wrapping up, and she said impulsively, "Would you like some? A hamburger?"

"Even uncooked! A little bit—yes." He extended a hand whose nails were filthy, and took what Michèle held out in the teaspoon. Paul shoved the meat into his mouth.

Michèle put the meat package back into the fridge, and nudged the door shut. The boy's hunger made her nervous, somehow. Of course if he were poor, his family wouldn't eat meat often. She didn't want to ask him about this. It was easier for her, a moment later, to offer Paul some cookies from a box that was nearly full. "Take several!" She handed the box to him.

Slowly and steadily, the boy ate them all, while he and Michèle watched the puppy licking the last morsels from his saucer. Then Paul picked up the saucer and carried it to the sink.

"Is this right, madame?"

Michèle nodded. She and Charles had a washing machine, and seldom used the sink for washing dishes. Now the boy was putting the empty cookie box into the yellow garbage bin. The bin was almost full, and the boy asked if he could empty it for her. Michèle shook her head a little, in wonderment, feeling as if a Christmas angel had wandered into her home. The boy and the white puppy! The boy so hungry, and he and the puppy so young! "It's this way—but you don't have to."

The boy wanted to be of help, so she showed him the gray plastic sack at the servants' entrance, where he could dump the contents of the garbage bin. Then they went back into the living room and played with the puppy on the carpet. Michèle had bought a blue rubber ball with a bell in it. Paul rolled the ball carefully for the puppy. He had politely declined to remove his coat or to sit down. Michèle noticed holes at the heels of both his socks. His shoes were in worse condition, cracked between soles and uppers. Even his blue jeans cuffs were tattered. How could a child keep warm in blue jeans in this weather?

"Thank you, madame," said Paul. "I'll go now."

"Aw-*ruff*!" said the puppy, wanting the boy to roll the ball again.

Michèle found herself as awkward suddenly as if she were with an adult from a different country and culture. "Thank you for your visit, Paul. And I wish you a happy Christmas in case I don't see you again."

Paul looked equally ill at ease, twisted his neck, and said, "And to you, madame, happy Christmas.—And you!" He addressed the white puppy. Abruptly he turned towards the door.

"I'd like to give you a present, Paul," Michèle said, following him. "How about a pair of shoes? What size do you wear?"

"Ha!" Was the boy blushing? "Thirty-two. Thirty-three maybe, since I'm growing, my father says." He lifted one foot in a comical manner.

"What does your father do?" Michèle was delighted to ask him a down-to-earth question.

"Deliverer. He takes bottles down from trucks."

Michèle imagined a sturdy fellow hauling down boxes of mineral water, wine, beer from a huge truck and tossing up empty crates. She saw such work all over Paris, every day, and maybe she had even glimpsed Paul's father. "Have you brothers and sisters?"

"One brother. Two sisters."

"And where do you live?"

"Oh—we live in a basement."

Michèle didn't want to ask him about the basement, whether it was a semi- or total basement, or whether his mother worked too. She was cheered by the idea of a present for him, shoes. "Come back tomorrow around eleven, and I'll have a pair of shoes for you."

Paul looked unbelieving, and wriggled his hands nervously in the pockets of his coat. "Yes, okay. At eleven."

The boy wanted to go down in the lift by himself, so Michèle let him.

The next morning at a few minutes past eleven, Michèle was strolling along the pavement near her apartment with the puppy on his leash. She and Charles had decided to name him Ezekiel last evening, a name already shortened to Zeke. Michèle suddenly saw Paul and a smaller figure beside him.

"My sister, Marie-Jeanne," said Paul, looking up at Michèle with his big dark eyes, then at his sister, whose hand he pushed towards Michèle.

Michèle took the little hand and they greeted each other. The sister was a smaller version of Paul, with longer black hair. *The shoes.* Michèle had bought two pairs for Paul. She asked them both to come up. The lift again, the apartment door opening, and the same wonder in the eyes of the sister.

"Try them on, Paul. Both pairs," said Michèle.

Paul sat on the floor and did so, excited and happy. "They both fit! Both pairs!" For fun, he put on a left and a right shoe of different pairs.

Marie-Jeanne was taking more interest in the apartment than in the shoes.

Michèle fetched Coca-Cola. One bottle each might be enough, she thought. Her heart went out to these children, but she was afraid of overdoing it, of losing control somehow. When she brought the cold drinks in, Zeke was starting to chew on one new shoe, and Paul was laughing. Quickly his sister rescued the shoe. Some Coca-Cola got spilled on the carpet, Michèle brought a sponge, and Paul scrubbed away, then rinsed the sponge.

Then suddenly they were both gone, each with a box of shoes under an arm.

That evening Charles could not find his letter-opener. It lay always on his desk in a room off the living room which was their library as well as Charles's study. He asked Michèle if she had possibly taken it.

"No. Maybe it fell on the floor?"

"I looked," said Charles.

But they both looked again. It was of silver, like a flat dagger with the hilt in the form of a coiled serpent.

"Genevieve will find it somewhere," said Michèle, but as soon as the words were out of her mouth, she suspected Paul—or even his sister. A throb went through her, akin to a sense of personal embarrassment, as if she were responsible for the theft, which was only a possibility, not yet a fact. But Michèle felt guilt as she glanced at her husband's slightly troubled face. He was opening a letter with his thumbnail.

"What did you do today, darling?" asked Charles, smiling once more, putting his letter away in a business folder.

Michèle told him she had argued with the telephone company about their last bill and won, this on Charles's behalf as he had queried a long-distance call, had looked in at the hairdresser's but only for an hour, and had aired Zeke three times, and she thought the puppy was learning fast. She did not tell Charles about buying two pairs of shoes for the boy called Paul, or about the visit of Paul and his sister to the apartment.

"And I hung the wreath on the door," said Michèle. "Not a lot of work, I know, but didn't you notice?"

"Of course. How could I have missed it?" He embraced her and kissed her cheek. "Very pretty, darling, the wreath."

That was Saturday. On Sunday Charles worked for a few hours in his office alone, as he often did. Michèle bought a small Christmas tree with an X-shaped base, and spent part of the afternoon decorating it, having put it on the dining table finally, instead of the floor, because the puppy refused to stop playing with the ornaments. Michèle did not look forward to the obligatory visit to Charles's parents—who never had a tree, and even Charles considered Christmas trees a silly import from England—on Christmas Eve Monday at 5 P.M. They lived in a big old walk-up apartment house in the 18th *arrondissement*. Here they would exchange presents and drink hot red wine that always made Michèle feel sickish. The rest of the evening would be jollier at her parents' apartment in Neuilly. They would have a cold midnight supper with champagne, and watch color TV of Christmas breaking all over the world. She told this to Zeke.

"Your first Christmas, Zeke! And you'll have—a *turkey* leg!"

The puppy seemed to understand her, and galloped around the living room with a lolling tongue and mischievous black eyes. And Paul and Marie-Jeanne? Were they smiling now? Maybe Paul was, with his two pairs of shoes. And maybe there was time for her to buy a shirt, a blouse for Marie-Jeanne, a cake for the other brother and sister, before Christmas Day. She could do that Monday, and maybe she'd see Paul and be able to give him the presents. Christmas meant giving, sharing, communicating with friends and neighbors and even with strangers. With Paul, she had begun.

"Oo-woo-woo," said the puppy, crouching.

"One second, Zeke, darling!" Michèle hurried to get his leash.

She flung on a fur jacket, and she and Zeke went out.

Zeke at once made for the gutter, and Michèle gave him a word of praise. The fancy grocery store across the street was open, and Michèle bought a box of candy—a beautiful tin box costing over a hundred francs—because the red ribbon on it had caught her eye.

"Madame—*bonjour!*"

Once more Michèle looked down at Paul's upturned face. His nose was bright pink with cold.

"Happy Christmas again, madame!" Paul said, smiling, stamping his feet. He wore the brown pair of new shoes. His hands were rammed into his pockets.

"Would you like a hot chocolate?" Michèle asked. A *bar-tabac* was just a few meters distant.

"Non, merci." Paul twisted his neck shyly.

"Or soup!" Michèle said with inspiration. "Come up with me!"

"My sister is with me." Paul turned quickly, stiff with cold, and at that moment Marie-Jeanne dashed out of the *bar-tabac.*

"Ah, *bonjour,* madame!" Marie-Jeanne was grinning, carrying a blue straw shopping bag which looked empty, but she opened it to show her brother. "Two packs. That's right?—Cigarettes for my father," she said to Michèle.

"Would you like to come up for a few minutes and see my Christmas tree?" Michèle's hospitality still glowed strongly. What was wrong with giving these two a bowl of hot soup and some candy?

They came. In the apartment, Michèle switched on the radio to London, which was giving out with carols. Just the thing! Marie-Jeanne squatted in front of the Christmas tree and chattered to her brother about the pretty packages amassed at the base, the decorations, the little presents perched in the branches. Michèle was heating a tin of split pea soup to which she had added an equal amount of milk. Good nourishing food! The English choirboys sang a French carol, and they all joined in:

> *Il est né le divin enfant . . .*
> *Chantez hautbois, résonnez musettes . . .*

Then as before they were gone all too suddenly—their laughter and chatter—Zeke barked as if to call them back, and Michèle was left with the empty soup bowls and crumpled chocolate papers to clear away. Impulsively Michèle had given them the pretty cookie box to take home. And Charles was due in a few minutes. Michèle had tidied the kitchen and was walking into the living room, when she heard the click of the lift door and Charles's step in the hall, and at the same time noticed a gap on the mantel. The clock! Charles's ormolu clock! It couldn't be gone. But it *was* gone.

A key was fitted into the lock, and the door opened.

Michèle seized a box—yellow-wrapped, house slippers for Charles— and set it where the clock had been.

"Hello, darling!" Charles said, kissing her.

Charles wanted a cup of tea: the temperature was dropping and he had nearly caught a chill waiting for a taxi just now. Michèle made tea for both of them, and tried to seat herself so that Charles would take a chair that put his back to the fireplace, but this didn't work, as Charles took a different armchair from the one Michèle had intended.

"What's the idea of a present up there?" Charles asked, meaning the yellow package.

Charles had an eye for order. Smiling, still in a good mood, he left his first cup of tea and went to the mantel. He took the package, turned towards the Christmas tree, then looked back at the mantel. "And where's the clock? You took it away?"

Michèle clenched her teeth, longing to lie, to say, yes, she'd put it in a cupboard in order to have room for Christmas decorations on the mantel, but would that make sense? "No, I—"

"Something the matter with the clock?" Charles's face had grown serious, as if he were inquiring about the health of a member of the family whom he loved.

"I don't know where it is," Michèle said.

Charles's brows came down and his body tensed. He tossed the lightweight package down on the table where the tree stood. "Did you see that boy again?—Did you invite him up?"

"Yes, Charles. Yes—I know I—"

"And today was perhaps the second time he was here?"

Michèle nodded. "Yes."

"For God's sake, Michèle! You know that's where my letter-opener went too, don't you? But the clock! My God, it's one hell of a lot more important! Where does this kid live?"

"I don't know."

Charles made a move towards the telephone and stopped. "When was he here? This afternoon?"

"Yes, less than an hour ago. Charles, I really am sorry!"

"He can't live far from here.—How *could* he have done it with you here with him?"

"His sister was here too." Michèle had showed her where the bathroom was. Of course Paul had taken the clock, then, put it in that blue shopping bag.

Charles understood, and nodded grimly. "Well, they'll have a nice Christmas, pawning that. And I'll bet we won't see either of them around here for the next many days—if ever. How could you bring such hoodlums into the *house*?"

Michèle hesitated, shocked by Charles's wrath. It was wrath turned against her. "They were cold and they were hungry—and poor." She looked her husband in the eyes.

"So was my father," Charles said slowly, "when he acquired that clock."

Michèle knew. The ormolu clock had been the Clement family's pride and joy since Charles had been twelve or so. The clock had been the one handsome item in their working-class household. It had caught Michèle's eye the first time she had visited the Clements, because the rest of the furnishings were dreadful *style rustique,* all varnish and formica. And Charles's father had given the clock to them as a wedding present.

"Filthy swine," Charles murmured, drawing on a cigarette, looking at the gap on the mantel. "You don't know such people perhaps, my dear Michèle, but I do. I grew up with them."

"Then you might be more sympathetic! If we can't get the clock back, Charles, I'll buy another for us, as near like it as possible. I can remember exactly how that clock looked."

Charles shook his head, squeezed his eyes shut and turned away.

Michèle left the room, taking the tea things with her. It was the first time she had seen Charles near tears.

Charles did not want to go to the dinner party to which they were invited that evening. He suggested that Michèle go alone and make some excuse for him, and Michèle at first said she would stay at home too, then changed her mind and got dressed.

"I don't see what's the matter with my idea of buying another clock," Michèle said. "I don't see—"

"Maybe you'll never see," Charles said.

Michèle had known Bernard and Yvonne Petit a long time. Both had been friends of Michèle's before she and Charles were married. Michèle wanted very much to tell Yvonne the story about the clock, but it was not a story one could tell at a dinner table of eight, and by coffee time Michèle had decided it was best not to tell it at all: Charles was seriously upset, and the mistake was her own. But Yvonne, as Michèle was leaving, asked her if something was on her mind, and Michèle was relieved to admit there was. She and Yvonne went into a library much like the one in Michèle's apartment, and Michèle told the story quickly.

"We've got just the clock you need *here!*" said Yvonne. "Bernard doesn't even much like it. Ha! That's a terrible thing to say, isn't it? But the clock's right here, darling Michèle. Look!" Yvonne pushed aside some invitation cards, so that the clock on the library mantel showed plainly on its splayed base: black hands, its round face crowned with a tiara of gilded knobs and curlicues.

The clock was indeed very like the one that had been stolen. While Michèle hesitated, Yvonne found newspaper and a plastic bag in the kitchen and wrapped the clock securely. She pressed it into Michèle's hands. "A Christmas present!"

"But it's the principle of the thing. I know Charles. So do you, Yvonne. If the clock that was stolen were from my family, if I'd known it all my life, even, I know it wouldn't matter to me so much."

"I know, I know."

"It's the fact that these kids were poor—and that it's Christmas. I asked them in, Paul first, by himself. Just to see their faces light up was so wonderful for me. They were so grateful for a bowl of soup. Paul told me they live in a basement somewhere."

Yvonne listened, though it was the second time Michèle had told her all this. "Just put the clock on the mantel where the clock was—and hope for the best." Yvonne spoke with a confident smile.

When Michèle got home by taxi, Charles was in bed reading. Michèle unwrapped the clock in the kitchen and set it on the mantel. Amazing how much it did look like the other clock! Charles, behind his newspaper, said that he had taken Zeke out for a walk half an hour ago. Otherwise Charles was silent, and Michèle did not try to talk to him.

The next morning, Christmas Eve, Charles spotted the new clock on the mantel as he walked into the living room from the kitchen, where he and Michèle had just breakfasted. Charles turned to Michèle with a shocked look in his eyes. "All right, Michèle. That's enough."

"Yvonne gave it to me. To us. I thought—just for *Christmas*—" What had she thought? How had she meant to finish that sentence?

"You do *not* understand," he said firmly. "I gave the police a description of that clock last night. I went to the police station, and I intend to get that clock back! I also informed them of the boy aged 'about ten' and his sister who live somewhere in the neighborhood in a basement."

Charles spoke as if he had declared war on a formidable enemy. To Michèle it was absurd. Then as Charles talked on in his tone of barely repressed fury about dishonesty, handouts to the irresponsible, to those who had not earned them or even tried to, about hooligans' disrespect for private property, Michèle began to understand. Charles felt that his castle had been invaded, that the enemy had been admitted by his own wife—and that she was on their side. Are you a Communist, Charles might have asked, but he didn't. Michèle didn't consider herself a Communist, never had.

"I simply think the rich ought to share," she interrupted.

"Since when are we rich, really rich, I mean?" Charles replied. "Well, I know. Your family, they *are* rich and you're used to it. You inherited it. That's not your fault."

Why on earth should it be her fault, Michèle wondered, and began to feel on surer ground. She had read often enough in newspapers and books that wealth had to be shared in this century, or else. "Well—and as for these kids, I'd do the same thing again," she said.

Charles's cheeks shook with exasperation. "They insulted us! This was thievery!"

Michèle's face grew warm. She left the room, as furious as Charles. But Michèle felt that she had a point. More than that, that she was right. She should put it into words, organize her argument. Her heart was beating fast. She glanced at the open bedroom door, expecting Charles's figure, expecting his voice, asking her to come back. There was silence.

Charles went off to his office half an hour later, and said he would probably not be back before 3:30. They were to go to his parents' house between four and five. Michèle rang up Yvonne, and in the course of their conversation Michèle's thoughts became clearer, and her trickle of tears stopped.

"I think Charles's attitude is wrong," Michèle said.

"But you mustn't say that to a man, dear Michèle. You be careful."

That afternoon at four, Michèle began tactfully with Charles. She asked him if he liked the wrapping of the present for his mother. The package contained the white tablecloth, which she had shown Charles.

"I'm not going. I can't." He went on, over Michèle's protestations. "Do you think I can face my parents—admit to them that the clock's been stolen?"

Why mention the clock, unless he wanted to ruin Christmas, Michèle thought. She knew it was useless to try to persuade him to come, so she gave it up. "I'll go—and take their presents." So she did, and left Charles at home to sulk, and to wait for a possible telephone call from the police, he had said.

Michèle had gone out laden with Charles's parents' presents as well as those for her own parents. Charles had said he would turn up at her parents' Neuilly apartment at 8 P.M. or so. But he did not. Michèle's parents suggested that she telephone Charles: maybe he had fallen asleep, or was working and had lost track of time, but Michèle did not telephone him. Everything was so cheerful and beautiful at her parents' house—their tree, the champagne buckets, her nice presents, one a travel umbrella in a leather case. Charles and the clock story loomed like an ugly black shadow in the golden glow of her parents' living room, and Michèle again blurted out the events.

Her father chuckled. "I remember that clock—I think. Nothing so great about it. It wasn't made by Cellini after all."

"It's the sentiment, however, Edouard," said Michèle's mother. "A pity it had to happen just at Christmas. And it was careless of you, Michèle. But—I have to agree with you, yes, they were simply little urchins of the *street,* and they were tempted."

Michèle felt further strengthened.

"Not the end of the world," Edouard murmured, pouring more champagne.

Michèle remembered her father's words the next day, Christmas Day, and on the day after. It was not the end of the world, but the end of something. The police had not found the clock, but Charles believed they would. He had spoken to them with some determination, he assured Michèle, and had brought them a colored drawing of the clock which Charles had made at the age of fourteen.

"Naturally the thieves wouldn't pawn it so soon," Charles said to Michèle, "but they're not going to drop it in the Seine either. They'll try to get cash for it sooner or later, and then we'll nail them."

"Frankly, I find your attitude unchristian and even cruel," said Michèle.

"And I find your attitude—silly."

It was not the end of the world, but it was the end of their marriage. No later words, no embrace if it ever came, could compensate Michèle for that remark from her husband. And, just as vital, she felt a deep dislike, a real aversion to her within Charles's heart and mind. And she for him? Was it not a similar feeling? Charles had lost something that Michèle considered human—if he had ever had it. With his poorer, less privileged background, Charles should have had more compassion than she, Michèle thought. What was wrong? And what was right? She felt muddled, as she sometimes did when she tried to ponder the phrases of carols, or of some poems, which could be interpreted in a couple of ways, and yet the heart, or sentiment always seemed to seek and find a path of its own, as hers had done, and wasn't this right? Wasn't it right to be forgiving, especially at this time of year?

Their friends, their parents counseled patience. They should separate for a week or so. Christmas always made people nervous. Michèle could come and stay at Yvonne's and Bernard's apartment, which she did. Then she and Charles could talk again, which they did. But nothing really changed, not at all.

Michèle and Charles were divorced within four months. And the police never found the clock.

A Shot from Nowhere

The hotel room in which Andrew Spatz lay was yellowish and vaguely dusty, like the dry little plaza beyond his single window, like the town itself. The town was called Quetzalan. Three days ago, Andrew had taken a local bus from the city of Jalapa, not caring where the bus wandered to, and he had got off with his suitcase and box of oil paints, brushes and sketch pads in this town, because it had pleased him at his first glimpse through the bus window. It looked like a town that nobody knew of or cared about. It looked real. And on the plaza he had found the Hotel Corona, maybe the only hotel in the town.

Now, unfortunately, he was suffering from the usual intestinal cramps, and since yesterday he thought he had a fever, though in the heat it was hard to tell. In the early mornings, he set out and walked up in the hills around the town and made sketches to be used later, possibly, for paintings. He sketched everywhere, from an iron bench in the plaza, from a curb, from a table in a bar. But when noon came, and after he had had a simple meal of tacos and beans and a beer, it was time to hide from the sun for a few hours, like everyone else. Quetzalan fell silent as a ghost town from half past twelve until nearly four every afternoon. And the yellow sun bore down with unnecessary force, as if to grind into the consciousness of man and beast and plant the fact that it had conquered, that rain and coolness were far away, maybe gone forever. Andrew had strange dreams when he dozed in the afternoons.

On one afternoon he awakened from a dream of red snakes in a cave in a desert. The snakes did not notice him in the dream, he did not feel in any danger, but the dream was disturbing. Andrew threw off the sheet he had pulled over himself against the inevitable fly or two, and went to the basin in the corner of his room. He took off his drip-dry shirt, wet it again in cool water, and put it back on. His window was open about ten inches top and bottom, but no breeze came.

Andrew glanced at the window, and a movement outside caught his attention.

There was the boy again, with his milk pan for the kittens. The boy looked about thirteen, barefoot in soiled white trousers and white shirt with sleeves rolled up. He was only some six yards away from where Andrew stood in his room, so Andrew could see clearly the tin pie plate and the milk in it. Now as a skinny brindle kitten staggered from some bushes in the plaza, Andrew knew that the boy was going to draw the pan back, as he had done before.

A second kitten appeared, and as the two kittens hunched and lapped, the boy looked over his shoulder, grinning mischievously, as if to see if anyone were watching him. The plaza and the surrounding walks and streets were quite deserted. A grown cat, so thin its bones made shadows in its fur, galloped from the hotel side of the plaza towards the milk pan, and Andrew heard the boy giggle softly, and saw him scramble to his feet, spilling a little of the milk from the pan he was taking away. Why?

Andrew pulled on his jeans, shoved his feet into sneakers, and ran out of his room. Within seconds, he was outside the hotel door on the sidewalk. The boy was walking toward Andrew, but at an angle off to Andrew's right.

"*Porquè*—" Andrew stopped, hearing faint laughter from somewhere left of him.

The boy trotted away, dumping what remained of the milk on the street.

On his left, Andrew saw a group of three or four men, one with a hand camera of the kind that could make movies. Were they shooting a film? Was that why the boy had to repeat the cat-feeding scene? The men were middle-aged, and looked like ordinary Mexicans, though not peasants. Andrew saw one laugh, and wave a hand in a gesture that might mean "The hell with it" or "Muffed that one again." At any rate, they turned away, drifted out of Andrew's sight.

Back in his room, Andrew removed sneakers and jeans and again lay on his bed on his back. What was the meaning of it? Why were three or four men, one with a camera, out in the hot sun at 2 P.M.? Was the boy an actor or was he a little sadist? Strange.

Andrew felt that the whole past month had been strange. The girl he was in love with in New York, the girl he had thought would last, had met someone else a month ago. This had so thrown him, he hadn't been able to attend classes at the Art Students League for two or three days, and he had felt a bit suicidal or at least self-destructive. He had telephoned his married sister Esther in Houston, and she had invited him to come and stay for a few days. He had not talked much to his sister, but she had been cheering. And there was Mexico which he had never seen, so near when one was already in Houston, so he had taken a slow, cheap train south. Everything he had seen was different, fascinating. But as yet Andrew didn't know what to make of his life, or of his feelings now.

His nap was ended by the jukebox of the Bar Felipe starting up in a corner of the square, which meant it was around four. The jukebox would play nonstop till nearly midnight. Andrew washed at the basin, dressed again, and gathered his sketching equipment. The hotel lobby was deserted as usual when he walked out, though there were a couple of other guests in the hotel, Mexican men, both very quiet.

At the Bar Felipe, Andrew treated himself to an iced tea, and kept an eye out for the men or any one of them whom he had seen watching the boy with the kittens. And for the boy himself. None of these came in through the open doors or walked past on the sidewalk. Other customers of Felipe, workmen with tattered sombreros, wearing tire-soled sandals, came up to the bar to drink a bottle of beer or the brightly colored orange drink that seemed very popular, and they all glanced at Andrew, but didn't stare at him as they had on his first day in town. A dog, thin as a whippet but of indeterminable breed, came up to Andrew's table hopefully, but Andrew hadn't ordered any potato chips or peanuts.

Andrew was pleased with his work of that afternoon. He had sketched two landscapes with color pencils, introducing a lot of purple in the yellow and tan hills. One drawing showed the cluster of tan and pinkish houses that formed the town.

He dined at a tiny restaurant he had discovered in a side street off the plaza, a place hardly bigger than a kitchen, with only four tables. It catered to laborers, Andrew had observed, plus a couple of men of sixty or so who were unshaven and always slightly drunk. Andrew ordered *frijoles refritos,* tortillas, and a mug of boiled milk. The smell of peppery meat in the place sickened him.

The next day repeated the day before it. Sketching in the morning, a light lunch, an orange in his room afterwards. Fruit you had to peel was free of germs, Andrew remembered, and the sweet juice was wonderfully refreshing. Beads of sweat stood on his forehead and seemed to return as soon as he had wiped them away.

Gradually, then all at once, the silence of the siesta period fell outside his window. Not a footstep sounded, not the twitter of a bird. It was the sun's time, and the time lasted nearly four hours while life cowered in little rooms like his, in shade anywhere. Andrew was lying on his back with a wet towel across his forehead, when he heard the *tink* of metal on cement. With nervous energy, and out of curiosity, he got up to see what might be moving outside.

The boy was there, in the same clothing, in the same place, and with the same pie tin of milk. And here came one kitten shakier than yesterday. And there was the boy's smile over his shoulder, quick and furtive.

Andrew's sun-bleached brows drew closer together as he stared. Now—yes, *now* the boy was sliding the pan back from the kitten who had been joined by the second kitten, and the boy set one foot under him, ready to rise with the pan.

There was a crack like a gunshot, not loud, but shocking in the silence.

The boy sagged at once, the pan made a little clatter and the milk spilled. The kittens lapped greedily. And here came the galloping older cat, the skinny brindle, as before.

A film, Andrew thought, still staring. Then he saw a red spot on the boy's shirt. It spread downward along the boy's right side. A plastic paint container that the boy had opened? Was the camera turning? The boy did not move.

Andrew got into his jeans and sneakers with crazy speed and left his room. He stopped on the sidewalk and looked left, expecting to see the camera crew again, but the corner there was deserted. No one was in sight, except the boy.

Andrew wet his lips, hesitated, then took a couple of steps in the direction of the boy, looked again to his left for the camera crew, then went on. The blood, or whatever it was, had reached the sidewalk and was flowing towards the street gutter. One of the kittens was in fact interested in it.

"Hey!" Andrew said. "*Hey,* boy!" Andrew stretched a hand out, but did not touch the boy's shoulder. The boy's eyes were half open. Andrew now saw the bullet hole in the white shirt.

He trotted towards the Bar Felipe, thinking that Felipe would be more easily aroused than the hotel proprietor, who seemed to close himself behind a couple of doors at the back of the hotel during siesta time.

"Hey!—*Felipe!*" Andrew knocked on the closed wooden doors of the bar. "Open!—*Por favor! Es importante!*" After a few seconds, Andrew tried again. He banged with his fist. He looked around the square. Not a shutter had opened, not a head showed at any window. Crazy!

"*Qué quiere?*" asked Felipe, having opened his door a little. He wore only pajama trousers and was barefoot.

"*Un niño—herido!*" Andrew gasped, pointing.

Felipe took two cautious steps on to the hot sidewalk, so he could see along the plaza's side, and at once jumped back into the shade of his doorway, waved a hand angrily and said something which Andrew took to mean "Don't bother me with that!"

"But—a doctor—or the police!" Andrew pushed against the doors which Felipe was trying rapidly to close, then heard a bolt being slid on the other side. Andrew trotted back to his hotel.

The hotel desk was deserted. Andrew banged his palm a couple of times on the little bell on the counter. "Señor *Diego!*"

There was nothing to stop him from using the telephone behind the counter, but he didn't know the police number and didn't see a directory.

"Señor *Diego!*" Andrew went to the closed door to the left of the counter and knocked vigorously.

He heard a grumbling shout from behind the door, then house-slippered footsteps.

Señor Diego, a middle-sized man with gray in his hair and mustache, looked at Andrew with surprise and annoyance. "What's the matter?" he asked, pulling his cotton bathrobe closer about him.

"A boy is dead! Out there!" Andrew pointed. "Didn't you hear the shot? A couple of minutes ago?"

Señor Diego frowned, walked a few paces across his lobby, and peered through the open doors of the hotel. The boy was quite visible from here. The three cats, the two kittens and the older cat, were still lapping at the blood, but with less enthusiasm, as the blood was drying or not flowing any longer. "Bad boy," Señor Diego commented softly.

"But—we telephone the police?"

Señor Diego blinked and seemed to ponder. It was the first time Andrew had seen him without his glasses.

"The police or a doctor!—Or we carry him in?"

"No!" Señor Diego gave Andrew a scathing glance—as if he detested him, Andrew felt—and moved towards the door of his living quarters. Then he turned and looked at Andrew. "The police will find him."

"But maybe he's not *dead*!" Andrew felt torn between an impulse to carry the boy into the hotel, and to leave him as he was for police detectives to determine where the shot had come from. Andrew went behind the counter to the telephone, picked it up, and was looking at the disk of emergency numbers on the telephone's base, when Señor Diego yanked the telephone from his hands.

"All right, the police! *Then* you will see . . ."

Andrew could not understand the rest.

Señor Diego dialed a number. Then he mumbled several words into the telephone. "*Sí-sí,* Hotel Corona. Okay." He hung up, and shook his head nervously. "Do not move from this hotel!" he commanded, scowling at Andrew.

Anger flowed through Andrew, and his face felt as if it were going to explode. He went off down the hall to his room, whose door was slightly open still. *Do not move from this hotel!* Why should he? Andrew let cold water run in his basin. His face looked dark pink in the mirror. He took off his shirt again, wet it, and put it back on. At once he was too cool, even shivering. He had been listening for the sound of a car motor, and now it came. Andrew went to his window, but his eyes were drawn first to the boy in white who lay on the plaza's sidewalk, in sun and shadow. No cats now. A car door banged shut.

He heard voices in the lobby, then the creak of a couple of shutters in the plaza. A policeman in faded khaki and a visored cap bent over the boy, touched the boy's shoulder, then straightened and walked towards the hotel door.

Two policemen and Señor Diego came into Andrew's room. Suddenly all three seemed to be talking at once, but quite calmly, as in a dream, Andrew thought. The policemen questioned him calmly. Andrew kept saying, "I *heard* the shot, yes . . . I was *here* . . . Just ten minutes ago . . . No, no. Not me, *no!* I have no gun. I saw the boy fall! . . . Ask Señor Felipe!" Andrew pointed. "I went—"

"Señor Felipe!" said the oldest of the policemen, who now numbered three, and threw a smile at Señor Diego.

Andrew knew that he had not made his story clear. But why hadn't he? What he was saying was quite simple, even if his Spanish was primitive. He watched the policemen conferring. His ears started ringing, he wanted to sit down, but instead went to his window for some air. Three or four people now milled about the fallen boy, not touching him. Curious townspeople had at last emerged.

"You come with us," said a mustached policeman, reaching towards Andrew as if to take him by the wrist.

Andrew was suddenly conscious of the fact that each of the policemen carried a gun at his hip and a nightstick at his other hip.

"But I can tell you everything *here,*" Andrew said. "I *saw* it, that's all."

"But if you shot?" said one cop.

Another policeman made a gesture as if to shut him up.

Señor Diego was smiling, murmuring something to the oldest policeman.

A handcuff snapped on one of Andrew's wrists as if by magic, and the policemen seemed to be arguing about whether to put the other wrist in the second handcuff or to attach that to a policeman's wrist, and they decided on Andrew. He was walked out between two policemen with his wrists together in front of him. The boy lay as before, and the people around him now gave their attention to Andrew and the police, who were emerging from the hotel door into the sunlight.

"My tourist card!" Andrew cried, jerking his arm away from a policeman who had hold of him. In English he said, "I demand to have my tourist card with me!"

"Hah!" But this same policeman, after a word with a colleague, seemed to agree that they take Andrew back to his room.

Andrew took his card from the pocket in the lid of his suitcase, and a policeman took it from him, glanced at it with the air of not reading a word, then stuck it in his own back pocket.

The tan police wagon was a decrepit Black Maria with metal benches inside. Cigarette butts littered the ridged metal floor, along with stains that looked like blood and what might have been dried vomit. The car had no springs, and potholes jolted them up from the benches. The vehicle, though open to the air with its heavy wire mesh sides, seemed to hold heat like a closed oven. The policemen's shirts became darker with sweat, they took off their caps and wiped their foreheads, talking all the while merrily.

Then suddenly Andrew was on the ridged floor. He had almost fainted, had lost his balance, and now the two policemen were hauling him back on to the bench. Andrew had no strength, as in a dream in which he couldn't escape from something. It's all a dream, he thought, because of the fever he had. Wasn't he really lying on his bed in his hotel room?

The wagon stopped. They all went up a couple of steps into a yellowish stone building and into a large room with a high ceiling, maybe formerly the anteroom of a private dwelling, but which was now unmistakably a police station. An officer in uniform approached an unoccupied desk at the back of the room, beside which hung a limp and faded flag on a tall staff.

Andrew asked for the toilet. He had to ask twice, had to insist, and insist also that his handcuffs be undone. A police officer accompanied him and stood indifferently near the doorless toilet—a hole in a tiled square on the floor—while Andrew attended to his needs. There was no toilet paper, not even any newspaper scraps on the nail in the wall beside the hanging chain, which produced no water when Andrew tugged at it. It was during these unpleasant moments that Andrew became sure that he was not dreaming.

Now he was standing before the desk in the large room, with a policeman on either side of him. One policeman narrated something rapidly, and handed the man at the desk Andrew's tourist card. This was valid for a three-week stay in Mexico, and Andrew was so far well within that limit.

"Spatz—Andrew Franklin—born Orlando, Florida," the officer murmured, and continued with his birth date.

Suddenly Andrew had a vision of his blonde sister Esther, happy and laughing, as she had looked just two weeks ago, when she had been trying to hold her two-year-old son still enough for Andrew to make a sketch. Andrew said in careful Spanish, "Sir, there is no reason why I am here. I saw a boy—shot."

"Hererra—Fernando," said a policeman at Andrew's elbow, as if performing a detail of duty. The name of the boy had already been uttered a few minutes earlier.

"*Sí-sí,*" said the desk officer calmly, then to Andrew, "Who shot?"

"I did not see—from where the shot came."

"It was just outside your hotel window. Ground floor room you have. You could have shot," said the desk officer. Or was it, "You have shot?"

"But I have no gun!" Andrew turned to one policeman, then the other. "You have *seen* my room."

One policeman said something to the desk officer about the Bar Felipe.

"Ahah!" The desk officer listened to further narration.

Was the cop saying he'd got rid of a gun between his hotel room and the Bar Felipe? The shot must have come from a rifle, Andrew thought. What was "rifle" in Spanish?

"The boy had robbed you," said the desk officer.

"No! I did not say that, never!"

"He was a very bad boy. A criminal," said the desk officer weightily, as if this altered the facts somehow.

"But I simply wanted to tell his death—to the Bar Felipe, to—" Andrew's hands were free, and he spread his arms to indicate a length. "With a gun so long—surely."

"You saw the gun?"

"*No!* I say—because of the *distance*—There was no one but the boy in the plaza when he—shot," Andrew finished lamely, exhausted now.

The desk officer beckoned, and the two policemen came closer to the desk. All three talked softly, and all at once, and Andrew hadn't a clue as to what they were saying. Then the two policemen returned to Andrew, and each took him by an arm. They were leading him towards a hall, towards a cell, probably. Andrew turned suddenly.

"I have the right to notify the American Consulate in Mexico City!" he shouted in English to the desk officer who was on his feet now.

"We shall notify the Consulate," he replied calmly in Spanish.

Andrew took a step towards the desk and said in Spanish, "I want to do it, please."

The desk officer shrugged. "Here is the number. Shall I dial it for you?"

"All right," said Andrew, because he didn't know the code for Mexico City. He didn't entirely trust the desk officer, but he was able to stand on the officer's left, and he saw that the number he dialed corresponded to the number in the officer's ledger beside EE UU Consulado.

"You see?" said the desk officer, after the telephone had rung at the other end eight or nine times. "Closed until four."

Andrew's watch showed ten past three. "Then again at four—I try."

The officer nodded.

The two policemen took him in charge again. Down the hall they went, and stopped at a wooden door in which a square had been cut at eye level.

The cell had one barred window, a bed, and a bucket in a corner.

"At four!" Andrew said to his escort of two, pointing to his wristwatch. "To telephone."

They might not have heard him. They were chatting about something else, like old friends, and after turning of locks and sliding of a couple of bolts, Andrew heard them strolling down the hall, and their voices faded out and were replaced by a moaning and muttering much closer. Andrew looked around, half expecting to find another person in the cell with him, in a corner or under the bed, but the drunken or demented voice was coming from the other side of a brick wall that formed one side of the cell.

A crazy, boastful laugh came after a stream of angry-sounding Spanish.

The town drunk hauled in to sleep it off, Andrew supposed. Andrew sat on the bed. It felt like rock. There was one sheet on it, maybe to protect the blanket, a more valuable item, from being pressed too hard against the coarse wire that was the bed's surface. He felt thirsty.

"Ah—*waaaaah!*" said the nonstop voice in the next cell. "*Yo mi 'cuerdo—'cuerdo*—woooosh-la! *Oof!*"

Of all strange things to happen, Andrew thought. What if it were all a show, all pretense, as in a film? Why hadn't he told the officer at the desk about the three (or four?) men he had seen yesterday, apparently photographing the boy who had been shot today, laughing even, as the boy drew the pan of milk back from the kittens? Were those men of significance? Was someone filming a "candid" movie, and could he even be part of it? Could there be a hidden camera filming him now? Andrew glanced at the upper corners of his unlit cell, and became aware of the smell of old urine. He himself stank of nervous sweat. All he needed now was fleas or lice from the blanket. He snatched the blanket from the metal bed, and took it to the only source of light, the barred window opposite the brick wall. He didn't see any lice or fleas, but he shook the blanket anyway and a thin cockroach fell out. Andrew stepped on it, with a feeling of small triumph. The floor was of rather pretty gray stone slabs. This might have been a home once, he thought, because the floor was handsome, as was the stone floor in the big room in front. The red brick wall between him and the mumbling inmate had been recently put there. Reassured somewhat about the blanket, Andrew lay down on his back and tried to collect himself.

He could explain himself in one minute to an English-speaking person at the Consulate. If that didn't work, Mexico City was only about two hours away by car. A man from the Consulate could get here by six or so. And though Andrew had a New York address just now, his sister was next door in Houston, Texas. She could find a Spanish-speaking American lawyer. But surely things wouldn't get *that* bad!

Andrew gave a tremendous sigh and closed his eyes.

Hadn't he the right to a glass of water? Even a pitcher of it to wash with?

"Hey!—*Hey!*" he yelled, and banged on the door a couple of times. "*Agua—por favor!*"

No one came. Andrew tried the yelling and banging again, then gave it up. He had a response only from the drunk next door, who seemed to want to engage him in conversation. Andrew glanced at his watch, lay down again, and closed his eyes.

He saw the fallen boy, the spreading red on his white shirt, the dusty green of the plaza's trees. He saw it sharply, as if the scene were six yards in front of him, and he opened his eyes to rid himself of the vision.

At four, he shouted, then shouted and banged more loudly. After more than five minutes, a policeman said through the square aperture:

"Qué pasa?"

"I want to telephone!"

The door was opened. They walked to the desk in front, where the desk officer sat, in shirtsleeves now, with his jacket over the back of his chair. The air seemed warmer than before. Andrew repeated his request to telephone the American Consulate. The officer dialed.

This time the Consulate answered, and the officer spoke in Spanish to a woman, Andrew judged from the voice he heard faintly, then to a man.

"I must speak to someone in English!" Andrew whispered urgently.

The officer continued in Spanish for a while, then passed the telephone to Andrew.

The man at the other end did speak English. Andrew gave his name, and said he was being held in a jail in Quetzalan for something he did not do.

"Do you have a tourist card?"

"Tourist card," Andrew said to the desk officer, not having memorized his number, and the officer pulled a manila envelope from a desk drawer and produced the card. Andrew read the number out.

"What are you being held for?" asked the American voice.

"I witnessed a shooting outside my hotel." Andrew described what had happened. "I reported it and—now I'm being accused of it. Or suspected of it." Andrew's throat was dry and hoarse. "I need a lawyer—someone who can speak for me."

"Your occupation, sir?" asked the cool voice.

"Painter. Well, I'm a student."

"Your age?"

"Twenty-two. Is there someone in this area who can help me?"

"Not today, I'm afraid."

The conversation dragged maddeningly on. The Consulate could not possibly send a representative until tomorrow noon. The slant of the man's questions gave Andrew the feeling that his interrogator was not sure whether to believe him or not. The man told Andrew that he was being held on suspicion, and that there was a limit to what the American Consulate could do at a moment's notice. Andrew was asked if he possessed a gun.

"No!—Can I give you the phone number of my sister in Houston? You can call her collect. She might be able to do something—faster."

The man patiently took her name and telephone number, repeated that he was sorry nothing could be done today, and as Andrew stammered, wanting to make sure the man would telephone his sister, the desk officer pulled the telephone from Andrew's grasp and came out with a spate of Spanish in a good-natured, even soothing tone, added a chuckle and hung up.

"Noon tomorrow," the desk officer said to Andrew, and turned his attention to some papers on his desk.

Had the desk officer told the Consulate that he had been drunk and disorderly? "Can you not ask Señor Diego of the Hotel Corona to come here?"

The desk officer did not bother replying, and gestured for the policemen to take Andrew away.

Andrew asked for water, and a glass was brought quickly. "More, please." Andrew held his hands apart to indicate the height of a pitcher.

The pitcher arrived a few minutes after Andrew was back in his cell. He washed his face and torso with his own wet shirt, letting the water fall on the stone floor. He was angry, and at the same time too weak to be angry. Absurd! He lay on the bed half awake and half asleep, and saw a series of visions, lots of people rushing (as he had never seen them) along the sidewalks of the plaza, and the grinning mouth, the big white fangs, the bulging eyes of the Aztec god he had sketched a few days ago near Mexico City. The atmosphere was menacing in all these half-dreams.

Supper arrived around six, rice with a red pepper sauce in a metal bowl, another bowl of beans. The rice dish smelled as if the bits of meat in it were tainted, but he ate the rice and beans for the strength they would give.

Andrew spent a chilly night, curled in his blanket. He was still cold at ten in the morning. At a quarter to noon, he clamored for the door to be opened. After several minutes, a different policeman from the ones Andrew knew arrived and asked what he wanted. Andrew said he was expecting a man from the American Consulate now, and said he wanted to speak to the "Capitano" at once, meaning the desk officer. All this was through the square in Andrew's door.

The policeman strolled away without a word, and Andrew didn't know whether he was going to be ignored or whether the policeman was going to return. The policeman returned with a second policeman, and they opened his cell door.

The desk officer had gone off to lunch, and Andrew was not allowed to use the telephone.

"I waited until twelve as I was told!" Andrew said, feeling that his Spanish was improving under his difficulties. "I demand—"

The two men took his arms. Andrew squirmed around to look at the wide open door again, hopefully, but it was empty save for the figures of two police guards standing facing each other, or rather leaning, in the doorway.

"You wait in your cell," said one policeman.

So Andrew was back in his cell. He had thrown up his breakfast of watery chocolate and bread hours ago, and now there was a smelly plate of something on the floor by his bed. He picked up the plate and tried to throw its contents through the barred window, but half of it fell on the floor.

"*Ah—tee-eee—ta—coraz—zón* . . ." sang the idiot in the next cell. "*Adiós, mujeres . . . des al . . .*"

Very likely he'd have to wait out the siesta period till four! Andrew uttered the worst curse he knew in English. The fact that he had the strength to curse cheered him. He would telephone his sister at four. He fell on his bed, not caring if he slept or not, wanting only the hours to pass until four.

Andrew was asleep when he heard the clink and scrape of various closures on his door being undone. Ten past four, he saw by his watch, and he got up from the bed, blinking.

"You come," said a policeman.

Andrew followed the one policeman to the front room again. The desk officer was on the telephone now. Andrew had to stand for several minutes while the officer made a few calls one after the other, one a personal call: the officer was asking about somebody's baby, and spoke about a dinner next Saturday night. At last the desk officer looked at Andrew.

"Spatz Andreo—you are to leave this building, leave your hotel, leave the United States of Mexico—for your safety," he said.

Andrew was puzzled, but leaving this building sounded pleasant. "I am free?"

The desk officer sighed, as if Andrew were not completely free of suspicion, or even guilt. "You have my orders," he murmured.

Andrew had nothing of his own in the cell, so he did not need to go back. "The *señor* from the American Consulate—"

"No one from the Consulate is coming."

Had the Consulate telephoned? Andrew thought it wise to ask no more questions.

"You will leave the country within twenty-four hours. Understood?" The desk officer handed Andrew his tourist card and a square of paper which he tore from a block and of which he had a carbon copy. "Please give this paper to the Mexican border police or the passport control at the airport before eighteen hours tomorrow."

Andrew looked at the form, which had his name, tourist card number and 18:00 written in with a pen. It was an order to leave, but in the list of "reasons" nothing had been indicated.

"*Adíos,*" said the desk officer.

"*Adíos,*" Andrew replied.

Two policemen, one of whom drove the wagon, took Andrew to within two streets of the Hotel Corona, and asked him to get out and go straight to his hotel. Andrew started walking. He was aware that he looked filthy, and wavering from weakness he might appear drunk also, so he avoided the eyes of a couple of the townspeople—a woman with a basket of laundry on her head, an old man with a cane. They both stared at him. Had he imagined that the old man had nodded and smiled at him?

"*Señor!*" said a small boy on the sidewalk near the hotel door. This was a greeting, the boy had smiled shyly, and dashed on at a run.

Señor Diego was standing behind the counter in the hotel lobby when Andrew entered.

"*Tardes,*" Andrew said in a weary voice, and waited for his key.

"*Buenas tardes, señor,*" replied Señor Diego, laying Andrew's key on the counter. He nodded slightly, with the hint of a smile.

A contemptuous smile? Did Señor Diego know already, having been informed by a telephone call from the desk officer, that he had to leave the country in twenty-four hours? Probably. "Can I have a bath, please?"

He could. Señor Diego went at once to the bathroom, which was down the hall from Andrew's room. Andrew had had a couple of baths there; one paid a little extra, that was all. Andrew unlocked his room door. The bed was made. Nothing seemed changed. He looked into the top of his suitcase and saw that his folder of traveler's checks was still there. His billfold was still in the inside pocket of his jacket in the closet, and he looked into it: several thousand pesos still, and maybe none at all had been removed.

Andrew took clean clothes with him into the bathroom. The humble but tidy bathroom looked luxurious. He soaped himself, washed his hair, cleaned the tub with a scrubbing brush he found in a bucket, then soaked his jeans, shirt and underpants in more hot water, soap and cleaning powder, and rinsed his hair at the basin. Life had its sweet moments! And goddamn the Consulate! A fat lot of help *they'd* been!

Or, Andrew thought a moment later as he pulled on clean Levi's, had the American Consulate rung up this morning, said or threatened something unless the police station made itself clear? Andrew decided to keep his resentment or his gratitude to himself until he learned something definite.

He hung his damp clothes on hangers at the window in his room, and put some old newspapers on the tiled floor below them. Andrew did not know what attitude to take with Señor Diego, whether to consider him friend or foe or neutral, because certainly he hadn't been helpful yesterday when the police had come and taken him away. Andrew decided to be merely polite.

"Señor Diego," he began with a nod. "I leave tomorrow morning. On the first bus for Mexico City. So—I should like to pay you now."

Señor Diego reached for Andrew's note in a pigeonhole behind him, and he added the item of the bath with a ballpoint pen. "*Sí, señor.* Here you are.—You are looking better now!"

Andrew smiled despite himself, as he pulled limp pesos out of his billfold. He watched Señor Diego count his money, then get some change for him from a locked drawer under the pigeonholes. "*Gracias.* And—the boy out there—" He went on, "He is dead?" Andrew knew he was dead, but he had to say it, in the form of half-question, half-statement.

Señor Diego's eyes grew small and sharp under his graying brows, and he nodded. "A bad boy. *Muy malo.* Someone shot him," he finished softly, with a shrug.

"Who?"

"*Quién sabe?* Everyone hated him. Even his family. They threw him out of the house long ago. The boy stole. Worse!" Señor Diego pointed to his temple. "*Muy loco.*"

Señor Diego's tone was friendly now, man to man. Andrew began to understand, or he thought he did. Someone with a grievance against the boy had shot him, and maybe the whole town knew who, and maybe the police had had to find someone to take the blame or at least be suspected for a while, to keep up a show of justice. Or perhaps, he thought, if he hadn't been naive enough to insist on reporting the shooting, the body would have simply lain there for hours until somebody removed it. Now

Andrew understood Felipe's pushing him out of his bar, not wanting to hear what he had to say. The town had had to shut him up.

"Yes," Andrew said, putting his pesos into his billfold. "A bad boy—with the little cats."

"The little *cats!* With people—shopkeepers! A thief! He was *all* bad!" Señor Diego spoke with fervor.

Andrew nodded, as if he agreed absolutely. He went back to his room, and slept for several hours.

When he woke up, it was dark. The Bar Felipe's jukebox played a mariachi song with xylophone, guitars, and an enthusiastic tenor. Andrew stretched and smiled. He smiled at his good luck. Twenty-four hours in a Mexican jail? He had read about dirtier jails, worse treatment in jails in books by Gogol, Koestler and Solzhenitsyn. He was ravenously hungry, and knew the little restaurant off the plaza would still be open, if Felipe's jukebox was playing. Andrew put on his cotton jacket against the evening cool. When he dropped his key on the counter, one of the men guests in the hotel said good evening to him, looked him in the eye, and gave him a friendly smile.

Andrew walked towards the little restaurant whose jukebox music he could hear before he reached the corner where he had to turn, the music overlapping for a few seconds with that from the Bar Felipe. There was no table free, but the young woman who served, who Andrew thought was the daughter of the woman who cooked, asked one man to move to a table with his friends, to whom he was talking anyway. Andrew was aware of more glances than on former evenings, but these glances seemed more friendly, as if the men knew him now, as if they were not merely curious about a gringo in the town.

"*Salud!*" A man of about fifty bent over Andrew's table, extending a hand. In his left hand he held a small, heavy tequila glass.

Andrew swallowed some of his first course of stuffed green peppers, put his fork down, and shook the man's thick hand.

"*Un tequila!*" said the man.

Andrew knew it would look rude to refuse. "Okay!—*Gracias.*"

"Tequila!" the man commanded.

"Tequila!" echoed the others. "*Andre-o!*"

It was "*Andre-o!*" again when the tequila arrived. In a discreet way, the dozen men in the restaurant toasted him. The young woman waitress suggested a special dish, which she said was ready in the kitchen. It turned out to be a substantial meal. When Andrew pulled out his billfold to pay, the waitress said:

"No, *señor.*" She wagged a finger and smiled. "You are invited tonight."

A few of the men laughed at Andrew's surprise.

At a quarter to eight the next morning, Andrew's bus, which had been half an hour late, rolled away from the plaza on the road to Jalapa, where he would board a larger bus. The town of Quetzalan looked sweet to him now, like a place he would like to return to one day. He smiled at his recollection of a man and woman, American or English tourists he had seen getting off the bus one afternoon in the plaza: they had gazed around them, conferred, then got back on the bus. Andrew shied away from the memory of the dead boy, though the vision of his white-clad body came now and then, quick and brief as a camera flash.

In Mexico City he rang Houston. He could catch a plane and be in Houston at 6:15 that evening, he told his sister. Esther sounded delighted, but she asked why he was coming back so soon. He would tell her when he saw her, he said, but everything was fine, quite okay.

Esther's husband Bob picked Andrew up at the airport. Houston was another world: chrome and glass, Texas accents, the comforts of home at his sister and Bob's house, containers of milk and ice cream in the fridge, a two-year-old tot who was learning to call him "Uncle Andy."

After dinner, Andrew told them about his last couple of days in Mexico. He had to tell them, before he showed them his drawing and painting efforts, which they were eager to see. Andrew had expected to narrate it smoothly, making it a bit funny, especially his time in the old jail-formerly-palace. But he found himself groping for the right words, particularly when trying to express what he had felt when he realized that the boy was dead.

Esther's face showed that he had made his story clear, however, in spite of his stammerings.

"How awful! Before your eyes!" she said, clasping her hands in her lap. "You should try to forget that sight, Andy. Otherwise it'll haunt you."

Andrew looked down at the living room carpet. Forget it? Should he? Why? Or forget the jail also, just because he hadn't realized why he was there, because the jail happened to have no toilet paper? Andrew gave a laugh. He felt older than his sister, though he was a year younger.

"Any news from—the girl you liked up in New York?" asked Bob.

Andrew's heart jumped. "In Mexico? No," he replied casually, and exchanged a glance with his sister. He had told his sister that he had had a bad time with a girl he liked, and of course Esther had said something to Bob. *Lorrie* was what he had to forget. Could he? Any more than he could forget the instant when he had realized that the patch of red on the white shirt was blood?

In New York, Andrew returned to his friends' apartment in SoHo, where he had a room of his own. Someone had been sleeping in his room in his absence and had paid rent, so the main owner of the apartment, Phyllis, didn't charge Andrew for the three weeks he had been gone. Andrew got his part-time job back, as the arrangements were informal and he was paid by the evening. He checked in again at the Art Students League. He made several sketches of the boy lying on the sidewalk of the plaza, and tried a gouache in green, gray and red. He did an oil of it, two oils, then paintings based on the sketches he had made of the Mexican hills. He worked afternoons at his painting, and all day on the days when he did not go to the League in the morning.

One night in the SoHo restaurant where he worked, Lorrie was sitting at a table with a big fellow with dark hair. Andrew felt as if a rifle bullet had gone through him. He spoke to another waiter, who agreed to serve Lorrie's table, which was in Andrew's assigned area. Andrew continued working, but he felt disturbed and avoided glancing at Lorrie, though he was sure that she had spotted him carrying trays, moving back and forth past her table. He loved her as much as ever.

That night Andrew could not sleep, and got out of bed and started another painting of the dead boy. Death, sudden death at thirteen. The jagged and pointed leaves of the palm trees were dusty gray-green, outlined in black, as if in mourning. A curious pigeon flew into the picture, like a disappointed dove of peace, maybe soon to be converted to a bird of prey. A ghostly and skinny kitten stood amazed on stiff legs, confronted by the milk and the blood which had just reached the cement of the walk. One of the boy's puzzled eyes was open, as was his mouth, and there was the pie pan inches from his fingers. How would the colors look by daylight? Andrew disliked painting by electric light. No matter, he had felt like painting it once more.

The dawn was coming when he fell into bed.

The
Stuff of Madness

When Christopher Waggoner, just out of law school, had married Penelope, he had known of her fondness for pets, and her family's fondness too. That was normal, to love a cat or dog that was part of the household. Christopher had not even thought much about the stuffed little Pixie, a white Pomeranian with shiny black artificial eyes, which stood in a corner of her father's study on a wooden base with her dates of birth and death, nor of the fluffy orange and white cat called Marmy, also preserved, which sat on the floor in another corner. A live cat and dog had lived in the Marshalls' house during his courting days, Christopher recalled, but long ago they had fallen into the taxidermist's hands, and now stood and sat respectively on an outcrop of rock in his and Penny's Suffolk garden. These were not the only animals that peopled, if the word could be used, the garden at Willow Close.

There was Smelty, a feisty little black Scotch terrier with one foot raised and an aggressive muzzle extended with bared teeth, and Jeff the Irish sheep dog, whose coat stood up the best against the elements. Some relics had been in the garden for twenty and more years. An Abyssinian cat called Riba, a name Penny had derived from some mystic experiment, stared with greenish yellow eyes from a tree branch, crouched as if to pounce on anyone walking in the path below. Christopher had seen guests catch a glimpse of the cat and recoil in alarm.

All in all, there were seventeen or eighteen preserved cats and dogs and one rabbit, Petekin, placed about the garden. The Waggoners' two children, Philip and Marjorie, long grown up and married, smiled indulgently at the garden, but Christopher could remember when they winced, when Marjorie didn't want her boyfriends to see the garden and there'd been fewer dead pets then, and when Philip at twelve had tried to burn Pixie on a bonfire, and had been caught by Penny and given the severest scolding of his life.

Now a crisis had come up, attentively listened to by their present dog and cat, Jupiter, an old red setter, and Flora, a docile black cat with white feet. These two were not used to a tense atmosphere in the calm of Willow Close. Little did they understand, Christopher thought, that he was taking a step to protect them from an eternal life after death in the form of being stuffed and made to stand outdoors in all weathers. Wouldn't any animal, if it were capable of choosing, prefer to be a few feet under the ground, dissolving like all flesh, when his time had come? Christopher had used this argument several times to no avail.

The present altercation, however, was over the possible visit of some journalists who would photograph the stuffed animals and write up Penelope's lifelong hobby.

"My old darlings in the newspaper," Penny said in a beseeching way. "I think it's a lovely tribute to them, Christopher, and the *Times* might reprint some of it with *one* photograph from the Ipswich paper anyway. And what's the harm in it?"

"The harm," Christopher began calmly but trying to make every word tell, "is that it's an invasion of privacy for me and for you too. I'm a respected solicitor—still going up to London once or twice a week. I don't want my private address to be bruited about. My clients and colleagues for the most part know my London whereabouts, only. Would you like the telephone ringing here twenty times a day?"

"Oh, Christopher! Anyone who wants your home address can get it, and you know that."

Christopher was standing in the brick-floored kitchen with some typewritten pages of a brief in his hand, wearing house slippers, comfortable trousers and a coat sweater. He had come in from his study, because he had thought the last telephone call, which Penny had made a few moments ago, might have been to give the green light to the journalists. But Penny told him she had been ringing her hairdresser in Ipswich for an appointment on Wednesday.

Christopher tried again. "Two days ago, you seemed to see my point of view. Quite frankly, I don't want my London associates to think I dwell in a place so—so whimsical." He had sought for a word, abandoned the word "macabre," but maybe macabre would have been better. "You see the garden a bit differently, dear. For most people, including me sometimes, it's a trifle depressing."

He saw he had hurt her. But he felt he had to take a stand now before it was too late. "I know you love all those memories in the garden, Penny, but to be honest Philip and Marjorie find our old pets a bit spooky. And Marjorie's two children, they giggle now, but—"

"You're saying it's only *my* pleasure."

He took a breath. "All I'm saying is that I don't want the garden publicized. If you think of Pixie and old Marmy," Christopher continued with a smile, "seeing themselves as they look now, in a newspaper, they might not like it either. It's an invasion of their privacy too."

Penny tugged her jumper down nervously over the top of her slacks. "I've already agreed to the journalists—just two, I think, the writer and the photographer—and they're coming Thursday morning."

Oh, my God, Christopher thought. He looked at his wife's round, innocent blue eyes. She really didn't understand. Since she had no occupation, her collection of taxidermy had become her chief interest, apart from knitting, at which she was quite skilled and in which she gave lessons at the Women's Institute. The journalists' arrival meant a show of her own achievement, in a way, not that she did any taxidermy herself, the expert they engaged was in London. Christopher felt angry and speechless. How could he turn the journalists off without appearing to be at odds with his wife, or without both of them (if Penny acquiesced to him) seeming full-blown cranks to hold their defunct pets so sacred, they wouldn't allow photographs of them? "It's going to damage my career—most gravely."

"But your career is made, dear. You're not struggling. And you're in semi-retirement anyway, you often say that." Her high, clear voice pleaded pitiably, like that of a little girl wanting something.

"I'm only sixty-one." Christopher pulled his abdomen in. "Hawkins's doing the same thing I am, commuting from Kent at sixty-nine."

Christopher returned to his study, his favorite room and his bedroom for the last couple of years, as he preferred it to the upstairs bedroom and the spare room. He was aware that tears had come to his eyes, but he told himself that they were tears of frustration and rage. He loved the house, an old two-story manse of red brick, the corners of its overhanging roof softened by Virginia creeper. They had an interesting catalpa in the back garden—on one of whose limbs unfortunately Riba the Abyssinian cat sat glowering—and a lovely design of well-worn paths whose every inch Christopher knew, along which he had strolled countless times, working out legal problems or relaxing from work by paying close attention to a rosebush or a hydrangea. He had acquired the habit of not noticing the macabre—yes, macabre—exteriors of pets he and Penny had known and loved in the past. Now all this was to be invaded, exposed to the public to wonder at, very likely to chuckle at too. In fact, had Penny a clue as to how the journalists intended to treat the article, which was probably going to be one of their full-page spreads, since the stuffed animals were in their way so photogenic? Who had put the idea into the heads of the *Chronicle* journalists?

One source of his anguish, Christopher knew, was that he hadn't put his foot down long ago, before Penny had turned the garden into a necropolis. Penny had always been a good wife, in the best sense of that term. She'd been a good mother to their children, she'd done nothing wrong, and she'd been quite pretty in her youth, and still took care of her appearance. It was he who had done something wrong, he had to admit. He didn't care to dwell on that period, which had been when Penny had been pregnant with Marjorie. Well, he had given Louise up, hadn't he? And Louise would have been with him now, if he had parted from Penny. How different his life would have been, how infinitely happier! Christopher imagined a more interesting, more richly fulfilled life, though he'd have gone on with his law career, of course. Louise had passion and imagination. She had been a graduate student of child psychiatry when Christopher met her. Now she had a high position in an institution for children in America, Christopher had read in a magazine, and years before that he had seen in a newspaper that she had married an American doctor.

Christopher suddenly saw Louise distinctly as she had looked when they'd had their first rendezvous at the Gare du Nord, she having been at the station to meet him, because she'd got to Paris a few hours before. He remembered her young, happy eyes of paler blue than Penny's, her soft, smiling lips, her voice, the round hat she wore with a beige crown and a black fur rim. He could recall the scent of her perfume. Penny had found out about that affair, and persuaded him to end it. How had she persuaded him? Christopher could not remember Penny's words, they certainly had not been threatening or blackmailing in any way. But he had agreed to give up Louise, and he had written as much to Louise, and then he had collapsed for two days in bed, exhausted as well as depressed, and so miserable, he had wanted to die. With the wisdom of years, Christopher realized that collapsing had been symbolic of a suicide, and that he was rather glad, after all, that he had merely spent two days in bed and not shot himself.

That evening at dinner, Penny remarked on his lack of appetite.

"Yes. Sorry," Christopher said, toying with his lamb chop. "I suppose old Jupiter may as well have this."

Christopher watched the dog carry the chop to his eating place in the corner of the kitchen, and Christopher thought: another year or so and Jupiter will be standing in the garden, perhaps on three legs, in a running position for ever. Christopher firmly hoped he wouldn't be alive to see it. He set his jaw and stared at the foot of his wine glass whose stem he twisted. Not even the wine cheered him.

"Christopher, I am sorry about the journalists. They looked *me* up, and begged me. I had no idea you'd be so upset."

Christopher had a feeling that what she said was not true. On the other hand, Penny wasn't malicious. He decided to chance it. "You could still cancel it, couldn't you? Tell them you've changed your mind. You won't have to mention me, I trust."

Penny hesitated, then shook her head. "I simply don't want to cancel it. I love my garden. This is a way of sharing it—with friends and with people I don't even know."

She probably envisaged letters from strangers saying they were going to take up the same method of preserving their pets in their houses or gardens—God forbid—and what was the name of their taxidermist? And so Christopher's will hardened. He would have to endure it, and endure it he would, like a man. He wouldn't even quit the house while the journalists were here, because that would be cowardly, but he was going to take care not to be in any photograph.

Wednesday, a pleasant and sunny day, he did not set foot in the garden. It was ruined for him. The blossoming roses, the softly bending willow, chartreuse-colored in the sunlight, seemed a stage set waiting for the accursed journalists. His work, a lot of it, making that garden so beautiful, and now the vulgarians were going to trample over the primroses, the pansies, backing up and stepping sideways for their silly photographs.

Something was building up inside Christopher, a desire to hit back at both the journalists and at Penny. He felt like bombing the garden, but that would destroy the growing things as well as part of the house, possibly. Absurd! But an insufferable wrath boiled in him. The white coat of Pixie showed left of the catalpa even from the kitchen window. A brown and white collie called Doggo was even more visible on a stone base near the garden wall. Christopher had been able to cut these out of his vision somehow—until today.

When Penny went to the hairdresser's on Wednesday afternoon, fetched by her friend Beatrice who went to the same hairdresser, Christopher took the car and drove rather aimlessly northward. He'd never done such a thing before. Waste of petrol, he'd have thought under usual circumstances, since he hadn't even a shopping list with him. His mind dwelt on Louise. *Louise*—a name he'd avoided saying to himself for years, because it pained him so. Now he relished the pain, as if it had a cleansing and clarifying power. *Louise* in the garden, that was what Penny needed to bring back to her what the past was all about. Louise, worthy of being preserved if any living creature ever had been. Penny had met her once at a cocktail party in London, while the affair was still going on, and had sensed something and later made a remark to Christopher. Months later, Penny had discovered his three photographs of Louise—though to give Penny credit, she had not been snooping, but looking for a cuff link that Christopher said he had lost in the chest of drawers. Penny had said, "Well, Christopher—this is the girl who was at that party, is it not?" and then it had come out, that he was still seeing her. With Penny pregnant, Christopher had not been able to fight for Louise. For that he reproached himself too.

Christopher turned the car towards Bury St. Edmunds, to a large department store, and found a parking place nearby. He was full of an unusual confidence that he would have his way, that everything would be easy. He looked in the windows of the store as he walked towards the entrance: summer clothing on tall mannequins with flesh-colored legs, wearing silly smiles or equally silly pouts, flamboyant with hands and arms flung out as if to say, "Look at me!" That wasn't quite what he wanted. Then he saw her—a blonde girl seated at a little white round table, in a crisp navy blue blouse rather like a sailor's middy, navy blue skirt and black patent leather pumps. An empty stemmed glass stood on the table before her, and around her dummy men reared back barefoot in white dungarees, either topless or wearing striped blue and white jumpers.

"Where might I find the manager?" Christopher asked, but received such a vague answer from a salesgirl, he decided to push on more directly. He barged into a stockroom near the window where the girl was.

Five minutes later, he had what he wanted, and a young window dresser called Jeremy something was even carrying her to his car, the girl in the navy blue outfit, without a hat and with very dead-looking strawy straight yellow hair. Christopher had offered a deposit of a hundred pounds for an overnight rental, half to be paid back on return of the dummy and clothing in good condition, and he had added encouragement by pushing a ten-pound note into the young man's hand.

With the dummy installed in the back seat, Christopher returned to shop for a hat. He found more or less what he was looking for, a round hat trimmed with black velour instead of fur, and the crown was white and not beige, but the resemblance to Louise's hat in the photograph, which he was sure Penny remembered, was sufficient and striking enough. When he returned to the car, a small child was staring curiously at the mannequin. Christopher smiled amiably, pulled a blanket (used to keep Jupiter's paws off the back seat when he went to the vet for arthritis shots) gently over the figure, and drove off. He felt a bit pressed for time, and hoped that Penny had decided to have tea at Beatrice's house instead of theirs.

He was in luck. Penny was not home yet. Having ascertained this, Christopher carried the dummy from the car into the house via the back door. He set the figure in his chair in front of his desk and indulged in a few seconds of amusement and imagination—imagining that it *was* Louise, young and round-cheeked, that he could say something to her, and she would reply. But the girl's eyes, though large and blue, were quite blank. Only her lips smiled in a rather absent but definite curve. This reminded Christopher of something, and he went quickly up the stairs and got the brightest red lipstick he could find among several on Penny's dressing table. Then down again, and carefully, trying his best to steady his hand which was trembling as it never had before, Christopher enlarged the upper lip, and lowered the under lip exactly in the center. The upturned red corners of the lips were superb.

Just then, he heard the sound of a car motor, and seconds later a car door slamming, voices, and he could tell from the tone that Penny was saying good-bye to Beatrice. Christopher at once set the dummy in a back corner of his study, and concealed the figure completely with a coverlet from his couch. At any rate, Penny almost never looked into his study, except when she knocked on the door to call him to tea or a meal. Christopher put the bag with the hat under the coverlet also.

Penny looked especially well coifed, and was in good spirits the rest of the afternoon and evening. Christopher behaved politely, merely, but in his way, he felt in good spirits too. He debated putting the effigy of Louise out in the garden tonight versus early tomorrow morning. Tonight, Jupiter might bark, as he slept outdoors in this season in his doghouse near the back door. Christopher could take a stroll in the garden, if he happened to be sleepless at midnight, tell Jupiter to hush, and the dog would, but if he were carrying a large object and fussing around getting it placed correctly, the silly dog just might keep on barking because he was tied up at night. Christopher decided on early tomorrow morning.

Penny retired just after ten, assuring Christopher cheerfully that "It'll all be over so quickly tomorrow," he wouldn't know it had happened. "I'll tell them to be very careful and not step on the flower beds." She added that she thought he was being very patient about it all.

In his study, Christopher hardly slept. He was aware of the village clock striking faintly at quite a distance every hour until four, when the window showed signs of dawn. Christopher got up and dressed. He sat Louise again in his desk chair, and practiced setting the hat on correctly at a jaunty angle. The extended forearm, without the glass stem in the fingers of the hand, looked able to hold a cigarette, and Christopher would have put one there unlighted, except that he and Penny didn't smoke, and there were no cigarettes in the house just now. Just as well, because the hand looked also as if Louise might be beckoning to someone, having just called out someone's name. Christopher reached for a black felt pen, and outlined both her blue eyes.

There! Now her eyes really stood out and the outer corners turned up just a little, imitating the upturn of her lips.

Christopher carried the figure out the back door with the coverlet still over it. He knew where it should be, on a short stone bench on the left side of the garden which was rather hidden by laurels. Jupiter's eyes had met Christopher's for an instant, the dog had been sleeping with forepaws and muzzle on the threshold of his wooden house, but Jupiter did not bother to lift his head. Christopher flicked the bench clean with the coverlet, then seated Louise gently, and put a stone under one black pump, since the shoe did not quite touch the ground. Her legs were crossed. She looked charming—much more charming than the longhaired Pekinese called Mao-Mao who peeked from the foliage to the left of the bench, facing the little clearing as if he were guarding it. Mao-Mao's tongue, which protruded nearly two inches and had been made by the taxidermist out of God knew what, had lost all its pink and was now a sickening flesh color. For some reason, Mao-Mao had always been a favorite target of his and Penny's dogs, so his coat looked miserable.

But Louise! She was fantastically smart with her round hat on, in her crisp new navy outfit, her happy eyes directed towards the approach to the nook in which she sat. Christopher smiled with satisfaction, and went back to his study, where he fell sound asleep until Penny awakened him with tea at eight.

The journalist and the photographer were due at 9:30, and they were punctual, in a dirty gray Volkswagen. Penny went down the front steps to greet them. The two young men, Christopher observed from the sitting-room window, looked even scruffier than he had foreseen, one in a T-shirt and the other in a polo-neck sweater, and both in blue jeans. Gentlemen of the press, indeed!

Christopher had two reasons, his legal mind assured him, for joining the company in the garden: he didn't want to appear huffy or possibly physically handicapped, since the journalists knew that Penny was married and to whom, and also he wanted to witness the discovery of Louise. So Christopher stood in the garden near the house, after the men had introduced themselves to him.

"Jonathan, look!" said the man without the camera, marveling at big Jeff, the Irish sheep dog who stood on the right side of the garden. "We must get this!" But his exclamations became more excited as he espied old Pixie, whose effigy made him laugh with delight.

The cameraman snapped here and there with a compact little machine that made a whir and a click. Stuffed animals were really everywhere, standing out more than the roses and peonies.

"Where do you have this expert work done, Mrs. Waggoner? Have you any objection to telling us? Some of our readers might like to start the same hobby."

"Oh, it's more than a hobby," Penny began. "It's my way of keeping my dear pets with me. I feel that with their forms around me—I don't suffer as much as other people do who bury their pets in their gardens."

"That's the kind of comment we want," said the journalist, writing in his tablet.

Jonathan was exploring the foot of the garden now. There was a beagle named Jonathan back to the right behind the barberry bush, Christopher recalled, but either Jonathan didn't see him or preferred the more attractive animals. The photographer drifted closer to Louise, but still did not notice her. Then, focusing on Riba, the cat in the catalpa, he stepped backward, nearly fell, and in recovering glanced behind him, and glanced again.

Penny was just then saying to the journalist, "Mr. Taylor puts a special weatherproofing on their coats with a spray . . ."

"Hey Mike!—*Mike,* look!" The second Mike had a shrill note of astonishment.

"What now?" asked Mike smiling, approaching.

"Mao-Mao," said Penny, following them in her medium-high heels. "I'm afraid he's not in the best—"

"No, no, the figure. Who is this?" asked the photographer with a polite smile.

Penny's gaze sought and found what the photographer was pointing at.

"Oh!—Oh, *goodness!*" Then she took a long breath and screamed, like a siren, and covered her face with her hands.

Jonathan caught her arm as she swayed. "Mrs. Waggoner! Something the matter? We didn't damage anything.—It's a friend of yours—I suppose?"

"Someone you liked very much?" asked Mike in a tactful tone.

Penny looked crushed, and for brief seconds Christopher relished it. Here was Louise in all her glory, young and pretty, sure of herself, sure of him, smack in their garden. "Penny, a cup of tea?" asked Christopher.

They escorted Penny through the back door and into the kitchen. Christopher put the kettle on.

"It's Louise!" Penny moaned in an eerie voice, and leaned back in the bamboo chair, her face white.

"Someone she didn't want us to photograph?" asked Jonathan. "We certainly won't."

Before Christopher could pour the first cup of tea, Mike said, "I think we'd better call for a doctor, don't you, Mr. Waggoner?"

"Y-yes, perhaps." Christopher could have said something comforting to Penny, he realized—that he had meant it as a joke. But he hadn't. And Penny was in a state beyond hearing anything anybody said.

"Why was she so surprised?" asked Jonathan.

Christopher didn't answer. He was on his way to the telephone, and Mike was coming with him, because Mike had the number of a doctor in Ipswich, in case the local doctor was not available. But this got interrupted by a shout from Jonathan. He wanted some help to get Penny to a sofa, or anywhere where she could lie down. The three of them carried her into the sitting room. The touch of rouge on her cheeks stood out garishly on her pale face.

"I think it's a heart attack," said Jonathan.

The local doctor was available, because his nurse knew whom he was visiting just now, and she thought he could arrive in about five minutes. Meanwhile Christopher covered Penny with a blanket he brought from upstairs, and started the kettle again for a hot water bottle. Penny was now breathing through parted lips.

"We'll stay till the doctor gets here, unless you want us to take her directly to Ipswich Hospital," said Jonathan.

"No—thank you. Since the doctor's on his way, it may be wisest to wait for him."

Dr. Dowes arrived soon after, took Penny's pulse, and at once gave her an injection. "It's a heart attack, yes, and she'd best go to hospital." He went to the telephone.

"If we possibly could, Mr. Waggoner," said Jonathan, "we'd like to come back tomorrow morning, because today I didn't get all the pictures I need to choose from, and the rest of today is so booked up, we're due somewhere in a few minutes.—If you could let us in around nine-thirty again, we'd need just another half hour."

Christopher thought at once of Louise. They hadn't got a picture of her as yet, and he wanted them to photograph her and was sure they would. "Yes, certainly. Nine-thirty tomorrow. If I happen not to be here, you can use the side passage into the garden. The gate's never locked."

As soon as they had driven off, the ambulance arrived. Dr. Dowes had not asked if anything had happened to give Penny a shock, but he had gathered the journalists' purpose—he knew of the stuffed animals in the garden, of course—and he said something to the effect that the excitement of showing her old pets to the public must have been a strain on her heart.

"Shall I go with her?" Christopher asked the doctor, not wanting at all to go.

"No, no, Mr. Waggoner, really no use in it. I'll ring the hospital in an hour or so, and then I'll ring you."

"But how dangerous is her state?"

"Can't tell as yet, but I think she has a good chance of pulling through. No former attacks like this."

The ambulance went away, and then Dr. Dowes. Christopher realized that he wouldn't have minded if the shock of seeing Louise had killed Penny. He felt strangely numb about the fact that at this minute, she was hovering between life and death. Tomorrow, Penny alive or not, the journalist and the photographer would be back, and they would take a picture of Louise. How would Penny, if she lived, explain the effigy of a young woman in her garden? Christopher smiled nervously. If Penny died, or if she didn't, he could still ring up the Ipswich *Chronicle* and say that under the circumstances, because his wife had suffered such emotional strain because of the publicity, he would be grateful if they canceled the article. But Christopher didn't want that. He wanted Louise's picture in the newspaper. Would his children Philip and Marjorie suspect Louise's identity, or role? Christopher couldn't imagine how, as they had never heard Louise's name spoken, he thought, never seen that photograph which Christopher had so cherished until Penny asked him to destroy it. As for what their friends and neighbors thought, let them draw their own conclusions.

Christopher poured more tea for himself, removed Penny's unfinished cup from the living room, and carried his tea into his study. He had work to do for the London office, and was supposed to telephone them before five this afternoon.

At two o'clock, the telephone rang. It was Dr. Dowes.

"Good news," said the doctor. "She's going to pull through nicely. An infarction, and she'll have to lie still in hospital for at least ten days, but by tomorrow you can visit . . ."

Christopher felt depressed at the news, though he said the right things. When he hung up, in an awful limbo between fantasy and reality, he told himself that he must let Marjorie know about her mother right away, and ask her to ring Philip. Christopher did this.

"You sound awfully down, Dad," said Marjorie. "It could have been worse after all."

Again he said the proper things. Marjorie said she would ring her brother, and maybe both of them could come down on Sunday.

By four o'clock, Christopher was able to ring his office and speak with Hawkins about a strategy he had worked out for a company client. Hawkins gave him a word of praise for his suggestions, and didn't remark that Christopher sounded depressed, nor did Christopher mention his wife.

Christopher did not ring the hospital or Dr. Dowes the rest of that evening. Penny was coming back, that was the fact and the main thing. How would he endure it? How could he return the dummy—Louise—to the department store, as he had promised? He couldn't return Louise, he simply couldn't. And Penny might tear her apart, once she regained the strength. Christopher poured a scotch, sipped it neat, and felt that it did him a power of good. It helped him pull his thoughts together. He went into his study and wrote a short letter to Jeremy Rogers, the window dresser who had given him his card in the Bury St. Edmunds store, saying that due to circumstances beyond his control, he would not be able to return the borrowed mannequin personally, but it could be fetched at his address, and for the extra trouble he would forfeit his deposit. He put this letter in the post box on the front gate.

Christopher's will was in order. As for his children, they would be quite surprised, and to what could they attribute it? Not to Penny's crisis, because she was on the mend. Let Penny explain it to them, Christopher thought, and had another drink.

Drink was part of his plan, and not being used to it, Christopher quickly felt its soothing power. He went upstairs to the medicine chest in the bathroom. Penny always had little sedatives, and maybe some big ones too. Christopher found four or five little glass jars that might suit his purpose, some of them overaged, perhaps, but no matter. He swallowed six or eight pills, washed down with scotch and water, mindful to think of something else—his appearance—while he did this, lest the thought of all the pills made him throw up.

In the downstairs hall looking-glass, Christopher combed his hair, and then he put on his best jacket, a rather new tweed, and went on taking pills with more scotch. He dropped the empty jars carelessly into the garbage. The cat Flora looked at him in surprise when he lurched against a sideboard and fell to one knee. Christopher got up again, and methodically fed the cat. As for Jupiter, he could afford to miss a meal.

"M'wow," said Flora, as she always did, as a kind of thank-you before she fell to.

Then Christopher made his way, touching doorjambs, fairly crawling down the steps, to the garden path. He fell only once, before he reached his goal, and then he smiled. Louise, though blurred at the edges, sat with the same air of dignity and confidence. She was alive! She smiled a welcome to him. "Louise," he said aloud, and with difficulty aimed himself and plopped on to the stone bench beside her. He touched her cool, firm hand, the one that was extended with fingers slightly parted. It was still a *hand,* he thought. Just cool from the evening air, perhaps.

The next morning the photographer and the journalist found him slumped sideways, stiff as the dummy, with his head in the navy blue lap.

Not in This Life,
Maybe the Next

Eleanor had been sewing nearly all day, sewing after dinner, too, and it was getting on for eleven o'clock. She looked away from her machine, sideways towards the hall door, and saw something about two feet high, something grayish black, which after a second or two moved and was lost from view in the hall. Eleanor rubbed her eyes. Her eyes smarted, and it was delicious to rub them. But since she was sure she had not really seen something, she did not get up from her chair to go and investigate. She forgot about it.

She stood up after five minutes or so, after tidying her sewing table, putting away her scissors, and folding the yellow dress whose side seams she had just let out. The dress was ready for Mrs. Burns tomorrow. Always letting out, Eleanor thought, never taking in. People seemed to grow sideways, not upward any more, and she smiled at this fuzzy little thought. She was tired, but she had had a good day. She gave her cat Bessie a saucer of milk—rather creamy milk, because Bessie liked the best of everything—heated some milk for herself and took it in a mug up to bed.

The second time she saw it, however, she was not tired, and the sun was shining brightly. This time, she was sitting in the armchair, putting a zipper in a skirt, and as she knotted her thread, she happened to glance at the door that went into what she called the side room, a room off the living room at the front of the house. She saw a squarish figure about two feet high, an ugly little thing that at first suggested an upended sandbag. It took a moment before she recognized a large square head, thick feet in heavy shoes, incredibly short arms with big hands that dangled.

Eleanor was half out of her chair, her slender body rigid.

The thing didn't move. But it was looking at her.

Get it out of the house, she thought at once. Shoo it out the door. What *was* it? The face was vaguely human. Eyes looked at her from under hair that was combed forward over the forehead. Had the children put some horrid toy in the house to frighten her? The Reynoldses next door had four children, the oldest eight. Children's toys these days—You never knew what to expect!

Then the thing moved, advanced slowly into the living room, and Eleanor stepped quickly behind the armchair.

"Get out! Get away!" she said in a voice shrill with panic.

"Um-m," came the reply, soft and deep.

Had she really heard anything? Now it looked from the floor—where it had stared while entering the room—to her face. The look at her seemed direct, yet was somehow vague and unfocused. The creature went on, towards the electric bar heater, where it stopped and held out its hands casually to the warmth. It was masculine, Eleanor thought, its legs—if those stumpy things could be called legs—were in trousers. Again the creature took a sidelong look at her, a little shyly, yet as if defying her to get it out of the room.

The cat, curled on a pillow in a chair, lifted her head and yawned, and the movement caught Eleanor's eye. She waited for Bessie to see the thing, straight before her and only four feet away, but Bessie put her head down again in a position for sleeping. That was curious!

Eleanor retreated quickly to the kitchen, opened the back door and went out, leaving the door open. She went round to the front door and opened that wide, too. Give the thing a chance to get out! Eleanor stayed on her front path, ready to run to the road if the creature emerged.

The thing came to the front door and said in a deep voice, the words more a rumble than articulated, "I'm not going to harm you, so why don't you come back in? It's your house." And there was the hint of a shrug in the chunky shoulders.

"I'd like you to get out, please!" Eleanor said.

"Um-m." He turned away, back into the living room.

Eleanor thought of going for Mr. Reynolds next door, a practical man who probably had a gun in the house, as he was a captain in the Air Force. Then she remembered the Reynoldses had gone off before lunch and that their house was empty. Eleanor gathered her courage and advanced towards the front door.

Now she didn't see him in the living room. She even looked behind the armchair. She went cautiously towards the side room. He was not in there, either. She looked quite thoroughly.

She stood in the hall and called up the stairs, really called to all the house, "If you're still in this house, I wish you would leave!"

Behind her a voice said, "I'm still here."

Eleanor turned and saw him standing in the living room.

"I won't do you any harm. But I can disappear if you prefer. Like this."

She thought she saw a set of bared teeth, as if he were making an effort. As she stared, the creature became paler gray, more fuzzy at the edges. And after ten seconds, there was nothing. *Nothing!* Was she losing her mind? She must tell Dr. Campbell, she thought. First thing tomorrow morning, go to his office at 9 A.M. and tell him honestly.

The rest of the day, and the evening, passed without incident. Mrs Burns came for her dress, and brought a coat to be shortened. Eleanor watched a television program, and went to bed at half past ten. She had thought she would be frightened, going to bed and turning all the lights out, but she wasn't. And before she had time to worry about whether she could get to sleep or not, she had fallen asleep.

But when she woke up, he was the second thing she saw, the first thing being her cat, who had slept on the foot of the bed for warmth. Bessie stretched, yawned and meowed simultaneously, demanding breakfast. And hardly two yards away, he stood, staring at her. Eleanor's promise of imme-diate breakfast to Bessie was cut short by her seeing him.

"I could use some breakfast myself." Was there a faint smile on that square face? "Nothing much. A piece of bread."

Now Eleanor found her teeth tight together, found herself wordless. She got out of bed on the other side from him, quickly pulled on her old flannel robe, and went down the stairs. In the kitchen, she comforted her-self with the usual routine: put the kettle on, feed Bessie while the kettle was heating, cut some bread. But she was waiting for the thing to appear in the kitchen doorway, and as she was slicing the bread, he did. Trembling, Eleanor held the piece of bread towards him.

"If I give you this, would you go away?" she asked.

The monstrous hand reached out and up, and took the bread. "Not necessarily," rumbled the bass voice. "I don't need to eat, you know. I thought I'd keep you company, that's all."

Eleanor was not sure, really not sure now if she had heard it. She was imagining telling Dr. Campbell all this, imagining the point at which Dr. Campbell would cut her short (politely, of course, because he was a nice man) and prescribe some kind of sedative.

Bessie, her breakfast finished, walked so close by the creature, her fur must have brushed his leg, but the cat showed no sign of seeing anything. That was proof enough that he didn't exist, Eleanor thought.

A strange rumbling. "Um-hm-hm," came from him. He was laughing! "Not everyone—or everything—can see me," he said to Eleanor. "Very few people can see me, in fact." He had eaten the bread, apparently.

Eleanor steeled herself to carry on with her breakfast. She cut another piece of bread, got out the butter and jam, scalded the teapot. It was ten to eight. By nine she'd be at Dr. Campbell's.

"Maybe there's something I can do for you today," he said. He had not moved from where he stood. "Odd jobs. I'm strong." The last word was like a nasal burr, like the horn of a large and distant ship.

At once, Eleanor thought of the rusty old lawn roller in her barn. She'd rung up Field's, the secondhand dealers, to come and take it away, but they were late as usual, two weeks late. "I have a roller out in the barn. After breakfast, you can take it to the edge of the road, if you will." That would be further proof, Eleanor thought, proof he wasn't real. The roller must weigh two or three hundred pounds.

He walked, in a slow, rolling gait, out of the kitchen and into the sitting room. He made no sound.

Eleanor ate her breakfast at the scrubbed wooden table in the kitchen, where she often preferred to eat instead of in the dining room. She propped a booklet on sewing tips before her, and after a few moments, she was able to concentrate on it.

At 8:30, dressed now, Eleanor went out to the barn behind her house. She had not looked for him in the house, didn't know where he was now, in fact, but somehow it did not surprise her to find him beside her when she reached the barn door.

"It's in the back corner. I'll show you." She removed the padlock which had not been fully closed.

He understood at once, rubbed his big yellowish hands together, and took a grip on the wooden stick of the roller. He pulled the thing towards him with apparently the greatest ease, then began to push it from behind, rolling it. But the stick was easier, so he took the stick again, and in less than five minutes, the roller was at the edge of the road, where Eleanor pointed.

Jane, the girl who delivered morning papers, was cycling along the road just then.

Eleanor tensed, thinking Jane would cry out at the sight of him, but Jane only said shyly (she was a very shy girl), " 'Morning, Mrs. Heathcote," and pedaled on.

"Good morning to you, Jane," Eleanor answered.

"Anything else?" he asked.

"I can't think of anything, thank you," Eleanor replied rather breathlessly.

"It won't do you any good to speak to your doctor about me," he said.

They were both walking back towards the house, up the carelessly flagged path that divided Eleanor's front garden.

"He won't be able to see me, and he'll just give you useless pills," he continued.

What made you think I was going to a doctor? Eleanor wanted to ask. But she knew. He could read her mind. *Is he some part of myself?* she asked herself, with a flash of intuition which went no further than the question. If no one *else* can see him—

"I am myself," he said, smiling at her over one shoulder. He was leading the way into the house. "Just me." And he laughed.

Eleanor did not go to Dr. Campbell. She decided to try to ignore him, and to go about her usual affairs. Her affairs that morning consisted of walking a quarter of a mile to the butcher's for some liver for Bessie and a half-chicken for herself, and of buying several things at Mr. White's, the grocer. But Eleanor was thinking of telling all this to Vance—Mrs. Florence Vansittart—who was her best friend in the town. Vance and she had tea together, at one or the other's house, at least once a week, usually once every five days, in fact, and Eleanor rang up Vance as soon as she got home.

The creature was not in sight at that time.

Vance agreed to come over at four o'clock. "How *are* you, dear?" Vance asked as she always did.

"All right, thanks!" Eleanor replied, more heartily than usual. "And you? . . . I'll make some blueberry muffins if I get my work done in time . . ."

That afternoon, though he had kept out of sight since the morning, he lumbered silently into the room just as Eleanor and Vance were starting on their second cups of tea, and just as Eleanor was drawing breath for the first statement, the first introductory statement, of her strange story. She had been thinking, the roller at the edge of the road (she must ring Field's again first thing in the morning) would be proof that what she said was not a dream.

"What's the matter, Eleanor?" asked Vance, sitting up a little. She was a woman of Eleanor's age, about fifty-five, one of the many widows in the town, though unlike Eleanor, Vance had never worked at anything, and had been left a little more money. And Vance looked to her right, at the side room's door, where Eleanor had been looking. Now Eleanor took her eyes away from the creature who stood four feet within the room.

"Nothing," Eleanor said. Vance didn't see him, she thought. Vance can't see him.

"She can't see me," the creature rumbled to Eleanor.

"Swallow something the wrong way?" Vance asked, chuckling, helping herself to another blueberry muffin.

The creature was staring at the muffins, but came no closer.

"You know, Eleanor—" Vance chewed, "—if you're still charging only a dollar for putting a hem up, I think you need your head examined. People around here, all of them could afford to give you two dollars. It's criminal the way you cheat yourself."

Vance meant, Eleanor thought, that it was high time she had her house painted, or re-covered the armchair, which she could do herself if she had the time. "It's not easy to mention raising prices, and the people who come to me are used to mine by now."

"Other people manage to mention price-raising pretty easily," Vance said as Eleanor had known she would. "I hear of a new one every day!"

The creature took a muffin. For a few seconds, the muffin must have been visible in midair to Vance, even if she didn't see him. But suddenly the muffin was gone, being chewed by the massive, wooden-looking jaw.

"You look a bit absent today, my dear," Vance said. "Something worrying you?" Vance looked at her attentively, waiting for a confidence—such as another tooth extraction that Eleanor felt doomed to, or news that her brother George in Canada, who had never made a go of anything, was once more failing in business. Eleanor braced herself and said, "I've had a visitor for the last two days. He's standing right here by the table." She nodded her head in his direction.

The creature was looking at Eleanor.

Vance looked where Eleanor had nodded. "What do you mean?"

"You can't see him?—He's quite friendly," Eleanor added. "It's a creature two feet high. He's right there. He just took a muffin! I know you don't believe me," she rushed on, "but he moved the roller this morning from the barn to the edge of the road. You saw it at the edge of the road, didn't you? You *said* something about it."

Vance tipped her head to one side, and looked in a puzzled way at Eleanor. "You mean a handyman. Old Gufford?"

"No, he's—" But at this moment, he was walking out of the room, so Vance couldn't possibly have seen him, and before he disappeared into the side room, he gave Eleanor a look and pushed his great hands flat downward in the air, as if to say, "Give it up," or "Don't talk." "I mean what I said," Eleanor pursued, determined to share her experience, determined also to get some sympathy, even protection. "I am not joking, Vance. It's a little—creature two feet high, and he talks to me." Her voice had sunk to a whisper. She glanced at the side room doorway, which was empty. "You think I'm seeing things, but I'm not, I swear it."

Vance still looked puzzled, but quite in control of herself, and she even assumed a superior attitude. "How long have you—been seeing him, my dear?" she asked, and chuckled again.

"I saw him first two nights ago," Eleanor said, still in a whisper. "Then yesterday quite plainly, in broad daylight. He has a deep voice."

"If he just took a muffin, where is he now?" Vance asked, getting up. "Why can't I see him?"

"He went into the side room. All right, come along." Eleanor was suddenly aware that she didn't know his name, didn't know how to address him. She and Vance looked into an apparently empty room, empty of anything alive except some plants on the windowsill. Eleanor looked behind the sofa end. "Well—he has the faculty of disappearing."

Vance smiled, again superiorly. "Eleanor, your eyes are getting worse. Are you using your glasses? That sewing—"

"I don't need them for sewing. Only for distances. Matter of fact I did put them on when I looked at him yesterday across the room." She was wearing her glasses now. She was nearsighted.

Vance frowned slightly. "My dear, are you afraid of him?—It looks like it. Stay with me tonight. Come home with me now, if you like. I can come back with Hester and look the house over thoroughly." Hester was her cleaning woman.

"Oh, I'm sure you wouldn't see him. And I'm not afraid. He's rather friendly. But I *did* want you to believe me."

"How can I believe you, if I don't see him?"

"I don't know." Eleanor thought of describing him more accurately. But would this convince Vance, or anybody? "I think I could take a photograph of him. I don't think he'd mind," Eleanor said.

"A good idea! You've got a camera?"

"No. Well, I have, an old one of John's, but—"

"I'll bring mine. This afternoon.—I'm going to finish my tea."

Vance brought the camera just before six. "Good luck, Eleanor. This should be interesting!" Vance said as she departed.

Eleanor could tell that Vance had not believed a word of what she had told her. The camera said "4" on its indicator. There were eight more pictures on the roll, Vance had said. Eleanor thought two would be enough.

"I don't photograph, I'm sure," his deep voice said on her left, and Eleanor saw him standing in the doorway of the side room. "But I'll pose for you. Um-hm-hm." It was the deep laugh.

Eleanor felt only a mild start of surprise, or of fear. The sun was still shining. "Would you sit in a chair in the garden?"

"Certainly," the creature said, and he was clearly amused.

Eleanor picked up the straight chair which she usually sat on when she worked, but he took it from her and went out the front door with it. He set the chair in the garden, careful not to tread on flowers. Then with a little boost, he got himself on to the seat and folded his short arms.

The sunlight fell full on his face. Vance had showed Eleanor how to work the camera. It was a simple one compared to John's. She took the picture at the prescribed six-foot distance. Then she saw old Gufford, the town handyman, going by in his little truck, staring at her. They did not usually greet each other, and they did not now, but Eleanor could imagine how odd he must think she was to be taking a picture of an ordinary chair in the garden. But she had seen him clearly in the finder. There was no doubt at all about that.

"Could I take one more of you standing by the chair?" she asked.

"Um-m." That was not a laugh, but a sound of assent. He slid off the chair and stood beside it, one hand resting on the chair's back.

This was splendid, Eleanor thought, because it showed his height in proportion to the chair.

Click!

"Thank you."

"They won't turn out, as they say," he replied, and took the chair back into the house.

"If you'd like another muffin," Eleanor said, wanting to be polite and thinking also he might have resented her asking him to be photographed, "they're in the kitchen."

"I know. I don't need to eat. I just took one to see if your friend would notice. She didn't. She's not very observant."

Eleanor thought again of the muffin in midair for a few seconds—it must have been—but she said nothing. "I—I don't know what to call you. Have you got a name?"

A fuzzy, rather general expression of amusement came over his square face. "Lots of names. No one particular name. No one speaks to me, so there's no need of a name."

"I speak to you," Eleanor said.

He was standing by the stove now, not as high, not nearly as high as the gas burners. His skin looked dry, yellowish, and his face somehow sad. She felt sorry for him.

"Where have you been living?"

He laughed. "Um-hm-hm. I live anywhere, everywhere. It doesn't matter."

She wanted to ask some questions, such as, "Do you feel the cold?" but she did not want to be personal, or prying. "It occurred to me you might like a bed," she said more brightly. "You could sleep on the sofa in the side room. I mean, with a blanket."

Again a laugh. "I don't need to sleep. But it's a kind thought. You're very kind." His eyes moved to the door, as Bessie walked in, making for her tablecloth of newspaper, on which stood her bowl of water and her unfinished bowl of creamy milk. His eyes followed the cat.

Eleanor felt a sudden apprehension. It was probably because Bessie had not seen him. That was certainly disturbing, when she could see him so well that even the wrinkles in his face were quite visible. He was clothed in strange material, gray-black, neither shiny nor dull.

"You must be lonely since your husband died," he said. "But I admit you do well. Considering he didn't leave you much."

Eleanor blushed. She could feel it. John hadn't been a big earner, certainly. But a decent man, a good husband, yes, he had been that. And their only child, a daughter, had been killed in a snow avalanche in Austria when she was twenty. Eleanor never thought of Penny. She had set herself never to think of Penny. She was disturbed, and felt awkward, because she thought of her now. And she hoped the creature would not mention Penny. Her death was one of life's tragedies. But other families had similar tragedies, only sons killed in useless wars.

"Now you have your cat," he said, as if he read her thoughts.

"Yes," Eleanor said, glad to change the subject. "Bessie is ten. She's had fifty-seven kittens. But three—no four years ago, I finally had her doctored. She's a dear companion."

Eleanor slipped away and got a big gray blanket, an army surplus blanket, from a closet and folded it in half on the sofa in the side room. He stood watching her. She put a pillow under the top part of the blanket. "That's a little cozier," she said.

"Thank you," came the deep voice.

In the next days, he cut the high grass around the barn with a scythe, and moved a huge rock that had always annoyed Eleanor, embedded as it was in the middle of a grassy square in front of the barn. It was August, but quite cool. They cleared out the attic, and he carried the heaviest things downstairs and to the edge of the road to be picked up by Field's. Some of these things were sold a few days later at auction, and fetched about thirty dollars. Eleanor still felt a slight tenseness when he was present, a fear that she might annoy him in some way, and yet in another way she was growing used to him. He certainly liked to be helpful. At night, he obligingly got on to his sofa bed, and she wanted to tuck him in, to bring him a cup of milk, but in fact he ate next to nothing, and then, as he said, only to keep her company. Eleanor could not understand where all his strength came from.

Vance rang up one day and said she had the pictures. Before Eleanor could ask about them, Vance had hung up. Vance was coming over at once.

"You took a picture of a chair, dear! Does he look like a chair?" Vance asked, laughing. She handed Eleanor the photographs.

There were twelve photographs in the batch, but Eleanor looked only at the top two, which showed him seated in the straight chair and standing by it. "Why, there he *is!*" she said triumphantly.

Vance hastily, but with a frown, looked at the pictures again, then smiled broadly. "Are you implying there's something wrong with *my* eyes? It's a chair, darling!"

Eleanor knew Vance was right, speaking for herself. Vance couldn't see him. For a moment, Eleanor couldn't say anything.

"I told you what would happen. Um-hm-hm."

He was behind her, in the doorway of the side room, Eleanor knew, though she did not turn to look at him.

"All right. Perhaps it's my eyes," Eleanor said. "But I *see* him there!" She couldn't give up. Should she tell Vance about his Herculean feats in the attic? Could she have got a big chest of drawers down the stairs by herself?

Vance stayed for a cup of tea. They talked of other things—everything to Eleanor was now "other" and a bit uninteresting and unimportant compared to *him*—and then Vance left, saying, "Promise me you'll go to Dr. Nimms next week. I'll drive you, if you don't want to drive. Maybe you shouldn't drive if your eyes are acting funny."

Eleanor had a car, but she seldom used it. She didn't care for driving. "Thanks, Vance, I'll go on my own." She meant it at that moment, but when Vance had gone, Eleanor knew she would not go to the eye doctor.

He sat with her while she ate her dinner. She now felt defensive and protective about him. She didn't want to share him with anyone.

"You shouldn't have bothered with those photographs," he said. "You see, what I told you is true. Whatever I say is true."

And yet he didn't look brilliant or even especially intelligent, Eleanor reflected.

He tore a piece of bread rather savagely in half, and stuffed a half into his mouth. "You're one of the very few people who can see me. Maybe only a dozen people in the world can see me. Maybe less than that.—Why should the others see me?" he continued, and shrugged his chunky shoulders. "They're just like me."

"What do you mean?" she asked.

He sighed. "Ugly." Then he laughed softly and deeply. "I am not nice. Not nice at all."

She was too confused to answer for a moment. A polite answer seemed absurd. She was trying to think what he really meant.

"You enjoyed taking care of your mother, didn't you? You didn't mind it," he said, as if being polite himself and filling in an awkward silence.

"No, of course not. I loved her," Eleanor said readily. How could he know? Her father had died when she was eighteen, and she hadn't been able to finish college because of a shortage of money. Then her mother had become ill with leukemia, but she had lived on for ten years. Her treatment had taken all the money Eleanor had been able to earn as a secretary, and a little more besides, so that everything of value they had possessed had finally been sold. Eleanor had married at twenty-nine, and gone with John to live in Boston. Oh, the gone and lovely days! John had been so kind, so understanding of the fact that she had been exhausted, in need of human company—or rather, the company of people her own age. Penny had been born when she was thirty.

"Yes, John was a good man, but not so good as you," he said, and sighed. "Hm-mm."

Now Eleanor laughed spontaneously. It was a relief from the thoughts she had been thinking. "How can one be good—or bad? Aren't we all a mixture? You're certainly not all bad."

This seemed to annoy him. "Don't tell me what I am."

Rebuffed, Eleanor said nothing more. She cleared the table.

She put him to bed, thanked him for his work in the garden that day— gouging up dandelions, no easy task. She was glad of his company in the house, even glad that no one else could see him. He was a funny doll that belonged to her. He made her feel odd, different, yet somehow special and privileged. She tried to put these thoughts from her mind, lest he disapprove of them, because he was looking, vaguely as usual, at her, with a resentment or a reproach, she felt. "Can I get you anything?" she asked.

"No," he answered shortly.

The next morning, she found Bessie in the middle of the kitchen floor with her neck wrung. Her head sat in the strangest way on her neck, facing backwards. Eleanor seized up the corpse impulsively and pressed the cat to her breast. The head lolled. She knew he had done it. But why?

"Yes, I did it," his deep voice said.

She looked at the doorway, but did not see him. "How could you? Why did you do it?" Eleanor began to weep. The cat was not warm any longer, but she was not stiff.

"It's my nature." He did not laugh, but there was a smile in his voice. "You hate me now. You wonder if I'll be going. Yes, I'll be going." His voice was fading as he walked through the living room, but still she could not see him. "To prove it, I'll slam the door, but I don't need to use the door to get out." The door slammed.

She was looking at the front door. The door had not moved.

Eleanor buried Bessie in the back lawn by the barn, and the pitchfork was heavy in her hands, the earth heavier on her spade. She had waited until late afternoon, as if hoping that by some miracle the cat might come alive again. But Bessie's body had grown rigid. Eleanor wept again.

She declined Vance's next invitation to tea, and finally Vance came to see her, unexpectedly. Eleanor was sewing. She had quite a bit of work to do, but she was depressed and lonely, not knowing what she wanted, there being no person she especially wanted to see. She realized that she missed him, the strange creature. And she knew he would never come back.

Vance was disappointed because she had not been to see Dr. Nimms. She told Eleanor that she was neglecting herself. Eleanor did not enjoy seeing her old friend Vance. Vance also remarked that she had lost weight.

"That—little monster isn't annoying you still, is he? Or is he?" Vance asked.

"He's gone," Eleanor said, and managed a smile, though what the smile meant, she didn't know.

"How's Bessie?"

"Bessie—was hit by a car a couple of weeks ago."

"Oh, Eleanor! I'm sorry.—Why didn't you—You should've *told* me! What bad luck! You'd better get another kitty. That's always the best thing to do. You're so fond of cats."

Eleanor shook her head a little.

"I'm going to find out where there's some nice kittens. The Carters' Siamese might've had another illegitimate batch." Vance smiled. "They're always nice, half-Siamese. Really!"

That evening, Eleanor ate no supper. She wandered through the empty-feeling rooms of her house, thinking not only of him, but of her lonely years here, and of the happier first three years here when John had been alive. He had tried to work in Millersville, ten miles away, but the job hadn't lasted. Or rather, the company hadn't lasted. That had been poor John's luck. No use thinking about it now, about what might have been if John had had a business of his own. Yes, once or twice, certainly, he had failed at that, too. But she thought more clearly of when *he* had been here, the funny little fellow who had turned against her. She wished he were back. She felt he would not do such a horrid thing again, if she spoke to him the right way. He had grown annoyed when she had said he was not entirely bad. But she knew he would not come back, not ever. She worked until ten o'clock. More letting out. More hems taken up. People were becoming square, she thought, but the thought did not make her smile that night. She tried to add three times eighty cents plus one dollar and twenty-five cents, and gave it up, perhaps because she was not interested. She looked at his photographs again, half expecting not to see him—like Vance—but he was still there, just as clear as ever, looking at her. That was some comfort to her, but pictures were so flat and lifeless.

The house had never seemed so silent. Her plants were doing beautifully. She had not long ago repotted most of them. Yet Eleanor sensed a negativity when she looked at them. It was very curious, a happy sight like blossoming plants causing sadness. She longed for something, and did not know what it was. That was strange also, the unidentifiable hunger, this loneliness that was worse and more profound than after John had died.

Tom Reynolds rang up one evening at 9 P.M. His wife was ill and he had to go at once to an "alert" at the Air Base. Could she come over and sit with his wife? He hoped to be home before midnight. Eleanor went over with a bowl of fresh strawberries sprinkled with powdered sugar. Mary Reynolds was not seriously ill, it was a daylong virus attack of some kind, but she was grateful for the strawberries. The bowl was put on the bed table. It was a pretty color to look at, though Mary could not eat anything just then. Eleanor felt herself, heard herself smiling and chatting as she always did, though in an odd way she felt she was not really present with Mary, not really even in the Reynoldses' house. It wasn't a "miles away" feeling, but a feeling that it was all not taking place. It was not even as real as a dream.

Eleanor went home at midnight, after Tom returned. Somehow she knew she was going to die that night. It was a calm and destined sensation. She might have died, she thought, if she had merely gone to bed and fallen asleep. But she wished to make sure of it, so she took a single-edged razor blade from her shelf of paints in the kitchen closet—the blade was rusty and dull, but no matter—and cut her two wrists at the bathroom basin. The blood ran and ran, and she washed it down with running cold water, still mindful, she thought with slight amusement, of conserving the hot water in the tank. Finally, she could see that the streams were lessening. She took her bath towel and wrapped it around both her wrists, winding her hands as if she were coiling wool. She was feeling weak, and she wanted to lie down and not soil the mattress, if possible. The blood did not come through the towel before she lay down on her bed. Then she closed her eyes and did not know if it came through or not. It really did not matter, she supposed. Nor did the finished and unfinished skirts and dresses down-stairs. People would come and claim them.

Eleanor thought of him, small and strong, strange and yet so plain and simple. He had never told her his name. She realized that she loved him.

I Am Not As Efficient As Other People

The shutters were the beginning of the crisis. Ralph's depression, his sense of failure, had been going on long before the shutters, of course, maybe since he had bought the house, if he thought about it, but the shutters seemed glaringly to illustrate his incompetence.

Ralph Marsh worked in Chicago, had an apartment there, but he had also a country house which he called sometimes his cottage, sometimes his shack, twenty miles outside of Chicago. He was a bachelor of twenty-nine, and a salesman of hi-fi equipment. He had had raises and promotions in his four years with Basic-Hi, he knew his job and was his company's best salesman, or so his superior had told him. Ralph knew the intricacies of a stereo set, and even considered himself reasonably good with his hands— not a genius do-it-yourself man, perhaps, but maybe better than average.

However, across Ralph's ten yards of lawn lived the Ralstons, Ed and Grace, who bustled about every weekend, doing not merely useful and necessary tasks such as lawn cutting, fence painting and hedge trimming (their hedge was young and low, and Ed kept it cropped with the sharpest of corners), but more difficult jobs such as cement mixing for bricklaying, which in the Ralstons' case had not meant simply piling one red brick on another: Ed had chipped into rectangles a number of large beige stones to create a low wall on the road side of his property. Part of the Ralstons' garage was a workshop, whence came the buzz of Ed's Black & Decker many hours every weekend. Ralph imagined Ed making furniture, repairing broken pipes, welding, doing things that Ralph would be afraid to attempt. Yet Ed Ralston, Ralph knew, was only a car salesman, probably hadn't finished university. Ralph was not chummy with the Ralstons, they only nodded greetings in a neighborly way when they saw one another.

Ralph had realized, since his first weekend at his cottage, that he was going to be envious of Ed. For one thing, Ed had a wife, and a wife was certainly a help in a house. The Ralstons also had an apartment in Chicago, they had told Ralph on their first meeting, and they said they had bought their country place for next to nothing, because it had been an empty barn. Ed and Grace had chipped away at the stone façade of the barn to expose beautiful old masonry, had put in windows, and installed heating and electricity with the help of a couple of chums of Ed's. They had bought their barn six months before Ralph acquired his house, and they were still at it every weekend, improving and adding things. Grace Ralston was as active as Ed, forever shaking out a doormat, hanging a wash on their plastic four-sided clothesline, or polishing windows.

Only when Ralph was tired around 7 P.M., wishing that he had someone to call him to a dinner already prepared, did he feel a little sorry for himself. Most of the time, he preferred to consider himself lucky. Ralph was at least six years younger than Ed, he earned more, and for all Ed's expert stonelaying, Ed was stuck with a wife who was certainly a boring type, and stuck too with a tantrumy four-year-old daughter who didn't look quite bright, in Ralph's opinion, whereas Ralph was free as the breeze and had a mobile girlfriend of twenty-four who was fun and made no demands on him. She was a dark blonde named Jane Eberhart, married to an airline pilot. Most weekends she was able to come out to the country house and stay the night, perhaps three Saturday nights out of four. They could manage a few dates in Chicago, too.

But the shutters. Ralph had painted three shutters on three windows, meaning six panels in all, in matte black. Because of other chores, Ralph had had to take three swats at the shutters on various weekends, but finally they were done, and he meant to say casually to Jane, "How do you like my shutters? They look neater, no?" which he did say one Saturday morning around eleven, when Jane arrived. Then when he folded back the third pair, he saw that he had missed one upper third of what would be the inside of a shutter when it was closed. It was like a visual joke, the former sickly pale brown which he had not painted contrasting with the black, and Jane appropriately laughed.

"Ha-ha!—Ralphie, you're a doll! *Very* funny! Hope you've got some paint left. But otherwise—sure, they look great, darling." Then she strolled in her mustard-colored slacks and clogs towards the house door.

Ralph felt a letdown, an embarrassment, as if he were on a stage and something had gone badly wrong. He folded the shutters back, so Ed Ralston wouldn't possibly see his blotch, but of course Ed would have his nose bent over some task of his own now, which he would complete perfectly. Absurd to feel like this, Ralph told himself, and deliberately smiled, though no one saw the smile. Ed Ralston would *not* have left an unpainted spot, or his wife would have noticed it in the course of Ed's painting, and called his attention to it.

Jane prepared lunch. She liked cooking for him more than for her husband, she said, because Ralph's taste was more catholic. Her husband was allergic to oysters, for instance, and disliked liver. That day, Jane made a delicious dish of fried shrimp with her own mayonnaise and tomato paste dressing, and Ralph had a bottle of cool white wine to accompany it. Usually after lunch he and Jane went to bed for an hour or so. After lunch and early morning, those were the times they both preferred.

Then Jane said during lunch: "So silly of you, that little unfinished spot on the shutters!" She laughed gaily again, as she bit into the last shrimp. "I bet old Ralston wouldn't've missed it! What's he up to today?—Remember the time he unplugged the kitchen sink with that electric gadget?" Jane shrieked with mirth at the memory.

Ralph remembered. Well, he hadn't a Roto-Rooter among his tools, and most people who were not professional plumbers didn't have one, in Ralph's opinion. "He's probably a health faddist, too," Ralph said. "Can't imagine him smoking or drinking a beer. Marches around with his back straight as if he's on parade somewhere. So does his wife."

Jane giggled, in a good mood, and lit a cigarette. 'I have to admit their place looks nice though—from the outside."

She'd never been in, though, and Ralph had. You could eat off the floor, as the saying went, but the furniture was not his style or Jane's, Ralph was sure. The Ralstons had an ugly, modern glass-top coffee table, and machine-made varnished furniture of rustic design or intention, suitable for the country, Ralph supposed the Ralstons thought. Grace Ralston had shown him with pride the brown and white tiles her husband had laid on the kitchen floor, and the cabinets with revolving corner sections which her husband had not made but had bought and sawed to measure and installed. Their rooms looked like sample rooms in a department store, not even a magazine out of place anywhere. Ralph had politely admired, but the Ralstons were not the kind of people he cared to cultivate, and he was sure Jane would feel the same way if she saw the inside of their house.

That afternoon, Ralph was not a success with Jane in bed. It was the first time in the four months they had known each other that this had happened, so Jane didn't take it seriously, and Ralph tried not to. One failure was unimportant, normal, Ralph told himself. But he knew otherwise. Jane's remarks comparing him with Ed Ralston had struck deep at his ego, even at his self-respect and his manliness, somehow. Ralph pictured Ed Ralston in bed, doing just the right thing with his plump, dull wife, because Ralston would never doubt, never hesitate. He probably had a technique as unvarying as the manner in which he changed the oil in his car, but at least it worked, and in this department Ralston would be labeled efficient also.

As they smoked a cigarette after their unsatisfactory lovemaking, dread thoughts swept through Ralph's mind. They all concerned failures. He recalled the simple two shelves he had started to put up in an alcove in the kitchen (before he met Jane), a project which he had abandoned when his drill hit a water pipe and caused a small flood. This had necessitated a plumber to solder the pipe, then the replacement of a piece of wall there, followed by Ralph's repainting of the plastered spot, which in turn had caused him to repaint the entire kitchen. Then the fixing of the towel rack in the bathroom: one end of it was still not as steady or strong as it should be, because the damned plaster didn't hold well enough, despite the length of the screws he had put in. Nothing he did was perfect. Jane wasn't perfect, if he thought about it, or her, because she was married, and her main allegiance was of course to her husband, whose schedule varied, and a few times she'd had to cancel a date with him, because her husband was unexpectedly due home for the weekend. Her husband Jack must be more efficient, or more highly trained, than he, Ralph realized, because he was an airline pilot. Ralph up to now had enjoyed his relationship with Jane, just because it wasn't binding or heavy, but that afternoon it seemed second-rate, incomplete, inferior to other men's relationships with girls, whether they were married or not. Couldn't he do better than Jane if he tried?

Instantly, Ralph reproached himself for this thought. Jane had many good qualities, such as discretion, patience, poise. She was rather pretty, and she liked to cook. But he wasn't top dog, or man, because Jane's husband was. Politics and economics bored Jane, while Ralph found them constantly interesting. She wasn't as intelligent as he could have wished a girlfriend to be, but that wasn't it, Ralph knew. He could imagine himself quite happy with an even less intelligent girl than Jane, if he could only hold up his end of things by properly coping with the odd jobs around his house, the repairs that a house always needed. Ed Ralston even got on a ladder and straightened roof tiles! Ralph wasn't afraid of heights, but he didn't care to risk breaking an arm, since he had to drive, and he wasn't sure he knew how to put right a tile that was out of place. His one achievement, he remembered with a flash of pride, had been sneaking into Jane and her husband's apartment, with Jane, and replacing a broken element in their stereo set. If her husband had come in, Jane had intended to say that Ralph was a repairman, but her husband hadn't come in. The replacement had been simple, but Jane had been most grateful and impressed. Could Ralston have done that? Ralph doubted it! Ralston wouldn't have known what was the matter, even after reading a brochure and an instruction book. Yet that triumph had been so long ago, three months or more now, and so brief.

" 'You're getting bored with me. Well—that happens," Jane said the next morning, when they were lying in bed.

"No. Don't be silly, Jane." Smiling, Ralph got out of bed, and put on his dressing gown.

But it was the end, and they both knew it, although they didn't mention it again that day. Jane left in her car before six in the evening, as her husband was due home before nine, and expected dinner. Ralph closed his house after Jane had gone, left a clean sink, and looked with bitter amusement at the vertical rafter or kingpin that extended from the middle of the living room floor up to the ceiling, and farther up through the top floor to the roof. Symbol of substantiality? What a laugh! The shutter discrepancy was on the inside, now that the shutters were closed, but Ralph was still aware of it as he drove off for Chicago. He thought it wisest and best if he didn't ring Jane again, and he was pretty sure she was not going to ring him.

A gloom settled over him, so large, so many-sided, that Ralph didn't know how to analyze it, much less get rid of it. He had no pep, no confidence. It was as if he had taken a sleeping pill, which he seldom did, though at the same time his thoughts came in nervous stabs: should he tell the office he needed a week off? They'd grant him that. But what good would it do? Should he visit a singles bar and look for a new girlfriend? With his lack of zest now, would he get one? On Wednesday of that week, he failed on a sale to a three-store chain in Chicago for a Basic-Hi product, because of his own lack of enthusiasm. The sale should have been a cinch, almost to be taken for granted, but a rival company with the same innovation in their line of gadgets won it. The day after his visit to the chain store, Ralph learned of his defeat from his boss, Ferguson. These things sometimes happened, but Ralph knew that Ferguson had noticed his depression that week.

"What's the matter, Ralph?—Had a tough weekend?" The weekend was four days past, but Ralph had been drooping all week. "Want to take tomorrow off? Sleep it off?" Ferguson grinned, knowing Ralph wasn't a big drinker, but perhaps thinking that Ralph had exhausted himself with a harem of girls last weekend at his country place.

"No, no. Thanks," Ralph said. "I'll shake it off. Just a mental attitude."

"Mental attitudes are important."

That day Ralph had lunch with Pete Barnes, another salesman of Basic-Hi, with whom Ralph was on closer terms. Ralph didn't mention his state of mind, and didn't need to, he supposed, because it showed. Pete also asked him what was the matter, if he'd had bad news, and Ralph told him about breaking with a girlfriend.

"Certainly not a tragedy," Ralph said. "For one thing, she's married. And we weren't in love. But of course for a couple of days, it's a letdown." Then Ralph turned the conversation to something else, their work, but even as he listened to Pete's news about their advertising budget, Ralph realized that it was the Ralstons' eternal bustling and efficient presence and proximity in the country that was gnawing at him far more than the loss of Jane. The Ralstons had the strange power to make him feel like a worm.

By Thursday evening, Jane had not telephoned. She always phoned at least by Thursday in regard to the weekend. Ralph thought it not fitting for him to ring, so he didn't. Ralph was sure the information about a breakup with a girlfriend reached Ferguson's ears at once via Pete Barnes, because the next day Ferguson asked if Ralph could come for dinner Saturday night, and added, "A very nice girl's coming—Frances Johnson. She's a personnel director for a bank, I forget which. You might enjoy meeting her."

Enjoy meeting her. What a phrase! You could meet somebody in five seconds, but *enjoy* it? Nevertheless, Ralph accepted graciously, and forewent his usual excursion to his country house that Saturday. His shack would only have depressed him further.

Ralph was bowled over by Frances Johnson. She was nearly as tall as he, with longish blonde hair—more blonde than Jane's—cool, slender, and long-legged, wearing a trouser suit that might have been made by the highest of haute couture, Ralph wasn't sure. Even the scent she wore was different and fascinating. Why was a girl like this free? And maybe she wasn't. Unless she had just broken with somebody too.

"Ralph's our number-one representative," Stewart Ferguson said to Frances during dinner, and Ferguson's wife nodded agreement.

The evening went well. When Frances was taking her leave, Ralph asked if he could see her to a taxi. She acquiesced, and he rode with her, as they had to go in the same direction. Frances's apartment house came first, and Ralph got out and held the door for her. By then, he had a date with her on Tuesday evening for dinner. She smiled as she said, "Good night, Ralph."

Ralph watched a gray-liveried doorman touch his cap and open a big glass door for her. Now that girl was nice, and maybe she liked him. Maybe she was important. She was a Smith graduate, plus having a degree in a business school whose name had escaped Ralph, maybe because when Ferguson had mentioned it at the table, Ralph had been looking into Frances's eyes, and she into his.

Tuesday evening, Frances still remained cool and collected, though Ralph fancied he felt a warm glow from her. She inspired him to be gallant and masterful, and he liked that. He had gone to his country place the preceding Sunday, tidied it more than he usually troubled to, with an idea of asking Frances if she would like to come out the following Saturday and stay overnight, if she cared to.

"I have two bedrooms," Ralph said, which was true.

Frances accepted. She knew how to drive, she said, but hadn't a car now. Ralph said it would be a pleasure to pick her up Saturday morning around eleven, and they could drive out together.

However, Ralph spent Friday night at his country house, did the shopping early Saturday morning, then drove the twenty miles to fetch Frances. He was in good spirits, and his work had gone well that week. Maybe he was in love with Frances, in love as he had never been with Jane. Maybe he could win Frances. But he hardly dared think of that. Frances was not the type to say "yes" quickly to anybody, about anything. But for the moment, her nearness was exhilarating.

As soon as he drove with Frances into the lane that curved towards his and the Ralstons' properties, Ralph was aware of the Ralstons' prettier, better-tended front lawn, better-clipped roses (it was already autumn), and he at once told himself to put such negative thoughts out of his head. Was Frances going to judge him as a man, as a possible lover, or even husband, by the way he clipped three rose bushes in front of his house?

In fact, Frances paid his shack a few compliments. She said the fireplace was just the right size. She liked his kitchen—yellow-walled, everything visible on shelves or pegs, and just now very clean and neat. Ralph put another log on the fire. They had a gin and Dubonnet. Frances did not want a refill before their lunch of cold lobster. They talked a little about their work, about their childhood and parents, and the minutes swam by. Ralph had forgotten his query to himself, was Frances free? She appeared free to him, she seemed to like him, but Ralph counseled himself not to move too fast, or he might lose all. As it was, that afternoon, he felt in a happy glow of expectation, as if the wine had gone to his head, though he had drunk less than he usually did.

"You did all this yourself?" Frances asked, as she stood with her coffee in the living room. She had been looking at the pictures on his walls, the bookcases.

"This shack? Well, I furnish it. I can't say much more for myself. I—" He broke off, thinking that all he could say was that he had painted the kitchen. He had bought his bookcases. She had seen his two bedrooms and bath, and put her overnight case in the bedroom with the single bed.

"It's very nice and cozy," said Frances, smiling, tossing her long hair carelessly back with one hand. But she shivered.

Ralph's start of pleasure at her compliment at once gave way to concern about her comfort. "Just a sec, I'll turn up the heat." He went and did so, in the broom closet off the kitchen where the heating control was. Then he poked the fire into greater action. His next little chore was a final touch to his weather stripping, which he had nearly completed that morning. This was to drive a small wedge of wood into a gap at the upper corner of a door in his living room, a door which opened on his small back garden in summertime. Ralph had just the piece of pine board that he needed, plus a hatchet in his lean-to shed, so he said, "Back in two minutes, Frances," and went out the front door.

He took the piece of wood, held it on end, and gave its edge a whack at its lower end. The point of the hatchet hit the cement threshold of the shed, but only a curled shaving came off the wood.

"What're you doing?" Frances asked.

Ralph had been aware of her approach. "Nothing serious," Ralph said with a smile, still stooped with his hatchet and wood. "I need a wedge for the door in the living room. The door never did fit at the top corner." Ralph struck again with the hatchet. This time a larger piece came off, but so large that it was not usable for his purpose. Ralph tried to laugh. Was he going to fail again? On a primitive little job like this?

"How big do you want it?" Frances asked, stooping nimbly beside him.

"Oh—like this." Ralph held his finger and thumb not half an inch apart. "That thick. Then tapering."

"I see," she said, and was ready to take the hatchet from him, but Ralph said:

"I'll try it again." He lifted the hatchet and tried to come down with direct aim and the right degree of strength, and once more his result was a useless shaving. He banged again more vigorously, which simply put an indentation in the side of the board.

Frances laughed a little. "Let me try. It's fun!"

"No." Quickly, as Frances drew her slender hand back, Ralph hacked again. He had it—but it was an oversized wedge, too long, and not worth the effort to shorten.

Frances was still smiling. "My turn." She succeeded with the first stroke. The hatchet had not even touched the cement threshold. She held up the wedge. "Something like this?"

"Perfect," said Ralph, rising. A faint sweat came over him.

In the house, he stood on a chair and banged the wedge into the top crack of the door with the hammer side of the hatchet. It went in perfectly, closed the door corner flush with the jamb, and didn't even stick out. "Makes a lot of difference with the draft," Ralph said.

"I'm sure." Frances was watching him. "Excellent. Good."

A hotter sweat came over Ralph, as if his banging in the wedge had caused him to expend a great deal of muscular effort. But he knew that was not the cause of his physical warmth. He was experiencing some kind of crisis. And Frances was smiling at him, casually but steadily. She liked him. Yet he felt at that moment like a wretch, worthless and inferior. What was it? He reminded himself, in a quick flash of reality, of his job, his "position"—not bad at his age, and even enviable for a man ten years older. His self-congratulation vanished at once. *It was the Ralstons. It was the wedge.* If, with some tact and finesse tonight, he might persuade Frances into his bed (he had changed the sheets that morning), he knew he would not be able to make it. And was he going to impose that failure, yet another failure, upon himself?

"What's the matter?" Frances asked. "You're all pink in the face."

"Blushing maybe?" Ralph tried to smile, and laid the hatchet on the floor by the front door to remind himself to take it back to the shed. When he turned to Frances again, she was still looking at him. "I'm cracking up, that's all," Ralph said.

"What?—Why?"

Suddenly words came bubbling out of him. "Because I can't do anything efficiently! Really, it's true! I'm not sure I could change a washer on the kitchen sink!—I—The fellow next door, Ed Ralston, even his wife—" Ralph gestured in the Ralstons' direction with a wave of his arm. "—they can do *everything!* You'd be amazed! He's a mason, plumber, electrician, and she's a gardener and *super* housekeeper. They never stop working—and doing things efficiently. Whereas I can't. I don't." Here Ralph was aware that he was or might be boring Frances, because she was looking at him with a puzzled frown, even though she smiled a little, but he plunged on. "It's—I don't expect you to understand. You've just met me. I've got to get out of this house or—" Or collapse under it, Ralph had been about to say.

Frances's calm, beautiful gray-blue eyes looked in the direction of the Ralston house, visible through the window.

She seemed lost in her own thoughts for a few seconds, and her gaze, to Ralph, seemed the gaze of a person who wished to escape (and who could blame her?). He had lost her. Ralph took a quick, deep breath. He could have collapsed with defeat, with unhappiness, and yet at the same time an insane energy boiled within him.

'I think you'd better leave," Ralph said in a hoarse but gentle tone.

"Leave?—Well—of course I will, if—" Now her eyes grew wider, with fear.

Because I'm going to destroy this house, Ralph thought. But he didn't want Frances to be crushed under it, just himself, perhaps.

"If you're so upset—"

"Yes," Ralph said. "I'm sorry. I can drive you—home." He stood rigid, boiling with heat and purpose again, ashamed of his behavior, yet ashamed as if he saw himself from a distance, as if he weren't himself, standing here, looking at the girl.

"All right. I'll get my case."

"Oh, no, I'll do it!" Ralph dashed past her and up the stairs. Her overnight case was still closed on the floor near the single bed, and a glance into the bathroom showed that she had not put out any toothbrush or cosmetics. Ralph went down with the case.

Now Frances had lit a cigarette, and she seemed calmer, standing where she had been before. "You know, it's absurd—thinking that you're inferior somehow—just because you're not a mason."

A mason was not what he meant. Ralph meant that he couldn't do *anything* properly. "I am not as efficient as other people," he said tensely, gasping. He could have leapt to the ceiling as easily as he had just run up the stairs. He twitched with repressed brute strength. "Can you—perhaps leave me alone for a minute or two? Could you take a little walk for five minutes?"

She had mentioned the woods across the road, said something about taking a walk there when they had arrived today. Now she said, "But of course."

When he saw that she had crossed the road, he took her suitcase and set it outside the house by his car. Then he fetched his large saw with the bow-shaped handle from his shed, and attacked the vertical rafter in the center of his living room. This was a blissful outlet for his energy. The wood seemed to cut like butter, though after a moment the saw stuck with friction, so he attacked the post from the other side, which would result in a V-shaped incision a little lower than his waist as he stood.

Done! He could see through the V even, yet the damned house didn't fall. "Curse you!" Ralph said.

He took a few steps backwards, rubbed his palms together, bent and charged.

His right shoulder struck the top part of the severed rafter, and he pushed harder against it, aware of a crackling, deep yet sharp, over his head. He was aware of pain in his shoulder, then a brief roar as of an avalanche. Then he blacked out.

When Ralph was next aware of consciousness, or of thought, he seemed to be floating, weightless, horizontal perhaps, and on his back. Frances was beside him, the beautiful Frances, and she was sitting by his bed. Of course he was on a bed, or in a bed, in a hospital. He remembered. What he saw through drugged, half-open eyes was a gray-white. He tried to lift his hands, and couldn't. But there sat Frances, he saw when he groggily looked to his left.

"I've come to see you—but I think I shouldn't see you again, Ralph. You frighten me. I hope you'll understand."

Ralph opened his dry lips to reply, and nothing came. Of course he understood. He was a failure, and worse, he had lost his head. He remembered, he had tried to blow up his house. No, not bomb it, but wreck it. He had attacked it with a sledgehammer. No, a *saw*. He remembered now. No wonder Frances had fled! He wondered if she were all right? And he hadn't the power to ask her. His eyes when he turned them to the left, whence came her voice, would not even bring Frances into focus. But there was her voice again:

"Ralph, I'm sorry. But I'm afraid of you. You must understand."

Ralph tried to nod in a pacific, polite and reconciled way. Could she see his nod? Ralph squeezed his eyes shut, wanting to weep, detesting himself, and feeling in agony at the loss, the predictable, inevitable loss of Frances. He wanted to die. And so he gave a groan.

"*O-oh-h!* A–ah–h!"

And Frances fled out the door. Who could blame her? And a nurse arrived quick as lightning, her figure a vague cloud at the left side of his bed, and she made a motion which Ralph knew was the injection of a needle into his arm, though he didn't feel anything.

Once more, consciousness stirred, he imagined that he saw things, such as the upper corners of his room, Frances somewhere on his left again, maybe sitting on a chair, leaning forward.

"You're going to be all right," said Frances in a soft voice. "Things—it's not so bad. Just a broken collarbone and a bang on the head."

"It is hopeless," Ralph murmured, mumbling like a drunk, and sleepy unto death. Maybe he was already dead? "I'm—hopeless."

"No!—Ralph, I understand why you did it. It's just a house. So what?" Frances's voice said with more conviction.

Now Ralph felt a pressure on his left hand. Frances might have been holding his hand in both hers. "I can't—" Ralph stopped, wanting to make the statement that he was not efficient, *not* efficient. "I can't do *anything.*"

"Who cares?" Frances's blonde personage or aura bent and kissed him on the lips.

Ralph blinked. "Are you real?" His vision of her was still fuzzy at the edges, but he felt the pressure on his hand.

"I am *real*. And I love you, Ralph."

Ralph sighed, and relaxed in a mingling of pleasure and pain. It was real. Frances was really here, and his earlier vision had been a dream, an hallucination. "Stay with me," he whispered.

"I will! I can stay all night in the next room. It's already two in the morning now!" she said with a laugh. "Oh, Ralph, I'm not very efficient either, except a little bit in the kitchen. I mean, I can't change a washer. Does it matter?" She kissed him again on the lips.

This was real. Ralph smiled, felt like dying again, but in a different way. The nurse came in, shooing Frances away. Did that matter? She would be near him, all night, in the next room.

Ralph saw her wave, as she went out the door. Ralph tried to look firmly at the nurse, steadily, and as usual, he failed. It didn't matter any more.

The Cruelest Month

Odile Masarati was having a boring, ordinary day. That was the way she thought of it, meaning everything was "the same as always." She was sitting at her desk (really just a table with a drawer) on its low platform in front of a class of fifteen- and sixteen-year-olds, all with heads bent as they scribbled away at their English exam. Noticing a movement out of the corner of her eye, Odile looked up from her book.

"Philippe?" she said gently, her mind still on what she had been reading.

Philippe's head ducked back into line, and bent again over the paper.

The little rat had been trying to cheat again, peering at the paper of the girl next to him! Odile returned to Graham Greene. She had read the novel at least twice before, but she never tired of it. How she admired his writing! Such economy, such intellect! She recalled that she had written him two or three highly complimentary letters, care of his publishers, but he had never replied. Well, he wouldn't reply. He was one of the Pantheon. But no matter. She had a correspondence going now with three of her idols, two men and one woman, so her life was not exactly empty. In fact, what cheered her at that moment was the thought of hurrying home at three and dashing a letter off to Dennis Hollingwood of Essex, England, a writer of adventure novels.

On the dot of three, Odile stood up and said mechanically, "Very good, boys and girls. It's three o'clock. *Merci—et bon après-midi!*"

"Ou-u-u!" moaned one boy.

Others giggled in sudden release, called to friends, stood up, or threw their pens down like angry businessmen.

The students deposited their papers on a corner of Odile's desk, and these she gathered up, stuck into a folder and stuck the folder into her briefcase. Odile walked briskly to her locker down the hall, barely saying *"Bon soir"* to a couple of colleagues whom she passed, but then half the time the teachers were feuding with her or among one another, and some were jealous of her, Odile suspected. Why bother keeping track of it all? Provincials, Odile thought, stupid and mediocre. Odile knew she was a born linguist, Italian being her mother tongue, French a close second, because of her family's moving to France when she was four, Spanish had been a piece of cake, and her German wasn't bad either, and as for English, she loved English literature so, that that language might as well have been another mother tongue. She tugged on her raincoat. It was raining again. Odile unlocked her Deux Chevaux, and drove off down a street bordered with cropped plane trees that reminded her of freshly trimmed tails of poodles. She might write that to Dennis Hollingwood, though his prose wasn't inclined to similes, but rather to blunt narration and action. She passed the one butcher's shop of the town, not open till four, and reminded herself that she must buy some *viande hâchée* for her father either on her way to or coming from the ecology meeting at 4:30. Odile was almost a vegetarian, but her father liked his meat.

She turned left on to a smaller road at almost the edge of town, and now farm fields spread to right and left, and the few houses were stone farm dwellings and barns. Odile's house was a bit grander, formerly a small château, though one wing of it had suffered fire and collapsed long ago and had never been rebuilt. Her parents had bought the place for a song thirty years ago, when her father had fled from Italy because of a business scandal due to his brother, who had been a crook, whereas her father was merely naive. The Masarati house was a two-and-a-half story, as Odile described it to her penpals and when she sent photos, which she often did to brighten up her letters, the half at the top being now their two attic rooms, but formerly the rooms of servants. Abominable ivy had been allowed to grow in ages past, and resisted Odile's vigorous efforts to oust it, though she cut through the thick stems at their base. She and her mother, a really energetic soul, might have conquered the ivy together, but her mother had been killed in a stupid car accident seven years ago, right here in Ezèvry-la-Montagne where the lane joined the main road into town. Her mother had been on foot.

Now Odile lived with her father alone, stuck with him, as she put it in many of her letters, though her feelings about the old man were mixed. Michel wasn't unintelligent, he had had a respectable career as hydraulic engineer, until Parkinson's syndrome had struck him about two years ago. Lately he had not been able to walk at all, and lived in a wheelchair, not an electrically propelled one, but one that he could maneuver all over the ground floor where he lived and slept. Bars beside the toilet and over the tub in the downstairs bathroom enabled him to use both these facilities without assistance. Michel read a lot, but the pills he took made him sleepy, and in Odile's opinion he slept more than their dog, Trixie, which was fifteen hours in twenty-four according to the dog books.

"Hello, Papa!" Odile cried, having let herself in with her key.

Her father sat in the living room in his wheelchair, reading under the yellowish light of the standing lamp, which always struck Odile as insufficient.

"Hello, my child. You had a nice day?" The old man always said this.

"Ye-es, thank you." Odile hung her raincoat on a peg in the dim hall, slipped out of her boots and went in stockinged feet up the stairs to her room, greeted Trixie who was asleep in her basket by the radiator, and opened her briefcase. "Ready for your walk, Trixie?" Odile asked, as she laid the folder of exam papers on a clear spot on her desk. She put on loafers. She wasn't going to walk any distance in this rain, just let the dog out on the back terrace to pee.

Trixie followed her, having yawned and groaned a little. The dog was eleven years old, a little plump, though Odile was strict about food and exercise when the weather permitted, taking walks of two miles with Trixie in the lanes and fields around. It was just that dogs who were part dachshund and part cocker (both these breeds being famous for overeating, Odile thought) needed discipline or they gained too much weight. Odile was back in her room with Trixie in five minutes, and sat down at her desk to spend a happy twenty minutes or so.

She addressed an envelope to Dennis Hollingwood at Five Oaks. She knew the rest of the long address and its postal zone by heart.

Dear Dennis,

What a day! Two English exams today, morning and afternoon for my little beasties, one of whom I caught cheating! If I find any amusing bloopers in the exams, which I have to start on later this afternoon after an ecology meeting of the locals, I shall regale you with same. Meanwhile it rains incessantly, reminding me of the old English soldiers' song, First World War: "Raining, raining, raining, always bloody well raining . . ." I hope weather is nicer at Five Oaks.

Did you receive my last letter with photos of my ivy which I've told you so much about? It fairly obscures all sunlight, when we have any, in downstairs living room. Must cut again around the windows.

She paused, ballpoint pen's end against her upper lip. She had sent Dennis cuff links at Christmas, for which he had written a note of thanks (they were a bit pricey), and he had added, "I hope you'll forgive me, but I haven't the time to answer every letter you write or in fact any of them just now." That had been Dennis's second and last letter, his first having been in response to a carefully wrought letter of praise from Odile in regard to *Devil's Bounty*, which Dennis Hollingwood had deigned to acknowledge with the remark, "I don't usually receive such intelligent fan mail, so yours was a pleasure—though I hardly fancy myself the equal of Conrad." This first letter had made Odile spin with joy (after all, Dennis Hollingwood was rather famous, and two of his eight novels had been made into films), and Odile had responded with a spate of letters to him, all of which she wrote in a light vein, but she had told him a lot about her own life, and about Stefan, a married man she had fallen in love with when she had been twenty-seven, and with whom she had had an affair for five years, until Stefan broke it off. Stefan Mockers was a doctor, a nose and throat specialist, dashing and handsome when she had met him, an Adonis to many women and girls, Odile had known, but she had also known that she had been his only mistress while their affair had lasted. The sad sequel to her five years of bliss with Stefan was that three months after Stefan had broken it off, he had been in a car accident (Stefan had been driving but it hadn't been his fault) on the Corniche near Marseille, had suffered broken legs and a head injury that had done him permanent brain damage. Stefan had had to abandon his practice, and was now not even a shadow of his old self, lived at home with his wife and their two teenaged children, and occasionally Odile saw Stefan and his wife shopping in Ezèvry, Stefan creeping around with a cane as if he were ninety instead of fifty-five, and Odile always looked the other way and was sure Stefan never saw her. On her cluttered, ever-changing desktop, Odile still found room for a small photograph of Stefan, virile and smiling, with dark hair and mustache (now his hair was all gray), in a frame which stood up. Odile believed that Stefan had been the love of her life, that she might, just might, meet another man with whom she might fall in love, but no one would ever be able to hold a candle to the brilliant Stefan in his prime.

However, back to Dennis Hollingwood. She had told Dennis (whom she had started addressing as Dennis after his thank-you letter for the cuff links) about her first meeting with Stefan, their discretion in making rendezvous in the area, Stefan's fantastic wit and charm, the tragedy of his breaking it off, followed so soon by his accident—and all this flashed through her head again like a recorded tape, and she experienced it all again in a matter of seconds, as if indeed it were a tape that she couldn't switch off until it played itself out.

Odile had realized that Dennis's letter saying he hadn't time to answer her letters had been a brush-off, but she had felt that silence on her part after that would have looked as if she were hurt or sulking, so she had gone on writing to Dennis every two weeks or so, as if he had said nothing of this kind. Odile didn't see that an occasional cheerful letter could be annoying. She wasn't telephoning him, which she had once tried to do and discovered that he had an unlisted number which the English operator had refused to give out.

> I wonder what you're working on now? I hope another master-piece like *Devil's Bounty.* I shall never forget the scene in which Ally learns the truth about his sister . . .

Odile went on for a few lines, glanced at her watch and saw that she still had time to inform Dennis that she was about to go off to the ecology meeting concerning tree care today, on which *she* would be expected, as town workhorse, to write a report of four or five hundred words, the report to be dropped into the post box of *La Voix d'Ezèvry* before she went to bed tonight.

She attended the ecology meeting—ten people, nearly all women—in the rundown bourgeois house of Mme. Gauthier of the village. Odile was bored, though she took notes on what was said. Ecology interested Odile, but the town was doing all right in the tree department, and Odile was more concerned about animal protection, the local rabbits and deer during the hunting season.

Soon she was back at her desk at home, and the letter to Dennis had to be put aside while she dashed off the ecology report on her French type-writer. Always best to get it done while it was fresh in her mind.

Then it was time to prepare dinner. She had picked up the mince. The

kitchen was old like the house, but it had a modern gas stove and a refrigerator. Her father had set the table, as he always did, and he hovered in the
hall in his chair, leaving her room to pass to carry things to the table.

"Anything new happen today?" asked her father.

"Ha! What's ever new? No, indeed! Nothing!" Odile replied cheerfully, stirring butter into her cooked fresh spinach.

She and her father spoke in French, though Odile had the habit of
speaking Italian to Trixie, Italian being cozier than French, in Odile's opinion, and more suitable for children and animals. She gave Trixie her dinner
of raw diced steak and a couple of dog biscuits, then she and her father sat
down. Odile had a good appetite and ate more rapidly than her father,
who of course dallied because it was his only social event of the day, and
Odile always sat on as long as she could stand it.

'You ought to get out more, Odile," said her father.

"Oh? And where?" Odile replied, eyebrows raised, smiling. "And with
whom? Do you know the people around here have never heard of Céline
even? You expect me to have intellectual conversations with these hicks?"
She laughed good-naturedly, and so did her father. "You took all your pills
today, Papa?"

"Ah, yes, I don't forget," he answered with resignation. As Odile was
pouring her father's *décaféiné* at half past nine, the telephone rang.

"And there's Marie-Claire," said her father calmly, just to be saying
something.

Odile, who had poured her cup of real coffee, good and strong, excused
herself and took the cup to the telephone on the other side of the room.

Marie-Claire Lambert rang nearly every evening between nine-thirty
and ten. She was Odile's best friend, almost her only friend in Ezèvry. They
had made acquaintance a couple of years ago at an ecology meeting.
Marie-Claire was also unmarried, about thirty-two, raised in Paris, and she
had inherited a large property on the southeast edge of town, including a
château, part of which she rented to a married couple, plus two houses in
which working-class families lived, paying Marie-Claire a rent that was
rather low, because the families tended the garden and the grapevines and
generally looked after things, not to mention that one of the wives was a
full-time housekeeper in the part of the château where Marie-Claire lived.
One thing Odile and Marie-Claire had in common was boredom with the
town and its inhabitants. They could at least make each other laugh with
their stories of tedium, stupidity, inefficiency, or whatever other local
drawbacks they might have encountered in the course of the day.

That evening, after their usual chitchat, Marie-Claire proposed a trip to England during Odile's Easter vacation in April. "Six days. I just happened to see this special rate in Hercule's window this morning." Hercule was the tiny travel agency of the town, based in a shop which sold electrical appliances.

Odile was interested. Her mind fixed at once on Dennis Hollingwood, whose face she knew from photographs on the jackets of his books. She wondered if she could somehow wangle a meeting with him, or at least see the outside of his house?

". . . Brighton, ha-ha," Marie-Claire went on, reading from the brochure. "Hotel's not included, you understand, this is just the *aller-retour,* but my God it's cheap!"

They both had to watch their pennies, Marie-Claire considerably less, but Odile appreciated her friend's sympathy for her smaller income and thought it rather noble of Marie-Claire to be concerned with economizing. Marie-Claire had a great-aunt in England, Odile knew, and Odile had gathered from Marie-Claire's description of her big country house that the great-aunt had money. Was Marie-Claire deriving some money from her? Odile had never asked and never would.

"Got time for a bite of lunch on Sunday?" asked Marie-Claire, switching to English as she often did.

"Dunno why not," Odile replied. "With pleasure. What time?"

Odile did not turn her light out that night until two in the morning, as usual. She had corrected and graded seven of the nearly one hundred English exam papers which she had to finish by Monday, and indulged in starting a letter to Wilma Knowles, an elderly writer of romance novels who lived in Canada, and who now and then answered a letter from Odile, which Odile admitted to herself was more gratifying than writing to a stone wall like Graham Greene. She and Wilma Knowles led rather the same kind of quiet lives in small towns, Odile thought. Wilma Knowles had written, at Odile's request, a description of her daily life, work in the mornings, maybe some shopping in the afternoons, she lived alone with two dogs in a country house a mile from town, and she still did her own housework and drove her car at the age of seventy-two.

The next morning when Odile stopped at the post office just after eight to collect her post and buy stamps, she received, besides an Eléctricité de France bill, a letter from Ralph Cowdray of Tucson, Arizona. This gave Odile a lift. She read it, sitting in her DC.

Dear Miss Masarati,

Can't write French but it's plain your English is great. Thanks for writing me. Glad you enjoyed *A Dead Man's Spurs* so much. Not my best in my opinion. Sorry I took so long to answer your letter but I've been busy doing research for my book-in-progress. You asked what color hair I've got? It's slightly red, not what we call carrot red here but still red.

Sorry your life is so boring in that little town which ought to have some pretty spots, if you look for them. Your story about your mother being hit by a car and about your lost love (if I may venture to call it that) touched me very much. Maybe you should write all this tragedy out some time, just for your own sake and kind of get it out of your system.

Meanwhile I'm pretty flattered that someone in a small town in France has discovered my books and likes them. My publishers still publish my stuff (paperback only of course) but I still can't make ends meet without the waiter's job I told you about in first letter, summers and Christmas in a hotel here.

> Best of luck, keep your chin up,
> Ralph Cowdray

This was Ralph Cowdray's second letter, and Odile answered it that very evening. Her letter was four foolscap pages long, written on both sides in her flowing, legible hand.

The Sunday lunch on Marie-Claire's handsome terrace (which faced in the right direction for sun, unlike Odile's) made Odile more excited about the coming trip to England. Marie-Claire had booked them at the Hotel Sherwood near the British Museum. And Easter holidays were just a few days off!

"Have some more oysters, dear," Marie-Claire said, gesturing towards the well-filled platter garnished with parsley and lemon halves in the middle of the table.

Odile did. They were lunching on oysters only, thin bread and butter, a good chilled white white, to be followed by Marie-Claire's early *fraises des bois* now in a bowl on a silver tray of ice. Marie-Claire looked pretty and animated today, her light brown hair fluffy and fresh. Like Odile, she wore a sweater, slacks and flat shoes. After lunch, they were going for a walk across the fields. Odile had brought Trixie.

"Do you know, I saw Alain going into the bar with that blonde whore this morning when I was buying bread?" Marie-Claire said during the *fraises*.

Odile knew the two she meant: Alain the recently married son of the grocery shop owner, and the blonde whose name Odile thought was Françoise. "Oh, she's not a whore. Is she?" They were talking in English, and Odile thought the word a bit strong.

"Well, everybody's girlfriend, shall we say? Alain's drinking more *pastis* than he can hold. He'll lose his wife and his job, if he doesn't watch out. And his wife's pregnant, did you know?"

Odile knew, and thought it all too boring, though she didn't say so. Her thoughts were of England, the huge city of London, the old buildings, its accents that she had to make an effort to understand sometimes, its theaters, lights.

Then the day came. Odile was up before dawn. One of the two women at Marie-Claire's, the one who was not Marie-Claire's housekeeper, had agreed to look in at the Masarati house twice a day, to see that Odile's father had everything he needed, to tidy the house, and to walk Trixie a little because all her father could do was let Trixie out on the terrace.

This same young woman, Jolaine, arrived in her car at six in the morning with Marie-Claire to drive them to Marseille for the train. Then the train from Marseille to Paris, very fast indeed and more thrilling than an airplane, then the train from Gare du Nord to Calais, and the Channel ferry on which they dozed on bench seats part of the time. Victoria Station at dusk in a light rain evoked Sherlock Holmes stories for Odile, hansom cabs, gas lights. The lovely, grimy English cruddiness! Was that the word? If so, Odile meant it affectionately.

They slept like logs in the high-ceilinged room at the Sherwood. Then a morning at Foyle's, which Marie-Claire loved too, but not with such passion as Odile, a walk to Trafalgar Square and to Piccadilly, where Odile fell in love with a tan raincoat at Simpson's, but the price really was sky-high, considering what she had just spent in orders from Foyle's, so she ended by buying a cheaper though much the same kind of raincoat at Lillywhites.

"Got to think of my aunt, you know?" said Marie-Claire that evening when they were in their hotel room. She frowned a little as if she suddenly had a stomach pain. "May as well ring her now."

"Want me to leave the room?" Odile asked, giggling.

"My great-aunt? Ha-ha."

Marie-Claire made the call while Odile looked at the *Evening Stan-*

dard. She heard Marie-Claire making a date for "tomorrow afternoon" and getting the times of trains out of Victoria. Marie-Claire chose an 11:20.

"No, no, Aunt Louise, thank you anyway. I'm with my friend Odile and we're in a hotel, so—Thanks, I'll ask her." She addressed Odile with her hand over the receiver. "Want to come for lunch?"

Odile screwed her eyes shut and shook her head. 'Tell her thanks."

"Odile says many thanks, but she has a date somewhere," said Marie-Claire.

By noon the next day, Odile was at Liverpool Street Station, having seen Marie-Claire off at Victoria. Odile had bought a hardcover copy of *Devil's Bounty* for Dennis Hollingwood to sign, if she were lucky enough to meet him. No matter, to glimpse his house would be enough! She bought a day-return ticket to Chelmsford, and boarded a train.

At Chelmsford, she was told that there was no transportation to Little Starr, Dennis's village, except a bus at 4 P.M., but it was only five and a half miles away, Odile knew from a detailed map she had at home, so she took one of the taxis at the station. The driver asked where she wanted to go in Little Starr.

"The main square," she replied. "The center, please."

They sped through a couple of communities that were towns, judging from their name-markers at the edge of the road, then the driver came to a halt in a village square bordered by two-story houses and shops and graced by several elms. Odile paid and got out, realizing that she would have to ask someone for Five Oaks, otherwise she could go marching off in quite the wrong direction. She saw a plump and cheerful-looking man arranging apples in front of his fruit shop.

"Five Oaks," he repeated. "Mr. Hollingwood's place." He looked at her with more attention and what might have been surprise. "That's—" He swung round, pointing. "—down that road about a mile. On the left."

"Thank you very much." The man probably thought she had a car, but Odile didn't look back to see if he were watching her. She had decided to walk.

Along the curving two-lane road, Odile passed a few houses which became ever fewer. She well knew how long a mile was, and when she saw on her left a two-story house of whitish stone with two chimneys and a climbing rose at the doorway, set a hundred yards or more back from the road, she felt sure that it was Five Oaks. She saw four oaks. There was a garage to the left, nearly concealed by trees and bushes.

Was Dennis Hollingwood at this moment bent over his typewriter, composing first draft prose, his handsome face frowning? Or was he wandering into the kitchen for another cup of coffee or tea to take back to his desk? A window to the right of the door was half raised. Could that be the window of Dennis's study or workroom? Could he see *her* now if he looked out?

A pang of shame and excitement struck Odile. She would be visible, just, if Dennis looked out, even though a hedgerow would conceal half her figure. She knew Dennis was not married, and she presumed he lived alone.

But the minutes went by and nothing happened. The spring wind blew softly in Odile's ears, and seemed to whisper friendliness and courage. Odile advanced along the smooth gravel driveway that wound towards Dennis's garage. A flagstone path went off to the right and led to the house. Odile would of course not go to the door. But as a matter of fact she did have her brand-new hardcover of *Devil's Bounty* in her big handbag which she pressed hard against her side out of nervousness. Her steps grew smaller, slower. Couldn't she dare knock on his door—she saw a brass knocker—and ask him for an autograph? Since his telephone number was unlisted, she couldn't have rung him, and he would realize that. When she was some five yards from the house, the front door opened.

Dennis Hollingwood stood in the doorway, tall, blondish, frowning in the bright sunlight!

"Afternoon," he said. "Help you?"

"Good afternoon. I'm—" Odile's eyes devoured his figure, and she realized that she was trying to memorize every detail as if he might vanish in a split second: he wore brown corduroys, a white shirt with sleeves rolled up, a dark green sleeveless sweater. "I'm Odile Masarati. I've written you once or—" She stopped, because he had thrust his fingers through his hair with an air of irritation. "I don't mean to disturb you. I have a book of yours with me and I'd—"

He nodded, and came down the two steps on to the path. He had a pen in his right hand. But suddenly he stopped and looked at her, still frowning. "How'd you find my house?"

"I asked. In the village." She was fumbling with the first pages of *Devil's Bounty*, looking for the title page, so Dennis could sign below his printed name. "I'm sorry if—"

He ruffled his hair again and tried to smile. "No, it's just that—Right here on my property, you know—" He signed his name rapidly with a hand that shook slightly.

His hand shook with repressed anger, Odile knew. She saw a muscle in his jaw tighten. "Thank you!" she said, taking the book back.

"I hope you'll understand—I can't answer those letters of yours. Too many, too often, you know?" He took a step back from her. "Good-bye, Miss—"

"Masarati," she said. She added in a feeble voice that was a ghost of her own, "Good-bye, Mr. Hollingwood." Then she turned and walked towards the road.

He had turned away first, and she heard his door close firmly.

She walked back towards the town of Little Starr in a daze of shame and confusion. He had detested her! And she had nourished a fantasy of being invited in for a cup of tea, invited to take a look at the desk where he worked! Odile felt that she had just made the worst social gaffe of her life. She had intruded, like a piece of riffraff off the street! She walked with her eyes on the ground, never looking up until she found herself in the square of Little Starr again, and she set about finding a taxi to take her to the station at Chelmsford.

In the taxi, her tears came, though she held her head high. It was as if Dennis Hollingwood had suddenly died, had suddenly been erased from— what? From her circle of friends and beloveds, anyway. No letter that she might write him could ever explain or excuse her advancing up the path to his house. Maybe he'd been having difficulties with his work today, but no matter, *she* had been the invader of his privacy, unannounced and uninvited.

Even after the train journey, Odile's mood was no better and no different. She felt that her guilt must be visible, as if she wore a hair shirt.

She was supposed to meet Marie-Claire at their hotel around six. That didn't matter any more. Eschewing the taxis at Liverpool Street Station, Odile walked on towards the tube station called The Angel, where she could either look for a taxi or take the tube in the direction of her hotel, or even just keep on walking. Then at a corner near The Angel station, she deliberately stepped out in front of a taxi which was making a turn quite fast. Odile had wanted to injure herself, perhaps kill herself, though she had realized this only a few seconds before she leapt into the taxi's path.

Odile woke to find herself lying on her back in a bed, and she felt pain all along the right side of her head and face. She lifted her right hand, and her fingertips encountered thick bandages that extended under her chin. The light was dim, but she could make out beds on either side of her and more beds against an opposite wall. Palely-clad nurses came and went.

One nurse, noticing her arm movement, perhaps, turned with a tray to look at her.

"Waking up now? Want another painkiller?—You speak English?"

"Oh, yes," said Odile in a faint voice.

She was given a pill. Odile learned that she had suffered a concussion and a "laceration" down her right cheek. She was asked where she had been staying in London. The hospital had found her passport in her handbag. Odile told them the Hotel Sherwood, and they rang Marie-Claire Lambert, who came at once, even though it was nearly midnight by then. Marie-Claire was both shocked and relieved. She had thought Odile might have been kidnapped and maybe also murdered.

"*Me* kidnapped? For what?" Odile could still joke.

Odile had to remain in the hospital another five days at least, and Marie-Claire wanted to stay on in London and wait for her, but Odile insisted that she go back on her return ticket. Odile had some money with her, and could pay her hospital bill with a transfer of money from her father, which Marie-Claire promised to arrange. Marie-Claire pressed Odile's arm, and departed, promising to come again the next day.

Odile watched her friend tiptoe towards the door of the ward, then turn back.

"Odile, I can't go home without you. I'll stay till you can leave this place and we'll go back together." Tears rolled down her cheeks. "It's unbelievable!" she whispered in French. "What on earth has happened to your *face*, my darling?"

Odile said nothing. She was prepared for the worst and expected it, a broad, gravelly scar, perhaps, going from her temple down to her jaw.

She was still bandaged lightly and had not seen her wound when she and Marie-Claire made their way home six days later. Odile was rather weak, and Marie-Claire was sure it was from shock. She did not tell Marie-Claire that she had seen her literary idol Dennis Hollingwood that fateful day. That was Odile's secret and would always remain her secret.

In due time, two days after her return home, Odile's loose bandage was changed by the Masaratis' doctor, Dr. Paul Resquin, who shook his head solemnly and murmured some words about the incapacity of English doctors. Odile, sitting in his office for this, nearly fainted even in that position, and she did not ask for a mirror. She imagined the wound bright pink, and rough, an inch and a half or four centimeters broad, slanting across her cheek to well under her jaw, horrid and repellent, making people wince and look away.

When she did have the courage to look at her scar on another day at the doctor's, when he removed the bandage for the last time, she saw that it was not as broad as she had feared, nor as rough (Dr. Resquin had deplored its "unnecessary roughness"), but still it was shocking enough. The doctor gave her smelling salts, and made her lie down on his sofa for ten minutes. Then she got into her DC and drove straight home.

Marie-Claire was sympathetic and at the same time cheerful about it. "It won't always be pink, Odile. With a little make-up, you'll hardly see it!"

This of course wasn't true. Even with make-up, the roughness made shadows in most lights, no doubt even in candlelight, Odile thought with grim humor, and when would she ever have a romantic dinner by candle-light again? The days of stolen rendezvous with Stefan seemed now to have taken place in prehistoric time, the girl she had been then not even herself, not even related to the woman she was now. Her love life was finished, over, just as surely as Dennis Hollingwood was finished, any further corre-spondence with him or hope of meeting him again one day in happier circumstances. Oddly, the loss of Dennis Hollingwood, his profound exas-peration with her, was to Odile almost as weighty a thing as the loss of her beauty. The word "beauty" might not ever have applied to her, she realized, but she had had a freshness in her not-bad-looking face which now was gone for ever.

Odile had managed her return to school, the stares and questions and kind words from colleagues, with a quiet courage. But in those first days of facing the public with the big pink scar that lost itself under her jaw— Odile's mind churned.

Sometimes she felt almost glad that she had the scar, felt that it was a mark of honor, an announcement to the world that she had paid for her sins. But what sins? Wanting to meet a writer whom she admired? Then her thoughts would become lost, because for one thing, she would realize that Dennis Hollingwood per se hadn't been worth it, as a writer. There were other writers, Graham Greene, for instance, whom she definitely admired more, and who hadn't replied at all to her letters. *Pride,* she thought, it was all nothing but pride on her part. True enough, but good writers, writers of great talent, were worth it all. In a sense, it was these good writers who had rebuffed her, not Dennis Hollingwood himself or per se. Odile felt that she had turned an important corner in her life, because of the brand she bore on her face, and that her ignominy, her abysmal shame of her appearance, now, had made her someone different, humbler, but maybe even stronger, who knew? Time would tell that.

At other moments, even when she was taking Trixie for a long walk in the fields, Odile would believe that her conspicuous blemish was due to the hand of fate striking her yet again, as it had with her mother's early death, with the loss of Stefan, and now excluding her from any future happiness with lover or husband. Then she would feel depressed, like a leper who couldn't ever be cured, like someone even doomed to die in a short time. Odile then saw herself, as she strode vigorously up a slope or leapt a ditch more gracefully than Trixie, growing old with this same scar, and the scar becoming part of her by the time she was forty, for instance, all her friends accustomed to it, accustomed to her solitary existence, for surely it would be by then, with her father likely to die within the next two or three years.

Odile continued to write to Wilma Knowles, the writer who lived in Canada. She wrote fan letters to two more writers with her old zest and her old genuine admiration—one an Australian, the other American, both novelists. Such correspondence, even if doomed to be one-sided, was Odile's real life and joy, she realized. And so be it.

In spring of the next year, her father was laid to rest, as the priest said, in the little cemetery in Ezèvry-la-Montagne, and after the funeral, Odile invited some twenty villagers including Marie-Claire, of course, to the house for food and wine, what the English called funeral meats. Odile was a cheerful and efficient hostess. She was not yet thinking about her father's absence, but rather that one day she would likely be lowered into the same ground here. Life was nothing but trying for something, followed by disappointment, and people kept on moving, doing what they had to do, serving—what? And whom? Odile felt wise and calm that day, and shed not a tear for her dear old father.

The Romantic

When Isabel Crane's mother died after an illness that had kept her in and out of hospitals for five years and finally at home, Isabel had thought that her life would change dramatically. Isabel was twenty-three, and since eighteen, when many young people embarked on four happy years at college, Isabel had stayed at home, with a job, of course, to help with finances. Boyfriends and parties had been minimal, and she had been in love only once, she thought, or maybe one and a half times, if she counted what she now considered a minor hang-up at twenty on a married man, who had been quite willing to start an affair, but Isabel had held back, thinking it would lead nowhere. The first young man hadn't liked her enough, but he had lingered longer, in Isabel's affections, more than a year.

Yet six weeks after her mother's funeral, Isabel found that her life had not changed much after all. She had imagined parties, liveliness in the apartment, young people. Well, that could come, of course. She had lost contact with a lot of her old high school friends, because they had got married, moved, and now she didn't know where to reach most of them. But the world was full of people.

Even the apartment on West 55th Street had not changed much, though she remembered, while her mother had still been alive, imagining changing the boring Dubonnet-and-cream colored curtains, now limp with age, and getting rid of the nutty little "settles," as her mother had called them, which took up space and looked like 1940 or worse. These were armless wooden seats without backs, which no one ever sat on, because they looked fragile, rather like little tables. Then there were the old books, not even classics, which filled more than half of the two bookcases (otherwise filled with better books or at least newer books), which Isabel imagined chucking, thereby leaving space for the occasional objet d'art or statuette or something, such as she had seen in magazine photographs of attractive living room interiors. But after weeks and weeks, little of this had been done, certainly not the curtains, and Isabel found that she couldn't shed even one settle, because nobody she knew wanted one. She had given away her mother's clothes and handbags to the Salvation Army.

Isabel was a secretary-typist at Weiler and Diggs, an agency that handled office space in the Manhattan and Queens areas. She had learned typing and steno in her last year at high school. There were four other secretaries, but only Isabel and two others, Priscilla (Prissy) and Valerie, took turns as receptionist at the lobby desk for a week, because they were younger and prettier than the other two secretaries. It was Prissy, who was very outspoken, who had said this one day, and Isabel thought it was true.

Prissy Kupperman was going to be married in a few months, and she had met her fiancé one day when she had been at the front desk, and he had walked in. "Reception" was a great place to meet people, men on the way up, all the girls said. Eighty percent of Weiler and Diggs's clientele was male. A girl could put herself out a little, escort the man to the office he wanted, and when he left, ask him if his visit had been successful and say, "My name is Prissy (or whatever) and if you need to get a message through or any special service, I'll see that it's done." Prissy had done something along these lines the day her Jeff had walked in.

Valerie, only twenty and a more lightweight type than Prissy, had had several dates with men she had met at work, but she wasn't ready for marriage, she said, and besides had a steady boyfriend whom she preferred. Isabel had tried the same tactics, escorting young men to the office they wanted, but this so far had never led to a date. Isabel would dearly have loved "a second encounter," as she termed it to herself, with some of those young men, who might have phoned back and asked to speak with Isabel. She imagined being invited out to dinner, possibly at a place where they had dancing. Isabel loved to dance.

"You ought to look a little more peppy," Valerie said one day in the women's room of the office. "You look too serious sometimes, Isabel. Scares men off, you know?"

Prissy had been present, doing her lips in the mirror, and they had all laughed a little, even Isabel. Isabel took that remark, as she had taken others, seriously. She would try to look more lighthearted, like Valerie. Once the girls had remarked on a blouse Isabel had been wearing. This had been just after her mother's death. The blouse had been lavender and white with

ruffles around the neck and down the front like a jabot. The girls had pronounced it "too old" for her, and maybe it had been, though Isabel had
thought it perky. Anyway, Isabel had never worn it again. The girls meant
well, Isabel knew, because they realized that she had spent the preceding
five years in a sad way, nursing her mother practically single-handed.
Isabel's father had died of a heart attack when Isabel had been nineteen,
and fortunately he had left some life insurance, but that hadn't been
enough for Isabel and her mother to engage a private nurse to come in
now and then, even part-time.

Isabel missed her father. He had been a tailor and presser at a dry
cleaning shop, and when Isabel's mother's illness had begun, her father had
started working overtime, knowing that her cancer was going to be a long
and expensive business. Isabel was sure that this was what had led to his
heart attack. Her father, a short man with brown and gray hair and a modest manner that Isabel loved, had used to come home stooped with fatigue
around ten at night, but always able to swing his arms forward and give
Isabel a smile and ask, "How's my favorite girl tonight?" Sometimes he put
his hands lightly on her shoulders and kissed her cheek, sometimes not, as
if he were even too tired for that, or as if he thought she might not like it.

As for social life, Isabel realized that she hadn't progressed much since
she had been seventeen and eighteen, dating now and then with boys she
had met through her high school acquaintances, and her high school had
been an all-girls school. Isabel considered herself not a knockout, perhaps,
but not bad-looking either. She was five feet six with light brown hair that
was inclined to wave, which made a short hairdo easy and soft-looking.
She had a clear skin, light brown eyes (though she wished her eyes were
larger), good teeth, and a medium-sized nose which only slightly turned
up. She had of course, checked herself as long as she could remember for
the usual faults, body odor or bad breath, or hair on the legs. Very important, those little matters.

Shortly after Prissy's remark about her looking too serious, Isabel went
to a party in Brooklyn given by one of her old high school friends who
was getting married, and Isabel tried deliberately to be merry and talkative.
There had been a most attractive young man called Charles Gramm or
maybe Graham, tall and fair-haired, with a friendly smile and a rather shy
manner. Isabel chatted with him for several minutes, and would have been
thrilled if he had asked when he might see her again, but he hadn't. Later,
Isabel reproached herself for not having invited Charles to a drinks party
or a Sunday brunch at her apartment.

This she did a week or so later, inviting Harriet, her Brooklyn hostess, and her fiancé, and asking Harriet to invite Charles, since Harriet must know how to reach him. Harriet did, Charles promised to come, Harriet said, and then didn't or couldn't. Isabel's brunch went quite well with the office girls (all except one who couldn't make it), but Isabel had no male partner in her efforts, and the brunch did not net her a boyfriend either.

Isabel read a great deal. She liked romance novels with happy endings. She had loved romances since she had been fourteen or so, and since her mother's death, when she had more time, she read three or four a week, most of them borrowed from the Public Library, a few bought in paper-back. She preferred reading romance novels to watching TV dramas in the evening. Whole novels with descriptions of landscapes and details of houses put her into another world. The romances were rather like a drug, she realized as she felt herself drawn in the evenings towards the living room sofa where lay her latest treasures, yet as drugs went, books were harmless, Isabel thought. They certainly weren't pot or cocaine, which Prissy said she indulged in at parties sometimes. Isabel loved the first meetings of girl and man in these novels, the magnetic attraction of each for each, the hurdles that had to be got over before they were united. The terrible handicaps made her tense in body and mind, yet in the end, all came out well.

One day in April, a tall and handsome young man with dark hair strode into the lobby of Weiler and Diggs, though Isabel was not at the reception desk that day. Valerie was. Isabel was just then carrying a stack of photostatted papers weighing nearly ten pounds across the lobby to Mr. Diggs's office, and she saw Valerie's mascaraed lashes flutter, her smile widen as she looked up at the young man and said, "Good morning, sir. Can I help you?"

As it happened, the young man came into Mr. Diggs's office a minute later, while Isabel was putting the photostats away. Then Mr Diggs said:

". . . in another office. Isabel? Can you get Area-six-six-A file for me? Isn't that in Current?"

"Yes, sir, and it's right here. One of these." Isabel pulled out the folder that Mr. Diggs wanted from near the bottom of the stack she had just brought in.

"Good girl, thanks," said Mr. Diggs.

Isabel started for the door, and the eyes of the young man met hers for an instant, and Isabel felt a pang go through her. Did that mean something important? Isabel carefully opened the door, and closed it behind her.

In less than five minutes, Mr. Diggs summoned her back. He wanted more photostats of two pages from the file. Isabel made the copies and brought them back. This time the young man did not glance at her, but Isabel was conscious of his broad shoulders under his neat dark blue jacket.

Isabel ate her coffee-shop lunch that day in a daze. Valerie and Linda (one of the not-so-pretty secretaries) were with her.

"Who was that Tarzan that came in this morning?" Linda asked with a mischievous smile, as if she really didn't care. She had addressed Valerie.

"Oh, wasn't he *ever!* He ought to be in movies instead of—whatever he's doing." Valerie giggled. "His name's Dudley Hall. *Dudley.* Imagine."

Dudley Hall. Suddenly the tall, dark man had an identity for Isabel. His name sounded like one of the characters in the novels she read. Isabel didn't say a word.

Around four that afternoon, Dudley Hall was back. Isabel didn't see him come in, but when she was summoned to Mr. Diggs's office, there he was. Mr. Diggs put her on to more details about the office space on Lexington Avenue that Mr. Hall was interested in. This job took nearly an hour. Mr. Hall came with her into another office (used by the secretaries, empty now), and Isabel had to make four telephone calls on Mr. Hall's behalf, which she did with courtesy and patience, writing down neatly the information she gleaned about conditions of floors and walls, and the time space could be seen, and who had the keys now.

As Mr. Hall pocketed her notes, he said, "That's very kind of you, Miss—"

"Isabel," she said with a smile. "Not kind. Just my job. Isabel Crane, my name is. If you need any extra information—quick service, just ask for Isabel."

He smiled back. "I'll do that. Could I phone my partner now?"

"Indeed, yes! Go ahead," said Isabel, indicating a telephone on the desk. "You can dial direct on this one."

Isabel lingered, straightening papers on the desk, awaiting a possible question or a request from Mr. Hall to note down something. But he was only making a date with his partner whom he called Al to meet him in half an hour at the Lexington address. Then Mr. Hall left.

Had he noticed her at all? Isabel wondered. Or was she just another face among the dozen or so girl secretaries he had seen lately? Isabel could almost believe she was in love with him, but to be in love was dangerous as well as being pleasant: she might never see Dudley Hall again.

By the middle of the next week, the picture had changed. There were a few legal matters that caused Mr. Hall to come to Weiler and Diggs several times. Isabel was called in each time, because by now she was familiar with the file. She typed letters, and provided Dudley Hall and Albert Frenay with clear, concise memos.

"I think I owe you a drink—or a meal," said Dudley Hall with his handsome smile. "Can't make it tonight, but how is tomorrow? There's The Brewery right downstairs. Good steaks there, I've tried 'em. Want to make it around six or whenever you get off? Or is that too early?"

Isabel suggested half past six, if that was all right with him.

She felt in the clouds, really in another world, yet one in which she was a principal character. She didn't mention her date to Valerie or Prissy, both of whom had commented on her "devotion" to Dudley Hall in the last days. Isabel had made the date for 6:30 so she would have time to get home and change before appearing at The Brewery.

She did go home, and fussed so long over her make-up, that she had to take a taxi to The Brewery. She had rather expected to see Dudley Hall standing near the door inside, or maybe at the bar, but she didn't see him. At one of the tables? She looked around. No. After checking her light coat, Isabel moved towards the bar, and obtained a seat only because a man got up and gave her his, saying he didn't mind standing up. He was talking to a friend on an adjacent stool. Isabel told the barman she was waiting for someone, and would be only a minute. She kept glancing at the door whenever it opened, which was every fifteen seconds. At twenty to seven, she ordered a scotch and soda. Dudley was probably working a bit late or had had difficulty getting a taxi. He'd be full of apologies, which Isabel would say were quite unnecessary. She had tidied her apartment, and the coffeemaker was clean and ready, in case he would accept her invitation to come up for a final coffee at the end of the evening. She had brandy also, though she was not fond of it.

The music, gentle from the walls, was old Cole Porter songs. The voices and laughter around her gave her cheer, and the aroma of freshly broiled steaks began to make her hungry. The décor was old brown wood and polished brass, masculine but romantic, Isabel thought. She checked her appearance in the mirror above the row of closely set bottles. She was wearing her best "little black frock" with a V-neck, a slender gold chain that she had inherited from her mother, earrings of jade. She had washed her hair early that morning, and she was looking her best. In a moment, she thought, glancing again at the door, Dudley would walk in hurriedly, looking around for her, spotting her and smiling when she raised her hand.

When Isabel next looked at her watch, she saw that it was a couple of minutes past 7:30. A painful shock went through her, making her almost shudder. Up to then, she had been able to believe he was just a little late, that a waiter would page her, calling out "Miss *Crane*?" to tell her that Mr. Hall would be arriving at any minute, but now Isabel realized that he might not be arriving. She was on her second scotch, which she had been sipping slowly so it would last, and she still had half of it.

"Waiting for somebody?—Buy you a drink in the meantime?" asked a heavy-set man on her left, the opposite side from the door side, whom Isabel had noticed observing her for several minutes.

"No, thanks," Isabel said with a quick smile, and looked away from him. She knew his type, just another lone wolf looking for a pick-up and maybe an easy, unimportant roll in the hay later. Hello and good-bye. Not her dish at all.

At about five minutes to eight, Isabel paid for her drinks and departed. She thought she had waited long enough. Either Dudley Hall didn't want to see her, or he had had a mishap. Isabel imagined a broken leg from a fall down some stairs, a mugging on the street which had left him unconscious. She knew these possibilities were most unlikely.

The next day Dudley Hall did telephone to make his excuses. He had been stuck at a meeting with his partner plus two other colleagues from six o'clock until nearly eight, he said, and it had been impossible to get away for two minutes to make a phone call, and he was terribly sorry.

"Oh—not so important. I understand," said Isabel pleasantly. She had rehearsed her words, in case he telephoned.

"I thought by seven-thirty or so you'd surely have left, so I didn't try to call The Brewery."

"Yes, I had left. Don't worry about it."

"Well—another time, maybe. Sorry about last night, Isabel."

They hung up, leaving Isabel with a sense of shock, not knowing how the last few seconds had passed, causing them both to hang up so quickly.

The following Sunday morning, Isabel went to the Metropolitan Museum to browse for an hour or so, then she took a leisurely stroll in Central Park. It was a sunny spring morning. People were airing their dogs, and mothers and nurses—women in uniforms, nannies of wealthy families—pushed baby carriages or sat on benches chatting, with the carriages turned so the babies would get the most sun. Isabel's eyes drifted often from the trees, which she loved to gaze at, to the babies and toddlers learning to walk, their hands held by their fathers and mothers.

It had occurred to her that Dudley Hall was not going to call her again. She could telephone him easily, and invite him for a Sunday brunch or simply for a drink at her apartment. But she was afraid that might look too forward, as if she were trying too hard.

Dudley Hall did not come again to the office, because he had no need to, Isabel realized. Nevertheless, meeting him had been exciting, she couldn't deny that. Those few hours when she had thought she had a date with him—well, she'd *had* one—had been more than happy, she'd been ecstatic as she'd never been in her life that she could remember. She had felt a little the way she did when reading a good romance novel, but her date had been real. Dudley had meant to keep it, she was sure. He could have done better about phoning, but Isabel believed that he had been tied up.

In her evenings alone, doing some chore like washing drip-dry blouses and hanging them on the rack over the tub, Isabel relived those minutes in The Brewery, when she had been looking so well, and had been expecting Dudley to walk through the door at any second. That had been enchantment. Black magic. If she concentrated, or sometimes if she didn't, a thrill went over her as she imagined his tall figure, his eyes finding her after he came through the big brown door of The Brewery.

Eva Rosenau, a good friend of her mother's, called her up one evening and insisted on popping over, as she had just made a sauerbraten and wanted to give Isabel some. Isabel could hardly decline, as Eva lived nearby and could walk to Isabel's building, and besides, Eva had been so helpful with her mother, Isabel felt rather in her debt.

Eva arrived, bearing a heavy iron casserole. "I know you always loved sauerbraten, Isabel. Are you eating enough, my child? You look a little pale."

"Really?—I don't feel pale." Isabel smiled. The sauerbraten was still a bit warm and gave off a delicious smell of ginger gravy and well-cooked beef. "This does look divine, Eva," said Isabel, meaning it.

They put the meat and gravy into another pot so Eva could take her casserole home. Isabel washed the big pot at the sink. Then she offered Eva a glass of wine, which Eva always enjoyed.

Eva was about sixty and had three grown children, none of whom lived with her. She had never had a job, but she could do a lot of things— fix faulty plumbing, knit, make electrical repairs, and she even knew something about nursing and could give injections. She was also motherly, or so Isabel had always felt. She had dark curly hair, now half gray, was a bit stocky, and dressed as if she didn't care how she looked as long as she was covered. Now she complimented Isabel on how neat the apartment looked.

"Bet you're glad to see the last of those bedpans!" Eva said, laughing.

Isabel rolled her eyes upwards and tried to smile, not wanting to think about bedpans. She had chucked the two of them long ago.

"Are you going out enough?" asked Eva, in an armchair now with her glass of wine. "Not too lonely?"

Isabel assured her that she wasn't.

"Theo's coming for Sunday dinner, bringing a man friend from his office. Come have dinner with us, Isabel! Around one. Not sauerbraten. Something different. Do you good, dear, and it's just two steps from here."

Theo was one of Eva's sons. "I'll—That's nice of you, Eva."

"Nice?" Eva frowned. "We'll expect you," she said firmly.

Isabel didn't go. She got up the courage to call Eva around ten on Sunday morning and to tell a small lie, which she disliked doing. She said she had extra work for the office to do at home, and though it wasn't a lot of work, she thought she should not interrupt it by going out at midday. It would have been easier to say she wasn't feeling well or had a cold, but in that case, Eva would have been over with some kind of medicine or hot soup.

Sunday afternoon Isabel tackled the apartment with a new, calmer determination. There were more of her mother's odds and ends to throw away, little things like old scarves that Isabel knew she would never wear. She moved the sofa to the other side of the room, nearer a front window, and put a settle between window and sofa to serve as an end table, a much better role for that object, and Isabel was sorry she hadn't thought of it before. "Settle" was not even the right word for these chair-tables, Isabel had found by accident when looking into the dictionary for something else. A settle had a back to it and was longer. Another, one of many, odd usage of her mother's. The sofa rearrangement caused a change in the position of the coffee table and an armchair, transforming the living room, making it look bigger and more cheerful. Isabel realized that she was lucky with her three-room apartment. It was in an old building, and the rent had gone up only slightly in the fifteen years since her family had had it. She could hardly have found a one-room-and-kitchenette these days for the rent she was paying now. Isabel was happy also because she had a plan for that Sunday evening.

Her plan, her intention, kept her in a good mood all the afternoon, even though she deliberately did not think hard about it. *Play it cool,* she told herself. Around five, she put a favorite Sinatra cassette on, and danced by herself.

By seven, she was in a large but rather cozy bar on Sixth Avenue in the upper 50s. Again she wore her pretty black dress with the V-neck, a jade or at least green-bead necklace, and no earrings. She pretended she had a date around 7:30, not with Dudley Hall necessarily, but with somebody. Again she sat at the bar and ordered a scotch and soda, sipped it slowly while she cast, from time to time, a glance at the door. And she looked at her watch calmly every once in a while. She knew no one was going to walk in who had a date with her, but she could look around at the mostly jolly crowd with a different feeling now, quite without anxiety, as if she were one of them. She could even chat with the businessman-type on the stool next to hers (though she didn't accept his invitation to have a drink on him), saying to him that she was waiting for someone. She did not feel in the least awkward or alone, as she had finally felt at The Brewery. During her second drink, she imagined her date: a blond man this time, around thirty-four, tall and athletic with a face just slightly creased from the cold winds he had braved when skiing. He'd have large hands and be rather the Scandinavian type. She looked for such a man when she next lifted her head and sought the faces of three or four men who were coming in the door. Isabel was aware that a couple of people around her had noticed, without interest, that she was awaiting someone. This made her feel infinitely more at ease than if she had been at the bar all by herself, as it were.

At a quarter to eight, she departed cheerfully, yet with an air of slight impatience which she affected for any observer, as if she had given up hope that the person she was waiting for would arrive.

Once at home, she put on more comfortable clothes and switched on the TV for a few minutes, feeling relaxed and happy, as if she'd had a pleasant drinks-hour out somewhere. She prepared some dinner for herself, then mended a loose hook at the waist of one of her skirts, and then it was still early enough to read a few pages in her current romance novel, *A Caged Heart,* before she went to bed, taking the book with her.

Valerie remarked that she was looking happier. Isabel hadn't realized this, but she was glad to hear it. She was happier lately. Now she was going out—dressing up nicely of course—twice a week on her fantasy dates, as she liked to think of them. What was the harm? And she never ordered more than two drinks, so it was even an inexpensive way of entertaining herself, never more than six or seven dollars an evening. She had a hazy collection of men with whom she had had imaginary dates in the past weeks, as hazy as the faces of girls she had known in high school, whose faces she was beginning to have trouble identifying when she looked into her graduation book, because most of the girls had been only a part of the coming and going and dropping-out landscape of the overcrowded school. The Scandinavian type and a dark man a bit like Dudley Hall did stand out to Isabel, because she had imagined that they had gone on from drinks to dinner, and then perhaps she had asked them back to her apartment. There could be a second date with the same man, of course. Isabel never imagined them in bed with her, though the men might have proposed this.

Isabel invited Eva Rosenau one Saturday for lunch, and served cold ham and potato salad and a good chilled white wine. Eva was pleased, appreciative, and she said she was glad Isabel was perking up, by which Isabel knew she meant that she no longer looked under the shadow of her mother's death. Isabel had finally thrown out the old curtains, not even wanting to use them for rags lest she be reminded of drearier days, and she had run up new light green curtains on her mother's sewing machine.

"Good huntin'!" Valerie said to Isabel, Valerie was off on her vacation. "Maybe you've got a secret heart interest now. Have you?"

Isabel was staying on at the office, taking her vacation last. "Is that all you think makes the world go round?" Isabel replied, but she felt the color rise to her cheeks as if she had a secret boyfriend whose identity she would spring on the girls when she invited them to her engagement party. "You and Roger have a ball!" Valerie was going off with her steady boyfriend with whom she was now living.

Four days before Isabel was to get her two weeks' vacation, she was called to the telephone by Prissy who was at the reception desk. Isabel took it in another office.

"Willy," the voice said. "Remember me? Wilbur Miller from Nebraska?" He laughed.

Isabel suddenly remembered a man of about thirty, not very tall, not very handsome, who had come to the office a few days ago and had found some office space. She remembered that he had said, when he had given his name for her to write down, "Really Wilbur. Nobody's named Wilbur anymore and nobody comes from Nebraska, but I do." Isabel said finally into the telephone, "Yes."

"Well—got any objections if I ask you out for dinner? Say Friday night? Just to say thanks, you know—Isabel."

"N-no. That's very nice of you, Mr. Miller."

"Willy. I was thinking of a restaurant downtown. Greenwich Street. It's called the Imperial Fish. You like fish? Lobster?" Before she could answer, he went on. Should he pick her up at the office Friday, or would she prefer to meet him at the restaurant?

"I can meet you—where you said, if you give me the address."

He had the address for her. They agreed upon seven.

Isabel looked at the address and telephone number of the Imperial Fish, which she had written down. Now she remembered Wilbur Miller very well. He had an openness and informality that was unlike most New Yorkers, she recalled, and at the same time he had looked full of self-confidence. He had wanted a two-room office, something to do with distribution of parts. Electronic parts? That didn't matter. She also remembered that she had felt an unusual awareness of him, something like friendliness and excitement at the same time. Funny. But she hadn't put herself out for him. She had smothered her feelings and even affected a little formality. Could Willy Miller of Nebraska be Mister Right? The knight on a white horse, as they said jokingly in some of the romances she read, with whom she was destined to spend the rest of her life?

Between then and Friday evening, Isabel's mind or memory shied away from what Willy Miller looked like, what his voice was like, though she well remembered. She was aware that her knees trembled, maybe her hands also, a couple of times on Friday.

Friday around six, Isabel dressed for her date with Willy Miller. She was not taking so much trouble with her appearance as she had for Dudley Hall, she thought, and it was true. A sleeveless dress of pale blue, because it was a warm evening, a raincoat of nearly transparent plastic, since rain was forecast, nice white sandals, and that was it.

She was in front of the Imperial Fish's blue-and-white striped awning at five past seven, and she glanced around for Willy among the people on the sidewalk, but he was probably in the restaurant, waiting for her. Isabel walked several paces in the uptown direction, then turned and strolled back, under the awning and past it. She wondered why she was hesitating. To make herself more interesting by being late? No. This evening with Willy could be just a nice evening, with dinner and conversation, and maybe coffee back at her apartment, maybe not.

What if she stood him up? She looked again at the awning and repressed a nervous laugh. He'd order a second drink, and keep glancing at the door, as she always did. He'd learn to know what it felt like. However, she had nothing whatsoever against Willy Miller. She simply realized that she didn't want to spend the evening with him, didn't want to make better acquaintance with him. She sensed that she could start an affair with him, which because she was older and wiser would be more important than the silly experience—She didn't know what to call that one-night affair with the second of her loves, who hadn't been even as important as the first, with whom she'd never been to bed. The second had been the married man.

She wanted to go back home. Or did she? Frowning, she stared at the door of the Imperial Fish. Should she go in and say, "Hello, Willy. Sorry I'm late"? Or "I'm sorry, Willy, but I don't want to keep this date."

I prefer my own dates, she might add. That was the truth.

A passerby bumped her shoulder, because she was standing still in the middle of the sidewalk. She set her teeth. *I'm going home,* she told herself, like a command, and she began to walk uptown in the direction of where she lived, and because she was in rather good clothes, she treated herself to a taxi.

About the Author

Born in Fort Worth, Texas, in 1921, Patricia Highsmith spent much of her adult life in Switzerland and France. She was educated at Barnard College, where she studied English, Latin, and Greek. Her first novel, *Strangers on a Train,* published initially in 1950, proved to be a major commercial success and was filmed by Alfred Hitchcock. Despite this early recognition, Highsmith was unappreciated in the United States for the entire length of her career.

Writing under the pseudonym of Clare Morgan, she then published *The Price of Salt* in 1953, which had been turned down by her previous American publisher because of its frank exploration of homosexual themes. Her most popular literary creation was Tom Ripley, the dapper sociopath who first debuted in her 1955 novel, *The Talented Mr. Ripley.* She followed with four other Ripley novels. Posthumously made into a major motion picture, *The Talented Mr. Ripley* has helped bring about a renewed appreciation of Highsmith's work in the United States.

The author of more than twenty books, Highsmith has won the O. Henry Memorial Award, the Edgar Allan Poe Award, Le Grand Prix de Littérature Policière, and the Award of the Crime Writers' Association of Great Britain. She died in Switzerland on February 4, 1995, and her literary archives are maintained in Basel.